Harlequin
Omnibus

3 Great Novels by

Iris Danbury

Harlequin Books

TORONTO • LONDON • NEW YORK • AMSTERDAM
SYDNEY • HAMBURG • PARIS

These books by Iris Danbury were originally published as
follows:

RENDEZVOUS IN LISBON
Copyright © 1967 by Iris Danbury
First published in 1967 by Mills & Boon Limited
Harlequin edition (#1178) published February 1968

DOCTOR AT VILLA RONDA
Copyright © 1967 by Iris Danbury
First published in 1967 by Mills & Boon Limited
Harlequin edition (#1257) published December 1968

HOTEL BELVEDERE
Copyright © 1961 by Iris Danbury
First published in 1961 by Mills & Boon Limited
Harlequin edition (#1331) published September 1969

Cover photograph © Larry Dale Gordon/The Image Bank of Canada

ISBN 0-373-70318-X

First **Harlequin Omnibus** edition published September 1975

Second printing May 1977
Third printing December 1978

Contents

Rendezvous in Lisbon

Janice Bowen was a competent secretary, but even she found Everard Whitney impossibly difficult to work with.

Small wonder her surprise when Mr. Whitney asked her to accompany him on a business trip to Portugal.

Janice was thrilled at the opportunity of seeing attractive Clive Dickson again. But strangely enough it was another man who turned out to be the important one in her life.

CHAPTER ONE

SHE KNEW that she was a few minutes late this morning and as she hurried from the elevator to her own office she hoped that her chief had not yet arrived. It would be typical of Mr. Whitney to come unpredictably early on the very morning when there had been a subway holdup.

A quick glance into his room assured her that he was not there, and she walked across the wide expanse of thick blue carpet to adjust the calendar on the massive, flat-topped desk, and place the diary at his elbow.

Janice Bowen stood back and sighed. To work for Everard Whitney in his lush executive suite was the ambition of almost every girl in this prestige block of offices—until each one discovered his sharp temper, his impatience and the impossibility of pleasing him.

Janice gazed around the big room, more like a club lounge with its comfortable armchairs and settee, glass-topped tables and houseplants. The view from the wide window always excited her. From this fifteenth floor it seemed that half London lay dwarfed below, square mile upon square mile stretching away into the mist, punctuated by tall office blocks and lesser church spires, the towers of the Abbey and the Houses of Parliament with toy bridges across the gleaming curve of the Thames. The roar of traffic was filtered out though at this height it would have been no more than a subdued hum.

Mr. Whitney seemed blind to all external interests. At the first slant of sunshine through the window, Janice would operate the venetian blinds and switch on concealed artificial daylight lighting that remained conveniently constant and did not cause distracting gleams or set the dust motes that were present even in this air-conditioned apartment dancing.

It was rumored downstairs in the typing pool that once a girl had daringly introduced a large aspidistra among the fashionably exotic houseplants and Mr. Whitney had failed to notice any difference.

In her own private office Janice sorted the mail, found the necessary files for reference, then took a quick look at herself in the full-length mirror inside the coat closet.

Not even Mr. Whitney could complain that she used excessive makeup—a mat finish to her creamy skin and a light touch of shadow and mascara around her sherry-brown eyes. Lately she had taken to piling up her glossy brown hair into a swept-up coil. She felt it gave her more dignity that way.

The day began as usual. Mr. Whitney grunted and barked his instructions, gave Janice an enormous amount of work to do, then went out at midday, no doubt to harry other people. Certainly it was impossible to imagine him daw-dling over a leisurely business luncheon. He never relaxed, it seemed.

At lunch in the firm's own restaurant another girl spoke to Janice. "You're lasting out well. How long have you been working for Whit?"

"Three weeks," Janice answered. "Seems like three years."

The other girl laughed. "And hard labor at that! Oh, he soon got tired of me and packed me back to my de-partment."

"You rush around, you type your fingers down to the knuckles, but you can't please him," said Janice crossly.

"I wonder which of you will win?"

Janice laughed in spite of her resentment. "No prizes for guessing! Anyway, I'm not giving him the chance to send me packing. I shall ask for a transfer back to Mr. Pickering's department. I didn't realize how happy I was there."

"But think of the glamour," reminded the other girl. "Secretary to the smartest executive in the company. At least, he thinks he is."

Janice nodded. Perhaps Everard Whitney was justified in having a high opinion of himself and his qualities. He had joined the company only a year ago and streaked his way to the top, so that now he was one of the four most important men in this huge building and civil-engineering concern, and Janice judged that he might not yet be thirty.

When he returned late in the afternoon and she took him the letters requiring his signature, as well as the reports and telephone messages, she studied him. As he sat hunched over the massive desk his broad shoulders belied his height of at least six feet. He had a mannerism of thrusting his fingers through his thick chestnut hair, then patting it down again. Always he gave an impression of high-powered concentration on the job in hand.

Now he paused after signing one of the letters, leaned back in his chair and regarded her with cool gray eyes.

"You're very conscientious, aren't you, Miss Brown?"

"Bowen," she corrected. It irritated her that he couldn't even remember her name.

"Oh, yes. Bowen. I seem to have had several Miss Browns from other departments."

Now, of course, was the moment to tell him that she wanted a transfer back to Mr. Pickering. He frequently demanded a change of secretary, so why shouldn't she ask for a change of chief?

She began to frame the words in her mind—*could I please*—but the words were never uttered.

"Miss Brown, er, Miss Bowen, I mean, can you be ready to go to Lisbon in two days from now?" His voice startled her.

"To Lisbon?" she echoed stupidly.

"Yes. You've heard of it, haven't you?" he demanded impatiently. "Capital of Portugal."

"Yes, Mr. Whitney."

"Have you a passport? Valid?" he asked.

"Yes. I went to Switzerland last year."

"We'll be flying the day after tomorrow and staying several weeks, possibly longer. I've been telling the chairman today that someone must coordinate work on those two hotels the company is building in Portugal or they'll never be finished in time and we shall be let in for penalty clauses. I've decided to go myself and I need a secretary. You're possibly the most reasonably promising girl I've had so far.''

"Thank you, Mr. Whitney.'' She was bowled over by his announcement, by the prospect of a trip to Lisbon and, most of all, by his grudging praise of her work.

"I understand you have no particular ties in London?''

How did he know that? He had never asked her the slightest personal question.

"Well, no,'' she answered. "I live in an—''

"An apartment in Highgate. Your parents are dead and you have an aunt in Norwich. You've been working in London for three years and with this company for two. You're not married and, as far as is known, not engaged.''

She stared at him in consternation. "How do you know all this?''

"I asked for the details from personnel records. I like to know something of the background of my employers. Are you engaged?''

"No,'' she answered firmly.

"Good. I can't afford untidy complications if we're going to work together.''

She nearly laughed. Untidy complications! That was certainly a new term for one of the highlights of the average girl's life.

She picked up the folder of signed letters, but as she reached the door of her own office he called out, "Oh, yes, one more point. Your salary will be increased and I've suggested to the cashier what I think is a reasonable figure. All your expenses in Lisbon, of course, will be charged to the company.''

"Thank you,'' was all she could murmur.

"And, Miss Bowen, no discussion of our visit, please, until we leave. You understand?''

"Of course. I treat all your affairs as confidential.''

He grunted, but whether with displeasure or amusement it was impossible for her to tell.

When she had finished for the day and left the building she paused to glance back at the huge skyscraper block built by the company for its head offices. From this center its worldwide-building projects were directed: office blocks, hotels, hospitals, schools, department stores, universities—everything on the grand scale. Janice wondered sometimes what the company's reaction would be if it were asked to build a small weekend bungalow.

At home in her apartment she prepared a meal, then lingered over her coffee, only now allowing her mind to dwell on the new and exciting possibilities that might develop from a business trip to Lisbon.

She was not compelled to go, of course. She could tell Mr. Whitney tomorrow morning that she was refusing to accompany him, but then she would lose the chance of meeting Clive Dickson again, and for that reason alone half the girls in the office would have been eager to travel much farther afield than Portugal.

Clive's attraction lay not so much in his undeniably handsome features and carefree social personality as in his ability to make a girl feel that she mattered at the moment more than any other girl in the world, even though sensible girls knew that the moment was fleeting.

He avoided entangling himself by allowing it to be known that his invitations to dinners, dances, parties or quiet afternoons in art galleries were not to be regarded as seriously binding. There were to be no farewells, no "end-of-the-affair" tears, for, indeed, the affair had never started. Clive offered his company equally to girls he had known a couple of years and those whom he had met only a week earlier.

"He picks us up and puts us down as though we were chessmen," one girl had declared wrathfully when she had been dropped, ostensibly for expecting too much from Clive.

Janice had been more levelheaded. She, too, had enjoyed a few outings with him until his transfer three months ago to the Lisbon branch office. Rumor declared that he had asked for a transfer to avoid scenes with a girl in his own department or that the management had considered it discreet to remove him and let him dally with foreign girls at a safe distance.

Without his cheerful magnetism the office had certainly been a duller place, and Janice looked forward eagerly to meeting him again. She was honest enough to admit that in spite of his capricious temperament she liked him and that, perhaps, with less of the wholesale London competition around her, he might develop a strong liking for her.

But that was all in the future and Mr. Whitney would probably give her little time for social distractions.

IN THE AIRPORT LOUNGE two days later Mr. Whitney handed Janice a small portable typewriter.

"You might look after this. I don't want to put it down somewhere and forget it," he said.

Janice swallowed the exclamation that sprang to her lips and merely gave him a brief smile. So he was all set to use the plane journey for business purposes! Trust Mr. Whitney never to lose a single moment of his secretary's time.

She was wrong, however, for the typewriter occupied a spare seat and the bulging briefcases full of reports and summaries were never opened. Instead, Mr. Whitney appeared almost human, even consulting Janice as to her preferences at lunch.

"This is not your first flight, is it?" he asked.

"I flew to Geneva last year, but that was a night flight."

With the plane now crossing the Bay of Biscay, it was rather late in the day, she thought, for any misgivings about her capacity to travel by air, but she forgot her irritations when later she saw the Tagus River spread out below, the harbor, the docks and the clustered mass of pink and white and gray buildings that was Lisbon.

She was delighted with the suite of rooms reserved for her chief and herself at the Hollandia, a luxury hotel facing a park. A porter showed her into a large and superbly furnished bedroom, one side of which was occupied by a range of built-in units in honey-colored wood with dark horizontal bands. A thick pale green carpet gave a touch of coolness and wide French windows opened onto a balcony. A private bathroom was handsomely equipped with shower, a turquoise and black bath and mirrors with strategically placed lighting.

The porter indicated that a side door in the lobby led into the adjoining sitting room and he stood aside, waiting for her to enter.

Mr. Whitney was already there. She supposed that his bedroom on the far side was similar to her own, with the sitting room between.

Her eyes sparkled with pleasure. "What lovely rooms!" she exclaimed enthusiastically after the porters had gone.

Mr. Whitney stood before her, hands thrust into his trouser pockets. "And do you suppose they were reserved for us by magic or thought transference?"

She stared blankly at him.

"You should have attended to the matter," he continued.

"I'm sorry. I didn't know," she murmured.

"Well, you didn't even ask if anything had been fixed, did you? It's fortunate that I made arrangements through the company's travel department, but you should have checked that. You'll have to learn to look after me, not let me do all the running about for myself."

"I'll remember in future," she answered quietly, all her pleasure quenched.

"I'm sure you will." He smiled frostily. "We shall use this sitting room as our office. You'll find it more pleasant than a room in the company's quarters and we shall waste less time in taxi rides."

"Yes."

He picked up one of the briefcases. "I'm going now to our Lisbon office. If anyone telephones for me, give vague answers. Say you don't know when I'll be here. I shall be back about seven and we'll have dinner sent up here. If you want anything in the meantime—tea, coffee or cold drinks— then telephone. I don't want you to go down into the public rooms."

Janice knew better by now than to query his reasons. She was glad of his absence so that she could unpack her case, then take a shower in the handsomely appointed private bathroom leading out of her bedroom. Already the afternoon heat was overpowering after the cool English summer at home.

She changed out of her lightweight traveling suit into a

cool sheath of deep geranium linen and ordered coffee and cakes.

In the sitting room her hand went out several times to the telephone. Should she call Clive and let him know she was here? But Mr. Whitney had gone to the branch office where Clive worked and Janice was fearful of interrupting some important conference. Perhaps it was better to wait until tomorrow when she could choose her opportunity.

She chafed now at spending the sunny afternoon indoors, when, but for Mr. Whitney's instructions, she might have been exploring Lisbon streets. It was surprising, too, she thought, that he had omitted to leave her some work to do in his absence.

When the waiter brought the coffee, she settled herself comfortably in one of the long chairs on the balcony, nibbled little cakes and reflected uncharitably on all her companions in the London office working madly to finish by five o'clock.

Her smugness was soon shattered by Mr. Whitney's arrival, and at the sound of his voice calling from the sitting room she hastened to assume a less indolent attitude.

She hurried into the room and found him sprawled on the settee, briefcase on the floor and his jacket flung carelessly across a chair.

"Can I get you anything?" she asked. "Coffee? Tea?"

He opened his eyes and glared at her. "I need something stronger."

Almost immediately a waiter knocked and entered, pushing a tea wagon with several bottles of brandy, Bacardi, tonic water and a bowl of ice cubes.

Janice watched the waiter prepare the Bacardi and tonic and hand it to Mr. Whitney.

After a few moments the drink seemed to have restored Mr. Whitney to his customary level of energy, for he sat up and said briskly to Janice, "We'll start work now."

As she settled herself with notebook she thought wryly that she should have known that an hour's slacking in the afternoon would certainly be offset by several hours of steady work during the evening.

Apparently nothing had gone right for him at the Lisbon

office. The people he particularly wanted to see had been out and those he had seen hadn't managed to give him the right information.

As he dictated notes and instructions his voice was as sharp as if he had been directly addressing the people concerned.

"I've ordered dinner for eight," he told her when he had finished dictating. "Please be ready by then, for at nine I'm expecting someone from the branch office."

She worked as hard as she could for the next hour or so, breaking off only in time to shower, apply fresh makeup and put on a sleeveless lime-green dress.

Dining with Mr. Whitney in the private sitting room might have the air of intimacy, but Janice remembered that eating strange dishes and sipping wine was still only part of the businesslike formality she was expected to maintain.

When the meal was finished Janice suggested that she should take the typewriter into her bedroom and continue with the letters and memoranda. She naturally assumed that her chief would prefer to see his visitor alone.

"No," he said abruptly. 'I want you here so that you can take notes of the conversation if need be."

It was nearer ten o'clock than nine when the telephone rang, and Janice answered it.

"Mr. Whitney's visitor is here," the clerk said in English.

"Please send him up," she instructed.

She went out to the balcony to tell Mr. Whitney and almost as soon as she entered the room again, the visitor, Clive Dickson, came toward her.

"Janice! Of all the wonderful things to happen! I'd no idea you were here."

"Clive!" she exclaimed.

He seized both her hands and bent down to kiss her cheek.

She pulled herself away, aware that Mr. Whitney was standing almost immediately behind her.

"So you've arrived at last, Dickson. I see that you don't need an introduction to my secretary. You apparently know each other very well." Mr. Whitney's voice was cold and dampening.

Clive rubbed his hands confidently. "I think it's a marvelous piece of luck that you've brought Janice—er, Miss Bowen—with you."

"Luck for you? Or Miss Bowen? Sit down. What will you drink?"

"Brandy, please," Clive answered.

Janice, who had been temporarily stricken with horror because Mr. Whitney had witnessed Clive's unnecessarily enthusiastic greeting, was glad to serve drinks to the two men.

"Have one yourself, Miss Bowen," Mr. Whitney said. "Try Bacardi."

She poured herself a very small glass of the clear white rum and sipped it while the two men became involved in a discussion of technical details.

"Miss Bowen, bring me the file of the Lisbon hotel—the rebuilding job."

As she handed Mr. Whitney the paper, Clive looked up and gave her a cordial smile. She glanced away hastily before her employer could notice.

"Now listen, Dickson," Mr. Whitney began. "There's no doubt that you've been slacking on the job. No coordination at all. Materials have been delivered and dumped anywhere, so that when they were really needed, they were mislaid or else tons of stuff had to be shifted from place to place."

"But, Mr. Whitney," Clive protested, "you've no idea how difficult it is here to get deliveries made in the right order. Sometimes we have to take all the baths and plumbing fittings long before we have the rooms ready for them."

"That's your job," declared Mr. Whitney. "It was the reason you were sent here—or so I gathered," he added dryly. "Why were you out this afternoon when I called?"

"I had to go to several suppliers," Clive answered. "If I'd known you were in Lisbon, I'd have stayed in, of course."

"I'm sure you would have—instead of going off to swim at Estoril beach."

Clive shook his head vehemently. "I certainly wasn't there."

"No matter where you actually were, your staff said you

usually worked only in the mornings and took the after-noons off.''

Clive waved his empty glass. "Oh, that's just jealous talk. I have to visit all kinds of people. I'm often doing the company's business late at night and in the evenings.''

"In cafés, most likely.''

Janice was embarrassed at being forced to listen while Clive was reprimanded by his boss, but just when she was wondering if she could creep out to the balcony, Mr. Whitney spoke to her.

"Take down these notes, Miss Bowen.''

When she had typed out the summaries and given a copy to Clive, Mr. Whitney said, "I'll meet you at the hotel site tomorrow morning, Dickson, not later than nine, and I shall expect you to bring me exact information as to the position of every piece of material. Good night.''

Clive seemed in no way downcast by Mr. Whitney's acrid remarks, and on his way out murmured to Janice, "Good night. I'll phone you in the morning.''

As soon as he had gone, Janice turned to face Mr. Whitney.

"You should have been honest with me, Miss Bowen, and told me that you were very friendly with Clive Dickson.''

"But I know him only slightly. When he was in the London office, he . . . .''

"Slightly?'' Everard Whitney's eyebrows went up. "By the way he greeted you tonight I thought I was seeing the reunion of a pair of—very close friends.''

She knew he had been going to say "a pair of lovers.''

"Oh, that's just his rather genial way,'' she murmured.

"I would certainly not have brought you here if I'd known you and he were on such a friendly footing, then. I'd have asked for someone else and made sure that she had no connection with Clive Dickson.''

He walked away from her across the room, then suddenly turned. "If you're going to be of any use to me,'' he said, "then I must have your complete loyalty.''

"But naturally you have that already,'' she asserted.

"At this moment, possibly. If different circumstances arise, whose side will you take?'' he demanded.

"Yours," she said unhesitatingly.

"Good. I hope I shall always be able to rely on that."

There was a long silence. Janice wanted to protest that she hadn't begged to accompany him. He had arbitrarily commanded her. Was it her fault that he had omitted to ask her if she knew Clive?

It was better to remain silent, though. The air seemed to vibrate with his censure, but at last she forced herself to speak.

"Is there anything further you wish me to do tonight?"

"No, thanks. It's late and we've both had a long and tiring day. You'd better get your sleep. Good night."

Before she prepared herself for bed she went out to the balcony of her room to breathe in the warm night air. Across the avenue below were the dark massed shadows of the park, and, way beyond, part of the city glittered with lights.

She reflected that she had been in Lisbon a whole afternoon and evening and so far had not yet set foot in its streets. She might as well have been in a mining town or on a remote island. She hoped Everard Whitney did not intend to monopolize all her time so that she saw nothing of this reputedly beautiful city. Besides, she was surely entitled to some free time, and the thought of occasional invitations from Clive gave her a thrill of exultation. At least he had given her a warm welcome. A few oases in the desert of Mr. Whitney's demands would be something to look forward to if it meant dancing with Clive or sunbathing on one of the nearby beaches.

Mr. Whitney had told her that he preferred to breakfast alone in his room. Janice welcomed this information, for it gave her the opportunity to eat hers on her balcony next morning and start the day with crisp rolls and toast, fresh fruit and what someone had once told her was "the best coffee in Europe."

When she went into the sitting room, Mr. Whitney was already there, studying a lengthy report.

"Oh, good morning, Miss Bowen," he greeted her. "Had your breakfast?"

"Yes, thank you."

He nodded and seemed to be gazing at the slender turquoise shift she was wearing, but no doubt he was thinking of something else.

"I've kept your nose to the grindstone these last few days. You might like to spend an hour or so exploring the city, looking at the shops and so on."

She smiled delightedly at this unexpected favor.

"I know you couldn't bring many clothes with you on the plane," he continued, "so you'll probably want to add a few items to your wardrobe." He fished in his jacket pocket and handed her a bundle of hundred escudo notes. "Since you can't buy anything unless you have some Portuguese currency, here's an advance on your salary."

His thoughtfulness and gracious manner were so surprising that she could hardly stammer out her thanks. "What time do you want me back here?"

"One o'clock will do. I shall be out, but I'll leave some notes for you. You might ask the reception desk to fix up a tape recorder for us as soon as they can."

"Yes, I'll do that," she promised. Evidently this morning he did not object to her being seen in the hotel.

She hurried out of the hotel before her employer could change his mind and haul her back for some urgent task.

The sunshine was dazzling and she guessed that she might find it necessary to buy a shady hat. Mr. Whitney had not thought to tell her where the main shopping center was and she found that she had to walk the length of the Avenida de Liberdade, a broad, tree-lined street with open-air cafés, before she came to several squares and then a maze of narrow streets full of shops.

She gazed in the windows, working out the exchange prices in her mind. After a coffee in a nearby café it occurred to her to try to telephone Clive. Surely there could be no harm in that.

When the call was put through and she heard his voice, speaking first in Portuguese, she said gaily, "Janice here. Am I interrupting anything?"

"Not this morning—yet," he replied. "Where's the boss?"

"I left him in the hotel," she answered, "but he said he was going out. To the rebuilding job, I think."

"And he let you off the chain?"

Janice giggled. "I'm down here in the city, spending escudos like water, dozens of them at a time!"

Clive made a few noncommittal noises. Then he said, "Janice, look! I'd like to take you out tonight, but I can't. I've, er, got to see someone and chat business with him. But how are you fixed for tomorrow?"

"Well, I don't know," she confessed. "You know what Mr. Whitney is. He wants to work all hours when it suits him."

"Yes, I do know," Clive replied grimly. "But I happen to know that his lordship has an engagement tomorrow evening and you should be free. I'll call at your hotel about, say, seven-thirty?"

"Thank you, Clive."

"And we'll have a quiet little dinner at a restaurant I know. We've a lot to talk about."

When he hung up, Janice was in a warm, dreamy state. How lucky she was to meet Clive again and that he was willing, even eager, to pay some attention to her! On the strength of her inner delight she bought herself a glittering silver lurex sheath, recklessly disregarding the cost and promising herself to economize on other items. She realized that she was not yet sure how much her salary was going to be.

Back at the hotel she found that Mr. Whitney had left her enough work to keep her busy for a day and a half and during the heat of the afternoon she thought longingly of lounging on golden beaches in sight of a sparkling sea. She had to make do with iced drinks and at five o'clock a pot of strong coffee to revive her flagging energies.

At seven Mr. Whitney telephoned to say that he would probably not return until about midnight.

"Have your dinner when you like," he told her. "You might prefer to take it in the hotel restaurant. There's no need to stay in the room in solitary state."

"Oh, thank you." So apparently he had no objection to

her being seen now in the public restaurant. The need for secrecy was over.

She was glad that he had given his gracious permission, for it was more lively in the restaurant, but although the waiters showed her to Mr. Whitney's reserved table and treated her with excessive courtesy and attention, she would have been happier eating a simple snack in a modest café with Clive for company.

Afterward she walked in the park opposite the hotel. From the top of a triumphal way flanked by two floodlit columns the view stretched right down the main avenue to the harbor and across the estuary, which was pinpointed with lights.

All next day as she worked she was buoyed up by the thought of the evening out with Clive, and she hoped that Everard Whitney would not keep her too late.

He had insisted that she take a siesta in the middle of the afternoon. "This isn't like Spain where they shut everything from twelve to four, but it's just as hot, and I don't want to tire you out."

His apparent consideration for her well-being was probably self-seeking, she thought mutinously. If she fell ill from overwork and exhaustion he would have to find another secretary, and she was not as expendable as all that.

All the same she had finished all his work by six o'clock and hoped he would release her.

"Is that the lot?" he asked, glancing through the reports and lists of materials delivered to the hotel sites.

"Yes. Everything."

"Pour yourself a Martini and flop in a chair for a few minutes," he advised her.

After a few moments, when she had followed his instructions and also handed him a drink, he said, "I take it you've no plans for this evening?" Without giving her time to reply, he continued, "I shall want you to accompany me to the house of some friends I have here. We'll have a light meal before we go, as we shall have to eat there, as well."

She gave a little gasp and he looked across the room at her.

"I I didn't think you'd be wanting me this evening, so I

made an arrangement." She could hardly disclose that Clive had said that Mr. Whitney would be going out, too.

"You've lost little time in making dates, I see." Then he smiled. "I suppose it's Dickson."

"Yes. I didn't think you'd mind," she said humbly.

"I mind very much on this occasion. You can go out with him some other time, but tonight I particularly want you with me."

After a slight pause she said coldly, "Very well, I'll be ready at whatever time you say." She thought he might at least have told her sooner about his plans for her.

"Hadn't you better telephone Dickson and tell him?" he suggested.

"I'll do that from my room telephone," she answered. She was not going to let him listen to her one-sided conversation, although he could probably listen to both sides on the sitting-room telephone if he chose.

She was annoyed to find that Clive had already left his office. What could she do now? If she told Mr. Whitney that Clive had gone home there might be more trouble for Clive.

She returned to the sitting room. "Mr. Dickson has already left the branch office," she said in her most formal manner.

Everard Whitney's gray eyes glinted and his mouth curved in a smile. "Of course! Dickson keeps English office hours and doesn't believe in staying as late as his Portuguese staff. Don't you know his hotel telephone number?"

"No."

He scribbled down the name of the hotel. "He may not be there. He probably stops at a café on the way home to gossip with his friends."

Janice took the paper and found the number. Fortunately Clive had arrived.

"Well, I'm darned!" Clive exclaimed when she had explained the situation. "He's done this on purpose. Oh, naturally, you'll have to tag along with the Big Chief."

"You said you knew where he was going. Where is it? Tell me."

"It's a private house. Belongs to a family named Carvalho. Well, it can't be helped. You go with him and have a good time. Don't worry, poppet. We'll make another date.''

She was left with a slight feeling of disappointment that Clive had treated the matter in so casual a way, but she supposed that since he had been in Lisbon for more than three months he would have no difficulty in filling in a broken date.

She decided that it might be out of place to wear the new dress of shimmering silver. Mr. Whitney no doubt expected her to wear something more sober. As she pulled the lime-green dress over her head she counted it as one more slight that she had been cheated out of even wearing her new dress tonight.

Yet he was wearing dinner jacket and black tie, so evidently the visit was not wholly concerned with business matters.

After a snack at the hotel, she accompanied her chief down to a waiting taxi.

''You'll like this house we're going to,'' he said conversationally, ''that is, if you have any feeling for domestic architecture. Actually, this was once a small palace, and the same family has lived there for two hundred years.''

From the street there was little to see—a high white wall with a pair of black wrought-iron gates. A manservant was there to let in the visitors and Janice walked with Mr. Whitney across the narrow garden toward the house. She glanced critically at the outline—long and three-storied, glowing now with a soft pink light where the sun caught it. A handsome house, perhaps, but hardly a palace, she thought.

Mr. Whitney was greeted by a maid who curtsied, then led the way through a corridor and out to the back of the house. Janice now realized that this was probably the front, opening onto a wide paved terrace and facing a secluded garden with lawns and tall trees and a tiny lake with a fountain.

''Everard! Oh, you've come at last!''

A slim girl with blue eyes and dazzlingly fair hair approached him and held out her hand.

''Why at last? I could hardly come sooner,'' he answered.

He turned toward Janice. "Selma, this is my secretary from England, Miss Bowen." He indicated the fair girl. "Miss Selma Carvalho."

The two girls murmured acknowledgements, then Selma linked her arm in Everard Whitney's and, with a smile, took him off in the direction of a knot of people at the far end.

A servant offered Janice a drink from a tray and she took one from the varied assortment, hardly knowing what liquid it was. She sipped the drink and gazed around her. There were probably between twenty and thirty people dotted around in little groups, some sitting at umbrella-shaded tables, others sitting companionably on wide stone benches placed near the edges of the garden.

Why on earth, she wondered, had Mr. Whitney insisted on bringing her here to this reception, cocktail party or whatever it was, then left her stranded immediately on arrival?

A voice behind her said quietly, "Forgive me, we have not been introduced, but I see you are alone. Has your escort deserted you?"

Janice turned to face a slender, dark-haired young man.

"Perhaps he has, but only for a few moments, I think," she answered.

"I think you're wrong about that, but no matter. Allow me to present myself. I am Manoel Carvalho." He bowed to her.

"My name is Bowen. Janice Bowen," she said.

"And you are in Lisbon with Everard?" he queried.

"Yes. I'm his secretary." Janice was determined that there should be no misunderstanding as to her position and status.

Manoel nodded. "Then now we are well known to each other. Shall we find a seat somewhere?"

He guided her towards a corner of the terrace where a curved stone seat looked inviting.

"I'd better not wander too far away in case Mr. Whitney comes back to look for me," said Janice.

Manoel smiled and his dark eyes twinkled with amusement. "At the moment he is occupied. Tell me, how long have you been in Lisbon?"

"Only three days."

He grimaced. "And you have been sightseeing?"

"Not very much." Janice laughed. "I really came here to work."

"Yes, of course. The English take work very seriously, or at least they pretend they do. I spent three years at Cambridge and some of my student friends put on a very good show of working hard while they managed to enjoy themselves most of the time."

"Not all of us can afford to idle," Janice said with a laugh.

"Except on evenings like this when there is nothing to do except talk and laugh and drink wine."

He hissed to a passing manservant carrying a tray of drinks and offered a glass of white wine to Janice.

"Try this wine, please," he commanded, and watched her face as she tasted it. "Do you like it?"

"It's delicious. What's it called?"

He smiled with satisfaction. "Amarante, the wine of love, so they say. One of our best Portuguese wines from the north."

In an effort to jerk the conversation back to a more mundane level, she said, "You told me your name is Carvalho. Is Selma Carvalho your sister?"

"No. My cousin. Selma is only half-Portuguese. Her mother belongs to the English colony in Lisbon and has married into our family."

She was curious to know whether the Carvalhos were guests or the hosts of this party. Perhaps the direct approach to this amiable young man was best. "And this is your home?" she queried.

"Of course," he answered. "That is why when I see a guest sitting alone, I must approach her and see that she is happy and enjoying herself."

"It was very kind of you."

"Not in the least. You must come here often with Everard. No doubt he will take every opportunity to see our beautiful cousin, Selma. He's very interested in her."

"Oh, is he?" Janice was surprised at finding this unexpectedly human characteristic in Mr. Whitney.

"Selma has many admirers, naturally," Manoel continued.

"She's very beautiful, although I only caught a quick glimpse of her."

"So is her younger sister, Leona—in a different way. Unfortunately, I am not interested in her and certainly she has no time for me. A pity, for our fathers expect us to marry and thus draw together two branches of the family. Look, there is Leona now, talking to an Englishman."

Janice glanced in the direction Manoel indicated and saw a dark-haired girl in a long, slinky dress of white lace, ankle length but slit to above the knee.

Then she caught her breath in a slight gasp as she saw that the girl's companion was Clive Dickson.

Was this an extraordinary coincidence, Janice wondered, or had Clive come there to find her this evening?

The girl seemed to be talking angrily, waving her hands and tossing her black hair out of her eyes. Clive was apparently listening sympathetically. Finally Leona gave him a little friendly push and scampered across the lawn as fast as her impeding skirt allowed her.

Clive turned and came toward Janice and her companion.

Manoel rose instantly to his feet. "You want to be introduced to my English friend?"

Clive waved away the offer. "No need, Manoel. Janice and I are old friends. We've known each other for years in England."

Manoel bowed. "In that case, I'll leave you both to your reunion. Excuse me, I must have a word with other guests."

When he had gone, Clive laughed softly. "Sorry if I disturbed your little chat with Manoel. I'll bet he's been telling you all the gossip and scandal of the neighborhood."

"Not really," Janice replied. "He told me about his two pretty cousins, Selma and Leona."

"Leona was pouring out her troubles to me a few moments ago."

"Yes, I saw you. Manoel told me who the girl was."

"Poor Leona! As you probably know, many of the families here, both English and those intermarried with the Portuguese, send their children to England for part of their education, although they grow up bilingual. Leona has endured one year in an exclusive boarding school and now that she's home for the vacation she's refusing to go back for a second dose."

"How old is she?" asked Janice.

"Eighteen, but about forty-five in some respects. Sometimes very sophisticated and at others like a rebellious six-year-old."

After a moment Janice asked, "How did you manage to be here this evening?"

"I knew that Whitney was coming here tonight, so I thought you and I could have a quiet evening to ourselves, but when milord insisted on yanking you along with him, I decided that I might as well get myself invited, too. I had only to telephone Leona as if I was making sure that the party was tonight. So here I am."

"Mr. Whitney broke up my plans for the evening, but almost as soon as we arrived here, he was carried off by Miss Selma Carvalho and I haven't seen him since."

"Oh, if Selma has beckoned him, he'll forget all about you," Clive assured her.

"It never occurred to me that he'd be interested in women," Janice said thoughtfully. "I imagined that he was absolutely dedicated to his work."

"So he is," agreed Clive. "But every man has some chink, however strong the armor. Every time he visits Portugal, the Carvalhos prepare for the great news of Selma's engagement to the handsome English tycoon."

At that moment the "handsome English tycoon" came striding toward Janice and Clive.

"I'm sorry I had to leave you so long, Miss Bowen," Everard Whitney began, "but I see you've found company." He turned toward Clive. "I thought you had a previous engagement for this evening, Dickson."

Clive stood up, faced his superior with easy assurance. "You're right, but at the last moment it was unfortunately canceled. So I chose to fill in an idle evening here."

For a moment Mr. Whitney glared at Clive, then he turned toward Janice. "Come with me, Miss Bowen. We are staying here for dinner, so I'll wish you good-night, Dickson. And I'd like you to be at the rebuilding job tomorrow morning at eight."

Janice murmured a quiet good night to Clive and gave him a glance of sympathy at being so brusquely dismissed.

Dinner was served in a secluded courtyard at the side of the house and Janice took stock of the two Carvalho sisters.

Selma's parentage was easily revealed in her English wild-rose coloring, her smooth fair skin, brilliantly blue eyes and pale gold hair.

Leona, with her dark hair and flashing brown eyes, her challenging mouth with full, richly red lips, appeared wholly Portuguese in spite of an English mother.

As the evening darkened, small lanterns hanging on the courtyard walls were switched on and glowed like jewels against the dark background of climbing plants, camellias, roses, and clematis.

At dinner Janice had been marooned between two elderly ladies, members of the Carvalho family no doubt, who were interested more in their immediate neighbors on the other side of Janice. When the meal was over Manoel came and spoke consolingly to her.

"Please forgive us all that we did not provide you with more congenial partners," he apologized. "Next time I will personally do better. I will see that I sit next to you."

When Mr. Whitney indicated that he was ready to leave, Janice went into the house to pick up her gold chiffon stole. Coming from somewhere in an adjacent room she could hear women's voices.

"Who was the girl with Everard? The one in the green dress?" a woman asked.

Janice stood still and a moment later another voice replied, "His secretary—so I understand. Perhaps he has brought her from England for his protection."

A sudden spurt of laughter drowned any further words, and Janice could not linger. She was slightly ashamed of having stopped to listen at all.

In the taxi back to the hotel she recalled the words with

amusement. The idea that Everard Whitney needed protection at any time was ludicrous; the suggestion that she might be the one to afford that protection was even more ridiculous.

CHAPTER TWO

JANICE HAD NEVER BEFORE been allowed to explore a palatial hotel where the foyer and ground-floor public rooms—all marble, chandelier lights and soft carpets—gave no hint that extensive rebuilding was in progress four floors above where there was the chaos of half-finished rooms, and gaps in floors and workmen shouting amid the noise and dust of machinery.

She followed Mr. Whitney and Clive on this inspection tour of the Castelo hotel, taking notes of everything she thought her chief might find useful. Sometimes when he spoke in Portuguese to the foreman or an electrician, Clive translated for her and gave her the gist of the conversation, for which she was grateful.

Sometimes she had to grope along dark passages lit by isolated naked bulbs strung on random loops of cord. Pools of water on uneven floors had to be negotiated and occasionally the only way to move from one level to another was by a short ladder, for neither staircase nor elevator shaft had yet been completed.

The two men were dressed in preparation for such rough conditions, for both Everard and Clive wore thin fawn Terylene trousers and dark checked shirts. Janice, unaware of what was in store for her, wished that Mr. Whitney had given her some guidance, for although she wore sensible sandals, her blue cotton dress was already marked and stained where she had rubbed against plastered walls or a grease-stained pipe.

On ground level at the back of the hotel Janice wondered

why in this dry, sunny climate there should be a sloppy sea of yellow mud.

"The men have to keep hosing down," Clive explained. "Otherwise they'd be choked with dust."

Stepping over girders and skirting trucks unloading cement was more fun than just doing paperwork in an office or even a luxurious hotel sitting room.

Here, Mr. Whitney's comments and criticisms made sense.

"Get the baths and showers put in as soon as the floors and ceilings are done. Why isn't the new service elevator working? All the electrical wiring for this side of the block should have been finished by now."

His orders and questions were endless and Janice could begin to see why he had thought it necessary to make this personal visit to Lisbon.

Clive came in for a share of instructions, too. "See that the material is delivered in the proper order. It's your job to coordinate all the supplies. It's no use stacking thousands of wall tiles before the plastering is done. They take up valuable space and in the end we shall find half of them broken."

Clive made a note of it, but when a few minutes later Everard walked to inspect a pile of drainpipes, Clive smiled at Janice and shrugged his shoulders.

"Tomorrow he'll be raging at me because something isn't delivered," he said. "Oh, well, here comes something to moisten our parched throats."

A waiter from the hotel brought a tray with glasses and two large carafes of wine.

"Quick!" Clive whispered, as he handed Janice a glass. "Before his lordship comes striding back. How about this evening? Are you free?"

"How do I know?" queried Janice. "I thought our arrangement was all right for last night, but he made me cancel it."

"I'll ring you at the hotel just before six o'clock," Clive said quietly, "and you can tell me then."

Janice's eyes sparkled. "All right. Thank you."

When she returned to the Hollandia hotel her first

thought was to shower away the dust and heat of the morning and change into a clean dress.

She started typing out the morning's notes, when Mr. Whitney put in an appearance, now spruced up and wearing a clean shirt and trousers.

"I see that you've had to change your clothes," he said. "I hope your dress wasn't too soiled. Some of our work turns out to be very dirty and dusty."

"My dress will wash quite easily," she assured him. "And I was very interested to see the building in progress. It makes a lot of figures and details come alive when you have to step over pipes or see baths piled up ready to be installed."

She glanced in his direction and caught a surprising expression of approval in his eyes.

"Finish that page," he instructed. "Then we'll go downstairs and have our lunch."

This was the first time they had appeared together in the hotel restaurant, and Janice was slightly flattered that apparently she had passed the test where he did not object to being seen in her company.

He studied the menu, recommended a Portuguese fish dish to her, then leaned back in his chair.

"What are you doing this afternoon?" he asked.

"Working, I expect, on this morning's notes." She thought his question was unnecessary.

"Not meeting Dickson?"

Warm color surged into her face. "No. Not this afternoon," she answered.

He half smiled. "I see." He waited for her to choose items from the hors d'oeuvres cart. Then he asked, "Have you been in the park opposite the hotel?"

"Yes. I walked there a day or so ago."

"Then go in the Estufa Fria for a couple of hours this afternoon. It's very cool and pleasant in there. Come back about four o'clock and put in a little work for me. Then you can dress up for your evening date with Dickson."

She supposed that her tone of voice had given away the fact that Clive was taking her out this evening and not this afternoon, but there was nothing to hide. Mr. Whitney had not forbidden her to see Clive or go out with him. She was cheered by this new and most reasonable attitude on Mr. Whitney's part and determined that in return she would work very hard indeed for him.

After lunch, as she walked through the hotel foyer, a dark young man came toward her. It was Manoel Carvalho.

"How lucky that I should meet you," he greeted her. "But surely you're not going out in the afternoon sun?"

"Only into the park for an hour or so," she answered. "Mr. Whitney recommended a visit to the Estufa Fria, whatever that is."

Manoel smiled. "He has a good idea there. May I accompany you?"

"Of course."

Stepping out from the cool, air-conditioned hotel into the burning sunshine was like entering a baker's oven.

"Fortunately it is no distance," said Manoel, fanning himself with his hand, "and I know the shortest way."

They walked along shady paths through shrubberies until a small lake opened out and at the side was the entrance to the mysterious Estufa Fria.

"What does it mean?" she asked. "A cold what?"

"The only translation I can give you is a 'cool hothouse,'" Manoel answered.

Janice saw now that the enclosure was a natural hollow, roofed over with narrow slats of wood that let in air and rain but kept out direct sunshine. A comparatively small area had been cleverly landscaped to make use of different natural levels; there were flowering shrubs, groups of soaring palm trees, rockeries, and water gurgling everywhere. Paths and steps twisted up or down unexpectedly leading to small grottos or caves, pools or fountains.

"In Brazil," Manoel told her, "this would be a natural rain forest where the trees shut out the sun. In Europe our Estufa Fria is unique," he added with pride.

"It's like an enormous enchanted cave, something out of *Peer Gynt*," she said.

Orchestral music came from amplifiers high in the trees and, recognizing part of a movement from Beethoven's *Pastoral Symphony*, she hummed along.

"Sometimes they play records of Debussy or Handel," Manoel said, "but not the 'pops.' That would not be appropriate."

"It's impossible to believe that we're in the middle of a large, busy city," Janice said as she and Manoel sat on little chairs under the tree. "I shall come in here every moment I can spare. It's conveniently close to our hotel."

"Then I shall also come often," returned Manoel. "So you must telephone me when I can meet you here."

She shook her head. "I won't know in advance. It's only a fluke that I came here today. Mr. Whitney gave me a little free time."

Manoel turned toward her, his arm across the back of her chair, the light of admiration in his dark eyes. "I'm glad I had to come to your hotel today. Actually I had to come to escort my cousin Selma. She wanted to see Everard at the hotel."

"I see." Janice certainly saw now why Mr. Whitney had given her part of the afternoon off. He was expecting Selma Carvalho and his secretary would have been in the way.

After a while she and Manoel left the Estufa Fria and climbed the slope to the café where umbrella-shaded tables were ranged alongside a narrow lake.

Manoel ordered coffee and spoke of places he had visited in England. "You must let me take you sightseeing here," he suggested. "Have you been up in our famous street elevator?"

"Not yet. I saw it from the main avenue."

"There, you see!" he exclaimed. "Everard will never bother to tell you of places to visit."

"But I don't want to take up your time," she protested. "Besides, I'm not here on holiday, but to work."

"My time?" he echoed. "Oh, I have nothing to do."

"You mean you haven't yet started any kind of work?"

"Work is not for me. At least, not a regular job. I'm a Carvalho—and we direct others to do the work. In September we shall go for the grape harvest to our *quinta*, our estate, where we have our vineyards. You must ask Everard to let you come and see the winepressing. It's a festival."

"September? I shall probably be back in England by then."

"Oh, no! Surely not." Disappointment lengthened his face.

Janice glanced at her watch. "It's nearly four o'clock. I have to go back to the hotel now and work. Thank you for showing me the Estufa."

Manoel frowned. "If I'm to have only five minutes of your company, perhaps you'll dine with me tonight?"

"I'm sorry, I can't tonight."

"Why? Is Everard taking you out somewhere?"

"Oh, no," she answered hastily.

"Then of course it's the Englishman, Dickson," Manoel gave a long drawn-out sigh. "That man is like a juggler who knows how to keep all the plates spinning at the same time." He gave her an oblique glance. "Of course you must accept an invitation from your compatriot, but after that it's my turn."

At the entrance to the Hollandia hotel, Manoel said in parting, "Have a good time tonight. Rest assured I won't tell Leona. I'll telephone you tomorrow."

Janice pondered on the reference to Leona as she went up to her room. Had Clive become so friendly with Leona Carvalho that the girl would be jealous if he showed attention to anyone else?

Mr. Whitney was not in the suite. Probably he had taken Senhorita Selma out to tea.

Janice concentrated on the typing and finished everything by six. After a shower she took special care with her hair and makeup and put on the new silver dress.

The telephone rang and a reception clerk informed her that Senhor Dickson was waiting.

"*Obrigado,*" Janice thanked him. "I am coming now."

At that moment Mr. Whitney entered the sitting room and stopped abruptly, eyeing her up and down. Whether he was flinching from the brightness of her dress or was struck dumb in admiration she could not tell.

"I've finished all the work." Her tone was hastily defensive.

"And you're now ready to go. New dress?"

She colored swiftly. "Yes. I bought it here."

"M'm," he murmured. "Quite eye-catching."

So he thought it was too showy. She was sorry now that she had not escaped a few minutes earlier.

Then he added, "You look very charming. Don't let Dickson keep you out too late. I want all your time tomorrow. We're going to Estoril."

Clive had a taxi waiting, but not until they were bowling down the Avenida da Liberdade did he and Janice turn to each other and laugh.

"Oh, I thought he'd haul me back for some last-minute job," Janice confessed.

"And I wouldn't dare come up to your suite in case he nabbed me for a long discussion on my shortcomings!"

They laughed again and Clive rested his arm lightly around her shoulders and gave her a gentle hug.

Janice sighed with happiness and contentment. She knew that she must not overvalue these little attentions from Clive, or build up false hopes of a permanent future, but for the moment it was sheer delight to be in his company, sharing the enjoyment of a few hours' freedom as though they were two excited children let off the leash.

After a leisurely aperitif at a café in the Rossio Square, the crowded center of Lisbon, Clive took her to a famous fish restaurant in a narrow street nearby.

Janice was delighted to sample small shellfishlike limpets and accepted Clive's recommendation of suckling pig to follow.

"What is Whitney's real purpose in coming here?" Clive asked her.

"To find out about the progress of the hotels," she replied.

For a moment he paid attention to his food. Then he said, "I wonder."

"You'd know better than I do if he has any other reasons." Her curiosity was already aroused.

"I'd like to know what's in his mind. My opinion is that he'd like a closer tie-in with the Carvalho family."

"Because of Selma Carvalho?" Janice queried.

"Selma is only one of several considerations. The Carvalhos are a very important family, extremely wealthy and respected, and they have their fingers in all sorts of pies.

They're connected with the wine trade, of course, but that's only incidental. They own shipping fleets and factories and estates, and, of course, a number of hotels, including those our company is building or rebuilding.''

Janice gave him a surprised look. "I didn't realize that. Oh, so that's why it was important to go to the Carvalho's house to dinner last night.''

"Partly. I think Whitney is aiming at a sort of double harness. Selma's father is probably the most important member of the family—he's chairman of this board and director of that—and there's Selma herself. If Whitney could land the pair, father and daughter, he'd be made for life.''

"Is he in love with Selma?" Janice asked.

"It's difficult to know how much he's attracted to her for the sake of her inheritance. She's marvelous to look at, but naturally Whitney has any number of competitors.''

Janice laughed softly. "I can't imagine Mr. Whitney ever being in love.''

Clive laughed, too. "No, it's a grim thought. You imagine him dishing out orders and instructions all the time and giving the girl an absentminded peck on the cheek when he remembers who she is.''

"Perhaps one day he'll meet his doom," Janice suggested.

"Every man has his weakness somewhere," Clive said. "With him it may be Selma, but I think it's more likely his ambition will drive him to marry into the right sphere, as long as the girl is tolerably presentable.''

Janice found herself faintly disquieted by these cynical remarks from Clive. She had no difficulty in accepting such estimates of Mr. Whitney's aspirations, but did Clive also look to a brilliant marriage to further his own ambitions?

"Well, now that we've got away from Mr. Whitney, don't let's talk about him," she said easily. "Tell me about yourself. What are your ambitions?''

Clive did not reply at once. Then he said, "I've altered my ideas quite a bit since I've been in Portugal. At first I was furious when I was shipped off from London. I was supposed to be promoted, put in charge of part of the Lisbon office and all that, but it seemed like banishment.''

Janice did not mention the gossip he had left behind, but waited for him to go on.

"Now I've begun to make the best of it," he continued. "There might even be more opportunities than I first thought. A great deal depends on what sort of report Whitney sends back to the company in London. It's irritating to think that perhaps my whole future depends on him and what sort of mood he's in when he sends that report."

"At least he's fair," Janice objected. "He wouldn't do anything out of spite."

Clive scoffed. "Oh, wouldn't he? You don't really know him. Whitney can be utterly ruthless when he likes."

She remained silent and Clive put his hand over hers.

"You've nothing to worry about, poppet," he said in a tone that lifted her drooping spirits. "Of all the girls Whitney might have brought with him, you're the one I'm glad he chose."

She laughed lightly. "Is that your stock phrase that you'd have said to whoever the girl was?"

"Not in the least. I mean it, Janice. Oh, I can see that we're going to have good times together, in spite of Lord High and Mighty."

He raised his wineglass to her. "Let's drink to happy times in Lisbon."

When she set down her glass, Clive folded his arms on the table and leaned toward her. "And you know, Janice, you might be very useful to me now that you're working with Whitney."

"How can I help?" she asked.

"Oh, in lots of ways," he replied airily. "At least you could let me know about some of his comings and goings so that I know when you're free."

Janice sighed. She had been afraid that Clive might ask her to hand on confidential information which she would be forced to withhold.

"Would you like to go dancing somewhere?" he asked, when he had paid the bill.

"Yes, I'd like that very much."

He took her to an imposing hotel where the dance floor was on the roof, enclosed on three sides by glass.

"What a wonderful place!" Janice exclaimed, enchanted by the views over the city in so many directions.

"I'm more interested in the view I'm holding in my arms," whispered Clive, as they danced. "You look marvellous in that dress."

"Thank you." Her eyes sparkled with pleasure. "Even Mr. Whitney noticed it, so it must be dazzling."

"Whitney?" echoed Clive, holding Janice away from him almost at arm's length. "What business is it of his what his secretary wears when she's going out?" he demanded with mock indignation. "The man must be falling for you if he notices your clothes."

Janice laughed happily. "I don't think that's likely. It's just a very showy dress, so loud that it talks by itself."

Clive hugged her close to him.

In the taxi going back to her hotel, he held her in his arms and kissed her, tenderly, but with all the practiced art that she knew he possessed.

"Oh, Jan," he whispered. "You must let me take you around everywhere while you're here."

Enclosed within his arms, her head on his shoulder, she murmured, "Yes, Clive. But I shall be in Lisbon only a very few weeks, perhaps only a month. When I'm back in England, you'll forget me," she said with a hint of provocation.

"Never! How could I?" he protested, sealing her mouth with his kisses.

When the taxi drew up at the hotel, Clive said urgently, "See how you're fixed for the weekend. We might be able to go to one of the seaside places. Let me know, darling."

She agreed. She crept quietly into her bedroom, avoiding the sitting room in case Mr. Whitney was there. She was aware that her hair was mussed and that her face probably did not match its immaculate look of the early evening.

Before undressing she stepped out onto her balcony. A few minutes spent in the tranquillity of the gentle night air might calm down her excited senses, her joyful exhilaration at being on such friendly terms with Clive. She refused to dwell on the prospect of returning to England and leaving Clive in Lisbon, ready and willing to take out the next girl who presented herself. After all, she told herself, he had been in the city for more than three months and had evidently not formed any permanent attachment to another girl.

Almost she began to bless, if not deify, Mr. Whitney for his good sense in choosing her to accompany him to Portugal. Lucky chance? Perhaps it was more like fate pointing in the right direction.

She turned to go into her bedroom and noticed that the sitting room and Mr. Whitney's bedroom were both in darkness. Then she saw the glowing tip of a cigarette from the end room, his room, and knew that he had been there in the darkness, waiting no doubt to see if she arrived home by midnight, watching her as she stood on the balcony with the lights of her own room behind her.

It irritated her that he would check so precisely on her movements. Why couldn't he trust her to come home at a respectable hour? She was about to call out a loud "Good night, Mr. Whitney," but prevented herself from revealing that she knew he was there.

Far from tiring her, her evening out with Clive had given her a certain zest, and next morning she was dressed and eating breakfast on her balcony at an early hour.

Yet Mr. Whitney was already in the sitting room sorting out bundles of documents when she entered.

"Ready?" he queried, without looking up.

"Yes," she answered, not quite knowing the exact purpose for which she was to be ready.

"I've ordered a car from our office here. Telephone and see if it has arrived," he said.

After inquiring, she told him that the car was waiting.

"Good. Then we'll be off. Have you everything you want for the day?" he asked.

She picked up the large woven straw handbag she had bought in Lisbon. In addition to her usual cosmetics and personal oddments, it held her notebooks, half a dozen pens, a diary for Mr. Whitney and a steel measuring tape, which he habitually used for checking everyone else's measurements of hotel rooms and equipment.

"D'you want to bring your swimsuit?" he asked. "Or don't you care for the sea?"

"Of course. I didn't know we'd have time for such frivolities." The words slipped out before she could stop them and she shot off into her room to get her bathing things before she could receive his reproving glance.

On the drive through the Lisbon suburbs and out along the coast road to Estoril she remained quiet while Mr. Whitney sat next to her in the back of the car and studied the plans and specifications of the new Hotel Mirador being built at Estoril.

She watched the land on the opposite side of the Tagus estuary slip away until there was only open sea. On the land side there were glimpses of villas half-hidden in the trees, the rising line of distant hills, and everywhere flowers massed in a lovely confusion of colors.

Suddenly Mr. Whitney pushed his papers into a briefcase and stretched his long legs in a relaxed attitude.

"Did Dickson come up to your expectations last night?" he asked Janice abruptly.

Her thoughts had been engrossed with the scenery and his sudden question jerked her back to the reality of answering with some degree of coherence.

"I enjoyed the evening out with Clive," she said as smoothly as she could. She was not going to admit to him that her expectations had been more than fulfilled.

"Where did you go?" he queried.

She wondered if he were really interested or merely wanted to find out where Clive had taken her so that he might have some grounds for criticism or rebuke.

Janice told him about the fish restaurant and later the hotel with the rooftop ballroom.

"Oh, yes, the goldfish bowl." He smiled and added, "Still, it's a very handsome place for dancing."

They had arrived at Estoril, and Janice stepped out onto the dusty rubble surrounding the uncompleted hotel.

The Mirador was not as huge as Janice had expected, especially when she saw the enormous size of some of the new hotels built alongside of the beach.

Mr. Whitney seemed to read her thoughts. "Our idea is to

make this one only a moderate size, large enough to be run efficiently but not so vast that the guests lose their identity and become mere room numbers.''

"Aren't they just room numbers even in a place like this?'' she asked doubtfully. "It's only in small boarding-houses or villas that the management often recognizes the guests.''

Mr. Whitney gave her a sharp glance. "Perhaps you're right, and anyway the holiday population changes too frequently for memorizing.''

"Holiday population explosion,'' she murmured. "I wonder what Estoril was like before the invasion.''

"Oh, it's always been a very elegant resort—fashionable and gay. It has a casino, all-the-year-round attractions, a superb climate and is only fifteen miles from Lisbon. It's expanded considerably, of course, and fast electric trains have taken the place of streetcars along the coast from Lisbon. My mother once told me that a friend recommended the place to her for her honeymoon, but she and my father chose Lucerne.''

Momentarily Janice's thoughts were switched from the beauties of Estoril and its magnificent surroundings to Mr. Whitney's reference to his family. Somehow one tended to believe that Everard Whitney had been born grown-up and executive-minded.

The inspection tour was long and exhausting, and after a couple of hours' plodding from room to room, floor to floor, up and down innumerable stairways, in and out of service elevators, Janice was relieved to sit down outside under a temporary awning.

"You'd better buy yourself a large sunhat of some sort,'' Mr. Whitney advised her. "I don't want you getting sunstroke at some crucial moment.''

"I'll try not to be ill at any time,'' she answered coolly, nettled that his thoughts were always slanted toward his own concerns.

She took a long draft of the iced fruit drink in front of her and watched with amazement a gang of workmen lowering a very tall palm tree into a deep pit.

"How can they plant a tree as tall as that?" she said. "It must be quite old. Won't it die if it's transplanted?"

He shook his head. "That at least is something many countries have learned. It's an expert art, of course, but we don't always have to plant little bushes or saplings and wait fifty years for them to grow."

She watched the crane swinging the carefully wrapped tree into position in what would eventually be the front garden of the hotel.

Elsewhere other men were planting bushes, oleanders, magnolias, and two workmen were experimenting with a small fountain, turning the water on and off, soaking each other to their mutual delight.

On the seaward façade of the hotel, men on scaffolds plastered the outside walls with a pale salmon pink that glowed with color but was less dazzling than stark white.

"White is too eye-wearying," Mr. Whitney remarked when Janice admired the color. "Also the upkeep is more expensive."

After they had finished their drinks he started off again with redoubled energy, but mercifully for only a short spell.

"Now for lunch," he said, and took her to a small restaurant with a cool, shady terrace overlooking a park.

The food and wine restored her vitality and after the meal she suggested that she would take his advice and buy herself a wide-brimmed hat.

The last thing she had expected was that Mr. Whitney would accompany her to the shops, but she relected that he knew them better than she did and also that he could speak fluent Portuguese, although many shopkeepers spoke English or French.

In one shop she tried on several but he shook his head. "Something with a more fluent line," he said, waving his hand to indicate a sweeping curve.

I should have known, she thought, *that he'd see hats in terms of architecture.*

But his advice was useful. Janice was shown a collection of beautiful hats of fine straw with wide curving brims, hats fit to grace a royal garden party as well as serve as beach sunshades.

Unconsciously, as she tried on each one, Janice waited for Mr. Whitney's approval. Finally her choice rested on a hat with a comfortable crown, the brim edged with a fuchsia piping, and wide fuchsia ribbons to tie under the chin, or behind her dark hair.

"Yes, that suits you," Mr. Whitney remarked as she paid the woman and counted her change.

Janice was glad of the wide brim to hide her face, knowing that she was blushing in a most stupid manner, especially as the shopkeeper beamed first at Mr. Whitney, then at Janice, obviously mistaking them for very close friends, if nothing else.

Mr. Whitney's genial mood lasted throughout the afternoon. Janice was pleasantly surprised to find him so relaxed and companionable when they sat together on a small, quieter beach at Cascais, a fishing village beyond Estoril.

"Don't overdo the suntanning," he warned her. "Take it in easy stages."

She nodded, rubbed suntan oil on her legs and lay down on her towel, with the new hat shielding her face.

Covertly she could watch this extraordinary man whose moods changed so rapidly from the censorious businessman to a restful beach companion. She was only now beginning to realize that Everard Whitney did most things according to his own pattern. He worked intensively with demon concentration, but when he took time off he relaxed as easily as a kitten.

Under the hat her mouth twitched in an uncontrollable smile. Likening Mr. Whitney to a playful kitten was a grotesque simile. Sunlight put reddish tints into his chestnut hair and his gray eyes seemed warmed by the Portuguese climate. Certainly she was no longer withered by that cold hard stare nor the uncompromising line of his mouth. It was a firm, sensitive mouth that could close into a ruthless line or smile with upturned corners. His body was already well tanned, and she marveled that he had found time during the English summer to acquire such a golden shade. But perhaps he had already spent short holidays in sunny places.

"What is your ambition?"

His question startled her. She sat up quickly and looked at

him. He had rolled over, one elbow half-buried in the sand, his chin resting on his open hand. For a moment the fleeting expression in his eyes disconcerted her.

"My ambition?" she echoed, playing for time.

"Yes. What d'you want to do with your life? Haven't you any plans at all?" The old impatient, arrogant tone of voice had returned. His eyes were mockingly cold.

Why did he want to know? What business was it of his? Yet she was flattered by his interest.

"Well, I'd like to be a really first-class secretary," she began.

"As a stepping-stone? To what?"

She looked down in her lap. "If you're a good secretary, there are all kinds of opportunities."

He half smiled. "Precisely. Sometimes they lead to foreign travel."

"Yes." She smiled in return. "I was glad to come here with you. One day I'd like to try for a job with one of the world organizations in Geneva or Brussels. I could improve my French."

"No more than that?" he asked. "Doesn't marriage come into your future plans? You're twenty-one."

"It comes into every girl's ideas about her future," she answered slowly.

"And young Dickson? Is he going to be part of your future?"

"Oh, I don't know about that." She moved her head so that her dark hair, loose around her shoulders, swung across her face. "Clive and I are good friends and as he happens to be the only other Englishman I know here in Lisbon, it's natural that we should see each other sometimes, but he knows that I'm not trying to trap him into anything."

How would Mr. Whitney like it, she wondered, if she pried into his plans and ambitions? For instance, was he going to marry Selma Carvalho? Why, he'd freeze at once.

She put on the hat, thus doubly obscuring her face from his searching gaze. For a few moments she stared at the sea, which was almost the same color as her blue swimsuit. Then she decided to go into the rented tent to dress.

When she came out Mr. Whitney had disappeared and

after a while she saw that he was swimming out beyond the raft. Later he came in and dressed quickly in the tent.

"Would you like some tea? We could go to the hotel facing the bay, or there's an English tearoom up the street."

"I prefer Portuguese coffee," she said.

He nodded approval. "One step nearer to becoming the true European?"

She hardly knew how to take that little gibe, but she let it go. It was better to make the most of these rare occasions when Mr. Whitney was in a semiholiday mood. At the bay hotel she yielded to the enjoyment of coffee and pastries on the wide, shaded terrace facing the fishing harbor. Brightly colored boats with high curving prows bobbed on the sparkling water; dark-skinned fishermen mended their nets and paid no attention to the throngs of holidaymakers. Janice almost began to believe that she, too, was on holiday in an idyllic setting and not on a working assignment with a difficult and temperamental employer.

That illusion fell apart on the drive back to Lisbon.

"You haven't a date for this evening, have you?" Mr. Whitney asked.

His negative way of asking the question meant that if she had any plans for the evening's enjoyment she'd better cancel them immediately.

"No. D'you want me to work?" she asked.

"For an hour or two. After that I've a job of my own to do and I shall need the typewriter."

Janice was careful not to show her surprise that apparently he could type, even if it was the two-fingered method adopted by inexpert typists.

"If you go out of the hotel afterward, I'd like to know. I'm not exactly prying, but I feel responsible for you in a foreign city. Don't go roaming about by yourself."

"I'll take the opportunity to have my hair done in the hotel's own salon," she said demurely, but with a slightly sardonic edge to her voice.

She supposed that she ought to take his concern for her welfare as a compliment, yet she chafed at the restrictions he placed on her movements. There were pavement cafés in the streets nearby. What possible harm could come to her if she spent an hour at one of them and watched the world go by?

When she returned to her room after having her hair shampooed and set she went to her balcony, but drew back immediately. Only a few feet away and illumined by the light streaming out from the room behind, Mr. Whitney and Selma Carvalho were sitting in lounge chairs. Their voices came clearly.

"Why did you bring this girl with you?" Selma asked.

"I needed a secretary," was Mr. Whitney's answer.

"She is just a secretary?"

"Of course."

"Surely it would have been more discreet if she were staying in another hotel? Not in the room next to yours."

"Next but one," he corrected.

Selma's laughter floated out on the warm night air. "I think you've brought her here just to spite me," she said. "D'you believe you can make me jealous that way?"

Mr. Whitney's reply was inaudible.

Janice closed her windows as quietly as she could and pulled the curtains across. Mr. Whitney had instructed her to stay in the hotel, but he must not imagine that she was eager to listen to his conversation with the Senhorita Selma.

Yet Janice was undeniably intrigued by the situation. She had already concluded that Mr. Whitney was attracted to Lisbon as much by the beautiful Selma as by the urgency of his company's business affairs.

To marry into the enormous Carvalho empire might be Everard Whitney's present and most cherished ambition.

Evidently Selma was exerting some of her pulling power, for Mr. Whitney announced next morning that he was spending the weekend at the Carvalhos' seaside villa at Guincho.

"I've left you some work on the tape and I'd like you to file these papers in the confidential folders." He handed her a few sheets of foolscap documents. "After that your time's your own. You might like to do some sight-seeing. The hotel reception desk will fix that for you."

Janice was astounded. Only last night he had said she was

not to roam around by herself. Now he was leaving her for a whole weekend, indifferent to what might befall her.

"If you go out at night, I'd prefer you to have an escort," he continued. He gave her a cool smile. "I've no doubt that Dickson might oblige in that way."

"He may have other arrangements," Janice answered stiffly. One minute Mr. Whitney deliberately broke up her outings with Clive, the next he was thrusting her into his company.

"That's possible," Mr. Whitney returned.

As soon as her chief had left the hotel for his weekend jaunt, Janice settled down to polish off the work as quickly as possible. She debated whether to telephone Clive and tell him that she had a free weekend, but hesitated. She preferred the initiative to come from him or he might believe that she was trying to cling to him.

When the telephone rang during the morning, she picked it up eagerly. It was sure to be Clive, who had no doubt heard of Mr. Whitney's absence.

Instead, it was Manoel's voice, offering to take her around sightseeing or for a day at the sea—anything she fancied.

"It would give me much pleasure," he told her warmly. "You will be in safe hands. Even your boss will admit that."

In spite of herself, she smiled. At first she tried to hedge, saying that she was not sure how much time she had, but in the end she agreed to meet Manoel for lunch.

She finished typing the tape, put everything away, then attended to the files. There were various reports on the progress of work on the hotels and the preliminary details of a new hotel to be built on the south side of the Tagus. Then there was the carbon copy of a long two-page report on an unnamed individual.

Janice read the list of faults and omissions and her cheeks burned with indignation. So this was why Mr. Whitney had needed the typewriter last night! To make this utterly damaging report on Clive Dickson! She read:

This man has no sense of responsibility. He is hopeless at even the simplest of coordination tasks .... whole months have been wasted while he has neglected his duties ... the financial side is not above suspicion. It is obvious that he has taken bribes to accept faulty materials. He might do well in some other kind of job, but he is no use to us and I recommend that he be dismissed at the earliest moment, even if that involves the company in compensation for a broken contract. In the long run this would be the cheaper method. ...

The report was comprehensive and every word was an indictment of Clive. Of course there was no name on this carbon copy. Mr. Whitney had taken care of that and filled in Clive's name on the copy sent to the company in London.

Janice sat down on the elegant settee. Mr. Whitney could afford to be at his most charming all day yesterday at Estoril and Cascais, treating her like a holiday companion, helping her to choose a hat and all the rest.

Certainly he had spared her the humiliation of having the report dictated to her and it was too dangerous to put on tape, but now he had gone away for the weekend so that he need not face her for a couple of days.

Her first thought was to telephone Clive and let him know that his world was crumbling under his feet, that his job with the company was practically ended, thanks to a cowardly, arrogant boss sent from England to spy on him. She asked for the number of the Lisbon office, but remembered that, as Mr. Whitney's confidential secretary, she was in a position of trust and couldn't disclose what she knew. She canceled the telephone call.

She regretted now that she had accepted Manoel's invitation to lunch. She needed the day to think out the best course, to try to warn Clive what was in store for him, without actually betraying her chief. She searched her mind for a pretext, but when she telephoned the Lisbon office, she was told that Senhor Dickson was not there today. She knew the name of the small hotel where he lived, but a telephone call there elicited the information that Senhor Dickson was away for the weekend.

Away! Had Clive already got wind of what was to come?

For the moment she could do no more. She filed the appallingly offensive report in the "Confidential: Personnel" folder, and locked it in the spare briefcase.

The telephone rang and reception informed her that Senhor Carvalho was waiting for her. She would be down in five minutes, she said.

She tidied her face and hands, but she had no appetite for lunch or for Manoel's carefree brand of gossip.

CHAPTER THREE

MANOEL TOOK considerable trouble to show Janice some of the sights of his city without reducing her to exhaustion in the afternoon heat. She was aware of his desire to please her, and as she could neither share her worries with him nor get in touch with Clive, by degrees she gave herself up to the enjoyment of the day.

Lunch at the sumptuous Avenida Palace Hotel, a boat trip on the Tagus, a leisurely climb to St. George's Castle—Manoel had mapped it out very well.

"From this point the view over the city and the river is worth the climb," Manoel pointed out, when they had reached the crenellated towers of the old fortress.

Janice agreed with him as she looked down on the clustered roofs below, the wide sweep of the Tagus and the small towns on the other side.

They walked through the flower-filled gardens where peacocks screeched like old women being tortured. Manoel told her interesting scraps of history, of battles and sieges. "Whoever holds this fortress on the hill holds Lisbon," he said.

But there was nothing warlike about the place now as its pale yellow stones slept in the sun.

Manoel suggested that he and Janice should rest for half an hour under the shade of a huge chestnut tree. "Then we will go down to the most interesting quarter of all Lisbon, Alfama, the old Moorish part," he said.

When they left the castle grounds Janice saw that a tiny village square opened out at the foot of the hill. "It could be miles out of town," she said, "right out in the country."

Manoel smiled, pleased that his efforts were meeting with some success.

An ice-cream stall in one corner of the square was surrounded by small children pestering the vendor to let them have popsicles at half price. Janice's faint grasp of Portuguese enabled her to understand part of their clamor.

"Oh, let's treat them for once," she said impulsively, and before Manoel could warn her of the consequences she had gestured to the ice-cream man to serve the children and she would pay.

The man shrugged, convinced that she was yet another mad foreigner, and started to hand out small ice-cream cones and popsicles to a never-ending stream of children who now came running, most of them barefoot, into the square from the streets below.

"There!" exclaimed Manoel, aghast at this treatment of Janice's generosity, "they will come twice or three times and then tell their friends in Benfica." He spoke first to the children, then to the ice-cream vendor, tossed the man a couple of notes, then took Janice's hand and pulled her down the first street from the square.

"I'm sorry about that, Manoel," she apologized. "I thought it would be a little pleasure for them. They look so poor."

She was embarrassed that he had not allowed her to pay.

"They are not so poor as you think," he said tersely. "They run barefoot because shoes are not necessary here, except in the winter, and their clothes are ragged because they climb and fight and tear them."

Janice realized that she had offended him by the implied criticism that the city was overrun by neglected children. "Yes, I can see that they look happy and well fed," she murmured in an attempt to placate him.

They were walking down the steepest, narrowest streets Janice had ever seen. Stairways slanted around unexpected corners, through archways to cobbled courtyards, only to rise again up another flight of stone steps. There were lamps on elegant wrought-iron brackets, lines of washing, lattice windows with flower boxes, even whole walls covered with flowers, and Janice felt that she had left the sophisticated capital city and been transported to this exotic confusion of former mansions and tiny taverns, markets and overhanging balconies.

Manoel guided her through the maze of streets that twisted and spiraled like a town-planner's nightmare until he and Janice came out onto the Santa Luzia belvedere, a wide terrace paneled with handsome glazed tiles. Marble columns supported a trellis covered with bougainvillea and other climbing plants, and Janice was glad to sit on one of the side marble benches in the shade and gaze down on the red and white sea of Alfama houses and, beyond, the blue green Tagus.

"The view from up here gives no idea of what it's really like down on the streets," she said. "If I came alone I should certainly lose my way."

Manoel laughed. "Not really. All you have to do is climb up in any direction until you can see the river."

In the evening they went on the ferry to Cacilhas, a small town on the opposite side of the Tagus.

"When it is really dark," said Manoel, "you will see Lisbon glowing like a million fireflies."

"I've seen more of Lisbon today than in the whole time I've been here," Janice said gratefully.

"Then I don't make too bad a guide?" he queried.

'Excellent," she answered.

But during dinner in the Floresta restaurant she remembered her employer's ruthless methods and that Clive was in peril of being dismissed.

"What are you doing with yourself tomorrow?" Manoel asked when they had finished the meal. "Your boss is safely out of the way."

Janice did not want to appear coquettish, but she hesitated to let Manoel monopolize her time. There was apparently no chance, however, of seeing Clive.

"I hadn't thought of any plans," she answered, "but because I have a free weekend I don't expect you to spend your time with me. I can go sightseeing. I have guidebooks and a map."

He smiled. "Guidebooks and maps are no substitute for a

Lisbon citizen who is only too anxious for you to take up his time."

"Gallantly spoken," she commented. "I thought you might want to spend tomorrow with your family."

"Oh, no. There's nothing to do at our town house and if I go to the villa at Guincho I shall certainly be in the way. Selma will contrive to have Everard in attendance wherever she goes and her sister, Leona, will divide her attention between your English friend Clive and any other young men she may have invited."

"Clive?" Janice echoed. "Is he at your villa?"

"Yes. Leona finds him very attractive, although how long that state of affairs will last remains to be seen. She's quite unpredictable. At the moment she has to prove to her parents and mine that she will never marry me."

Janice was silent for a few moments. So that was where Clive had gone for the weekend. Yet earlier in the week he had promised to spend part of it with Janice if she were free. Was Leona's invitation a sudden last-minute plan?

Then it occurred to her that at the Carvalhos' villa Mr. Whitney would be staying in the same house as the man on whom he had written such a damaging report. How would they face each other? Surely Mr. Whitney would have the decency to tell Clive what was likely to happen, or give him some hint of the situation.

"How long has Clive known your cousin?" she asked.

"Only since she returned from her English school a couple of months ago." Manoel laughed with enjoyment. "She's fighting like a young Amazon to stop her father sending her back there. She hated it, she said. In fact, she told me that rather than go back she would prefer to marry me. So it must have been very tough for her."

But what would happen, Janice reflected, if Clive were recalled to England? Leona might not find her school quite so forbidding.

Janice gladly accepted Manoel's offer of a drive next day over the Arrabida mountains south of the Tagus. There was no sense, she decided, in staying in the hotel to mope. Repeatedly she told herself that she could not expect to be the single object of Clive's undivided devotion. Yet she was hurt that he had not bothered to let her know that he had been invited to the Carvalhos' villa.

She made an effort to enjoy the day and was surprised to find how well she succeeded, remembering Mr. Whitney only when she sat with Manoel on the beach at Portinho where the sea resembled a stretch of blue silk. Thoughts of Clive came into her head only at the end of the day when she was eating the small limpetlike shellfish to which Clive had first introduced her. In spite of her worries she was amused by the notion of connecting Clive only with food.

Next morning, however, the atmosphere was quite different. Mr. Whitney returned from Guincho at eleven and immediately started work on a mass of figures and estimates.

Janice felt that she could hardly bear to be in the same room with him, but since he required her to check quantity specifications and lists of material with him she had no choice. Twice she had tried to telephone Clive at the Lisbon office and at his hotel, but he had apparently not yet put in an appearance at either place.

"Did you enjoy yourself with Manoel?" her chief asked abruptly when they had stopped work to take a breather on the balcony and share a pot of coffee.

"Yes, I did," she acknowledged. "I suppose the Carvalhos have a grapevine."

Everard Whitney laughed. "Very little goes on in that family that isn't immediately known to all of them. Manoel isn't a bad chap and he'll be quite pleased to take you about and entertain you lavishly. He'll end up, of course, by marrying his cousin Leona to cement the family alliances yet more strongly."

Janice gave him a sidelong glance. "Am I being warned not to take him too seriously?" she queried, with a smile. "I didn't think we'd be here long enough for me to form any violent attachments."

Mr. Whitney put down his coffee cup and faced her with an amused, interested expression. "I think coming to Lisbon has had a good affect upon you. You're more self-assured and independent."

It was not very self-assured, she thought, to feel herself

blushing at this unexpected compliment, if that was what it was. In some of his moods Mr. Whitney was a man one could almost like, but then his next words recalled her to the thorny situation that existed.

"I suppose you didn't see anything of Dickson during the weekend?"

"No. I understood he was a guest of the Carvalhos." She spoke stiffly, wondering what he was up to now.

"Yes, Leona invited him. I think he's often been to their house in Lisbon, but I was surprised to find him at Guincho."

That must have been an unpleasant shock for you, she thought with some satisfaction.

"Did you know about it?" he continued.

"Not until Manoel told me," she answered.

Was he using some subtle means of inducing her to inform him in advance of Clive's movements? If so, he would find her very noncommunicative.

But he said no more on the subject and the rest of the day passed in hard work with a short siesta in the afternoon.

Mr. Whitney went out before dinner, and as Janice was taking a shower, she heard her bedroom telephone ringing.

"Darling!" came Clive's voice, when she answered. "Is His Lordship there?"

"No. He's gone out. I don't know where or for how long."

"Listen, sweet. Can you meet me and we'll have a meal somewhere?"

"Yes, of course. Where?" She longed to see him, although she dreaded what effect the news of his impending dismissal might have had on him, for surely he knew by now of Mr. Whitney's ruthless decision. Yet she could disclose nothing and was powerless to help him.

"Come down to Black Horse Square and take the ferry to Cacilhas. You know the quay?" he asked.

"Yes. Any particular time?"

"As soon as you can. I've news. Can't stay now. 'Bye, darling."

She was mystified. Whatever his news, he seemed in a

cheerful mood, but why didn't he want to come to the hotel or even meet her in the foyer of a restaurant?

She was glad that by the time she left the hotel Mr. Whitney had not returned. She took a taxi to Black Horse Square, the nickname given by the English to the elegant Praça do Comercio facing the river. The ferry boats were crowded with people going home from work. She was not sure whether Clive meant to meet her here on the Cacilhas side, but she pushed her way onto a boat as soon as she could and stood in the bow so that she could see him if he were already on the quay.

He emerged from nowhere, it seemed, as she stepped off the gangway.

"What's the mystery?" she asked. "I've always heard that Lisbon was a center of intrigue, but—"

"Let's go up the street," he interrupted, and took her arm. "Good news should be told over a bottle of wine."

He led her across the square and up a winding street to a café. A narrow staircase provided access to a balcony with three or four umbrella-shaded tables overlooking the street. As soon as he had ordered wine he leaned on his folded arms and said to Janice, "I said there were plenty of opportunities here, and I was right. I've landed—or I think it's pretty certain—a new job." His eyes shone and he was smiling.

Instantly Janice's fears leaped to her mind. "A new job?"

He raised a finger in caution as the waiter brought a bottle of *faisca* and poured the slightly sparkling wine into their glasses.

"Cheers! *A vossa saude! Skoal* and *prosit* and all the rest of the good-health jargon. I'm joining the Carvalhos' organization."

For the moment she could say nothing, for too many conflicting thoughts were chasing through her mind.

"Well? Haven't you anything to say?" he chided her. "Aren't you going to wish me luck?"

"Of course!" She raised her glass. "Best of luck!"

"This is going to be my big chance, Janice," he spoke rapidly. "I've just been marking time messing about in the London company. But here I've had a chance to learn

Portuguese, not that I speak it very well, but enough to get along with. I've seen the methods used here and I've a bit of know-how of my own. I've been offered a job in their wine-shipping company. That'll suit me fine, with a few trips now and again to their various *quintas* to break the monotony."

"It sounds wonderfully interesting," Janice murmured, managing a smile with her cold lips and hoping that it disguised the bleakness she felt.

"There's one snag," Clive continued, barely noticing her comment. "I have a two-way contract with our company in London and I don't know whether they'll release me as soon as I want. D'you think you could put in a good word for me there, Janice?"

She gasped. It was obvious that he did not yet know of Mr. Whitney's report or that the contract might be terminated.

"I wouldn't think there'd be any trouble about that," she said guardedly.

"Whitney's been anxious to get rid of me ever since he came to Lisbon. I've always known that I could expect no favors from him. He's probably sent back a scathing report on me already."

"Then a bad report wouldn't be a blow to you now, would it?"

Clive looked intently at her. "You mean he has already done that? Oh, good! That's going to let me out in the best possible way."

"But, Clive, I didn't mean that—I was only thinking that you're not altogether dependent—that you've something else in view." She tried desperately to retrieve that neutral standpoint that she had momentarily forsaken.

But Clive was in full flow again, bubbling over with accounts of what the new job would mean in terms of status as well as hard cash. "I'll be able to run a car of my own, live in a decent apartment or flat somewhere instead of my back-street hotel. As for Whitney, the tables are going to be turned on him." Clive's handsome face took on an expression of slightly malevolent triumph. "He's been able to tread me down in the past, but in the future he'll need to be more careful." Clive suddenly exploded with laughter. "Oh,

I'd give anything to see his face when he finds that I've gone over to the firm who are virtually his bosses here!''

Janice was bewildered at the speed with which Clive was rushing into the future, even if only in his mind. He had not yet left one company to start with the other.

"Does this mean that you'll stay permanently in Portugal?" She forced herself to ask the direct question without circling around it first.

He stroked his chin thoughtfully. "Not altogether, perhaps. I don't know." He shrugged. "Actually, I might stay here for a year or two, and then go off somewhere else. Of course, I'm glad now that I was practically banished—exiled, in fact. I might have been stuck in London until it was time to retire and draw my pension. This way I shall see something of the world apart from the odd fortnight's holiday in Majorca or Tunisia."

"Perhaps you're the rolling-stone type," she said quietly.

"Maybe," he conceded. "I'm not as old as Whitney, and he doesn't want to settle down anywhere yet." He laughed again. "What a lark it would be if eventually the fair Selma tied the noose around his neck! He'd become one of the Carvalho family. He'd probably have to change his name to theirs anyway, instead of the other way around."

Clive's attention was caught by someone below in the street and he waved. "Come on up!" he cried.

Janice wondered who the newcomer might be and if Clive wanted her to leave.

Leona Carvalho emerged from the top of the staircase and Clive stood up to greet her.

"You know Leona, I think, Janice," he said. "Miss Janice Bowen from England."

Leona inclined her head. "We have officially met," she said in cool, precise tones, "and I have heard much about you from many quarters."

"Oh?" Janice raised her eyebrows. "I hope nothing that was bad."

Leona's initial primness vanished. She giggled. "It's extraordinary that English girls want to be regarded as very wicked and shocking, and for most of them it is quite impossible."

Clive ordered more wine and Leona sat next to him, almost dismissing Janice from the scene.

Leona wore a smart two-piece of strawberry pink, the collar edged with a narrow band of dark fur. She was evidently the type who could take a golden suntan without looking like café au lait. Her hair was intensely dark, but not quite black, for it held brown gleams. Now she flashed on Clive the full force of her beautiful dark brown eyes as she spoke rapidly to him in a voice deliberately hushed, but intense and vibrant.

"I've been telling Janice about—about the new venture," Clive said, trying to draw Janice back into the threesome.

Leona frowned. "But it was to be a secret!" she exclaimed. "You told me that nobody was to know yet."

Clive smiled indulgently. "Oh, yes, I know. But Janice is different. She's closely connected with all that goes on."

Leona glanced swiftly in Janice's direction, an appraising look as though to weigh her value. "Naturally she works for Everard and therefore knows his secrets." She turned toward Clive. "But you should be careful," she told him, "that you are not giving away information that might be useful to your enemies."

Clive flung back his head and laughed. "Oh, Leona! You talk like a very bad spy novel. What d'you think Janice is? A double agent?"

The carelessly spoken words struck Janice like the point of a dagger. Double agent? She was now beginning to see that she might be in a very dangerous position, and Clive's next words served only to make that situation clearer still.

"Actually Janice has been very helpful," he said. "I may be able to clear matters up much sooner than I thought, thanks to her."

"But I haven't done anything really," she protested, trying yet again to disavow that she had given him any real information.

"Well, it will all come right in the end, and very soon, too," Clive said comfortably, refilling all the glasses with wine. "We must eat. What would you like, Janice?"

She shrugged. "I leave it to you. You will know better what this café serves."

"Oh, but we're not eating here!" Leona's voice was shocked. "Clive will take me to the Floresta."

"I'm taking you both to the Floresta," Clive said firmly, and Janice was grateful for that little gesture of inclusion when Leona was so determined to cold-shoulder her.

All the same it was not a merry meal, for Janice had little appetite, but as Leona talked to Clive throughout the meal about people and parties and happenings of which Janice had no knowledge, the other two did not notice her silence.

"When do you go back to England?" Leona turned suddenly to Janice.

"Nothing has been decided yet," Janice answered, aware that she was being warned not to linger. "Mr. Whitney will probably let me know when the work is finished here."

"Of course, it is tempting to stay in Lisbon," Leona said with a sweeping gesture of her hand that nearly sent the wine bottle off the table. "Our climate is very attractive, and yours is not good."

"I gather you don't like England?" queried Janice, refusing to be thrust aside by this spoilt younger daughter of a wealthy family.

Leona shrugged. "It has some advantages, perhaps. London has some interesting buildings and there is much entertainment going on—but oh, it is so cold everywhere in your country. It is winter all the time or else it is raining."

"English schools think it's good for our morale not to have too much central heating," Janice returned.

But Leona was now bored with the conversation and turned her attention to Clive.

Leona had parked her car in the open space near the quay and grudgingly offered Janice a lift back to Lisbon. She drove very fast but with confidence and skill, and slowed down only on approaching the new bridge over the Tagus, opened only a few weeks before.

Clive sat in front with Leona. Janice in the back watched the wide panoramic view of the sparkling piece of jewelry that was Lisbon, the dark curving sweep of the river, and the colossal illuminated statue of *Christ the King*. She was still wondering what purpose Clive had in asking her to meet him in Cacilhas to give her news of his new job and then confronting her with Leona Carvalho. Leona's arrival had been no chance meeting, for she had known exactly where to find Clive.

It now occurred to Janice that perhaps he had telephoned Leona asking her to meet him in Cacilhas at an obscure café, but had not disclosed that Janice would also be there. What was he trying to do?

If he had succeeded in entering the Carvalhos' business organization through Leona's efforts, was he demonstrating to her that he had certain other interests outside the firm and that one of them was Janice?

Alternatively, and Janice had already convinced herself of this, it was more likely that he was proving to her that he was on very cordial terms with Leona Carvalho and trying to show all that might mean to his future progress.

Janice felt extremely depressed. Leona dropped her outside her hotel, but Clive reentered the car and gave her a cheery "Good night" and a smile before Leona impatiently drove away, no doubt to a café or nightclub or some other place where they could be alone without Janice's restricting presence.

Yet as she prepared herself for bed, Janice had to admit to herself that her own thoughts had not been too creditable, for if Clive had been sent back to England she would also have been there after Mr. Whitney's business trip was over. It was unworthy of her to believe that perhaps she might have profited by Clive's setback. In her mind she knew she was flattering herself, for in England there would be formidable competition against her.

For a couple of days she was still extremely nervous in case Clive had already involved her in wanting to be released from his contract, but nothing happened and on the last day of August she was lifted out of her low spirits.

Mr. Whitney handed her a salary slip and she was astounded at what seemed to her a huge amount. In London her salary had been reasonable, even high, for a secretary of her age, but this was nearly double.

"It's wonderfully generous," she said. "Thank you very much indeed."

He permitted himself a small, friendly grimace. "Well, you've worked well and at all kinds of hours. Perhaps I'll demand even more of you in future."

"I'll be willing," she promised. At this moment she would have worked all around the clock to please him.

"Your hotel and other expenses here cost you nothing, but part of that sterling amount will have to be credited to you at home," he explained. "I've opened an account for you with the Bank of London and South America—they have an office close by—and they will deal with all the currency regulations for you, provide you with travelers' checks and so on."

"Oh, thank you. That's very helpful of you." She gave him a shy, upward glance. He smiled, and in his gray eyes was an expression of indulgent amusement.

"I've sized you up," he said, "and I thought you'd prefer to be independent about your spending money rather than have to ask me for a handful of escudos every other day."

"Yes, your guess was accurate," she agreed.

For the rest of the day she was in high spirits and longed to tell someone of her good fortune, but there was only Clive and she had heard nothing from him since that meeting in Cacilhas. She did not even know if he were working every day at the Lisbon office or had already left. Even Manoel failed to contact her, although after the previous bout of sight-seeing he had promised to telephone her.

Several times she accompanied Mr. Whitney to the Castelo hotel that was being rebuilt and worked with him over the figures and estimates.

It was only afterward that she realized that this short peaceful period was the flat calm that presaged a storm.

Janice was finishing a long report that Mr. Whitney had put on tape, when he came striding into the hotel sitting room.

She glanced up and quailed before the angry glare in his eyes, the tight set of his mouth. He had spent the morning at the docks supervizing the unloading of a shipment of electrical fittings and she wondered what catastrophe had happened there to put him in such a furious temper.

"Miss Bowen!" he shouted, although he was only a yard

away from her. "Where is the confidential file on personnel?"

"In the special briefcase," she answered, but the color had fled from her cheeks.

"Then get it for me," he snapped.

She unlocked the case, took out the file and handed it to him.

"Is this the report you filed last week?" he demanded.

She nodded dumbly.

"Then read it—unless you're already so familiar with it that you know it by heart."

She took the carbon copy, but the words blurred before her eyes.

"Do you see a name mentioned there?" he asked.

"No."

"Then whom did you think it referred to?"

"I—I don't know," she muttered.

"That's a lie!" he retorted. "You thought you knew. You jumped to the conclusion that it was Dickson, didn't you?"

"Yes, I did."

"Exactly. Will you please look at the reference number at the top of that report. Well? What does it say?"

She saw the figures "1593. L."

"If you'd ever paid the slightest attention to the Lisbon office file, you'd have known that the number referred to Alfonso Columbano, the head clerk in that office."

Janice gasped. She remembered how eagerly Clive had seized on that half-sentence in the café at Cacilhas.

Everard Whitney began to stride around the room. "You're so infatuated by Dickson that you'll go to any length to bolster him up, even when it's not necessary. Did you telephone him as soon as I had left for Guincho?"

"No." She recalled, though, that she had indeed attempted to do so, but failed to get in touch with Clive only because he had already gone to the Carvalhos' villa at Guincho.

"Then you must have been in touch with him since then or in some other way." He flung the words savagely at her.

"No, I did not tell him!" His furious anger was already stiffening her resistance and she knew it would be fatal to cringe before this fierce, relentless man who brushed aside denials and excuses as though they had not been spoken.

"Then why does Dickson come to me with a tale that he can break his contract with us because I've already sent to England a report that's a virtual dismissal?"

Janice saw now where her unthinking words had led her. She had let slip a couple of phrases intended to buoy up Clive and he had completely misconstrued them into a definite loophole for his own ends.

It was useless to reiterate her denials. Between them, the two men had trapped her into an awkward position.

"Dickson was expressly sent to the office here to keep men like Columbano in order and see that all the rest of the staff did their work properly. He's been as bad as the rest, and everything has been neglected." Everard Whitney flung himself into a chair. "Now," he continued, "I'd be glad to get rid of them both, Dickson and Columbano, but I'm not sure which I can let go first. If Columbano were efficient, I could easily spare Dickson. In fact, he need never have been sent here, but I can't do without both together until I can get adequate replacements."

He was on his feet again, restlessly pacing between the balcony and the sitting-room door. "You've created a situation of havoc, Miss Bowen," he stormed. "I shall probably have to stay in Lisbon much longer than I intended."

When she remained silent, he came toward her and towered menacingly over her. "That may suit you very well, and you'll no doubt be pleased to have opportunities to see Dickson, but it interferes with my plans."

"I'm sorry if I've failed you, Mr. Whitney," she managed to say at last.

"Don't you understand? You're in a position of trust. I must compel absolute secrecy. I told you in the first place that I didn't want emotional tangles or complications. Yet since you've been here you've let Dickson pick you up whenever he had nothing better to do or wanted some information out of you."

"Oh, no, Mr. Whitney, Clive has never asked me for any information of any kind," she protested.

Everard's mouth curved in a sneer. "Unnecessary! He had only to channel the conversation in the right direction and you'd tell him all he wanted to know."

Cold shivers ran down her spine. She couldn't believe that Clive had been deliberately prodding her into admissions.

There was a long silence, but the room seemed to echo with taunts and accusations.

At last he said, "Miss Bowen, you have your choice. You can either go home on the first available plane and I'll do without help until I can get another girl—" he paused "—or you can continue here until my job is finished if I have some assurance of your complete integrity. My kind of work is too important to be at the mercy of a girl's infatuation, particularly when a man like Dickson is involved, and more essential still, if and when he gets this job with the Carvalhos that he boasts is coming up."

Every word he said hurt her like a whiplash. How could she continue to work for this tyrant who showed no mercy for moments of human weakness, who believed what suited him just as much as Clive?

"Take the afternoon off and think it over, Miss Bowen," he said more quietly. "We'll have dinner here tonight—unless of course you have a date with Dickson—and you can tell me your decision. Whichever way it is, I'll accept it."

His brutal tone stirred all Janice's resentment. She would meet his challenge with her own.

She stood up. "I don't need the afternoon off, Mr. Whitney," she said in a tensely controlled voice. "I can give you my answer now. I'll stay."

For a moment their glances met across the room, opponents measuring each other's stamina. Everard Whitney's cool gray eyes momentarily softened. She could not be sure, but she imagined that his mouth lifted in the hint of a smile. A smile of triumph? Or mere satisfaction in her defeat?

CHAPTER FOUR

EVERARD WHITNEY'S THREAT—it could scarcely be termed an invitation—that Janice was to have dinner with him that evening in their suite was not fulfilled. She could have made only a pretense of eating, anyway.

His anger had quietened down when he returned to the hotel about six o'clock and he spoke quite mildly to Janice about the work in hand.

After a shower, she put on a primrose-yellow dress of fine cotton, its only decoration bands of horizontal tucking. The sitting room was empty and Mr. Whitney called from the balcony.

"Out here!"

He handed her a martini, mixed a drink for himself and sat absorbed reading the Lisbon evening paper. Below in the street the traffic hummed, and the cool breeze that swirled through Lisbon's valleys every night toward sunset was pleasant after the day's heat. Only the atmosphere between Janice and her chief was tensely watchful and subdued.

The silence was shattered by an exclamation from the interior of the sitting room. "Oh, there you are, Everard! I thought there was no one at home."

Selma Carvalho came out to the balcony as Everard rose to his feet.

"I'd no idea—" he began.

"Oh, I thought it was time I came to prize you out of your hermit existence." Selma broke off to glance disdainfully at Janice. "At least you always *claim* that you're busy working."

"I think you've met my secretary," Everard said coolly.

"Have I?" Selma shrugged her beautiful shoulders. She was wearing a turquoise evening dress, low cut with gossamer shoulder straps, the bodice thickly embroidered with crystal beads that flashed and sparkled like splinters of ice. Her pale gold hair was dressed high in a sculptured chignon held in place by a jeweled band.

Janice decided that it was not her place to remind the Senhorita Carvalho of the previous meeting in the Carvalhos' town house. "Good evening, Senhorita Carvalho," she said politely.

Selma smiled coldly and turned away toward Everard, who was bringing a third chair out to the balcony.

"Janice, will you get a drink for Miss Carvalho?" he said, as Selma settled herself in the cushioned chair.

"Certainly," she answered quickly. "What would you like?"

Selma stretched one hand behind her head. "Everard knows what I like. He's just being lazy."

"Benedictine and brandy, half and half," he whispered to Janice. "And a dash of Angostura."

Janice hurried into the room to prepare Miss Carvalho's favorite beverage.

"Quite the little handmaiden, isn't she?"

Janice heard Selma's sarcastic voice behind her, but she could not catch Mr. Whitney's reply if he made one. Then suddenly she stopped in midstir and stared into the swirling golden liquids in the tall glass. Mr. Whitney had called her Janice. Until now he had never used her Christian name, not even on that day at Estoril when they had bathed and sat on the beach. Mr. Whitney did not lightly shed the conventions with his clothes.

Janice blinked, shook herself back into her immediate surroundings and took the drink out to Selma.

She hovered uncertainly in the sitting-room doorway, not knowing whether to go away or stay, but she was sure that there would be no dinner-for-three in the suite tonight. Selma had not come dressed in an exquisite gown merely to sit in an hotel suite with Everard accompanied by his secretary.

"Go and get yourself dressed, Everard," Selma ordered when she had tasted her drink and made a wry face for Janice's benefit.

Mr. Whitney was comfortably attired in dark trousers and a white shirt.

"Later," he said. "Unless you're going to an embassy ball?"

"You're driving me out to the Estoril-Sol," she said lazily, with an upward provocative glance.

"Oh? Am I? Who else is in the party?"

"Just you and me," Selma replied.

"Supposing I have business matters to attend to?" He gazed down on Selma and smiled.

"This is important business," she retorted. "There's someone I want you to meet at the Estoril-Sol."

She was irresistible, thought Janice, and she knew it.

Everard Whitney shrugged, bowing apparently to the inevitable.

Janice hastily withdrew into the sitting room out of the way, and when Mr. Whitney came in she said quickly, "If you don't mind, I think I'll go out for a walk before dinner."

He nodded. "Yes. I have to go out, as you see."

But there was no smile on his face as he went into his bedroom.

Janice walked in the Edouard VII park, glad enough to have escaped from an uncomfortable meal with her chief. Let him take out the glamorous Selma. Perhaps the evening in her company would soothe him and make him less contentious tomorrow. Yet Janice felt a wisp of scorn that so forceful, so domineering a man as Everard Whitney should capitulate so easily to a pretty woman. Then she remembered that Selma was a Carvalho and even if she had been grotesquely ugly, the family backing would no doubt have made her attractive to many men.

Janice was in two minds whether to have a snack at the park café and pass a little time watching the people. Then she decided to return to the hotel, have dinner in the restaurant and go to bed early and read.

As she left the restaurant and crossed toward the elevator, someone touched her elbow.

"Clive!" she exclaimed as she spun around. "Where did you spring from?"

"I was waiting for you to finish your dinner," he explained.

"Have you had yours?"

He shook his head. "I'll have something later. Let's go in the bar."

They sat at a corner table and he ordered brandies.

Janice was being cautious this time and waited for him to start the real conversation after the small talk.

"What was the old man like today?" Clive asked after a long pause.

Janice regarded him steadily. "If you mean Mr. Whitney, he was in a boiling rage and took it out on me. You let me down, Clive."

"I? How was that?"

"Over your contract. Mr. Whitney thinks I told you about a bad report on you."

Clive frowned with perplexity. "Well, I didn't even mention you. All I said to Whitney was that if he was sending an unfavorable report on me, that would let me out of the contract. I still don't know whether he has or hasn't."

"But you jumped to the conclusion that it had been sent," Janice pointed out, aware that she had also fallen into the same trap.

Clive gave her a deprecating smile. Then he looked away and down into his brandy glass. "You must admit, Jan, that you did give me that impression."

"Indeed I did not," she protested. "You grasped at a half sentence because you wanted it to fit in with your new plans. Mr. Whitney was so furious with me that he offered me the choice of going home immediately—"

"But no, Janice! You can't do that!" Clive's alarm surprised her.

"What difference would it make to you if I went home to England tomorrow?" she asked, longing to hear his answer that he did not want to be parted from her.

"Well, it would, er, matter quite a lot. I mean I would feel that I'd upset your job and lost you the chance of an extra bit of near holiday in a nice climate."

Janice wanted to say, *No more than that?*

Clive leaned nearer to her. "Besides, I might want your help soon."

"How?" she queried, alerted to danger.

"Oh, I don't know," he answered casually. "You never know what's going to crop up, and I'd be glad to have you around."

"Thank you," she said stiffly. "You talk as though I were a handy little tool on a work bench."

Clive laughed delightedly. "Don't bridle, darling. You're no handy little tool. You're a spirited little pony."

"I don't know that you've improved matters comparing me to a horse. I'm tired and I was intending to have an early night. I'll say good-night, Clive."

"No, don't do that." He was on his feet in an instant. "Let's go out somewhere. Would you like to hear some *fado* singing? I know several good places, quite respectable."

Janice was torn between maintaining her pride and wanting his company.

"Would you take Leona there?" she asked.

His face showed complete surprise. "I couldn't take her anywhere alone, not even to this five-star luxury hotel. No girls of good Portuguese families are allowed to go out to dinner or anywhere else unchaperoned."

"And Selma? Is she different?" Janice was careful not to mention that her employer had been bulldozed into taking Selma to Estoril.

"Not in the least. I happen to know already that she came to collect Whitney tonight, but she's sure to have told him that others will be in the party. Otherwise he wouldn't have taken the risk of offending her parents. Selma knows, though, that she has only to bring an acquaintance to the table, chat with him for a few seconds, then she can have Whitney to herself for the rest of the time. But she wouldn't be seen dining alone with him here in Lisbon."

"Was that why Leona could come to see you in Cacilhas?" Janice asked. "Did you tell her I would be there?"

"Certainly."

"But you didn't tell me," she retorted.

"There was no need. Actually, Leona would have risked it in a small café on the other side of the river."

After a few moments, Janice said, "I don't think I fancy the idea of being chaperone."

"Don't be so silly. You and I are different. We're English and no one takes any notice of us. Come, let's go to hear the *fado*."

On the way to the Machado, Clive explained that the "*fado*" was a typical Portuguese folk song, a lament against fate, a nostalgic yearning.

The big room was filled with plain chairs and tables. On a low dais sat two men: one with a Spanish guitar, the other nursing a six-stringed *guitarra*; one instrument for the melody, the other for the strumming accompaniment.

A woman, clad in black and with a black shawl, stepped onto the platform and put one hand on the guitarist's shoulder as though she were a sad and tragic outcast who needed support. When she sang her voice held all the sorrow of the world; it would have been sorrowful in any language and it was unnecessary to understand Portuguese to comprehend her grief.

After three songs she received the applause and chatted to the musicians and friends in the audience; then she sang a second group of songs, even more mournful than the first.

There was nothing of the gaiety and dramatic color of Spanish flamenco about these performances, thought Janice. In a way, the melancholy heartsickness of the atmosphere was more attuned to her present mood than a gloriously joyful evening would have been.

About midnight Janice asked Clive if they could leave. "I have to be up early in the morning," she said, "unlike you who can stroll into your offices at any hour. I work on the premises where I live."

"That has advantages," he answered, giving her hand a light squeeze. "How much longer I shall be occupying my desk in the Lisbon office is anyone's guess. If you could do anything for me when Whitney is in a good frame of mind—"

"Clive, I'm too tired to go into all that again," she said

wearily. He seemed to have no idea of the intensity of Mr. Whitney's anger.

Wisely, Clive said no more, but when they were in the taxi returning to her hotel, he took her gently in his arms and kissed her with tenderness.

"You worry too much about business affairs," he told her soothingly. "Don't take everything so seriously or you'll be an old woman before your time."

"It's not so easy for me," Janice said, half sobbing. "You don't have to—"

"Here, you've got the wrong idea!" he contradicted. "In a year or so you'll get married, say goodbye to typewriters and all that, but I've got to make a living somehow. How can it be so easy for me?"

"Yes, perhaps you're right," she sighed, disengaging herself gently from his embrace.

"Look, if we're both free this weekend, how about coming to Cascais or Sesimbra or somewhere with me on Sunday? We could buy a picnic lunch probably and swim and laze and have a nice time. How about it?"

"I'll have to let you know," she temporized, unwilling to commit herself.

"Don't be a goof and throw away chances of a bit of pleasure just for the sake of Whitney and his slave driving. Besides, you want to make the most of being in a country where the weather's reliable. None of this—'oh, we'll see if it's fine on Sunday'—it won't rain here until October, if then."

Just before she stepped out of the taxi, she turned to him. "I suppose you're not also inviting Leona so that I can act as her chaperone?"

Clive pulled her against him and kissed her full on the mouth. "You're sweet, Jan, but you're a terror for being jealous. All right, I'll assure you. We won't tell Leona a word about it. It shall be a dark secret just between us. Good-night, darling."

In her room she pottered in and out of the bathroom and finally flung herself into bed with a long sigh of relief. It had been an exhausting day, mentally and emotionally, and now that she was alone her despondency returned. She had been so happy about the large increase in her salary, more so because it meant that Mr. Whitney was satisfied with her than merely because of the extra money. Now she felt she had let him down, although in her turn she could not be sure that Clive had not done the same to her.

Clive puzzled her. As she lay in bed pondering over his conversations, seeing again the fleeting expressions on his handsome face, the gleams of fun or tenderness in his eyes, she wondered how much any girl meant to him at this period in his career. He chose his girl friends so that they could be of use to him. There was Leona who had been able to draw him into the Carvalho organization. Janice was probably useful only in being close to Mr. Whitney and knowing his intentions, although her guesswork about Clive's contract had proved utterly disastrous.

A good night's sleep, a sunny morning and the pleasure of taking breakfast on her balcony refreshed Janice considerably. She sniffed the cool morning air and was glad that Mr. Whitney had chosen such a heavenly climate for this trip abroad. A drizzily day in England would have been depressing.

Even Mr. Whitney himself was in better spirits and temper, but probably that was the result of his evening out with Selma.

Halfway through the morning's work, he stood up, ruffled his thick chestnut hair, and walked toward the open sitting-room windows leading to the balcony.

"You all right this morning, Janice?" he queried.

She glanced up, wondering what had given him the impression that she was not all right. "Yes, thank you," she said.

"I'm sorry I pitched into you like that yesterday," he said quietly. "I admit I was pretty mad at the way things had turned out, but there was no justification for saying what I did. You were not the only one to blame."

She stared at him, hardly daring to believe that he was actually apologizing for storming at her.

"I think you were justified in putting at least part of the blame on me," she said. If he could be magnanimous, then so could she. "I guessed badly and jumped to a wrong conclusion, but I didn't tell Clive anything."

He nodded. "No, I believe that. Dickson is capable of twisting any little half-phrase to his own advantage."

He came around the back of the chair and put a hand lightly on her shoulder. "So I'll apologize for my rough treatment. But you will be very careful what you say to outsiders, won't you?"

She gave him a weak smile. She knew she was trembling and her hands felt cold, in spite of the warm, sunny morning.

"Yes, I'll be careful," she said, schooling herself to speak calmly. But she was not referring only to business matters.

He moved to his chair opposite her and picked up some papers from out of a file. Then he grinned. "It was just as well that we didn't have dinner together last night. You might have thrown the food at me."

For some time he was silent. Janice was grateful for a few moments' breathing space, for she was deeply disturbed by Everard Whitney's touch. It was not possible, she told herself, aware of the deafening clamor of her thoughts. It was absurd, ridiculous, any adjective one could think of. To fall in love with one's boss was a worn-out cliché, a hackneyed, trite situation that most girls at least guarded against. If it happened, then sensible girls recognized it as a worthless infatuation born of propinquity and a common interest in a particular kind of work.

If it had been mere infatuation that she felt for Clive, it had never frightened her. She had usually been happy in his company and had always looked forward with delighted anticipation to meeting him. But now, with this new strange emotion for Everard Whitney surging over her, she knew she was afraid. She recoiled from a lonely future without Everard. Love had crept up beside her, without her knowing it, until she was forced to face the bitter fact of a one-sided devotion.

She was nearly blinded by tears as her fingers struck the typewriter keys. She made mistakes, and on the pretext of searching for another eraser, she managed to blink away the threatening overflow, blow her nose and at least try to appear the normal, efficient secretary with no ardent designs on her chief.

Mr. Whitney was engrossed in a long report and for a time he turned the pages, and made notes in the margins.

"And what did you do with yourself last night after all?" he asked suddenly, without looking up.

"I had dinner down in the restaurant here," she answered.

"Did you see Dickson?" He was looking at her now across the table.

Her sherry-brown eyes met his cool gray stare with honesty mingled with a touch of bravado. "Yes, I did," she answered. "I met him downstairs in the hotel after dinner." If he were going to catechize her, it would be preferable to tell him everything voluntarily. "He took me to a café where there was *fado* singing."

"I see." He put the tips of his fingers together. "I hope he came to make amends for landing you in a mess."

Janice was uncertain how to reply. If she admitted that she and Clive had touched on business matters, Mr. Whitney would seize the chance again of warning her not to discuss anything with Clive. By the time she had thought of an innocuous reply, he was speaking again.

"For the time being, I'd rather you didn't meet Dickson," he said. "It may not be possible for you to avoid him altogether, but at least you need not accept his invitations or go out to places with him."

Janice flushed. "I would have done that in the first place, Mr. Whitney, if you had instructed me that you didn't want me to meet Clive socially." The words rolled out before she could stop them, or before she could control the fiery, resentful tone of her voice. "There's no need to treat me like a schoolgirl forbidden to meet a boyfriend outside the school gates!"

"The fact that you're so easily offended over him seems to indicate that your emotions are not very stable where he's concerned," he said, and there was almost a sneer in his tone. "Surely you can see that if I've decided to let him go to Carvalhos as soon as he likes and if I keep Columbano for the time being, the position could have its dangers. I don't want it said or hinted that I let my secretary act as a companionable go-between now that Dickson is going to work for the Carvalhos, in the hope of getting information that might be useful."

She raised a startled face, but before she could speak, he continued, "I can see that you hadn't thought of that possibility. But it exists, I assure you."

She looked down at her hands in her lap. "Very well, Mr. Whitney, I'll do as you ask. I certainly don't want to get involved in any secret-agent intrigue."

He began to chuckle, and she stared resentfully at him. How dared he laugh at her when she had knuckled under to him in the most humiliating way?

"I wouldn't put it on the high plane of international espionage," he murmured. "All I'm asking for is a little discretion in your choice of escorts on your outings."

This time she could not trust herself to speak, for it seemed that whatever she said could be twisted to suit Mr. Whitney's purpose. Obviously, men were all alike—Clive, Everard Whitney, the whole lot of them—manipulating everything to their own ends. A life of solitude would be preferable, thought Janice, visualizing herself as a stern, dedicated career woman, antipathetic to men except in the realm of business. It was a noble, if sobering, prospect.

When she was calmer, she realized that Mr. Whitney had evidently agreed to release Clive in place of the head clerk, Columbano.

After dinner that evening, Janice sat with Mr. Whitney on the balcony of their suite. He smoked a cigar, drank brandy, and told her about the process of grape harvesting. The Carvalho family owned several *quintas*, or estates with vineyards, in different parts of Portugal, so that they could grow and ship various kinds of wines, apart from port.

"It may be possible, while we're here, to fit in a visit for you to one of the *quintas*," he said. "It's a chance to see something interesting firsthand."

"Yes, I'd like that," she said. He was evidently keen to provide diversions for her so that she would not go running around after Clive. As though it mattered now! Even tonight he was determined to keep her a semiprisoner on the hotel balcony; one part of her mind acknowledged dreamily that she liked it and would not object, while another part rebelled at his lack of trust.

He suddenly moved his feet from the balcony rail. "Would you like to go out somewhere tonight? I haven't spent much time showing you the sights or introducing you to the real Lisbon."

He was excelling himself in trying to be a thoughtful host, she reflected, but at the same time she could scarcely restrain her eagerness to be out and about with him, anywhere.

"I don't think I expected you to spare time to take me sightseeing," she said demurely. "I can be ready in five minutes." After a slight hesitation, she asked, "Is this dress all right?"

She was wearing a lime-green cotton dress that accorded well with her hair and her now slightly tanned skin. She inquired because she did not want to put on a dress obviously meant for dancing, only to find that she was too conspicuous in the streets.

He stood gazing at her without speaking for a moment or two and under his level scrutiny she felt herself blushing.

"Yes," he said at last. "You look very charming."

Outside the hotel he took a taxi. Janice had glimpses of long wide boulevards, but there were fewer people walking around than down in the crowded squares and streets nearer to the river.

"Is this the business district?" she asked.

"Mm'm," he answered. "Our own office is farther back. We've passed it. It's really an old palace and has a fine staircase."

The taxi had stopped and Janice alighted outside what looked like a row of single-story sheds, which were gaily decorated and lit.

It turned out to be a fair with sideshows and stalls, but totally unlike anything Janice had ever seen. The noise of canned music and booming invitations to try one's luck, the shouts of stallholders cooking sardines and other fish, the murmur of thousands of Lisbon inhabitants milling around in the wide gangways between the stalls, all merged into a volume of sound that battered the eardrums into insensibility.

A fat woman staggered along, carrying a set of three aluminum saucepans, a trophy she had just won somewhere. Men carried bottles of wine or boxes of assorted groceries and children danced gleefully in and out of the crowds, yelling and clamoring for their parents to choose the stalls where the prizes were large packs of chocolate.

Janice gasped. Who would have thought that Everard Whitney would bring her to a fair like this?

He held her elbow tightly. "I'd hate to lose you in this crowd," he said with a grin. "Do you fancy smoked sardines cooked in this fashion?" He pointed to a stall where thousands of sardines were being grilled over a charcoal burner.

"Not at the moment," she answered, thinking that the smell was overpowering, let alone the taste.

"I must have a go at this," he said suddenly, stopping in front of a stand where mechanical horse racing was in progress.

Janice, watching as he furiously turned his particular handle, found herself cheering him on with wild cries, though probably her shouts were lost in the general din. At the third attempt, his horse came in second and his reward was a couple of cigars, which he pocketed with a flourish.

There were numerous small shops selling furniture, radios and household goods; dozens of kiosks with cheap jewelry and pottery, and souvenirs of all kinds.

"It's like a fair and a market and a pinball-machine parlor all rolled into one," she said breathlessly, as she and Everard Whitney struggled along a less crowded avenue.

At a stand which announced in jazzily flickering lights Travel the World, Everard stopped to play a game involving colored balls that had to travel along the correct air routes to reach Lisbon. Janice tried this, too, but was still in Newfoundland when someone else won.

"*Tourismo o Mundo* indeed!" she grumbled. "I've only just started from New York."

"Don't despair," Everard encouraged her. "Try again. Have you any more small change?"

She gave him several centavos and was delighted when he won by skilful playing. The prize was a fairly presentable doll, dressed in Minho costume, which he shoved into her hands.

"Let that be a lesson to you in gambling," he said as they moved away and took deep breaths of air heavily laden with the pungent odor of smoking fish. "If you lend money for stakes, your luck will change immediately, so if the other person wins, then keep your own money in your pocket—or borrow from him when he's winning. Then he'll start losing."

"A seesaw of luck," she muttered, but his attention was drawn to another booth.

Even though the din gave her a headache and she was hoarse through shouting, Janice was thoroughly enjoying herself. She was in a daze, spending an evening with a man she did not know, an Everard Whitney who was altogether different from the ruthless, tyrannical boss for whom she worked. He was a man who had shed his inhibitions to become a boy out for a spree with a girl to share his enthusiasm.

She was almost asleep on her feet when at last they left the fair. She clutched the doll and a tin of sweets. Everard dangled a straw basket that he had been forced to buy to hold the four bottles of wine and two dubious-looking vases he had won at various stalls.

The taxi driver, far from being surprised, helped Everard to stow his trophies in the cab, congratulating him on his good luck.

At the hotel the commissionaire permitted his impassive features to slip a little when he saw the results of this late-night shopping expedition. The Hollandia's five-star luxury exclusiveness was slightly affronted, but Everard carried the situation with such nonchalant arrogance that not even the manager himself would have had the courage to point out that it was not really the thing for hotel guests to bring in bottles of wine they had won at a fair.

But in the privacy of their suite, Everard dumped the basket and its contents on the sitting-room table.

"Give these to the chambermaid or someone tomorrow,"

he said to Janice. "Yours, too, if you don't want to be cluttered."

"Oh, no," she answered quickly, in spite of her tiredness. "I shall keep mine. The doll, anyway."

She would never tell him that the doll in Portuguese costume would be more than a cherished souvenir. It would be a reminder of one joyous evening she had spent in his company when he had shown her an entirely different facet of his complex nature.

IN THE MIDDLE of the following morning, when Everard Whitney had gone out on one of his inspection visits and Janice was alone in the suite, a telephone call came from Selma Carvalho.

"Isn't Everard there?" asked Selma.

"No, I'm afraid not. Is there any message?"

Selma did not reply for a moment. Then she said, "Please remind him that he's coming to us at Guincho for the weekend."

"Yes, I'll do that," promised Janice. "I've made a note of it."

"And Miss, er, I've forgotten your name. . . ."

"Bowen. Janice Bowen."

"Oh, yes, of course. Would you also like to come for the weekend?"

Janice was astounded by Selma's invitation and mumbled rather incoherent thanks.

"Everard can bring you with him," came Selma's cool voice. "But we shall expect you both for lunch on Saturday. Goodbye."

Janice hardly knew what to make of this sudden offer. Should she have refused? Everard might be embarrassed by having his secretary staying as a guest in the same house as Selma Carvalho to whom he was apparently strongly attracted.

At the first opportunity as soon as he returned, Janice mentioned the telephone call.

"Miss Carvalho very kindly included me, but if you don't want me to be there—" she broke off.

"Why on earth shouldn't I want you there?" he demanded, giving her a fierce, frowning look. "It's thoughtful and considerate of Selma to invite you." He walked a couple of steps toward the balcony. "Actually, I wasn't going to Guincho this weekend. I had other plans in view, but if she's made a special call about it, then we'll both go."

Janice remained quiet, although she wondered what other plans had been in his mind. She wanted to protest that he need not put himself out to take her to Guincho, that she could quite easily amuse herself if he wanted to go alone, but for once she was wisely silent. Besides, the prospect both allured and repelled her at the same time. Apart from a couple of days in a pleasant seaside villa, she was intrigued to know which of the various Everards would be uppermost at the Carvalhos'.

On the other hand, she recoiled at the vision of Everard's tender, loving glances toward Selma and hoped she would not be forced to watch Selma being capricious or Everard cheapening himself by being too anxious to please.

Janice remembered only as an afterthought that Clive had half promised to take her out on Sunday to one of the seaside resorts. Nothing definite had been arranged, and an invitation to the Carvalhos' was almost a command. She hoped that Clive would forget his vague suggestions, but in this she was disappointed, for he telephoned her at a time when he knew that Everard Whitney would not be in the hotel.

"I'm sorry about it, Clive," she said mildly, when he wanted to fix a time. "I—I find I'm not free."

His laughter came over the telephone. "Not free? Don't tell me the old slave driver is making you work on Sundays as well as overtime half the night all the rest of the week. What's he up to? Or rather, what are you up to?"

"Nothing," she replied. "I've just got to go somewhere else."

"You're being very mysterious. Where?" he demanded.

"Clive! I don't ask you where you spend all your weekends or other free times. I think it's not my business."

"Oh, dear me! I *am* being warned off." His tone was unpleasantly derisive. "Is it permitted to ask if you're going to this—this place alone?"

"Not alone. There'll be other people there." She wished with all her heart now that she had said openly in the first place that she had been invited to Guincho, but she would not tamely surrender now to his importunate questions.

"I see," Clive said smoothly. "So you're going with him. With Whitney. Well, well, well! Who would have thought, my dear Janice, that you would slide off for a quiet weekend with him? I must admit I'm surprised. Not about him, but I thought you were a little different. Oh, well, we all have wrong opinions about people sometimes. Go and enjoy yourselves."

"Clive, you're insulting—" she began, but the telephone was already dead.

Her cheeks flamed. His insinuations were very plain, and they disgusted her. She reflected, however, that perhaps she was to blame as much as Clive. If she had said openly that Carvalhos' villa was her destination, Clive would never had made those abominable remarks. But then if she had told him the truth, she might have been in trouble with Everard, especially if Clive invited himself through Leona.

Janice was now completely uncertain whether it would be a good thing or not if Clive were also a member of the Carvalhos' weekend party. Either way, his presence or absence had already debased what had promised to be a restful and interesting couple of days, even if, from Janice's point of view, they became a crucial test of how deep or superficial her feelings were toward Everard.

CHAPTER FIVE

THE CARVALHOS' SEASIDE VILLA at Guincho was more or
less as Janice had expected—a white building, green roofed,
with cool, shady rooms, a patio where fountains gurgled,
and gardens full of flowers and exotic shrubs with towering
palm trees for shade.

The surprise was the great change in the coast. Here, open
to the Atlantic, the breakers surged against the rugged
coast, reminding Janice of Cornwall rather than the quiet
seas and sheltered beaches of the Tagus estuary.

On arrival at the villa, Janice had been unsure of her
welcome, but if Selma was no more than the impeccably
courteous hostess, Manoel was there to greet Janice cordially and apologize for his neglect of her.

"It was discourteous of me, but my father took me to one
of our *quintas* in the Douro," he explained. "We have to see
about the grape harvest. I couldn't get back sooner."

Leona was not present at lunch and Janice was immensely thankful that Clive had not so far arrived. Manoel
suggested that after lunch they should all visit *Boca do
Inferno*—Hell's Mouth.

Selma said languidly, "You can take Miss Bowen, but
there's simply no reason why Everard and I should have to
trudge around that place."

Janice took no part in the argument, willing to fall in with
whatever plans were eventually made.

Everard, instead of wearing his usual businessman's
clothes, was dressed in a light blue sports shirt and pale
fawn Terylene trousers.

"We'll all go," he decided, and ignored Selma's pouting grimace.

Manoel drove along the road toward Cascais and parked at the top of a flight of winding stone steps leading down to the sea. The force of the wind was astonishing, and from the balustraded platform below, Janice watched the sea booming and hissing into the great sea cavern. The rocks, fretted and gnawed into fantastic shapes, made a marine orchestra, while ceaselessly the sea broke its fury on the razor edges, to pour into cavities and galleries with roars and grunts and sighs. Every wave was a living, determined creature bent on destruction by battering the land into fragments until it could gain passage.

"It's unexpected," Janice murmured, "to see such a wild sight here."

Manoel invited her to accompany him down to a lower level, but Everard called sharply, "Don't go down there, Janice. It's too risky in this wind."

Janice, glancing upward, caught the surprised expression on Selma's face. Before starting out this morning, Everard had said, "Probably you'd better start calling me Everard. Mr. Whitney sounds overly formal for a weekend jaunt."

But Selma would not know this, nor that this use of the Christian name would last only a couple of days.

Obediently, Janice retraced her steps to the platform. When Manoel joined them, Everard said severely, but with a smile, "You ought to have more sense, Manoel, than to take Janice down that far. D'you think I want to lose her?"

Manoel merely shrugged, but Selma put in playfully, "Of course you must take care of your secretary, Everard. Most unfortunate if anything should happen to her."

There was not the slightest hint of malice on Selma's lovely face, but she had triumphantly succeeded in putting Janice firmly in her place, as Everard's secretary—invited for courtesy's sake.

Presently, the four drank coffee at the elegant new restaurant near the road, but Selma showed impatience to return to the car.

Dinner that night was a very formal affair, it seemed to Janice. Senhora Carvalho, Selma's mother, arrived from

Lisbon, with Leona and several other members of the family.

By changing places and upsetting his aunt's table arrangement, Manoel managed to sit next to Janice, and she was glad of his comforting chatter, for Everard was placed far down the table next to Selma.

Janice was able to study Senhora Carvalho, the English mother of Selma and Leona, for since that first glimpse of her in the garden of the Carvalhos' town house, Janice had not met her again.

With delicately colored, rounded features and blond hair only slightly darker than Selma's she looked almost too English to be true and, apart from her fluent Portuguese, would have caused no stir in any town from Bath to Harrogate.

On the wide patio where coffee and liqueurs were served, she asked Janice about her home in England.

"Of course, a tiny apartment," she commented, when Janice told her. "Every girl's dream nowadays, no matter how much more comfortable her own home might be. But independence is precious when one is young. You must get in touch with Leona when she returns to school in Sussex and when you are back in England."

Janice smiled in acquiescence, although she was sure that if by some malevolent force of destiny Leona were thrust back to her English school, she would not exactly yearn for Janice's company.

Someone suggested that they should make up a party for the casino at Estoril and Janice waited to take her cue from Everard, but he seemed to take it for granted that she would go with the others. In fact, he practically forced her into one of the cars, much to the evident disgust of Selma who had expected to have him to herself. There was no room for Manoel, who suggested that it would be better for Janice to ride with him in Leona's car.

"Not likely," muttered Everard. "Not the way that young maniac drives."

But they all arrived at the handsome casino without mishap.

The evening flashed by like a dream, Janice thought, but

a dream that held a brilliant high spot. Of course it was fun to gamble a little, lose a few escudos, and watch an entrancing floor show, but when she danced with Everard, she was in a dizzy heaven, unconscious of anything except that she was held in his arms, his face so close above her own.

Manoel was eager to claim her as often as he could and she could hardly tell him that however charming a partner he made, she would rather be with Everard.

"Enjoying yourself?" Everard asked her as they walked across the floor toward their table.

Janice, aware of Selma's hostile gaze focused on her and Everard, looked up defiantly into his face and smiled.

"Every moment!" she answered gaily. "Something to remember."

Then, for a fraction of a second, there was an expression in his eyes, a dancing gleam that warmed her and, in other circumstances, might have emboldened her to pursue this heady course. But the place was too public, Selma was too near, and Janice lowered her glance quickly before Everard could see any answering flash. He must not assume that on the strength of a single social weekend she was trying to flirt with him.

Manoel complained bitterly that he was being frozen out. "Everard has you to himself every day in the hotel," he grumbled. "Why must he dance with you now? Come, Janice, will you give me the pleasure?"

She obeyed, secretly amused by his old-fashioned courtesy, but then he was Portuguese. Everard, in his casually blunt, Anglo-Saxon way, merely said, "Let's dance this one, Janice."

"You must come and visit us more often," Manoel told her as they danced. "Everard ought to bring you to one of our *quintas*. We have several country estates."

Her answer almost tumbled out that Everard had promised to arrange a visit for her to a *quinta* somewhere, but she remembered in time to be discreet and gave Manoel a vague answer.

There was hardly a moment during the following day when Manoel was not closely beside her, down on the beach, in the beautiful grounds of the villa, or on the cool patio.

Evidently this did not escape Everard's attention, for after dinner he said to Janice, "You've made quite a hit with Manoel, haven't you?"

Janice reddened. "Well, I suppose he feels that he has to pay me some attention while I'm a guest here," she said with a smile.

"I'm not so sure," he returned, and his mouth lifted in that little curve that Janice found maddeningly incomprehensible, for she was never sure if he were amused or being ironic. "I think Manoel may be playing a subtle game. He wants to show Leona that he'd be quite happy not to marry her, as all the family want to arrange. She's inclined to be single-minded and see only her own point of view."

Janice was vaguely ruffled. It seemed that Everard had to go out of his way to spoil any scrap of pleasure that she might find in the well-mannered companionship of an attractive young man. In the next minute he would be warning her against taking the handsome Portuguese too seriously.

"You mustn't believe all that Manoel says," Everard continued.

Janice laughed sharply, then immediately composed her face. "I'm not quite as susceptible as that," she said in her chilliest tone, frankly not caring whether Everard liked it or not. When she glanced at him, she saw that he was staring at her, a perplexed frown creasing his forehead, but there was only cold hostility in his eyes.

Janice became aware that Selma was approaching with Leona following close behind. Leona dashed past her sister and all but flung herself into Everard's arms. "I've had the most brilliant idea," she exclaimed, drawing away from him, but still grasping his wrists. "Tomorrow I will take Janice sightseeing," she declared. "I'm quite sure that you haven't given her much free time to see our lovely city. With you, it's all business, business, money, telephoning big deals."

Everard laughed indulgently. "Some of your family have

to put time into business, business and big deals, if you're to be provided with the clothes and amusements you want.''

"Naturally. But you can do without Janice for one day more," she asserted.

He raised his eyebrows and looked at Janice, who was standing a yard or two away, an onlooker of the scene.

"I don't know that I can spare Janice," he said after a moment. "We have appointments fixed and can't break them at a moment's notice."

"You can keep your appointments yourself." Leona tossed her long dark hair over her shoulder. "I'm not conducting *you* on the sight-seeing tour." She shrugged her slim shoulders. "It's your fault if you haven't been to places by now. You've been to Portugal often enough."

"Oh, don't pester Everard," interposed Selma in her languid manner. "I don't suppose Miss Bowen wants to spend her time tramping around a lot of museums."

Leona whirled around on her sister. "Who said we would go to the museums?" she demanded. "But that's a good idea. There's the Coaches Museum. Now, that is really something. Have you been there, Janice?"

"No, not yet. I intend to, when I have time." Janice was wondering why Leona was suddenly so friendly and eager.

"Now listen, Leona," Everard began. "Janice and I have a very busy day tomorrow, but—wait, Leona, let me finish! The day after, Tuesday, that is, you can take Janice out for the day. In any case, as you should know, many of the museums and other buildings are closed on Mondays."

Leona left it at that and made no further argument. As Everard explained when he and Janice had returned to the Lisbon hotel, "I have this Arrabida trip to inspect sites for possible new hotels and I really need you with me. I hope you don't think I deliberately prevented you from going out with Leona."

"Oh, no." She was more than prepared to forget those previous occasions when he had deliberately, it seemed, made her cancel arrangements with Clive. She was only too glad of the chance to accompany Everard.

He warned her that site inspecting was a tiring process

and however much one could use a car, there was still a lot of walking involved.

Janice took the hint and put on comfortable shoes in place of the sandals she usually wore. A pair of serviceable dark blue trousers and a lemon shirt, she decided, were more appropriate than a dress for clambering about sandy beaches or rocky headlands or whatever kind of ground it turned out to be.

On arrival across the peninsula, she waited while Everard and a surveyor from the Lisbon office measured and paced, and consulted plans and land documents. This was the place where Manoel had brought her a week or two ago, and she wondered if more hotels and hordes of visitors would spoil its peaceful charm and its quietness, with the sea like silk gently ruffled by the ghost of a breeze.

She wrote down in her notebook details and figures concerning the aspects and distances from the beach. "When all the necessary hotels are built," she said to Everard, "a different sort of people will come here for holidays. Those who liked it quiet and unspoilt will go to other places and those who like liveliness and noise will bring more noise with them."

Everard gave her his characteristic amused glance, as though she were a child to be humored. "They'll also bring a lot of cash to this country. Now that the new bridge over the Tagus is opened, all this peninsula south of Lisbon is ready for development."

"Exactly. That beautiful bridge has put all this part of the country at the mercy of developers."

He laughed quietly. "You should know by now—and since you've been working for our company—that there is good development as well as bad. In fact, I've been trying to persuade the Carvalhos that several smaller hotels, each in its own grounds, and all close enough together to come under a unified management, are going to be a much better future proposition than one enormous matchbox stuck up on end."

She thought this over for a moment or two. Then she said, "Is it more expensive to build them that way?"

"To some extent, yes, but I believe that the capital costs

would soon be offset by better profits with all-the-year-round visitors."

"How do the Carvalhos react to your suggestions?" she asked.

He turned toward her and there was an oddly suspicious expression in his gray eyes. "Nothing has been decided yet," he said brusquely, then abruptly changed the subject.

Janice felt snubbed. It seemed that as soon as she showed an intelligent interest in Everard Whitney's work, his ideas and ambitious planning, he slammed a door in her face. Then it occurred to her that perhaps he imagined that she wanted information to pass on to someone else—Clive, for instance.

The surveyor came back to the car where Janice and Everard had been sitting for a few minutes. The two men spoke in rapid Portuguese, with Everard pointing to the various parts of plans and rough sketches. "We'll go to Sesimbra now," Everard decided at length. "We'll have our lunch first and meet the Carvalhos' representative afterward."

Sesimbra, too, was fast developing from the quiet fishing village it had been to a resort with much to offer to tourists. The part around the fish quay was old and boats with high curved prows jostled in the harbor alongside smart white yachts and squat fishing boats with funnels painted in stripes like soccer jerseys. A medieval castle dominated the skyline, and below, white houses dotted the rising cliff.

In contrast, the modern development extended along the shore with an esplanade and bathing beach curving as far as the rocky headland. One elegantly designed hotel stood alone on the new road facing the sea. Everard had chosen it for lunch, and Janice, entering the cool, dim restaurant, was temporarily blinded by the sudden contrast between the dazzling sun outside and this shady interior.

She stood for a moment, the two men behind her, the waiter ahead ready to convey the party to their table, when she saw Clive rise and come toward them.

Clive here? It couldn't be. Even Everard seemed surprised.

"Hello, Janice!" Clive greeted her. "How nice to see you!"

"I'm sorry, Dickson," Everard broke in, "but I'm here on business today."

"So am I," returned Clive smoothly. "Won't you sit down?" He indicated the table laid for four to which the waiter had directed Everard and his assistant.

Everard glared at Clive. Janice waited expectantly, but did not sit down.

Clive was smiling, a peculiarly self-satisfied smile. "You don't understand, do you," he mocked. "You're meeting me today. I'm the new representative for Carvalhos.'"

Everard's attitude astounded Janice. For a fraction of a second he seemed dumbfounded. Then he recovered his poise.

"Of course, I understand now. Why didn't you say so at first?" Everard waved to Janice to sit where the waiter was patiently holding her chair. "There's evidently some lack of coordination. I came prepared to meet Almeida. I think I should have been told by telephone of the change—as a matter of courtesy."

Janice's spirits rose. Clive had initially scored a point by surprise tactics, but Everard was not an easy opponent and already in a sentence he had reduced Clive to an inferior position.

During the meal the three men talked business, mostly about the new hotel sites available on this part of the coast, but when Clive asked to see the plans and drawings, Everard replied, "Later, Dickson. I prefer to eat my lunch without having the plans mixed up with my lobster."

Not even when the four went out to the umbrella-shaded terrace for coffee and liqueurs would Everard produce any documents to show Clive. He now seemed perfectly at ease in this extraordinary situation where a young man who had been his subordinate in his company's Lisbon office was now in a position to negotiate on behalf of the Carvalhos.

In due course Janice accompanied the three men to the possible site for a new Carvalho hotel. When Everard was talking to Clive's assistant, the surveyor, Clive took the opportunity of whispering to Janice, "Why didn't you tell me where you were going for the weekend?"

"Was it your business?" she snapped back in a quiet voice.

"Well, it was pretty obvious that I'd soon find out," he retorted.

"Then your curiosity was soon satisfied?" she told him with a coolness that seemed to surprise him.

"You're different, Janice," he said slowly. "You're becoming hard and sophisticated. Must be due to Whitney's influence."

At some other time she would have laughed at the idea of anyone saying that she was hard and sophisticated, but now she did not want to be on genial terms with Clive. Instead, she answered his thrust about Everard.

"Perhaps I'm getting a more businesslike attitude, thanks to Mr. Whitney's training."

She moved away from him, but Clive stepped toward her.

"If you'd told me that you were going to Guincho for the weekend, I'd have come there, too. It would have been quite a joke to see Whitney's face when he had to be polite to me as a guest in the same house." Clive laughed softly. "Really, I believe he took you there to keep an eye on you so that you were definitely away from me."

She stared at him, unable to believe that this was the man to whom she had once been so attracted. "You flatter yourself, I think, Clive. Mr. Whitney doesn't stoop to that kind of low cunning. Why should he?"

"I'm not sure," he muttered. "I wouldn't put any kind of horse trading past him."

Janice now made a determined effort to leave Clive and rejoin the other two. The discussions continued about soil depth, access to beaches, southern aspects and the rest, and Janice diligently noted down the conversations, often verbatim.

Several times Clive asked to see the projected plans, but always Everard refused. "How can I tell old Joaquim what's decided if I don't see what you—your company, that is—have in mind?" Clive queried.

"Nothing will be decided until Senhor Joaquim Carvalho has the reports on the nature of the sites, their values and whether they are worth considering," Everard said smoothly. "Then we shall produce our plans and sketches for inspection. If at that time you are still empowered to act on behalf of the Carvalhos as their accredited representative—" he paused significantly before he went on "—no doubt you will see all the necessary documents."

Clive began to bluster. "This is damnably unfair. You've got your knife into me, but you'll regret it, Whitney. I'm already inside the Carvalho organization and you're not. Don't rely too much on Selma to drag you in. Soon I shall be in a position to say yes or no to all your company's projects."

Everard gave Clive a long, measured glance. Then he took a cigar out of his pocket and lit it with the deliberation of a connoisseur before he spoke again. "I'm glad you've reminded yourself, Dickson, that you no longer work for my company. I regret, though, that during the time you stayed with us, you learned so little about the art of timing. Come, Janice, I think we've finished business for the day."

She and the surveyor followed Everard back to the rough road where the car was waiting. Janice looked back over her shoulder. Clive stood where the others had left him, slightly dejected, she thought. But he had deserved Everard's harsh treatment. He should have known better than to threaten or try to bully anyone of Everard's steely caliber.

Janice took a taxi next day to keep her appointment at the Coaches Museum with Leona. As it happened, there was a great deal of work for Everard, and Janice had been diffident about taking the afternoon off. "Perhaps I could telephone Senhorita Carvalho," she suggested, "and arrange another day?"

"No, no, you go along," was Everard's slightly testy answer. "You made a promise and you must keep it. The work will keep."

Leona had not arrived at the appointed time, and after twenty minutes spent in walking up and down the street Janice decided to go into the museum. Perhaps Leona had meant that they should meet inside.

At that moment, as Janice approached the entrance,

Leona drew up with a screech of brakes and thrust her head out of the window. "Wait one moment, please! I have to park the car."

She slid off toward a square where she might find space and a few minutes later came back on foot.

"I apologize for being late."

"It didn't matter," Janice hastened to assure her.

Janice already knew that this famous Coach Museum housed a collection of royal and other coaches from a former riding school belonging to one of the royal palaces.

In style, the two long lines of state coaches of the eighteenth and early nineteenth centuries were more ornate than Cinderella's godmother could ever have conjured up. Gilded, embellished with classical figures and enormous statuary, upholstered in richly-colored velvets and brocades, they were a dream of pageantry and splendor.

"They must have needed strong horses to pull these weighty affairs," remarked Janice, standing before a magnificent coach built for a Portuguese ambassador to Rome. "The passengers must have had a rough ride over the roads as they were at that time."

Leona laughed. "In those days people had to put up with having their bones shaken about. Imagine! No other way. No cars, no planes, no trains."

"In spite of all the padding, it must have been very tiring to be important enough to ride in one of these."

Janice paused to look at an Italian type with a roof upholstered in pale blue brocade.

"Tell me, Janice," Leona said quietly, "are you in love with Clive?"

Janice turned a startled expression to her companion. "In love with Clive?" she echoed, just as quietly. "Why do you ask?"

"Because I wish to know," said Leona. "Do you want to marry him?"

"He hasn't asked me," replied Janice.

"Now here is a beautiful coach," Leona had strolled to the next. "This was used for the coronation of one of our kings."

Since Janice could quite well read the card identifying the vehicle, Leona's guidebook explanation was unnecessary.

"And if Clive should ask you to marry him, what would be your answer?" pursued Leona.

"A very definite no." Janice's tone was chilly.

The two girls walked in silence around the exhibits. In a corner of the great hall were several small two-seater carriages, high in the body. Mysterious leather hoods with rimmed portholes provided protection from the weather and gave the carriage the appearance of a sinister insect of terrifying size.

"What fun it must have been to drive in one of these," murmured Leona. "Especially accompanied by a lover."

"The lover would have his work cut out to see where the horse was taking him," retorted Janice.

"If it is not Clive that you are in love with, then perhaps there is someone else? At home in England?" Leona persisted.

"That could be a possibility," returned Janice, determined to remain cool and not very informative.

Leona did not speak for several moments. Then she walked around to the other side of a coach so that she was facing Janice across the gilded back axle. "Then you are likely to marry soon?" was her next query.

"Why are you asking all these questions, Leona?" Janice decided that it was her turn now to inquire into Leona's motives.

Leona flashed her a dazzling smile.

"Did you suggest this meeting just so that you could cross-examine me?" continued Janice.

"Naturally," answered the other. "You understand that I couldn't do so during the weekend when you were a guest in our house. Nor could I do so if we met in the presence of others or at your hotel. So I chose this way."

"*Toujours la politesse*," murmured Janice rather acidly.

"Exactly. Conventions must be observed. Oh, I have learnt in England to do some of the right things." Leona came to Janice's side. "I like you very much, Janice."

"Thank you."

"But you understand that you make situations awkward for us."

"Do I? How?" demanded Janice.

Leona shrugged as though unwilling to continue with the explanation, which she knew must follow. "This weekend, for example, Everard brought you so that he knew where you were and what you were doing."

"Oh? Did he?" Janice felt obliged to make some non-committal reply, but only yesterday Clive had said something to the same effect."

"It's likely that he wanted to keep an eye on you," continued Leona.

Janice realized instantly that Leona had been in touch with Clive during the weekend and told him that Janice was at Guincho. He had used the same phrase about "keeping an eye on her."

"And you see, Janice, that if you are at Guincho, then I can't invite Clive."

"Why not?"

Leona's dark eyes flashed with irritation. "Oh, no! When Everard has taken the trouble to separate you from Clive, it would not be right to bring him to our villa."

"I don't really follow your reasoning, but perhaps you'll allow me to ask you a question, Leona. Are you in love with Clive? Do you want to marry him?"

Leona's lovely face first lost its animation, then quickened into a derisive grin. "Of course not! Clive is very sweet and handsome. He's lively and good fun, but I'm not at all in love with him and he doesn't love me."

"Then why are you so anxious to make sure that I'm not a possible rival?" Janice wanted to know.

"It's surely very plain. To me, it's most obvious. If I am to avoid being betrothed to Manoel for the sake of the family business, then I must be madly in love—for the time being—with someone else. If the man were Portuguese, that could make a bad complication, but Clive is an Englishman. Many of our family have married English men or women, so that's not strange. But Clive must at least pretend, also for the time being, that I am his entire world and that he would like very much to marry me. If he is attracted to another girl, such as you, then my position is not so strong.''

Janice smiled with amusement. "You make it sound very intriguing.''

"Also there is the question that I might be sent back to England to that hated school on your south coast. Let me say that it is no *Costa do sul*. Oh, so cold in the winter and so much rain all the summer! Only when I am at home for holidays do I see the sun at all.''

"I expect you're right about that, but sometimes our climate can be quite agreeable.''

"Not at boarding schools,'' said Leona emphatically. "Besides, I speak English quite well. Our mother has seen that we were bilingual since we were babies. What polish can an English school give me?''

"I see your point,'' conceded Janice. Irritated though she was by the afternoon's catechism on highly personal matters, she found some aspects of Leona's character very likable. The girl was young and impulsive, yet restrained when there was a sufficiently good reason; she had a delicate sense of time and place, choosing neutral ground for her merciless inquisition.

The two girls left the Coach Museum and walked to Leona's car. "I shall now take you to the Tower of Belem,'' Leona announced. "It is not far.''

"And will you ask me a further set of questions when we arrive?'' asked Janice with a smile.

Leona turned her head and laughed, alarming Janice by such inattention to the traffic. "No. I have discovered what I wanted to know—for the time being,'' Leona answered.

Possibly there was a latent threat there, but Janice remained silent, aware that there was a great deal that she would like to know. Would she have the courage to ask Leona point-blank whether her sister Selma intended to marry Everard?

The Belem Tower, a fortress built like a wedding cake, was set in the sea to guard the entrance to the Tagus. It was a romantic place with rooms full of solid old English furniture and doors opening onto balconies as though it were a house with a river view.

But as the two girls toured the rooms, with Leona acting as guide, Janice let her impulsive tongue guide her and asked that vital question before she could even frame it properly.

"Your sister Selma—does she intend to marry Mr. Whitney? Oh, please forgive my curiosity, Leona," she was constrained to add.

Leona paused on the balcony. There were few visitors today and no one else on this level. She looked at the water gently flowing below. "Selma?" she murmured. "Oh, I don't know. She has dozens of offers because she's very beautiful and very English-looking, so that makes her different from the average Portuguese girl. Of course, Everard has always been madly in love with her since he first met her. That's why he comes to Portugal whenever he can."

"But Selma is not in love with him?" Janice strove to make her voice utterly casual, keeping out the faintest trace of hope.

"I think she was about a year ago," Leona answered. "Then she grew tired of him—and he went back to England, so she forgot him. There are always plenty of other men to come to our house. My father is an important man and sometimes we wonder how much our young men love us or our family business," Leona ended on a slightly wistful note.

Janice laughed lightly. "That doubt will never trouble me. I've no wealthy family connections."

They finished exploring the tower. Leona suggested going to a café for tea, but instead of taking Janice to one of the large open-air garden cafés, she chose a small place in a back street. The two small tables on the pavement outside were deserted and the proprietor came hurrying out to take the order.

"Tea? Coffee?" asked Leona of Janice.

"Coffee, please. I like Portuguese coffee and one can have tea anytime at home in England."

Perversely, it seemed, Leona chose tea. For some time she nibbled the little cakes that accompanied the pots of tea and coffee, and Janice noticed how frequently she glanced along the street.

Janice looked at her watch. "I don't want to seem in a hurry," she began, "but I must go soon. I promised Everard that I'd be back at the hotel to do some work for him before dinner."

Leona waved her hand airily. "There's plenty of time. I can drive you there in fifteen minutes or less."

After a further half hour had elapsed, it occurred to Janice that Leona had chosen this particular café because she had arranged a meeting with someone. Clive? Whoever it was had not turned up. Automatically, Janice knew that it must be a man, for Leona would have mentioned the matter if a woman had been expected. So again Janice was cast in the role of chaperone for Leona's meetings with Clive.

"I could easily get a taxi back to the hotel," suggested Janice. "You don't have to drive me."

Leona pouted, heaved a dramatic sigh, and hissed to the waiter that she was ready to pay. "We'll go, then," she said.

"Not if it's inconvenient to you," began Janice tentatively, but Leona was already speaking to the café proprietor, telling him what to say if her friend called. Janice caught the words "*senhor*" and the phrase about "not being able to wait any longer."

Leona drove through the park Monsanto, avoiding most of the Lisbon rush-hour congestion. As Janice alighted on the sidewalk outside her hotel, she saw Everard standing under the portico, talking to two men. Leona evidently saw him, too, for she got out of the car and went toward him.

While Janice was thanking her for a pleasant afternoon, Leona waved a greeting to Everard and he excused himself from his companions. "Hello, Leona! So you've brought Janice back in one piece, I see. D'you want a drink?"

"Of course," she returned.

"I'd better go up to the suite and start work," said Janice.

"Not yet," Everard decided. "You need to celebrate a lucky journey in Leona's driving hands." He led the way to the hotel bar.

Leona decided that she wanted *sangria*, the long, delicious concoction of red wine, brandy, mineral water, ice and lemons. This meant that she intended to stay longer than courtesy demanded of a dry martini, for *sangria* comes in a tall jug with a wooden spoon for stirring and reviving the flavors glass by glass, throughout a long sitting.

But Janice did not reckon on Leona's capriciousness. She chattered to Everard about the afternoon's sight-seeing. "We did more than tourist stuff," she confided to him across the top of her glass. "We had some fascinating exchange of confidences. Mostly about men, of course."

"Of course," agreed Everard dryly.

"Did you know that Janice has someone in England, a young man she is very fond of?"

Janice felt a deep flush staining her face and neck. How could Leona so maliciously misconstrue a simple remark so vaguely made?

"I—I didn't exactly say that . . ." she began.

"It's very wrong of you, Leona, to betray confidences spoken in the warmth of a sunny afternoon," Everard said lightly.

"Oh, I'm not!" Leona declared. "All I meant was that—"

"Never mind what you meant. Janice and I have work to do this evening." Everard's tone was indulgent as though he were speaking to a small child.

Leona jumped to her feet. "Yes, I am to go! I never understand why you're so quick to take offense, Everard. Selma must be an angel to put up with you." She picked up her gloves and bag. "Goodbye, Janice. I hope I haven't offended you, too."

"No, of course not," Janice managed to say. "Good-night and thank you—for this afternoon."

While Everard went out to see Leona to her car, Janice fled upstairs to her room. By the time he came up to the suite, she was already banging away at the ill-used typewriter.

Everard prowled around the room, now and again giving her a vague instruction, asking if she understood his corrections and marginal notes. Janice wished he would take himself off so that at least she could have a good cry in peace. Her throat ached with the effort of controlling her tears.

Finally he came and stood close to her. She hated anyone watching the typewritten lines appearing on the page and inevitably lost control of her fingering and made mistakes.

"Janice, why didn't you tell me about this—man—this friend you have at home?"

His nearness almost suffocated her. She found the eraser and started to rub out the spelling mistake.

"Should I have done so?" she muttered, not looking at him.

"I tried to make sure that you were, er, unattached, only to find that you were very friendly with Dickson when we arrived here. Now it seems you've left someone at home eating his heart out for you. Apart from all that, Manoel Carvalho almost tucks you into his pocket when he has the chance and oozes the liquid Latin look all over you. I'd no idea that when I asked you to come with me, I was bringing such a magnet." He moved away from her, then turned. "Why must you complicate everything so?"

"I didn't know that I was making complications," she answered. "I haven't let any of these—diversions interfere with your work. I'm willing to work at all times to make up for afternoons off. At home in England you wouldn't know or be interested in what I did after office hours."

"You're right," he admitted. "I'm not entitled to question how you spend your time, except that I feel responsible for you." He was standing behind her and suddenly began to chuckle. "You're not doing that sheet of typescript any good, are you?"

She saw that she had rubbed a hole right through one of the thin tissue carbon copies. She snatched the whole set out of the typewriter, recklessly wanting to throw the lot in his face.

For a fleeting moment he put his hands on her shoulders, and electric prickles ran through her body. "Calm down, Janice," he said softly. "I apologize for probing into your private life."

She wanted to fling herself into his arms, to tell him that any attraction she might have felt for Clive was now definitely on the wane, that Manoel was an amiable acquaintance and that there was no one, not even a shadow of a man anywhere in the world for whom she cared more than a couple of lemon pips, except Everard himself.

She wanted to outrage him with tempestuous behavior. Then he would send her home in disgrace and she would be free of this tormenting longing, this day-by-day craving for a man who regarded her only as a 'responsibility' in a foreign city.

It was better to deny nothing and let him believe that there were half a dozen men with whom she was ready to flirt, rather than let Everard imagine that his lightest touch had the power to fire her blood and set her nerves tingling. It was better to let herself remain no more than a temporary responsibility.

CHAPTER SIX

"HOW MUCH HOLIDAY is due to you, Janice? You haven't used all your leave for this year, have you?" Everard asked the question suddenly when Janice was checking a long list of figures.

"No, I have one week left," she replied.

"Had you planned anything special?"

"No. I hadn't thought about it."

For the last week Everard and Janice had been on polite noncommittal terms—not the frigid courtesy which denotes a large icy area between two people, but a strictly business-like attitude that allowed occasional cordial interludes.

He had not asked any further questions about her friends and was obviously now exploring only very tentatively the matter of another holiday.

"I wondered if you'd like to spend a week or even a few days at one of the *quintas* and see something of the grape harvest, the wine pressing and so on," he suggested.

"Yes, I would." Was he intending to spend any time on the *quinta*, too? That was a question she could not ask him.

"All right, I'll fix it for you," he offered.

"Thank you." She was uncertain whether the trip to a Portuguese estate was being held out as a peace offering or whether it was part of a plan into which she was expected to fit.

She had not seen Clive since the day when he had tried to ride roughshod over Everard in the matter of planning the sites for new hotels.

Everard had referred only once to that episode.

"Dickson thought he was going to take me down quite a

few pegs," he said. "But he needs to know more about the Carvalho business than he does at present. As soon as I mentioned the matter to Selma's father, Senhor Joaquim, he laughed. Said he'd never given Dickson any kind of authority and in fact didn't know he'd gone to meet me. I suppose Dickson must have told Almeida some tale or other to get him out of the way."

Janice remembered Clive's eagerness to see the plans and sketches. If he had no authority from the Carvalhos, what ulterior motive was in his mind?

On several occasions Janice worked at the Lisbon office when Everard went there to try to sort out the tangle of estimates and contracts that Clive had left in chaos. The head clerk, Columbano, was overeager to please and hurried obsequiously in and out of the rooms where Everard happened to be at work. He was the man about whom that critical report had been written, when Janice had mistakenly concluded that the subject was Clive. She wondered if Columbano had been given a warning, either hinted or open, that he would be dismissed if he did not improve his efficiency.

Everard made a point of doing most of his telephoning, especially calls to his company in London, from his hotel suite. "I can't be sure," he told Janice, "that the hotel is free from hidden microphones or other devices, but at least fewer people in the hotel are interested in my conversations. Our Lisbon office has too many extensions on which people can listen."

So evidently Clive had introduced a note of suspicion into the atmosphere of the Lisbon office.

For some days Everard and Janice really slogged hard at the work. Endless estimates, reports on sites, progress reports and correspondence kept Janice busy through long days when she and Everard took their meals in the sitting room to save time. Yet, in a way, Janice had never found such satisfaction before in her relationship with Everard. True, he was still impatient and demanding, but even his instructions were less curt. He was more solicitous in many ways, insisting that she have short restful breaks between the tiring sessions at the typewriter, stressing that it was better to loll on a long chair on the balcony for twenty minutes than continue working until fatigue slowed down the output.

"That's factory technique," observed Janice, resting as he had ordered, a long cool drink at her elbow. "If workers are compelled to do very long stretches, without a break, they start making mistakes and damage themselves or the machine. 'Impaired efficiency' is the correct jargon, I think."

Everard looked down at her, having just fetched himself another drink. His unwavering glance almost turned her bones to water. "You're wearing a cap that wasn't intended to fit you," he said gravely, but his eyes laughed. "But it's perfectly natural that if I overwork you, I shall suffer, as well as you."

"Then for your sake chiefly I'll try not to break down." It was easy enough to return an occasional flippant remark as long as she could keep her voice steady and a blank expression in her eyes.

In the end the work was finished with a day to spare. Everard had an important conference to attend, a meeting of international tourist boards, at which he would present a resumé of all the present and future projects planned so far by his company.

"I wonder if you'd go to Estoril today, Janice," he suggested on the opening day of the conference. "Two of the tourist board officials from Sweden are staying there at the Hotel Estoril-Sol. I'm sure they'd like to have some of these reports to study beforehand, but try to deliver them personally. I don't want them lying about in the reception office for days."

Janice was pleased at the prosepct of an unexpected jaunt to Estoril, especially alone, for she had not had the opportunity so far to potter around on her own.

"You can take the rest of the day off," Everard continued idly. "Go swimming or do whatever you like. But you must be back here in the hotel by six. At that time there's a phone call from London with the additional figures for the estimates we asked for. Take them down, type them in duplicate and bring me one copy to the Avenida Palace."

"Yes, I'll be sure to be here for the call," she promised.

She decided to go by train to Estoril and after delivering the package of reports into the hands of one of the delegates, prepared to enjoy one day of luxurious freedom. She walked along the promenade as far as Cascais and wandered about the little streets, into the small shady garden and then along one of the new main streets. Inevitably, road widening had been necessary for the traffic demands and one side was so obviously new that Janice wondered how big a slice of picturesque old buildings had been destroyed to make way for cars.

She bought savory pastries, cakes and fruit for a picnic lunch, added a bottle of wine and set off toward a small secluded cove that she had noticed from the road to Guincho.

In her mind, as she walked along, she planned her day. One swim before lunch, then a rest on the sun-baked rocks, for by now, September, the fire had gone out of the midday heat. Another swim to freshen up, then it would be time to start the return to Lisbon. A pleasant, idling program, she reflected, a day's holiday sandwiched between periods of concentrated work.

But her plan did not work out quite so smoothly. A pale green car came flashing around the curving road and pulled up with a violent screech of brakes.

Leona, of course. Who else would stop so sharply without regard for her passenger, her tires or herself?

Clive leaned out of the window. "Janice!" he exclaimed. "What are you doing here? Is this the way you laze about in your employer's time?"

"Ha! I might ask you the same question," she retorted.

"Doesn't follow," he said. "I'm free to work how I will in my own time. I'm not under Whitney's thumb anymore," he added with a touch of mingled rancor and smugness.

"I was just off for a swim and a laze on the beach," Janice explained more to Leona than to Clive. She made a tentative move as though to walk on.

"Splendid idea!" Clive sounded enthusiastic. "D'you mind if we join you?"

Leona leaned back in the driving seat, her mouth unsmiling, but with a lively gleam in her dark eyes.

"But that might upset your plans," protested Janice, seeing her idyllic dream of solitude vanish like smoke. "Besides, I've brought a picnic lunch and you wouldn't want to—"

"We'll certainly enjoy a picnic lunch with you," said Leona emphatically. "Come, Janice, step in the car and we'll go and buy provisions for ourselves."

"Good," agreed Clive. "That's much better than a boring lunch at a restaurant."

Janice still hesitated, but Clive nimbly stepped out and held the door open for her. She had little chance, she thought, but afterward she wondered why she had been so supine. She should have marched off and left them to their own devices.

Leona drove smartly toward the center of Cascais, parked her car near a cluster of shops and then in the slickest Continental manner purchased a variety of foods and wine.

Janice noticed with amusement that while she herself had been expected to wait her turn in the shops, the proprietors now broke off serving other customers to attend to Leona and her imperious demands. Because she was a Carvalho? Or because she was so flamboyantly eye-catching?

When the boxes, packages and bottles were all stowed in the car, Leona drove down the narrow street to the harbor square, then along the Guincho road.

"I know a better cove farther along," she said to Janice. "Very secluded and quiet."

Janice nodded agreement, although she was sceptical of any place that Leona judged quiet, but this time the description was true. There were few people in the cove—a family party with small children, two or three couples and four young men amusing themselves with horseplay in and out of the clear water that lapped gently against the labyrinth of rocks.

It seemed that Leona always carried bathing towels and a bikini in her car. Clive, too, had a pair of trunks on the back seat.

"Always useful," he commented. "You never know when

you want to stop and take a plunge." He went off to undress behind some sheltering rocks so that the girls could use the car for changing.

Leona's red-and-white spotted bikini contrasted excellently with the smooth satin of her tanned body. Beside her, Janice was aware that her own tan was patchy, according to the various swimsuits and bikinis she had worn, but then she didn't have the same opportunities as Leona who had the use of a private pool at the Guincho villa apart from all the beaches on the coast.

When Leona set out almost enough food for a party buffet after their prelunch swim, Janice again felt at a disadvantage, but determinedly ate some of her own patties and insisted on sharing her bottle of sparkling *vinho rose*. Leona must not be allowed to think that her own wealth could buy everything else.

Afterward the three stretched out on the soft sand. Janice tilted her wide-brimmed hat over her eyes and was surprised to hear Clive say, "I recognized you by the hat, Janice. Quite a fetching cartwheel, isn't it?"

Leona asked sharply, "D'you know the hats of all your girl friends?"

Clive chuckled. "I know this one of Janice's."

Janice deemed it diplomatic to pretend to be asleep.

After a pause Leona said, "We mustn't stay too long. I have to go home and change."

Janice removed her hat and leaned on one elbow to look at Leona. "Of course. You probably have something important you want to do. I have the afternoon free for lazing."

"We're going to some garden party affair at the embassy," Clive explained.

"Sounds nice," murmured Janice.

"But surely you're going, too?" His eyebrows shot up in surprise. "Isn't Whitney going?"

"I haven't heard anything about it," answered Janice, noting the triumphant look in Leona's eyes.

"Seems as if Whitney kept it dark from you," Clive teased. "Now I wonder who else he's taking. Could be Selma, I suppose?" He tossed a questioning glance at Leona.

"Selma has a good choice of men to take her to all the parties," Leona snapped with obvious satisfaction.

There was a short pause. Then Clive said to Janice, "Isn't today the big day for the start of the conference?"

"I expect you know as much about it as I do," Janice replied cautiously.

"Well, I daresay I'll be seeing you if you're bobbing about at Whitney's elbow."

Leona stretched herself out and closed her eyes to indicate that the conversation no longer interested her.

Janice tilted her hat over her face, leaving Leona and Clive to their own devices. In a way she wished they would go soon. After all, she had been perfectly willing to spend the afternoon alone. It was they who had intruded on her.

Leona was a restless creature, forever altering her position or addressing an occasional remark to anyone who cared to listen, and eventually Janice gave up trying to doze. She sat up.

"Are you going to swim again?" Leona asked her.

"Perhaps. What's the time, Clive?" Janice asked.

He glanced lazily at his wrist. "Just turned half-past two."

"But you wear a watch," Leona said idly, touching Janice's wrist where a lighter patch of skin outlined a watchband.

"Yes, It's in my handbag in case I forget and wear it in the sea. Coming in?" She looked down at Leona.

"In a moment, when I'm ready."

Janice sauntered off to the stretch of water between the rocks and swam out beyond to deeper water. Presently she turned over to float, idly watching the blue canopy of the sky and sensing the gentle cushioning of the glittering water under her body. Why had those two almost insisted on spending the afternoon with her? By telling her about a garden party in one place was Clive trying to prompt her to say exactly where Everard could be found in another?

She lay there on the water musing on embassy-garden receptions, wondering if Everard would be there escorting Selma. Was that why he had sent Janice out to Estoril to deliver documents, then take the rest of the day off, well out of his way? Naturally this would spare him the embarrassment of having his secretary tagging along at his elbow and being forced to introduce her.

After a while she turned to see if Clive and Leona were near, but could not see them. Oh, well, apparently they hadn't bothered.

She swam back and waded ashore to the spot where she and the other two had been sitting. Her towel and hat were there along with her white handbag conspicuously lying on a dark rock. But Leona and Clive had gone. There were no signs of them at all. She called out, "Leona! Clive!" One or two other people on the beach glanced at her with only momentary interest.

Surely Leona hadn't gone off in the car without a word? Why hadn't she or Clive called out that they had to leave? Janice peered behind several rocks. Then she picked up her belongings and scrambled up the rough path to the road. Perhaps they were waiting for her there. But the only car standing on the road was a dusty black sedan, empty. Certainly there was nothing resembling Leona's smart green car.

Now the true nature of her plight hit Janice between the eyes. Her clothes were in Leona's car! All she had left to cover her white bikini was one large towel, and she could scarcely ride home in the Lisbon train clad like that. Well, there was nothing to do but to buy a cheap dress in Cascais. Fortunately, she had kept her sandals to walk around more comfortably on the beach, otherwise she might have been barefoot, as well.

She sat down on the side of the road and opened her handbag to count her money. Also she must keep an eye on the time. She must be back at Lisbon hotel for Everard's important telephone call from London.

Panic now clutched her throat as she scrabbled among the contents of her handbag. She tipped everything out onto the towel, but no brown leather purse was there. All her money, her return ticket to Lisbon, the gold watch, which she had put into a compartment of the purse, were gone.

Clutching the towel around her, she dashed back to the beach and again searched the spot where she and the others had eaten their lunch. Leona had apparently collected most of the litter of boxes and bottles, leaving only Janice's wine bottle and one empty carton.

Janice glanced around the beach. Almost everyone else had left except a young couple sitting on the rocks. She walked across to them and asked in halting Portuguese if they knew the time. The man shrugged apologetically and indicated that he had no watch with him.

She tried to tell him that her purse had been stolen from her handbag, but he failed to understand. Janice spoke in French and the woman replied that she had seen no one suspicious.

Janice thanked them and returned to make yet another useless search in the sand and in the hollows between the rocks in case the purse had merely fallen out of the handbag.

How on earth was she now to get back to Lisbon with no ticket, and no money? Any other day it would not have mattered what time she arrived, but today of all days, with Everard's warning echoing in her ears that she must be in the hotel before six o'clock, it would be a disaster if she were not there.

She stopped the first person she saw on the road and asked the time. "*Que horas são?*"

When the boy showed her his wristwatch, she was appalled at the lateness. "A quarter to five?" she echoed. "*Obrigado.*"

She hurried down to the harbor in Cascais, then paused, trying to decide the best thing to do first. Report the loss to the local police? Perhaps they would lend her enough money to return to Lisbon. They could easily check that she really was staying at the Hotel Hollandia there.

She explained her plight to the first policeman she met and he courteously directed her to the local police office, but she soon realized that she could not afford the time to explain her situation to officials who might not understand English or her own still poor Portuguese.

She thanked the man and started walking toward Estoril, hoping that she might find a taxi and persuade the driver to trust her until arrival at the Lisbon hotel. Perversely, all the taxis seemed either full or purposefully going in the opposite direction. Ideas flashed through her mind. If only she'd had a few odd bits of change loose at the bottom of her bag, she might have telephoned the Carvalhos' villa at Guincho and asked Leona what sort of prank it was to leave Janice without her clothes. She might have demanded that Leona came down to Estoril in the car and give her a lift back to Lisbon. Or if Manoel were there he might have been able to help her with transport.

She was becoming more self-conscious about her appearance on the Estoril promenade, even though it was not particularly unusual for girls to walk along swathed in bathing towels. She decided that carrying her hat would tend to make her less conspicuous, and once again her anger rose that Leona and Clive together should play such a dirty trick on her. Or was it a mere accident? Sheer thoughtlessness on Leona's part?

Janice couldn't be sure. All she knew was that with neither time nor money she was on the edge of calamity. If her return to Lisbon had not been so imperative, she would have walked into Estoril and explained her situation to one of the big tourist companies there. They could have advised her, telephoned the local police and checked her statement that she was staying at the Hollandia. She might even have been able to telephone Everard if he were already at the conference hotel, although she flinched from what he would say when he learned that she had let him down like this.

At last she secured a taxi, telling the driver in French that she had lost her money, but would pay him immediately on arrival at the Hollandia. The journey was excruciatingly slow. Twice they were held up at railway level crossings and Janice wished fervently that she had secreted a little money in another pocket of her handbag or guarded her return rail ticket more carefully. At least there were trains at frequent intervals.

Outside Lisbon the taxi driver tried a shortcut, but was held up in a traffic jam caused by a truck in collision with a car. In Lisbon itself there were crowded streets and traffic lights to add to the delay. Finally, when the taxi drew up outside her hotel, Janice leaped out and spoke to the reception clerk, asking him to pay the driver and add a generous tip on her behalf.

"Make it double or treble," she said breathlessly. "It was good of him to trust me."

The desk clerk looked slightly scandalized at the sight of hotel visitors running around draped only in towels, but Janice had to linger a few more moments.

"Have there been any telephone calls?" she asked. "Mr. Whitney was expecting a call from London. Urgent."

The clerk made inquiries of a colleague. "Yes," he answered after a maddening delay. "There was no one in your suite to take the call."

The time was now nearly half-past six. "Did they say if they would ring again?"

The man shook his head. "I don't know. I was not on duty."

Two of the head reception clerks hovered close to her, trying to usher her quickly into the elevator before too many eyebrows were raised in alarm.

She shot out of the elevator, hurried into the suite and dressed quickly, leaving her room door open so that she could hear the telephone. Dumbly, she went to sit by the telephone, almost willing it to ring. When suddenly the bell shattered the silence, she grabbed the receiver eagerly, but the call was only a query as to whether she or Mr. Whitney required dinner to be served in the suite or wished to take it in the restaurant.

She paced the room, walking out to the balcony and back again. What was she to do? There was no point in going to the Avenida Palace unless she had the figures Everard wanted. She decided it was better to take the bull by the horns and telephone him, admitting her failure to do her job properly.

She reached out a hand to pick up the receiver when a call came through. In a moment she knew it was Everard.

"Oh, at last!" he exclaimed angrily. "Where on earth have you been? I've called you three or four times in the last hour."

Before Janice could even formulate the words of explanation, he continued, "Well, have you got the figures? If you haven't time to type them, then read them out to me now and I'll jot them down.''

Janice drew a deep breath. "I haven't—the figures," she said jerkily.

"What d'you mean? Didn't London call you?"

"I think so, but I wasn't here to take the call," she admitted, reddening with shame even though he could not see her.

"Not? Oh, Janice!" He made her name sound like an imprecation. "Oh, really! Why weren't you back in time? Dammit, I gave you practically the whole day to do whatever you wanted! Surely you could have managed to do this one thing that I asked you. I told you how important it was to me.''

"I'm sorry, Mr. Whitney," she said, swallowing a great lump in her throat. "I—I had some bad luck at Cascais. I lost my watch and my—"

"Then next time stay where there's a clock in view," he snapped explosively. "Here am I down here, promising exact estimates and all the rest. Well, you'd better stay there and see if London makes another call. If nothing happens in the next ten minutes, then put in a call to them, although it's unlikely that anyone will stay on there to receive it. You should have done that already.''

"Yes, Mr. Whitney," she mumbled. To continue to call him Everard in these circumstances seemed unpardonable.

He banged down the telephone, leaving Janice to reflect on her own stupidity and her lack of common sense. She dreaded her next encounter face-to-face with Everard, for this time he would be fully justified in severely reprimanding her.

While she waited she tried to piece together how her purse could have been stolen. The last time she had looked at the watch was when she had taken it off before swimming. That was before lunch. It was true that while she was in the water with the other two, Clive and Leona, their possessions were left unattended. Could someone else on the beach have helped himself, choosing his time carefully when they were all absent?

It was a pity she had asked Clive the time instead of

looking for herself. She might have discovered the loss then; she could have borrowed money from Clive or Leona and she would have been here at the Hollandia in good time.

A wisp of suspicion came into her head, insidious like a trace of smoke creeping into the mind. Clive and Leona must have left the beach in a hurry, apparently without sparing a moment to get Janice's clothes from the car and leave them where she could find them. Janice pushed these thoughts aside. She would not believe yet that today's loss had been anything but an unfortunate accident, the kind of carelessness that made temptation easy, although it was doubly unlucky that Leona had left Janice's handbag stuck so obviously on top of the rocks.

When the telephone rang again, she picked it up with relief. London this time, surely. But it was only reception saying that Senhor Dickson was here and would the *senhorita* receive him.

"Please tell him to call another time," said Janice hastily. She could not possibly cope with Clive at this moment.

"Very well, *senhorita*," the clerk replied.

Then it occurred to her that Clive might have come to apologize for deserting her this afternoon. She picked up the telephone and asked for Senhor Dickson to be shown up to the suite immediately.

"What made you change your mind?" asked Clive as he came into the sitting room. "Lucky I hung about for a minute or two."

"Perhaps you might have hung about for a minute or two this afternoon," she said angrily, "instead of leaving me absolutely stranded. D'you realize that my clothes were in Leona's car? What made you two go off like that without a word?"

"Your clothes? Good lord, I'd no idea. I'm terribly sorry, Janice. Leona wanted to get back to the villa and I realized I'd made a mistake about the time when I told you. It was really half-past three, not half-past two. We called out that we were going, but you probably didn't hear. How on earth did you manage? About your clothes, I mean."

"They weren't the only things missing," she said coldly. She told him of the loss of her watch and money and how difficult it had been for her to return from Cascais. "Even my return railway ticket was in the purse," she added.

"That was darned bad luck," he said sympathetically. "I didn't realize that your clothes would be in Leona's car."

"It could hardly have escaped her notice," she retorted.

"I'll ask her, of course, to return them to you immediately."

"Don't bother. I have other dresses to wear." She was furiously angry with both Clive and Leona, the one here in front of her, the other absent. "It was awkward walking without a dress through the streets of Cascais and Estoril, but I'm glad Leona managed to leave me my towel. That at least was useful. Money would have been better still. I could have bought a cheap dress."

"Did you lose much money?" he asked. "I can lend you some if you need it."

"No, thanks." Janice waved her hand in a gesture of dismissing the importance of the money. "No, no, it wasn't much. Not more than three or four pounds in sterling. I don't carry much about with me. It was my watch that I minded about. I took it off for swimming, then left it inside my purse so that sand wouldn't blow into it. It seems that I left it most conveniently for the thief."

"Was it a valuable watch? Did you have it insured?"

"Yes, it was insured," she answered. "But I haven't had time to report the loss to the police or anyone. It was more important to me to know the time because I was anxious to get back here." She gave him an angry glance. "It wasn't particularly helpful when you misled me about the time, telling me it was an hour earlier."

"Sorry, Janice, that was pure accident. Just the way I looked at my own watch." He was lounging in a chair near the open French windows. "What was the hurry?"

"I—I had some work to do for Mr. Whitney," she said lamely, and watched the disbelieving look spread over Clive's features. In haste she unzipped the cover from the typewriter, but before she could make a show of working, he rose and came toward her.

"That wasn't the real reason, was it?" he queried, his hand on her shoulder. "I suggest that the delay in getting back here stopped you from being ready to go with Whitney to the conference at the Avenida Palace.''

"No, it was nothing of the sort. There was no question of my going there,'' she said coolly.

He put his hand under her chin and turned her face toward him. "Weren't you going there after the call from London?''

She twisted her face away from his grasp. "I don't know what you mean. There was no call from London.''

"Oh, yes, there was. You weren't here in time to receive it.''

She stood up and faced him. A devastating suspicion roared through her mind. Had Clive in some way or other managed to take that call and get hold of the vital figures? Why else should he be hanging around the hotel?

"And were you here to take it?'' she demanded. "You seem to have left that garden party rather early. Or was that only make-believe?''

"Janice, you're all upset by this afternoon. You don't know what you're saying,'' he said.

"Clive, be honest with me! Did you take my watch and money—just temporarily—so that I'd be delayed?''

"Janice!'' He stepped back from her, appalled by her accusing question. "You don't really believe that I've sunk as low as that? Stealing a girl's purse?''

He turned away and stepped out onto the balcony.

After a long pause, Janice moved toward him. "I'm sorry, Clive,'' she mumbled. "I didn't mean to offend you. I apologize for what I said. But it did seem rather odd that you and Leona should take the trouble to spend part of the day with me on the beach when you were due to go to this garden party affair.''

"Why shouldn't we?'' He whirled around on her. "I'll be more careful next time—''

"And so shall I!'' she flung at him. "It'll be a long time before I accept invitations from you or Leona.''

"Please yourself. D'you think—?'' He broke off as the telephone rang.

Janice rushed to pick up the receiver, but almost instantly Clive snatched it out of her grasp.

"Clive!" she exclaimed. "It's my call! Let me take it."

"I'm just as interested as you are," he said, smiling.

"No, no!" With both hands she grabbed the earpiece, but heard nothing but a jumble of voices before Clive regained it and replaced it on the rest.

She stared at him for a moment. "How dare you cut me off like that when it was probably an important call?"

"At this time of night?" he queried smoothly. "You don't expect another London call now, do you?" He smiled at her. "Don't panic, Jan. It was only a reception clerk asking when you want your dinner."

"I don't know that I believe you." Supposing it had been London on the line and again she failed to listen? But whatever her suspicions of Clive, the last few moments had almost convinced her that he hadn't yet obtained the vital figures that Everard was waiting for.

Now Clive's eyes danced with admiration. "I'm enchanted by you when you're in one of these spirited moods. I'd no idea you could be so vivacious, especially about business matters. Come, Janice, forget this fictitious work you're supposed to be doing for Whitney and come and have dinner with me. I'll take you to one of the nicest places Lisbon can offer and afterward we'll dance. After all, I'm trying to make amends for what happened this afternoon."

"No, thank you," she answered stonily. "I don't want your invitations."

He sighed loudly. "Obstinate girl! What must I do to coax you?"

"Nothing," she snapped.

He came behind her and dropped a light kiss on the back of her neck. Furiously she whirled around to elude him, but he seized her arms and pinioned them behind her back.

"What's gone sour with us, Jan?" he whispered. "You used to like me a little, didn't you?"

"That was before I knew you so well," she said in a low, angry tone. "Let me go!"

"In due course," he murmured. He held her so tightly she could not escape his relentlessly savage kisses as he forced her head back.

Suddenly Clive relaxed his grip and she stumbled backward, putting up her hand to her bruised mouth. Only then did she become aware that Everard Whitney was standing in the middle of the room, his face ominous as thunder.

"What in heaven's name does this mean?" he demanded, looking from Clive to Janice.

Clive sat negligently on the arm of a chair. "Perfectly simple situation, I should have thought. I suppose I don't have to ask your permission if I want to kiss Janice?"

"Get out!" Everard said tersely.

"Oh, you can't order me about now, Whitney. I'm not under your thumb now, you know," retorted Clive.

"This is my apartment, and I'm ordering you to get out before I have you thrown out."

"I'm afraid we didn't expect you back so soon from the conference," Clive continued. "What went wrong?"

Janice, almost paralyzed with shame and humiliation that Everard should have caught her with Clive in such a compromising situation, now stared at Clive. He was making it sound as though she had specially invited him into the suite in Everard's absence.

Everard loomed over Clive. "Are you going now or must I throw you out with my own hands?"

"Please go, Clive," Janice said in a tremulous whisper.

Clive rose and straightened the crease on his trousers. "All right." He glared defiantly at Everard. "As Janice invited me here, I'll go only when she says the word. Good-night, Whitney. Sorry if I've interrupted some big business deal you had cooking—but then you interrupted my tête-à-tête with Janice, didn't you?"

The door closed behind Clive and silence filled the room with a stifling fog of doubt and bewilderment.

Janice was the first to speak. "If you'll excuse me, I'll go to my room." She knew that she must look a disheveled, frightful sight, but, more important, she was bruised in spirit.

"You won't go anywhere until I have some explanation," Everard said harshly, arresting her when she was already halfway to her bedroom door.

"I'm sorry for what happened," she said slowly, "but I didn't invite Clive here."

"No?" he queried in disbelief. "I doubt if he climbed up from the street to the balcony. Or are you trying to tell me that he forced his way in?"

"No, I didn't mean that. When the reception clerk said he was here, I said Clive could come up. I thought he might be able to help me about my watch. He—he might have seen someone suspicious on the beach."

Everard stared at her, contempt in his eyes. "D'you mean to say he was with you all this afternoon? Oh, well, I gave you the time off, so I suppose I must expect you to meet him as often as you can."

"No, it wasn't like that," she said hastily. "I met Clive and Leona near Cascais. They were in her car and they decided to join me and picnic on the beach. They went off earlier because they were due at the embassy garden party."

"Embassy party?" he echoed. "Oh, yes, I believe there was something on at the Venezuelan Embassy." He moved away from her across the room. "I still don't understand why you came back here so late. Hadn't you any sense of time?"

When she explained that all her money and return ticket had also gone—she said nothing of the loss of her clothes as well—he drew a deep breath as though he were trying to prevent himself from exploding. A faintly cynical smile curved his mouth. "I really did pick a nitwit didn't I?" he said quietly. "Not only is it probable that you have lost the company a very important contract, but you can't even look after your own money."

Janice raised her head. She longed to crumple and burst into tears, but the spiritless way was the wrong way with Everard Whitney. He brushed aside excuses as though they were specks of dust.

"I deserve all the names you can call me," she said firmly. "I was careless and inefficient. At my age I ought to have more sense. But I really am sorry about missing your telephone call."

"H'm." He leaned against the balcony window. "And how did you get back here after all? I doubt whether you walked all the way."

"By taxi. I had to ask the driver to wait for his money until a reception clerk at the hotel could pay him."

"Didn't it occur to you to go to our new hotel at Estoril? You could have telephoned from there and had the London call transferred."

"I wasn't clever enought to think of that," she admitted. "I hadn't a single escudo even for a telephone call anywhere."

She couldn't tell him that the thought had crossed her mind, but that she couldn't face the stares and winks of gangs of men working on the hotel if they suspected she had lost her clothes.

"It wasn't money you needed, Janice, but common sense." He sighed and flung himself on the settee. "Well, what are we going to do with you now?"

"Send me back to England, I would think, at the first opportunity."

He glanced swiftly at her. "And leave Dickson? You know that he's going to be here for some time—that is, as long as the Carvalhos will tolerate him."

"I'm not interested in Clive, or whether he stays here or returns to England."

Everard pressed his fingertips together. He was rumpling his dinner jacket, his black tie was crooked and his hair looked windblown. Janice wanted to kneel down by his side and beg his forgiveness for letting him down so badly.

"So that was the great farewell scene that I interrupted?"

"Certainly not!" she said hotly. "I wanted him to go."

"After you'd invited him up to the suite?" Everard's tone was disbelieving. "Didn't you know his real reason for calling here?"

"To try to intercept those figures?" she queried.

"Perhaps he hoped to, either by listening to the call, or persuading you to let him see what you'd taken down."

"I would never have disclosed the figures to anyone, least of all Clive," she protested.

He gave her a steady glance, then rose from the settee, straightened his hair, his tie, his jacket. "I have to go to this banquet now at the Avenida. You'd better stay here in case a call from London comes through. Have your dinner sent up, and you can while away the rest of the evening packing your belongings.''

So he was sending her home in disgrace!

"Telephone the airline and book a flight on any plane to London leaving after midday," he continued.

She was to be given no time to dwell on her shortcomings or regret her mistakes. She was to pack up the briefcases according to his instructions, with the confidential papers and files.

"I'll take them tomorrow to the Carvalhos' house here, on my way to the airport," he told her.

"On your way to the airport?" she echoed, sure that she had misunderstood what he said.

"Yes. I'm flying to London tomorrow. I'll be able to deal with those figures better on the spot."

"And am I to wait here until you come back?"

His gray eyes were cold, even menacing, yet somewhere lurking in their depths was a gleam of sardonic amusement.

"You're going to the *quinta*. I promised you a week's holiday at one of Carvalhos' *quintas*, so you'd better grab the chance. I'd intended you to go after this conference was over, but you might as well go now."

"But will the Carvalho family mind if I arrive—wherever it is—out of the blue?"

"You won't be arriving out of the blue or any other color. Manoel will be delighted to escort you at a moment's notice."

"Oh, I see. So we're vacating this suite from tomorrow?" she queried, striving to get his exact instructions and leave nothing to chance.

"That's right. I'll telephone you at the *quinta* as soon as I return," he said.

"Thank you—for the holiday." Her voice was choked with emotion, for she knew that she scarcely deserved this reprieve unless Everard had an important ulterior reason for keeping her in Portugal.

"I'm off now to the Avenida," he said, glancing at his watch. "You'd better report your loss of watch and money and other things to the British Embassy. Otherwise you won't have much chance of claiming on the insurance.''

She watched him walk toward the door, where he turned to her with a smile. "Enjoy yourself at the *quinta*, Janice. And of course, it's quite probable that you might find Dickson there for a few days. Good-night."

Janice stood in the middle of the room, motionless, numbed by what had happened in the last few hours. Instead of seeing the door that had closed behind Everard, she saw only his mocking face when he referred to Clive.

She could not comprehend Everard's line of action—his apparently sudden decision to fly home, his arranging for her visit to the *quinta*. But she knew that between her and the unpredictable man was a great barrier. She remembered seeing on one of her own sight-seeing trips the *Casa dos Bicos*, the House of the Pointed Stones, where the entire façade was composed of pyramid-shaped stones. Just such a curtain of defensive points had erected itself in a single day between her and Everard.

CHAPTER SEVEN

"WILL IT DELAY YOU very much if I call first at the British Embassy?" asked Janice when Manoel came next morning to the hotel.

"Not in the least," he answered. "Is it some trouble with your papers?"

She explained about the loss of her watch and money. "Everard advised me to go there as quickly as possible and report the loss, otherwise the insurance company at home may not believe that the watch actually disappeared."

As he drove through the city and down a long avenue giving perspective to the Basilica Estrela at the far end, she realized that he was unusually silent.

"There's a little park I hadn't seen before," she remarked conversationally. "I suppose it's the Estrela Gardens?"

Manoel nodded.

Janice wondered if perhaps he were put out because some of his own arrangements had been altered by the sudden visit to the *quinta*.

"I hope all this journey wasn't inconvenient for you," she began. "I really had no choice in the matter when Everard said—"

"Oh, don't think that," he said quickly. "I'm delighted to take you to our most beautiful *quinta*, the best we have. I'm sad because now you will think that all the Portuguese are dishonest and ready to steal."

"Not at all," protested Janice. "I could as easily have lost everything, handbag and all, on an English beach. It was my own carelessness."

Manoel flashed her a smile of gratitude and she felt his spirits lighten.

The embassy visit did not take long, but while Janice filled in a long form with particulars, then waited for the typed declaration, she had time to glance beyond the windows to what looked like a delightful garden. No doubt garden parties took place here as well as at the Venezuelan Embassy, and Leona and Selma strolled around with their escorts—Everard and others. She was seized with a sudden pang of jealousy at the thought that Selma and Everard would walk about those green lawns when yet another Englishman married into the Carvalho dynasty.

When Janice and Manoel started off again, it was some time before she noticed that he was driving due north on a road well inland and far from the coast.

"Where is your *quinta*?" she asked. "I thought it was not far from your villa at Guincho."

"That is at Colares, where the wine is very good. Our really important one is near the Douro."

"The Douro?" she echoed. "But that's a long way—right up in the north."

Manoel smiled and handed her the map.

"Good heavens!" she exclaimed. "It's almost the other end of the country."

He laughed. "You forget that Portugal is only a comparatively small country. We shall arrive before dark, I hope. I must make good time or the family will not receive our signals."

What did he mean by "signals," she wondered. She understood now, though, that having to visit the embassy first had really delayed him.

He stopped at an hotel in Santarém for lunch, apologizing for the fact that he could not show her the sights of the town.

"Another time, we must break our journey here when we have half a day to spare. It's an interesting town," he told her.

The landscape became more mountainous on the way north, and far away over to the right the bare gray brown peaks ranged toward the Spanish plateau. Sometimes the road wound through a valley hemmed in by vine terraces.

"Porto is another city that you really must visit," Manoel said, when they came to the outskirts, "but not today."

Only when he was driving up a steep, narrow road, with a valley on one side, did Janice realize what the "signals" were, for he blared his horn continuously, although there was often little other traffic in sight, not even an oxcart.

"In a moment, when we turn the bend, you will see our *quinta*," he explained. He pointed across the valley and Janice saw what looked like a doll's house crouching at the foot of a hill.

"Take the glasses," he said, "and see if they are answering."

Mystified, she picked up the field glasses and focused them on the white house, obscured now and again by a bush or tree as Manoel swerved along the road.

"Are they waving back?" he asked.

"I can see some white sheets flapping at a window," she answered. "That's all."

He laughed. "You don't understand. Keep watching. Soon you will see that from many windows they will flap towels and sheets and tablecloths. Shirts, perhaps. It is the answer to us. They know we're coming and it's to say 'Welcome!' "

Manoel ceased to use his horn, for apparently the household had been thoroughly roused and from almost every window linen of one sort or another, indistinguishable at this distance, fluttered violently.

Manoel descended almost onto the floor of the valley, crossed a river by a narrow bridge, then began to climb the other side. Before the house came in sight again, he stopped the car at the beginning of a rough track, where already several maids and one strong-looking boy were waiting.

"We have to walk to the house. It's too rough even for me to drive," he explained. "But one day we will pave the path and then we can arrive at the house in style."

Janice wondered how even carts could manage such a stony path, but Manoel took her arm and helped her over the worst bits. Bobbing behind them, completely undeterred

by the rough track, came a small procession of maids with
the luggage, suitcases or baskets of supplies nonchalantly
balanced on their heads on top of the flat circlet of sacking
worn like a crown.

"It seems effortless for Portuguese women to carry most
things on their heads," Janice murmured, "but I tried it
once in my hotel room with only a small bag." She laughed.
"I nearly shot the thing over my balcony rail out onto the
pavement."

"But then you do not need to carry anything," Manoel
assured her. "We have many people to do those things for
us."

She sighed, resigning herself to the acceptance of the
Carvalhos' way of life, where wealth could command service on almost a feudal scale.

The house was no doll's villa now, but a long, rambling
white building. A ceiling of wisteria covered the pillared
porch and the wide steps which led to the front door.

Inside all was noise and bustle. There were greetings from
various members of the Carvalho family whom Janice had
not met before. Maids scurried around to look after rooms,
refreshments, luggage. Dogs and small boys pattered
through the rooms. Janice was relieved to be shown to her
room and for a few moments she stood gazing entranced at
the vista outside her windows. The hills across the valley
had turned to wine red in the slanting evening sun and
farther distances lay like purple smudges on the horizon,
until twilight engulfed both mountains and sky.

Even up here she could hear the chatter in the kitchens,
and what sounded like turkeys or ducks squawking. Somewhere along the road a bullock cart squealed with the thin,
plaintive scream of a wooden axle rubbing in its sockets.
The "music of the Douro" they called it, so Everard had
told her.

Her thoughts turned to him and she wondered if he had
arrived safely in England and how soon he would be
returning to Portugal. What then? Was this holiday at the
quinta intended to be an easy rounding off of a business trip,
notable from his point of view as a series of disasters?
Perhaps he would bring someone else back from England to

replace her? Someone who would not be so foolish as to fall in love with her chief?

Speculation was useless, for Everard was completely unpredictable, and in the meantime she had better enjoy the little unexpected holiday.

Manoel was the only Carvalho she could identify among the dozen or so relatives at dinner, for being introduced to so many new faces all at once had only confused her, especially as they were now all wearing different clothes. It seemed that most of the family was gathered at this, the most important *quinta*, for the grape harvest and pressing.

"Tomorrow," Manoel promised, "I'll take you to the shed where we've started treading the grapes. Many growers have gone over to machinery and maybe we shall do the same at some future time, but at present we still crush grapes—or cut—in the old traditional way—with the human feet."

"Does it take a long time to tread grapes into a mush?" she asked.

Manoel grinned. "Longer than you think. Grapes are cold and hard to start with, like small pebbles. They resist the foot, as though they're reluctant to give up their juice."

"You've done it yourself?"

"Oh, yes, when we're small boys, we long to ape the men. But when we begin to grow up, we soon realize that it's work for the men and not us."

Manoel took her next day to the shed where the *lagares* stood, a huge gray granite tank in which five men linking arms trod rhythmically in a sea of grapes up to their knees. An old man played folk songs on his concertina and one or two bystanders sang lustily, but the cutters, as the treaders are called, needed their breath and energy for the grapes. At intervals, the foreman gave them strong brandy to keep them going and the concertina player struck up a livelier tune.

The air was thick and heady with the fumes of brandy and the fermenting grapes, and Janice realized how easily one might feel intoxicated even on the smell of wine that was slowly coming alive.

"You'll see now," said Manoel, "that the foreman has to

decide the exact moment when to stop the fermenting process. This vat is for port, so large quantities of brandy have to be poured in to fix the wine.''

He had taken Janice now to another shed where the grapes had already been trodden and the fermented juice seethed and bubbled like a witch's cauldron.

"This is what makes port different from other wines,'' Manoel explained. "For the other lighter table wines, the sugar has to ferment itself right out, but for port it must be stopped by adding brandy.''

Later in the day he took her to the vine terraces where women were gathering the grapes and loading them onto wooden trays, which they then carried on their heads to one or other of the sheds at the farmhouse.

"In the spring and early summer there are whole fields of mimosa,'' he told Janice, "like a sea of fluffy mustard. We don't need the flowers but we use the stalks for the vines to twine along, so that the bunches of grapes are kept off the soil and mud.''

"The early part of the year must be a wonderful season here,'' murmured Janice, visualizing the mimosa fields and the orange and lemon groves in blossom, with the sharp clear light of spring etching the mountains against a blue sky.

"But of course you will be here again to see it for yourself,'' Manoel said easily. "What does Everard plan to do? Stay here most of the winter and watch his hotels being built?''

"I don't know,'' Janice answered cautiously. "I doubt if he could stay long at any time.''

"Ah,'' sighed Manoel. "He's so very much the typical English business slave. He'll wear himself out by the time he's forty-five and he won't have seen anything except the inside of planes, hotel rooms in every world capital and everlasting boardrooms. Why doesn't he relax sometimes?''

Janice shrugged without answering. She was remembering those occasions when Everard had at least seemed to be relaxed: that day on the beach at Cascais when she had first worn the hat he had practically bludgeoned her into buying; the evening at the fair where he was delighted to win ridiculous prizes. Surely he had shown then that he could throw off the businessman's rigid mentality and enjoy idle moments.

When she and Manoel returned to the house in the late afternoon Leona had arrived, and immediately Janice sensed that the atmosphere had changed. Leona's presence almost anywhere brought a restless irritation, a kindling of tension, a flame of vitality threatening to devour anything in its path.

This at any rate was the effect she had on Janice, who now saw that she had thoroughly enjoyed being in Manoel's company all day. His easy, undemanding companionship and gentle, courteous manner had soothed her after the frets and jagged emotional outbursts on that last day in Lisbon. She had been wonderfully relieved that Clive was not at the *quinta*, but Leona soon put an end to any hopes Janice might have had that he would not come while she was there.

But first there was a bone to pick between the two girls. Leona had come to Janice's room on the initial pretext of seeing if the guest had all she wanted and was comfortable.

"Also I came to return your clothes which were in my car when we went to the beach the other day. I am so sorry, Janice, I didn't realize—"

"How could you fail to realize?" demanded Janice. "When you dressed in the car you must have seen my belongings there."

Leona shrugged. "No, indeed. That was it. I didn't dress. I just put a towel over my shoulders and drove home."

Janice was silenced. Leona's temperament and the climate she lived in were enough to make even an outrageous idea sound plausible.

"Please pardon me," continued Leona in what was for her a sweetly humble voice. "I had no wish to offend you."

Janice was about to smile forgiveness when Leona's tittering laughter bubbled out.

"It must have been quite an adventure to parade in your bikini—" Leona giggled.

"It wasn't a laughing matter at all," declared Janice crossly. "If the same thing happened to you in England, you wouldn't have been amused, especially if you'd been left

with no money to buy anything or even pay your fare back
to Lisbon.''

Leona's face sobered. "Oh, yes, Clive told me. I searched
in my car, but there was no purse. Perhaps it dropped out of
your bag on the sand.''

"No," denied Janice flatly. "If it had I'd have found it. I
dug about everywhere.'' She kept her glance firmly away
from Leona in case the latter should imagine an accusing
light in Janice's eyes.

"It was a sad accident,'' murmured Leona. "But you're
insured?''

"Yes fortunately.'' Janic was irritated by the assumption
that all contingencies would be canceled if only the insurance value were paid.

There was a long pause. Then Leona said, "Tomorrow
Clive is coming.''

"Oh, is he?'' Janice tried to sound neutral, neither dis-
mayed nor enthusiastic.

"So you will please occupy yourself with Manoel?''
Leona continued, her dark eyes flashing with laughter. "He
is very safe for you, like a brother.''

"What exactly d'you mean?'' asked Janice. "Take him
off your hands?''

"Precisely.'' Leona nodded vehemently. "Here at the
quinta there is more freedom for us than in Lisbon, so it's
not indiscreet if I go out for a day with Clive into the
country or to show him our estate. But please do not make
up the party of four.''

Janice began to laugh. "I do admire your utterly direct
way, Leona. Sometimes I think we would never get our love
lives into a tangle if we were all as outspoken as you are.''

"And what is your tangle with your love life?'' Leona
demanded.

"No tangles at present,'' Janice answered quietly.

"Then all is settled? You are to marry the young man in
England?''

"What young man?'' queried Janice, forgetting that
Leona had jumped to this wrong conclusion on an earlier
occasion.

"But you told me that you loved this man in England.

Have you changed your mind again? You won't come back to Clive, will you?''

Janice smiled. "No need to worry about that. Clive and I are only two people who knew each other some time ago. Nothing more.''

"Perhaps it has been very good for you to be away for a time from this young man," pursued Leona with some smugness, but Janice only smiled in reply. The less said about this fictitious young man the better.

After Leona had gone, Janice shrugged off her resentment. It was no use pursuing any kind of vendetta with Leona, who was far too skilful in escaping the consequence of any awkward situation she had contrived.

Janice opened the large dress box Leona had left. Inside was the dress she had worn that disastrous day. With her own underwear, all now carefully laundered and pressed, was another set with a new lace bra and panties and a lovely salmon-pink shift in lacy openwork wool. Under the tissue wrappings was a note scrawled in a large, flamboyant hand. "A thousand apologies. Please accept this small gift. Leona.''

Janice, hating to bear a grudge, was instantly charmed. She determined to forget the whole incident as far as Leona was concerned. The girl was criminally thoughtless, but not malicious.

When Clive arrived for the weekend, it appeared that Leona's plans for monopolizing his company were not going to be easy for her to carry out. Opposition seemed to come from several directions.

Senhora Carvalho, Leona's mother, welcomed Clive with some enthusiasm and seemed to take it for granted that Janice would be unduly glad to meet her compatriot again.

"So nice to have someone really English here for you, Janice," she said to the girl. "Then you won't feel alien among us.''

Then there was Clive's own attitude. On every possible occasion he sought out Janice, practically elbowing Manoel out of the way and certainly ignoring Leona's attempts to entice him into some secluded corner.

Janice was not only puzzled but definitely angry that after

the last stormy scene in the hotel suite only a few days ago, Clive should expect her to be willing to reinstate a friendship that had, from her point of view, been irrevocably damaged.

On the first possible occasion she spoke to him abut his obvious tactics. "I'm not particularly flattered by your persistent attentions," she told him. "Naturally I'm prepared to be polite to you while we're staying here, but no more than that."

Clive smiled lazily at her. "I find you adorable when you go all distant and haughty on me," he murmured. "Leona's exciting and charming, but she does pursue a man so. She has a lot to learn."

"I thought you saw Leona as a pleasant means to a great end—marriage with the important Carvalho family and your future permanently assured."

"Who said anything about marriage?" he demanded, his eyes glittering with amusement. "Leona isn't as innocent as that."

"So you don't hope to marry her, in spite of Manoel?" she queried.

"I don't think I'm ready for marriage yet and I'm certainly not going to have it thrust on me," he answered. "Besides, I might eventually find that you're the one, although you'll have to wait until I've carved out a satisfactory career for myself."

Janice stared at him for a moment. Then she jumped to her feet. She and Clive had been sitting on a stone bench under a eucalyptus tree.

"Don't flatter yourself, Clive, that I'm going to hang around while you dally with a string of attractive girls. I'm not interested in your career or your future."

He took a step toward her and grasped her wrist. "Janice! Leona says that you've a boyfriend in England, one you're very smitten with. Anyone I know?"

"I don't think so," replied Janice.

Clive swung her around to face him. "So that's your way of stirring up jealousy, is it? You've taken a leaf out of Leona's book. She plays off Manoel against me and probably one or two more men we don't know about."

"How wrong you are!" a voice behind Janice observed in a casual tone.

Manoel stood there, immaculately dressed, his cream suit dappled with shade from the faintly moving tree branches above.

"Leona is very attracted to you, Clive," he continued. "In fact she is asking that you go to her now. She's in the patio waiting for you."

Clive hesitated, a scowl crossing his face as he glared at Manoel. "I wonder if she knew where I was and that Janice was with me, and sent you to break it up."

"Nothing could be further from her thoughts," Manoel assured him with mock concern.

When Clive was well out of earshot, Manoel laughed softly.

"Did Leona really send you with that message?" Janice asked.

"No, of course not. I thought you might like to be rescued, so that was the best way of getting rid of him."

She shared his laughter as they sat on the bench under the eucalyptus tree. "I'll never understand how to deal with your family. It would take me a hundred years."

"It will also take Clive quite a long time to keep up with Leona. For all his experience, he is really a new boy when it comes to handling my cousins. Even I who've known them both most of my life know that they're a pair of very slippery eels."

Janice laughed afresh at the idea of the two Carvalho sisters, so contrasted in coloring, but both so elegantly sophisticated, being likened to eels.

"Let's forget both Leona and Clive for a while. I must take you about to places." Manoel looked suddenly serious. "We can't let you waste all your time here and see nothing."

So during the next three days Manoel became Janice's tour guide, taking her first for a day to Porto, as he had previously promised.

"In England you call it 'Oporto,'" he reminded her as they walked by the quays. "For us it was just 'the port.'"

"Oh, trust the English to mutilate some piece of foreign

language," Janice admitted, "or run the two words together." She began to laugh. "I found that Portuguese 'O'
meaning 'the' very confusing at first. You see it perhaps in
the newspaper headline like 'O sport' or 'O sol' and it seems
like a cry wrung from the heart."

"English is worse," declared Manoel, "for the spelling.
All those words with 'ough' and hardly one alike!"

"Oh, give thanks to be born English and learn the
spelling as you grow up!"

In Manoel's company, as always, she could feel happy
and relaxed, and she wondered if he sought her out sometimes because he felt the same way about her, a sort of mild
rest cure from the turmoil of dozens of conflicting Carvalhos.

On the other days he took her for long drives through the
breathtaking scenery of the Minho province, where in the
villages women wore the most colorful peasant costumes.

On some of the higher slopes the olive harvest was being
gathered, and Manoel and Janice alighted from the car to
watch a group of women spread a large canvas under the
tree while men with sticks climbed the branches and
knocked down the olives to the canvas for the women to
pick up and sort, discarding leaves and small twigs.

"Our landscape looks quite different in spring," Manoel
told her. "It rains then, just like England, and everything is
gray or brown, waiting for the sun. The Douro isn't exactly
a river of gold, but one of mud, bringing down the rains
from the mountains. The vine terraces are bare and leafless.
Suddenly one morning everything is alive, the first pale
leaves are on the vines flickering like shimmering light, the
sky is clear with a blue so sharp that it cuts like a knife edge
and the wisteria on our porch makes a complete ceiling so
that when the wind shakes the blossoms, you feel you're
under the sea in a blue cavern."

Manoel ceased talking and turned a slightly embarrassed
face toward Janice. "Forgive me, I didn't mean to—to bore
you with these long descriptions," he muttered.

"But go on, Manoel. I couldn't possibly be bored when
you tell me about your country. Tell me some more," she
said encouragingly.

As he drove along the twisting roads, he told her of the occasional wolves in the High Douro, where in winter shepherds lit fires to keep themselves warm and keep away the stray wolf. He talked of dawns he had watched over the mountains where the colors were unbelievable; he spoke of the wild flowers—the gay tulips of the Serra, the white broom, the clumps of wild lavender with dark purple flowers.

"I think you only pretend to be a town playboy," she said presently when he became silent. "Your heart is really here in the wild mountainous country among things that grow. You like to watch the cycle of the year. Why must you live in Lisbon?"

He shrugged. "Perhaps I like both worlds. The life of the capital is worthwhile for its culture and its amusements, and our country is small enough for us to come to the north in a day."

"Is that all you're going to do with your life?" she asked. "Commute between Lisbon and the Douro?"

"Who knows?" He smiled obliquely at her. "Much depends on how all our various business interests flourish. Perhaps, also, and even more important, it may depend on my wife and what she likes best."

The expression in his dark eyes forced Janice to look away. It was all a pleasant game, of course, no more, but she did not want to cause complications among the Carvalhos by encouraging Manoel to flirt with her.

Janice had, however, underestimated the communal strength of the Carvalhos when danger threatened from outside. Senhora Carvalho, Leona's mother, had evidently decided that she was best fitted to handle the situation. Manoel's mother, Senhora Ernesto Carvalho, was Portuguese and although she spoke English very well, she could not claim a common nationality with Janice.

Senhora Joaquim Carvalho, her English fairness untouched by countless Portuguese summers, tactfully and casually invited Janice to her own private sitting room almost as soon as the girl had returned from the day's outing with Manoel.

The room was cool and spacious and held a dappled

greenness where the setting sun filtered through the narrow slatted blinds. Janice thought it was like being enclosed in a house under the sea, but the smiling matronly figure opposite was no mermaid.

"I'm sure you'll forgive me if I speak plainly, Janice," began the Senhora.

"Of course."

"Then may I ask you a very personal question?"

Janice smiled and nodded.

The Senhora settled herself. "I understand that you were a—a special friend, shall we say—of Clive Dickson. You knew him in England when he worked in your company there."

"Yes. I knew him quite well. But we were never exactly *special* friends," Janice answered with a deprecating smile.

Senhora Carvalho played with the handsome rings on her fingers. "But since you have met him here again?"

"Senhora Carvalho," began Janice gently, "let me be frank with you. Clive and I are not in love with each other and there's no question of our becoming engaged or married."

"I see." After a pause, the Senhora continued, "He seems to have a remarkable effect on Leona. She, of course, is much too young to know her own mind, but she declares that she wants to marry him. This would naturally be absurd."

"Because he's English?" queried Janice unthinkingly.

"Oh, no." The Senhora gave a quiet laugh. "But one doesn't let one's daughter marry the first attractive Englishman who hovers around. Besides, there is Manoel." Janice realized that the initial chat about Clive was only a finesse approach to the real reason for this interview.

"Leona and Manoel are extremely well suited to each other," Senhora Carvalho asserted, not emphatically, but more with the air of one who has discovered this affinity for the first time. "I would be very sorry if you mistook Manoel's companionship for something stronger."

"Please be reassured, *senhora*," Janice said quickly. "I enjoy Manoel's company. He's charming and it's very pleasant to be taken to interesting places. But when I'm back in England, I shall think of this holiday as one of my happiest memories.''

Senhora Carvalho smiled graciously. "How very sensible you are! But then you have your fiancé waiting for you in England, so Leona tells me.''

Janice let it go at that, neither agreeing nor denying. She had received the full warning that she was not in any way to disrupt the excellent future union of two Carvalho branches within the empire. Yet she longed with all her heart to be able to say that the only young man in England in whom she had the slightest interest was Everard. Deep down, she wondered what electrifying effect this would have had on Senhora Carvalho, who was supposedly quite ready to welcome Everard Whitney as Selma's husband into that same vast Carvalho empire.

Janice tried to talk to Leona alone, but she had no opportunity until late in the evening, when she visited Leona's room.

"Did you tell your mother that you were afraid I might be falling in love with Manoel?'' Janice asked abruptly, having found this the best way of dealing with Leona.

"My mother has good eyesight and can see for herself what is going on,'' returned Leona smoothly.

"Well, I was only carrying out your wishes. You suggested that I might take Manoel off your hands, so that you could gad about with Clive.''

"Clive went back to Lisbon yesterday morning. Didn't he say farewell to you?'' queried Leona.

"As long as he said farewell to you, that's all that matters, isn't it?''

Leona made no reply, but picked up a nail file from her dressing table.

"You're younger than I,'' continued Janice, "but I don't understand the game you play. You know that you don't want to marry Clive and that you'll end by marrying Manoel. Why do you create such difficulties for everyone else?''

Leona swung around on the dressing stool. "English girls are very naive. Here we learn to pull first this string, then that one. It is one of the pleasures of life.''

"It may be for you, but I seem to have received no thanks at all for helping you, if that's what you wanted. All I've done now is offend your mother, who probably thinks I've behaved very badly as a guest in her house."

Leona put out her hand and touched Janice's arm. "No, no, you mustn't think unkindly of me." She raised her eyes and stared at Janice. "I like you better when you argue. You're more interesting. Perhaps you're more a danger to Selma than to me."

"What d'you mean by that?" demanded Janice quickly, aware in a flash that in her own mind she constituted the third point of a triangle between herself, Everard and Selma, even though the other two knew nothing of it.

Leona waved her hand in a sweeping arc. "Oh, nothing. We'll be friends, eh?" Before Janice could reply, the other girl rushed on. "Tomorrow we'll go out by ourselves and make sure we leave Manoel at home. That'll reassure my mother."

"All right." Janice saw, too, that it would be very undiplomatic to go out alone with Manoel on yet another tourist trip.

"But don't tell anyone," warned Leona. "We'll start early—eight o'clock. Have your breakfast in your room, then come down to the gate at the end of the track. You know, where the servants come to collect our luggage and so on."

"Yes, I know the place."

"If anyone sees you, say you're out for a morning walk," Leona instructed. "I'll have the car ready."

It was only when Janice returned to her room that she remembered Leona's madcap way of driving. The ludicrous thought entered her head that perhaps Leona had a drastically effective way of removing nuisances from her life by plunging them over the nearest precipice.

But next day Janice was pleasantly surprised when Leona showed respect for the narrow, twisting, mountainous roads and the delays caused by plodding oxcarts. Leona suggested spending a little time exploring the old town of Vila Real.

"There's also one of the most beautiful manor houses in all Portugal."

Janice agreed to every suggestion, believing that toward the end of her holiday at the *quinta*, Leona had decided there was little to gain by annoyance, especially now that Clive had already left.

The two girls lunched at a *pousada*, one of several special inns built by the state in remote places, often in the mountains where there was little accommodation for the traveler.

At one point, later, high in the mountains, Leona stopped the car where a clump of pine trees clung precariously to the edge of a cliff which fell hundreds of feet below to the river valley.

Janice ventured cautiously to the edge when Leona called her.

"I love standing on these heights," exclaimed Leona, while the wind tore at her long dark hair. "Don't you?"

"No. I get dizzy," Janice lied. She had a good head for heights, but she could not trust Leona one hundred percent. Some vague speck of mistrust constantly warned Janice that today's version of Leona was rather too good to be true.

Back in the car and with Leona driving through a pass between soaring peaks of purple and sapphire, Janice asked, "Where are we now? Where's the map?"

"We're near a small town called Mirandela."

Janice found the place marked on the map and realized that Mirandela was a long way from the Carvalho *quinta*. It was already dusk. Did Leona intend to career gaily through these mountain roads in the dark? Fortunately Janice saw that Mirandela was on a main road, though she sometimes winced when she saw in the car's headlights the crumbling edge of the unfenced road. A cluster of lights blinked far ahead, but the road turned and snaked so many times that it took Leona some time to reach what was obviously not a town, but a small, scattered village.

"It doesn't matter," she said airily. "Mirandela is farther on, but now it's dark, so there's not much to see there."

"Wouldn't it be best to turn back and go home?" queried Janice.

Leona was driving slowly and peering around her. "I'm

looking for somewhere for us to eat. Then, as you say, we'll go home.''

Janice would have preferred to stifle her hunger, but Leona insisted that there was sure to be a small inn or tavern where they could have a simple meal.

After a moment or two she stopped outside a dimly lit house. "Stay here while I inquire," she told Janice, and disappeared through a dark doorway.

She returned within a couple of minutes and beckoned Janice to follow her.

"It will be only a simple meal, but quite good.''

The two girls were shown into a small lamplit room from which evidently other customers had been ejected. An elderly woman came to wipe down a table where drinks had been spilled, then laid a cloth and cutlery.

Leona spoke to her in rapid Portuguese and the woman answered, but the speech was too quick and the accent too difficult for Janice to follow.

"She says they have a nice *caldo verde*. That's a sort of cabbage soup. Then there is ham and other cold meats. But first she will bring us some wine.''

"Won't your mother be anxious after you've been out all day and we haven't returned to the *quinta* for dinner?'' Janice asked.

"Not at all. She knows that when we're at our *quinta* I must have more freedom than if I were in Lisbon.''

To Janice it seemed an odd reply, without logic, but there was no point in trying to pin down Leona to a straightforward argument. She drank the sparkling *vinho rose*, enjoyed the soup and cold meats, followed by yellow cheese, which was slightly tacky but deliciously flavored.

"Good cheese?'' queried Leona. "It's called 'Serra' and comes from farther south in the Serra da Estrela.''

Janice had not realized how hungry she had been when they arrived at this village, but the food and wine put new life into her.

"In a moment we will go,'' said Leona, "but first you must try their special brandy.''

Janice almost choked on the raw, white spirit. "So strong!'' she gasped:

"Nonsense!" exclaimed Leona. "It's better after the first sip. Try some more."

"Glad I'm not driving," Janice murmured, hoping that Leona would be restrained at least in how much she drank.

The walls suddenly began to shimmer and dissolve, to spin around fast. Janice tried to stand, but her feet were made of feathers and were useless.

"Leona! I—I—I think I'm—" she muttered incoherently, and saw the other girl's face swinging in a confused circle.

There was nothing more to see. Darkness reached out and took Janice down into a void.

CHAPTER EIGHT

JANICE OPENED HER EYES and stared at the blackened ceiling above her. She raised her head and a sledgehammer blow seemed to hit her between the eyes. More cautiously she sat up and peered across the room. It was apparently a kitchen with a large black cooking stove on one wall.

Janice saw that she was lying on a rough bench with a cushion at her head and a heavy shawl covering her. For a few moments she held her aching head in her hands, trying to recall what had happened.

Gradually the mist cleared. Of course, she and Leona had stopped at a village inn last night. Obviously they had stayed there for the night.

"Leona!" she called, and a woman came into the room.

She glared malevolently at Janice and spoke in Portuguese, but so quickly and with such a different accent that Janice was unable to understand one word in ten.

"Where is my friend?" she asked slowly.

The woman shook her head, and Janice stood up, but almost immediately sat down again. Her legs seemed to give way under her.

"What happened?" She spoke carefully in Portuguese. "Was I ill?"

For the first time the woman's face broke into a smile. She made a coarse gesture of tipping a bottle to her mouth and pointed slyly at Janice.

"I see. Too much wine." Janice rose again to her feet, determined not to fall this time. "Where is my friend Leona Carvalho?" she asked.

A spasm of terror crossed the woman's face. "Carvalho?"

she echoed. Then she clapped her hand to her mouth and dashed out of the room.

"What's the matter with her now?" muttered Janice, exasperated.

By holding onto the table and a chair she managed to reach the door. *Leona must be somewhere about, surely.*

Janice found herself in a dark passage, but at the end a door was open and she stepped out into a yard. The sunlight hurt her eyes and she craved for shade, for a wash in cold water, for a cool drink to ease her parched throat.

In a corner the woman she had been talking to was now speaking in a very agitated manner to a stout dark man. As soon as she saw Janice again, she gave a shriek and vanished through the doorway of a barn.

The man came toward Janice, giving her an amiable smile and a "*Bom dia, senhorita.*"

He listened carefully to her questions which she repeated all over again.

From his deliberately slow speech Janice gathered that Leona had gone home by car after supper, saying that her friend was too ill to be driven along rough roads, so if she could stay the night at the inn, Leona would return for her in the morning.

Janice thoughtfully digested this piece of news, nodding to the man to show that she understood.

"What made me ill?" she asked.

The man smiled sympathetically. "The brandy was too strong for you. We are more used to it."

She remembered the fiery spirit that seemed to explode in her head. She asked the innkeeper now for a glass of Luso mineral water. When she had drunk it and washed her face in a bucket of water in the yard, intense anger took the place of her former muzziness.

Leona had tricked her again! Here she was miles and miles away from the *quinta* and no idea how to return there. Luckily she was still wearing some clothes, rumpled though her dress and shoes might be, but where were her handbag and money?

She asked the innkeeper and he produced it immediately

from a small locked cupboard behind his bar. "I kept it safe for you," he told her.

Well, this time at least she also had money to provide herself with transport back to the *quinta*.

She made an effort to remember the name of the town that Leona had been making for. Mirandela—that was it!

"Mirandela?" the innkeeper echoed. "Many kilometers. Behind the mountains."

He told her the name of the tiny village in which his inn was situated, but it conveyed nothing to her.

"Then how far is it to the *Quinta Carvalho*?"

He considered for a moment. "About three kilometers."

"Three? But that's only two miles."

He took her to the street and pointed out the road, but warned her that it was very rough.

She handed him a couple of twenty-escudo notes, thanked him for his kindness and set off.

"But your friend?" he called after her.

"It's all right," Janice called back. She knew how much the "friend" would be calling for her this morning. She saw the woman who had behaved so strangely at the inn and seemed terrified at the mention of the name "Carvalho." From a side door of the inn the woman watched Janice, then she crossed herself and darted indoors.

As she marched up the steep road, Janice was more angry than ever. So Leona had only pretended that they were a long way from home and must have a meal. Of course it was the strong wine, probably doped even, and the stronger brandy that had knocked Janice out for the time being, and Leona had marooned her there for the night.

Possibly that was why the woman was terrified at the mention of the Carvalhos' name. No doubt Leona had bribed her not to disclose where the inn was.

But what tale had Leona told last night when she had returned to the *quinta* minus Janice? Was it possible that no one had even missed a guest? It was quite likely that members of the family and their friends were going and coming all the time and no one took much notice of a vacant seat at the dinner table.

The road was certainly rough and stony as she had been

warned, and after about a mile Janice sat down to rest. This morning a light mist obscured the sun and since she had no watch for the time being she had no idea of the time, but she judged it to be fairly early by the slight chilliness in the air.

She wondered again why on earth Leona indulged in such stupid pranks. What had she to gain? Leona's nature was too twisted for Janice to fathom, but the latter blamed herself for being hoodwinked a second time after that first painful experience of Leona's thoughtlessness—or was it a malicious lark, as this latest escapade seemed to have been?

After another half-hour's plodding, Janice was relieved to see some distance ahead the white house with the large letters "*Quinta Carvalho*" painted on the side.

As she neared the gate, she saw Manoel hurrying down the rough path toward her. He ran the last few steps and caught her in his arms. "Janice! What happened to you?"

She smiled. "Nothing much."

"But we were worried about you."

"I suppose it's no use saying that I went out for an early morning stroll?"

"I came home very late last night," he explained, "and naturally I didn't know until this morning when the maid said you were not in the house."

"What did Leona say about it?"

"Leona? Was she with you yesterday?"

"Of course. I went in her car to—to several places."

Manoel shrugged. "Oh, we can sort that out later. Let me take you back to the house."

It was too much to hope that her entry into the house might be unobtrusive, and in this instance Manoel was no help. He called out loudly for maids to come and attend to Janice, although by now she was quite capable of walking up to her room and looking after herself.

Several of the Carvalho family greeted her either coolly or with mystification, not perhaps knowing why she should appear so disheveled early in the morning.

Then Janice found herself facing Selma Carvalho, who suddenly appeared and gave her a frosty smile.

"We thought you had quite deserted our humble country

home," she said smoothly, but with an acid edge, "to go back to Lisbon."

"Where is Leona?" asked Janice, determined to challenge that archtrickster here and now.

"Leona? She is somewhere in the house, or perhaps she may have gone out. I don't know."

"But surely she must have explained that—" began Janice.

"Please forgive me," Selma interrupted softly but firmly as steel, "I have something important to do for my mother. Tell me later about your adventures." She hurried away along a corridor and into another room, leaving Janice standing at the foot of the staircase.

Janice felt that it would be better to face the rest of this inexplicable family after she had showered and dressed. She asked a maid to bring her a pot of strong black coffee and half an hour later, wide awake now, groomed and with fresh makeup, she sought out her hostess, Senhora Carvalho.

But the Senhora was occupied with her cook arranging the catering for the score or more of relatives and guests in the house. Eventually Janice was shown into Senhora Carvalho's personal sitting room—a cool, shady cavern of green and gold.

"I came to offer my sincere apologies," began Janice, as soon as she sat down.

"For what, Janice?"

The girl looked up, startled at this bland imperturbability. Was it possible for even such an English matron to remain unruffled by events?

"For not coming home last night, but you understand it wasn't my fault."

"Of course not." The Senhora smiled her understanding and waited.

"Leona," Janice began, choosing her words carefully. "Leona and I went out for the day, but intended to return for dinner. Then it became dark and—"

"You say Leona was with you?" queried the older woman.

"Of course. She drove the car. We went to a town called Vila Real and—"

"I don't understand, I'm afraid. Leona said she was at home all day yesterday."

Janice was appalled. Of course, Leona had given her account first, removing herself from any hint of blame.

Senhora Carvalho rang a bell and as soon as a maid appeared requested her to find Senhorita Leona.

An oppressive silence invaded the room until the maid returned with the news that Senhorita Leona was not in the house.

Senhora Carvalho rose, indicating politely that she had further hostess tasks requiring her attention.

"Please think no more of the incident," she said smoothly.

Janice realized that she had timed this interview badly. She should have waited until she was sure that Leona would be present.

In the end Leona's presence did not help Janice at all. At the *quinta*, lunch was an informal meal to be taken in the house, the patio, the garden or wherever two or three people wanted to eat. Maids would bring cooked dishes, or salads and fruit, large carafes of wine, cheese or sweet cakes to suit the mood or appetite of the guests. Only the evening dinner was a more formal affair.

Janice was thus able to escape the feeling that she was under a cloud of disgrace in the eyes of the Carvalho clan until she sat at the huge oval table in the dark paneled dining room.

Leona sat between Manoel and one of her uncles and was equally sparkling to both. Janice, sandwiched between two elderly aunts, felt that even Manoel had temporarily deserted her.

After the meal Janice would have been glad to drift away somewhere alone, but a maid told her that Senhora Carvalho would like to see her.

Leona was in her mother's room this time and Janice was elatedly convinced that the truth would now be brought out.

"Janice, I think you are not well," was Leona's first surprising remark.

"I'm perfectly all right—now," returned Janice.

"But why did you tell my mother that we went together to Vila Real yesterday?"

"Because it was true," replied Janice. "Perhaps it is you, Leona, who are suffering from loss of memory." Those impulsive words were a mistake, for they recoiled on her in a manner she had not bargained for.

Leona laughed. "I never went near Vila Real yesterday. Someone else took you there—if that's where you went."

"But we lunched at a *pousada* and then you drove all through those corkscrew mountain roads," repeated Janice. "Then when it was dark, you saw a village, so we had a meal there—and—"

"Yes?" prompted Senhora Carvalho.

"I felt ill," continued Janice, "and I—I went to sleep—and when I woke up, Leona had gone."

Leona shook her head slowly. "It's well known that at grape harvest even the air is full of fancies. People imagine things that have never happened."

"These events certainly happened to me," declared Janice.

"And when you woke up—your friend who was with you in the car had driven off?" Senhora Carvalho asked.

"Leona had driven off."

"But my car is still in Lisbon," Leona protested. "How could I have taken you in it yesterday?"

It now dawned on Janice that Leona had not used her familiar green car, but a small black one.

"You were driving a different one," Janice muttered.

Leona restlessly moved across the room. "Ridiculous! In any case, Selma knows that when she arrived we sat in her room talking for a long time."

Senhora Carvalho glanced from her daughter to Janice. "I do appreciate," she said evenly, "that English girls nowadays have a tremendous amount of freedom, especially when they are completely independent as you are, earning your own living and so on. But if you wanted to go off for a day—or stay longer—it might have been better to mention it to me."

Janice was crushingly rebuked by the Senhora's cool,

gentle words. Yet she still struggled to make herself believed.

"But the whole point was secrecy," she said. "That was how Leona wanted it."

Leona, who had so far seemed in admirable control of her fiery temper, now whirled around on Janice. "Secrecy?" she exlaimed. "What sort of secrecy should I practice here in my own home?" She turned toward her mother. "Janice is ill with delusions. The other day she accused me of taking her purse and hiding it!"

"Indeed I did not!" stormed Janice. "I only blamed you for taking my clothes home in your car after we'd been bathing."

"There! You see!" Leona was exultant in her triumph. "One accusation after another."

"Leona!" her mother called. "Please don't shout like a fishwife!"

The inference was not lost on Janice, who rose, mustered what dignity she could and said, "I'm sorry, Senhora Carvalho. I have nothing more to say. Please forget what happened." After a hesitant moment, she went on, "If you would like me to pack, I'll do so tonight. If someone will drive me tomorrow to Oporto, I can go back to Lisbon by train."

Senhora Carvalho smiled in her usual unruffled way. "There's no need, my dear Janice. Everard is coming tomorrow and he'll probably make arrangements for you."

Janice went out of the room into the garden, then decided to go to her room. She sat on the bed and reviewed her position. Undoubtedly, Everard would be regaled with a lurid version of recent incidents. Oh, what did it matter? He thought of her as a nitwit, a stupid lump of inefficiency. Now when he left her in charge of his friends at their country villa, she even managed to get herself into a reckless scrape. His opinion could hardly fall lower than zero. Yet she wished with all her heart that she could have done something, performed some small action that might have put her on the credit side.

She was unprepared for Leona's call later that night.

"Have you come to apologize for all those lies you told

your mother?'' asked Janice. ''If you haven't, I've no wish
to discuss anything further.''

Leona's dark brown eyes gazed at Janice. ''You were
quite foolish to tell my mother your story.''

''Why? You had already told her your version. Why
shouldn't I tell her the truth?''

Leona suddenly sat down on Janice's bed. ''Janice, d'you
think I could really tell her the truth—that you were—well,
that you had drunk too much?''

''And whose fault was that?''

''Your own entirely,'' was Leona's innocent answer. ''I
warned you that the wine was strong.''

''On the contrary, you continually persuaded me to have
more and then finish up with raw brandy—the kind they
give to the grape treaders to keep them going when they're
cutting the vintage. In any case, why did you leave me at the
inn? How did you know I wouldn't be robbed or something
even worse happen to me?''

''Nothing bad would have happened there to you. I know
the old couple who keep the place.''

''Of course. That's why you bribed them.''

''Janice, you don't remember how violent you were. You
were yelling and shouting 'I want to go to Mirandela.' ''

Janice was not impressed by this further tissue of invention. ''And instead of being near Mirandela, as you said, we
were only a couple of miles from your home. How can I ever
believe another single word you say?''

When Leona was silent for a couple of moments, Janice
said quietly, ''What was the real purpose, Leona? I'm
asking because I want to understand why you play these
senseless pranks.''

''If I told you, you wouldn't believe me. You've just told
me so.''

''Quite probably I wouldn't believe you,'' Janice admitted. ''All I can see is that you want to do everything you can
to discredit me with Everard, don't you?''

''If you say so, perhaps it is true. You should go back to
England as soon as possible and marry your young man
there. Then we shall not feel unhappy, Selma and I.''

''Selma? D'you really think I could come between her

and Everard if he's the man she wants?'' Janice forced herself to say the words in the most derisive tone she could manage. There was no possibility that Leona would give even a qualified yes.

"Everard has been here to Portugal many times,'' Leona said slowly, "but he has never brought a secretary with him before. We think that is very strange.''

Janice laughed shakily. Whatever the cost Leona must not discover the way Janice felt about Everard.

"Not very strange,'' she said crisply. "He needed someone to work with him all the time. When he returns he'll probably bring a new girl with him to take my place, someone more efficient and businesslike.'' She paused, then could not resist the chance of a dig at Leona. "She might turn out to be a real rival, very formidable, to your sister.''

Leona's face brightened. "Then you're going home soon?''

"I don't know. Nothing has been arranged. Let's wait until Everard comes.''

When at last Leona had gone, Janice stretched on her bed, yielding to the delicious anticipation of Everard's arrival the next day. No matter what anyone told him about her misadventures, she would see him again.

IT WAS LATE AFTERNOON the next day before Everard arrived, having flown in to Oporto, but Janice made a point of not being on the doorstep to greet him. From her balcony she saw the car arrive, the chauffeur alight, then Everard, his thick hair none too tidy. The sight of him made her heart turn over with a sickening yet delightful lurch, but she calmed herself. Soon, now, the whole adventure of her stay in Portugal would be over, a high spot to look back on during the years when she continued a more sober business career.

She was in the lantern-lit patio with a dozen other people gathering for a drink before dinner when he came toward her. She had prepared herself for this moment, but now she was stuck by an agonizing shyness and could utter only the most mundane remarks. "Did you have a good trip? Was it a success?''

He smiled at her over the top of his sherry glass. "Very good indeed. And your holiday?"

"I've enjoyed it very much. Wine pressing, olive harvest, all sorts of things."

"Back to work tomorrow." His eyes held a mock threatening light.

One of the senior Carvalho uncles led him away to a shadowed corner, no doubt to talk business. Poor Everard! In demand as soon as he arrived from England. But of course if he was leaving for Lisbon tomorrow, there would be few other opportunities.

After dinner when she hoped to at least join the fringe of the companionable circle of guests which surrounded Everard, Manoel suggested a stroll in the garden.

"Janice, please come with me. I understand that Everard intends to whisk you back to Lisbon at first daylight, so it's your last night here."

Manoel had exerted himself to make her holiday a pleasant one, so, after a moment's hesitation, she allowed him to guide her away from the patio into the more secluded part of the garden.

"After Lisbon, what follows?" he asked.

"I don't know," she confessed. "Everard hasn't had a chance to tell me his plans."

Manoel sighed in the darkness. "I wish it could all have been different," he said softly.

"In what way?"

"That you could stay here permanently."

"But you know I can't," she pointed out.

"Not if you married a Portuguese? I've become very fond of you, Janice."

"I like you, too, but when I go away you'll soon forget me."

"No, I shall always remember you. When I first met you I thought Clive was the rival for me to stumble over. But I soon found that that wasn't so."

When he paused Janice remained silent, for the trend of this conversation was making her apprehensive.

"I need never have worried about Clive," Manoel went on. "There was someone else."

She laughed gently. "Leona has been telling you about a man I know in England."

"Leona talks as the birds fly and often with no more direction. Sometimes I think I'm in love with you, Janice, but then I remember this other man and I know you will never love me."

"I've told you—I like you very much," protested Janice, "but it's not love."

"No. You have love for him, but is he as indifferent as he tries to appear?"

"How d'you mean? You don't know him."

"Oh, yes, very well indeed. Your eyes light up when he comes toward you." She turned her head away from him, although under the eucalyptus and tall magnolia trees it was dark.

"Is it so obvious?" she whispered. She valued Manoel's friendship too much to fence with him and pretend that she didn't know he was referring to Everard.

"Only perhaps to me."

"Then keep it a secret between us," she begged. "He's a difficult man to understand and I—"

"Courage, Janice. You must open his eyes. At present he's blind."

She shivered. "No, there's nothing I can do. But please promise that you won't ever let him know."

Manoel laughed softly. "Of course I promise." He took her hand and pressed it to indicate the bargain. "If he can't help himself why should I guide his footsteps?"

After a long pause, she said, "We seem to have got ourselves into some ill-assorted pairs, haven't we? What of Leona? You'll eventually marry her?"

"No." His answer was brusque and direct and she feared that she had offended him. "At least you've saved me from that. Some day she'll meet a man who'll tame her and then she'll be very happy."

Janice agreed with this perceptive remark of his. Leona would never respect a gentle, considerate man like Manoel whom she could twist into a knot and flaunt in her hair.

"Leona fights everyone because she is still fighting herself," he continued. "When she grows older, she'll relax."

Janice laughed. "I wish I'd met her when she was rather older. She does the craziest things—and as for the truth—"

He patted her hand. "At this moment we take everything she says with a very large handful of salt. She is so opposed to going back to school in England that she'll do anything to prove what a bad influence an English girl can be."

"Including making me tipsy—and abandoning me for the night!"

"If I'd known of the adventure sooner I'd have come to the inn and brought you home," he said.

After a few moments Janice asked, "Have you any ideas about your own future?"

In the darkness she could feel that he merely shrugged. "In our family there are several pretty cousins—also there are daughters belonging to many other important business concerns in Lisbon or Oporto. Marriages are intended, of course, to strengthen the inheritances, but first I shall put more of my time into the affairs of our various *quintas*. And who knows? Perhaps I shall end up by bringing an attractive peasant girl into the family circle."

"That might be a good thing instead of so much intermarrying. Besides, I would hate you to be dragged into an arranged marriage for the sake of finance."

They walked back toward the patio, now almost deserted, and a tall figure detached itself from the shadow of an archway.

"Oh, there you are, Janice," Everard said coolly. "I was beginning to wonder if I'd see you again tonight, with Manoel luring you off into the enchanted wood. I'm afraid it's an early start tomorrow. Will you be ready to leave by, say, nine o'clock?"

"Easily," she answered. "Anytime you say."

"Right. Then I'll leave you and Manoel to your wanderings again, but don't stay up too late, Janice. Good night."

He went abruptly into the house, and it was only then that she realized that she and Manoel had been standing there hand in hand.

"We are dismissed," laughed Manoel, "so come! We might as well take his advice and exchange a good-night kiss and wish each other the best of luck."

A few minutes later when Janice entered the house there was no sign of Everard or indeed of either Selma or Leona.

Wryly, Janice wondered if Everard was also exchanging a good-night kiss with Selma, to seal this brief reunion and comfort her for tomorrow's parting.

CHAPTER NINE

JANICE WAS UNEXPECTEDLY CHEERED next morning when she discovered that Everard was driving her back to Lisbon and there were to be no other passengers.

Some of the family and guests were at the front door to wave goodbye. Manoel came out to give Janice a small parting gift, but Selma did not put in an appearance and Leona stood leaning over the balcony of an upstairs room.

Everard seemed unusually talkative during the first part of the journey. Then he asked suddenly, "Aren't you going to open your present from Manoel?"

She picked up the flat package from her lap. "If you're impatient to see it, I'll open it."

"Perhaps you already know what's inside."

"No. I don't." She undid the wrappings and took out an embossed leather purse with a matching notecase and wallet all in warm pale brown. Her initials were stamped on both wallet and purse.

"M'm," commented Everard. "Excellent. Now why didn't I think of giving you a new purse to replace the one you lost?"

"It didn't occur to you, I expect." This morning, after his week's absence in England, she felt more on equal terms. She could give him slightly flippant answers without chewing the words over first.

He slowed down to pass a cart drawn by a pair of blond oxen linked by an elaborately carved wooden yoke. When the road was clear, he said casually, "Manoel is quite a decent fellow, a good companion and all that, but—"

"But I'm not to fall in love with him?" She gave Everard

a quick smile. "All right, I've been warned—several times. Don't worry. Manoel isn't in love with me either."

"Glad to hear it." His tone seemed a trifle brusque. "Heaven knows what further complications might arise if he decided not to marry Leona because he'd found someone else."

"Manoel says he isn't going to marry Leona anyway. She doesn't want him either."

"Oh?" Everard momentarily turned his head toward her. "Have you put an end to that arrangement?"

"I don't think I had any effect. Manoel is too nice to be pushed into marriage with his cousin merely for the sake of family money."

Everard began to laugh. "So you've taken an interest in Carvalho futures? What about Leona? Is she too nice also?"

Janice did not reply for a few moments and Everard went on, "I heard about some strange incidents concerning you two."

"I wonder if you heard the truth," Janice said.

"I don't know. You tell me your version."

She stared stonily ahead. "No. Whatever I tell you, you'll either laugh at me or storm at me."

He drove for several miles without speaking, and Janice realized she had gone too far in her blunt speech. They stopped at a wayside inn for coffee and cokes, then strolled in the surrounding garden before entering the car again.

A cloud of gloom had descended on them, for which Janice blamed herself. When she settled herself in the car, he tossed a small twig with a few silvery leaves into her lap.

"Come, Janice," he said, "we have a long drive before us and I'd like to hear all about your holiday at the *quinta*. I promise I'll neither laugh nor storm. Fair enough?"

She smiled at him. Then she launched into an account of the day-by-day trips with Manoel and finally with Leona.

"And you say she left you at this inn?"

"Yes. Fortunately, I found that instead of being miles away from the *quinta*, it was quite near."

"Leona's a strange creature," Everard murmured. "She behaves like a spoilt child one minute and an old harridan the next." After a pause he said, "You didn't tell me that

the day at Estoril when you lost your purse she'd left you
without your clothes.''

"I wish she hadn't told you now!" Janice said quickly.
"At least I managed to keep that to myself when you were so
cross with me for getting back late.''

"But I'd have been more sympathetic over that.''

"I think she knew what she was doing," declared Janice.
"Just another of her merry pranks.''

His gaze was fixed on the curving road ahead. "The
people at the hotel must have been rather—surprised—when
you emerged from your taxi.''

There was just the faintest trace of amusement in his
voice, and she looked quickly at his face to find his lips
curving in a smile.

"You see? I knew you'd laugh. Men find the idea irresist-
ibly funny. At least I was wearing my large hat," she
finished crossly.

"I'm not laughing," he protested, unable to control his
guffaws. "It's just that you're such a complete goose.''

The effect on Janice startled even herself, for she burst
into tears. For the first time in Everard's presence she was
crying—quietly, yet with the tears raining down her face.

He stopped the car at once. "What's the matter? What
have I said?''

"Nothing. It's just—that . . . that you treat me like a
stupid child!''

With his arm around her shoulders, he dabbed at her
tears with his handkerchief.

"Not true, Janice. Not true. I'm very much aware of you
as, well, certainly not a child. Where's your sense of humor
gone?''

Now that she was calmer, her head cradled on his
shoulder, she reflected that women in love can't always see
the funny side of events concerning the man in question.

Even now he was still treating her as a child that must be
soothed—smoothing her hair away from her face, even
planting a light kiss on her cheek.

"Janice, there's something I want to say—'' he began.

She glanced upward and saw in his eyes that same
intense, dancing light that had wrought such mischief in

her, the look that was both demanding and pleading at the
same time. He was holding her in a close embrace, his face
only inches from her own.

"I—for a long time I—" he began again.

A violent screech of car horns jerked the moment apart.

"Damn!" said Everard. A glance through the rear window showed him that a truck wanted to pass and apparently
his car was half blocking the road.

He started the car and drove off at a furious rate, out-
distancing the truck in no time.

Janice remained quiet, wondering what Everard had
been about to say, wondering if she had only imagined that
leaping light in his eyes, telling herself that she was merely
guilty of wishful thinking. Idly she picked up the twig that
had fallen between the seat and the car door, twiddled it for
a few moments in her fingers, then tossed it through the
open window.

Everard seemed intent on driving to Lisbon in the
shortest time, stopping for lunch at a restaurant in Coim-
bra, then driving off again without delay. While he did not
remain silent, he spoke mainly of impersonal matters as
though he were an acquaintance she had just met who was
politely giving her a lift to Lisbon.

Only once did he mention business matters. "By the
way," he said casually, "those figures for the new hotel, the
estimates I wanted for the conference—I did better by
returning to England. They got out a new set of estimates
and we've been able to cut down on some of the costs, so
perhaps it was just as well that you weren't available for
that telephone call."

In spite of his grudging tone of voice, Janice accepted this
as a compliment, even though it was only by accident that
she had been missing at the appropriate moment. "I'm glad
of that," she smiled. "So we shall get the contract for the
new hotel?"

"The company will get it, no doubt."

His correction was like a douche of cold water. She
realized that she must not associate herself with the company as "we." Now it flashed across her mind that possibly
Everard had been on the verge of sacking her when the

impatient truck driver interrupted him. Of course, he would
try to wrap it up nicely—*Take her in your arms and be ready
to kiss away the next flood of tears when you tell her the sad
news. Dear Janice! Utterly sweet, but impossible to work with,
always getting herself into appalling scrapes. . . .* She could
fancy the words going over in his mind. Now he would have
to make another opportunity to tell her of her impending
dismissal, but next time she'd be ready for it, braced with a
smile and certainly no tears.

As they approached Lisbon, Janice remembered that she
had done nothing about reserving accommodations.
Everard had scolded her that first day when they had
arrived at the Hollandia. What should she have done? She
had received no instructions from him.

Tentatively she asked, "Are we going back to the Hollandia? Do they know?"

"We're staying at the Carvalhos' house for a day or
two," he answered. "Then we'll move elsewhere."

The news surprised her, but she was thankful that Selma
and Leona were still at the *quinta*.

When Everard drove into the stone-flagged courtyard
that had been built for horse carriages, a manservant came
immediately to take the suitcases.

Almost immediately a familiar voice floated out of the
house. "Everard! Oh, you've arrived." There was Selma
with her cool English rose fairness, superbly dressed in a
sapphire blue silk edged with white, her slender arms bare
to the cutaway shoulders.

Janice could see now why Everard had been in such a
hurry to get here.

Selma took Everard's arm in a proprietorial manner,
giving Janice a brief smile and nod of acknowledgement.
"Everything's ready," Selma was saying.

Janice, following several paces in the rear, thought this
was almost a repetition of that first meeting with the
Carvalhos, when Selma had drawn Everard away, leaving
Janice alone in a strange garden.

Not precisely the same though, for history repeats itself
only inexactly. Now Everard turned toward Janice. "Janice
and I will be staying here only a couple of days. You know

that," he explained to Selma. "We could have gone straight to the hotel, but—"

Selma laughed in her well-bred, musical manner. "But my mother insisted on your staying here."

At dinner several members of the Carvalho family were present, although Janice could scarcely remember having met them before.

Everard had been given a room in which to work and next morning he and Janice started on a pile of estimates and reports concerning the various jobs in hand.

After a week's lazing and sight-seeing, Janice was ready to concentrate on the hard realities of hotel property, building specifications and the shortcomings of bureaucratic officials. In this way she had less time to dwell on the situation between Everard and Selma.

By late afternoon Everard had decided that the work could be safely left for a short time. "Let's take a breather," he said to Janice. "We've slogged long enough." He put on his jacket and led Janice to a part of the Carvalho garden that she had not previously seen.

"Oh, it's exquisite!" she exlaimed. A double archway led to a small, oblong pool, the borders massed with flowers, zinnias, canna lilies and exotic shrubs with unfamiliar names. At regular intervals thin jets of water curved into the pool, the light catching them against the dark background of the dense camellia hedge that walled in this hidden water garden.

"It's really Spanish style," Everard explained, watching her delight. "A small copy of gardens in Granada. The Moors introduced them. One of the Carvalhos was Spanish from Andalusia and he made most of the gardens here."

"Water bracelets," murmured Janice, listening to the music of water splashing and running in hidden channels.

Placed conveniently here and there were benches covered with *azulejos*, the handsome blue and white tiles found in many parts of Portugal and Spain. Sometimes the patterns were formal, geometrical arrangements of leaves or flowers; others told narratives in pictures of animals or humans. Janice paused before one where dogs and chickens, bullocks and birds were apparently engaged in some festive gala.

"The quick brown fox jumps right over the lazy dog in this one," she said with a laugh.

"Let's sit down on this sporting piece," Everard suggested. For a few moments they sat in silence, contemplating the darkening garden. Yet Everard seemed totally unrelaxed, as though he were wrestling with a complicated problem. Surely he could leave his business worries behind him for half an hour, Janice thought. He fidgeted uneasily, then said suddenly, "I suppose you know, Janice, that Dickson is going to Brazil in a month or two?"

She turned her face toward him. "No, I didn't know. Are the Carvalhos sending him?"

"No. He's taken a job with another firm."

Was this the momentous announcement that had apparently given him so much concern? She wanted to laugh and tell Everard that wherever Clive went was no more than a triviality to her.

To prove this point to him, Janice deliberately changed the subject. "Do you want me to reserve a hotel accommodation for you at the Hollandia—or elsewhere?"

This, surely, would give him the chance of saying outright that he would make his own plans, plans that did not concern her, that he was sending her back to England or whatever it was he had in mind.

He gave her a measured glance as though he were first weighing his words. "There's a suite at the Castelo—the hotel we're rebuilding," he said at last. "It'll be ready tomorrow—but you might check that." Once more he was her business chief.

As they walked back to the house, Selma came out. "Everard! I've been looking everywhere for you. Where have you been?"

"In the garden—with Janice," he answered, accenting Janice's name in case Selma could not guess the fact herself.

"I want to talk to you," Selma said. "I'm sure that Janice won't mind."

Janice went to her room, convinced that Selma's real intention was to break up anything that looked like a tête-à-tête unless it were for strictly business purposes.

They were all in the middle of dinner when one of the maids waiting at the table spoke to Selma.

"Telephone?" queried Selma. "Ask them to leave a message. We're at dinner."

The maid glanced at Everard. "Is it for me?" he asked her. When she nodded he rose at once, excusing himself.

"Don't bother, Everard," exclaimed Selma impatiently. "Surely business can wait while we eat!"

In less than a couple of minutes he returned to the dining room. "The Castelo hotel is on fire. Janice, get a coat and come with me."

"But—Everard—" Selma's voice followed them as Janice hurried after Everard. She ran upstairs for a coat and came down at full speed. He was already waiting in a car and as soon as she slammed the door shut, he turned out of the gate and down the street.

Janice was too sensible to ask Everard if he knew how the fire had started, or whether it was serious. On the telephone he could not yet have received many details.

The Castelo occupied a corner site and both streets were cordoned off, with police and firemen guarding the barriers.

Everard spoke to one of the policemen and was allowed through along with Janice.

It was a spectacular fire with smoke pouring out of windows on some of the upper floors, several of which were ablaze.

In the hotel vestibule crowded with visitors who had been forced to leave their rooms, Everard questioned the anxious manager and several of his subordinates while Janice jotted down answers.

"Are all the visitors and staff clear of the top floors?" Everard insisted. "You're sure of that?"

"Quite sure," the manager agreed, but Everard was not satisfied until he had the word of the fire chief that no one remained.

"You've checked the service elevators in case someone is trapped?" queried Everard.

"Yes, all the elevators and all the stairs."

At midnight the crowds in the streets had melted away, for there were no more orange flames against a blue black sky. Only smoke still wreathed around the blackened upper stories of the hotel; the streets were still cluttered with fire appliances, ambulances, and police cars. Everard and Janice had found a couple of chairs and were taking a few minutes' rest while they munched bread rolls and slices of ham and wedges of cheese washed down with cool white wine.

"See if you can get me some brandy, Janice," Everard said. "The barman has probably run out of stock with all these hotel visitors demanding it for the shock to their nerves. Try, anyway."

She pushed her way through the crowd of guests refusing to leave through the crush of press photographers and reporters. When she returned triumphantly with two large *ballons* of cognac Everard had disappeared, but he was suddenly at her elbow a few minutes later.

"Good girl! This'll save my life."

"You'd better drink both glasses," she said, laughing up at him.

"You need it, too," he urged.

"No fear! Not after what happened when Leona wished me 'good health.'"

"This isn't the same. That was raw spirit." He looked at her and burst into laughter. "You look comical, Janice. You've a large smudge down one side of your face and your lipstick's gone to pot."

"Pooh!" She grimaced at him. "You don't look too *soigné* yourself. *Your* face is dirty all over, your shirt's a mess and you seem to have lost your tie."

With the brandy glass in his hand he stood laughing helplessly, and after a moment's hesitation she joined in. She realized what satisfaction there was in working in emergencies for this demanding man. When things went wrong he seemed to be at his best in overruling the circumstances that had caused disaster, and she was touched with pride that tonight he had chosen her to accompany him when he could so easily have come alone or asked Selma.

It was past three in the morning when at last most of the vestibule was cleared and hotel guests had been persuaded to go to rooms that had been found in adjacent hotels.

"Make sure, Janice, that we have a list of people boarded

out for the night. You can get it from the hotel receptionist who has attended to the reservations. We shall need that information to put it on the claim for the insurance company.''

A loud crash like thunder above their heads made them both glance up.

''Another ceiling gone, I fear,'' was Everard's comment. ''Possibly the suite of rooms they had ready for us.''

''Am I to reserve a suite somewhere else?'' she queried.

''Wait until tomorrow,'' he advised. ''We can always get in at the Hollandia, I think.''

He drove her back to the Carvalhos' house in the gray dawn and, apart from the fact of the fire disaster itself, she thought she had never enjoyed an evening with Everard so much—except, perhaps, that other night at the amusement park.

How different he was when he allowed that businesslike veneer to peel off and reveal the boyish attitude underneath! Was that how he behaved with Selma all the time? Janice was too tired even to be jealous as she slipped off her clothes, cleaned her face and tumbled into bed.

CHAPTER TEN

JANICE FOUND A MESSAGE on her breakfast tray next morning. She was to go down to the Castelo hotel about midday. She realized at once that this was Everard's tactful way of letting her sleep late, but as soon as she had showered, dressed, and eaten her rolls and coffee, she took a taxi to the Castelo and arrived there before eleven.

"I've brought the typewriter down here," Everard told her, "and I think we can squeeze into the manager's office. The insurance people are sending an inspector this morning, so grab yourself a little desk space and I'll give you the damage reports as the inspector and I do them piecemeal."

Two of the senior Carvalhos were in consultation with the hotel manager when Janice entered the office and she subsided into an unobstrusive corner.

The damage by fire and subsequent hosing was extensive, and Janice thought how heartrending it must be for Everard and the Carvalhos to find most of their new reconstruction work ruined.

There was a pervading odor of water-soaked, charred furnishings throughout the hotel; carpets were being taken up to be dried and cleaned; furniture was assembled in some ground-floor rooms to be inspected.

"Half the main staircase has gone," Everard told Janice when she came into the office again. "Curious thing, the fire seems to have started on the fifth floor, Suite 500. That was the one I'd reserved for us."

She glanced quickly at him. "Could it have been an accident? Perhaps the electricians working on it?"

He bent toward her. "Sabotage, I think, but say nothing yet."

For the next two days she and Everard worked all day and half into the night on the long, detailed reports, which had to be corroborated by insurance assessors, the Carvalho company and Everard himself.

At the end of that time Everard decided that he and Janice needed a break.

"We'll take tomorrow off and do simply nothing," he said.

"Thank you."

"And then we'll move to the Hollandia. We've stayed here with the Carvalhos long enough."

Janice was ready to leave the Carvalho house at any time, although in the last few days she had seen little of it or of Selma.

On the way home in the taxi, Everard decided to alight at the Avenida Palace. "There's someone I might see there if I'm lucky. The taxi will take you to the Carvalhos'. See you later."

When the taxi stopped outside the street entrance to the Carvalho house, Janice alighted, then hesitated as a maid opened the iron gate. A man hurried out, looking furtively around him, then walked quickly down the street.

Her curiosity mounted and she followed the man at a discreet distance. There was a vaguely familiar look about his figure, yet she could not place him.

He turned the corner where café tables curved along the pavement, and as the light streamed out from the café she saw the man's face—Columbano, the head clerk at the company's Lisbon office—the man whom Everard had been ready to sack if only Clive had not left, as well. What was Columbano doing skulking around, visiting the Carvalhos?

She soon had the answer. Dawdling in the shadows and avoiding the shop and café lights, she saw Columbano join another man at an outside table. Probably no more than a casual meeting between friends, she thought, but then a roll of notes changed hands and went into Columbano's pocket. A waiter brought drinks and the two men raised their glasses to each other.

Janice walked back to the Carvalho house very slowly, pondering this strange incident.

Indoors she was immediately greeted by Manoel, who had returned to Lisbon because he had heard of the fire.

"You're tired, Janice," said Manoel solicitously. "Everard's been slaving you to death."

"There certainly has been a lot to do," she agreed. "but the worst is over now and he's given me a day's holiday tomorrow."

"Good. Then come out with me. We'll just amble about the city or go wherever you like."

"All right," she answered, seeing no point in arguing. She might as well make the most of whatever time was left to explore Lisbon.

She thanked Manoel for the leather purse and wallet. "They're both beautiful," she said, "and I'm delighted to have them."

Leona had also returned to Lisbon, but this fact did not particularly delight Janice.

When she went up to her room her attention was suddenly arrested by something on the dressing table—a brown leather purse. Janice opened it. Inside were her gold watch, the Portuguese money, and a few stamps. She sought Leona before dinner and demanded to know the truth.

"One of the chauffeurs found the purse in my car," Leona explained in her airy, nonchalant manner.

"But how did it get there?"

"You must have dropped it when you undressed in the car. I told you the purse must have fallen from your bag."

Janice drew a deep breath. Leona's explanation was plausible.

"Thank you, Leona. I'm glad to get back the watch at least."

Everard returned later in the evening, long after dinner, and Janice was eager to tell him about Columbano's café appointment.

"Columbano?" Everard echoed softly. "Of course! He has a grudge against me personally. I sacked him, but he'd seen that coming, especially as Clive Dickson had also told him to watch out."

"What would he be doing in exchange for the money?" asked Janice.

"He gambles heavily. His salary doesn't allow for that, so he has to make a bit in other ways. Bribes for information, a commission here, a rake-off there. Oh!" exclaimed Everard. "Oh, I see daylight now. That fire at the Castelo started in our suite, the one we were to occupy. What Columbano didn't know was that I had changed the date of arrival. The Carvalhos insisted on our staying at their Lisbon house for two or three days. That suited the Castelo manager who said the rooms were not quite ready. But Columbano thought we were already there and went ahead with his original plan."

"D'you think he intended to injure you?"

"I doubt if he cared, but at least he hoped to cause me a great deal of trouble if all our business documents were destroyed." After a pause, Everard continued. "There was another point, too. I found out some time ago that the insurance policies for the reconstruction work at the hotel hadn't been renewed at the proper times. That was Columbano's responsibility—probably he'd swindled the premium money one way or another. So if damage had occurred in any way—fire, explosion, water—we wouldn't have a leg to stand on with the insurance if the policies had lapsed."

"Another black mark against our company," commented Janice.

"And a big hole in the profits of the job," added Everard grimly.

"I wonder why he was here at the Carvalhos' house," said Janice.

"Somewhere on the staff here he has a contact, but Columbano slipped up over the dates and he may have imagined that someone was double-crossing him."

"You wonder who really gains by all this," Janice said. "Columbano seems to have got his money, but the man who paid it—what does he gain?"

Everard shrugged. "Just another form of gambling. Sometimes win, sometimes lose." He gave a long sigh, then lit a cigar. "That's enough of business headaches. I said we'd take the day off tomorrow."

"You haven't changed your mind?" queried Janice with a touch of apprehension.

He laughed. "You think the slave driver is regretting his promise? No, Janice. I thought we might potter around together, spend the day at Sintra or Queluz, perhaps. Most of the tourists have gone and places are quieter."

She closed her eyes in misery. Why hadn't he suggested this before she committed herself to going out with Manoel? Then it occurred to her that Manoel would understand if she broke her promise to him. She'd explain that Everard's time was more limited.

"Yes, I haven't been to either place yet," she said now.

"We'll start fairly early in case some telephone call or urgent message pins me down here. Then we can visit Queluz first and go on leisurely to Sintra."

As soon as she could she planned to find Manoel and tell him of the change of plans; then, at that moment Manoel himself came toward the corner of the patio where Everard and Janice were sitting.

The two men talked first of the hotel fire, the aftermath of clearing up the debris and the details still to be settled.

Then Manoel said suddenly before Janice could warn him, "I hear you've given Janice a day off tomorrow, so I'm taking her out, in case you change your mind and glue her to the typewriter."

In the silence that followed, Janice was aware of Everard's complete withdrawal from her as though he had removed to another planet. Janice began helplessly floundering, "Manoel—I—I—"

Then Everard's steely voice broke in. "I see, Janice. I didn't realize you had a previous engagement for tomorrow. You should have told me. Of course you must go with Manoel."

He rose, called a brief good-night and went into the house.

"What's bitten him now?" asked Manoel.

"I was going to tell you, but I hadn't a chance," she said hurriedly. "He wanted me to go with him to Sintra and I—I thought if I asked you, you wouldn't mind—" Her voice trailed away in despair.

Manoel was silent for a few moments. Then he said, "Well, I'd have minded, but I expect I'd have given way, for your sake if not my own. No use making the sacrifice now I suppose?"

"None at all," said Janice emphatically. "Everard won't make the offer twice."

"I'm sorry I've made a mess of it," said Manoel contritely. "Shouldn't have blurted it out like that, but I'd no idea. Anyway, I'll do my best to give you a wonderful time tomorrow, Janice."

Tears rose in her throat, choking her, and she wanted to rush away, careless of dignity or anything else, but what would be the use now? When she could control her voice, she spoke of other subjects—the beautiful garden hidden alongside the Carvalho house, the fact that her watch and purse had been mysteriously returned to her, any topic that came to her mind.

"So you needn't reproach yourself now about Portuguese honesty," she told him.

But when eventually she reached her room, she stuffed her head into the pillow and wept for her own impulsive inanity and her power to offend the one man in all the world with whom she longed to be in loving harmony.

MANOEL, TRUE TO HIS PROMISE, exerted himself next day to be the thoughtful host and Janice responded, believing it churlish to vent her disappointment on him. She made suggestions or fell in with his ideas and partly succeeded in forgetting her grief over the missed day with Everard.

"Let's go up in the street elevator," she said. "I don't seem to have had time to do that yet."

Where Lisbon's hills rose too sharply for trams or buses, funiculars and street elevators served to convey people from one level to another. At the top of the Santa Justa elevator shaft a covered passage led over rooftops and courts below to the Largo do Carmo, an irregular-shaped square from which streets veered off at unexpected angles. Standing in the cobbled space with Manoel, Janice had the illusion of being suddenly transported to a different town. Close by were the ruins of the old Carmo Church, open to the sky with its nave and aisles turned into a well-kept garden where cats sunned themselves on broken pillars.

"You've been shopping, of course, in the Rua Garrett," Manoel said as he and Janice left the Carmo. "Known as our Bond Street or Via Veneto."

"Yes, but I arrived there from the other end, toiling up an impossible hill. I didn't know this was the easy way."

For a time they gazed in windows at the beautiful jewelry and silverware, the elegant clothes, the vast rows of books; they sauntered through streets down to the Cais do Sodre where a banana boat had just unloaded and barefoot women shouted raucously, offering the curving yellow fruit at ridiculously low prices.

"Today's banana day," murmured Janice. "Last time I was here all the women had lemons. Good ones, too. I bought some."

Apart from the fruit sellers, the fish women known as *varinhas* were always there with their baskets on their heads and their incessant cries of "Fresh fish!"

Manoel suggested lunch at the riverside restaurant on the opposite side of the Tagus at Cacilhas and they took the ferry.

Janice had visited the Floresta restaurant on previous occasions, but it was still a delight to sit by the windows watching big and little ships glide by. Best of all was to view Lisbon looking like a city of washed marble rising in irregular tiers from the river, towers and church steeples breaking the skyline.

It became a day of small pleasures, a savoring of the charming delights that Lisbon could offer, and Janice was thankful that Manoel sensed her mood so well and did not try to hustle her around in tourist fashion.

They returned across the river to Belem, the fortress with the wedding-cake tower and spent a little time in the Jeronimos Church where the cloisters were like lacework carved in white stone.

In the early evening when they sat at one of the crowded cafés in the Rossio Square, Janice said, "That's a sound that startled me when I first came to Lisbon. I thought someone was being shot."

Manoel was having his shoes cleaned by one of the shoeshine boys who roamed hawk-eyed through the cafés, seeking dusty, mud-stained shoes. The buzz of conversation was punctuated by the staccato crack as they flapped their cloths against the shoes to give a glowing mirror shine.

"If you would like to go home to our house and change for dinner early," Manoel suggested, "we could slip out somewhere by ourselves."

"I wonder if we need to do that," she said. "Would you mind if we stayed here and then later have dinner at a restaurant?"

Manoel agreed instantly. Janice did not want to run the risk of meeting Everard in the Carvalhos' house, nor did she want to be waylaid by Selma or Leona or anyone else.

It was nearly midnight when Manoel and Janice returned to the house and walked through the quiet, dark garden.

"Thank you, Manoel," she said, "for a really perfect day." That was true. The day itself had been perfect. The only flaw was that she had chosen the wrong companion.

"Perfect for me," whispered Manoel. "I wish we could spend the days like this forever."

"Gallantly spoken, but then what would the *quintas* do without you? Where would your family business be if you didn't pay occasional attention to it?"

Manoel chuckled softly. He had paused as though he were searching for something in the flower beds. "Ah, yes, this is it," he muttered.

He put a short twig into her hands, but in the dim light from the house she could not see clearly what it was.

"What is it, Manoel?"

"An olive branch, of course. It means peace between us. You must forgive me for taking you away today from Everard."

"An olive branch?" she whispered. She walked toward the nearest lantern in the courtyard and looked at the small silvery leaves. "Oh, how foolish I was!" she murmured, pain twisting her heart at the memory of that other olive branch Everard had thrown into her lap.

"We have here in our garden one small olive tree for this

purpose. It doesn't grow well in a town, but it's useful when we have family quarrels.''

"It's a charming thought,'' she said.

"But you realize that you must never hand on to someone else what has been given to you,'' Manoel continued. "You must always pick a branch specially for one person.''

She was silent until they were inside the house. Then she said, "Thank you, Manoel. Thank you very much.''

She wondered if he understood that she was thanking him for considerably more than a day's enjoyment. He had shown her the way to make at least some gesture to Everard.

She rose very early next morning, packed her belongings ready for the move to the hotel, gathered up all Everard's business documents, then went quietly downstairs and out into the garden. She was sure she could remember roughly where the olive tree was. She turned a corner and almost ran slap into Everard.

"Hello! Out for a morning stroll in the rain?'' he queried.

She had scarcely had time to notice that a fine drizzle was falling. "I've packed everything,'' she said, ignoring his idle question.

"Good. Have you had breakfast?''

"Not yet.''

"Then we'll have it inside. There're quite a number of points I want to discuss with you.'' Even at this hour of the morning he was implacably businesslike.

"I'll bring my notebook,'' she said, with a touch of sarcasm.

There was no chance at this moment of finding the olive tree, but later she would search again. She could always ask Manoel where exactly it was.

Ill luck chased Janice that morning and by the time she and Everard stepped into the car that was to take them to the Hollandia hotel she had not been able to seize a single opportune moment to find the olive tree.

The goodbyes echoed in her ears as the chauffeur moved out of the courtyard. Mechanically she waved to Selma and others of the household, but all the time she was glancing nervously out the window for signs of an olive tree.

"Did you have a pleasant day yesterday?" Everard asked her.

"Yes, thank you. Very good indeed."

They were like strangers embedded in separate ice blocks. Janice was glad that there was a busy day ahead while they settled in at the Hollandia in a different suite from the one they had formerly been given.

"They caught Columbano," he told her later, "at the docks. He was trying to get away on a ship to West Africa."

"Oh? Was he the only one involved?" She was not wildly interested but had to make a pretense of being concerned.

"No. Columbano soon squealed and put the police on to several more important men mixed up in the game."

"Was it deliberate sabotage?" she asked.

"I'm afraid so."

IT WAS NEARLY SIX in the evening before Everard showed signs of halting work. "Let's have a drink and call it a day," he said without enthusiasm.

"I want to go out for a short time," she said quickly. "I've some shopping to do."

"Why on earth didn't you say so?" Exasperation sharpened his voice. "You could have gone out long ago."

"Don't worry. I can get what I want now." She went into her bedroom, flung on a coat and left the suite before he could argue further. As she waited for a taxi to draw up outside the hotel she glanced up at the fourth floor suite. Everard was on the balcony watching her, but she gave no sign. *Let him think what he likes,* she thought.

At the Carvalho house she waited outside the wrought iron gates until a maid let her in. "I think I left something in my room this morning," she explained. She had thought up that excuse in the taxi. She made the futile journey to the room she had occupied, waited a minute or two, then went downstairs again. Oh, if only she could find Manoel; when she asked for him, however, she was told that he was not at home.

"Thank you. I'll go out through the garden," she said.

She paused at about the spot where Manoel had picked the branch the night before, but in the darkness she could not distinguish one shrub from another. She saw one of the garage men in a lighted doorway. If she hesitated much longer someone would think she was loitering in the garden for no good purpose. Boldly she asked him where the olive tree could be found and he took her straight to it. He was about to pick the branch, but she said hastily, "No, let me do it."

Poor little olive tree, she thought. *No wonder it doesn't grow well, with everyone plucking bits off it every time there is a quarrel.*

She thanked the man.

"*Sim, senhorita,*" he said, and escorted her to the outside gates, and called a taxi for her.

Clutching the precious emblem, she returned to the hotel, but realized she must hide it under her coat in case she met Everard.

He was not in the sitting room. Perhaps he had gone out.

She took a shower, then for no reason except that she wanted to cheer herself up, she put on the glittering silver dress she had bought soon after she first came to Lisbon. She brushed her dark hair, piled it high and added a twist of sparkling braid to the chignon.

Then she went into the sitting room, quivering with apprehension, her palms damp with tension. Everard glanced up at her almost automatically, then gave her a second sharp look.

"Gala night?" he queried. "Who's the lucky man this time?"

"Why? Must I ask you which dress I can wear and when?" To answer so sharply had been far from her intention, but his sardonic tone drove her to return cut for cut.

"I merely wondered." Then he took a step toward her. "We can't go on like this," he said fiercely. "Either let's be civilized or part company. If you want to go home, say so. What I can't stand is—your dishonesty"

She stared at him. "My dishonesty? When have I been "

"There was yesterday, for instance. Oh, yes, you'd come out for the day with me, when all the time you'd arranged to spend it with Manoel. Then again, tonight, you pretended to go shopping. Tell me the truth, Janice. You did nothing of the sort, did you?''

She remained stubbornly silent.

"Who was so important that you had to go tearing off in a taxi to meet him?''

Still she did not answer. Then as his eyes roamed impatiently away from her, he saw the small sprig of olive. For a long moment he stood motionless. Then he picked up the branch.

"Where did you get this?'' he asked softly.

"Does it matter?'' Tears were threatening to choke her.

"Of course it matters!'' he thundered at her. Then, more quietly, "Does it mean peace between us?''

She looked at him with stormy sherry-brown eyes.

"It looks like it, doesn't it?'' she blazed at him. "Yes, you'd better send me home. It's impossible to work with you anymore.''

He came toward her. "It's impossible for me, too. You've done that to me. I swore I'd never fall in love with any girl who worked for me, but you crept under my defenses.'' He put his hands on her shoulders. "I love you, Janice.''

She raised her face and stared at him. The expression in his eyes set her heart thudding so that she trembled, but she refused to believe yet the truth she so longed to hear.

"What about Selma?'' she forced herself to say.

"Selma? She's a sparkling piece of ice. Oh, I admit I admired her very much. Her very coldness was a challenge to me, the same as to all the other men she gathers around her. There was a time when I thought I wanted her, mainly perhaps because she was remote and unapproachable. So I brought you to Lisbon with me—''

"To make Selma jealous?'' she queried when he paused.

"In a way. I know it was shameful to use you like that, but I didn't know then that I was going to be caught in my own trap. At first when you went around with Dickson I was glad, but I soon found that I was the one who was jealous.''

He held her closely in his arms and rested his cheek against hers.

"I can't believe it,'' she whispered.

"That I love you, darling?''

She smiled at him. "It's wonderful to hear you say it."

He kissed her lips, her temple, her cheek with tenderness. "But why did you throw away my olive branch?" he wanted to know.

"I didn't understand," she answered. "You have to thank Manoel for that. He told me how it was symbol— although of course I ought to have known."

"Manoel!" he repeated. "He took you out, he gave you small presents—all the things I hadn't the wit to do for myself. But, Janice, I'll begin right now to make amends if only you'll say you love me."

"D'you need to be told?" she countered, her self-confidence surging back. "Why else d'you think I hared off in a taxi to the Carvalhos' little personal olive tree?"

He laughed joyously. "So that's where you got it?"

"You'd have had it sooner if only you'd given me two minutes this morning instead of hovering and fidgeting at my elbow."

He laughed again, then held her close. "That's what I love about you, Janice. You don't mince your words. You may be softhearted sometimes, but you go straight to the point with that peppery tongue of yours. Oh, I can see I shall have to watch out when we're married!"

"Married?"

"Well, yes." He looked down at her face so close to his own. "Didn't you hear me the first time?"

"A good secretary always gets her facts verified."

Some time later when they had made a pretense of eating dinner and had toasted each other with champagne, Everard said, "I don't know if you want to go out, Janice, but I've two tickets for a concert in the Estufa Fria. D'you want to go or shall I tear them up?"

She looked into his eyes. "You already had them, hadn't you?"

"Yes," he admitted. "Then I saw you togged up in that damned dress and I thought—"

"Let's go." She cut his explanations short. She had seen the beautiful little concert hall tucked away in the Estufa Fria, but had not visited it until now. In the darkened gardens, there were small lights edging the paths, exquisite little patches of floodlighting to illumine the tops of trees or a mysterious grotto. Then there was the blaze of light from the concert hall where all one side was window. Inside at the back was a rock garden, where water glistened but fell without sound.

The evening went by like a dream. Janice was conscious only of music that transported her to another world and of her hand held firmly in Everard's warm clasp, anchoring her to his world.

When they returned to the hotel, he said, "We'll have that day together at Sintra. Tomorrow."

"But the work—"

"I've worked enough for ten men in the last few days. Let them whistle for me!"

To Janice the next day seemed a hazy blur. There was the setting out in a rented car for the pink and cream miniature Versailles at Queluz in the hills behind Lisbon. There were cool rooms with small fountains in the middle, a ladies' drawing room with magpies pointedly decorating the ceiling and, surrounding the former royal home, vast gardens and dark, water-stained sculpture.

Then to Sintra where the palace in the town resembled a Kentish coasthouse with its funnel chimneys, and halfway up the hill almost hidden among pine woods was a mansion like a pale stone cruet, all knobs and pepperboxes.

Everard parked the car and hired a horse-drawn carriage to amble up the hill to Pena. Perhaps this was really the way to see the scenery, Janice thought dreamily. When the heart was so full of happiness, beautiful surroundings added the gloss.

"We shall have to go back to England soon," Everard told her as they descended into the small town of Sintra again. "Oh, yes, I forgot—who's this chap at home that you're supposed to be tied up with?"

She laughed. "He isn't in England now. He's sitting next to me. That was just another wrong conclusion of Leona's."

"A fabrication just to keep me on the hooks?"

"Not intentionally."

"We'll come to Portugal again," he promised. "For both

business and pleasure. I shall have to make many visits with all these hotels on the move.''

"Will you bring a secretary with you?'' she asked, her eyes dancing.

"I'm not sure. I shall have to ask my wife about that.''

He pulled her close and kissed her, then drew her head onto his shoulder. The carriage driver slowed down his horse. It was unkind to disturb young couples who were in a dream world of their own.

DOCTOR AT VILLA RONDA

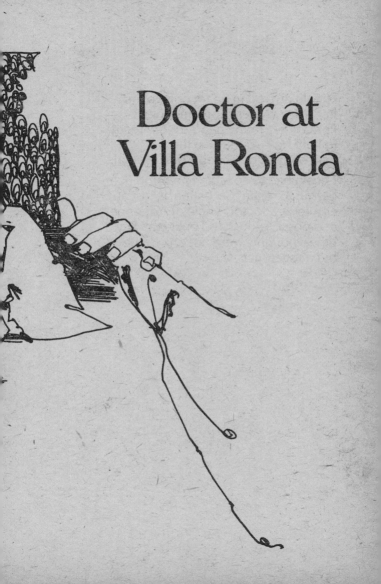

Doctor at
Villa Ronda

Nicola arrived in Spain only to find her sister mysteriously missing. Fortunately many people were ready to help her—including the handsome Doctor Sebastian Montal.

Nicola had to constantly remind herself to regard Sebastian as just an employer, doctor, uncle of Adrienne and possible husband of Elena. Any other thoughts were not only futile but dangerous!

CHAPTER ONE

NICOLA WAS COMPLETELY UNABLE to understand the situation. A slim girl above average height, with light brown hair and intensely blue eyes, she stood now in the vestibule of the block of apartments, trying to decide on her next step.

It was disconcerting enough to arrive in Barcelona and fail to find her sister, Lisa, at either the airport or the city terminal to meet her, but to come now by taxi to Lisa's address only to be told that the English *señorita* had left the apartment some days ago was bewildering.

"Do you know when she will return?" Nicola had asked the woman in the neighboring apartment. The woman shook her head and shrugged, leaving Nicola uncertain as to whether her question had been understood.

Again she checked the address Lisa had given her. There might be other English girls living in the same block.

The only alternative now seemed to be to find a hotel in Barcelona and hope that Lisa would return very soon.

Her thoughts were almost completely occupied with anxiety about Lisa's mysterious absence, yet Nicola could not fail to appreciate the wide expanse of sapphire sea under a cloudless sky, the dazzling new promenade and blocks of modern apartments that had replaced the old unsightly wharves and warehouses along the seafront.

As soon as a vacant taxi appeared, Nicola handed the driver her one suitcase and told him to take her to one of the well-known travel agencies, where she explained her situation.

"My sister is probably away on business," she said. "I can't get into her apartment, of course, so perhaps you'd recommend an inexpensive hotel I could stay at for a night or two."

She produced her passport and after a few minutes the clerk told her that a room was booked in her name at a small, comfortable hotel just off the main *rambla*.

In the privacy of her hotel, Nicola changed out of her traveling suit, freshened her makeup and put on a light-weight blue dress.

She read again Lisa's recent letter.

. . . Why don't you give up your work and come here? You could easily take over my job. It bores me, but you'd probably like it. In any case I'm leaving soon. I've had a modeling job offered me and that sounds much more fun . . . at least come here for a week or so and see how you like Spain. . . .

Nicola had not seen her younger sister for nearly a year and Lisa wrote at irregular intervals, but this particular letter had come at a crucial point in Nicola's own career.

The firm where she worked as secretary to the assistant manager had been taken over by a larger concern, her boss had found himself a position elsewhere and Nicola had to work for three men instead of one. From a comparatively peaceful, responsible position she had been pitchforked into an atmosphere of haste and chaos where each of her three bosses clamored for his own work to be done first, testily interrupting her before she could finish each task.

Nicola was not in the habit of accepting Lisa's usually wild suggestions, but this time she had acted on impulse and replied that she had given notice and would come to Barcelona for two or three weeks.

" . . . Perhaps I needed this shake-up," she wrote to her sister, "to get me out of a rut. I'm sure I can get another job when I come back . . . ."

Lisa's reply, dated only a week ago, had been brief, merely asking when Nicola would arrive. Nicola had already sent this information before Lisa's second letter arrived.

But now, with Lisa's nonappearance, Nicola was not sure

how long she could stay in Barcelona. She calculated the cost of her hotel room, added what she imagined to be the price of meals, a few pounds for minimum sight-seeing, and reached the conclusion that she could probably manage something less than a fortnight.

Surely during that time she would be able to contact Lisa.

It now occurred to her that Lisa might be ill and helpless in the apartment with no one to attend her. The neighbor might be wrong in believing that the English girl had gone away.

Nicola found the telephone number of the block and asked to be put through to Señorita Brettell's apartment, as Lisa's name was not in the directory.

There was no reply to Nicola's call and after half an hour she tried again with no result. Then what about the firm for which Lisa worked? That was where she was most likely to be if she had merely changed her home address.

Nicola now realized that she did not know the name of her sister's employers, except that they were wine shippers and had an English-sounding name. Even if Lisa had already changed her job, they might know where she had gone.

By the time Nicola had found a local post office and hunted through a classified trades directory it was past seven o'clock, but she tried two of the most likely firms, knowing that Spanish working hours usually ran later than English ones because of the long afternoon siesta.

Neither firm had ever employed a Miss Brettell, they said.

Dispirited, puzzled and hungry, Nicola decided that a good dinner might revive her. After a meal in a small restaurant facing the Rambla Capuchinos, she strolled across to the wide tree-lined center of the *ramblas* where, it seemed, half the population of Barcelona was milling around, hurrying, strolling, buying newspapers and lottery tickets at the kiosks, drinking coffee at tables grouped under the trees.

She paused to watch an artist at his easel surrounded by a small knot of bystanders. She compared his canvas replica with the long vista of plane trees in their fresh May foliage, the darkening sky, street lamps pricking the distant dusk, the hurrying or leisurely figures, now caught by the painter in a moment of arrested motion. He seemed unconcerned by onlookers or their comments.

Nicola was luckier next day in her inquiries, for when she telephoned the only other likely firm on her list, an English voice answered.

"Yes, there was a Miss Brettell here, but she left some time ago," the man said.

"Some time ago?" Nicola echoed. "But—but I thought—well, d'you know where she works now?"

"No, I'm afraid not."

"Then d'you know her present address?"

"If I did," he replied, "I don't know whether she'd like me to give it. I think she stayed somewhere off the Paseo de Gracia, but she's moved around quite a bit. May I ask why you're interested?"

"I'm her sister and I've come for a holiday," Nicola explained, "but I can't seem to get in touch with her."

There was a pause. Then the man spoke. "I'm sorry I can't help you at present, but would it be possible for us to meet? My name is Patrick Holton and I work for this firm. If you'd like to have dinner with me tonight—or tomorrow—I might be able to help you in some way."

"That's very kind of you," Nicola said impulsively. When she put the telephone down she wondered if she had been wise in accepting a dinner invitation from a man she didn't know and had never seen. She reminded herself that she was nearly twenty-four and even if she were alone in a foreign city it was not so very different from being on holiday alone in Bournemouth.

She was ready, wearing a new cream suit, when Patrick Holton called at the hotel at half-past eight. He took her to a restaurant near the Plaza Cataluna and during the meal she had opportunities to study him.

She judged him to be in his middle twenties, but with his pleasant, smiling face he could easily have been older. Tall and slim with fair hair, he looked completely English, and his friendly manner soon put her at ease.

"You're not at all like your sister in looks," he observed.

Nicola smiled. "Oh, no, I'm not in the same street as Lisa. She's the pretty one and I'm ordinary."

Against Lisa's small, dark-eyed, vivacious appearance Nicola had often felt at a disadvantage.

"Tell me what made you decide to come to Barcelona," he suggested. "We might be able to find a clue that will lead us to Lisa."

Nicola explained about the letters that had passed between her and her sister, the sudden decision to leave the now unattractive London job, but she did not mention Lisa's idea that Nicola should take over the job in the Barcelona wine shippers! That could come later, although she doubted whether there was a vacancy now if Lisa had left some time ago.

"I went to the apartment on the Paseo Maritimo and a woman told me that Lisa had left a few days ago," Nicola said.

Patrick's eyebrows shot up. "The Paseo Maritimo? Those apartments are quite stylish. Wish I could afford one."

"When did Lisa leave your firm?" she said.

"I checked that before I left tonight," he answered. "End of March, roughly six weeks ago."

"Six weeks?" Nicola instantly suppressed the dismay she felt. That meant that Lisa had already changed jobs before she had suggested Nicola's visit. Why hadn't she said so?

After a long pause Nicola asked, "What was Lisa's work in your firm? Was she satisfactory?"

Patrick took a few moments to answer. "She typed invoices, and I gather she wasn't exactly the darling of the department. She was very unpunctual and apparently took a day off when she fancied."

Nicola smiled. It sounded so typical of Lisa, who had jumped from one job to another ever since she had left school. Aloud she said, "My sister doesn't like monotony."

"I don't think she liked any kind of work, either," he observed.

He had shrewdly summed up Lisa's attitude to earning a living. Nicola was barely twenty and Lisa eighteen when their father died suddenly three years ago. Their mother had died some years before.

Nicola naturally assumed responsibility for her younger sister, but at eighteen Lisa had already planned what she wanted out of life. "Luxury, clothes, gaiety—and no hard work," she had told Nicola many times over in different words.

She was disappointed that their father had left so little money. "Let's sell this house," she had suggested to Nicola, "and take a small apartment in central London. We're so far out here at Richmond."

On the lawyer's advice, Nicola had insisted that part of Lisa's half-share of the proceeds was to be held in trust until she was twenty-one, but the rest had been speedily exhausted, and it was Nicola who usually had to pay the expenses of the small apartment the two girls shared in Bayswater.

Courses at a drama academy, then a modeling school, had proved both expensive and unfruitful in furthering Lisa's career and she found it impossible to settle in a job for more than a few weeks. As soon as she was twenty-one and could claim her trust fund she was off, first for a prolonged holiday with friends in Italy and Corsica. Then she wrote to Nicola that she was working in Barcelona and having a wonderful time.

But where was Lisa now?

"You could try the British Embassy," Patrick was saying, "and see if they have news of your sister. Or, of course, the police, the *policía.*"

Nicola sighed. "If Lisa's gone away for only a few days, she'd be furious if I did that."

"I think you ought to try to get into that apartment of hers," he continued. "You might find some sort of clue there. She may even have left a letter for you."

"How simple! I see that I ought to have insisted on being let in yesterday."

"Somewhere in the building you'll probably find a caretaker who has master keys," Patrick told her.

He promised to keep in touch with her and next morning she went early to the apartment block on the Paseo Maritimo.

She tried Lisa's door hopefully and rang the bell, but

there was only silence. Only after a heated argument with
the woman caretaker, with Nicola brandishing her passport
to prove her identity, was the girl at last allowed to enter the
apartment, accompanied by the caretaker.

Nicola gazed at the fine spacious room with modern
furniture, a bathroom with shower, a small alcove ostensibly for cooking, but the apartment was as impersonal as a
hotel suite. There was not a single possession anywhere:
empty wardrobe and drawers, no cosmetics on the dressing
table. There was nothing to prove that Lisa had ever lived in
the apartment.

"You knew my sister?" Nicola asked the caretaker.

"*Si, señorita*." A composed, shut look crossed the woman's face.

"No address?" pursued Nicola.

"*No, señorita*."

Nicola's knowledge of Spanish was no more than elementary, but she managed to understand from the woman
that the apartment rent was paid until the end of the month.
Then if the Señorita Brettell did not return, it would be let
again.

Nicola made a swift, impulsive decision. Why should she
stay in the hotel for the rest of her holiday when she could
take over the apartment for the next two weeks? She would
be here on the spot, too, if Lisa returned suddenly.

She thanked the woman, gave her a few pesetas and told
her that she would be returning tomorrow to stay for a week
or two.

Back in the hotel Nicola sat on her bed to consider her
next step. Even staying in Lisa's apartment was only a
negative measure incapable of solving by itself Lisa's
disappearance.

The fact that Lisa had apparently cleared out all her
possessions seemed to indicate a planned, if hasty, flight.
But why? Over and over again Nicola asked herself that
question.

After lunch she went out to explore the cathedral and the
old quarter of Barcelona. So far she had not had much time
for sight-seeing.

Returning down the Calle de Santa Ana, she saw a notice

advertising an art exhibition. Last Day, announced a strip pasted across the board outside the small salon. She went in, received a program and toured the two rooms. Evidently the exhibition was for young painters under twenty-five, and Nicola thought how encouraging it was that so many of the pictures indicated that they were sold.

Out of several stylish portraits, Nicola's gaze was drawn to one of a man with harsh, eaglelike features, black hair and a somber expression in his brown eyes. In the black cloak with silver fastenings, the head slightly downbent as though he were considering an intricate problem, he looked like one of the original Inquisitors.

She looked for the artist's name and checked with the catalog. Adrienne Montal.

Nicola moved away, stared at landscapes and still lifes, but found herself drawn back to the portrait by the young artist Montal.

"You like it?" a voice spoke to her in English.

Nicola turned to face a girl of about seventeen, fair skinned, with pale golden hair and an attractive, youthful candor in her gray eyes.

"Very much," Nicola answered.

"He's my Uncle Sebastian," the girl explained. "Not really handsome, but one does one's best."

"Then you're the artist Adrienne Montal?"

The girl nodded. "Do you paint?" she asked Nicola.

"No, but I like looking at pictures. You must be very talented to have your work here when you're so young."

Adrienne giggled. "I really cheated," she admitted. "I have been well commended for my painting of the cloak and the background, but Sebastian, my uncle, was difficult. He was impatient and would not wear a nice expression, so I made him happier than he really is."

Nicola's fleeting thought was that the unknown Sebastian must be an extremely bitter-looking individual.

"The cloak one paints afterwards," Adrienne continued. "It is easy to drape it on a hanger."

Nicola laughed. "Perhaps you ought not to be telling me all these trade secrets."

"Oh, I am very glad to talk to someone who will praise me. I do not like criticism," Adrienne added disarmingly.

Nicola studied her catalog. "You have other pictures here?" she asked.

The girl shrugged. "No others." She grimaced. "I offered some landscapes, but the judges did not like them."

"Bad luck."

As Adrienne conducted Nicola to some of the best exhibits, again Nicola's glance covertly returned to the portrait of the unknown Uncle Sebastian.

There were few people at this time in the salon, but suddenly Adrienne turned to greet a tall man coming across the room.

"Oh, here is my uncle," she exclaimed. "He has come to collect me now that he has finished his work at the hospital. He is a doctor." She grinned mischievously at Nicola. "Now you can see for yourself if my portrait is good or bad."

But Nicola's interest was aroused not so much by comparing the man with the picture as by the fact that he was connected with hospitals. Why hadn't she thought of inquiring for Lisa at some of the city hospitals?

"D'you think I could—that is, I mean—" she began incoherently, but Adrienne was already making introductions.

"Pardon me," she turned toward Nicola, "but I do not know your name. This is my uncle, Dr. Sebastian Montal."

Nicola supplied her name and realized even while Adrienne explained her meeting with an English girl that after the usual conventional greetings uncle and niece would leave and that would be the end of the matter.

Nicola had to act swiftly, if perhaps discourteously.

"Dr. Montal, I believe you are connected with the hospitals here?"

He inclined his head in agreement.

"Then forgive me if this is not the correct thing to do, but my sister . . . ." She gave a brief account of Lisa's disappearance. "How can I find out if she is in hospital somewhere?"

"First I could find out if your sister is in the hospital I

attend," Dr. Montal answered. "Then there are several convent hospitals."

"Thank you very much." Nicola wrote her address on a slip of paper and handed it to him. "Today I'm still at the hotel in Santa Ana, but tomorrow I will be staying at the apartment for perhaps a fortnight. After that—I don't know."

His strong, eaglelike features softened for a moment.

"I will do what I can," he promised. Then he turned toward his niece. "Adrienne, if you're ready?"

He gave Nicola a formal bow and moved away toward the exit of the salon.

"Goodbye, Miss Brettell," Adrienne said breathlessly. "We live at Orsola de Mar. You must come and see us."

She followed her uncle out of the salon and as Nicola watched the two disappear, the tall man in a light gray suit, the blond girl in a hyacinth-blue dress, it seemed as if they had taken light and vitality with them, leaving the exhibition salon dim and lifeless in spite of the glowing pictures on the walls.

Nicola waited a few minutes before leaving. She did not want to appear to be following the Montals, but when she stepped out into the narrow street where practically all the second-floor balconies were decorated with flowers in window boxes and tubs, there was no sign of the doctor and his niece.

In the lobby of her hotel, Nicola studied the large map of Barcelona, but could not find the place mentioned by Adrienne.

"Orsola de Mar?" the receptionist echoed. "About forty-five kilometers from Barcelona. You can go by train."

"Oh, I see. Thank you." Nicola had imagined that the Montals lived in a suburb, but the place Adrienne had mentioned was nearly thirty miles away.

For the time being Nicola gave no more thought to Adrienne's casual suggestion. She had to pack her clothes and pay her bill in readiness for leaving early the next day.

She found time to telephone Patrick Holton to tell him about the move.

"The rent is apparently paid, so I might as well move in,"

she said, and then continued with an account of her meeting with Dr. Montal and his niece.

"It never occurred to me that poor Lisa might actually be in hospital," she went on. "I know it was stupid, but she's hardly ever ill."

"Well, a doctor should be able to trace her, if she's ill. I've no further news at this end," Patrick told her. "Look, let's forget your sister for a bit. Tomorrow's Saturday. How about coming out with me somewhere? You ought to see something of Barcelona while you're here."

Nicola hesitated. Then she said, "I don't want you to feel obliged to take me around just because I'm English—and Lisa's sister."

"That hadn't entered my head," he retorted. "All right. What shall we say? Three o'clock I'll meet you at the foot of the Columbus monument, the Colon. That suit you? It's handy for both of us."

Although Nicola agreed, she was to some extent worried that an urgent message might come when she was out enjoying herself, but then, she reflected, one could not stay in all the time.

It took only an hour or two next day to settle herself in Lisa's apartment and she persuaded the caretaker to provide her with a key.

As she unpacked and put underwear into the dressing-table drawers, a small hard object rattled around. Nicola recognized it at once—a small topaz brooch in antique silver setting that one of Lisa's friends had given her for her birthday.

So Lisa had really stayed here. Nicola stood with the brooch in her hands, cold shivers chasing up and down her spine. Four days in Barcelona and still no news of Lisa, who must have known exactly when Nicola was expected to arrive. Even if for some reason Lisa did not want to meet her sister yet, surely she could have sent a reassuring message. Or was Lisa in some particularly bad scrape and afraid to make even that contact?

About midday a letter was delivered, addressed to "Señorita Brettell." Nicola eagerly tore it open without examining the postmark. This might be the clue she had been seeking.

Instead, the note was a cordial invitation from Adrienne to spend the next day, Sunday, at the Montals' villa in Orsola.

If you can take the ten-o'clock train from the main station, I will come to meet you and take you to our home. Adrienne.

So it had not been one of those meaningless phrases—"Do come and see us." Adrienne's intentions had been sincere.

Nicola told Patrick of the invitation when she was walking with him in the city park.

"Orsola de Mar? Yes, I know it. A very pleasant fishing village up the coast."

"You don't know anything of this doctor, I suppose?" she queried.

Patrick grinned. "Actually I haven't been ill—yet!"

They spent the afternoon on the sandy beach farther along the promenade. "How long have you been in Spain?" Nicola asked.

"Nearly two years."

"Why did you come in the first place?"

Patrick smiled. "I'd spent a couple of holidays in Spain and I suppose I liked the climate. The firm I work for is partly British, and somehow you feel that shipping wine and importing foreign spirits is more interesting than selling soap or breakfast foods."

"Especially in a country where you buy good wine so cheaply," Nicola observed.

"What are you going to do if Lisa doesn't turn up before your holiday runs out?" he asked.

She hesitated. "Go home, of course. I couldn't stay here indefinitely."

"But you've no job to go back to?" Patrick sat up and spoke earnestly. "Look, I could probably get you a job here—either in my own firm, or recommend you somewhere else where you'd be comfortable."

"That's very kind of you, Patrick, but I can't really make any plans yet. I must wait and see."

"Well, let me know how you feel. You'll need a work permit and one or two other documents, but I could help you there."

"Thank you."

Nicola thought it unlikely that she would need Patrick's assistance. It might have been possible to step into Lisa's position, but it seemed that her sister had left behind a rather unsatisfactory reputation where work was concerned and the firm might not relish employing another Miss Brettell.

Then, too, there was the apartment in Bayswater. Nicola had struggled to keep it on without Lisa's contribution on the assumption that sooner or later Lisa would return to London and need a place to live.

It was inconceivable that Lisa had disappeared without trace. She had probably had to switch her plans at short notice and even now there might be letters or telegrams at home telling Nicola of some new address.

All the same Nicola was eager next day to see Dr. Montal in case he had news of her sister.

Adrienne met her at Orsola station and led the way to a long white car.

"It is only a short drive to our house," she told Nicola.

Nicola had a glimpse of the harbor as the road climbed out of the village and Adrienne took the fork that led away from the main road, drove through a pair of open gates and halted before a large white house with an arcaded front. Nicola followed the young girl through the center archway to a courtyard, massed with flowers and trees, feathery palms, trellises laden with foliage and splashed with color.

"We must immediately have something to drink," declared Adrienne.

When a young manservant appeared, Nicola decided on iced lemonade rather than wine. Half-past eleven was rather too early in the day for her, whatever the Spanish habits might be.

"My uncle will not be home until nearly lunchtime,"

Adrienne informed her, "so we have time for bathing. You swim?"

"Yes, but actually I haven't brought bathing things with me today," Nicola answered.

"Oh, that is no matter. We have a selection of swimsuits for our guests. Also we have our own pool in case we do not want to go down to the seashore."

After resting in the cushioned wicker chairs for a while, the two girls walked through part of the extensive gardens surrounding the Montals' villa.

The pool, lined in azure blue tiles, was surrounded by a flower garden and completely secluded, yet within easy reach of the main part of the house.

Nicola enjoyed swimming in the warm pool.

"Much warmer than bathing around our icy shores at home," she called to Adrienne, who was floating lazily on her back.

"There is no sense in plunging into freezing water," Adrienne replied.

Nicola reflected that her hostess probably did not realize how few opportunities the average English girl had of swimming in private pools in flower-scented gardens.

Dr. Sebastian Montal arrived home only a few minutes before lunch and Nicola was anxious to ask him if he had learned any news of Lisa, but she restrained herself until the meal had begun. The three sat at a table in a corner of the main courtyard in the dappled shade cast by the canopy of three dwarf palm trees.

After an impressive selection of hors d'oeuvres, from which Nicola had to choose between some twenty or more tempting dishes, Adrienne said, "I hope you can eat *calamares*. They are small squids. If not, we will offer you something else."

"I would like to try," replied Nicola. "What's the use of eating everything English when you could at least try Spanish food?"

She glanced at the doctor and saw that for one swift moment an expression of approval flitted across his stern features. It seemed the moment to ask for information.

He shook his head in answer to her query. "Nothing so

far, I'm afraid. No young woman has been brought in during the past week or ten days. No girl, that is, answering to your description or of that name."

Nicola's face fell, although to hear that Lisa was in hospital was the last thing she wanted to hear.

"But I shall make inquiries elsewhere," the doctor promised.

After lunch Dr. Montal withdrew, probably to enjoy his siesta, while Adrienne conducted Nicola to a terrace that gave a panoramic view of the harbor. Here there were more tables and chairs and Nicola was commanded to lie full length on one of the mattressed lounge chairs.

"I'm not used to going to sleep in the afternoon," she protested mildly.

"In Spain it is necessary," said Adrienne firmly. "This is only May. In July and August our sun is too strong for us to move about after lunch."

"I understand that the Spanish take their siesta all through the winter, too." Nicola could not keep the teasing note out of her voice.

"Ah, but that is because we have our nightlife here and in England perhaps you go to bed at ten in the evening. That is just when we have finished our dinner and are waking up for the evening's entertainment."

After a pause to settle herself, Nicola asked, "Have you always lived here?"

"Oh, yes," returned Adrienne. "Except when I was away at school, of course. This house, the Villa Ronda, is also my father's house, but he is away, very far away, in South America." Adrienne's tone became sad.

"But he'll come home soon?"

Adrienne shook her head. "That we do not know. He has been there for more than three years. He went abroad when my mother died. She was French, you understand. He is also a doctor and he was sad that all his skill could not save her."

"Oh, I'm sorry," Nicola sympathized.

"We do not know when my father will come back. He has not written for nearly two years. Sebastian believes that he is dead, but I know that my father will come home some time."

"So you have only your uncle as close relative?"

"There are branches of the family, of course, but they live elsewhere—in Barcelona, Tarragona, Madrid—all kinds of places."

Nicola remained silent, unwilling to probe further into the girl's tragic history, but she saw now the significance of Adrienne's name, her fairness and her correct, precise English spoken with a faint French accent.

The day passed quickly, but the doctor did not join his niece and her guest until shortly before dinner. Nicola had been slightly anxious about leaving after so late a dinner. "Will there be a train back to Barcelona?" she asked.

"Our chauffeur will drive you back," Sebastian Montal assured her.

"Oh, but I mustn't put you to that trouble," she began to protest, but Dr. Montal silenced her with a glance from his somber eyes.

"You could not be allowed to walk from the railway station to your apartment so late at night."

Nicola made no reply, realizing that his ideas about girls walking in strange towns late at night were different from her own carefree English attitude.

During the long, protracted dinner he asked questions about what work she had done and she gave him polite answers. When it was time to go, Nicola thanked both Adrienne and her uncle for an extremely pleasant day.

"You must come again," invited Adrienne eagerly, but there was no echoing support from the doctor, only the promise to telephone or write if he heard any news of Lisa.

It was nearly midnight when the chauffeur brought Nicola to the main entrance of the apartments. She thanked him and sympathized that he had to drive all the way back to Orsola, but she supposed that it was all part of his job.

As she mounted the stairs she was aware of the scrutiny of a young man who leaned against the wall. From the second floor she peered once over the banister, but apparently he had lost interest in her.

She had been in the apartment no more than a couple of minutes when there was a subdued knocking at the outer door. Her first instinct was to take no notice, but the knocking came again, this time louder.

She called out, "Who is it?"

A man's voice called back, "Lisa! Lisa!"

In a moment of panic she unlocked the door, thinking that Lisa might also be there. She was confronted by the man from downstairs. The smile on his dark face instantly faded as he began to say "*Al fin!*" Then he said, "Lisa?" followed by rapid exclamations and questions in Spanish, which Nicola failed to follow.

She gathered that he was asking for Lisa, believing her to be still living at the apartment.

Nicola shook her head. "Lisa—no. Who are you?"

"*Amigo,*" he declared. "*Dónde está Lisa?*"

Nicola shrugged her shoulders and spread her hands in a gesture of ignorance.

"*Inglesa?*" he queried.

"*Sí. No hablo bien Español. Parlez-vous Français?*" She did not like the look of him particularly, yet she was desperately anxious not to miss an opportunity of hearing something of Lisa.

"*Je suis la soeur de Lisa,*" she explained slowly. "*Hermana.* Understand?"

"*Hermana?*" he echoed. "*Buenas noches.*" He turned sharply, hurried along the corridor and vanished down the stairway before Nicola could even return his "Good night."

She shut the door quickly, locked it, then pondered on the man's odd and abrupt behavior. Evidently he had been waiting for Lisa to come home, expecting to find her still living in the apartment. Naturally, he had not connected Nicola with Lisa, since they were so different in looks.

Nicola was really too tired to cope with the problem now, but she sat on the bed and forced herself to think. Was Lisa in the habit of receiving visits from young men at such late hours? All the circumstances of Lisa's strange disappearance were beginning to build up into something sinister.

Nicola knew now that she could not go home to England without knowing what had happened to her sister. She was vexed with herself that she had made no attempt to ask the man's name.

She telephoned Patrick next morning and told him that she had changed her mind. "If there's a job going in your office, I'll be glad to take it. I can't explain in detail, but I need it now."

"Why? Have you found Lisa?"

"No. I've decided to stay here and go on looking for her, but I must work. Can you fix an interview for me?"

"With pleasure," he replied.

At Patrick's firm of wine shippers next day Nicola was interviewed by one of the English directors, but he held out no encouraging prospects.

"We filled the vacancy left by your sister, Miss Brettell," he told Nicola, "and at the moment I don't see where we could fit you in, especially as you say you're an experienced secretary. Your sister was only a copy typist." She could almost hear his thoughts—and a pretty poor one at that. "Still, if we have a vacancy here within the next few weeks," he promised, "I'll get in touch with you if you're still free or want a change."

Nicola thanked him, left her address and went out into the outer office. A man sat on a bench and glanced up as she passed, but looked away immediately. She was sure it was the man who had called at the apartment on Sunday night, asking for Lisa.

"*Señor!*" Nicola addressed him quietly. "Can you tell me anything about my sister, Lisa?"

As she said Lisa's name, the man jerked up his head, but stared blankly at Nicola.

"You came to her apartment in the Paseo Maritimo on Sunday night," she continued in a hushed voice, forgetting that he probably could not understand English except for a word or two.

He shrugged and turned his face away. "*No conozco a Vd,*" he muttered.

Nicola understood that he was refusing to recognize her or admit that they had ever met before. A young man was trying to conduct her out of the office and she gave up her attempts to contact Lisa's friend. If only she could have been able to ask him something about Lisa's life here in Barcelona, she might have obtained some sort of clue to work on. Unfortunately Patrick did not appear to be in the office or he could have acted as interpreter.

Dispirited, she returned to the apartment, prepared herself a light lunch and reminded herself that she must make her money spin out as far as possible. This afternoon she would buy local newspapers and find out how to get in touch with employment agencies.

She was just on her way out when the caretaker handed her several letters, all addressed to "Señorita Brettell." One bore no stamp or postmark and Nicola went flying up the stairs again to her apartment. Something from Lisa after all!

But instead it was a note from Adrienne.

Will you come on Thursday, day after tomorrow, if you can? Do not bother with the train. Ignacio, our chauffeur, will come for you at ten o'clock. If you have another engagement, will you telephone us?

In a way, Nicola welcomed the diversion, for she realized that after the next few days she would have little time for leisure except at weekends.

She opened the other letters and gasped in amazement. Nothing but bills! Items for dresses, hats, shoes, a leather handbag, an expensive suitcase. A long bulky envelope contained a further batch of accounts, together with a letter from a firm of lawyers, and even Nicola's tenuous grasp of Spanish was enough to comprehend the threatening tones.

What on earth had Lisa been doing, ordering all these articles and then failing to pay for them?

Nicola searched again among the envelopes. Was there no word at all from Lisa? She knew now that it was hopeless to expect anything. She understood clearly the reason for her sister's hurried flight.

Nicola stared bleakly out of the window at the azure sea and sky, the beach dotted with people, the sleek cars driving along the road. What was she to do now? Could she be held responsible for Lisa's debts? She had no idea how Spanish law might work or whether she could be called upon to pay because she happened to be in the country.

She moved restlessly around the room. Her problems weighed a ton and she wished with all her heart that she had never responded to Lisa's invitation to come to Spain.

She could, of course, do exactly what Lisa had done—pack her suitcases, leave the apartment and disappear. There was no proof that she had ever received the bills. She could leave Barcelona and stay somewhere else. But furtively moving from one obscure hotel to another, apprehensive every time she produced her passport, was no sort of holiday. It would be preferable to go back to England at the earliest moment.

Yet Nicola knew that she could not do that. Lisa's debts had to be paid somehow.

A vision of the Montals rose before her—Dr. Sebastian with his eaglelike features and stern mouth, Adrienne's impulsive gaiety. How would they regard her if they discovered that she had disappeared, leaving behind a mass of unpaid bills in the name of Brettell?

Patrick telephoned later in the day. "How did you get on with the interview? Sorry I had to be out."

"Only vague promises. There's no vacancy at present," she answered dully, wondering whether to spill the whole story to him.

"Pity," he commented. "I'll get in touch with one or two other men and firms I know and see what I can do."

She decided against unloading all her problems on Patrick. He was doing his best for her. She thanked him and ended the conversation as briefly as she could. She sighed. A job was now a more urgent necessity than ever.

First, however, she must call on all those shops where Lisa had run up accounts.

The managers listened attentively to Nicola's explanations and were helpful. Only one, a jeweler, seemed suspicious, but she remembered that he probably had to deal with fraudulent customers sometimes, although she would not allow herself to believe that Lisa had acted under false pretenses. Her sister was unduly extravagant, that was all.

"You understand, *señor*, that my sister may be very ill somewhere and unable to do anything about payment of your bill?"

"*Si, si,*" he agreed halfheartedly.

Finally, she visited the lawyer's office, where she explained that the shops and stores had agreed to give her time to pay if she could get herself a job.

"You have no idea where your sister is now?" the elderly lawyer asked.

"No. I've been trying to trace her ever since I arrived here. Dr. Sebastian Montal is also looking for her in the hospitals." Nicola regretted instantly that she had carelessly used his name.

"Dr. Montal? He would act as surety for you, perhaps?"

"Oh, no," she replied quickly. "I don't know him well enough for that."

The old lawyer gave her a piercing glance over the top of his gold-rimmed spectacles.

"Is there anyone else you could name as surety?" he asked.

"No one." She was not going to involve Patrick, either.

"Then at least you are more honest than your sister," he snapped dryly. "She apparently gave the names of several persons as references, but she did not have their permission."

At last it was agreed that as soon as Nicola landed a job, she would tell the lawyers the amount of her salary and they would fix a reasonable monthly sum to pay off Lisa's debts. The old man impressed on her that he was treating her as leniently as possible because both she and her sister were foreigners.

Nicola was surprised when she went to the Villa Ronda the following day that Dr. Montal was at home.

"Sebastian does not attend the hospital on Thursdays," Adrienne explained, "unless there is a very urgent case for him. But do not be worried. We can enjoy ourselves and keep out of his way." She gave a mischievous giggle.

The significance of being invited to Orsola on a Thursday became clear to Nicola only some time later.

At lunch she was aware of the doctor's intent scrutiny, while Adrienne kept up a lively conversation. Curiously, the young girl's English became fractured and stumbling whenever her uncle was present. Was that due to the nervous effect he had on her?

Certainly when Adrienne encouraged Nicola to practice speaking in Spanish, Nicola's few words and phrases completely deserted her if she had to reply to Sebastian.

After their siesta, the two girls bathed in the pool, sunned themselves on the marble edge and drank long iced drinks.

"Do you like my Uncle Sebastian?" Adrienne asked without warning.

"I hardly know him, do I?" countered Nicola. "I think he's very kind and helpful."

"Then you must come here often so that you can get well acquainted."

Nicola smiled apologetically. "I'm afraid that's not going to be possible. I've decided to stay for a few months in Spain."

"But that is excellent news!"

"No, listen. I have to work. I must get a job. I have the vague promise of one, but I must find some English firm who will employ me."

Adrienne stared, her gray eyes unfathomable, her smooth face immobile. At last she queried, "In Barcelona?"

"Probably. It's a large town with a lot of commerce and industry. I hope to find something suitable."

"We must tell Sebastian about it," decided Adrienne, "but we will wait until we have the aperitif."

Nicola failed to see why Sebastian must be informed, for her plans would not interest him except where the search for Lisa was concerned.

In the early evening the doctor joined the two girls on the balustraded terrace that gave such a breathtaking view over the harbor and coast.

Nicola sipped her sherry, then after a few minutes Sebastian said, "Adrienne, would you leave us, please? I wish to talk with Miss Brettell."

Contrary to Nicola's expectations, Adrienne rose obediently at once, leaned over her uncle and gave him a light kiss on the side of his head. "Of course, *cher* Sebastian. I promise not to listen and I will go far away."

He watched her as she walked away, a slight, youthful figure in a white dress, her long golden hair covering her shoulders. Then he turned toward Nicola and knocked the ash off his cigarette. "Adrienne has told me that you intend to stay here for a time and work."

"Yes." In a vague way, Nicola was disappointed. She had imagined that he had news of Lisa.

"What prospects have you?"

"The promise of a suitable vacancy at the firm where my sister worked for a time. But I won't rely on that. I can go to agencies or look at the advertisements," she added hastily.

"You have definitely left your job in England?" he queried.

"Oh, yes," she assured him. "I expected to have a holiday here with Lisa. Then I thought I could decide whether to take over her job at the wine shippers, if they would allow me, or I could go home to London and easily get another job there."

His dark eyes regarded her. "Even with your qualifications and experience, I doubt whether you would secure a job here as easily as you could in England."

After a pause, she said, "You're advising me to go home, then, even abandon my search for Lisa?"

"On the contrary." He stubbed out his cigarette. "I have a proposition to make. Adrienne, as you know, is my niece. Her mother is dead." A faint spasm of pain seemed to cross his face. "Her father, my brother, Eduardo, may be in South America, but we have heard nothing of him for almost two years. So you understand that Adrienne is my responsibility."

When he paused Nicola waited, wondering what was in his mind.

"Adrienne needs companionship. She's seventeen and sometimes rather wild and impulsive. She has opposed all my previous attempts to provide her with a companion near her own age, preferably slightly older, but it seems that she has become very attracted to you." He gave Nicola a slightly sardonic smile. "She would accept you. In fact, the suggestion has come from her. She asks me to persuade you to stay here."

Nicola was dumbfounded. "But I—I've no experience of being anyone's companion—not in the way you mean for Adrienne."

"One moment. I have put the cart before the horse, as I think you say in England. I would be glad to use your secretarial experience. When I have the leisure, I work on a medical book concerning heart diseases and I am doing the English translation myself so that it can be published in England and America as well as here."

"I've no experience of medical terms, either," she objected.

"We have an adequate supply of dictionaries here," he answered. "You must, of course, take time to think over what I've said. Later, if you accept, we can discuss terms, your salary and so on. You would live here in the house, of course. We have a competent staff and I must warn you that Rosana, our housekeeper, will tolerate no interference, not even from me. There is one important condition which you must consider carefully. I shall expect you to stay here for at least one year. I have strong reasons. Adrienne is still rather too young to marry, but in a year's time—no doubt she'll be betrothed. When she marries, then my responsibility is ended, or at least diminished."

Nicola finished her sherry. She felt she needed it. Her mind was whirling with the impact of this strange proposition from a man she had met only three times. To keep an eye on his niece and in her spare time type his medical notes—it sounded a fantastic situation.

The doctor poured her another sherry. "I will not rush you into a hasty decision, but I would like to know soon. If you stay here, you could still continue to look for your sister."

He had pointed out one of the strongest advantages of accepting his offer, but she could not disclose that it was just as important to her to earn sufficient money in the next few months to pay Lisa's debts.

She left the Villa Ronda after dinner as soon as she could do so with politeness, but as she stepped into the car, Adrienne came to wave goodbye.

"You will come and live with us, won't you? Please! Without you, my English will go to pieces, so at least you can make yourself useful."

"I'll think very carefully about it," Nicola promised.

"*Hasta la vista!*" called Adrienne as the car slid away.

Nicola spent a sleepless night, trying to work out her problem. The offer was attractive in the extreme, but could she bind herself for a year? Yet some immediate employment was an absolute necessity if she was to stay in Spain, and unless she could find a well-paid job, she did not know how she could manage to live economically and reserve a monthly sum to pay Lisa's debts.

Nicola began to see now that in undertaking her sister's responsibilities she had committed herself to a course from which she could not turn back.

CHAPTER TWO

NICOLA ROSE at first daylight, for there was no more sleep in her. She wrapped herself in a housecoat and, jotting figures on a piece of paper, she sat by the window.

Lisa's debts amounted to over twenty thousand pesetas, which sounded worse in Spanish money than sterling, but it was still well over a hundred and twenty pounds. Nicola had put most of her half-share of the proceeds of her father's house into an account with the bank and withdrawals needed six months' notice. In any case, she knew there would be difficulty in getting the amount transferred to Spain. The bank would help in transferring the currency, but it would all take time, and Nicola needed money now.

There was the apartment in London to dispose of, but she knew several friends who would jump at the chance to take it over. The rest of her clothes and other possessions—well, she would have to think about those details later.

She stood up suddenly, gazing out but not seeing the sunlit sea and turquoise sky before her. She realized that her decision had already been made, even forced on her by circumstances. Perhaps, subconsciously, she had made it last night before leaving the Villa Ronda, even at the moment when Dr. Montal had murmured a grave "Good night" and there had been just the faintest gleam of warmth in his dark eyes.

She would inform Patrick at the first opportunity, for she did not want him to waste his time looking for other openings for her.

First, though, she must write to Dr. Montal, agreeing to

accept his offer if he would let her have more details before she made a final decision.

His reply was prompt, for he suggested a meeting at the Avenida Palace hotel the following evening.

For the occasion Nicola wore her smartest dress, a pale lemon polyester, and carried a white and silver stole, for she had brought with her from England only one all-purpose lightweight coat.

The doctor was waiting for her in the hotel foyer and took her to a quiet corner of the bar. When he had ordered drinks, he spoke straight to the point.

"You will need references about myself. Here are the names of two of my colleagues at the hospital, and the prefect at the city hall. You can also inquire about me at the British Embassy. Our family is well known to them."

She was surprised by his formality. "I'm afraid I can't offer any references in return," she said, "except the firm where I worked in England."

He waved her apologies aside. "The case is not quite the same. You are coming to work in our house and you must be assured that you will be treated correctly." A hint of a smile crossed his face, lighting his eyes for an instant.

"Thank you," was all she could say.

"You will probably have expenses of one sort or another to settle," he continued, "both here in Barcelona and where you lived in London, so I am paying you two months' salary in advance. If you want extra money, then please ask me and I'll arrange it."

She found that her salary was generous in the extreme. With no living expenses of her own to pay for, she would be able to settle Lisa's debts more promptly than she had expected.

"We can discuss all the other details when you have settled in at the villa," the doctor told her. Once again the vestige of a smile lit his somber face. "I will try not to work you too hard, but obviously, we will have to arrange our working hours to suit us both."

Adrienne joined her uncle and Nicola for dinner at this deluxe hotel, so different from the modest little place where Nicola had spent the first few days in the city. But although

Adrienne maintained an easy flow of conversation and was plainly delighted that Nicola had agreed to accept Sebastian Montal's offer, the doctor by contrast seemed to relapse into a withdrawn silence, giving only an occasional answer when directly addressed by his niece.

It was arranged that Nicola should take three or four days to attend to clearing up her tenancy of the apartment and when she was ready, the Montals' chauffeur, Ignacio, would collect her and her belongings for the move to Villa Ronda.

She telephoned Patrick next day. "I've found a very interesting job," she told him. "Unusual, too. If you could meet me somewhere tonight I'll tell you all about it."

He was waiting for her at a table outside the Café Zurich near the Plaza de Cataluna.

When she told him of her good fortune he frowned and took a sceptical view of the whole venture.

"Why are you rushing into a strange sort of job like this?" he demanded. "You haven't given yourself time to look around yet."

Nicola hesitated, wondering how much of the truth to disclose to Patrick. At last she said, "I called at the hotel in Santa Ana on my way here. No messages. Nothing about Lisa."

"Oh, never mind her," he said brusquely. "I'm more concerned about you."

She sighed. "In a way the whole affair does concern Lisa as well as me." She looked away to the wide plaza with the traffic swirling around it. "You'd better know the truth."

He listened to her explanation and then burst out angrily, "But you can't take on these responsibilities for your sister! It's not the first time the shops have met a few bad debts. As for the lawyers, they know perfectly well that they couldn't possibly enforce payment from you."

"They're not enforcing. I'm doing it voluntarily. I have a moral obligation, especially as we're foreigners in this country."

"You should have let the shops whistle for their money if they were all daft enough to let Lisa run up accounts. And she'll never learn to stand on her own feet if you're going to bolster her up like this every time she gets herself into a mess,'' he protested.

"But d'you really think I could calmly go back to England knowing that she had cheated shops and stores out of their money? Actually, I don't even know that she intended to vanish without paying. I still think she may be lying ill somewhere in hospital.''

"Doubtful!'' was Patrick's terse comment. "And in your heart you know that, too, Nicola. From what I know of Lisa and her ideas about money—'' he broke off and picked up his coffee cup.

"What else were you going to say?'' she queried. "Lisa borrowed money from her friends? From you? Or others in your office?''

He refused to meet her glance. "Oh, she paid it back sometimes. I shouldn't have told you that. Forget it. Let's hear more about your new prospects. Isn't it rather odd that this Dr. Montal insists on your staying a year?''

"That's because of Adrienne,'' she replied. "He seems to think that when she's eighteen, she'll probably marry—or at least be engaged.''

"And then you'll be given the push, I suppose?''

Nicola laughed. "Oh, I don't know about that. I might acquire such a taste for living in a luxury villa in a sensible climate that if he doesn't want my services, I'll find some-one else who does.''

Patrick gave an amused grunt. "How your sister would envy you! This is just the sort of life that Lisa was looking for—oh, never mind the odd bit of typing now and again. Comfort, security and the chance to find plenty of amuse-ment. If I were you, Nicola, I'd keep out of her way.''

"Oh, Patrick! How unkind! I shall go on looking for her whenever I can. In fact, it's one of the advantages of my new job—although the doctor hasn't heard anything of her at any of the hospitals.''

"And be sure he never will,'' Patrick observed crisply. "Wherever she is, Lisa certainly isn't languishing in a hospital all this time.''

After a pause, Nicola said, "There was another reason for wanting a job here.'' She related how one of Lisa's friends

had called at the apartment one night and then she had seen
him again in the offices of Patrick's firm.

"Could he work there?" she queried.

Patrick was thoughtful for a few moments. "Lisa had
quite a few men friends."

"Of course! She's very attractive," put in Nicola.

"Several of the men at our place took her out sometimes," he said. "Once or twice I did myself. It's also
possible that she struck up friendships with some of the men
who call on the firm. There are plenty of those coming in
and out."

"I could have been mistaken," Nicola admitted, "and
perhaps he only resembled the man who called at the
apartment, but I was sure he recognized me the second time,
although he pretended not to. What was so odd was the way
he rushed off when I said I was Lisa's sister."

Patrick laughed. "Probably doesn't want contact with
any of Lisa's family. I've no doubt that Lisa herself was
enough."

"Maybe. But I keep wondering if there isn't something
really mysterious about Lisa's disappearance. Apart from
the debts, I don't think I could have gone home at the end of
a holiday without knowing what had become of her."

"I think she'll turn up at the exact moment when it suits
her." Patrick prophesied. "She may quite possibly know
every move you've made so far. Even sent you the bills."

Nicola did not reply, and after a long pause, Patrick said
moodily, "I suppose I won't be seeing you when you're
installed at Orsola."

"Why not?" she demanded. "I've been very grateful for
all your help. I will expect to have free time now and again
and come to Barcelona. I don't drop my friends as easily as
that."

His pleasant face cleared in a smile. "You certainly are
the opposite of your sister!"

For the first time it occurred to Nicola that perhaps
Patrick had become fond of Lisa, who had merely flirted
with him. Was that why he sounded so bitter about her?

"Well, I wish you luck," he said. "Let's keep in touch. I

can always take you sight-seeing when you've time. You haven't really seen much of Barcelona, have you?''

Nicola admitted that although she had come for a holiday intending to explore the place fairly thoroughly, she hadn't even seen the main buildings.

"We'll remedy that," Patrick promised. "We mustn't let the good doctor believe that he can have all your time just because you'll be under his roof. You'll have to stipulate that you want days off.''

"I'll tell him," laughed Nicola. "I'll have it all written down in the contract.''

"Well, if you don't like the job there, leave it, contract or no contract. There's no sense in working in bad conditions.''

On the day when Nicola was due to leave Barcelona for Orsola, Adrienne accompanied Ignacio, a courteous gesture, which Nicola appreciated.

"It was very kind of you to come," she said to Adrienne.

The younger girl laughed. "Oh, I came to make sure that you are really coming to us. Ignacio will carry all your luggage down for you to the car.''

"Thank you. There isn't much," Nicola confessed. "Only what I brought on the plane and a few more things I've bought here.''

When she handed the key of the apartment to the woman who seemed to act as caretaker, she impressed on her to be sure to send on any letters that might arrive. "Please do not forget," she said in Spanish. "Here is my new address.''

The woman took the half sheet of paper without glancing at it, but gave Nicola a slightly contemptuous look and muttered that the English girls always found rich friends.

Nicola's Spanish was now equal at least to that remark, but she made no answer.

At the Villa Ronda she was given an exquisite room with furniture in warm chestnut brown banded with intricate carvings. A pale water-green carpet made a cool contrast and curtains patterned in green and white with a hint of flame matched the bed covers. Gilded mirrors on the walls gave unexpected reflections of the room. The double windows opened onto a balcony overlooking a flower-decked patio that Nicola did not remember having seen before, but perhaps she was only viewing it from a different angle. The villa was set in extensive grounds that had been cunningly landscaped to provide surprises.

"I must take you on a tour of the house," Adrienne offered, "so that you do not lose your way."

Nicola was shown Adrienne's own suite, with her studio attached. "Here I can make an untidy mess and no one will dare to clean it up!" There was a vast salon with arched windows, a grand piano, an ornate fireplace and a tiled fountain at one end of the room.

"Next door is Sebastian's study," Adrienne pointed out, "but we must not go in uninvited. He will show you that himself."

Out-of-doors, Nicola found she had much to learn about the layout of the garden. Paths and steps led up or down everywhere, it seemed, and Adrienne conducted her down a long winding path that led to the sea.

"We have our beach house here," she said, indicating a handsome cottagelike structure set between the sea and a group of rocks enclosing a small cove.

Inside was a comfortably furnished sitting room and beyond that two small rooms for changing.

"Sometimes we have parties down here," Adrienne added. "We put tables on those rocks up there and lots of lanterns and the effect is quite charming."

Nicola laughed. "Not so charming, perhaps, for your staff who have to bring all the food down here."

"Oh, they don't mind," said the girl airily.

"I'd like to explore Orsola when we have time," said Nicola. "All I've seen of it so far is the part between the railway station and your villa."

"This afternoon we will go together," said Adrienne after a thoughtful pause. "Also we will go down to the harbor when the fishing boats come in. That is quite interesting to watch."

The doctor was evidently not at the villa today, and Adrienne and Nicola ate their lunch on the rounded terrace overlooking the sea. After the meal Adrienne focused binoculars on the scene in the harbor.

After a moment she murmured, "Yes, he has come. His yacht is there."

She handed the binoculars to Nicola. "You can see among the other boats a white yacht, very smart. Its name is *Clorinda*."

Nicola swung the binoculars in the direction Adrienne indicated, looking first for the name *Clorinda,* but she could not see which boat was so called. In the harbor several smart yachts rode at anchor.

"Tonight Elena will come ashore," Adrienne said, "and I think we will have a surprise for her."

"Friends of yours?" queried Nicola.

"Señora Elena is a neighbor of ours. She has a villa not far away." Adrienne had taken the binoculars again. "That's her brother, Ramon on board. It's his yacht." She put down the binoculars on the table and tilted her chair back at an alarming angle. "Sooner or later I am expected to marry Ramon."

"Oh?" Nicola's eyebrows rose. "Your uncle has already chosen your husband, then?"

"So he imagines. We will see." Adrienne's tone was a mixture of smugness and a subtle hint of duplicity.

"But you're not in love with him?"

Adrienne's light laugh rippled among the surrounding trees and bushes. "It is intended to be a good match. One does not ask whether love comes into the arrangement."

"But surely you won't be content with an arranged marriage like that, will you?" pursued Nicola.

The girl shrugged. "I don't know. If the arrangement suited me, then perhaps I might agree. If not—" she left the sentence unfinished.

"D'you like Señor Ramon?"

Adrienne raised her eyes in mock adoration. "He's charming! Handsome, accomplished, rich."

"But elderly?"

"Not at all. Twenty-eight. Elena is rather older. She is thirty and the same age as Sebastian." Adrienne's fair face broke into a wicked grin. She leaned across the table toward Nicola. "D'you know, if it so happened that I married Ramon and Elena could have her dearest wish granted to

marry Sebastian, do you understand how I would be related
to her? She would be my—what do you say?''

"Sister-in-law," supplied Nicola. "But also your aunt by
marriage." She joined Adrienne in a fresh burst of laughter.

"A droll position!" Adrienne exclaimed.

"Droll indeed," agreed Nicola, but she was intrigued by
the possibility of Sebastian's marriage.

"They will both come to dinner tonight or tomorrow, so
you will see them," Adrienne said. "Elena is a widow. She
lost her husband two years ago. He was ill for a long time."

Later in the afternoon the two girls went down to explore
Orsola. Adrienne parked her car near a square at the top of
the main street, a wide, tree-lined *rambla*.

Small shops and houses were mixed indiscriminately
along the sides of the street, cafés set out their clusters of
chairs and tables. Outside what was evidently a tiny school,
a group of small girls seated on kitchen chairs were busy
learning the art of lace-making under their instructress, a
gentle-faced nun. They sang local songs in high, childish
trebles as they twisted and twirled the bobbins on the lace
pillows.

The roadway was so wide that it seemed not all of it was
necessary for traffic and part was covered in thick reddish
brown dust; at one point a dark-skinned man and several
women had apparently set up a small camp and they sat
outside platting straw baskets.

"You realize," Adrienne explained, "that all these *ramblas* were at one time river beds. They have dried up. It's the
same in Barcelona.''

"I see. That's why it's such a vast width. Not like some of
our little streets in England where they're continually
knocking down one side to make room for traffic." Nicola,
not really paying attention to her feet, stumbled against a
disconcertingly high curb.

The two girls arrived at the fish quay on the farther side
of the harbor soon after the fishing fleet had arrived.

"You must watch the auction," Adrienne told her. "You
will not understand what he says, but the fish are pretty.''

A cryptic remark, thought Nicola, but she understood
when she went into the covered market shed where large

shallow baskets of fish were placed in the center of an enclosure. An assortment of tourists, fish buyers and idle spectators leaned over the iron railing of the ring while the auctioneer gabbled his patter in Dutch bids downward.

"Too fast for me," muttered Nicola.

"Me, too," confessed Adrienne with a grin. "He speaks in Catalan."

Occasionally above the din the auctioneer bawled "*Silencio!*" and cleared the ring of small, boisterous boys.

But it was the arrangement of fish in the trays that fascinated Nicola. Every tray was a work of art, fish arranged in patterns, star shaped or crisscrossed, dark or light iridescences placed as though they were rug designs. Frivolous borders of pink scampi or centerpieces of pale blue or silver fish of some strange Mediterranean species delighted the eye.

"If you could climb up to the roof and look down on each tray," said Nicola, "they'd look like medallions worked in *petit point*. How on earth do they have time to do all this?"

There was no reply from Adrienne and when Nicola shifted her position and looked around, her companion had disappeared.

She strolled across to the second ring where the same process was going on with another auctioneer, but it was almost distressing to see the exquisite symmetry of the fish tray ruined when the buyers tipped the contents into their boxes or buckets.

Nicola suddenly caught sight of Adrienne talking to a young, dark-haired boy wearing a faded blue shirt and denim trousers rolled up above his ankles. His bare feet were tanned to coffee color, matching his slim arms.

Adrienne's face was animated as she talked to the boy. Then she put her hand on his shoulder in an apparent gesture of farewell and came back toward Nicola. She did not enlighten Nicola as to who the boy was and Nicola judged it no business of hers to ask. For all she knew, Adrienne might be passing on the housekeeper's instructions as to the fish required at the Villa Ronda.

On arrival back at the villa, Adrienne said, "Evidently

Elena and Ramon are coming tonight to dinner. Wear your nicest dress and together we will impress them both.''

In any case, Nicola would have taken extra trouble with her appearance tonight, for this was the first time she had dined at the villa as a member of the household instead of as a guest. She chose a new dress she had bought in Barcelona, a turquoise blue cotton, which deepened the color of her eyes and accorded well with the gentle tan she had already acquired. She made up her face carefully, brushed her hair into its own loose waves and fervently hoped that she would not make some ghastly mistake during the evening.

Ramon Ventallo was introduced to her by Adrienne on the balustraded terrace that had the nickname of the "Mediterranean balcony.'' He was very broad shouldered and muscular-looking, with almost black eyes and a thatch of crispy curling hair. He bowed to Nicola and raised her hand to his lips.

"You are on holiday?'' he queried.

"Oh, no,'' Adrienne intervened before Nicola could reply. "Nicola is here to stay. She is to keep a watchful eye on me.'' She gave Ramon a provocative glance. "Any spare time she has left over from that task will be used by Sebastian. She is to help him with his book.''

Ramon regarded Nicola with rather more interest. Then he smiled. "You will have a full life here at the villa, I assure you. To look after Adrienne is more than enough. To cope with Sebastian, also—'' he broke off and shook his head in mock sympathy, his eyes twinkling.

In a few moments the trio were joined by Sebastian, accompanied by a fairly tall young woman wearing dark glasses. She wore a full-length dress of kingfisher blue and her jewels sparkled and flashed in the evening sun.

"Doña Elena, may I present Miss Nicola Brettell from England?'' Sebastian made the introductions, and Elena inclined her head graciously in acknowledgement.

During the round of predinner drinks, Nicola had the opportunity to study the two newcomers. Ramon did most of the talking with Adrienne chaffing and contradicting him. Sometimes he reverted to Spanish, then made a swift apology to Nicola.

Elena, whose face was effectively masked by the dark glasses, spoke quietly to Sebastian, who seemed much more genial than usual.

Ramon spoke of his trip to Tangier and Nicola gathered that Elena had accompanied him.

"I have been away too long from Orsola—and all its attractions," Ramon declared with a frank look at Adrienne and a sidelong covert glance at Nicola. "We must remedy matters. With your English friend staying here, we all have fine excuses for a season of gaiety and sight-seeing. What does it matter if we have seen the places already?"

"We'll take Nicola to Sitges for Corpus Christi," suggested Adrienne. "Now that's something worth seeing, but we will not tell you until you arrive," she said, turning to Nicola.

Nicola did not disclose that she already knew from colored postcards how the main streets of Sitges were literally paved with flowers. She was, however, a little apprehensive as to how Sebastian would regard these plans. She gave him a quick look of interrogation and was relieved when he smiled and nodded approval.

Dinner tonight was a more formal affair than the meals at which Nicola had been present. It was served in a rectangular dining room with arched windows leading to a shaded terrace. The furniture was black oak with high-backed chairs upholstered in dark red brocade. When the candles were lit on the table the shadows advanced from the rest of the room and only the women's dresses and the white dinner jackets of the two men made illumined contrasts. Two manservants and a maid seemed to appear at one's elbow by magic to serve the innumerable dishes or refill one's glasses with wine.

When the long dinner was over at last Nicola felt sleepy not only because of the food and wine, but because the day had been a full and tiring one. She would willingly have excused herself and left the others to their coffee and liqueurs on the lantern-lit terrace outside the dining room, but she thought it wiser to stay and remain unobtrusive.

Adrienne and Ramon were engaged in some bantering conversation, and it was only now that she noticed Elena and Sebastian had gone away. Nicola stared out at the dark midnight-blue sky spangled with stars, the gardens were full of scents and sighing trees. Then she heard Elena's voice from some adjacent room, which evidently opened onto the same terrace. Elena spoke in Spanish and Nicola could not follow, but she distinctly heard her own name mentioned, and the way Elena said "Señorita Brettell" was certainly not friendly.

Sebastian was answering in a low rumbling tone, and Nicola was in a way thankful that she did not understand enough Spanish to be guilty of eavesdropping.

Next morning Adrienne was in a wildly excited state. "Oh, Nicola, I told you we'd surprise Elena," she began. "Last night she was furious."

"About what?" queried Nicola, although she guessed the answer.

"About you. Elena has been quite anxious to provide me with a slightly motherly eye—or at least an aunt's eye—so that she could be more often in this house and with Sebastian. Now that she finds I am provided with a suitable companion, she is very angry indeed." Adrienne collapsed into a fit of laughter. "She says it was a plot behind her back while she was still away with Ramon," the girl continued after a pause.

"And wasn't it?" asked Nicola with a smile.

Adrienne's frank gray eyes looked into Nicola's face.

"Yes, of course. You understand now why I was so anxious to have the matter settled immediately."

"And does she think I'm a suitable companion for you?"

Adrienne laughed again. "No, she does not. You're too young and you're English, so you don't understand our Spanish ways. More than that, Sebastian knows nothing about you, except perhaps that you are good at typing and shorthand. Elena does not say so outright, but clearly she thinks you could easily be a very dubious character, glad to stay in Spain out of the way of any crimes you have committed elsewhere."

Nicola shivered. The assessment was so very near the truth, except that it was Lisa who was involved, not herself.

"So perhaps Doña Elena will keep an eye on us both," she murmured.

"Not at all!" declared Adrienne hotly. "I have fought her off for a whole year. I am not going to give in to her now. She expects to come here, choose my clothes, select my friends, tell me where I should go and not go, and I will not tolerate her. Besides, I must save Sebastian from her," she finished dramatically.

"But supposing he might like to marry her?" Nicola pointed out.

"He has more sense than that!" was Adrienne's scornful comment.

It was Nicola's turn to laugh quietly. "When it comes to love and marriage, men don't usually bother about sense— any more than women do."

Adrienne stared in some admiration at Nicola. "There! Now I see how right I was to want you for my confidante. You are practical and wise and you have the head wound on well."

"Screwed on, we say," Nicola corrected her.

Adrienne beamed. "Oh, I can see that we are going to have enjoyable times together, you and I, provided that Sebastian doesn't make you work too hard—and I will certainly see that he does not."

"I must be prepared to do some," Nicola reminded her. "That's partly why I'm here."

"That, at least, is something that Elena cannot do," the younger girl retorted.

"She has probably never had any need. I've had to earn a living."

"True." After a long pause, Adrienne said, "If Elena has a private talk with you, and I think she will try soon, then you must say as little as possible. Just be polite and no more."

"Very well," agreed Nicola. Doña Elena was not a woman to be underrated, she thought. Once or twice during dinner last night, when Elena had removed her concealing dark glasses, Nicola had caught an occasional glance from cold green brown eyes.

At four o'clock when Dr. Sebastian returned from Barce-

Iona, he came out to the little courtyard at the back of the villa.

"If I could have your attention, Miss Brettell, for an hour or two? That is, if my niece will kindly give me permission?"

Adrienne gave her uncle a friendly thump on his arm.

Sebastian's study was book lined, furnished with a large desk, chairs of embossed leather and a beautiful bronze statue of Apollo. There were long, complicated forms to fill in on her behalf in connection with her work permit, and the doctor completed all he could for her.

"You must attend in person first at your own embassy, then at the Ministry of Labor, but I will take you there tomorrow."

"Thank you."

He handed her what was evidently a chapter of his book. "Could you manage to retype that with all the alterations and so on?"

She studied the corrected pages for a few moments. "Yes, I'm sure I could do that. Now?" She looked around for the typewriter.

"Presently." He rose and walked around the room while Nicola waited.

"Miss Brettell," he said at last, "did you go to the village yesterday? With Adrienne?"

"Yes, Dr. Montal."

"And you visited the fish quay?"

Nicola's face lit with enthusiasm.

"Oh, yes. I thought it was wonderfully interesting. Those marvelous patterns they make with the fish!"

Sebastian's face grew more somber, if that were possible.

"Did Adrienne meet anyone there?" he asked.

"No, I don't think so," she replied.

"Not a young fisherlad?" he persisted.

"Oh, yes. I saw her talking to a young boy. I suppose he was a fisherman."

Sebastian nodded. "Exactly. Now, Miss Brettell, I want you to listen carefully. My niece is apparently forming a great attachment to this young man, Barto. He lives in a cottage farther down the road with his family. Actually, I own the cottage. Adrienne seems to find many excuses to call at his home or see him wherever she can.'' When he paused, Nicola waited in silence.

"I want you to do your best to prevent Adrienne from continuing this association and to report to me whenever she meets the young man.''

Nicola's face flamed. "But, Dr. Montal, you're asking me to spy on your niece!''

"Certainly. I cannot tuck her under my arm all the time. I am a busy man, but I must do something to stop her from making a fool of herself over Barto.''

"Surely there couldn't be much harm in a youthful friendship like that?'' she protested.

"Allow me to know whether harm might arise or not,'' he said coldly. "I'm not concerned only about any harm to Adrienne. There's the boy, Bartolomeo, also to be considered. The friendship must stop for his sake as well as hers.''

After a few moments Nicola said, "How am I expected to do that?''

"Adrienne is easily persuaded to a course of action if she likes the person giving the advice. She will probably accept advice from you that she would resent from me— or . . . or . . . others.''

She guessed that he had been going to say "Elena.''

"Wouldn't this . . . this undesirable friendship die of its own accord if no one interfered?'' Nicola felt bound to ask. "To forbid her to see him may only result in her rebellion.''

Sebastian smiled, but only with his mouth. There was no warmth in his eyes. "I see that you have common sense, Miss Brettell. That is why I think I can rely on you to carry out my wishes.''

"Supposing I am doing your work here, how am I to prevent Adrienne from doing whatever she chooses or going wherever she fancies?''

"Miss Brettell—may I call you Nicola—you are evidently extremely logical. Perhaps your business training has given you that. Of course you can't be in two places at once, but you can influence Adrienne to the extent that she won't disobey you.''

"I think you're crediting me, Dr. Montal, with more

powers than I possess, but I'll do my best for Adrienne—and for you.''

"I'm aware of the order in which you've placed us, but perhaps Adrienne should come first. It's really her future that's my concern. Her father may or may not be dead, but either way I must safeguard Adrienne.''

"How much of this am I to tell your niece?'' she queried. "Is she to be informed that I am her newly appointed watchdog?''

The doctor placed his hands on the back of a chair and looked down at her. "If you think it wise to do so. I admire your frankness, but Adrienne may like the truth disguised a little.''

The next hour or so was taken up with Nicola's instruction in how Sebastian wanted his typescript done, but when she left him in his study, she was glad to escape the claustrophobic atmosphere.

She went to her room and looked out over the flower-edged patio. Such lovely surroundings to a gracious house, yet there were discords and crosscurrents of opposition. She began to wonder whether she had been wise to sign away her own freedom for a year.

Where was Adrienne now? Down in Orsola chatting to her fisherboy? Nicola went out of the house to search, hating herself already that she had been forced into the position of a wardress. But Adrienne was chatting to Ramon on the Mediterranean balcony, a tall jug of sangría between them.

When the courtesies of kissing Nicola's hand had been observed by Ramon and she was invited to sample the deliciously cool sangría, he said, "We are making plans to go to Sitges for Corpus Christi. You will of course come with us?''

"Thank you, I'd like to,'' returned Nicola.

"Elena will come with us,'' continued Ramon, "but will Sebastian?''

"I doubt it,'' said Adrienne, who seemed rather subdued.

Ramon said he had matters to attend to on board his yacht, and as soon as he had left and was safely out of earshot, Adrienne leaned forward toward Nicola.

"Just imagine!" she said breathlessly. "Elena is home only one day and already makes trouble between me and Sebastian."

Nicola said "Oh?" in a questioning tone, aware of what she was to be told.

"She spied on me yesterday when we were at the quay and I was talking to Barto. Where she was I don't know—perhaps on the yacht. But she told Sebastian immediately, and now I am forbidden to see Barto." Adrienne thrust out her arms. "What could be the harm? But you, Nicola, will be able to help me, I know. I will not allow Doña Elena to rule me."

Nicola wriggled in her chair. Her conscience was wriggling, too, in sympathy. She saw that she was already in the unenviable situation of being between the devil and the deep blue sea, that her allegiance was being stretched in opposite directions. How much simpler it would have been to have returned to England and taken an ordinary job in an ordinary office! But that would have been duller and would not have solved the problem of Lisa's debts. Nicola had to admit to herself that perhaps she was a little bit keyed up by this intriguing development.

CHAPTER THREE

WHEN SHE WAS TAKEN to Sitges on Corpus Christi day Nicola had her first taste of the way in which her life with the Montals might be enlivened.

Ramon drove one car with Adrienne and Nicola accompanying him, while Sebastian escorted Doña Elena in his own car driven by Ignacio.

"Sebastian changed his mind at the last minute and decided to come with us," Adrienne confided to Nicola just before they started. "So he has the pleasure of Doña Elena's company and she is not inflicted on us."

Nicola merely smiled and was cautious enough not to make any comment. She realized that where Elena was concerned she must choose her words carefully and at least try to appear neutral.

"Now you must always pray that the weather will keep fine," Adrienne continued. "One year we started out in bright sunshine, but thunder clouds descended from the mountains. All Sitges was drenched with rain and the flower carpets were spoilt."

Nicola realized that all the rest of the party must have visited Sitges at Corpus Christi many times, yet Ramon and Adrienne at least were taking the trouble to show her one of the loveliest of their local sights.

The drive itself was exciting, sometimes hair-raising, for Ramon swung at top speed around sinuous bends along the winding coast road, where a slight error of judgment could send the car and its occupants plunging over the edge to the rocks below.

The little town of Sitges was crowded with tourists and

inhabitants alike. The narrow pavements served as margins from which to view the roadways completely carpeted with flowers, each street with its own individual pattern. Some designs showed giant cherries, nasturtiums and red and yellow canna lilies on a background of white jasmine. Another took the conventional geometrical motifs and worked them in green, yellow and red, so that the whole appeared like a huge stair-carpet unrolled in the roadway.

"The hours of work it must take," commented Nicola.

"Many days," agreed Adrienne. "But everyone helps. The inhabitants regard the *Alfombras de flores*—the flower carpets—as a kind of fancy dress for their town for this one day, and they put in their spare time and money making its costume."

After they had toured the various streets, Ramon suggested lunch at a restaurant in the old part of the town toward the end of the bay where a church on massive ramparts jutted out almost into the sea.

Dr. Montal became more genial during the meal, helping Nicola to understand the various dishes.

"You must try this white wine," he invited, showing her the label on the bottle, *Priorato blanco*.

Almost at once Doña Elena claimed his attention, and Nicola found when she looked across the table Ramon's dark twinkling gaze fixed on her.

"You are enjoying yourself?" he queried.

"Oh, yes," Nicola agreed easily. "Who wouldn't on a day like this?"

He nodded approval. "Together we must have many days of showing you places and interesting sights."

His smile was suddenly extinguished and he bent his head to concentrate on his food. Nicola, aware of the abrupt break, glanced beyond Sebastian who sat next to her to Doña Elena at the head of the table. Indoors, Doña Elena had discarded her usual heavily smoked glasses and now Nicola caught an expression of ice-cold dislike in those green brown eyes. Momentarily, Elena maintained her gaze, but Nicola looked away first. She felt that she was caught here in shafts of cross fire that she did not know how to parry.

After lunch and a long rest for coffee and liqueurs, Sebastian suggested that Nicola might like to visit two very interesting museums close by.

"One was originally a Basque-style house where three painters lived for a few years. One of the three was Picasso."

Touring the lovely old house with its typical Basque furnishings, Nicola stood entranced by those earlier paintings, gentle pictures of harmony.

The other small museum, Sebastian told her when they arrived, had been bought and completely restored by an American millionaire who then gave half to the town and the other half to his son.

"The division is curious," Sebastian said. "You see the blocked doorway ahead. It happens to be on a bridge across the roadway."

"Perhaps it was meant to be symbolic," Nicola observed. "A door between public property and private."

The doctor gave her a sharp questioning glance, but made no further comment.

When Sebastian and Nicola rejoined the others to walk along the palm-edged promenade, Ramon escorted her, leaving Sebastian to accompany Adrienne and Elena.

"How do you like Sitges?" Ramon asked.

"It's a charming town. Now I understand the views of a friend of mine at home who declares that when he retires he's coming to live here."

As she walked between the double row of palms with tops like green feather dusters, she saw how the regularly recurring shadows were cast on the roadway at the side.

"Look, Señor Ventallo," she said. "D'you think the people here took their inspiration for the flower carpets from the way the shadows fall? Each one makes a pattern."

"So it does. But you must not be so formal. Please call me Ramon. And you—may I address you as Nicola?"

She turned to smile at him. "Of course."

On the return journey Nicola was invited to share Sebastian's car. She agreed instantly, but she was vaguely surprised that it meant that Ramon and Adrienne would be allowed to drive home in his car unchaperoned. She sat with

Elena in the back while Sebastian drove, Ignacio beside him.

Doña Elena was graciousness itself during the drive, breaking a sentence only once when Sebastian met a large bus and had to back to the very edge of the rocky cliff.

On arrival at the Villa Ronda, Elena said, "Señorita Brettell, you must sit down and tell me about yourself."

Nicola realized now as she regarded this formidable young widow that Elena had urged Sebastian to include her, Nicola, so that they would be home before the other two, Adrienne and Ramon.

"Yes, Doña Elena," Nicola said gently, as they sat in one of the small patios of the villa. "What would you like to know?"

Elena removed her dark glasses. "About your family. Your life in London. Dr. Montal says you came here only for a holiday."

"Yes." Nicola decided that without being impolite or obstructive, she need not make it easy for Doña Elena.

"Then why did you stay?" asked the other.

"I had arranged to meet my sister, Lisa, in Barcelona, even step into her job, which she had given up. But I haven't been able to trace Lisa yet." Nicola realized that the doctor might already have given Elena some of these details.

"How very interesting!" Elena had replaced her dark glasses. "Are you still looking for her?"

"Of course."

Elena's lips curled into a faintly derisive smile.

"Have the police been able to help you?" she asked.

Nicola inwardly shivered. "So far I haven't asked for their help."

"I see. No doubt you have good reasons for that."

Nicola remained silent. This was no time to make hot protests or Elena would probe and suspect until she arrived at the truth about Lisa.

"I feel I must give you a friendly warning," Elena continued. "About Adrienne. At the moment she is very taken with you. She finds you a pleasant companion. But she is very young—and she changes her mind most rapidly. If you should suddenly find yourself on bad terms with her, that is something you must entirely expect.''

After a brief pause, Nicola said, ''Thank you, Doña Elena. I'll bear in mind what you say.'' She had no intention of revealing that she had pledged herself to stay for a year, and evidently Dr. Montal had not mentioned the fact to Elena. Of course, Nicola reflected, Adrienne might make the situation so impossible that Nicola would be glad to go and Sebastian only too willing to release her. It was obvious now that Elena would do everything in her power to sow trouble between Nicola and both Adrienne and her uncle.

Elena rose, a beautiful woman, slightly above the average Spanish height, with a regal carriage and a proud tilt of her head so that it showed the camellia-white pillar of her throat. Beside her, Nicola felt undistinguished and at this moment even grubby after the day's outing. She was longing to get away from Elena and take a cool shower. At last Elena dismissed her with a cool smile and a final warning: ''You will remember what I said, won't you?''

Nicola fled to her room. She was going to be no match for this elegant, sophisticated woman. In many ways, although she was older, she could not always follow Adrienne's sometimes tortuous reasoning and impulsive actions, but at least the young girl was frank about her intentions.

Elena and Ramon stayed to dinner at the villa, and although on the surface the atmosphere was gay and light enough, Nicola sensed an undercurrent of uneasy watchfulness. Ramon suggested that he might take Adrienne and Nicola out for a trip in the motorized dinghy, which he used with his yacht.

''Tomorrow?'' queried Adrienne. ''Oh, we would be delighted.''

Before Nicola could agree, the doctor interposed. ''Tomorrow is not a very convenient day for me.''

Ramon laughed lightly, his dark eyes twinkling. ''Forgive me, dear Sebastian, but I had no idea that you would want to come with us. But of course you're welcome.''

Sebastian's face did not relax. ''I was not thinking of wasting my time on boat trips. It was merely that I thought

Miss Brettell might be able to give some of her time to work for me."

"Oh, I see." Ramon gave Nicola an oblique glance accompanied by his most charming smile.

"But of course I'm available to work whenever you say, Dr. Montal," Nicola said hastily before any further remarks or significant pauses could complicate the situation.

"I protest!" exclaimed Ramon. "You must give Nicola a few chances to have leisure with us."

"Miss Brettell will not be worked unduly hard, I assure you," replied Sebastian. Now his face was lit with a smile that softened his forbidding features. *Why doesn't he look like that more often*, thought Nicola, *instead of keeping his smiles hidden away and unused?*

"I could accompany Adrienne," suggested Elena, who was immediately rewarded with a flashing angry look from Adrienne.

"Oh, no," put in Ramon quickly. "You know how you hate my small boats."

"It seems that we'd better compromise," Sebastian advised. "Ramon can take you two girls out in the morning and after lunch I will be home and Miss Brettell will then be free to assist me."

For a moment Ramon stared at his host. "As you arrange it, so it will be," he said politely with the merest nod. It was clear to Nicola that he was displeased with the cavalier way in which Sebastian had ordered the day's arrangements, but no doubt Ramon was familiar with Dr. Montal's moods and character.

On the way down to the harbor next morning, Adrienne giggled with amusement.

"Did you see Elena's face last night when she offered to chaperone me in the boat?" she asked Nicola. "She was divided into two pieces, one to be with me and Ramon and the other with you and Sebastian," Adrienne's laughter rang out joyously as she drove her white car down the winding lane toward the shore.

Nicola, too, was beginning to see that she must tread most warily in this circle where convention still had to be respected.

Ramon was waiting for the two girls where the road ran along by the harbor. His white shirt and shorts intensified the blackness of his hair, his tanned skin and dark, luminous eyes. He was undeniably handsome, Nicola had to admit, and his courteous manners added a new dimension to politeness. When he handed Nicola into the dinghy he became the courtier receiving his princess. She noticed that he held her hand in his firm clasp rather longer than was necessary.

He navigated carefully among the crowd of other vessels in the harbor, but once outside in the open sea, he opened the throttle and the boat skimmed along like a white bird, leaving a creamy wake of foam astern. The wind tore through Nicola's hair and she was thankful that she had recently had it cut into a shorter style for the summer. Adrienne's long fair hair blew and twisted into a tangle of untidy strands. Ramon steered away from the shore and the coastline diminished so that it became only an undulating line of blue gray shadow.

"Not so far out, Ramon!" called Adrienne. "You'll have us in Majorca in no time!"

He flashed his white teeth at her in reply, but soon turned the boat in a wide arc that brought the dinghy parallel to the shore. He slowed down so that the boat seemed to drift lazily on top of the scintillating waves.

He lolled against the thwart and lit a cigar.

"Why don't you have lunch with us on the yacht?" he asked.

"No. We promised we would be back at the villa at two o'clock," said Adrienne firmly. "Nicolà must be there for Sebastian, you remember?"

Ramon laughed. "I remember! His Imperious Excellency never lets an opportunity go by to play the Conquistador. You, Nicola, must preserve your Anglo-Saxon character and refuse to yield to his orders."

Nicola smiled. "I can hardly do that. I'm not just a guest. I'm paid to work for Dr. Montal."

Ramon took the two girls aboard the *Clorinda* in the harbor. Adrienne knew her way around the yacht, but Ramon conducted Nicola on a quick tour of inspection. She admired its trim luxury, shining white paint and gleaming brasswork. A steward served drinks at an elegant teak table where an awning stretched across the well deck made a cool patch of shade as the yacht rode at anchor.

Ramon renewed his invitation to lunch, protesting that he disliked eating alone. Adrienne wavered, but Nicola put in decisively, "It's very kind of you, Señor—I mean, Ramon." She felt herself blushing under his intense stare. "But perhaps another time when we have made the proper arrangements?"

"By all means! I shall be enchanted." He raised her hand to his lips, then preceded the two girls into the dinghy to take them ashore.

On the quay Nicola gazed again at the yacht *Clorinda,* a craft with beautiful clear-cut lines, well qualified to take her place among those other handsome luxury vessels from Los Angeles and Stockholm, London and Monte Carlo.

Ramon was about halfway between the quay and the *Clorinda* and he waved to the two girls, who waved back.

"You like Ramon?" queried Adrienne as she and Nicola walked toward the road.

"I think he's a very pleasant young man," Nicola said smoothly.

Adrienne gave a faint chuckle. "Yes, he has charm and much else besides. Perhaps you had better marry him."

"Hold on a moment! I've only met him two or three times."

"Does that matter?" asked Adrienne. "Me, I have known him too long—since I was a small child."

"So he is just like a brother to you." Nicola's voice held gentle sarcasm.

"Exactly so! There is no—how shall I say—no excitement, no turbulence. I would like a man to set me on fire with his glance and make me feel faint with his kisses."

Nicola hardly knew whether to laugh or take Adrienne seriously. "At your age every girl wants a man like that."

"Then why shouldn't we find him?"

"Be patient, Adrienne. One day you might find that Ramon sparks you off just like that."

Adrienne sighed. "Never, I think, with Ramon. Besides, he is most flirtatious."

"Then that ought to make you jealous. Doesn't it?"

"No," declared Adrienne crossly.

On the way back to the villa, she stopped the car outside a small cottage. "I want you to visit some friends I have here," she explained.

"But we shall be very late for lunch," Nicola objected.

"We shall stay only a few minutes."

Nicola followed Adrienne through the doorway of the pink-washed cottage. After the dazzling sunshine outside, it took her a moment or two to accustom her eyes to the dark interior. Then she became aware that two women had emerged from the shadows.

Adrienne was introducing her in Spanish.

"Señora Gallito—Señorita Micaela Gallito—Señorita Brettell, *mi amiga inglesa*."

The two women, evidently mother and daughter, bowed gravely in acknowledgement. The younger one hurried away and came back with a jug of wine. The two girls drank the rough wine from small stone goblets. Then Adrienne asked, "Barto?"

The young girl, Micaela, shook her head and replied in Spanish. Adrienne asked further questions.

Nicola was appalled. The Gallitos were evidently Barto's family, and here she was, at Adrienne's invitation, drinking wine in their house, when she had been most definitely instructed by Dr. Montal to keep Adrienne out of Barto's way.

How could she now persuade Adrienne to leave? She glanced pointedly at her watch and murmured "*Vamos*," then repeated in English, "Let's go."

Adrienne smiled. "*Momentito*. No hurry."

A few more minutes went by, then Adrienne rose, ready to leave, and Nicola sighed with relief. At that moment the doorway was blocked by a shadow and a young, slim boy came in, carrying a bucket of fish. Adrienne greeted him, then turned toward Nicola.

"This is Barto,"

"Bartolomeo Gallito," he announced with dignity as he bowed to Nicola.

Adrienne called out, "*Adiós,* Señora! Micaela!" then spoke rapidly to Barto in an undertone. "Come on, Nicola."

During the short drive between the cottage and the Villa Ronda, Nicola remained silent until Adrienne exclaimed irritably, "You are angry with me."

"Not exactly angry," countered Nicola. "But I think you took me there under false pretences."

"Not in the least," declared Adrienne. "Now you know what Barto's family is like. How can you say that they are not honest and charming people?"

"I don't doubt it, but you'll get Barto into trouble."

Adrienne laughed as she swung the car through the gates and along the curving driveway. "Sebastian won't know anything about our visit—unless you tell him."

Nicola alighted from the car. "That puts me into the position of a spy. I thought you disliked that sort of thing."

Adrienne stared at Nicola, her gray eyes wide with hurt bewilderment. "I really believe you would tell Sebastian!"

"I'd much rather not," admitted Nicola.

"But you think you have a duty to Sebastian."

Nicola shrugged and turned away. "Don't let's discuss it further. But please, Adrienne, don't make me your companion—" she had nearly said "accomplice" "—on these occasions."

It was a pity, thought Nicola afterward, that the doctor was home for lunch that day and required her services in the afternoon, for Adrienne's ill-temper would easily have evaporated had he been absent. But he was waiting with barely concealed impatience and when Adrienne and Nicola joined him, he said mildly, but in a reproving tone, "You're very late home, Adrienne. I thought you must have decided to stay to lunch on Ramon's yacht."

"We had some shopping to do on the way back," Adrienne answered casually. She glanced at her uncle, then at Nicola. "No, that's not true. Before Nicola can tell you, I will tell you myself," she said defiantly. "I went today to call on the Gallitos."

"For what purpose?" asked Sebastian coldly.

"Only to see them. Barto came home while I was there and I saw him for two whole minutes. So what can you do now?"

Sebastian put down his sherry glass. "I'm glad you've told me, Adrienne," he said calmly. "For Nicola's sake, more than your own. On the way up here I passed your car, which was standing outside the Gallitos' house." He paused, finished his sherry, then rose. "We'll begin lunch."

Adrienne jumped to her feet, fury in every line of her body, her face contorted in rage. "How hateful you have become, Sebastian!" she exclaimed. "You knew I was there, yet you tried to trap me into saying that we stayed late on Ramon's boat. No, indeed, I don't want lunch. I won't sit down and eat with you!"

She dashed away across the courtyard and was hidden by a clump of oleander and magnolia trees.

Nicola shot a questioning look at Sebastian. Should she follow Adrienne and pacify her if possible, or was her neutrality to be undermined by staying with the doctor?

"Come along, Nicola," he said, resolving her doubts. "No doubt you're hungry after the morning boat trip."

He led the way to the table placed under the three palm trees.

"I'm afraid I couldn't prevent that visit to the Gallito family," she said, after they had begun the meal. "I didn't at first realize who the women were, until I heard about Barto. Then I realized they were his mother and sister."

Sebastian smiled, that rare smile of his, which lit his face like a gilt-edged cloud after a storm. "Don't worry about it. You know now, so you will understand the position next time. It's an advantage to know where the dangers are. Then you can avoid them."

Nicola was silent. It was not always quite so easy to avoid complications even when the dangers were plainly in sight. She longed to say to the doctor that if he really wanted to stop his niece from seeing Barto, then he was going the wrong way about it.

He spoke of other subjects during the meal, his work at the big hospital in Barcelona, his clinic in the poorer part of

Orsola, and Nicola gave him her attention. There was no sense in letting her mind dwell on Adrienne's temporary fury.

Nicola would have been ready to start on the doctor's typing work almost immediately after lunch, but he always insisted on the siesta, although she suspected that he did not often take a real rest himself, but merely sat writing in his study.

At four-thirty, refreshed by lemon tea, she settled down to work in Sebastian's study and he came in some time later to settle any queries.

"By the way," he said suddenly, "I met a girl this morning who might possibly be your sister."

Nicola almost jumped up from the typewriter. "Lisa? Oh, where is she?"

"This girl is in a convent hospital in Barcelona."

"Is she ill?" Nicola asked.

"Not physically. Her trouble is more mental. She's had a shock of some kind, I imagine."

Nicola went cold with apprehension. If the girl were really Lisa, what could have happened to her?

"I must go and find out if she's Lisa," she said agitatedly.

"I'll take you there tomorrow," he promised.

"Tomorrow?" she echoed. "But—"

"I know," he interposed. "You're going to tell me that you want to go now, that you can't wait. There's nothing to be gained by going today. The nuns would not allow you to see the girl without my presence as a doctor."

Nicola choked down her disappointment. Sebastian Montal was hard and unfeeling. Had his profession as a healer taught him nothing of kindness and sympathy? To spring the news on her that Lisa might possibly be found and then to make her wait in excruciating suspense throughout the rest of the day and tonight, surely this was cruelty itself.

After a long pause she said quietly, "Why didn't you tell me sooner? You saw this girl this morning."

He came closer to her and stood on the opposite side of her desk. "You think it would have improved your appetite at lunch if I'd told you then? Even good news can be very disturbing at mealtimes, let alone something that is very uncertain."

Her hands rested idly on the typewriter keys.

"I'd better concentrate on your work, Dr. Montal," she said stiffly. "Thank you for telling me about this girl. I will be ready at whatever time you say tomorrow morning."

"You understand that I may be mistaken?" he reminded her.

"Of course."

He went out through the arched windows onto the terrace and Nicola was glad of his absence. She needed a few minutes to collect her thoughts. If the girl turned out to be Lisa, how could Nicola try to look after her? She could scarcely expect Dr. Montal to give Lisa a home and treat her as a patient.

Nicola turned back to the typing. Then she gave a half smile. The doctor had probably been right after all not to tell her until there was something else to occupy her mind. Work was the conventional antidote to worry.

Adrienne did not appear at dinner and Nicola was concerned about the girl.

"Will she be all right?" she asked the doctor. "She must surely be very hungry—and unhappy," she added quietly.

The doctor smiled. "Hungry? No. Rosana, our house-keeper, will keep Adrienne well supplied with whatever meals she fancies. As to her being unhappy, she has proba-bly forgotten her tantrum, but she wants to make certain that I know how displeased she is with me. I know Adrienne."

Nicola wondered if Dr. Montal knew his niece at all. Adrienne was no longer the gay schoolgirl, ready to agree to Sebastian's ideas. At seventeen she was half child, half woman, experiencing all the pangs and joys of growing up without maturing. With neither mother nor father to guide her through this phase with all its frustrations and heady discoveries, she needed more understanding and sympathy than her uncle was apparently willing to give.

Yet Nicola was secretly delighted to be dining alone with her employer out on the Mediterranean balcony. The last sunset colors of mauve and yellow, crimson and gray were fading, leaving the mountains sharply silhouetted like two-dimensional cardboard cutouts. Lights in the harbor came on first in ones or twos, then a small chain, and the sea intensified to a deep midnight blue. When the dusk on the balcony deepened, a manservant brought oil lamps to insert in iron sconces on the balustrade.

After the meal the warm night air and the aroma of Sebastian's cigar combined to make Nicola feel sleepy and presently she excused herself.

"Good night, Dr. Montal. I will be ready early tomorrow morning for our trip to Barcelona."

On the way to her room she paused outside Adrienne's suite. Courtesy and friendliness demanded that she should make inquiries in case Adrienne was really in distress, yet Nicola did not want to appear to be taking sides.

Adrienne called out, "Come in," in reply to Nicola's knock.

"Ah! So you have come at last. I wondered if you had been forbidden to visit the prisoner."

Nicola smiled. "Prisoner? I thought it was you who chose seclusion. You're all right?" The query, she knew, was unnecessary. Adrienne seemed in perfect health and spirits.

"Naturally. Why not?"

"When you didn't appear at dinner, I wondered."

"Oh, I have had an excellent dinner of bread and water." Adrienne declared. "I will continue to live."

"Fortunately for us all," Nicola said dryly.

Adrienne glanced up and burst into delighted laughter. "You have much sense, Nicola, not to take me too seriously. I fly into a rage, then it is all over in ten minutes, but I cannot then admit that it was not important, so I remain—what would you say—remote?"

"Aloof is perhaps the word that suits you." Nicola sat on the foot of the bed. "I have news. Your uncle thinks he may have discovered my sister, so tomorrow he's taking me to Barcelona. I didn't think to ask him whether he is also taking you."

"Oh, I'm not a toy to be picked up whenever he has the fancy. Besides, tomorrow I have plans of my own." Adrienne's face melted into a self-satisfied expression. "Sebastian will jump to the wrong conclusion," she continued, "that I will immediately go to see Barto. So I think he will invite dear Doña Elena to keep me company, and see that I don't stray." She giggled. "What frustration for her! Her day will not be at all happy."

"Why? What are you going to do?" Nicola was vaguely alarmed.

"Nothing wicked. Only what I am permitted to do. Good night, Nicola. Have a happy day tomorrow—and I hope you find your sister."

ON THE WAY to Barcelona next day Nicola was not certain whether she wanted this distressed girl in a convent hospital to be Lisa. To see her high-spirited sister mentally ill would be a painful experience, yet every day the anxiety of not knowing what had become of Lisa constantly gnawed at Nicola's peace of mind.

Dr. Montal lost no time in taking Nicola straight to the girl's bedside. Nicola looked at the pale face, the cloudy dark hair, and knew that the girl was not Lisa. When the patient opened her eyes and stared wildly at the doctor, Nicola was relieved that she was able to say definitely, "No, Dr. Montal, she is not my sister."

When they left the ward, Dr. Montal asked, "Have you a photograph of your sister?"

"Not here. I might be able to get one from home. A snapshot or one of those Lisa had taken for publicity."

"That might make it easier to trace her."

Nicola shivered. "You mean the police?"

"Yes, the police. Possibly in other directions, too," he answered.

She knew what he meant by "other directions." As a doctor he was naturally in touch not only with hospitals, but mortuaries, and the thought that Lisa might be dead was unbearable.

"I will be busy here and at another hospital," the doctor told her. "Can you amuse yourself until about five o'clock? Then I'll pick you up and take you back to the villa."

"Of course. I'll be glad of the time to explore Barcelona," she agreed without hesitation.

"You might go to the 'Spanish Village' at Montjuich," he suggested, "unless you've already been there. Take a taxi."

Outside the convent it occurred to Nicola that she ought to get in touch with Patrick. Today was Saturday and he would not be working this afternoon, although he might already have arrangements of his own and be unable to see her.

She took a taxi to the Plaza de Cataluna and telephoned his office. "I could meet you somewhere at about two o'clock," he told her. "I'm tied up until then. Where would you like to go?"

"Dr. Montal suggested the Spanish Village—whatever that may be," Nicola replied.

"Oh, yes, you ought to see that. All right, I'll meet you at the Plaza de España by the air terminal and we'll have a quick snack lunch and then go to the village. Quarter past two?"

"Thank you, Patrick. That would be fine."

She spent the morning idling in the shops, then strolled along the *ramblas* where flower stalls splashed brilliant colors beneath the plane trees and the air was vibrant with the chatter of crowds, punctuated by raucous cries from the lottery-ticket sellers.

When Patrick took her to the *Pueblo Español,* the Spanish village built inside Montjuich Park to illustrate all the various styles of Spanish architecture, she was delighted.

"What a marvelous place! I'm glad Dr. Montal suggested I should come," she said.

"I'd have brought you here anyway," retorted Patrick, "without waiting for your boss to mention it. We just haven't had time together for me to show you the sights before you went dashing off to live it up in a classy villa at Orsola."

She sensed that for some reason his feelings were ruffled. "Tell me about the buildings," she said tactfully, avoiding the personal element.

"They had an International Exhibition here in 1929," he explained, "and this village was part of the celebrations."

"And the houses have stood up all this time?" she queried.

"Oh, yes. They're solidly built, not just canvas and plaster."

As they walked through the various squares and up the narrow, twisting streets, he pointed out replicas of typical houses found in Andalusia and Catalonia, Castile and Navarre and all the other provinces of Spain.

"But they haven't made it a dead showpiece," Patrick said. "All kinds of crafts go on in the workshops and there are shops to sell the products."

Nicola was charmed to see leather purses actually being embossed and decorated and could not resist buying a couple. At a small printing shop she bought some Christmas cards illustrating scenes from Don Quixote.

"Look, Patrick, straight from a hand press. None of my friends in England would be able to match that."

Other shops sold handwoven textiles and there was even, tucked away under an archway, a blacksmith's forge where ironwork was fashioned.

"I could spend days here," she said happily.

"Why don't we?" returned Patrick.

She laughed. "Since both of us have to work, that's not a very sensible question!"

They returned to the miniature Plaza Mayor, which Patrick said was similar to the one in Madrid. One side was a balcony café and Nicola was glad of the opportunity to rest her feet and drink coffee.

"We must come here again when they have a *fiesta*," Patrick suggested. "Sometimes they dance the *sardana* in costume, or they have entertainments on Sundays for children. All kinds of shows go on here."

"Yes, we must make a date," she replied. After a pause, she added, "Dr. Montal found a girl in hospital whom he thought might be Lisa. I went to see her this morning. But she wasn't Lisa."

"Disappointing," he said almost curtly.

"Not really," Nicola said hastily. "This girl was in a very unhappy state. Mental breakdown, I think. I hope never to see Lisa like that."

Patrick was silent, and Nicola had the impression that in some way he was relieved that Lisa had not been traced.

"You didn't like Lisa, did you?" she questioned.

"If you must know the truth, no, I didn't."

"Any particular reason? Or shouldn't I ask that?"

Patrick sighed. "It doesn't matter. It's just that she was the kind of girl I don't care for. Too mercenary. Too eager to have a good time. You see, Nicola, you're paying for her good time, and if she knew about it she'd laugh and tell you what a fool you were."

Nicola smiled. "I think you're a little hard on her. Anyway, I shall be able to pay off the debts quickly, thanks to Dr. Montal's generous salary. After that, I will be able to enjoy my own good time with money to fling about like Spanish gold."

He gazed across the table at her, his eyes stared with an intensity that slightly disconcerted her. "Your idea of a good time isn't the same as Lisa's," he said at last. "But I'm glad you'll get a run for your money later on. I may not be here when you polish off the final debts. I'm due home in September."

"For a holiday?"

"In a way, yes. I'm getting married." He turned his head away to look across the *plaza*. "My fiancée lives in Sussex."

"But you'll come back here to your firm—with your wife?"

"H'm. I don't know. I have a contract with the firm, but it'll expire about that time and I don't know if we shall renew it. But we'll let the future take care of itself."

"Then let me wish you every happiness," said Nicola quietly with a smile.

He gave her a swift glance. "Thanks, Nicola," he said, but his tone was cool.

She caught sight of the clock on the opposite side of the square. "Heavens! Is that the time?" she exclaimed in dismay. "It's gone five o'clock and I promised to meet the doctor."

"What? At this hour?" Patrick queried.

"Yes, at five." She was gathering her handbag and the small parcels.

"If I'd known, we could have had a decent lunch. I thought you had the rest of the evening free and then we could have dinner together. Why didn't you say so?"

"It didn't occur to me," she said lamely. "Anyway, I don't want to take up all your free time."

He frowned. "Where are you meeting this all-important boss of yours?"

Nicola bit her lip in vexation. "I'm not sure. He didn't make any definite arrangement as to place—except that he suggested the Spanish Village."

"So therefore if you didn't accept his suggestion, he'd expect you to let him know by telephone where you'd gone?" Patrick raised his eyebrows mockingly. "He certainly keeps tabs on you. Doesn't like you roaming around Barcelona on your own."

Nicola smiled rather nervously. Patrick's acid comments had solved her problem. "Thank you for such a nice afternoon," she said hurriedly. "I've enjoyed it, but I apologize for leaving you so early. I ought to have explained."

He smiled, apparently having recovered his normal good humor. "Don't worry, Nicola. It's as I said. You're so different from Lisa. She wouldn't have cared two hoots about keeping a promise, employer or anyone else. I'll come out to the exit with you in case his lordship hasn't arrived."

But as soon as Nicola reached the exit and walked down to the road through the park she saw Sebastian Montal's car. She said goodbye to Patrick, thanked him again for a pleasant afternoon, and ran toward the car.

Dr. Montal opened the door without a word.

"I'm sorry I'm late, Dr. Montal," she said contritely.

"Who was the young man you were with?" he asked, ignoring her apology.

"He's English. He works at the firm of wine shippers where my sister worked for a time. He's been helpful to me."

"Oh? In what way?"

"Well, he had known Lisa for a short time and he was able to give me information about her. He was someone with whom I could discuss the problem. He even offered to find me a job in his firm if he could.''

''But I gather he was not successful. I believe you said there was no immediate vacancy there.''

''Yes, that's so. But it was kind of Patrick to try to help me.''

Dr. Montal had sounded so critical of Patrick that in turn her voice took on a defiant note.

''Are you in love with this man—Patrick?''

The question took her by surprise, but she did not hesitate in her reply. ''No, indeed! He's a good friend. Besides, he's engaged to a girl in England and later in the year he's going back to marry her.''

That should settle the doctor's uncertainties, she thought with satisfaction.

He drove for some minutes before he spoke again.

''I asked if you were in love with him—not he with you,'' he said brusquely.

''The situation doesn't arise, Dr. Montal,'' she answered stiffly. Why must he catechize her like this? What business was it of his if she and Patrick fell in love?

''Is there someone in England with whom you have—as the English so often say—an understanding?''

''No one at all,'' she snapped.

''Good. I like to know where we stand in these matters. I apologize for my curiosity.''

He gave her a warm smile and began to ask her about her visit to the Spanish Village.

She thought his change of mood entirely remarkable, but since there was no point in maintaining a hostile relationship with her employer Nicola matched his geniality.

It was only when she arrived at the Villa Ronda and went to her room that it now occurred to her why Patrick might be so hypercritical about her working for the doctor. Possibly he had been disappointed that he had not succeeded in obtaining a job for her with his own firm and therefore annoyed that she had grabbed at the first available chance elsewhere.

It could hardly matter to him now, for he would be returning to England in a few months' time. It was more important to Nicola that Dr. Montal seemed reasonably content with her secretarial services. How she succeeded in the other half of her dual post, as companion to Adrienne, was another matter. In this direction the doctor was easily displeased, and Nicola knew she must be careful not to make careless blunders.

CHAPTER FOUR

NICOLA WAS RESTING on her balcony overlooking the flowered patio when Adrienne approached from below.

"Come down and bathe!" she called.

"In the pool?" queried Nicola.

"No, in the sea. We'll go to the beach house."

A few moments later Adrienne came into Nicola's room. She was bubbling with high spirits.

"Oh, this has been a day!"

"You've been up to mischief, I can tell," Nicola said with mock severity.

"No, truly, I have been working hard painting all day. But tell me—did you find your sister?"

Nicola shook her head. "The girl was not Lisa."

"Ah. A pity." After a momentary pause, Adrienne continued, "Doña Elena called quite early, as I knew she would. Oh, she pretended it was pure chance, but I know Sebastian had warned her to come and follow me."

"Well, what harm was there in that?"

Adrienne exploded with laughter. "None to me. But poor Elena! She is so tired, walking all those kilometers. You see, when I am painting, naturally I have several canvases not finished. I wait for them to dry, so today I worked on numerous scenes. Elena had to follow where I went. Down to the beach, then up the hill, along the road, down again to the harbor."

"That was very naughty of you. Inconsiderate, too," said Nicola.

"Do not blame me! Blame Sebastian!" Adrienne was all pious indignation. "If he had told me that Doña Elena was to be my jailer in your absence, I would have treated her more politely, but when she came uninvited by me, then she must put up with my plans already arranged.''

On the way down to the beach house, Nicola told Adrienne of her own day and that she had met Patrick.

"You must invite this young man to our party," suggested Adrienne. "Then you will have more freedom to flirt with all the other young men there."

"How does that follow?" queried Nicola.

"Naturally. If you have no special companion of your own, then you are not free to capture someone else's admirer. But with a man to exchange, the position is simple."

The two girls had reached the beach chalet and Nicola stood for a moment outside the door, convulsed with helpless laughter at Adrienne's sophisticated philosophy.

"You make it sound like a French farce," she spluttered at last. "Tossing men about as though they were children's balls!"

"That is the true essence of a party," declared Adrienne.

As she changed into her swimsuit, Nicola reflected that now that she knew that Patrick was engaged it would be reasonable to invite him to a festivity at the villa. There would be no suggestion that she was trying to impose on a friendship and, after all, he had shown her a great deal of courtesy and hospitality.

The cove, which was apparently private property belonging to the Villa Ronda, was probably an ideal setting for a seashore party, thought Nicola, as she surveyed it from the gentle tossing waves. She could already imagine it, lit with lanterns, alive with music and the sound of laughter.

Tonight the two girls dined alone with Sebastian, this time in the shadowed dining room. Adrienne was all bubbling gaiety, but Nicola instinctively felt that under Sebastian's calm exterior a threatening storm was brewing.

"Tomorrow evening," he said casually, when the meal was nearly finished, "we will be dining on Ramon's yacht. I suppose, Adrienne, that if I give you a day's warning, you can manage to be ready by eight o'clock?"

She grimaced at him. "I will do my best."

Nicola did not jump to the conclusion that the arrangement included herself, but Sebastian, perhaps understanding that she could not ask such a question, said, "Of course you will come with us, Nicola."

"Thank you." She smiled at him, appreciating his tact.

The doctor himself drove the two girls down to the harbor next evening. Nicola supposed that the chauffeur, Ignacio, could hardly be expected to guess the time he would be required to bring the party home and Sebastian was too considerate of his staff to keep the man waiting there needlessly.

Nicola was doubly glad now that she had recently bought a new evening dress of dull satin in a glowing sapphire shade that enhanced her blue eyes and put highlights into her mid-brown hair.

Adrienne, in her turquoise and silver lamé dress, looked like a particularly innocent and vulnerable angel with her long fair hair and flawless complexion. Nicola was beginning to understand that a guileless appearance could often be belied by a single mischievous glance from Adrienne's eyes.

A member of Ramon's crew was waiting at the harbor with the *Clorinda's* dinghy and took the doctor and two girls out to the moored yacht where Ramon welcomed his guests aboard. He looked particularly smart in his white dinner jacket, but then, Nicola reflected, so did Dr. Montal, who was considerably taller and slimmer than Ramon.

Doña Elena was waiting to greet the others in the small cocktail cabin leading off the main dining saloon. She seemed surprised to find that Nicola was aboard, but immediately recovered her poise and good manners.

While she sipped her sherry and left most of the conversation to the others, Nicola's gaze wandered around the luxurious furnishings of the yacht. On that first hasty inspection tour a few days ago she had not had time to notice the magnificence of interior design. No space wasted, yet an air of complete comfort everywhere.

The dinner was long and leisurely and darkness had fallen by the time the coffee stage was reached. Ramon suggested that he might take Adrienne and Nicola on his next trip to San Fernando in about a fortnight's time.

"I've been there many times," Adrienne replied casually, "but Nicola has not visited the island. Have you, Nicola?"

"No."

Doña Elena rewarded Nicola with a hostile glance.

"Possibly you will have found your sister by then," she said smoothly, "and you will both have other plans."

"I don't know," muttered Nicola noncommittally, not daring to look at Sebastian. Evidently Elena still did not know that Nicola was expected to remain for a year, but it was not Nicola's responsibility to disclose that fact.

Ramon insisted on taking Nicola for a more thorough tour of the yacht. "Last time you were in such a hurry. Now you must allow me to show you my treasure in detail."

She was slightly apprehensive that Ramon's suggestion might not meet with the doctor's approval, but although he looked at Nicola, he gave no indication of agreement or otherwise.

Ramon showed her the well-furnished cabins with elegant beds instead of bunks, the galley that was as up-to-date and as efficiently arranged as the kitchen of a first-class hotel. He took her into the skipper's cabin. "I do not always pilot the yacht myself. If I am captain, then I have no time to spend with my guests on board," he explained. Finally he brought Nicola up a stairway to the upper deck and for a few moments she stood by the taffrail and gazed at the scene around her. Harbor lights twinkled in almost a complete circle, but there were few sounds except an occasional shout and the puttering of a motorized dinghy. Once or twice in the stillness Nicola was convinced that she could hear nightingales in the pines on shore.

"Are there nightingales here?" she queried.

"Oh, yes." Ramon lifted her hand and held it closely under his own on the polished wood rail. "We must plan many amusements for you. *Fiestas* in Barcelona, of course, and a trip to Tibidabo, but there is also sardine fishing at night. Now that is a wonderful sight."

Nicola turned toward him, a gentle smile on her lips.

"Fishing for sardines? But you can buy all the sardines you want, surely?"

"We go for the fun. When I was a young boy, I slipped out at nights to join the fishermen. Sebastian used to come, too. Eduardo was too old at that time. Now we take our guests to enjoy the spectacle."

Nicola was digesting the information that Sebastian had joined these simple pastimes when he was younger. Now he was so dignified, usually so withdrawn, that it was difficult to imagine he had ever enjoyed the natural pleasures and escapades of a boy.

Ramon added, "You will come to San Fernando with us, I hope? I have a house there in the north part of the island."

"I must wait until Dr. Montal gives me permission," she answered cautiously.

"Sebastian! Oh, you simply must not let him dictate to you. He always wants to rule people like an emperor."

"Ramon!" Doña Elena's voice cut sharply on the air. Neither Nicola nor Ramon had noticed her approach, but now they saw that Sebastian accompanied her.

"Adrienne is looking for you," Elena continued to her brother.

Ramon gave her a fiery scowl, then with deliberate slowness he raised Nicola's hand to his lips and bowed. He turned and marched swiftly along the deck, annoyance and indignation evident in every step.

Sebastian leaned his back against the rail and remained silent.

"I hope my brother has not been boring you," Elena said to Nicola. "You must forgive him. This yacht is his new one and he likes to show it off as though it were a toy."

"No, Doña Elena," Nicola answered hastily. "I've enjoyed being taken around." She was uncertain whether to remain on deck or go below, but Sebastian solved that problem by sauntering slowly out of sight.

"Señorita Brettell," began Elena in a low, but precise voice, "I think I must explain to you some of our traditional customs. When someone comes to our house and admires a picture or ornament or a piece of furniture, it is our courteous habit to say, 'Take it. It is yours.' But we do not expect our guest to wrap it up and take it away. Similarly, when invitations are tossed about, we do not always expect them to be accepted."

"I understand, *señora*. But how is the foreigner to know which invitations to accept and which to refuse discreetly?"

Elena smiled. "I can see that you are a sensible girl. In this case it is Ramon who has been to blame. When we go to San Fernando, I will be on board to be companion to Adrienne. You understand it will not be necessary for you to be with us?"

"Yes, *señora*, but I have to take my instructions from Dr. Montal," Nicola said coldly.

"Naturally," agreed Elena, and Nicola knew by her tone that she meant to persuade the doctor to exclude Nicola. "Of course, I do not wish to deprive you of the opportunity to visit San Fernando, but no doubt you will find your own chances. When you have found your sister, perhaps?"

"That would be something pleasant to hope for," replied Nicola, "but at present I have no news."

"So I understand from Sebastian, who took you on an unsuccessful search. But I am sure you will find her sooner or later—if that is possible."

Nicola barely caught that last whispered phrase, but now she understood clearly why Doña Elena so often referred to the missing sister.

"Do you believe, Doña Elena, that I have invented a missing sister? What purpose would I have?"

Elena shrugged her elegant shoulders. "Sebastian is kindhearted and a sympathetic doctor. He is easily taken in."

Nicola could have laughed aloud, but the moment was too tensely dramatic for her to indulge in laughter about Sebastian's gullibility.

"I am not staying in the doctor's house just so that he can help me search for Lisa," Nicola said firmly. "I am there to work for him as a secretary and sometimes act as a young companion to Adrienne."

"Exactly. Let us say no more about it. I think you understand the position."

Elena gave Nicola one of her most gracious smiles and turned away to walk to the stairway.

Nicola was seething with fury. It had not occurred to her that anyone would think that searching for Lisa was a fiction to enable her to stay in a comfortable villa and be well paid for a moderate amount of work. Did Sebastian think that, too? At a more opportune moment she would certainly ask him point blank.

It was nearly midnight when Ramon took his guests ashore in the dinghy. Nicola pretended that she was tired, although she had never felt more wide awake, but it gave her the excuse of keeping quiet on the drive up to the Villa Ronda, where Sebastian dropped the two girls, then took Doña Elena on to her own house farther up the hill.

Adrienne, too, was rather silent, for her, and as they went to their respective rooms, she said, "Nicola, you must watch carefully for Elena. She is hatching something very bad."

"Oh, never mind," returned Nicola carelessly. "Let's go to bed. I'm sleepy after that luscious dinner and all that wine." She yawned exaggeratedly.

She was just as certain as Adrienne, though, that Doña Elena was out to manipulate matters to suit her own purposes.

During the next few days, Nicola spent a great deal of her time working for the doctor on his book. Adrienne divided her days between painting, mostly in her studio, and arranging the forthcoming party on the beach.

"How lucky you are in this country," sighed Nicola, "to be able to invite people to an evening outdoor party and not have to worry about the weather. In England, we might have a week's beautiful summer before the party and on the night a thunderstorm would wreck everything."

"No thunderstorms until the end of September," remarked Adrienne. "That is when they come, so we do not make arrangements."

Nicola had diplomatically suggested that while she was engaged on her secretarial work, Adrienne could perhaps not visit the Gallitos' house or go out of her way to see Barto, and without actually mentioning the family, Adrienne had tacitly agreed.

"This young man, Patrick," Adrienne said, consulting her list of guests. "What is his address?"

"I've no idea where he lives," confessed Nicola. "I know only his office address. Perhaps I could telephone and ask him to the party?"

Adrienne wrote down his name. "Patrick Holton," she murmured.

"I am longing to meet him. Make sure, Nicola, that I do not snatch him from you."

"I thought you said that that was the object—to snatch each other's men," Nicola reminded her.

Adrienne giggled. "I will see that you have a wide assortment to choose from. There is Ramon, of course, and Felipe, Isidro and Vicente, Pablo and many others."

On the day of the party Sebastian gave Nicola more work than usual, and because she was anxious to finish quickly she made more mistakes and had to retype pages. There were queries for which she had to leave blank spaces and footnotes indicated too late to go on the appropriate page. When he came into the study at six o'clock and found her still hard at work, he seemed surprised.

"Aren't you attending Adrienne's party?" he asked.

"Of course. But I haven't finished the work yet."

He came to stand close by her side. "But I didn't intend you to finish the whole chapter. Have you no sense of proportion?"

A fine time to tell her now what his intentions were or were not when she had slaved all day long!

"My training as a secretary has made me conscientious," she said stiffly, "but I'll leave the rest if I may."

He smiled. "I'm sorry." Then he added, "Adrienne tells me you have invited your English friend from Barcelona."

"Yes. She suggested that I should ask Patrick." As the doctor made no reply, she continued hurriedly, "Perhaps I should have asked your permission, too?"

"Certainly not. You're quite free to invite anyone you choose."

Yet she still had the impression that he resented her friendship with Patrick, or perhaps he wanted all her interests concentrated within the Villa Ronda so that she would never neglect her various duties.

She took extra trouble with her appearance that night and put on the *sardana* costume lent her by Adrienne, a full-skirted dress of blue and white cotton, with a small fringed shawl in deep violet, an apron and flowing headdress to match, the latter secured with two pink roses on a velvet band. Rope-soled espadrilles tied with crisscross ribbons around the ankles completed the outfit, and Nicola looked in the mirror, well pleased with herself. The fact that she had as yet not the slightest knowledge of the *sardana,* Catalonia's own regional dance, did not matter, she thought. She would pick up the steps when she saw it being performed.

Adrienne had considerately fixed eight o'clock as the approximate time for guests to start arriving so that they could descend the rough path to the beach while it was still daylight.

Nicola decided to go down to the main patio in case Patrick had already arrived. On the way she remembered a further query in the current chapter of Dr. Montal's book and hurried to the study to make a note before she forgot the point. The doctor entered as she scribbled a note on the pad next to the typewriter.

"Oh! A *sardana* costume," he commented. "It suits you very well. D'you know our local dance?"

"Not yet, but I shall learn."

He stood facing her, his eyes showing a half-veiled, unwilling admiration, but his mouth was a taut line.

"Perhaps I should show you some of the steps now?"

She was aware that Patrick might be outside, alone, not knowing a soul, but she could not refuse Dr. Montal's offer.

He took her hand and began to hum a tune. She followed his intricate tiptoe pointings, occasionally making mistakes.

"The right foot there, to the center," he instructed.

What fun he could be when he unbent and threw off his somber surliness, she thought. Then the door of the study flew open and Adrienne was in the room.

"Tell me the meaning of this latest insult!" she exclaimed, her face flushed, her eyes stormy with tears. "Doña

Elena says you have invited her to stay in this house indefinitely.''

"And what are your objections?" asked Sebastian.

Nicola threw a wild look at the doctor and his distraught niece, then she dodged behind Adrienne and escaped through the arched window, but the girl's angry words followed her. ". . . Now I have two jailers . . . one young, one old. Elena is too old. Too old even for you!''

Adrienne then lapsed into a torrent of Spanish, and by that time Nicola was farther away. She hurried to the patio where Patrick was waiting, leaning against a pillar of the main archway.

"I'm sorry, Patrick. I ought to have been here to greet you when you arrived, but I was delayed. We'd better go directly down to the beach.''

"This is quite a place, isn't it?" he commented. "Take me on a tour first before we go down below.''

Nicola was agitated by the violent scene of which she surmised she had seen only the beginning. Probably it was still going on, with Adrienne becoming more intense and angry every moment. Nicola was not exactly in the mood to point out the beauties of the Villa Ronda and its setting, yet as she conducted Patrick through one patio, down flights of steps to another, showed him the swimming pool, she felt tranquility flow into her mind. It was usually easy to be companionable with Patrick and she was grateful to him for unwittingly giving her time to recover.

When she and Patrick arrived down by the shore, tables and chairs were already set out on the flat rocks, which formed a natural platform. Many of the tables were already occupied by groups of people and at one end a small band of musicians was settling itself. Lanterns and strings of colored lights in the shape of oranges, lemons or peaches were in position but not yet lit.

"So this is the Montals' private beach," said Patrick. "Their very own little piece of Spanish coastline.''

"Over there is the beach chalet," Nicola pointed out, "where there are several rooms for changing into swimsuits and so on.''

"All modern conveniences!" Patrick's tone was slightly derisive.

Ramon approached Nicola and she introduced him to Patrick.

"*Bienvenido!*" Ramon welcomed Patrick and raised Nicola's hand to his lips at the same time. He was dressed in a white shirt, black knee breeches with a wide orange sash and cap.

"Should I have come in fancy dress?" inquired Patrick when he and Nicola had moved away so that Ramon could greet a crowd of guests just arriving.

"Not at all," returned Nicola. "You look very smart. I wonder why men at home don't wear white dinner jackets, at least in summer?"

"Summer?" echoed Patrick. "After a couple of years in Spain, I don't really miss English summers. What frightens me is that I might even have to spend a winter there."

"You've gone soft!"

Patrick's eyes glinted with amusement, but he did not reply to her gentle teasing.

Adrienne's appearance was the signal for the party to start in earnest. Since most of her friends were Spanish, she spoke in that language, but with a minimum amount of help from Patrick, Nicola understood that everything was to be free and easy and nothing too formally arranged. The guests could swim or dance or eat or merely sit in secluded corners as they chose. The band struck up a gay tune, the villa staff and a few extra helpers were there to serve drinks and food, and Patrick nimbly lifted two glasses of wine from a tray momentarily set down.

"Here's to us," he said, toasting Nicola. "I can't tell you how glad I am that you decided to stay here after all."

Nicola supposed he meant that he thought her suitable and congenial company during the next two or three months until he returned to England. But surely he must know quite a number of other girls? Perhaps they were all Spanish and engaged to jealous and fiery young men.

At the back of her mind while she chatted and laughed with Patrick was the remarkable appearance of Adrienne, cool, poised, and smiling, the perfect hostess despite her

youth, and no trace of that stormy outburst less than half an
hour ago. To Nicola it was an example worth studying. *If
such a scene had happened to me*, she thought, *I wouldn't be
fit to be seen for hours*.

Adrienne also wore a *sardana* costume, but in different
colors to Nicola's—a pink and white dress, with deep green
shawl and apron, a green headdress with a filet of tiny pink
flowers.

Patrick decided that he would like to bathe in the Montals' private patch of the Mediterranean. "Coming, Nicola?"

She hesitated. She had taken some trouble with her
makeup and hairdo and was not particularly anxious to
swim just now, but she agreed for Patrick's sake.

"Afraid of mussing up your hair?" Patrick read her
thoughts correctly.

"It'll be all right," she assured him.

Together they went to the beach chalet and she pointed
out to him the men's changing room. Then Ramon seized
her by the waist and whirled her around.

"Come, please, and dance with me," he invited.

"But I was just about to go in swimming," she objected.

"Time for that later, when it is really dark and the moon
has risen."

By this time he had guided her away from the chalet and
toward the flat space below the platform where a number of
couples were already dancing.

"I don't know what Patrick will say," she murmured
doubtfully.

"The young Englishman? No doubt he will explore the
sea trying to find you, and that will occupy him for a short
while."

The dance was an unfamiliar one to Nicola, a cross
between a waltz and a gallop danced to *paso doble* time, but
she managed not to make too many mistakes, and Ramon
was such an energetic dancer that he practically lifted her
off her feet at every opportunity. By the end Nicola was so
hot that she would have welcomed a bath in the sea. Instead,
Ramon conducted her to a table in deep shadow, comman-
deered platefuls of food, a bottle of wine, and proceeded to

combine the business of eating with many exaggerated compliments. Sometimes he spoke in Spanish, then gave her a ludicrous translation.

"Tonight is for romance!" he exclaimed, raising his glass to her and thrusting his arm around her shoulders, so that she could scarcely raise her own glass. "I drink to your most beautiful eyes." He gave her his most genial smile.

"I will drink to the return of your sense, Ramon," she told him, laughing.

"Oh, no. Nonsense is for the nighttime and sense for the morning," he protested.

"The morning after?"

Yet it was exhilarating to be in his company and accept his nonsense.

Presently she said, "I ought to go and look for Patrick. He doesn't know anyone else here, and he's my guest."

"Have no fear. He will come to you, drawn by a magnet!" was Ramon's flowery answer.

As it happened, it was ridiculously true, for at that moment Patrick appeared close to Nicola's side.

"Patrick!" she called to him.

"Oh, there you are!" His glance took in Ramon's closeness to Nicola, his arm around her waist.

"Sit down, Patrick. You must be starving," Nicola said.

"I thought you were coming in to bathe. Or did you have a quick dip in and out again?"

Nicola began to giggle. "I was waylaid by Señor Don Ramon and marched here."

"But not against your will!" Ramon asserted.

Patrick sat down at the table and suddenly Doña Elena appeared, tapping Ramon on the shoulder. She said something quickly to him in Spanish and he rose, annoyance darkening his face. Doña Elena had already melted into the shadows. He bowed to Nicola, nodded to Patrick and deliberately and very slowly followed the direction Elena had taken.

"Well, that's got rid of him, whoever she was," said Patrick contentedly. "She looked like the Fairy Carabosse."

Nicola flung herself back in her chair and laughed. "It's fortunate she can't hear you. She's Ramon's sister, Doña

Elena Rabell, and not too fond of me. She thinks I'm an intruder.''

Patrick leaned across the table and grasped her hand. ''Perhaps you are.''

She gently withdrew her hand. ''I don't know what you mean.''

''I'm puzzled by you, Nicola,'' he said, when he had helped himself to an assortment of seafood and salads from a laden cart.

''What makes me an enigma?'' she queried. Perhaps it was the effect of the wine, but for once she felt both lighthearted and poised, ready to tackle any situation.

''Well, for one thing, you're not married. You say you're twenty-three, and nowadays most girls get themselves tied up at twenty-one or younger, sometimes much younger.''

''I suppose it isn't a crime? Or d'you think I'm halfway to ending up as an old maid?''

''I would think that's very unlikely,'' he said firmly.

''As gallant as Ramon himself,'' she commented lightly.

''Oh, I can't compete with the Spaniards, much as I like them.''

Soon people began to move from the tables down to the beach, there was a hissing of conversation and the band was now sounding only a drum.

''They're starting the *sardana,*'' Patrick told her. ''Let's go.''

The drummer stopped playing and now a shrill piping followed by a squeaking fiddle introduced the dance. Nicola had already noticed the curious combination of instruments that made up the small band; one double bass, a trombone, pipe, tabor, a fiddle and several instruments she did not recognize all combined to make harmonious or exhilarating noises.

On the beach where moonlight now flooded the shore and cast a silver pathway on the sea, people were arranging themselves into circles of eight or ten dancers. Nicola and Patrick took their places among one of the circles and the band launched into the tune.

In spite of the preliminary tuition she had received from Dr. Montal earlier in the evening and the fact that Patrick was by her side and she had only to copy his steps, she found this intricate, stately dance with its toe-pointings and mathematical tiptoe caperings very difficult to follow.

The music changed and Nicola found her hands suddenly lifted to head level by her two partners, then as rapidly lowered.

"I shall never learn this one, Patrick," she whispered. "I'd better try flamenco."

"Patience!" he answered. "Flamenco isn't your style, anyway, and you must keep a proper solemn face now or you'll be thrown out for rowdyism."

Moonlight flashed fitfully across the dancers' faces and she reflected that surely no dance was ever performed with more dignified gravity than the *sardana*. It would not have been out of place in church. But as soon as the band decided they needed a rest, there was clapping and chattering and delighted grins creased previously somber faces. After a short interval the band played a different tune, but to the same rhythm, a sort of brisk march overlaid with a hint of a more languorous style.

"You go, Patrick, with another partner," Nicola said. "I'll watch."

"You'll never learn it just by looking," he warned her. "Come along."

Ramon suddenly appeared on her other hand. "This is good fortune," he said with his usual flattering glance.

This time she progressed and at least knew when to raise her hands and move to right or left. Then another hand closed around her wrist, Ramon was pushed aside and she saw that Dr. Montal had taken his place.

"So now you know our local Catalan dance," he whispered to her.

"Not yet. I'm still making crowds of mistakes."

Until now she had been concentrating on the pattern of steps, but with Sebastian Montal deliberately interposing himself between her and Ramon and ousting him, she realized that perhaps this was the moment she had been unconsciously awaiting all the evening.

Her feet failed to respond to her direction and she felt clumsy and awkward, yet when he turned his face toward her and gave her an encouraging smile, her heart lifted and confidence flowed into her. At the end of the dance she introduced Patrick to the doctor, but the two men did not seem to have much to say to each other, beyond conventional polite remarks. The band demanded a rest and adequate refreshment, so the rings of dancers dispersed and Sebastian excused himself and disappeared into the shadows.

"H'm," Patrick muttered. "So that's your boss! Is he always as ruthless in throwing people out of his way?" He laughed. "I'm glad it was that chap, Ramon, that he chased away instead of me!"

Nicola shared his laughter. "Perhaps Dr. Montal didn't recognize my English friend until I introduced you."

The party continued with more dancing and singing, and Nicola realized that midnight must have come and gone long ago, for the moon now illumined a different part of the beach, leaving the platform in deep shadows, pricked out with its lanterns and fairy lights.

"I ought to try to find Adrienne," Nicola murmured. "She wanted to meet you."

"I can wait. Some other time." Patrick had drawn Nicola into the inky darkness made by a jutting rock. His arms went around her as he held her in at first a gentle embrace. "As long as I have you here, I'm not discontented," he said, seeking her face with his lips.

Perhaps, thought Nicola, it was a natural conclusion to a good party that Patrick should kiss her, but when she realized the fierceness of his demanding kisses on her mouth, her cheek, her neck, she tried to push him away.

"Nicola, my darling," he whispered, "you've bewitched me. I can't think of anything else when you're with me."

"Patrick!" she murmured. "This isn't you. It's the wine, the excitement, the party . . . ."

"It's nothing of the sort—and you know it. D'you think I haven't drunk plenty of Spanish wine before now?"

"But you're engaged to someone else, a girl at home," she protested.

"I'm supposed to be, and sometimes I wonder if Maureen

isn't enjoying herself with another man. It would be natural."

"But not very honest for either of you."

"Nicola, dearest, you take these things too seriously."

She drew away from him, although his arms still held her. "Then I won't take this incident seriously at all. It's just a good-night kiss after a party."

"Not on your life!" Patrick drew her against him with some violence. "I'm not too sure that I want to go home and marry Maureen."

"Because of a passing fancy?" she demanded angrily. "Patrick, you can't make me a party to this. You'll have to decide for yourself whether you're going to marry Maureen or not, but I'm telling you very plainly that I'll have nothing to do with it."

"But, Nicola, I thought you liked me."

"So I do. Very much—as a friend."

"And you can't possibly imagine that you might fall in love with me—as I have with you?"

"No," she snapped. "And if I thought that I might fall in love with you, I'd leave this place, leave Spain and never see you again."

Unconsciously he had relaxed his savage grip on her and his voice became more gentle. "What's Maureen to you?"

Nicola stared at him, although she could see only the vague outline of his features. "A girl who apparently trusts you. She doesn't deserve to be let down."

"Ah!" he murmured. "So that's it. Someone once let you down?"

"It's all in the past, over and done with."

"So because someone—some man hurt you, you're going to shut out all romance and love for the rest of your life?"

"I didn't say that. It's just that I couldn't bear to take someone else's fiancé."

"Doesn't it occur to you that engagements are made so that if necessary they can be broken before it's too late? Once the marriage takes place, things become more difficult."

"You have an easy philosophy, and up to a point I admit you're right about engagements."

"You won't tell me about this past episode in your life? If you're always going to bottle it up, you'll end by being bitter."

She was stung. "All right, you can have the truth. The man I was engaged to did exactly what you say you have in mind. He went on a six months' business trip to Australia, and a month before our wedding he wrote that he had met another girl and married her."

"Nicola, I'm sorry." Patrick's tone was tender enough now.

"Now perhaps you can understand how I feel about stealing another girl's man!" She was near to tears and she broke away from him and walked across the beach, leaving him to follow.

"I won't give up hope, Nicola," Patrick said quietly when he had caught up to her. "Who knows? Maureen might be glad to release me, and then—"

"Don't bank on anything," she said. "I can't encourage you to think that way. Let's go and find Adrienne if we can."

"Damn Adrienne," he muttered softly under his breath.

Nicola secretly hoped that she might also find Sebastian Montal, but among the small groups and knots of people, she could find no trace of either. Possibly they were both swimming among the half dozen bathers still amusing themselves tossing a ball to each other.

Patrick decided to leave. "I don't want to inflict myself on you any longer tonight," he said, "and I can't stand seeing that Ramon chap flirting with you, so I'll go."

"Did you come by car, or can I get you a lift with someone going back to Barcelona?"

"I borrowed a friend's car."

By the time he and Nicola had reached the villa, many of the other guests were straggling up the path.

"See you soon," Patrick said casually, as he entered his car. "Ring me some time. In the meantime, don't fall in love with anyone else, will you? Especially not that doctor boss of yours? He might be a menace."

In a moment he was gone, leaving Nicola standing there, her hand upraised in midwave. Around her a crowd of people were entering their cars, laughing, chattering, thanking someone for a lovely party, but Nicola heard nothing.

She was already overwrought by Patrick's sudden change from a companionable friend to a man demanding her love, but his last remarks had finally unnerved her. " . . . . Don't fall in love . . . that doctor boss . . . he might be a menace."

Nicola fled through the main entrance of the villa, raced up the beautiful staircase with its wrought-iron work, its spacious landings decked with flowers, and did not stop until she reached the safety of her own room. Even here she could not face this growing suspicion that of all men, it was Sebastian Montal who attracted and repelled her, rendered her nervous in his presence and overjoyed her with those rare moments when he laid aside his iron reserve.

She fought down these ridiculous fancies, yet she knew that if tonight it had been Sebastian instead of Patrick who showered on her those fierce, savage kisses and held her in his arms as in a vice, she would have yielded to his endearments, returned them kiss for kiss.

CHAPTER FIVE

NICOLA LAY AWAKE for what seemed like hours, then had only fallen into a doze when a tap at her door was followed not by Adrienne, as she had expected, but by the girl's maid, Iñez.

"Señorita, Adrienne is not here? You have seen her?" the maid asked in Spanish.

"No," Nicola answered sleepily.

"*Gracias.*" The maid went out and almost immediately Doña Elena came in.

"When did you see Adrienne last tonight? Where?" she asked urgently.

Nicola sat up in bed, wide awake now and already alerted to fears of some mishap. "Not since about the middle of the evening, I think."

"We cannot find her."

"She hasn't come home?" Nicola queried.

"No. You must please come downstairs."

Elena hurried out, and Nicola flung a housecoat around herself and followed quickly. The sound of voices coming from Dr. Montal's study directed her.

The maid Iñez was outside the door and motioned to Nicola to enter.

With the only lighting a desk lamp and a couple of wall brackets the grouping resembled a scene from a play. Ramon stood with folded arms by the book-lined wall. Doña Elena sat tensely in an armchair while Sebastian was giving instructions to Ignacio, the chauffeur.

When the man had gone, Sebastian came toward Nicola.

"Did you see Barto there tonight?" he asked.

She shook her head. "No, I didn't, but there were so many young people there, and a lot of them in costume."

"What was Adrienne wearing when you last saw her?"

"Her *sardana* costume," replied Nicola.

"We found those clothes in the beach chalet. Her swimsuit is missing."

Nicola gasped. "You don't think that—"

"We know nothing," snapped Sebastian. "We have sent men to search the sea for her."

"But she could be—somewhere else—in the grounds of the villa?" hazarded Nicola.

"She is not in the villa or the gardens," declared Sebastian. "It is possible that she has gone somewhere with Barto."

"Then that will be entirely your fault." Ramon spoke for the first time since Nicola had entered the room.

Sebastian stared, his cold, arrogant gaze fixed on Ramon.

"I've told you before, Sebastian, that you've driven her too hard. You should have had more sense than to interfere in a simple friendship with a fisherboy. If you hadn't pulled so tight all the time the affair would have worn itself out by now."

Nicola glanced at Ramon with quickened interest. His was a logical view to take, but in the circumstances she was surprised, considering that he was expected to marry Adrienne.

"And will you stand there as calmly if we find that my niece—"

"Barto would never harm Adrienne's little finger," Ramon interrupted before Sebastian could complete his dangerous sentence. "The boy knows that a Montal girl is not for him. Anyway, we do not know that they are together."

"If Adrienne had not been allowed always to do as she pleased," Doña Elena said, "this might not have happened." She shot a hostile glance at Nicola. "I understood that Señorita Brettell was *paid* to act as Adrienne's companion. Tonight she does not seem to have carried out her duties well."

Sebastian made an impatient gesture. "Do not let us start

blaming each other, Elena. After all, you were also at the beach party and you could have kept a friendly eye on Adrienne.''

Elena jumped to her feet, her eyes blazing. "You forget, Sebastian, that you asked me most definitely not to appear to spy on her. How could I know what thoughts she would have? Or where she would go?''

"I have my responsibility to her father," Sebastian said in a low tone.

"Adrienne is not only her father's daughter," declared Elena indignantly. "She also had a mother.''

Nicola, the unwilling witness of this stormy scene between Sebastian, Ramon and Elena, fidgeted in her chair, praying for a signal of dismissal from Sebastian, but he gave none. Perhaps she could slip out of the room unnoticed. She rose, but instantly Sebastian's dark eyes glared at her.

"You—you don't need me again?" she queried.

"Please stay, Nicola. I may want to ask further questions.''

She felt Elena's sharp turn of the head, probably at that easy use of "Nicola" instead of "Señorita Brettell.''

Suddenly Ramon exclaimed, "You don't think that perhaps Adrienne has gone to the *Clorinda*?''

"How would she get there without a boat?" demanded Elena.

"Barto would have a boat—or be able to borrow one," returned Ramon. "Of course! Stupid of us not to have thought of that before.'' He was halfway out of the room when Elena's voice halted him.

"Why would she go there? To remain on board without a chaperone would be very indiscreet.''

"Well, I'm going down to the harbor to find out," Ramon said finally. "I'll telephone you, Sebastian, if there is any news.''

Elena stood staring at Sebastian. Then, recovering her more usual dignity, she said, "I will stay here tonight as it was planned, but tomorrow I will return to my own house, even though I have let my servants go away for a holiday. I will send Iñez now to remain with you and Señorita Brettell, if you have other business to discuss.''

She walked out of the room, leaving the door open, and a pale-faced Iñez came timidly into the room. But Sebastian had changed his mind about any further questions, for he waved the maid away and said gently to Nicola, "Go back to bed now. There's nothing more we can do until I have news of some sort."

"I hope it's good news," Nicola answered.

In her room she noticed that it was now past five o'clock. Soon it would be daylight and there was little sense in trying to sleep. Instead, she took a shower and dressed, then sat on her balcony waiting for a dawn that might bring tragedy to the Montal household. Even then she must have dozed through sheer lack of sleep, for she became aware of full daylight and the pearly colors of sunrise fading into pale green and saffron.

She went through her room and downstairs to the main part of the villa. The servants were already hurrying around attending to their duties, but their faces were grave instead of smiling and they spoke in anxious whispers. Did they know what had happened to Adrienne?

She found Iñez who spoke a little English and good French through her association with Adrienne. "Any news of Señorita Adrienne?" Nicola asked.

The girl shook her head. *"No, señorita."*

Nicola wondered if Sebastian had remained in his study and with some hesitation she knocked on the door. There was no answer, and she entered. Sebastian was slumped across his desk, his dark head resting on his sprawled arms. The lights were still burning, the curtains drawn, the windows shuttered.

Nicola stood for a moment, uncertain, a great cloud of fear threatening to envelop her. She moved toward Sebastian, noting that he had flung his white dinner jacket on the floor. She picked it up, held it for a moment as she watched the rise and fall of his shoulders. Then a sigh of relief escaped her and she put down the jacket, pulled back the curtains, but found she could not manipulate the heavy shutters. Her efforts roused Sebastian, who dragged himself up to a sitting posture, rubbed his eyes, thrust his fingers through his tousled hair and stared dazedly at Nicola as though she were a ghost.

"Adrienne?" she whispered.

He shook his head and yawned.

"I'll have some coffee brought to you." She went out toward the kitchen, met Rosana, the housekeeper, and asked for coffee to be sent to the doctor's study.

"*Sí, señorita.*"

When she returned to the study, Sebastian had already opened the shutters and daylight revealed the grayness of his face. It was unnecessary to ask him if he had heard anything new. Her glance, as she looked away, fell on a framed photograph on his desk. She realized that it had been close to his hand when she first entered the room, and he did not adorn his desk with personal photographs. He moved toward the desk, picked up the silver-framed photograph and replaced it in a drawer, but not before Nicola had seen that it was a portrait of a young and beautiful woman. Elena? Nicola thought not.

A maid brought in the coffee tray and Sebastian poured cups for Nicola and himself.

"Thank you, Nicola." He spoke at last after the long silence. "It is good to have someone who does not ask stupid questions."

"I know that if there is anything to tell me, you will do so," she answered quietly.

"Let's take our coffee outside. I can't bear any more of this room now. Our house is old and the rooms have heard many bad announcements as well as good news, they have seen quarrels and gaiety."

Nicola nodded. She was overwhelmingly grateful that he allowed her to be with him at this agonizing time. She was about to pour more coffee when she heard steps coming along the patio. She jumped to her feet.

"Adrienne!" she cried out, and ran toward the girl approaching, accompanied by Barto.

Nicola flung her arms around Adrienne's neck but the girl gently disengaged herself and her face became composed and unsmiling. Nicola stood aside, aware that Sebastian was facing his niece and her companion.

"*Buenos días, Tío* Sebastian," Adrienne greeted her uncle calmly.

The boy Barto bowed to Sebastian. "*Señor.*"

"Well, Adrienne? Where have you been?"

Nicola was puzzled by Adrienne's black dress. Why had she changed into this, leaving her *sardana* outfit in the beach chalet—unless the reason was to cause as much anxiety as possible?

"In the church. All night," returned Adrienne.

"With Barto?" asked Sebastian.

Nicola walked a few steps away. She did not want to hear Sebastian forcing an explanation from Adrienne.

"Don't go, Nicola," Sebastian ordered. "You must hear Adrienne's explanation from herself and not secondhand. But we will go indoors to hear the story." In the study he turned toward his niece. "I asked whether you were with Barto."

"No, *señor,*" the boy answered quickly.

"Adrienne? I asked *you.*"

"I was alone. I met Barto this morning by the harbor."

"I want the truth," pursued Sebastian. "Not a parcel of lies."

"I am not lying." Adrienne answered coolly. "Nor is Barto. It's his unhappy misfortune that he insisted on accompanying me here so early in the morning."

Sebastian shook his head. "Leave Barto out of this. I will deal with him later." After a pause, he asked, "Why did you go to church? And when?"

"I warned you last night, *Tío* Sebastian, that I would not put up with Doña Elena residing in this house. It is enough that I have to suffer her visits."

"So you chose this childish way of making us all anxious about your safety." Sebastian's lip curled in derision. "If you want to be treated as a woman, you must learn to behave like one, not a spoilt baby."

Nicola reddened with shame that the doctor should so humiliate Adrienne in front of herself and the boy, Barto.

"We sent men down to search the sea for you, Ignacio

scoured the town looking for you, Ramon was worried and
Nicola has had no sleep."

Adrienne smiled. "And you, Sebastian? Were you anxious, or did you sleep soundly and not bother?"

"You haven't told me why you went to the church." He
ignored her gibe.

"I wanted to hurt you." Adrienne said vehemently. "To
run away and make you sorry. If I had wanted, I could have
gone to Barto's house, but that would have dragged him
into the affair, so I went to the church."

"After midnight? It's always locked before then. How did
you get there? Did you walk along the road and through the
streets?"

"No. Some of the guests gave me a lift in their car down
to the village."

"Without recognizing their hostess?" Sebastian's tone
was incredulous.

"I wore a black dress and veiled my face." Dramatically,
Adrienne withdrew from the pocket of the dress the black
lace mantilla that most Spanish women wore in church.

"And how did you get in the church? Or does your
imagination fail?"

"The door was not locked, and I pushed it open and went
inside." Adrienne was defiant.

"So you stayed there until a short while ago? Then you
decided to return here and on the way you happily met
Barto?"

"He had been out with the fishing boats and had just
landed, so he escorted me here."

Sebastian remained silent for a moment. Then his face
became darker than ever with anger. "Adrienne Montal,
you are not fit to be the daughter of my brother and your
mother. How dare you stand there and tell me this fairy tale
of nonsense!"

Barto, who did not understand the rapid English of
Sebastian and Adrienne, looked from one face to the other
and shifted on his feet restlessly, but he understood the
doctor's angry tone. Nicola wanted to cry out that surely
Sebastian could see Adrienne was telling the truth, what-

ever her mixed motives might have been for such alarming behavior.

"If you do not choose to believe the truth," Adrienne began, "then I really will disappear. Perhaps I will go to South America and look for my father. To be lost in the jungle would be better than staying under this roof."

Sebastian closed his eyes for a moment as though in pain at the reminder of his brother's unknown fate.

"Barto." He spoke quietly to the boy in what Nicola thought to be Catalan. The boy, his large eyes unwavering in their honesty, answered with polite dignity. There was nothing cringing nor servile about him, and Nicola reflected the truth of the saying that all Spaniards consider themselves the equal of kings.

There was a long pause, and then one of the manservants knocked and announced that Fr. Anselmo had called and would like to see Don Sebastian.

Adrienne smiled triumphantly. "Of course he must come in."

The priest hurried into the room. "Your pardon, Don Sebastian," he began in Spanish, "but these young people arrived here too quickly for my old legs. Señorita Adrienne has told you?"

"Sit down and let me hear your story," commanded Sebastian.

Nicola could scarcely follow the priest's rapid Spanish or Sebastian's questions, but she gathered that his account corroborated Adrienne's own story, and he had come up to the villa for that express purpose.

Sebastian sank heavily into the chair at his desk. In reply to Barto's questioning glance, he nodded and indicated that the boy could leave. Then he stood up.

"Adrienne, please offer Fr. Anselmo coffee and any breakfast he wishes to have. I am going out."

He went through the windows onto the patio and disappeared into the sunlit garden.

Nicola was uncertain whether to go or stay, but finally she said, "I'll be in my room, Adrienne. Perhaps later we can talk."

She wanted to rush after Sebastian, to comfort him in his

defeat, to reassure him that in future she would stay close to Adrienne, act as her shadow and see that she did not upset the entire household by her wildcat exploits. Instead, she went to her own room as she had promised and waited for Adrienne to come. The girl was not long in arriving. She had taken off her sober black dress and now wore a padded terylene housecoat embroidered with pink and white flowers.

"Why did you do this mad thing?" was Nicola's first question.

Adrienne sat on the dressing stool and peered at her face in the mirror. "I was very angry with the way Sebastian had allowed Elena to come here and practically act as *la madre* in our house. She must wait to do that when she marries Sebastian—if that should ever take place—and perhaps by that time she will be a very old woman!"

"But even allowing for your anger, why leave the villa and not come home?"

Adrienne swung around on the stool. "Perhaps it was a devil that entered me. I wanted to do something most desperate, to throw myself into the sea and swim far out so that I would be lost and not able to return. Then I wanted to throw Elena into the sea so that she would never come back and distress us. All this time the party was so gay, and underneath it all I was seething like a boiling pot."

"But the black dress?" queried Nicola. "Did you take it down to the shore with you so that you could conveniently leave your other clothes behind?"

Adrienne smiled. "No. It was when I was changing into my swimsuit that I saw the black dress hanging on a peg in the beach house. There are always spare dresses down there. Sometimes they are mine, sometimes they belong to Iñez or one of the other maids. So I had the idea that after my swim I would leave my *sardana* costume and slip away somewhere in the black dress. It did happen to be mine."

"But surely that was wrong of you! You were hostess at the party."

Adrienne shrugged. "In the house one could not leave the guests like that, but down on the shore it is different. Who will care whether the hostess is there or not? Everyone is enjoying themselves and in the darkness one cannot see where everyone is. I did not even meet your Patrick."

"Never mind about Patrick now. Go on. Tell me why you stayed so long in the church, and how was it that you weren't recognized in the car that took you there?"

"I spoke in Catalan, which, truth to tell, I don't speak very well, but in my black dress, the friends mistook me for one of the extra helpers we had engaged from the village, so it was natural they should give a lift home, and so I was deposited almost outside the church. Now I felt guilty and thought I should enter the church to ask forgiveness for all my black thoughts."

"It was not locked?"

"No. Fr. Anselmo does not have it locked usually. Only the big door is closed. The small side one is nearly always open. It was so peaceful there, the candles burning, very quiet, and I felt all my anger melt away."

"Then why didn't you come back to the villa then?" demanded Nicola. "Didn't you realize how anxious everyone would be, wondering what had happened to you?"

"I think I fell asleep," said Adrienne simply. "I heard the main door open and then Fr. Anselmo was talking to me. So I told him all that I had done. He was concerned that I had been out a whole night—or what was left of it after the party—and he promised to come and tell Sebastian the truth. As I passed the harbor Barto was just coming ashore and he offered to walk up with me."

"Poor Barto! You didn't think that he might have to take most of the blame for your escapade?"

"Why should he? Fr. Anselmo knew that he was speaking the truth. Only Sebastian disbelieved."

"It was a selfish prank, Adrienne," said Nicola gently, aware that she must not sound censorious.

"It has served its purpose, though." Adrienne's face was flushed with triumph. "Doña Elena will not, I think, take up her residence here."

"How can you be sure of that?" asked Nicola. "Both she and your uncle may feel that her supervision is all the more necessary. She has the power that I can't have obviously."

"She will not have power over me," returned Adrienne firmly.

After a pause Nicola said, "Will you tell me your plans for today? Then I can arrange the hours when I will do the doctor's typing work."

Adrienne impulsively sprang from the stool and kissed Nicola's cheek. "You are sweet and charming, Nicola. What you really mean is that I am not to go off on wild madcap trips while you are glued to your typewriter and cannot watch me." She laughed happily. "This I will freely promise. Today I shall busy myself in my studio and work on my pictures and you will have not the slightest cause for complaint."

"Thank you for that assurance. Perhaps you should also reassure your uncle. He spent a very unhappy and anxious night over your disappearance."

Adrienne nodded, "Yes, I will apologize to him. It is odd that when you scold me for my wrongdoing, I accept it, but Sebastian—oh, he must always play the heavy uncle and then I feel rebellious."

"Have you thought that it might be that he loves you very much? You're very dear to him."

"Yes, he is fond of me," Adrienne admitted. "But sometimes he tries to squeeze me into a little box and shut down the lid."

Nicola laughed. Adrienne's comment was an apt description of Sebastian's passion for orderliness. Was it because he was a doctor and had been trained to admire system? Even so, Nicola reflected, as a doctor he should understand that individuals cannot always conform to a rigid pattern.

"Is that why he hasn't married?" Nicola asked the daring question now because she doubted whether there would ever be a better opportunity. "Perhaps he wouldn't like the untidiness of being in love?"

"I think he was very unhappy in his first love affair," Adrienne answered after some hesitation. "So he has not tried again."

"But Doña Elena?" Nicola pursued. "Does she love him?"

"Doña Elena has no love for anyone but herself," Adrienne answered crisply. "But she is widowed and still young—almost young—so she is looking to Sebastian to console her. Actually, she is too old for him, but then he seems to fall in love with women older than himself."

"You said Doña Elena was only about his age."

"Of course, but women are always older than men at the same age. That is why we should marry men older, much older than ourselves, and young wives can, if they are clever, keep their men always at the end of the string."

Nicola flung herself back in her chair and laughed. "Oh, Adrienne! Sometimes I think you're seventy, not seventeen. You're so worldly-wise that you make me feel like a small child completely ignorant of what makes people tick."

Ramon called later, having already heard that Adrienne was home, and Nicola heard him greet her with both endearments and scolding. "*Querida!*" he murmured tenderly, then changed his tone of voice to give her a severe lecture.

Nicola wondered if Ramon really loved Adrienne or only thought of her as a highly suitable match. She was certain that Adrienne did not love him, and it was a pity that she was apparently to be married to him before she had time to discover a more exciting rapture.

Sebastian had gone this morning to his clinic in the village, so Nicola absorbed herself in further chapters of his book. Yet her concentration was not entirely unbroken, for stray thoughts, unconnected with medical subjects, came into her mind. She remembered Adrienne's remark that Sebastian had suffered an unhappy love affair and that he always seemed to like women older than himself. She remembered, too, that photograph which she had seen on his desk, a portrait of a woman. Was that why he had become so withdrawn, so remote from the warmth of an ordinary, companionable life? What of the woman? Had she jilted him? Married someone else?

Nicola scolded herself for wasting time on these trivial reflections. Her job was to make sense of what Sebastian had written about the medical aspect of hearts and their maladies, not what might be right or wrong with hearts in the more figurative sense.

Ramon stayed for lunch, but neither Sebastian nor Doña Elena appeared.

"Sebastian is probably delayed at the clinic," Ramon suggested. "I know there was a small explosion on one of the fishing boats and two or three men were injured."

"Has Doña Elena gone home?" asked Adrienne.

Ramon looked slightly embarrassed. "Well, it is rather awkward. She has shut our house, and sent the staff on holiday, except for Pedro who will act as caretaker. I am on the *Clorinda,* of course, and she can come there, but she does not care for living on the yacht unless we are sailing somewhere. So I think we'd better advance our plans for San Fernando. Then she will be at home in our house there."

Adrienne looked down at her plate. "Very well, Ramon. When do you suggest?"

"The day after tomorrow, perhaps." His amiable glance swerved toward Nicola. "Can you also be ready by then, Nicola?"

She flushed. "I could, of course, be ready, but I will have to ask permission from Dr. Montal."

"But naturally you must come with us," urged Adrienne. "Sebastian is planning to come, so you need not fear his work will be at a standstill." She laughed happily. "Indeed, perhaps you can persuade him to bring the typewriter and then you can clack away in one of the yacht's cabins."

But Nicola was cautious, remembering Doña Elena's warning. Even so, it would be Sebastian who would decide the matter and certainly not Elena.

If the rest of the party went off to San Fernando for a week or two Nicola considered that she could use some of her free time for visits to Barcelona and a further search for Lisa. She might even this time contact the *policia* or the British Embassy. She had previously hesitated to take these steps for fear of unwelcome publicity that might involve the Montals, but now she knew she must act more directly.

When Sebastian returned early in the evening he had recovered some of his normal reserve. He discussed the various queries in Nicola's work, made some amendments here and there. Everything was all strictly businesslike, and

Nicola was glad, for his cool attitude helped her to fight down that surging delight when she was alone with him.

But a casual remark from Adrienne after dinner upset all Nicola's calculated poise.

"But I couldn't possibly leave my work at the hospitals and the clinic and go to San Fernando now," Sebastian said.

"You promised to come," Adrienne pointed out.

"Yes, but not tomorrow or the next day. I need time to arrange matters with my colleagues. There's no reason why you shouldn't go with Ramon."

"And Doña Elena?" queried Adrienne stormily.

"Naturally. Obviously you cannot stay in Ramon's house in San Fernando unless Doña Elena is also there."

At that moment Sebastian was called to the telephone.

"I don't know whether I now wish to go on the yacht to San Fernando or anywhere else at all," muttered Adrienne.

Nicola murmured something vague in reply, but her whole mind was engaged with the entrancing vista ahead. To remain with Sebastian at the villa while all the warring elements cruised the Mediterranean was a heavenly prospect.

Sebastian did not return to the terrace to rejoin the two girls, and later Nicola found out that he had been called urgently to attend to one of the men injured in the fishing boat explosion.

"The man is in great pain and Sebastian must get him to a hospital quickly," Adrienne explained. "Well, we must wait until tomorrow to tackle the visit to San Fernando. Without Sebastian to keep Elena in her place I shall be miserable."

Nicola said nothing, hoping that her silence would indicate that she sympathized with Adrienne's point of view.

The next day added a completely different aspect to the project. Nicola took the opportunity to ask Sebastian if she might have an odd day or two off whenever it fitted in with his plans.

"You'll probably not need me to work the whole of every day and I could try to make more inquiries in Barcelona for my sister."

Sebastian stared at her. "But you won't be here. I thought it was understood that you were going to San Fernando with the others." He smiled. "In Adrienne's present state of mind you'll certainly be needed to keep the peace between her and Doña Elena."

"Señor Ventallo invited me, but I couldn't accept unless you knew it."

"But you assumed that I would prevent you? Don't you want to go on this fine yacht and visit Ramon's beautiful house? It will be a holiday for you—nothing to do except cast an occasional glance on Adrienne and possibly exchange messages between her and Doña Elena."

"Yes, I'd like to go," she said.

"But . . . ?" he prompted. "What's the obstacle? The young Englishman in Barcelona?"

"Certainly not!"

Sebastian laughed. "You are very quick to protest. Reassure him that you will not be away too long. No doubt he can survive two weeks or so."

"Patrick is only a friend . . . and . . . and he's not concerned in whether I'm away or not."

Sebastian's eyebrows lifted and she thought then that it was extraordinary how his whole face could betray amusement, yet his mouth did not smile, but remained the firm stern line it usually was.

"Really? At the beach party he seemed very closely concerned with you. You were so locked in each other's arms that you were unaware of passersby."

She flushed with fury that he had witnessed that incident. "Oh, I didn't know you'd seen us."

"You are really longing to say that I spied on you. All Montals spy on each other, but I did not deliberately do so in this case. I was looking for you, but then I realized that I had better leave you where you were—in safe company."

She remained silent, fearing to give him any more excuses for linking her with Patrick.

Then he spoke again. "Do you want any more money? To shop in Barcelona for clothes—or whatever you need—for San Fernando?"

She was touched by his thoughtfulness, then wondered if

he had noticed how few clothes she possessed in spite of an extremely generous salary.

"It's very kind of you. I have enough money for the time being, but I'd like to go to Barcelona today and buy one or two things."

"Of course. Ignacio will take you and then you can tell him what time you would like him to bring you back."

"I'll come back by train," she said quickly. She had reasons for not wanting to be tied to a return time.

She asked Ignacio to drop her at the Plaza de Cataluna in Barcelona. From that vast square with its twin fountains she knew her bearings and could visit the Paseo de Gracia with its elegant shops as well as the small side streets off the *ramblas* where less expensive clothes could be bought.

But first she had to visit the lawyer's office to pay the monthly installment against Lisa's debts. If she were going to be in San Fernando for a fortnight or even longer, payment might be delayed and until now she had made a special point of paying cash personally. She did not want letters from lawyers arriving at the Villa Ronda.

"You are a young lady of good method," the lawyer congratulated her, as he gave her the receipt.

"I've been lucky to get a well-paid job," she answered. "Soon I will have finished all the payments."

She bought a couple of dresses in a small shop then went to a café on the edge of the Plaza Real, an enchanting little square she had discovered one day by accident. Tall feather-duster palms soared over an ornate fountain and the surrounding buildings shut out the noise of traffic.

At the café Nicola wrote a note to Patrick, telling him that she would be in San Fernando for the next week or two with the Montals. She thought it unwise to add that she was traveling on Ramon's yacht, or else Patrick would tease her next time they met about "living it up."

She pondered as to what else she could say to him after that scene at the beach party. She did not want to encourage him to expect more than an ordinarily friendly relationship, yet at the same time it would be stupid to break with the only other English person she knew here.

Out in the streets today there was an air of impending

gaiety. Illuminations, decorations of all sorts, clusters of fireworks were being erected. She asked the waiter what *fiesta* was coming along. "The Eve of St. John," she was told— celebrations to greet the following day, Midsummer Day.

A pity she would miss it, she thought. She would have liked to sample a real Barcelona *fiesta,* but no doubt there would be other excitements in San Fernando.

On arrival back at the Villa Ronda she found that plans had been changed yet again.

"To sail tomorrow proved too hasty for Ramon to be ready with the yacht," Adrienne explained. "And we also have our own preparations. Then we remembered the *fiesta* in Barcelona tomorrow for San Juan, so we will take you there to show you the festival."

Nicola was delighted. "I'm glad I won't miss it," she said. "I saw them putting up strings of lights in the streets."

She was about to go to her room to dress for dinner when Iñez, Adrienne's maid, told her that Doña Elena would like to see her.

"Where is Doña Elena?" asked Nicola.

"In the salon."

Mystified, Nicola entered that vast apartment which seemed so rarely used, at least in summer. Portraits of Montal ancestors frowned from the walls. Certainly Sebastian had no monopoly of arrogant reserve when it came to facial expression.

Doña Elena was at the far end of the room and Nicola's heels tapped on the marble floor.

"I wanted to see you," Elena began graciously, "to invite you to join us on our visit to San Fernando."

Nicola's mind, for once, worked quickly. Evidently Elena did not know that she was already included.

"But you told me that I was on no account to accept such an invitation," Nicola said politely.

Doña Elena made a graceful gesture of her shoulders. "That was before all our plans had been properly made."

"And now you want me to come on the yacht?" queried Nicola.

"You are paid to be Adrienne's companion." Elena

never missed a chance of reminding Nicola that she was only a paid servant in the Montal household.

"May I inquire if you intend to accompany us?" Nicola asked.

"Naturally, although I would prefer to fly. I do not consider you suitable to be chaperone to Adrienne on the *Clorinda*. However, I am always willing to sacrifice my personal wishes in these matters."

"Then if you are accompanying Adrienne, there is no necessity for me to go, as well."

For a brief moment Elena was put out of countenance, but she quickly recovered and gave Nicola a charming smile.

"If Adrienne wants you with her, then you cannot speak of 'necessity.' Besides, it will be a good holiday for you."

"Thank you, Doña Elena. I am paid, as you say, by Dr. Montal, so I will accept his instructions, but I am glad to know that I shall be welcome aboard the *Clorinda* and in your house." Nicola smiled disarmingly but Elena did not respond this time.

"That is all," Elena said, dismissing Nicola with a gesture.

In her room where the gilded mirrors gave so many reflections of oneself, Nicola smiled and hummed a little tune.

Doña Elena had apparently belatedly discovered that Sebastian was staying at the villa and of course it would never do to leave the young English girl with him in the same house, alone except for half a dozen servants.

Doña Elena stayed to dinner, and although it seemed as though a truce had been called between herself and Adrienne, she gave Nicola some penetrating glances.

Afterward when Adrienne and Nicola were alone, Adrienne giggled softly. "Doña Elena is furious because we are leaving Sebastian behind. Oh, she imagined a wonderful time with him, sitting holding his hand, no doubt, under the stars!"

"Does a Spanish lady of Doña Elena's type hold hands with a gentleman not yet her husband?" asked Nicola slyly.

"You've been reading about our very ancient customs

when the ladies remained behind iron grilles," said Adrienne with mock severity. "We are more advanced now. To shake hands with a man does not give us the electric shock."

"Sometimes it ought to do just that—if it's the right man."

But Sebastian and Elena had returned to the patio, and Nicola wondered if they had indeed been holding hands under the stars. A wave of insane jealousy swept over her, but she crushed it ruthlessly. To think of Sebastian in any way other than that of employer, doctor, uncle of Adrienne and possible husband of Elena was not only futile but dangerous.

CHAPTER SIX

WHEN NICOLA was making herself ready for the *fiesta* she had no inkling that the Eve of St. John would remain in her memory as one of the highest peaks of ecstasy she had ever experienced.

In the first place she had not realized that the party would be a foursome, Ramon and Adrienne, Sebastian and herself. By what mysterious magic Doña Elena had been persuaded or even hoodwinked to stay away, Nicola neither knew nor cared. No doubt Elena had seen a surfeit of festivals.

The evening began soberly enough with dinner at the yacht club in Barcelona, the Real Club Maritimo, of which Ramon was a member. From this elegant setting overlooking the harbor they could see rockets from boats or quays lighting the dark blue sky in colored arcs of bursting stars over the water.

After dinner Ramon suggested they should all go to see the Montjuich fountains, which he explained to Nicola always put on a special display on the eve of holidays. "So many changes and colors you will never have seen before," he told her with pride.

A taxi took them as close as possible to the *Cascades*, Sebastian having sent Ignacio home.

A crowd stood around or sat on the wide flight of steps leading to the Palacio Nacional; families with children, laughing groups of young people, old couples who must have seen it all a hundred times. The changing colors and patterns of water almost mesmerized Nicola who could not take her eyes away.

"You have fountains like this in England?" Adrienne

queried with a touch of disbelief mingled with national pride.

"Not at all like this." Nicola watched the gradual shading from mauve to blue, through green to yellow, back to orange and red, and saw how the colors were reflected dazzlingly on the faces of the spectators.

After a while Sebastian guided her to a small cabin where they could see a man controlling the play of lights and water from a switchboard.

With a man's passion for the way things work, Sebastian explained, "The operator can see the whole of the fountain from here and he can make so many endless changes that he need not repeat himself once for over two hours."

"Let me go on believing that it's all done by magic," said Nicola, "with an army of goblins and elves to work this fairyland."

An hour slipped by while they watched the unbelievable display. Then Ramon asked, "What now?"

Adrienne's immediate answer was "Tibidabo!"

"Tibidabo?" echoed Sebastian. "But that's right out on the hill."

"I know exactly where it is," she retorted. "But remember we must show Nicola Spain in all its moods, and *fiesta* in Barcelona is not complete without Tibidabo."

"Very well. If you say so," agreed Sebastian.

"Besides, it will do you good to let yourself go at the amusement park," Adrienne continued in what Nicola had come to recognize as her "bossy" voice.

On the way the taxi driver slowed several times to allow his passengers to see spectacular fireworks in gardens; huge green ferns of fire; weeping willows in thin pink streams; set pieces in orange and green that whirled and disintegrated into a thousand stars.

On the top of Mount Tibidabo the huge church with the figure of Christ on top was floodlit.

"If we take the elevator to the top," Adrienne suggested, "we can see all the lights of the city."

It was a remarkable experience to step into an elevator and be conveyed silently to the high roof platform.

"In England we usually have to walk up hundreds of

worn steps," Nicola remarked, but she realized that several of these church buildings were completely new and in fact not quite finished yet. Out of the glare of the floodlight and the illuminations from the amusement park below, she gazed at the distant city sparkling like a piece of jewelry flung down on black velvet.

"You can see the *ramblas* and the *paseos* like long streaks of light," Sebastian murmured. "In between, the lights merge into each other, but you can see the harbor. Come here some time in daylight and you can see the most impressive view of the city."

There were steps to terraces above and below to be negotiated, and Nicola, temporarily blinded by a revolving floodlight on a tower, almost stumbled. Sebastian caught her, steadied her, then firmly linked her arm in his so that she might feel safe. She was glad to leave it there.

At the amusement park Sebastian cast off some of his inhibitions, it seemed to Nicola. He laughed at her when she was lost in the labyrinth and came up behind her and swung her around in a different direction. On the monorail Sebastian waited until they could secure front seats. "Are you frightened?" he asked.

She wanted to answer "Never with you," but thought better of that give-away remark and said, "I'll try to put up with it." But as the car lurched around a corner, she gave a little squeal of fright, believing for a moment that she was about to take off into space. Sebastian's arm went around her shoulders and she felt ashamed of her fears.

When doors loomed up ahead she braced herself for the terrifying impact, only to find that as they swung back the car raced through them to enter grottos sparkling with fairy lights. One grotto even had mermaids and an undersea atmosphere.

As soon as the trip was over Sebastian suggested that they should sample the seesaw, a contraption poised high on a transverse beam with two small cages at each end. Here again when their cage was high off the ground the wonderful view of Barcelona spread out before them, and Nicola was conscious of Sebastian's presence. Oh, if she could stay up here forever with him, close against his side in the slowly revolving iron cage! But impatient passengers in the car below on the ground were eager for their turn and reluctantly Nicola stepped out of the cage, when it returned to ground level. Ramon and Adrienne walked ahead, happier together, it seemed to Nicola, than they usually were. But perhaps that was the effect of the *fiesta* and Tibidabo.

Dotted all over the fairground were sideshows and stalls for games, for drinks and things to eat: *charros*, those curving, sausagelike lengths of batter fried in smoking oil, dishes of *paella* or potato omelets made to order.

Sebastian suddenly darted toward a confectionery stall and bought a dozen flat cakes with candied fruit and pine kernels. "They are called '*coques,*'" he told Nicola. "Special for San Juan's day. We should really eat them tomorrow, but it can't be far off midnight."

After the excellent dinner at the yacht club, Nicola was scarcely hungry, but the little cakes were delicious. Sebastian was munching away like a schoolboy in a forbidden kitchen.

Firecrackers exploded everywhere, a band vainly tried to compete with the general din, people yelled and shouted, laughed and punctured each other's balloons.

Nicola noticed a small merry-go-round with Ali Baba pots to stand in, so that children's heads popped up unexpectedly or disappeared when they crouched down to elude their parents watching for them.

"You have Ali Baba pots in your garden at the villa," Nicola said to Sebastian. "Are they just ornaments or do you use them for water or something else?"

He laughed at her question. "We don't keep the sherry in them, true. Oh, all over Spain everyone uses them for different purposes. Long ago, in Andalusia, people used them for baths. They climbed a small ladder outside, descended another inside and stepped into the jar half filled with water. Only their heads showed above the neck of the jar, so it was not only a private bath, but families or friends could continue their conversation if they had enough pots."

Nicola laughed in return, but was slightly sceptical about his tale until Ramon nodded and declared it was true.

Nicola was in a mood to accept any preposterous tale, for

she had never known until now that Sebastian Montal could relax and behave like a carefree man out on an evening's holiday. She was in a dreamlike cocoon of delight and was unwilling, even unable, to bother with the problems that surrounded her day-to-day existence.

When Sebastian had apparently exhausted all the side-shows and amusements he wanted Nicola to share, Ramon secured a taxi to take the party down to the yacht club by the harbor where he had parked his own car. Sebastian suddenly disappeared for a few moments and Ramon exclaimed, "Now where's he gone?" Sebastian returned almost immediately waving a block of *turrón*, a sweet made from honey, sugar and almonds.

"Are you afraid of starving?" Adrienne teased him.

"Nicola probably hasn't tasted the special Tibidabo brand of *turrón*," he retorted.

Nicola was tremendously flattered that he should go out of his way to offer these small thoughtful kindnesses, yet she forced herself to treat the matter lightly. "I'm surprised that a doctor should encourage such orgies of overeating," she said.

"It's a good thing occasionally to see how far one can tax the digestion," was his unexpected reply. "That way we find out our limitations. Eating is like sleeping. You can always rest next day."

"We'll certainly need to sleep all day tomorrow on the *Clorinda*," said Adrienne with a yawn.

The taxi driver declared that he could go no farther when he came to the old part of the city center. The streets were jammed with people, processions, bands and bonfires. Ramon and Sebastian accepted this view and said they would walk through the crowded part and pick up another taxi elsewhere. Adrienne grumbled that she was already dead on her feet, but Nicola had suddenly discovered a new lease on wakefulness.

At the Plaza de San Jaime a band was playing for *sardanas* and in no time Sebastian had whirled Nicola into one of the circles of dancers. At a moment when everyone raised their linked hands to head level, Nicola found herself staring at a man on the opposite side of her particular ring.

Surely it was the man who had come that night to Lisa's apartment, the same man who had denied knowing Nicola when she was in the wine shipper's office? Momentarily she lost step in the dance and Sebastian gently corrected her. When she looked up again the man had disappeared into the crowd of spectators lining the square.

The incident haunted Nicola all the way home when eventually the party left and were driven to Orsola by Ramon. She had to admit to herself that she could have been mistaken, but was it only a coincidence that the man had almost immediately left the *sardana* circle when Nicola met his eyes?

On arrival at the Villa Ronda Adrienne sleepily promised that she and Nicola would be ready by about five in the afternoon to go aboard the *Clorinda*. Ramon called out "Good night," and drove himself back to the harbor. Adrienne tottered through the arched entrance of the villa and went up the main staircase.

Sebastian hesitated a moment. Then he said with all that restrained dignity that Nicola knew so well, "I hope it was a night to remember, Nicola. Have you enjoyed your first taste of a *fiesta*?"

She wanted to dance up and down like a seven-year-old after a party, but she, too, restrained herself. "I will never forget it. The color, the light, the gaiety—and—" She stopped abruptly. She had nearly added, "And you in your merriest of moods."

"Good. I hope we will be able to take you to other festivities. We need the excuse of a stranger sometimes to prod us into enjoying our own way of life." Then he took Nicola's hand and raised it to his lips. "*Buenas noches,*" he murmured. "Enjoy yourself on the *Clorinda*. I may be able to come to San Fernando in a week's time."

In a daze she went up to her room, glancing once over the wrought-iron rail of the curving staircase. Sebastian was looking up at her. He smiled and raised his hand in salute. She was too disconcerted to do more than give a quick nod in return, then hurried along to her room.

Surely it was fortunate that she was due to leave for San Fernando within a few hours or she might have made a complete fool of herself. How stupid to believe that this one night's peak of enjoyment meant anything but a typical instance of Spanish hospitality!

Sebastian had said almost that himself; that having a visitor was an excuse for indulging in the local gaieties.

How could she be so naive, Nicola asked herself, as to imagine herself in love with Sebastian Montal because he had acted the jaunty host and kissed her hand in spontaneous farewell before she left his house for a week or so?

No doubt many other girls had deluded themselves in the same way, for he had everything to make him most eligible: distinguished career, wealth, handsome saturnine looks and a certain unapproachability that beckoned women toward him like a moth to a candle flame. Yet every one of those girls had been ineffectual against his withdrawn indifference. Who was the woman he had loved so much that now all he had to offer was a hard shell of refusal?

As she lay in bed and dawn lightened the room so that the furniture emerged as blurred shapes, she told herself that the emotion she felt for Sebastian could not be love. She was no stranger to love. She had loved David with all her heart, and the time of their acquaintance followed by engagement had been nothing but enchanting happiness, delight in each other's company, the sharing of simple pleasures and planning a home together. Not the faintest cloud had ever marred the sunshine of that period until he went on the Australian trip. Even then the weeks sped by, punctuated by his regular letters, until the final blow.

When he had broken the engagement by marrying another girl Nicola had resolved that she would never again be taken in by false infatuation or by a lightly exchanged love.

Patrick had tested her reserve at the beach party only a couple of nights ago and she had easily withstood his ardor. Yet she could not so smoothly dismiss this growing involvement with Sebastian. She refused to place it deeper than that. This painful longing, this ache that seemed like a heart full of unshed tears, surely this could not be real love, but only an unworthy hankering, an envy to possess something that could never be hers.

In a way it was both a disappointment and a relief that she did not see Sebastian again before she and Adrienne left the Villa Ronda to start their yacht trip.

Iñez, Adrienne's maid, who was to accompany them to Majorca had packed for Nicola as well as Adrienne, so there was nothing to do and Nicola went into Sebastian's study on the pretext of leaving everything tidy. The reality, she knew, was something different. She wanted to run her hands over the back of his chair, to touch the things he had touched, his pens, his papers. Most of all, she longed to pull open the desk drawer in which lay the framed photograph of the woman who still retained his heart to the exclusion of any other.

Nicola clasped her hands tightly, willing herself not even to try the drawer to see if it was locked. She could not stoop to this mean, despicable act. Even the thought brought a shamed blush to her cheeks and she ran out of the room as though a demon were pursuing her.

The prospect of a trip in the lovely *Clorinda* now riding at anchor in the harbor should have excited her, but she thought of the miles of sea separating her from Sebastian. Yet she welcomed the breathing space that a fortnight in San Fernando might provide. Perhaps by the time she returned she would have her emotions under better control and be able to view events in their proper perspective. She tried not to remember that Sebastian had promised that he might come later to Ramon's house in San Fernando. At this moment, Nicola hardly knew whether she would be glad or sorry.

The *Clorinda* sailed during the early evening with much hauling of ropes from the mooring buoys and clanking of anchor chains. Besides the crew of three or four men, Ramon had his skipper aboard, a stout, podgy man with a small dark mustache, expressive eyes and a gentle but authoritative manner. When the yacht glided out of the harbor and turned for the open sea, Adrienne pointed out to Nicola the Villa Ronda, a white patch set in a clump of green trees high up above the shore. Nicola wondered wistfully if Sebastian happened to be on the Mediterranean balcony watching the yacht's departure, but that was a silly, vain thought that should never have entered her head. He was probably not yet back from his hospital duty in Barcelona.

Since there was no timetable hurry Ramon decided on a leisurely cruising speed, and the night steamer from Barcelona to San Fernando soon passed the yacht with much waving from passengers on the steamer's crowded decks.

Nicola reflected on her good fortune to be traveling in such luxurious style, and Patrick's remark echoed in her mind. ". . . . The sort of life Lisa was looking for , . . comfort, security and plenty of amusement . . . ."

His words described Nicola's present mode of life. Surely she could be content with that and not sigh for the moon, as well!

Ramon's chef, Juan, had apparently spent all day concocting a celebration dinner for the party on board. Gazpacho, the delicious iced soup, was followed by a *zarzuela*, an assortment of fried fish and seafood in a sauce of laurel leaves, wine and tomatoes. Then, as this was still San Juan's day, the chef served his special version of the little round cakes appropriate to his "namesaint."

Elena as hostess to her brother was at her most charming and Nicola was only too eager to comply with her mood. To be staying eventually in Ramon's house and be at loggerheads with his sister would be undeniably uncomfortable.

Nicola's cabin was romantically elegant in turquoise and cream, while the adjoining bathroom, which she shared with Adrienne, was paneled in a blurred pattern of sea-green tiles, giving the impression that one was in an ocean cavern.

After a short walk around the deck after dinner to watch moonlight creaming the yacht's wake, to gaze at the stars in the vast arch of inky sky, Nicola was glad to retire to her cabin. Lulled by the murmuring hum of the yacht's engines, she fell asleep almost instantly and it seemed only a couple of minutes before Iñez, Adrienne's maid, brought in a breakfast tray of coffee and rolls and fruit.

When she bathed and dressed and went up on deck, she was amazed to see that the *Clorinda* was about to enter San Fernando Harbor, a vast sheet of water backed by blue sky,

the spires and towers of the ancient cathedral dominating
the hill. A crescent of dazzling hotels, white or golden
colored, swept along the harbor edge to the distant point.

"We will stay a day here," Ramon told her. "Then you
can see some of the fine buildings, visit the shops, the
markets, just as you choose."

Nicola smiled at him. "You think of everything for the
passengers' comfort and enjoyment."

He returned her smile, put his hand on her shoulder and
gave her a friendly shake. "That is my pleasure, as well as
my duty."

"But he does not tell you why he must first come to San
Fernando town," Adrienne's voice broke in behind them.
"He has to report to the authorities that he has arrived."

Ramon's face drooped scornfully. "Oh, Adrienne, *querida*, you must learn not to spoil my fine speeches." He put
an arm around each of the girls. "Come, you must prepare
for going ashore, and get out of my way or the skipper will
grumble at me."

Nicola thought, as she had on previous occasions, that
there was something about Ramon so engaging, so lighthearted and amiable, that it was a pity that Adrienne could
regard him only as her future betrothed and not as a man to
be adored and loved for his charming qualities.

The day was exciting enough with Adrienne to show
Nicola some of the attractions of San Fernando.

"You must see the cathedral another time," Adrienne
advised. "It is very beautiful and deserves a leisurely stroll
through it. Also, we will take you one day to the glassworks
near the harbor where you can see men making very lovely
pieces."

She conducted Nicola through some of the old streets
where the Arab quarter had once been and where it was
easy to imagine dark-eyed girls peering from barred windows. A long, winding flight of steps was edged with small
shops selling leather articles, souvenirs, baskets and shoes.
Suddenly at the top of the steps a large, arcaded square
opened out, with cafés at almost every point.

Nicola was glad of a long, cool drink of brandy and soda
with ice.

"After lunch," explained Adrienne, "we will look at the paintings in the open air down near the harbor. Painters arrange them under the palm trees."

Nicola smiled. "How fortunate the climate is so reliable! In England the artist would probably have to cover them three times a day because of the rain."

Adrienne laughed. "Also because of the fog?"

Lunch at one of the fashionable hotels along the *paseo* was a lengthy affair, especially when Adrienne insisted on a siesta in the hotel garden, but at four o'clock Nicola suggested, "Why don't we drive along the promenade in one of those basketwork carriages? They look as though they would be fun, and you can still finish your nap riding along."

Adrienne agreed, and the two girls found a sleepy driver with an equally sleepy horse, which consented to plod sedately along the *paseo* with the two girls in the woven cane carriage.

"I feel a mad desire to wave to the passersby," said Nicola. "You know, royal salute and all that."

"Then please choose only the very old men and the women," advised Adrienne, taking Nicola's remark seriously, "or else the young men will walk alongside and make *piropos.*"

Nicola laughed. "Oh, I know what they are. Extravagant compliments that mean exactly nothing. 'A man might die happy kissing your dear little elbow'—that sort of thing. All right, I won't wave to anyone."

The carriage took the girls to the far end of the promenade and had returned nearly to the starting point when Nicola, idly glancing along the *paseo*, suddenly saw a girl staring at her.

Her heart leaped with excitement. "Lisa! Lisa!" she cried out. Then without thinking she jumped out of the slow-moving carriage onto the roadway and ran back to the spot where she had seen her sister, but the girl had vanished.

Nicola stood bewildered, then dashed to the entrance of a small garden adjacent to one of the hotels. Two waiters, their feet resting on a table, regarded her with surprise.

"*Señorita*?" one asked.

Hurriedly in stammering Spanish she asked if they had seen a young girl in a red and white dress, dark hair, slim.

"*No aqui,*" the other waiter answered. Not here.

Nicola could see that for herself for there was no one else in the garden. She thanked them and went across the road slowly to where the carriage had stopped. Adrienne had alighted and now looked concerned as Nicola approached.

"What is the matter, Nicola?" she asked. "I was half asleep and suddenly you had jumped out of the carriage."

"I saw my sister. I'm sure it was Lisa. Then she disappeared."

"Come and sit in the carriage," urged Adrienne. "You look most white."

"The girl was exactly like Lisa," Nicola said in a dull toneless voice.

"But your sister would not run away when she saw you. You must have been mistaken."

"She had Lisa's face, her hair, her height, everything."

"While we are in San Fernando we could make inquiries," suggested Adrienne. "We could try the *policia.*"

Nicola shivered, then tried to recover her poise. "Oh, it was probably just a girl who resembled my sister. Think no more about it."

She had the best of reasons for not contacting the police if that could be avoided, reasons unknown to either Adrienne or Sebastian.

Adrienne instructed the driver to stop at the harbor end of the promenade and paid him off.

"Now," she said to Nicola, "we will inspect the pictures."

Under a double row of huge palm trees several artists had their open-air galleries, hanging their pictures on thin lines of stretched rope. Nicola strolled with Adrienne, who stopped now and again to study the pictures in detail, but Nicola's mind was far from appreciation of art at this moment. If that girl had really been Lisa why had she disappeared when there was everything to gain by being reunited with Nicola? Or had Lisa other reasons for avoiding any contact at all?

Adrienne's attention was caught by a glowing scene of

one of San Fernando's old streets, a painting that held all the pulsating color and mystery of what might lie within the walls. She nodded. "That is very good indeed."

The artist was at her elbow, unobtrusive but attentive. They began to talk in Spanish, discussing the points of first one picture then another.

Nicola moved away and sat on a bench by the edge of a flower bed where closely packed succulent plants substituted for grass turf, which would already have been scorched and withered by the hot sun. Was she beginning to see Lisa's face in other girls, as she fancied she had seen the young Spaniard who had once called at Lisa's apartment?

Adrienne concluded her deal with the artist and returned with the painting she had purchased wrapped in polythene.

"One artist must help another," she said. "Perhaps he does not really need the money, but it is pleasant to sell your work sometimes."

Nicola roused herself to make some vague remark in agreement.

"When we arrive at Ramon's house," continued Adrienne, "you should try your hand at painting. Perhaps you will be so good that I will be madly jealous of your talent."

Nicola managed a smile. "No fear of that! I've done very little since I left school except paint a couple of backdrops for a dramatic society."

"But that is very good for you. To paint something large makes you use broad strokes so that you do not . . . fidget—is that the right word?"

"I think you mean 'niggle,'" supplied Nicola, aware that Adrienne was making conversation to help her over the shock of even imagining that she had seen Lisa. Yet long after she and Adrienne had returned to the yacht for dinner the girl's face haunted Nicola. If only the *Clorinda* could have stayed in San Fernando Harbor for a few more days instead of leaving tomorrow for Cala Castell at the other end of the island! Ashore in the town of San Fernando there was a possibility that Nicola might see the girl again, but at Cala Castell that would be out of the question.

After dinner when the huge harbor was pricked with lights and shimmering reflections, Doña Elena announced,

"I am going tomorrow by car to our house at Cala Castell. Perhaps, Adrienne, you would like to accompany me with the Señorita Brettell? It is tedious to remain on the yacht. Ramon will bring that to Cala Castell."

Ramon smiled gently. "A ship is a lady. I will take *her* to Cala Castell."

Adrienne remained thoughtful for a moment. "As you wish," she said at last to Elena. "It will give Nicola a chance of seeing the interior of the island."

Nicola knew that she had no choice in the matter. If she could not stay indefinitely in San Fernando Town and search for Lisa, then it hardly mattered whether she went to Cala Castell by sea or land. Yet her common sense reminded her that searching for Lisa in San Fernando would be just as fruitless as in Barcelona. The towns were too big whereas a tiny village might have yielded results, but then Lisa would probably never be found in a small place. She liked life and gaiety, lights and dancing.

In spite of her depression Nicola found the drive to Cala Castell full of interest. Ramon's car with a driver was waiting at the harbor when she accompanied Doña Elena and Adrienne ashore.

There were districts of San Fernando that Nicola had not had time to see; the melon market; newly constructed streets to replace old congested alleys and buildings, but designed with care and artistry to blend with ancient surroundings. Out in the country they drove through small villages of golden stone where the houses were shuttered and few people appeared. Sometimes doors hung with chain curtains stood open and black-clad women sat outside on the sidewalk or dusty doorstep preparing vegetables or busy with some other household task.

After a time the road climbed away from the modest hills with small towns perched defensively on their summits and a range of mountains loomed in folds of mauve and slate blue. Pine woods stretched ahead in an apparently solid mass, but close up to them scattered white villas with splashes of yellow and crimson flower gardens were disclosed.

When the road wound through the pines the smell of

resin perfumed the air. Farther on was a small town with a few shops, a wine bar or two, and a square where the buildings on one side struck the eye with dazzling whiteness, while those opposite merged into deep slate-blue shadows. Then the car was running down a steep hill toward the sea until a sharp turn to the left brought it between pillared gates to Ramon's house. Here again were the brilliant contrasts of Moorish arches, cool and shadowed, and the pale pink walls covered with bougainvillea.

Doña Elena was greeted by half a dozen servants of whom she asked a few questions and apparently received reassuring answers that everything was ready for the family and their guests.

"You will find this house different from our own," Adrienne murmured to Nicola, who had already noticed that the Casa Margarita was built on less formal lines than the Montals' Villa Ronda. Stone floors with rugs, much simple wooden furniture, flowers in rough pottery bowls, all indicated the refreshing ease of a country villa.

Her room looked out over the trees to a part of the bay sheltered by a curving arm of the mountains.

"When will Ramon arrive with the yacht?" she asked Adrienne.

"Perhaps tomorrow. Maybe today," answered Adrienne with an indifferent shrug.

Nicola's query was an idle one for it made little difference to her whether he arrived one day or another, but she wished she could be as casual about Sebastian's visit for which she tried to quell her impatience.

She spent the next few days lazing, often with Adrienne and Ramon, either in the Casa Margarita's garden or down on the beach where straw umbrellas like wigwams mounted on poles provided shade. Each was furnished with a handy little shelf, fixed at a convenient height off the sand, for drinks and other odds and ends. Pines protected by stone walls came right down to the edge of the sandy shore and added further welcome patches of shade.

"A few days of this," murmured Nicola one morning, "and I will never want to do any work again."

"Perhaps you will not have to," retorted Ramon. "Stay

in Spain, marry a man who will give you a maid or two and your life can be pleasant and leisurely."

"Sound advice," agreed Nicola. "I'll think about it."

"You have your Englishman, Patrick," put in Adrienne. "He is one possibility."

"No!" Nicola spoke more sharply than she had intended. "Anyway he is soon going back to England and may not return."

"Undoubtedly he will return," protested Ramon. "Once a man has lived here he cannot help himself. Either he will stay or he is drawn back. You know that San Fernando is really the Land of the Lotus-eaters?"

"I can well believe it," said Nicola, her blue eyes twinkling. "It's as good an excuse as any."

"Ah, but no, it really is a fact. Odysseus came here and was so enchanted with the people because they were happy that he stayed and stayed."

"But eventually he tore himself away?" Nicola mocked. "At least, so I've read."

"With sadness and sorrow," agreed Ramon.

During this time Doña Elena was not only the thoughtful hostess but treated Nicola with more friendliness than she had hitherto shown. She made no further references to Nicola's missing sister, and Nicola had asked Adrienne not to mention the incident in the town of San Fernando.

But Elena's attitude changed sharply on the arrival of Sebastian. In the most subtle ways Nicola was made to feel that she was the fifth wheel in a quartet made up of Elena and Sebastian, Ramon and Adrienne. She found small tasks to occupy Nicola and prevent her from joining the others at beach parties or on drives to other parts of the island. Nicola accepted this role, part companion-governess to Adrienne, part unoccupied secretary to Sebastian, and remained in the background when the others went off somewhere.

Then one morning Sebastian asked her bluntly what was the matter.

"Matter?" she queried.

"Doña Elena says you have constant headaches. Have you been lying in the sun too long?"

"No. I've been careful not to overdo the sunbathing."

So that was the scheme, she thought. Poor Nicola has another of her headaches. . . .

"Then you'd better let me examine you and find the cause," he continued.

In his casual yellow shirt and beige trousers it was easy to forget that he was a doctor. She wanted to tell him that her headaches were nonexistent and a fiction on the part of Elena. Her only anxiety had been that he might not arrive.

"Truly I haven't a headache now," she protested.

"Then in that case you'll be able to come with us to the Dragon caves. Bring sensible shoes and a warm jacket with you. It can be cold down there."

Nicola, dressed as she had been instructed, came through the arched entrance of the Casa to join the others.

Elena asked in her most sympathetic tone, "How is your headache this morning?"

"I haven't one," replied Nicola, feeling more confident than usual. She was about to add that she rarely suffered from this complaint, but it was enough to see the chagrin on Elena's face, for Sebastian had come out at that moment.

Elena recovered and smiled. "I'm very glad." She did not add any invitation to join the party, evidently assuming either that Nicola would have the tact to stay at home or that she would efface herself in a corner of the car. But Sebastian put a restraining hand on Nicola's arm as she moved toward Ramon's car. "We'll take your smaller one, Ramon," he said. "You three go ahead. We'll soon catch you up."

Ramon smiled and nodded and immediately drove off before Elena could decide on any action. Nicola, watching the disappearing car, knew that Elena was too well bred to turn around and peer out of the back window but her disapproval could easily be imagined.

After the first moment of surprise Nicola had no room for any thought but that Sebastian had definitely indicated a preference for her company. Such a day might never come again and Nicola was determined to enjoy every moment of it, but in the small car with Sebastian driving she found herself tongue-tied or clumsy when she spoke at all. His very presence next to her robbed her of self-confidence, and mentally she kicked herself for behaving like a stupid schoolgirl.

She was undecided whether to tell him of that chance encounter with a girl who resembled Lisa, but then the words spilled out of their own accord.

"She made no attempt to recognize you or be recognized herself?" he asked, when she told him what had happened.

"None at all. She disappeared before I could catch up to her."

He was silent for a few moments. "Are you sure that you would now recognize your sister if you saw her? Remember it is well over a year since your last meeting and she may have changed."

"In small things, perhaps. Hairstyle, makeup, but not in her essential expression. This girl was exactly like that photograph that I showed you."

Some weeks earlier Nicola had acted on his suggestion that a photograph, even a snapshot, might help to locate Lisa, and one of the girls who had taken over Nicola's apartment in London had sent the only photograph she could find among Nicola's belongings, one that Lisa had used for modeling.

"I wonder if we're searching for a girl who does not now exist," he said at last.

"Doesn't exist?" she echoed hotly. "Do you also believe that I made up a missing sister—for my own ends?"

Momentarily he gave her a sharp glance, then turned his attention to the road. "I don't believe that at all, whoever may have put that idea into your head. What I meant was that your sister may have deliberately changed her appearance."

Nicola saw the logic of his argument. "So any girl who looks the way Lisa used to be probably isn't her at all," she said slowly. "That certainly makes it more difficult to find her."

"Have you made thorough inquiries in England? How do you know that she hasn't returned there and is now searching for you?"

This possibility had not occurred seriously to Nicola and

she soon dismissed it. "The apartment where I lived is now occupied by two friends of mine. They could soon give Lisa my address."

Eventually she realized that Sebastian must have at some time on this journey taken a different route from Ramon's road, for although he drove fast they did not catch up the other car, and again Nicola felt that warm feeling toward Sebastian.

Just before they reached the famous caves he asked, "D'you know anything about the caves?"

"Yes. They're full of stalactites and there's a lake at the bottom. We have similar ones in England—at Cheddar and other places."

"There are none in England like these," he returned smugly.

"Then I will have to find that out, won't I?"

He was slowing down the car at the entrance and now he turned to give her a long, sustained glance. As she, too, turned toward him she blushed and was the first to avert her eyes. For one ridiculous, fleeting moment she imagined she had seen in his dark eyes the same light, half merriment, half admiration, that long ago she had seen in David's eyes when she was engaged to him.

The other car with Ramon, Adrienne and Elena arrived within a few minutes and they all entered the caves with a guide who collected a few more people and sternly instructed his charges not to wander away from him or the paths.

Nicola speedily found that the caves were not quite like those at Cheddar or Wookey Hole. They were not only on a vast scale but miraculously lit as though for spectacular stage sets. Stalactites hung like waterfalls or tattered, windswept curtains; stalagmites reared from the ground in columns like pagodas or cacti, took the shapes of monks or fairies or groups of Dresden china—whatever the imaginative eye could invent.

Steps or gentle paths led up and down to various levels, and as Sebastian had warned her, Nicola was glad to put on the lightweight cardigan she had brought with her, for the temperature was much lower than in the blazing sunshine outside. At last they were down in a huge cavern where columns of stalactites and stalagmites met to form pillars apparently holding up the fretted scintillating roof. There was a glint of a mass of still, black water, and tourists were instructed to sit on the rough benches in front of it. Suddenly every light was dimmed and the blackness, intense and enveloping, seemed a palpable thing that could be held in the hand and folded like velvet.

The guides, having brought their individual parties to this point, called quietly for silence, but the visitors had already hushed themselves into an impressive stillness. Faintly, music came from a distant point, swelled as it approached, then a small boat decked with fairy lights emerged from a black tunnel, and the quartet of musicians was revealed. Boatmen dipped their oars without the slightest splash to disturb the Chopin nocturne and the boat with its two violins, viola and cello glided past the crowd and swung around for the return journey. Now they played the "Barcarolle" from *The Tales of Hoffmann,* and Nicola knew that she would never hear that well-known air in more appropriate surroundings.

Only now was she aware that Sebastian had taken her hand in his and was gently swaying their twined fingers to the rhythm of the music. Tears pricked her eyes because the moment was too emotional, too beautiful, to be borne.

When the musicians' boat had disappeared around the curving tunnel, Sebastian whispered, "We go out that way, too."

"By boat?" she asked.

"Yes."

The boats were small and took only half a dozen passengers at a time. When their turn came, Nicola selfishly hoped that none of the rest of Ramon's party would be in the same boat. Impersonal strangers would not break the fragile thread of this experience, but subdued chatter from friends would debase it to just another tourist attraction.

In the darkness with only the faintest illumination coming from somewhere along the rough stone walls of the lake Nicola could not discern Sebastian's face, but she did not need to be reassured that he was close by her side.

"What is the poem about the sacred river?" he asked her.

"'Kubla Khan,'" she whispered, "'. . . where Alph, the sacred river, ran through caverns measureless to man. Down to a sunless sea.'"

Another voice in the boat murmured, "This is like crossing the Styx with old Charon."

No doubt the boatmen were familiar with such sallies in half a dozen languages.

Daylight appeared with dramatic suddenness and the boat pulled in to a small platform for the passengers to disembark.

"But it isn't a sunless sea," said Nicola. "It's a sunlit one instead."

Sebastian was looking away from her and did not answer. When Ramon, Adrienne and Elena arrived in the next boat he waved to them and seemed anxious not to be separated from them or alone with Nicola.

For the rest of the day he was no more than his usual withdrawn self. Nicola wondered at times whether he regretted those friendly gestures in the dark secrecy of the caves, whether he had been influenced by the grimly romantic atmosphere as she had been. But to her it was a novelty, and Sebastian must have been, on many previous occasions, in the caves or in others like them elsewhere on the island.

She resolved not to let the slightest cloud of disappointment spoil this day of days, for there was still the return journey to look forward to. But here she had to suffer the inevitable.

Elena made sure that Sebastian and Nicola would not drive home alone together. "There is room for you in Ramon's car," she told Nicola when they were ready to return home.

Nicola hesitated, and Elena smiled. "I will accompany Sebastian. He will not have to drive alone. We have many matters to discuss."

CHAPTER SEVEN

IT WAS NOTICEABLE, too, during the next few days how many times Elena cornered Sebastian on the pretext of needing his advice or discussing business matters with him. All the same there were fleeting occasions when he seemed to escape from Elena's supervision, if that was what it was, and spend an odd half hour with Nicola.

She had accepted Adrienne's suggestion that she should try painting.

"Daub away as you feel," advised Adrienne. "What does it matter to spoil a canvas?"

"Who knows? Someone might think my effort much better spoilt and read genius into it, especially upside down."

"You must not mock art," Adrienne rebuked her. "One must look beneath the surface."

"I'll be content to paint the bay and the rocks and a chunk of blue sky," declared Nicola, "and hope that I won't have to put a caption underneath. 'This is a picture of Cala Castell.'"

Adrienne supplied Nicola with brushes and paints, a small portable easel and showed her how to carry a wet painting home without smudging it.

"I am most grateful to my art teacher," Nicola thanked her.

"You are not in the serious mood that one should be," grumbled Adrienne.

One evening before dinner Nicola was in a corner of the garden painting part of an archway between two courtyards and trying to catch the light and the long shadows. She heard footsteps approaching and was then instantly aware of Sebastian standing behind her. Her brush jabbed a splotch of color in the wrong place and she took a rag and wiped it out.

"Leave it alone," he commanded. "That gives the right misty look to the shadowed part." He took the brush from her hand, dabbed delicately at the canvas, then wound the rag around the handle end of the brush and wiped some of the paint away. "Even though the wall is in shadow, we must see what it is made of underneath," he said.

She gave him a swift upward glance. "I didn't know you also painted," she said.

"All Montals paint," was his brief reply, as he picked up a second brush. "My brother, Eduardo, was very good. He painted birds and flowers. Sometimes his work was used as illustrations for books."

"So that's where Adrienne gets her talent," murmured Nicola.

"Not entirely. Her mother was a brilliant artist and exhibited in Madrid. Unfortunately she died too young to achieve the reputation she deserved."

"That was very sad." Nicola longed to say something less trite, but feared that some clumsy remark might hurt or offend him.

"I'm going to the town of San Fernando tomorrow," he said, handing back her brush. "Would you like to come with me? I doubt if we shall see your sister by chance, but we could make inquiries."

Nicola eagerly seized the chance. She was flattered and delighted that he should ask her. But as soon as Elena heard of the plan she immediately declared that she had some shopping to do in San Fernando and would also accompany Sebastian.

Nicola's enthusiasm for the visit was soon quenched, but she realized that she might have expected this reaction from Doña Elena. The day was not entirely spoilt, however, for when Sebastian suggested that Nicola should accompany him to the British Consul and other official authorities, Elena protested that surely Nicola could do that alone.

"But Nicola may need someone to speak Spanish for her," Sebastian answered.

"At the British Consulate?" Elena's eyebrows were raised in disbelief.

"Of course not," retorted Sebastian irritably. "But we may have to talk to officials elsewhere."

"And you think your sister may have come here?" Elena asked Nicola.

"I thought I recognized her the day we arrived in San Fernando. I may have been mistaken."

"It is often the case that the memory of a lost person plays tricks," replied Elena. "We see their faces everywhere."

It was obvious that Elena believed that Nicola had invented this so-called chance meeting in order to induce Sebastian to take her to San Fernando. But this time Sebastian seemed determined not to give in to Elena, who had to be content with taking her siesta on the private balcony of the yacht club, where they all had lunch.

There was no information at the Consul's office, but they made a note of Lisa's name in case anything should be heard of her.

"Elisabeth Brettell is the name on her passport," Nicola told the official. "But she is usually known as 'Lisa.'"

Lisa had dropped her formal name even while she was at school except for official purposes. "Why I had to be named after some aunt or other beats me," she had once grumbled.

When Nicola and Sebastian left the Consulate, he said, "Why do you never want to contact the police? What are you afraid of?"

"Nothing," Nicola replied sharply.

"D'you think your sister may have had some trouble with the police?" he persisted.

"Certainly not!"

Sebastian smiled. "Your answer was too quick, Nicola. You don't want to go in case you learn the worst. It was the same in Barcelona. What sort of scrape makes you so cowardly that you can't bear even to find out?"

Nicola tried to smile back. "I just don't imagine for a moment that Lisa would be in any sort of trouble or scrape."

Sebastian sighed. "It's no use lying to me. I've been trained as a doctor to know sometimes, although not always, when people are not speaking the truth."

"Oh, very well then, we'll go to the police and make the fullest inquiries," she said in exasperation, forgetting how much she owed to Sebastian even as her employer.

"That's better," he commented. "Haven't you thought that if your sister is really in any serious trouble, she may believe that *you* have deserted *her*?"

"That's possible," she admitted quietly, although she thought the idea was far from probable.

There was nothing on record at the police headquarters, and Nicola was intensely relieved.

"Now that the doubts are off your mind," said Sebastian, "we will try to visit the glass factory and watch them blowing beautiful bubbles."

The men had just started work again after their siesta, and Nicola realized how much they needed rest in the hottest part of the afternoon for the furnaces radiated an almost intolerable heat. She watched men manipulating molten glass as though it were toffee, forming brandy balloons and fantastic, colored shapes. The long showroom of finished products seemed cool by contrast and Nicola sauntered along inspecting the pieces on the shelves and in showcases. She saw a sea-green ornament—one could hardly call it a vase or bowl—for its shape was like a large flattened doughnut upended on a stand. Yet it had a small opening near the base for flowers, and a demonstrator showed how flowers could be inserted and the water would reach its own level in the transparent double circle.

"Isn't it a remarkable piece!" she exclaimed to Sebastian at her side.

"Do you like it?"

"Oh, yes. I'll buy it."

"No," he said gravely. "I'll buy it for you."

She was too astounded to reply, undecided whether this was merely a generous Spanish custom to buy something that a guest admired or whether he was really meaning to make her a gift.

Whatever his motive she would treasure this piece of

green glass all her life. Although he did not ask her to accept this small present in secrecy, Nicola had enough sense not to disclose who had actually purchased it. Not even to Adrienne would she admit Sebastian's impulsive gesture, which might, Nicola reflected afterward, have been more in the nature of a consolation prize after the failure to learn any news of Lisa.

Sebastian's holiday was nearly up when he astonished Nicola and probably everyone else at the Casa Margarita by saying that he must fly back to Orsola the following day.

"If Nicola can tear herself away from this enchanted island, I'd like her to come back with me," he announced when they were all at dinner.

Nicola almost swallowed some food the wrong way and partly choked.

She looked across the table at Elena, whose already pale complexion seemed to have gone whiter.

"You're taking Nicola?" Elena managed to whisper. "But why?"

"Yes, why should you deprive Nicola of her hard-earned holiday?" asked Adrienne.

"Because I have work for her to do. I want that book finished as soon as possible," was Sebastian's reply.

Nicola knew that he was looking at her and she raised her head and smiled at him. "Of course I'll come back whenever you say," she said. She hoped her tone conveyed the dutiful secretary rather than the voice of a girl who knew she was now head over heels in love with him.

"What shall I do without my Nicola?" wailed Adrienne.

"What you did before she came, no doubt," returned Sebastian dryly. "You have Ramon to amuse you and Doña Elena as your hostess. What more could you desire?"

Adrienne opened her mouth to make further heated protests, then caught sight of Nicola's face and suddenly changed her mind. "It will be as you say. Life is full of unexpected happenings."

"Would you want it any other way?" asked Ramon gently. "You would complain that it was monotonous."

But if Adrienne had accepted for her own unknown reasons Sebastian's sudden decision, Doña Elena did not follow suit. After dinner, Nicola knew that a long argument developed between Elena and Sebastian. They sat on a bench in part of the courtyard behind the archway that Nicola had tried to paint. They spoke in Spanish and their voices only occasionally drifted Nicola's way, but she could easily gather the gist of Elena's angry sentences. Nicola in the midst of this flurry of changed plans hugged herself, dreamily reveling in the prospect of being at the Villa Ronda with Sebastian and, more than that, knowing that he wanted her there.

The plane trip in Sebastian's company, the welcome at the Villa Ronda, the three days that followed were all sheer joy to Nicola. Without the disturbing presence of Doña Elena or even the unpredictable vagaries of Adrienne, Nicola had the feeling of being home in an idyllic setting. Sebastian was out of the house most of the day, either at one or other of the hospitals, or at his clinic, yet she was conscious of his intangible presence in the rooms where he worked and lived. Dinner with him on the Mediterranean balcony or some other part of one of the patios was the focal point to which the rest of the day led, the moment to savor, the time when he seemed to relax, even recount anecdotes about his patients.

Nicola might have guessed that this brief passage of time was too fragile to endure the rough buffetings of daily life. It was shattered as suddenly as though it were a bubble of glass imperfectly shaped and deliberately smashed as she had seen in the glassworks at San Fernando.

She decided after lunch and her siesta on the fourth day to go down to swim in the sea instead of the villa's swimming pool. She went down the long path to the beach house, pushed open the door, which was rarely locked, and kicked off her shoes. She reached for a towel and a voice behind her said, "Hello, Nicky!"

Nicola spun around, her spine tingling with fear that reached the back of her head. Who would say, "Hello, Nicky," in English? Who but her sister, Lisa?

But this girl leaning nonchalantly against a cupboard, could she possibly be Lisa?

Nicola forced herself to move closer to the girl, peering at the blond hair, the deep suntanned features that somehow seemed coarser than Lisa's remembered face. Only the dark brown eyes seemed to belong.

"Well, can't you say something?" said the girl. "You seem bowled over, but I'm not a ghost."

"Lisa!" whispered Nicola in awed amazement. "Can it really be you?"

The girl smiled. "That's better! At least you can remember my name."

"But where—where have you been all this time? And why did you disappear?"

Lisa smiled. "It's a long story. Let's sit down and be comfortable." She moved toward a cane chair and sat down. Nicola remained standing for a few moments; she, too, felt the need of support for her trembling legs and sat on the long, cushioned settee.

"We can't stay here long," Nicola said, "in case someone else comes down here to bathe."

"Long enough," replied Lisa confidently. "In any case it doesn't matter who finds me here. I could easily be a friend of yours, or a new member of the staff, or a neighbor."

"How did you find this place down here on the beach? It's private."

"Oh, I know. It belongs to the Montals; Dr. Sebastian Montal and his family. But anyone can walk through the gates of the villa and down the path to this beach."

"It was lucky that I happened to come down here today," said Nicola, with a shiver of apprehension. "Supposing someone else had come!"

Lisa smiled. "I've been here since yesterday. As a matter of fact, I thought you were never coming."

"Since yesterday?" The words hit Nicola like a blow. "You mean you've slept here?"

Lisa nodded. "Not too comfortably, I must admit. And if you hadn't shown up today, I'd have been forced to call at the front door of the villa and ask for you."

"Why didn't you?" asked Nicola, and knew in that instant with burning shame that she was thankful that Lisa had not done so.

"I thought it would be easier to talk if I met you first

before you revealed all, that your missing sister had been found, and so on.''

Nicola held her head with both hands. "I don't understand a single thing. You invite me to come to Spain, then you disappear without a word, leaving no address. The job I was supposed to take over from you had also disappeared, for you left it weeks before.''

Lisa laughed softly. "That's the good Patrick who told you that.''

"Naturally. I was anxious about what had happened to you, and I still don't know.''

"For a sister who appeared so concerned over my disappearance, Nicola, you've shown remarkably little joy at my return. Not so much as a kiss of welcome!''

"I'm still trying to get over the shock,'' muttered Nicola, "but of course I'm glad to find you again.'' She rose and embraced Lisa, but again she was aware of a strange revulsion.

"I hope you are. Glad, I mean, at finding me—or perhaps at my finding you, for I promise you, Nicola, things are going to be different from now on.''

Nicola smiled for the first time at her sister with some affection. "Oh, Lisa, I hope so!'' she said warmly. "I really have been worried. All those debts . . . .''

"Oh, I can explain those. You see, when I came here and found that deadly job in the wine place, I only took it as a stopgap. You know me, Nicola. You know very well that it wasn't at all my type of job. All the men, too, were just as dull. Then I met Tony. He worked in one of the big tourist companies—oh, he was marvelous! Handsome, accomplished, lots of money. We went everywhere. He gave me a wonderful time.''

"Was he English?'' queried Nicola.

"Oh, yes. He spoke four or five foreign languages and he had friends of all nationalities. Then we became engaged.'' Lisa leaned toward her sister. "You know, Nicola, I thought I was smart where men were concerned. I thought I could see through those who were shams. Yet I believed Tony was different.''

"What happened?''

"On the strength of my engagement I launched out into some decent clothes for once. Tony gave me a beautiful ring, a large, square-cut emerald. Also at first he took care of all my bills. I took the apartment in the Paseo Maritimo and enjoyed myself hugely with entertaining all our friends."

"And then?" prompted Nicola.

Lisa sighed. "A sad disillusionment. He vanished. I received a letter breaking off our engagement owing to circumstances he couldn't control, he said. He was clearing out abroad somewhere else. I found out afterward that he'd taken some of the tourist agency's money with him—or so it was hinted. As for me, I was left flat broke, with no job and nothing but a few clothes not paid for and a lot of bills."

"Oh, I know something about the bills," Nicola said grimly.

"At first I was so angry that this sort of thing could happen to me! Then I remembered the emerald ring. That ought to fetch something." Lisa laughed harshly. "It did! About three hundred pesetas—a couple of pounds or so. It turned out to be glass rather nicely mounted. So now I was boiling with rage, and when I heard that he'd probably gone to San Fernando, I followed."

"San Fernando? But I was there until a few days ago."

"I know. I was there at the harbor when you arrived on that stylish yacht."

"So it could have been you I saw along the *paseo*? But that girl had dark hair."

Lisa shook her head. "That wasn't me. You practically looked straight at me and didn't recognize me. It's astonishing what a change of hair color can do. I've been blond a long time now."

Momentarily Nicola remembered Sebastian's words about " . . . searching for a girl who does not exist. . . ."

"And did you find Tony in San Fernando?" she asked.

"Not a hope. He probably let it be supposed that he'd gone there, knowing that I might follow. He's probably safely in South America by now." There was only the faintest trace of bitterness in Lisa's tone.

After a moment Nicola asked, "Why didn't you make yourself known to me if you saw me arrive from the yacht?"

"It wasn't discreet for me to do so then."

"But it is now? Why?"

Lisa hung her arm over the back of her chair and regarded Nicola with amusement. "I have to make my decisions as I go along and I thought it might be more advantageous—more advisable, shall we say—to wait until you were back here again at the doctor's villa."

"If you didn't find Tony, what were you living on in San Fernando?" demanded Nicola, sensing a premonition of danger.

"I wasn't doing too badly. I landed in a revue put on for the English and American tourists. Not the sort of show that your fine Spanish friends would patronize, of course, but quite respectable."

"And I suppose you've now walked out on that?"

"Nicky, you're taking a very schoolmarmish attitude. Forget you're my elder sister. In some ways you're still a ten-year-old, absolutely innocent of the evils of this wicked world."

It was on the tip of Nicola's tongue to retort that perhaps she hadn't taken the chance to explore the so-called wicked world and its evils, but that would have been unkind to Lisa who had been forced to fight her own battles for the last year or more. Instead, she asked a question that had been puzzling her for the last few minutes. "How did you find out where I was living?"

Lisa lit a cigarette before replying. Then she gave her sister an oblique glance. "No doubt the devoted Patrick always knows where you're likely to be?"

"You mean you've been in touch with him all the time? He didn't even know the address of your new apartment on the Paseo Maritimo."

"Of course he did!" Lisa's tone was derisive. "He came to parties there several times."

"I don't believe it," Nicola retorted abruptly. "Patrick isn't like that. He did all he could to help me to trace you."

"Naturally. That gave him the chance of seeing you whenever he wanted to."

Nicola was bewildered. Could Patrick have been in Lisa's

confidence all this time and only pretended that he disliked her?

"Tell me," continued Lisa, "have you fallen just a little for Patrick? He has a certain charm."

"I agree he has charm," returned Nicola steadily, "but I haven't fallen for him, and if I had it wouldn't be much use, would it? Didn't you know that he's engaged to a girl in England?"

Lisa's mouth curled in a smile. "Oh, yes. Whether he'll ever go back and marry her is quite another matter. Isn't it odd, Nicola, how men take refuge behind an engagement and use it as a kind of shield to fend off all the other attractive girls within reach? If they only knew, it makes them much more vulnerable."

"Perhaps only to girls like you. I'd prefer Patrick to be loyal to his fiancée."

"Oh, yes, of course, I'd forgotten. You had the experience of David marrying that other girl, didn't you?"

But Nicola was not eager to pursue the subject of that old heartbreak. "Was it also Patrick who told you that I was going to San Fernando? Or was it just a lucky coincidence that you happened to be at the harbor when I came ashore?"

Lisa shook her head. "Ruben, my faithful spy, let me know that you'd be coming with the Montals and others on a very expensive-looking yacht."

"Who's Ruben?" demanded Nicola.

"You saw him once when he called at the apartment."

"That dark young man who raced off when he found me there instead of you? I saw him again at least once and he refused to recognize me."

"You couldn't expect him to do that. Too dangerous."

"Dangerous? What danger was there in letting me know where you were, that you were safe, that I needn't worry about you?" Nicola's blue eyes blazed with anger and she tripped herself impetuously into a disclosure that she had not intended to make at that moment. "You left plenty of debts behind. Did the faithful Ruben also tell you who paid those bills?"

Lisa stared blankly at Nicola. Then she burst into

laughter. "Don't tell me, Nicky, that you were fool enough to pay them!"

"Fool or not, I *have* paid most of them."

"Good heavens!" exclaimed Lisa. "Whatever for? The sake of the family honor? Once I was out of the way, no one could have done a thing about payment. You're really greener than I thought you were."

"I shall never understand you, Lisa," Nicola said sadly.

"Don't try!" snapped the other. "We're two entirely different persons."

"Yes, we are," agreed Nicola. "With different ideas about living and occasionally having consideration for other people."

"You're afraid of life, Nicky. You're too timid to laugh out and challenge fate."

"I'm certainly afraid of living beyond my means and at other people's expense."

Lisa smiled. "Oh, a few debts to shops. They could afford it. Their prices were high enough." She stubbed out her cigarette. "Well, we must talk about my future."

"Yes," agreed Nicola. "Obviously you can't stay here in this beach chalet place. What are your plans?"

Lisa flung out her hands. "I haven't any. I thought you'd be able to form some for me."

"But, Lisa, how do I know what you want to do? You don't like working in an office. You've tried modeling, and you worked in this revue in San Fernando. Nothing pleases you for more than a short time."

Lisa smiled mischievously. "Nothing that sounds like work pleases me."

"Well, now that you're back here—and you've very little in the way of debts to hinder you—haven't you any friends who would help you? I don't suppose Patrick is of much use to you, but there are probably other people."

"Who could be of greater help than my own sister?" queried Lisa in her most innocent tone.

"You know I'll help you all I can, but how? What can I do?"

"You seem to have found a very comfortable post yourself. Trot around after Mademoiselle Adrienne, type a page or two for the doctor—and then enjoy yourself with all modern conveniences.''

"You can't expect me to find a similar job for you!''

"Why not? Preferably one without the work thrown in!''

"But, Lisa, be reasonable. I can't hide you here, but equally, I can't dump you on the Montals. It's not my house.''

"Who said anything about dumping me on the Montals?'' demanded Lisa, and her dark eyes glittered with indignation. "You've found yourself a nice soft living and I want to live in the same high style. Why shouldn't I? We're sisters. Surely you can share and share alike with me? If I were on top, you'd expect me to share my good fortune with you, wouldn't you?''

Lisa's outburst left Nicola amazed and perplexed.

"All right, then. Where am I supposed to have found you? Skulking in a beach chalet?''

"Oh, we can invent something better than that. My good friend Ruben can always act as go-between. We could stage a most dramatic meeting. Then you can take me to Dr. Montal's house and introduce me as your long lost and thankfully found sister.''

Nicola sighed. "You could stay there for a time, of course, but there can't be anything permanent.''

"We'll see.''

"I could give you a little money today. I've none down here, of course. You could go to one of the small hotels in Orsola and wait until I come. I could then ask Dr. Montal for permission to bring you to his house for the time being.''

"No, Nicky, that won't do.'' Lisa spoke coldly. "It seems to me that you've gone up in the world and now you're ashamed of this sister that you're supposed to have been searching for. I want to start living in the Villa Ronda straightaway.''

"That's impossible.''

"Why? You can't give me one good reason, except that you want to keep everything selfishly to yourself. I'll give you until the doctor comes home this evening, so that you can break the good news to him. I'll be sitting in a nearby corner of the garden and you can then invite me into the house and introduce me.''

When Nicola remained silent, thinking over this extraordinary proposition, Lisa continued, ''Of course, there is an alternative. I could just come to the front door of the villa and announce that I, too, am a Señorita Brettell. Spanish hospitality being what it is, I would certainly be welcomed, even if I were your cousin fourth removed.''

''No, it would be better for me to tell the doctor first,'' Nicola decided hurriedly. ''I'll go back to the villa now. D'you want anything to eat? How did you get on if you've been here since yesterday?''

''Oh, I didn't mean I'd been sitting here waiting for you to condescend to come down to swim. I roamed around Orsola, found out quite a bit more about the Montals, drank a coffee here, ate a snack there. I'm not absolutely destitute.''

''Have you any luggage? Where is it?'' asked Nicola.

Lisa pointed to a small overnight bag on the floor near a chair. ''A few essentials. The rest I can send for when I have a new permanent address.''

Nicola returned up the long path to the Villa Ronda, her mind in turmoil, her heart heavy with foreboding. Yet she took herself to task for an instinctive lack of the kind of spontaneous and cordial welcome that she had imagined she would give to Lisa when they eventually met.

''What's wrong with me?'' she asked aloud of the tree-bordered path. ''I ought to be overjoyed to see her again.''

She made excuses that Lisa had changed not only in appearance but character. Yet she knew that Lisa's nature had not really changed. It was only the circumstances that came into Lisa's life. Lisa had always been an opportunist.

In Sebastian's cool study, Nicola sat at the small desk and turned over the typewritten pages she still had to copy. She both longed for and dreaded Sebastian's return. How could she be sure that Lisa would stay down at the beach and amuse herself by swimming or sunbathing? It was just as likely that she would walk into the villa whenever she was tired of being alone.

Sebastian came home fairly early and Nicola plunged

straight into her news. She felt that if she put it off even for a single moment she would never have the courage to tell him. Yet she did not know why she should have this curious reluctance.

"But that's very good news," Sebastian commented. "You must be immensely relieved. How did you find her?"

In her distress Nicola had forgotten Lisa's suggestion that Ruben could act as messenger. "I—I think a friend was in touch with her and gave her this address."

"So she was not in San Fernando after all."

Nicola let that slip by. There was no point in complicating matters unnecessarily.

"No, apparently not."

"Then where has she been living all this time?" he asked.

"I'm not sure. I mean I haven't had time to find out."

"Where is your sister now?"

"In the garden," replied Nicola, hoping that Lisa would at least behave in a reasonable manner.

"Then bring her in here. I will be delighted to welcome her, for your sake, Nicola, as well as her own."

Nicola was glad of the opportunity to hurry out of the study and to brush away a few tears from her eyes.

At first Nicola could not find Lisa, and for a moment her disloyal heart lightened. Had Lisa already seen the impossibility of the situation? But as Nicola turned the curve of a row of oleander bushes she heard Lisa's voice talking in very bad Spanish.

Lisa reclined on a chaise longue, a long cool drink at her elbow, while Felipe, one of the gardeners, smiled down at her. *Oh, trust Lisa not to waste time sitting alone!* Nicola thought uncharitably.

"Ah, there you are!" exclaimed Lisa when she saw Nicola. The gardener bowed and went off to his tasks. "Well, how did the great man take the dramatic news?" she wanted to know.

"Come with me and meet him," replied Nicola, keeping a tight rein on her self-control.

Sebastian gave Lisa a smile of welcome and said, "I am very glad that you have been found. Your sister has been very anxious about you."

He placed a chair for Lisa, waited for Nicola also to be seated, then he sat at his desk as though he were in his consulting room. He pulled from a drawer the photograph of Lisa that Nicola had received from England and compared the picture with the original.

"You mustn't take any notice of the difference," Lisa pointed out immediately. "I've had my hair tinted a different color and I'm suntanned."

He nodded. "Have you been ill, Miss Brettell?"

For a few seconds Lisa did not reply, and Nicola held her breath, fearful of what revelations her sister might make.

Then Lisa said sweetly and patiently, "I think I must have been ill for some time, because I don't remember whole patches of events. I seemed to wake up and weeks and weeks had gone by."

So that was to be the tale, Nicola reflected. Loss of memory. Perhaps it was as good as any other.

"Did you have some kind of accident? A blow on the head? A car crash or something of the kind?"

Lisa appeared to ponder. "I don't remember. It could have been a car crash, I suppose."

"But you were not in any hospital in this part of the country," he said crisply. "Were you nursed privately?"

"I suppose I must have been."

Sebastian rose. "Then we must look after you, Miss Brettell, and see that there are no bad aftereffects. I may be allowed to examine you later on, perhaps? I am a doctor."

"Naturally. I would be most relieved to be examined and find out that I'm now all right."

Sebastian ordered a guest room to be prepared for Lisa, who came along to Nicola's room some time before dinner.

"I came to see what I could borrow to wear for dinner," Lisa explained. "I haven't any rags, as you know."

"I've one or two outfits in the wardrobe," Nicola offered.

Lisa inspected the contents and sniffed. "H'm. Not much here, is there? Everything's too long, anyway. You're taller than I and no one would ever call you an up-to-date fashion follower."

"There's a pink skirt there that you could hitch up a bit

by turning the waist over and wearing this little brocade jacket on top.''

"It'll do for one evening," observed Lisa grudgingly. "Tomorrow you must come with me to Barcelona and help me to do some shopping. I must have a few rags to stand up in.''

Nicola's first impulse was to say that she couldn't possibly spare the time, but second thoughts warned her that it might be desirable to watch Lisa actually spending the money and paying cash for the articles. Nicola would have to provide the money anyway.

Lisa was glancing around the room. "Not bad," she said. "I really wanted to see if mine was as good as yours, as I don't see why I should be fobbed off with anything less.''

"And are you satisfied with your accommodation?" asked Nicola coolly.

"For the time being, yes. I think, Nicky, that I'm going to enjoy myself in the Villa Ronda. Good girl, you chose a nice place. I'll say that for you.''

Nicola realized at dinner that those delightful tête-à-tête meals with Sebastian were at an end. Lisa made a lively but intrusive third, and Nicola was nervously on edge lest her sister should drop some hint of unpaid bills or visits to San Fernando or any other perilous subject. Sebastian was courtesy itself, conversing with Lisa in a way that both flattered and challenged her to sparkle. Eventually Nicola excused herself on the pretext that she wanted to finish some typing, but he rose quickly instead.

"No, Nicola, not tonight. You must stay and talk to your sister. You must have so much to say to each other after this long silence.''

When the two girls were alone on the lamp-lit patio, Lisa helped herself to a little more wine.

"Utterly charming," she said softly. "I'd no idea. D'you think you've any chance of marrying him?''

"No chance at all, I imagine," Nicola replied smoothly, grateful for the darkness that dimmed her face. "He's otherwise reserved for someone else.''

"Pity," commented Lisa. "You'd be in clover here. So might I.''

After a pause, Lisa continued, "I wonder . . . I wonder if I could—"

"Could what?"

"Manage to oust this other woman who has put a reserved label on him."

Nicola managed a chuckle that was half amusement, but half desperation. "It's rather early to make plans yet, Lisa. You don't really know what he's like."

"And do you?"

"To a small extent, yes," replied Nicola.

"Tell me about him."

Nicola stood up. "Some other time, Lisa. It's late and I'm going to bed. Coming?"

"This place isn't exactly a center of evening entertainment, is it?" grumbled Lisa. "Everyone off to bed before midnight."

"It's not Barcelona, if that's what you mean. It's not even San Fernando."

"Oh, well, maybe there'll be more excitement when the others return from the yachting trip." Lisa stretched and yawned. "All right, Nicky, I'll count my blessings, as you so often used to command me, and we'll see what tomorrow brings."

Long after Lisa had gone to her room after a final chat, Nicola lay awake, not only apprehensive and disquieted at the sudden reappearance of her sister, but bitterly ashamed at her own reactions. She would have been more content to know definitely that Lisa was safe and well and prosperous, but at some distance from the Villa Ronda. She did not want Lisa here in Sebastian's house and knew that her reasons were selfish and unworthy.

CHAPTER EIGHT

ON THE SHOPPING EXPEDITION next day to buy clothes for
Lisa, Nicola decided to be as generous as possible with
money, if only to salve her conscience and cancel those
distrustful feelings that Lisa's sudden reappearance had
caused. For her part Nicola was pleasantly surprised to find
Lisa's demands so moderate. "A couple of inexpensive
dresses, two pairs of shoes, some underwear—those will
probably do for the time being," she said as she walked
with Nicola along one of the shopping streets.

Sebastian had considerately given Nicola the entire day
off, so the two girls were able to lunch leisurely at a
restaurant in the Paseo de Gracia.

"We ought to telephone Patrick," Lisa suggested. "You
don't want him to go on searching for me, do you?"

Nicola smiled. "I thought you said he knew all about
your movements. If that's so, then he'll know that you're
now staying at the Villa Ronda."

Lisa made a grimace. "Still, there's no harm in talking to
him."

"I never like telephoning men at their office in business
hours," Nicola objected.

"Have it your own way." Lisa shrugged. "I can see why
David didn't come rushing back to marry you. You're too
diffident, Nicola. You've simply got to be more positive in
this world."

Nicola looked down at the tablecloth. "There was no
need to remind me of David. That's all over and finished."

"Well then, why don't you learn from experience? We all

make mistakes. I made one over Tony, but I'm not going to forget those hard lessons."

In the end Lisa telephoned Patrick, who agreed to meet the two girls when he had finished work.

"He's another like you," gibed Lisa. " 'When I've finished work. . . .' Any man worth his salt would just walk out of his office, take a taxi and arrive here in ten minutes."

Nicola laughed. "Perhaps he doesn't think either of us is worth getting into trouble with his boss." After a moment, she asked, "Wasn't he surprised to hear from you?"

"Well, yes, in a way, I suppose he was, but you heard me explain to him," Lisa answered vaguely.

Nicola had also heard Patrick's sharp exclamations of surprise at the other end. "Lisa!" he had shouted. "*Lisa!* I can't believe it. Nicola will be pleased. Oh, she's there with you."

When eventually he met the two girls at a café near the Plaza de Cataluna, Patrick's first reaction to Lisa was one of complete astonishment. "Lisa! I would scarcely have known you."

"I can see I shall have to go back to my uninteresting dark hair and peaky little white face, or else my friends won't know me," Lisa returned with self-assurance.

Over the coffee and cognac Patrick asked questions and Lisa answered vaguely or parried his queries neatly with irrelevant remarks.

"And how did you enjoy your yachting holiday?" he asked Nicola.

"Fine. I liked San Fernando, too. The others aren't back yet. I flew home with Dr. Montal, because he had to start work again. He can be away for only a very limited time."

Patrick smiled. "Well, you did right to pick a job like that. Think of the perks!"

"I'm going on the next yachting trip," declared Lisa. "It'll just suit me."

"Shouldn't you wait until you're asked?" teased Patrick.

"Oh, never fear! Nicola wouldn't dare go without me. Would you, dear?"

"Since the yacht belongs to Ramon, I suppose he can ask whom he likes," Nicola said lightly.

On the way home to Orsola in the train, Lisa said idly, "Patrick finds you very attractive, doesn't he?"

"I just happen to be English—and someone to talk to," Nicola answered noncommittally.

Lisa shook her head. "Not so! I know that look in their eyes. You might do worse than marry him, Nicky. I think he has a reasonable job with prospects, and at least you'd be living in a lovely climate."

Nicola laughed. "Don't try to arrange my future for me. Or even Patrick's."

For a few days Lisa behaved very well indeed, amusing herself down on the shore swimming or sunbathing when Nicola was busy with Sebastian's secretarial work. Then the *Clorinda* returned with Ramon, Adrienne and Elena.

At first Adrienne was as cordial in her welcome as her uncle had been.

"Oh, it is so good that Nicola has found her sister." she said when she heard the news, and was introduced to Lisa.

Doña Elena was far more restrained.

"She looked at me," complained Lisa afterward, "as though I were a particularly nasty-smelling piece of fish."

"That's her usual manner," soothed Nicola. "She doesn't do it deliberately."

"I don't like her," said Lisa, and there was something ominous in her tone. "It's a blessing she doesn't live here."

"You may be wrong in that. Doña Elena has shut up her house nearby for a few weeks and she may stay here, so don't go out of your way to offend her. She and Adrienne don't hit it off very well together, so we don't want the house in an uproar." Nicola spoke firmly, knowing her sister's capacity for stirring up indignation and resentment between people who were antipathetic to each other.

But it was Nicola who first became indignant and Doña Elena who started the explosive series of situations that seemed to detonate each other.

"Is she in truth your sister?" Elena asked Nicola one evening. "You are not at all alike."

"It's not unusual for relations to be entirely opposite in looks," answered Nicola mildly.

"It was very clever of you to insert this girl into Dr.

Montal's house," continued Elena. "Naturally, by maintaining that you had lost touch with her, that she was missing and might be in deep trouble, you were assured that when the time was ready, you would have no difficulty in bringing her here for an indefinite stay."

"Is that how it appears to you, Doña Elena?" asked Nicola. "I assure you that my sister was really missing. In fact, she has been ill with loss of memory."

Elena gave an unbelieving smile. "That is always the excuse. Loss of memory. So easy. Who could prove otherwise?"

"I suppose Dr. Montal could tell whether Lisa were shamming or not?" Nicola said coldly.

"He would *know,* but he might not *tell* you. He would not want to hurt your feelings."

"I can always ask him to let me know the truth," retorted Nicola, "and hope that my feelings can stand it."

Elena shrugged her elegant shoulders. "Surely it would be better now that you two sisters are reunited if you found work where you could be together?"

"I am still employed by Dr. Montal," Nicola reminded her, but did not add that she was bound by her promise to stay a year. "My sister will certainly find work as soon as she has had a short rest."

"But then you will still be separated, and if your sister is not in good health, it is your duty to look after her."

Nicola realized that it was hopeless to try to argue with Elena. "I agree with part of what you say, Doña Elena, but in all matters I must take instructions from Dr. Montal."

Nicola thought with a certain touch of mild savagery that Elena would lose no time in pouring her troubles direct into Dr. Montal's ear.

A few days later Adrienne was at war with Lisa. It appeared from Adrienne's impassioned outburst that she had caught Lisa snooping around in the upstairs rooms of one wing of the Villa Ronda.

"She had no right to be there!" declared Adrienne hotly. "Those rooms belonged to my parents. My father wanted my mother's suite kept exactly as it was when she died.

When he went away, we also kept his rooms as they were. They are not for strangers to roam about.''

Nicola could well understand Adrienne's indignation. ''But how could Lisa get into that wing?''

''Naturally the rooms must be cleaned sometimes. Possibly Lisa followed one of the maids. I don't know. I went there myself because today is my father's birthday anniversary and I wanted to be in his room. Lisa was there, picking over the papers on his desk.''

''I'm very sorry,'' Nicola said quietly. ''I'll speak to Lisa about it and see that it never happens again.''

Adrienne, whose gray eyes were full of unshed tears, seemed pacified by Nicola's gentle understanding, but there were other bones of contention.

''Also I do not like the way she is always making journeys to the yacht to see Ramon. Almost every day she is down at the harbor signalling for the dinghy to fetch her.''

Nicola smiled. ''A yacht is rather a novelty to Lisa. It was to me. I'd never been aboard one like Ramon's before.''

''Then perhaps she can explore other yachts instead of the *Clorinda*.''

At this moment, with Adrienne in a state of furious excitability, Nicola was too tactful to say what she thought, but in her opinion it might benefit Adrienne if Lisa provided some real or imagined competition for Ramon.

Nicola again promised to do what she could to prevent Lisa from becoming too friendly with Ramon. There was no opportunity that day, for Lisa stayed out all day and telephoned that she would not be at the villa for dinner. In one way Nicola was only too glad of Lisa's absence, but she could not help worrying in case some new mischief were brewing.

Ramon was there at dinner, so obviously Lisa could not be in his company, but Nicola guessed that Lisa would not be spending the evening alone. Patrick, perhaps? Or the faithful spy, Ruben?

When Lisa appeared about midmorning the next day, Nicola knew that she had to move warily.

''Did you have a good time yesterday?'' she asked.

Lisa, still looking sleepy, nodded.

"You must have come home pretty late," continued Nicola. "I wasn't in bed until after one and I didn't hear you come in."

"Does it matter what time I come in? This place is like a rest home for old ladies. I must have some gaiety and fun somewhere."

"All right. As long as you remember that the villa is not a hotel with a night porter. Someone has to get up and let you in."

"That's what they're paid for, isn't it?" said Lisa sulkily.

Obviously this was not the moment to reproach Lisa with causing upsets in the Montal household. Nicola thought it wiser to choose a more propitious moment. The delay did not help for when the mail was delivered just before midday as it usually was, Nicola took Sebastian's letters to his study, opened the circulars and then glanced at several letters addressed to herself.

She turned the envelopes over. "Señorita Brettell, Villa Ronda . . . ." She had given her address to so few people. Perhaps these were for Lisa.

She opened them. Bills for dresses, coats, shoes, all from expensive shops.

Nicola raged, fury in her heart. No wonder Lisa had been so modest in her initial demands on Nicola's purse! She had now gone in for a real shopping spree.

With the bills in her hand, Nicola rushed out to the patio where she had left Lisa, but her sister had disappeared. Lisa was not in her room and Nicola snatched open the wardrobe door. Half a dozen new dresses and two coats hung there. A pile of cardboard boxes and tissue paper had been tidied into one corner by the maid who attended to Lisa's room.

"Did the young Señorita Brettell say where she was going?" Nicola asked several of the staff. No one had seen her.

Nicola spent a little time searching the gardens, but there was no sign of Lisa. Adrienne was on the Mediterranean balcony with the binoculars glued to her eyes.

"I suppose you haven't seen my sister, Lisa?" Nicola inquired as calmly as she could.

"I'm looking for her!" snapped Adrienne wrathfully. "If I see her step on the *Clorinda,* I will go down and wait for her and then I will throw her into the harbor. I hope she cannot swim!"

Nicola controlled her smiles. "Luckily—or unluckily— she's a very good swimmer."

By lunchtime, Adrienne, too, had disappeared. Whether she was bent on throwing Lisa into the harbor Nicola did not know, but Nicola was relieved to lunch alone and be spared the necessity of making normal conversation. She could only pick over the food, anyway, for anger and worry robbed her of appetite. She was too keyed up to bother about a siesta and worked on Sebastian's book all afternoon.

Lisa did not put in an appearance until almost dinner-time and then Nicola had no opportunity of a private talk. Lisa was wearing a gold-lamé dress, her hair was newly set and long pendant earrings added a sparkle.

As soon as the meal was over, Lisa excused herself. Nicola rose, too, determined not to let Lisa escape so easily. She murmured her excuses to Sebastian and caught Adrienne's inquiring gaze. But there was more to discuss with Lisa than snooping in private rooms or trying to flirt with Ramon.

Nicola hurried after her sister. "Lisa! I want to talk to you for a few moments."

"Not now, please. I have an appointment." Lisa gave her sister a disarming smile.

"Your appointment can wait! I expect he will," Nicola added. "We'll go to your room."

"As bad as that? You're going to shout at me and you don't want half the servants to hear you. They might be surprised."

At the foot of the staircase Lisa turned, for once irresolute and half inclined to make a dash for it and get away from Nicola's scoldings, but Nicola's determined face decided against that.

"I can give you only two or three minutes, Nicky," she said, mounting the stairs. "I have to get a stole and then I'm off."

In Lisa's bedroom, Nicola shut the door and stood with

her back against it. Lisa began to dab her nose with powder, touch up her lipstick.

"Today I had a new batch of bills sent to me," Nicola announced.

"Oh, yes?"

"Bills for the dresses and coats in that wardrobe. Your bills, Lisa. I hope you're going to pay them."

"Give me a chance! I haven't said I'm not going to pay them."

"I haven't finished paying off the other lot," Nicola said harshly. "D'you think you're going to saddle me with this new collection?"

Lisa turned from the dressing-table mirror. "What are you making a fuss about? Nobody's asked you to pay them yet."

"Then why didn't you have the bills addressed to yourself? You were careful not to give your own name or initial, so that you knew I'd open them."

"Well, I must have clothes. It may not be as important for you. After all, you don't have much chance to wear them here in this quiet little place. Besides, you're only here as a secretary-companion, if that's the correct style, and it would be out of place for you to wear fashionable or impressive models."

Nicola stared disbelievingly at her sister. "And you? What are you in this house?"

"A guest, of course. I have far more freedom of action than you, my dear Nicola."

"Including freedom to spend my money? D'you realize that all the time I've been working for Dr. Montal a large part of my salary has had to be set aside to clear your debts?"

"I didn't ask you to pay them, and I told you before, you were a fool. Anyway, you really enjoy being a martyr, don't you?"

"Not enough to go on propping you up, Lisa, all your life. Some of these clothes you haven't worn. You can have them packed up and sent back to the shops."

"I'll do no such thing. D'you mean to tell me that you can't get plenty of money out of your dear doctor?"

"I haven't tried," retorted Nicola. "There are other matters, too."

"Oh, spare me the reproaches!" cried Lisa. "I'm late already."

"If you consider yourself a guest in this house, then try to remember that you shouldn't intrude into rooms where you're not invited. Adrienne was most upset at the idea of your prying into her father's study."

"How was I to know? The door was open."

Nicola was about to mention Ramon, but reflected that Lisa would deliberately tease and taunt Adrienne if given the slightest chance. She would take every opportunity to flirt with him, even though it was all part of a game to Lisa.

Lisa now draped a chiffon stole around her shoulders and approached the door.

"Nicky, will you please move out of the way? My date may already have decided that I'm not coming."

"That would be a pity." Nicola could not keep the sarcasm out of her voice.

"Don't let yourself become bitter because a man let you down once and now you're getting older all the time and have to watch younger girls attracting the men."

Nicola stood away from the door. "I'm not bitter, Lisa, but if I have different ideas I'm entitled to them. Go out and enjoy yourself. Is it Patrick? Or Ruben?"

"You mustn't be inquisitive. It might be someone you don't know. It could even be Ramon."

With a triumphant smile Lisa fled through the door, leaving Nicola churned up, her emotions so disturbed that she flung herself on Lisa's bed and wept for sheer relief from the unbearable tension of the last few minutes. After a while she became calmer, but still determined to teach Lisa a sharp lesson. She went to her own room, brought back bills that had come this morning and compared the items with the clothes in the wardrobe, the drawers and shoe racks. Fortunately, some had not yet been worn.

She called Iñez, Adrienne's personal maid, and instructed her to pack some of the garments very carefully into their respective boxes. She would have preferred to do the task herself, but Iñez had the professional touch. Nicola took the boxes to her room and next morning despatched them to the shops from which the articles had come.

When Nicola entered Sebastian's study after breakfast, Lisa was there, apparently ransacking the doctor's desk. Papers and notebooks were strewn everywhere.

"What d'you think you're doing?" demanded Nicola.

"Looking for those bills," snapped Lisa. "How dare you send back clothes I've bought!"

"Not bought *yet!*" Nicola reminded her. "And how dare you ransack among the doctor's papers!"

Lisa whirled around on her sister. "You're a fine one to talk of ransacking and snooping! I wonder you left me anything to stand up in."

"I couldn't return clothes that had been worn. The others you can do without until you're in a position to pay for what you want."

"Or find someone else to pay the bills for me!" retorted Lisa.

"If you want the rest of the bills, here they are!" Nicola tossed them across to Lisa. "Now perhaps you will kindly replace everything in the doctor's desk."

Nicola's gaze was riveted on the framed photograph that Lisa held in her hand. Nicola had seen it once before when Sebastian lay sprawled across the desk, clutching this photograph of a woman.

"Give me that portrait," she said.

Lisa glanced down at the photograph. Then she laughed. "Oh, so he keeps secret portraits in his desk! Is this the love of his life?"

Nicola snatched the frame from Lisa's hands. Then she became aware that Sebastian was in the room.

"Were you looking for something?" he asked in icy tones.

Nicola realized that she was still holding the photograph. In silence she replaced it in the drawer and began to gather the scattered papers from the top of the desk.

"I can explain," she began hesitantly.

"I am waiting," was his grim answer.

She noticed that Lisa was no longer in the room.

"My sister—" she stopped, knowing that every word of

plausible explanation would implicate Lisa. "Lisa," she began again, "mistakenly thought some papers were in your desk instead of mine. She was looking for them."

"And her habit is to toss everything out, including personal articles?" he queried.

"I apologize sincerely—for both of us. It was unforgivable."

"I would prefer the whole truth, Nicola. Tell me what your sister was looking for."

"These." Nicola pointed to the bills that Lisa had left on the desk.

He turned them over casually. "Yours?"

Nicola did not know what to answer. If they were for goods she had purchased, why the uproar? If they were on Lisa's behalf, why had Nicola taken them?

He construed her silence in a way she had not imagined.

"I'm beginning to see," he said at last. "When I gave you this post—if you could call it that—I believed you were genuinely distressed by the disappearance of your sister and by the fact that you needed to support yourself while you could continue to look for her. I made the condition that you should stay here a year, thinking that it provided you with a certain security."

"And I was very grateful to you," she said quickly.

"I can appreciate that," he snapped. "What I did not realize was that while you pretended that Lisa was missing, you knew perfectly well where she was and what had happened."

"Oh, no!" she exclaimed, aghast at this accusation.

"Financially I tried to treat you generously. I had no idea that I was also helping to support your sister. Oh, I know what you can say," he waved away her intended interruption. "You were at liberty to spend your salary exactly as you pleased. It isn't money, Nicola. It's the false pretenses, the gross deception that I find so distasteful."

"Sebastian, I assure you that—" she stopped, horrified because she had unwittingly addressed him by his Christian name. He appeared not to have noticed and she found the courage to continue. "When Lisa was found it was a complete surprise to me."

"You expect me to believe that? Every time it was suggested that you should contact the police or the Consul, you refused."

Nicola saw now that her diffidence in trying to protect Lisa had only blackened her own case.

"You allowed me to waste my time looking in hospitals and elsewhere when you knew positively that I would never find her," he stormed.

"I can only repeat that I'm sorry."

"Your sister boasted that she knew all your movements both here and in San Fernando. How can I believe that you were so much in the dark?"

Further explanations were useless, she thought. The way out of her present dilemma was clear. "Dr. Montal, the best thing is for me to leave your employ as soon as possible. Naturally, I shall take my sister with me, so you'll be rid of us both."

He had been standing at his desk, looming over her as she remained opposite. Now he strode menacingly toward her, put his hands on her shoulders and forced her into the chair behind her.

"No, indeed, Nicola. The solution is not as easy as that. My book is not yet complete, as you know. I've no intention of having it left unfinished because you choose to go. I will not hold you to your promise to stay a year, but in one month's time we will discuss the situation together. If the book is finished and you want to go, then we'll see what can be arranged."

She nodded agreement, sick at heart with the way things had turned out. So now she was virtually on a month's trial, in effect a month of forced labor, for at the end he would tell her that she was free to go and she would have no excuse to stay.

He went out of the study into the garden and Nicola took the opportunity to rush away to her own room. She did not feel up to facing anyone at this moment. But even the privacy of her room was no solace, for the first thing that met her gaze was the green glass vase from San Fernando. It lay on the carpet smashed into pieces.

How had that happened? No one came into the room

except the maid, unless—but Nicola would not allow herself even to imagine that Lisa would deliberately come here and smash an ornament.

Ironically, Nicola reflected that perhaps it was appropriate that the only article Sebastian had ever given her should now lie in fragments on the floor. His faith in her integrity had been equally shattered, even though he had chosen to believe his own logic rather than the truth.

Later in the day Lisa apologized to Nicola.

"That green ornament or vase in your room—it was an accident. I'm afraid I carelessly knocked it off the table."

"It doesn't matter," muttered Nicola, thankful that Lisa had not tried to put the blame onto one of the maids.

"Was it a valuable piece?" asked Lisa.

"No, not particularly valuable. Just treasured. It was given to me when we went to the glassworks in San Fernando."

"I see. Sebastian bought it for you?"

Nicola should have known that Lisa was unusually quick witted and always saw through with percipience the gaps in other people's conversations. She drew more satisfying conclusions from silences or vague phrases than from what was actually said.

"I hope you haven't become enamored of the good doctor, Nicky, when you're aware of his attachment."

"Oh, for heaven's sake be quiet, Lisa!" Nicola was at the end of her tether. "Listen, for once, to the real truth. Dr. Montal is so disgusted with the pair of us that he's given me the sack. I have the equivalent of a month's notice."

"You mean he's given you your salary and told you to go?"

Nicola thought wearily how often Lisa's first reaction was concerned with money.

"I don't mean that. I'm working to finish the book for him. So you'd better start looking for some sort of job, Lisa."

"I daresay I can find something. I've done it before. I can do it again."

"Then you'd better find it fast," urged Nicola.

"What's the hurry?" queried Lisa.

"Surely you don't imagine you can stay on here at the Villa Ronda when I've gone?"

Lisa stretched her pretty arms high above her head. "I suppose the kind doctor could throw me out through the villa gates and my pitifully few belongings after me. More than that, I can't see what he could do."

"Don't be ridiculous, Lisa. Don't make more difficulties than we already have to cope with. I'm already blamed for knowing that your so-called disappearance was a put-up job between us."

"Oh? That's too bad of Sebastian."

Nicola walked away a few steps. She was tired of Lisa's lighthearted acceptance of ease and comfort and that facile way of shifting all the troublesome situations onto someone else's shoulders.

"When I leave here, Lisa," Nicola said quietly, "you'll have to fend for yourself. I've been too willing and ready to help you out of all the scrapes, mostly money troubles. In future you'll have to extricate yourself."

"Soft living has made you hard toward others less fortunate," grumbled Lisa.

"You've benefited from my soft living," retorted Nicola.

She went to the swimming pool in the garden, changed into her white swimsuit and splashed around in the water. She had forgotten to bring a cap with her and her hair clung to her scalp. She floated on her back, staring up at the clear sapphire sky, the tips of dark cypresses and let the gently pulsing water soothe her irritations of the day.

A loud splash behind her made her turn sharply and she saw Sebastian's dark head emerge a few yards away. At once she flushed with embarrassment. It was a curious situation to be the target of his rebukes a few hours ago and now find herself sharing the intimacy of his swimming pool.

He trod water, his bare tanned shoulders glistening in the sun with crystal drops.

"Best part of the day," he called, making casual conversation as though this morning's outburst had never occurred. Nicola realized that only the fact that this had been the day when he stayed home had caused such an explosion. If he had gone to the hospital or been at his clinic, he would

never have witnessed that scene between her and her sister.
She clambered over the side of the pool and sat for a few
moments to let the water drain off her.

He passed her with strong overarm strokes, then turned
to gaze at her.

"You look like a mermaid," he said. Was it illusion or
was there a warm, tender expression in his dark eyes?
Nicola tried not to read too much into a fleeting glance, but
she could not help hoping that he was trying to soften his
hard attitude of this morning. At least he had known she
was in the pool when he arrived. He could easily have
withdrawn if he did not want to see her.

Then Doña Elena appeared wearing a beach coat over her
swimsuit. She greeted Sebastian, ignored Nicola and
plunged into the water more like a mermaid than Nicola
could ever hope to be.

Of course it was clear now. Sebastian had been waiting
for Elena to join him. Finding Nicola in the pool was
merely an accident, irritating perhaps but unavoidable
when the pool was there for anyone's use.

Nicola toweled herself, then with a wave went to the
changing cubicle, dressed as fast as she could and left
Sebastian and Elena together, as no doubt had been their
intention.

CHAPTER NINE

NICOLA WORKED hard at her part of the bargain during the month that had been agreed on between her and Sebastian, and was only held back from finishing the doctor's lengthy book by his revisions and additional chapters. It would have been flattering to pretend that he was reluctant to part with her or even her services, but with Doña Elena constantly in and out of the villa, although she had recalled her staff and opened her house farther up the hill, Nicola did not delude herself.

Lisa went out every day on some mysterious business of her own, sometimes dropping a casual remark that she was well on the way to getting herself a delightful job. Nicola worried about what kind of job it would turn out to be, but knew that if Lisa was not in the mood to answer questions there would be no information forthcoming.

A certain coolness seemed to have sprung up again between Ramon and Adrienne, and while he spent a lot of time on the yacht, Adrienne either painted or drove about the countryside in her own white car. Sometimes Nicola accompanied her on these jaunts, and secretly wished that Adrienne would not drive quite so fast, especially around blind corners and along twisting roads.

Nicola noticed how the long summer had already changed the colors of the landscape. The almond trees bordering the roads had lost their fresh green look and become dusty. Soon the pickers would come for the harvest, shaking down the nuts into large sheets spread below. In the villages the walls of houses were decorated with brilliant scarlet banners of pimentos hung from the windows to dry in the sun.

"When will your sister leave us?" Adrienne asked one day when the two girls were driving to a small seaside place farther up the coast.

"Soon, I think," returned Nicola. "She speaks of a job she has in mind."

"Soon, I *hope*!" retorted Adrienne, unconsciously putting her foot down on the accelerator and narrowly missing a donkey laden with pottery.

"Careful!" exclaimed Nicola.

Adrienne stopped the car. It was impossible to turn in the narrow road, but she began to reverse. The irate donkey owner was gesticulating and shouting.

"It is lucky that you possibly do not understand all he is saying," commented Adrienne, as she alighted and walked toward the man.

Nicola, sensing the curses and imprecations, could well imagine, but Adrienne's smile—and no doubt honeyed words—soothed him at once. He became all smiles and courteous bows as he displayed his wares. Nicola understood at once that Adrienne was about to purchase some small article as a peace offering. Nicola stepped out of the car and joined Adrienne.

"We must buy each other small presents," said Adrienne. "What would you like?"

Nicola had long been meaning to buy as a souvenir a small reproduction of the terra-cotta jugs commonly used everywhere in Spain for fetching water from wells or street fountains.

She chose one about nine inches high, faithfully made in all its details, the spout on the side, with a knob opposite for balance, and the curved top with its small pinhole.

"A mini jug," said Nicola. "And what would you like, Adrienne?"

This, of course, was coals to Newcastle, but Adrienne with innate courtesy considered the pots and baskets, the sacred pictures, and finally chose a small glazed bowl with a bird's beak for a spout and a curving tail for a handle.

"It is a piece I can use for still-life painting," she said. "A million thanks."

The picturesque hawker in his long, baggy red and black striped trousers, black waistcoat and wide-brimmed hat was determined to give good measure for custom and now took out his bagpipes decorated with red and white ribbons and wheezed out an air unrecognizable to Nicola's ears, but intended as a token of cordiality all the same. Eventually, with the exchange of many salutations and gracious bows, the two girls returned to the car.

In resuming the journey, Adrienne also continued the conversation. "I am sorry, but I cannot like Lisa. It is a pity that she had to be found. Oh, I do not wish to hurt you, Nicola, and it is very ill-bred of me to tell you, but she is not a good sister for you. She is a bad influence."

Nicola tried to smile. "I don't think she will influence me in wrong directions."

"That is just what she can do," declared Adrienne firmly. "She is selfish and is only anxious to have everything she wants. She is what I think you call a gold digger."

Nicola remained silent for a few moments, searching for words that were noncommittal. Finally she said, "Lisa hasn't always been very lucky. Things don't always come right for her."

"Why should she expect it?" queried Adrienne. "All of us must suffer sometimes."

Nicola knew that this was a dangerous discussion, especially when Adrienne continued, "She is too eager for men with money."

Nicola laughed. "Aren't we all?"

"No, I think you're different. The kind of man is more important to you than money."

Nicola reflected ruefully that it would not have mattered if it were Sebastian himself or his position that appealed to her. The result was the same.

ONE DAY Nicola made a strange discovery. She was in the salon of the Villa Ronda gazing idly at the portraits of former members of the Montal family. Most of the men looked as though they had stepped out of Velasquez groups, but the women were more like Goyas. Sebastian's portrait, painted by Adrienne and exhibited, hung at the far end next to one that seemed a slightly older edition of him. Would that be his elder brother, Eduardo? Nicola wondered.

Then she saw the portrait of the woman whose photograph Sebastian kept in his desk. Young, very beautiful, delicate features but not the Spanish type, her eyes brilliantly blue.

Adrienne said quietly, "That was my mother."

Nicola spun around. She bit back an exclamation of surprise and controlled herself to say, "What a beautiful woman!" She glanced at Adrienne. "You are almost exactly like her, except that your eyes are gray."

"And that is my father next to Sebastian," Adrienne pointed out. "Oh, I wonder if he will ever come back! Sebastian really believes that he is dead, but I am sure he is alive."

Nicola reflected that the Villa Ronda household had its full share of the anxiety caused by a missing member. Sebastian and Adrienne both knew the desolation of the long silence just as she, Nicola, had longed to hear even the smallest wisp of news about Lisa.

Possibly Sebastian had taken more trouble to search for Lisa because he sympathized with Nicola's similar position.

A perplexing thought niggled at the back of Nicola's mind. Why did Sebastian keep the photograph of Adrienne's mother in his desk? Why couldn't it be displayed openly on the top? Why didn't it belong in Eduardo's rooms? But then Nicola had no means of knowing what portraits or photographs were still in the elder brother's suite.

When she had free time Nicola painted local scenes while Adrienne helped and criticized her efforts.

"You must make the contrasts sharper," advised Adrienne, "or it does not look like our country, all sunshine and shadow."

"Yes, I'm more used to our own English gray greens."

One afternoon Nicola was painting in the patio of the villa. Her picture represented the arched entrance flanked by palms and one giant cactus that had suddenly burst into flower, scarlet and salmon-pink tassels hanging from the dark menacing leaves with their serrated edges.

Sebastian's car drove up, but Ignacio took it out of the way as soon as he could, and Sebastian came toward Nicola where she stood at her easel, protected by a large umbrella.

"I gather you don't want my car spoiling your picture," he said, gazing critically at her half-finished effort. "It's coming quite well," he continued, after a pause. "But you must put more yellow with the white. Just a touch, then it will dazzle much more than pure white."

"Yes, I see."

"I notice you have learnt the lesson I gave you about the shadow revealing what is underneath."

"I've tried to remember," she answered smoothly. He had taught her more lessons than how to paint shadowed brickwork. Some of those lessons had been painfully sharp.

"I cannot remember if anyone has ever painted the entrance to our villa before. What are you going to do with the picture?"

"Take it home with me, I expect, as a souvenir." She controlled her shaky embarrassment by searching for a tube of cadmium yellow.

"You've decided, then, to return to England?" he asked.

"It's probably the best thing I can do," she muttered, hoping that he would go away and leave her alone.

"When you've finished it, would you give me the picture, Nicola?"

She raised a startled face. "It won't be good enough. It's only a daub. I—I don't know enough about the technique."

"Let me be the judge of that." His smile was warm, with just a hint of amusement in his eyes.

When he had walked away, Nicola stared first after him, then at the painting, which would never be a success now, for he had made her nervous and inhibited. Still, it was something that he took any interest at all in what she did or what her future plans were.

Lisa did not return to the villa that night, but since she often came in long after midnight, Nicola did not know of her sister's absence until next morning. This time, however, Lisa lost no time in informing Nicola. A letter came at midday and the brief note explained that Lisa had gone on a short cruise somewhere in the Mediterranean.

> A yachting holiday appeals to me. Don't worry. Love, Lisa.

Nicola's first alarming thought was that Lisa had gone off with Ramon in the *Clorinda*, but a reassuring glance through Adrienne's binoculars verified that the *Clorinda* was still in harbor. As Ramon eventually arrived in the evening, it was evident that Lisa's yachtsman was someone else.

"I am delighted to hear that she has gone for a holiday," was Adrienne's frank reaction to the news of Lisa's absence.

Ramon began to chuckle and his dark eyes glinted with fun. He broke into hilarious laughter.

"Ah, the American has been trapped!" he managed to say at last.

"What American?" asked Nicola.

"There were many days when Lisa came to the harbor and signaled for my dinghy. When she came aboard the *Clorinda* I could not get rid of her."

"Did you try very hard? Or was it too difficult?" queried Adrienne acidly.

Ramon gave Adrienne a teasing glance. "Sometimes both," he declared, leaving the girl to make what she could of that answer. "But one day the American was on my boat and Lisa asked me many questions about him. She could see that his yacht was larger than mine, and no doubt his house in Florida, his apartment in New York, his ranch in Arizona are all most luxurious."

Nicola was uncertain whether Ramon knew these facts or had invented them to rid himself of Lisa's pestering.

"That was clever of you, *querido*," commented Adrienne.

It was the first time that Nicola had heard the girl call Ramon *querido*, although he often used the "darling" endearment to her.

Perhaps Lisa's intrusion had not been entirely in vain after all. If she had supplied the catalyst to spark off Adrienne's dormant jealousy and succeeded in awakening her love for Ramon, then Lisa had unwittingly contrived more good than harm.

Nicola excused herself and left Adrienne and Ramon to their own confidences. She was slightly uneasy as to the outcome of Lisa's new venture. Was this to be another Tony affair with nothing to show at the end except disappointment and a handful of unpaid bills?

When Nicola told one of the maids that her sister would not be at the villa for the next few days, it occurred to her to find out if Lisa had taken most of her personal belongings with her. The wardrobe was entirely empty, the drawers likewise. Not even an odd nylon stocking remained. Her brushes and cosmetic bottles were cleared from the dressing table, but in one of the compartments a small object was wrapped in an envelope. Inside was the topaz brooch that Nicola had found in the apartment occupied by Lisa on the Paseo Maritimo in Barcelona, the only evidence that Lisa had really stayed there.

Nicola had returned it to her sister soon after the latter had come to the Villa Ronda.

There was a screw of paper.

—You can have this, Nicola. Diamonds are more in my line.

Nicola stood there with the little brooch in her hand. So Lisa had been steadily and stealthily transferring her possessions elsewhere. No doubt this was the job, the professional assignment that Lisa had meant when she spoke of her efforts to make a livelihood.

Nicola turned the scrap of paper and found a few words on the other side.

I'm sorry about the green vase. I did smash it deliberately because I was so angry with you, but I'll make amends some day with a piece of real jade.

Nicola hurried from the room, unable to contain her grief mixed with contempt, her resentment mingled with pity. Lisa's ruthlessness might not eventually bring her the rewards she so longed for, yet Nicola could only hope that her restless, covetous sister would ultimately succeed in her ambitions.

Patrick had evidently heard vaguely of Lisa's new hopes, for when Nicola met him at the Café Zurich, he sighed his relief.

"This tycoon that she's picked up through Ramon is probably the best thing that ever happened to her," he said. "Also, she told me that having such a good address as the Villa Ronda and being a guest of the Montals was a great help." Patrick gave her a quizzical glance. "You don't seem to have made the most of your opportunities, Nicola."

"Perhaps I don't see the same things as opportunities," she replied. She had already decided when this meeting with Patrick was arranged that she would tell him of her impending return to England.

He seemed astounded. "But why on earth should you throw away the good life like that? What are you afraid of?"

"Nothing."

"D'you think Lisa will saddle you with another load of bills? Is that why you think it might be safer to be in England?"

Nicola smiled. "The thought may have crossed my mind."

"Oh, don't meet troubles more than halfway," he said impatiently. "What does the doctor think of your backing out of your year's contract like this?"

"The contract is being broken mutually," she said. "Probably Lisa didn't tell you this, but she ordered a lot of clothes, no doubt to impress the American yacht owner, but she sent the bills to me. I managed to return some of the articles, but the others I've paid for."

"All right, then, so you've nothing to fear."

"No, it wasn't all right. Lisa made a scene in the doctor's study, he came in, thought the bills were mine and that we'd both been having a high old time on the generous salary he paid me. He still believes that I knew where Lisa was all the time and that as far as I'm concerned she wasn't missing at all."

"I see," said Patrick thoughtfully. "So you've both decided to end the contract. That doesn't grieve me, but you're a fool not to stay here. A reference from him and you'd get a job anywhere."

"Possibly." Nicola looked into space.

"Then why go?"

"Maybe there's nothing to keep me in Spain."

"Nothing? Don't I count?" he demanded hotly.

"Well, yes. I've enjoyed your company. I always do. But you'll be going home soon."

"I'm not so sure. The firm I work for has offered to renew my contract on better terms."

"Good," she commented. "Then you'll be able to marry Maureen and bring her here."

He shook his head. "You haven't got the situation really weighed up properly. Maureen would never leave her family to come and live in a foreign country."

Nicola's eyes opened wide. "Foreign? But Spain is a charming country. Its very foreignness is part of its attraction. Besides, you can fly to England in two or three hours. Distance doesn't count so much nowadays."

"I know. We've been over all this scores of times, Maureen and I. But she's a girl who's used to visiting her relatives frequently. She has a couple of married sisters, one brother, a dozen aunts and uncles, apart from a sort of pattern of friends in the neighborhood."

"But she'd soon make friends here. Even in your firm there are a lot of English people."

Patrick frowned. "That would make no difference. Every time a problem or small difficulty arose, Maureen would want to go to her mother for advice and bypass me."

Nicola was silent. She understood from her own experience how many girls were reluctant to loosen the bonds between mother and daughter. But was Patrick telling her this to strengthen his own case for not returning to England?

He leaned back in his chair and smiled at her, a slow, quiet smile that said more than words. "Oh, well, let me know when you leave and we'll have a farewell dinner the night before. Unless, of course, you change your mind. You can always stay—and marry me.''

Nicola smiled in return. "No, Patrick. You know how I feel about that.''

He suddenly leaned toward her. "But what good reason can you give me? You like me, don't you?''

"Yes, but I don't love you.''

Nicola said the words lightly, for she felt that Patrick was not entirely seriously inclined. There was a mutual attraction between them, and had they met elsewhere, in England, say, at the local tennis club or a dance, they might easily have found more than mere companionship. But Nicola had irrevocably given her heart to Sebastian, and there was nothing to do but put a thousand miles between her and the doctor.

CHAPTER TEN

THE LAST FEW DAYS of Nicola's final month at the Villa Ronda became sultry and oppressive with heat. Everyone went around sighing and muttering that thunder was on the way, but no storm came.

Suddenly, with the impact of an emotional thunderclap, Adrienne's father, Eduardo, returned from his long exile in South America.

Nicola was in Sebastian's study when she was conscious of someone standing by the arched window. At first she thought it was Sebastian returning early from his clinic.

"*Buenas tardes, señorita.*" The man's voice sounded much older than Sebastian's.

"*Buenas tardes, señor,*" she returned, standing up ready to find out what he wanted. It was unusual for strangers to approach the villa through Sebastian's study windows. Then she saw the likeness. "Señor Montal?"

He nodded and asked in Spanish where his brother Sebastian could be found.

"*No aquí,*" she replied. "Not here. At the clinic."

She pulled out a chair for him, for he looked tired, his face was gray with fatigue; his almost white hair prematurely aged him so that he looked more like Sebastian's father than brother.

Nicola rang the bell and immediately a maid appeared. Nicola told her to fetch Rosana, the elderly housekeeper. She would certainly know what to do.

"Adrienne is out somewhere," Nicola told Don Eduardo, "but she will return to lunch."

Rosana came bustling in, her arms outstretched. She ran

to Eduardo, folded him in her arms and crooned broken phrases as though he were a child lost and now found again.

After that, pandemonium raged through the villa. Maids were sent scurrying around like feathers out of a ripped bolster. Menservants brought wine, dozens of bottles for Eduardo to make a choice. Food was set before him, with Rosana sitting beside him to tempt him to this morsel or that. Telephone calls were made to every possible place where Adrienne might be and to the clinic where Sebastian could not leave his patients unattended.

Nicola effaced herself again in the study. This was a family matter in which she had no part, yet she was delighted for Adrienne's sake that the girl's father had returned.

Adrienne did not return until early evening, and as Nicola saw her come across the patio, she ran out to warn her.

"My father? Oh, what happiness!" she exclaimed, rushing indoors, seeking Eduardo.

Dinner was a reunion at which Nicola felt she had no right to be present. Father and daughter smiled and gazed at each other, Doña Elena and Ramon had been hurriedly invited, Sebastian quietly surveyed the others. Was it Nicola's fancy that he was less cordial in his welcome to his brother, or was it merely that he was less demonstrative of his emotions?

"My faith was justified!" cried Adrienne excitedly. "I knew you could not be lost in the jungle."

"No, I was never lost."

"But you never communicated with us for more than two years," Sebastian pointed out.

Eduardo shrugged his frail shoulders. "It was difficult. I was in a remote village on a river bank. I set up my headquarters there and treated the Indians as well as I could in a simple way."

"But your supplies must have come to you," Doña Elena said. "Could you not have had your letters also sent out?"

"Oh, I did, but pieces of paper with words written on them do not seem important to such practical tribes. What supplies I could get from the nearest settlement I had to sketch, to indicate what part of the body they were for.''

Eduardo retired to his room immediately after dinner and Adrienne accompanied him, for she needed to talk with him.

Nicola again decided that she was *de trop* in this family celebration and went to the balcony of her room. A few more days and then she would never again see the gardens, the patios, the innumerable curves and arches and red-tiled roofs of the Villa Ronda.

Tonight the sky seemed dark and opaque with few stars and the trees were motionless. Somewhere below voices floated up.

''. . . . That was why Eduardo stayed away so long.'' Doña Elena was speaking in Spanish, but Nicola understood.

The listener replied, and now Nicola caught the tones of Ramon's voice. He and his sister were discussing Eduardo. Nicola could not avoid hearing fragments and isolated words that she could translate, '' . . . forgiveness . . . Sebastian . . . Héloise . . . .''

Surely Héloise was the name of Adrienne's French mother? Or had Nicola heard some other word that sounded like the name?

Next day Nicola made a sudden decision to leave quickly, without fuss or farewell. Sebastian's book was completely finished. She had fulfilled that part of the contract.

Ramon and Adrienne were now on the best of terms and ready to announce their betrothal. As Adrienne had confided to Nicola only a day or two previously, ''Your sister, Lisa, made me so furious about Ramon that I found I did not want her—or anyone else—to put hooks into him.''

''Poor Ramon! You make him sound like a fish that you want to land.''

''Well, Ramon is *my* fish!'' Adrienne declared possessively. ''We will be most happy. We love each other.''

The entire household was so involved with Eduardo that Nicola's departure would never be noticed. She would leave letters for Sebastian and Adrienne, explaining her action in going away a couple of days before the due date.

She would have to wait until after dinner before she could

slip away unobserved, and during the day she packed her suitcase. She included the terra-cotta water jug that Adrienne had given her and hesitated over the few pictures she had painted. The only one she wanted to take home with her was that of the villa, and Sebastian had asked for that. She propped the canvas on her dressing table and set the note for Sebastian by the side. It was not a very good picture, she thought critically, and probably later on he would laugh at it. The paint was not dry, anyway, and would only smudge.

After dinner, she managed to slip out of the villa gates and hoped no car would reveal her in its headlights. Suddenly, as she was halfway down the hill toward the village and the station, rain which had been threatening all day now began to fall in great drops, then in a curtain of such tropical intensity that Nicola was taken by surprise. Her thin nylon raincoat which she had brought from England and never worn while she was here was now in the bottom of her suitcase, and she was already soaked to the skin before she could even begin to unlock the case.

Lightning illuminated the road in a blinding mauve flash and thunder roared overhead. A figure bent almost double hurried past her as Nicola cowered against the wall of a house.

A voice shouted "*Venga aqui!*" and in the next lightning flash she saw someone beckoning her toward a house a few yards away. Nicola ran, glad of any shelter. *Downpours as violent as this never lasted long*, she thought.

The woman pulled Nicola into the house and banged the door shut, standing against it for a moment to get her breath back. In the dim light of a lamp, Nicola now saw that the girl was Micaela, Barto's sister.

Barto's mother, Señora Gallito, rose to help Nicola out of her soaked clothes, talking rapidly about the bad storm. Nicola gathered that Micaela had been down to the harbor to try to persuade Barto not to go out this evening with the fishing fleet, but he was obstinate and had gone.

Micaela gave Nicola a cup of hot soup and, glancing at the suitcase, asked if Nicola was leaving Orsola. When Nicola nodded, the girl asked why not by automobile.

Nicola answered vaguely that she had not wanted to bother anyone at the villa to take her down to the station.

"But there are no trains!" exclaimed Micaela in Spanish. "The last one goes at twenty hours."

Nicola mentally kicked herself for not finding this out sooner. Eight o'clock. The train had already gone before dinner at the Villa Ronda.

She had made the best of a bad job. "Perhaps when the rain stops, I can go to the station and wait until morning."

A glance passed between Micaela and her mother. "You must stay here," said Señora Gallito. "The storm will last a long time."

The two women made up a bed for Nicola and Micaela promised to wake her very early in the morning for the first train, but there was no sleep for anyone in the house.

Thunder shook the walls and the noise of heavy rain was like a waterfall. All the windows were shuttered and Nicola could see nothing, but she could hear the constant drumming on the roof. She was glad when at last, after only the most fitful dozing, she could see daylight through a chink in the shutters.

Micaela brought her hot coffee and rolls and explained that Nicola's clothes were not yet dry.

"*No importa,*" replied Nicola. She added that she could find dry clothes in her suitcase. She wondered how she could repay the Gallitos' hospitality and decided to leave a little money in an unobtrusive place where they would find it after she had left.

When Nicola said her thanks and goodbyes and stepped out of the door she was amazed at the scene. The road was still awash although the rain had stopped, the sun shone as though there had never been a storm. But boulders and stones had been washed down by the torrent and Nicola found it difficult to thread her way through the debris.

Micaela caught up to her, saying that she had to go to the harbor and wait for the boats to come in. Nicola guessed how anxious the girl was about her brother, Barto.

At the foot of the hill where the road led into the village the devastation was something that Nicola had only read

about or seen on newsreels. The harbor was dotted with
wrecked or capsized boats, the railway line was completely
submerged and down the wide *rambla*, normally a dusty
street, the river had returned to its old bed and was coursing
down lapping against the walls of shops and houses. Tree
trunks and boulders had acted as battering rams and
destroyed the footbridge over the lower end of the *rambla*.

Nicola and Micaela stared at the damaged village, then at
each other.

"There will be no trains," said Micaela.

"Nor anything else," replied Nicola quietly. Several cars
had been caught by the flood and were overturned or
jammed against a tree. The whole roadway that came
around the coast and led to Barcelona had risen in a great
bulge, then cracked with the force of water above and below
it.

Micaela said she must now join her mother at the harbor
to wait for Barto's boat, and Nicola stood disconsolately on
part of a wall from which the water had slightly receded.
What on earth was she to do now? She was unlikely to find
any kind of transport at all in this flood-devastated village,
and to crawl back to the villa was unthinkable.

It occurred to her that the floods farther up the railway
line might not have been so bad and perhaps there were
trains running along that part of the coast. If only she could
cross this roaring river somehow, she might be able to skirt
the worst flooded areas by keeping to the higher parts.

Encumbered as she was with the suitcase, it was not easy
to pick her way over the rough, slippery ground and when
she was faced with another fast-moving stream, she retraced her steps to the center of the village. Scores of men
and women were either barricading their shops and houses
against the rushing water, or they were bailing or pumping
out the basements and cellars where the water had receded.
One enterprising boatman was already ferrying people
from one side of the *rambla* to the other, and Nicola shouted
to catch his attention. She had to wait her turn until he had
made several journeys. Then she scrambled in, dragging her
suitcase with her.

Somebody shouted, "Nicola! Nicola!"

She shaded her eyes from the sun and peered up. Sebastian stood there, dressed in yellow oilskins.

"Come back! Come back!" he shouted.

But there was no turning back now, for the boatman had started his precarious journey. Nicola realized that the most sensible thing to do was to stay in the boat on its return journey. Naturally Sebastian would be down here at the earliest moment for as a doctor he was needed in such an emergency as this. Then the decision whether to return to safety or try to continue her crazy journey was taken out of Nicola's hands. A fully grown tree, its boughs turning and twisting helplessly, came swirling down the wide stream. Before he could evade the branches, the boatman was caught, his loaded boat pushed toward the walls of a house and jammed there.

Something hit Nicola a heavy blow on the head and the sun was blotted out.

NICOLA OPENED HER EYES. It was a curious sensation to imagine that she was back in her former room at the Villa Ronda, instead of on this jogging, throbbing train. How had she managed to get on the train, she wondered. There were floods and the line was torn up.

She blinked, trying to focus on the passing landscape, but the walls that enclosed her were cream. Here was the pale green carpet, the green and white curtains at the half-shuttered windows. She tried to sit up and the top of her head nearly jumped off.

A quiet voice said in Spanish, "Please lie still." Iñez, Adrienne's maid, was by the bedside. "You are safe at the Villa Ronda," murmured Iñez.

A few moments later, or perhaps it was hours, Adrienne came toward the bed.

"Oh, it was such a fright!" she exclaimed. "You are now much better?"

Nicola nodded, but even that hurt her head. She put up her hand to feel a bandage around her forehead.

"What happened? How did I get here?"

"We did not even know that you had gone away, but

Sebastian went to the village as soon as it was daylight. Many people have been injured, so he went to help."

"Of course." Nicola had a vague impression of seeing Sebastian in yellow oilskins, and he had shouted at her.

"Then," continued Adrienne, "I sent Iñez to your room to find how you had slept through the terrible storm. You had gone and there were your letters. My father—" and even in her present vague state, Nicola noticed the pride in Adrienne's voice "—my father advised us to send someone down to the harbor to find Sebastian so that he could look for you."

"Micaela took me to her house when the storm began. I stayed there all night."

Adrienne sighed. "They have trouble, too. Barto is missing and all the men on his boat. Other boats are also missing."

"Poor Barto," murmured Nicola. "His family was very kind to me."

"You must now sleep or else Sebastian will scold me for talking," said Adrienne.

Nicola must have dozed, for when she was next awake she became aware of someone holding her hand in a firm grip. Sebastian sat by the bedside and his clasp was totally unlike that of a doctor taking a patient's pulse.

"*Querida!*" he said softly. "Darling Nicola!" She could not believe her ears. She was still dreaming. Then he spoke again. "Why did you run away? And why did you choose such a stormy night? Did you *want* to drown?"

"No." She gave him a timid smile. "I started out before the storm broke."

"Then why didn't you turn back?" he demanded, his eyes bright with concern.

Her gaze fell. "I—I hadn't the courage, I suppose."

"But you knew how much I wanted you to stay here for always. Couldn't you see that I loved you?"

Nicola's heart thumped around so much that she was sure that Dr. Sebastian Montal could hear it.

"I thought you'd be glad to be rid of me—both of us, my sister and me."

"I loved you long before your sister came here. Oh,

Nicola, there is so much to tell you, but it can wait. First I must hear something from you.''

"Yes?"

"Do you love me? Enough to marry me and stay here at the villa?"

Nicola's face became radiant. "How could you doubt it? Of course I do!"

He stood up, then stared down at her. "It is most improper for a doctor to embrace his patient, but perhaps he may be allowed to kiss his future wife?"

With his arms around her, his lips against hers, his tender words of endearment, she forgot her aching head, her foolish, false pride, and remembered only that her own love for him had brought far more than its just reward. She was luckier than she had ever imagined in her wildest dreams.

"What happened to my head to give me such a knock?" she asked.

"The boat crashed into a building at the foot of the *rambla*. Luckily no one was drowned, but most of the passengers were knocked about and you were thrown against the wall."

"Have they found Barto yet?"

He nodded. "Yes. All the others, too. The three boats kept together and decided to go far away from land and ride out the storm. But they're home now, although Barto has a broken arm."

"I'm glad he's safe, for his mother's sake and Micaela's."

"Not Adrienne's?" he teased.

"Not now. She's happy enough with Ramon, her fish."

"Her fish?" he echoed, puzzled.

But she would not explain to him, fearing that he might also believe that he had been successfully hooked and landed.

It was another two days before Sebastian would allow Nicola to get up, and then only to sit in the garden. She did not rebel, for she realized that he had scores of casualties to attend to in the village.

Her suitcase had been irrevocably lost when the boat crashed, so it was fortunate that she had not taken quite all her clothes with her, for she still had two or three dresses at the villa, and Adrienne was glad to provide her with whatever else she needed.

Nicola was relaxing in a long garden chair on the Mediterranean balcony when Sebastian came to her at the end of another grueling day of attending his injured patients and inoculating hundreds of others against typhoid owing to the lack of drinking water.

She had already seen for herself the damage in the Villa Ronda gardens, the magnolia cracked and broken, the flower beds scoured and swept clear of bushes and plants, the red mud left behind. Even the swimming pool had to be emptied and cleaned, for mud and debris had been swept into it.

Adrienne came bustling up behind him and he frowned slightly at her.

She bent to kiss Nicola. "At last he has fallen in love with someone young!" she cried at the top of her voice for the whole landscape to hear. "I was so afraid he would let Doña Elena choose him."

"There was no question of that," murmured Sebastian.

"No?" Adrienne queried disbelievingly. "If Nicola had not arrived here, I would have had Doña Elena for both aunt and sister-in-law. Now Nicola shall be my aunt. Dear Tía Nicola!" Adrienne made an elaborate curtsey. "When it is possible, Nicola, you must give Sebastian a small medal—a decoration. He fished you out of the water when the boat sank. Of course, he could not save everyone, but you were special."

Adrienne whisked away leaving behind her a momentarily silent couple.

"Why didn't you tell me?" asked Nicola at last.

"There was so little to tell. When I saw what had happened, I was able to get into another boat, then clamber along the small bridge, which was wrecked. Then I brought you here," he ended simply. After a pause he asked, "Why didn't *you* tell me about those bills of your sister's?"

"I thought it better not to."

"And all the time you were here, your salary was going to pay all those debts for your sister. You must forgive me for believing that you were like her."

"Of course." She stretched out her hand to him.

"But there is still a long story to tell you," he said.

"Not unless you want to tell me," she said quietly.

"I must. Otherwise you will never understand why I was so angry because a mere photograph had been pulled out of a drawer. Eduardo is much older than I, more than ten years. He married in France, then he and Héloïse spent some time there, then in the Pyrenees and other parts of Spain. When I had qualified as a doctor and returned here for a short time, I fell in love with Héloïse. Until then I had not known her very well, a few meetings, a few visits. But now—she was so beautiful, so gay and accomplished. She made my world, but she was my brother's wife. She loved Eduardo and she had a child, Adrienne."

He paused, and Nicola recalled that fragmentary mention by Ramon and Elena of "Héloïse."

"I decided that I must go away, although no other woman would ever mean as much to me. But it was Eduardo who asked me to stay. He wanted to go on a long expedition to the Pyrenees. So I stayed. But Héloïse was wise. She absented herself for long periods, painting in the mountains or in Andalusia. Then she became ill and in due course Eduardo returned. We treated her, trying to find out what was wrong. We brought other doctors for consultation, but with no result. Only when she died after several years of suffering was it possible to know that she had a very rare disease of the heart."

Nicola laid her hand over his in a sympathetic gesture. "So we had both lost her," continued Sebastian. "But Eduardo blamed me as well as himself for not recognizing the symptoms until it was too late to cure her. Now, Nicola, you know why I have written a long book on these unusual heart conditions. It is dedicated to Héloïse and in a way it is a kind of atonement for my longing for her." He gave her a sudden, warm smile that illumined his somber expression. "But now it is finished. The book, I mean. My attachment to Héloïse—now I know it was only a boy's infatuation. Even Eduardo has realized that life is not finished for him, although he needed time to know that."

"Thank you for telling me," said Nicola.

"You understand, of course, that now that Eduardo has returned, I am no longer the head of our house. If it should happen that he marries again, then his wife will be *la madre*, and not you, Nicola. Will you mind being the second—of less importance?"

"Second fiddle?" she queried happily. "I will be content to play any instrument at the Villa Ronda or anywhere you happen to be."

"Bless you!" He cradled her head on his shoulder.

Tonight was calm, but with only a few lights pricking the velvet dusk, for not all the electricity services had yet been restored. The storm, the nightmare waters might never have happened, except that Nicola had returned to the Villa Ronda and Sebastian.

"Adrienne has her fish," she murmured, "and I have my second fiddle."

"What is this joke about Adrienne's fish?" he asked.

She laughed. "One day I will share it with you, dear Sebastian." As she would also share with him everything else that life had to offer.

"If we are speaking of fish," he said, "I must take you out one night for the sardine fishing. It's interesting and exciting."

"I would like that," she murmured. What a man! To find romance not in roses and moonlight, but in the hazards of sardine fishing.

Life with Sebastian would be full of surprises, and that was the way Nicola wanted it.

HOTEL BELVEDERE

Hotel
Belvedere

Andrea wasn't sure she'd done the right thing when she'd accepted a position at the luxury hotel where her aunt was head housekeeper. So many strange things had happened since.

Still, the job had its compensations. Keir Holt was one of them—and when he asked Andrea to "play the part of a girl who might even like me a little," she found she didn't really need to act!

CHAPTER ONE

ANDREA STEPPED into the revolving door of the Hotel Belvedere. A vigorous thrust from behind her sent the door whirling and catapulted her into the entrance hall, where she landed full length on the thick carpet.

She was aware of somebody's grasp on her wrist as she scrambled to her feet and a very tall man was murmuring apologies.

"I beg your pardon. I'm afraid I didn't see you. Are you all right?"

"Yes, thank you. The door caught the heel of my shoe. You pushed the door rather sharply." The statement sounded like an accusation.

"It was entirely my fault. I'm sorry." One of the hotel porters gravely handed Andrea her shoe and handbag as though it were a normal part of his routine to attend to visitors who fell flat on their faces.

She moved toward the reception desk. "I have an appointment with Mrs. Mayfield. I am Miss Lansdale."

"Will you wait a moment, please?" The receptionist picked up a telephone and then smiled at the man behind Andrea.

"Good afternoon, Mr. Holt." As the porter handed him his key, Andrea glanced quickly at the man who had so violently shot her into the hotel. Against the light, his features were indistinct, but she received an impression of a stern, almost scowling face, a slight beaked nose and straight mouth.

A bellhop took her up to Mrs. Mayfield's sitting room.

"Good afternoon—Aunt Catherine." The greeting came

awkwardly on Andrea's tongue, for she had not met her aunt for more than six years, not since the death of her own mother, Catherine's sister. Now that her father had been killed in a tragic accident, crashing a car into a stone wall while trying to avoid a small child, Aunt Catherine was probably the only close relative she had.

"You've grown up, Andrea. You were still a schoolgirl the last time I saw you."

Mrs. Mayfield thought that her niece appeared hardly more than a schoolgirl now, in spite of the plain black suit and white blouse. The girl was small, with tawny hair and gray eyes—not in the least like her mother, Leonie, who had possessed much greater height and a Scandinavian fairness.

"How old are you?" she asked Andrea.

"Nineteen."

Catherine Mayfield sighed. "Yes, it's a tragic age to be left to fend for oneself."

Andrea remembered with compassion that her aunt, too, had known grief and tragedy, for her husband had died, leaving Catherine to carve out a new life for herself, working in hotels, until she had risen to the responsibility of head housekeeper in this large provincial hotel, the Belvedere.

"Have you any plans for the future?" Mrs. Mayfield asked. "Anything you specially want to do?"

"I'm not really sure."

"But you must have been working at something since you left school."

"Oh, yes. I learned shorthand and typing and worked in an estate office in Stowchester. That's our nearest town, about five miles away. But I don't think I like office life enough to stay there indefinitely."

"You don't like routine work?"

"I suppose that's it."

"That was a characteristic of your father."

Andrea resented this immediate attack on her father, but before she could protest, Mrs. Mayfield asked, "What d'you want to do?"

The girl hesitated before replying. "I've been taking cooking lessons at evening classes. I thought if I worked hard I might eventually become some kind of demonstrator.''

"That sort of job requires a lot of training and plenty of stamina. D'you think you have the right temperament and enough confidence?''

Andrea sensed the underlying hostility in her aunt's smooth question. "Perhaps that's something I have to find out.''

A waiter brought in a tray of tea and as Mrs. Mayfield poured Andrea studied this woman who had invited her to visit. Andrea had, of course, written with the news of her father's death in an accident, and although Aunt Catherine had not attended the funeral, she had replied sympathetically and cordially, inviting Andrea to come to the hotel in Millbridge and stay a few days.

Six years ago, Aunt Catherine had loomed as a tall, slender pale-faced woman, with a set expression that rarely broke into a smile. After her mother's death, Andrea vaguely remembered the bitter quarrels between her father and Aunt Catherine, but she'd been too young to understand their significance.

Now, Aunt Catherine looked almost the same. The plain black dress enhanced her pallor so that her dark eyes seemed more deeply set. Her dark hair was beginning to gray. A marcasite brooch and earrings were her only pieces of jewelry and her firm mouth was outlined in the most discreet of lipsticks.

As she handed a cup of tea to Andrea, Mrs. Mayfield adroitly changed the subject to her niece's career. "Tell me about these people with whom you and your father have been living. Was he really only their chauffeur and handyman?''

"Yes he was." Andrea's defiance rose again. "He took the job of chauffeur to Mrs. Dennistoun because he thought it was probably the only way he could afford to provide a home for me for a year or two after I left school until I earned enough to keep myself. We had the apartment over the garage and we managed comfortably. Mrs. Dennistoun treated my father as a friend more than an employee. She knew that he was an educated man.''

"Educated?" Catherine put down the cup that had been halfway to her lips. "Of course he was educated! And he threw away all his talents for the sake of his whims. With his degrees, his knowledge of Latin and Greek, history, archaeology and the rest, he could have had a brilliant career and given your mother a comfortable home and surroundings, instead of dragging her to wild places and forcing her to lead a poverty-stricken existence in foreign slums."

"But they were happy together, and mother enjoyed wandering around Europe with him."

"You don't realize how much your mother suffered. Ill health and poverty broke her spirit, so that she didn't care about anything, not even when she caught a terrible germ in some hovel in Greece and died in misery. Oh, yes, it was exciting and interesting for your father to roam around Greece and Turkey and Persia, but he didn't care what happened to poor Leonie."

"He did care!" retorted Andrea. "He often spoke about her and always blamed himself for not looking after her better."

Aunt Catherine smiled coldly. "It was too late then."

Andrea stood up, indignation and anger warring with her sense of courtesy to an older woman. "Why must you attack my father like this? Why do you dislike him so much? What injury had he done to you?"

"None—except what he did to Leonie."

"Perhaps in the end he paid for all his shortcomings." Andrea spoke vehemently. "He gave his life for a child." Her voice broke and tears welled into her eyes.

Catherine's hand reached out toward the girl. "I'm sorry, Andrea. I shouldn't have allowed my own feelings to carry me away like that. Tell me what you intend to do now. Could you stay on with these people, the Dennistouns?"

Andrea sat down again. "Mrs. Dennistoun will need a new chauffeur and he'll want the apartment, especially if he's married. In any case, I wouldn't want to stay there without father."

"No other ties there, I suppose? A boyfriend, perhaps."

"Oh, no. Nothing like that." Andrea smiled.

"Then you could probably get a job as a typist here in Millbridge, just as well as the other place. You'd earn more money, too, and might find something more interesting than your dull estate office."

"I haven't made any plans yet." Andrea was disappointed that this interview had taken on such a stormy character.

"You'll stay here a few days, won't you? The change might do you good, after the shock of the past week or so."

A few moments ago, Andrea had been on the verge of dashing out of the room, vowing never to see Aunt Catherine again, but now she recognized a more gentle note in the other's voice.

"I'll stay tonight, of course. Thank you very much. But I'll go home, that is, I mean, back to the Dennistouns tomorrow. I'll decide what to do and then write and let you know." Andrea spoke quietly, with a cool dignity that made Catherine glance sharply at her niece.

"You have Leonie's spirit." She smiled with almost unwilling approval. "If you're really interested in domestic science, how would you like to train for a hotel career? Live here and work under my supervision?"

Andrea caught her breath. "I—I don't know what to say."

Catherine was surprised at her own sudden yielding to a momentary impulse. "You can think it over and let me know. But I must warn you that if you agree to come here and train seriously for some kind of hotel or catering job, I shall expect you to stay at least twelve months, no matter how tedious the routine may be."

Andrea gave her aunt a straight, level glance. "If I decide to accept your very kind offer, I'll undertake to stay of course. That's why I'd like a little time to make up my mind."

A faint smile played around Catherine's mouth. It was a rare experience for a woman who was one of the half-dozen most important people concerned in the running of a large hotel to find her quite generous offer the subject of consideration. Twenty girls with more qualifications and probably greater aptitude than Andrea would have jumped at the chance.

"One point I haven't mentioned. You'll be treated exactly the same as any other trainee. No special privileges because you are my niece."

Andrea nodded. "I understand. And I'd resent special or favored treatment."

"Good. I have dinner here in my room at half-past seven. I'll ring for somebody to show you to your room, and then perhaps you'd like to go out and look at the shops and amuse yourself until then."

"Thank you. I'll be back in good time."

When Andrea had gone, Catherine wondered what rashness had urged her to make such an unnecessary offer to Leonie's daughter. Yet she could hardly have done less.

She had so bitterly resented losing Roger, her husband, after only two years of marriage. More than that, jealousy of other women's children had raged within her for many years, making it impossible for her to visit or have any contact with Andrea after Leonie died.

Now she had made this extraordinary and quixotic offer, knowing that if the girl accepted, Andrea would be a constant and grievous reminder of the daughter Catherine had never borne. She doubted, though, whether Andrea would stay. The girl had almost certainly inherited her father's restlessness, his revolt against discipline and inability to persevere at humdrum tasks. She would find hotel life exacting and decidedly less glamorous than the luxurious furnishings of the public rooms might lead one to believe.

Andrea, on her way back next day to Howden Hall, the home of the Dennistouns in the small village of Knight's Croome, thought a great deal about her aunt's generosity, but she was not yet sure whether she was going to accept the offer of a position as hotel trainee.

Mrs. Dennistoun was surprised at Andrea's sudden return. "I thought you were staying several days," she commented.

Andrea, confessing to herself that she was in an unusually sensitive mood, ready to hear the slightest tinge of criticism in the most harmless words, explained that she had not wanted to stay longer because if she decided to go back, there were many small arrangements to make here in the village.

"I think it's a splendid offer," Mrs. Dennistoun opined. "It solves all your problems at one stroke. Provides you with a change of occupation, somewhere to live, a promising new career, and above all, a friendly aunt to advise you when you're in difficulty."

The girl was not so optimistic. She saw that in solving one set of problems, she was likely to encounter a number of different ones, not the least of which would arise from a clash between herself and the "friendly aunt."

"Please don't think, Andrea, that I'm anxious for you to go," Mrs. Dennistoun continued. "You're most welcome to stay here until you decide your future."

"Yes, I know that, and I'm grateful to you. I'm going to think matters over for a day or two." After a moment she added, "I'll tidy the apartment and pack up my possessions. I know you'll be wanting to have it ready for a new chauffeur."

"There's no hurry. Your father will not be very easy to replace, and in the meantime, Trevor can drive me wherever I want to go."

Mrs. Dennistoun's mention of her son was an unnecessary underlining of the older woman's true reasons for hoping that Andrea would find a job and a home elsewhere—anywhere away from Howden Hall.

Andrea had glibly told her Aunt Catherine that she had no ties in the village, no boyfriend, and indeed, that was entirely true. But Trevor Dennistoun, twenty-six, attractive and eligible was a source of anxiety to his mother, who feared that he might marry the wrong girl. Several in the district were interested. Daughters of neighbors, his secretary at the department store—which his father had founded and which was now the largest and most exclusive in Stowchester—any of these girls would have been delighted to become Mrs. Trevor Dennistoun. But so far, Trevor had shown no eagerness to marry any of the girls whose excellent qualities his mother presented in a most subtle manner.

At first, Andrea had regarded him only in a friendly way as the son of her father's employer, and a young man with an easy, natural manner. He had certainly never given her the impression that he was attracted to her, and Andrea was quietly amused that Mrs. Dennistoun should even consider her as a disastrous possibility. Gradually, though, as she came to know him, she recognized that she was only a step away from being in love with him. Occasionally he brought her home from her weekly evening classes in Stowchester, although one or two other young men who did not possess cars would have been glad to walk with her down the lane from the bus stop.

Later in the day, Andrea went out for a solitary walk along the Gloucestershire lanes, taking her problems with her for company. The day was hot and sultry and eventually she branched off through a gap in the hedge, leading to a tiny glade carpeted with lush grass and fringed with bushes tangled with honeysuckle and traveler's joy. At the foot of the slope a shallow river trickled.

She flung herself down full length by the water's edge and gazed at the hazy sky. She need not accept her aunt's offer, she reasoned. She could change jobs, leave Stowchester, strike out for herself in London, perhaps, where no doubt she could earn enough to keep herself in modest comfort even if, at first, it meant living in a hostel.

Yet she was not sufficiently interested in any aspect of commerce to overcome her distaste for what seemed to her the cold impersonality of office life. Other girls might like the atmosphere, but to Andrea there was nothing more chilling and forlorn than the sight of an empty office after six when typewriters were covered, desks cleared and only the echoing clatter of a cleaner's bucket broke the silence. Surely there must be something warmer about hotel life, a sense of continuity and shared communal interests?

She returned through the village, averting her eyes from the stone wall into which her father had crashed. A cyclist overtook her and then swerved violently, just missing a child who darted across the road, almost under his wheels.

"Jennifer! Jennifer!" A woman appeared at an open door of one of the row of cottages. "Come in this minute!" Then she saw Andrea and her expression changed.

Andrea had been standing motionless, her anger mounting in a passionate tide as she recognized both child and mother.

"Your Jennifer nearly caused another accident! Lucky it was a cyclist and he wasn't going fast, but he might have been injured and Jennifer, too. Don't you think, Mrs. Carter, that you ought to take more care of your child for her own sake and for the sake of others?"

The woman pushed back her untidy hair, and from within the cottage came the wail of a baby.

"I know how you feel, miss, seeing it was your father that other time, but the traffic along here is cruel—"

Andrea, ashamed for her flaring outburst, turned toward the small girl, now squatting down by the roadside and playing with a handful of dusty leaves and an empty cigarette carton.

"Come along, Jennifer," she urged, and gently took the child's hand and led her across the road.

"I don't know what I can do, miss," the woman whined. "Living on the road like this, no front garden or nothing! Soon as my back's turned, that Jennifer's out, no matter how I try to stop her." She bent down now and smacked the child's arm so spitefully that Jennifer immediately began to bawl.

"Couldn't you have a gate fixed across the door—or something that would prevent Jennifer running out into the road?"

The woman laughed with derision. "Easy to see you haven't got mites of your own. Our Jennie would climb over anything like that in no time."

Andrea turned away, knowing it was useless to argue with a woman like Mrs. Carter.

Later, during the evening when she was telling Mrs. Dennistoun of her decision to accept her aunt's offer of training at the Hotel Belvedere, she reflected how curious it was that the sight of a small girl whose sudden dash across the road had caused Mr. Lansdale's death should swing her in favor of the hotel.

"I think it's the best thing to get away," she told Mrs. Dennistoun. "There are too many associations here in the

village. I'd like to remember the pleasant incidents and
forget the uncomfortable ones."

Approval shone in Mrs. Dennistoun's shrewd brown
eyes. "You're young, and it's easy enough to make changes
at your age," she observed.

When Trevor heard the news, he seemed more concerned
than Andrea had imagined he would be and for a moment
she was exhilarated.

"I'll miss you, Andrea," he told her, but immediately she
recognized that there was no more than friendliness in his
voice.

"Not for long. Quite likely the next chauffeur will have a
daughter."

"Or a schoolboy son who'll cast a longing eye on my
newest car and yearn to drive it on the M.I."

When Andrea did not answer, he said, "You wouldn't
like a job in the store, I suppose? You could do something
other than shorthand and typing. Sell cosmetics or dresses—
anything you fancy."

She was both surprised and touched by his offer, especially as she was sure it was being made without the
knowledge or approval of his mother, and for a silly
moment she was tempted to accept, chancing Mrs. Dennistoun's wrath.

But she had the sense to shake her head and smile. "No.
It's wonderfully kind of you, but I want to get away." She
told him briefly of Jennifer's second escape. "So, you see,
I'd be reminded all the time of my father."

His hand closed over her wrist. "All right. If you want to
go, we can't stop you. But remember that if you get in a jam,
you have friends here."

CHAPTER TWO

ANDREA ARRIVED at the Hotel Belvedere about a fortnight later, after working her week's notice at the estate agent's in Stowchester. There, too, her employers had declared that if she needed a job, they would gladly try to find her a vacancy.

On this stifling Saturday afternoon the hotel's revolving door was fixed open, so, she thought grimly, there was no chance of being propelled through it by some careless man behind her.

Aunt Catherine helped her to settle in, giving her a number of details about her work as a chambermaid on the fourth floor.

"You'll have to pick up the routine a little at a time. Telling you everything now won't make sense," her aunt said. "But you'll find Miss Wyvern, the floor housekeeper on fourth, will put you right on details. And one other point—it will be better for you, Andrea, if our relationship is not known. It's not that I mind, but it might make your position very difficult as a newcomer."

Andrea saw the sense in that. She wanted to accept no favors, so there was no point in claiming the relationship of aunt and niece.

"You'll be sharing a room with a French girl, Huguette Cloubert. She's here in England to perfect her English and probably you'll be able to improve your French."

Andrea was relieved to find that she had at least half a room; she had imagined that the less important members of the staff would sleep in dormitories.

Huguette, a dark-haired girl with mischievous brown

eyes and a curvy figure, which she exploited in a flattering
way, seemed disposed to be friendly when she came off duty.

"You have worked in hotel before?" she asked.

"No. But I know how to make beds and clean bath-
rooms," Andrea replied.

Huguette's little trill of laughter soon punctured Andrea's
confidence. "You have much to learn. Hotel is not the same
as home. But on fourth floor, perhaps it does not matter so
much. Me, I am on second and I have two private suites."

"What are they like?" Andrea asked eagerly.

"*De luxe*" was the succinct reply. "The one Miss Jensen
has is the best. She is a very beautiful Danish girl, very
rich." Huguette shrugged her shoulders under the flimsy
nightdress. "One must be—oh, *superbly* rich to stay there.
There is a fine bedroom with beds padded in blue silk and
blue carpet to match. All the furniture is pale wood, like
honey, with small black bands and stripes and silver han-
dles. The bathroom is yellow and then there is a sitting
room with armchairs and tables for when your friends
come." Huguette dramatically slapped her chest. "But the
bill downstairs! Oh, climbing up and up!" She waved her
fingers like a bird in flight. "One night to stay there and pay
the bill myself—and I would die of shock!"

Andrea burst into delighted laughter. "But if somebody
else paid the bill, what then?"

"That is different. But even then, one can spend someone
else's money better than that."

By the time Andrea had observed this streak of true
Gallic practicality in her new friend, Huguette had switched
off the light and thumped herself into her own bed with
much jangling of springs.

Next morning Andrea realized that she had, indeed,
much to learn. Being called at six, with a deafening thump
on the door, dressing hurriedly in the pale mauve check
uniform and white apron and dashing to the end of a
corridor on fourth floor to sign on at half-past six under the
watchful eye of Miss Wyvern was an unfamiliar routine.

Miriam, the head chambermaid with whom she was to
work for the time being on Block C, took her to the
housekeeper's station on their floor, gave her a cup of

scalding tea and showed her how to prepare the early morning teas and room breakfasts.

"You do your *mise-en-place* the night before—that's French—means putting things ready," explained Miriam, a girl in her late twenties, with lank mousy hair and light eyes set in a pasty face.

Andrea read the call list sent up by the night porter, and eventually helped to set the trays in order of time, ready for Miriam to take them to the various bedrooms.

"Sunday's a quiet day," Miriam told her. "Always is, in city hotels. But we have to do D block today, as well as our own, because some of the other girls are off duty."

In between trays of tea being required, there were several breakfasts to be served in the rooms. "I'll show you how to order those. Several of the staff have bedrooms on our floor and they're a bit particular how they're treated."

By the time she was free to go to breakfast in the women's staff hall, Andrea was wilting with fatigue. Some of the other girls laughed, but not too unsympathetically.

"Just as well you've started on a Sunday," said one. "Wait until Tuesday morning, when the place is full of businessmen ringing bells and roaring their heads off."

Miriam, for all her unprepossessing appearance, was a friendly and helpful person, and as the two girls made beds, tidied washbasins and showers, vacuumed carpets and dusted dressing tables, she recounted to Andrea almost her entire life history.

"So I got fed up with this boy, you see, and gave him the push. After that, I met a chap who had his own garage. Plenty of money. Treated me very handsome, he did. But not the marrying kind, as you might say. Not that I'd have wanted to settle down with him."

The saga continued from room to room along C and D blocks, but Andrea was more intent on memorizing the routine and remembering the layout of passages, cupboards and stairs.

Toward the end of her first week, she had a fairly clear picture of her duties and responsibilities, although she was not overconfident that she could carry them out to the satisfaction of her superiors, especially for Miss Wyvern, the floor housekeeper.

Andrea soon discovered that it was far from easy to balance a loaded tray and unlock bedroom doors at the same time. Once when she placed the tray on the floor, Miriam hissed disapproval.

"Don't you let Wyvern catch you putting things on the floor! Only the empties, mind!"

Andrea had already experienced a few critical comments from Miss Wyvern, but accepted these as part of learning her job. She was mildly surprised that she had seen Aunt Catherine only once during the whole week, but she didn't realize that her aunt's firm management included a great amount of trust in her floor housekeepers, and a minimum of supervision.

As a newcomer, Andrea was given two free days at the weekend. "But next week," Miss Wyvern told her, "your free day will be the Monday following, and you realize that you won't always get alternate Saturdays and Sundays. You have three days in a fortnight and the roster is always pinned up in the staff hall, so you'll know well in advance. If you want to come in later than eleven-thirty, you must ask me beforehand for a late pass. The staff entrance is closed and you come in by the front door and have your pass checked by the night porter."

Andrea found plenty to do, washing and ironing her personal clothes before going out to shop on Saturday afternoon while the stores were still open. She bought a gray linen dress, marked down at a knockout price in a mid-August sale, and was sure that her father would not wish her to continue wearing black for him; he had been far too progressive in his views to pander to such conventions.

Besides, she had to wear black every night at the hotel when she was on duty.

The next day, Sunday, she went to morning service at a church whose steeple she had seen from the top windows of the Belvedere. It stood in a dusty, barren square at the foot of a long street of offices and warehouses. Georgian porches and fanlights remained on a few buildings as evidence that the square had once been a collection of dignified private residences that were now turned into offices or small factories.

In the afternoon the closed shops and hushed business quarters of the city emphasized her own loneliness and she was glad to take a bus to one of the parks, where at least crowds of people enjoyed themselves.

She was conscious of a wistful regret at leaving a known way of life with its companionships, job, familiar people and surroundings for the uncertainties of hotel life, all rush and bustle for periods of the day, followed in off-duty hours by the feeling that one was merely a fish flipped out of a pool. But she told herself that this despondency would fade, that it was too soon to expect to be integrated into the concerns of others, that eventually she would find companions and friends among those with whom she worked.

At about nine o'clock she returned to the Belvedere and was about to pass the main door and turn down the side street where the staff entrance was discreetly tucked away, when a man alighted from his car.

He glanced at her, then smiled in recognition, as he crossed the sidewalk. "Aren't you the young lady I sent flying through this door a week or so ago?"

She was aware that a porter had come out to take the man's suitcases.

"Yes."

He was still smiling at her. "Then this time I promise to be extra careful and not tread on your heels." He stood waiting for her to precede him, but color rose furiously into her cheeks. It was against all the rules to be chatting familiarly with a hotel guest and she could no longer use the front entrance, even if she were off duty and wearing a gray linen dress and a silly white hat swathed in spotted tulle.

"I, er, if you'll excuse me—I have a call to make."

She gave him the nervous smile of a frightened rabbit and fled around the corner and down to the staff entrance. Safely inside, she recovered some of her wits. Now why on earth couldn't she have said she worked at the Belvedere and had to use a different door? As she walked up the back stairs to her room she remembered his name, Mr. Holt; the name she had heard the receptionist address him by.

During the next week she had little time to dwell on anything but her work. Whether Aunt Catherine knew it or not, Andrea was out to prove that she could be painstaking and diligent in even the most trivial tasks.

One evening when she and Huguette were preparing for bed, Andrea asked, "Do you know a Mr. Holt who comes here?"

Huguette, engrossed in massaging her face, peered into the dressing-table mirror. "Huh? Who?" Then, as the name registered she swung around toward Andrea. "Holt? Keir Holt?"

"I don't know his Christian name."

"But you know him?"

"Well, no. I've just heard his name, that's all."

"He is very tall, very dark and oh, so excitingly 'andsome."

Andrea frowned a little. "Tall and dark, yes, but I don't know that I'd call him handsome."

Huguette waved her hands triumphantly. "Then you do know him quite well. You have studied his face. Where did you meet him?"

Andrea sighed. "If you must know, he pushed the revolving door on me when I first came to see Mrs. Mayfield and I fell flat on my face. He and the porter picked me up."

Huguette raised her hands and eyes to heaven. "Such luck!"

"What's so lucky about being knocked down?" Andrea demanded.

Huguette ignored the question. "My good Andrea, you must throw away foolish—what do you call them—fancies about this man."

"I haven't any foolish fancies. I tell you I don't even know him. All I asked was—"

"Mr. Holt comes here many times. I do not know his profession, but he does something for new buildings in the city. Big new blocks of offices and shops. I think he is very rich, and such men as Monsieur Holt do not have time for chambermaids, not even when they are as pretty as you."

"I didn't say—"

"Listen to my advice!" Huguette interrupted. "These

men stay in hotels, they smile at us, flirt a little, squeeze us by the waist—"

"*Around* the waist," corrected Andrea.

"Put their hands under our chins and maybe try to kiss in a dark corner—but no, my Andrea, they are always married already. If not, they do not marry us."

Andrea rocked with laughter. "Just like a French girl! Why should I care if Mr. Holt is married or not? Perhaps his wife is here, too."

"Ah, no. She is not here."

Andrea smiled triumphantly. "*You* know that, do you?"

"But of course. He likes to have the Somerset suite. That is on my floor, but I do not attend to it. It is Margaret's."

"And you and Margaret and the rest of you exchange gossip about all the guests? Nobody who comes to stay here dare have a secret."

Huguette put on her Mona Lisa smile of mysterious complacence. "Understand, *ma chérie*, that our floor has the most important guests. You must wait a little before you can come down from the top."

Andrea chuckled. "I realize already that in hotels you work your way up by coming down from the top."

On Saturday afternoon Andrea entered her bedroom to change into her black dress for the evening. Huguette, who was off duty, was already dressed to go out and turned sharply. She wore a nylon raincoat over her dress.

"It isn't raining," Andrea observed.

Huguette hastily picked up bag and gloves. "One does not want to soil a good dress going down the back stairs," she said, not looking at Andrea.

"But you're wearing a fur stole as well—under the coat."

Huguette smiled. "That is why I wear the coat. I do not want to spoil the fur." She whisked out of the room before Andrea could make any further comment.

Whomever Huguette was going to meet, she was certainly determined to make an impression, Andrea thought. Evidently she had a weekend pass, for she did not return that night.

Next morning, as Andrea came out of a bedroom on

fourth, Miriam handed her a note. "You got a boyfriend?" she asked.

Andrea stuffed the note in her apron pocket, for she had seen Miss Wyvern at the end of the corridor.

"Thank you, Miriam. It's probably from the manager, asking me to lunch with him." Andrea hurried into the next bedroom, left the door wide open and waited until Miss Wyvern had glanced casually in then passed on.

She opened the envelope and took out the single sheet. Even before she saw Huguette's signature, she recognized the French style of handwriting.

> Ma chère Andrea,
>   I am in a small trouble. Come to this address in your off duty today *without fail.* I trust you, but do not tell anybody where you are coming. A million million thanks and my love. Huguette.

Andrea was concerned. The words "without fail" were heavily underlined. What scrape had Huguette landed herself in? And where on earth was Barnbattle Green? Wherever it was, Andrea hoped she would be able to get there and back in her three hours free time this afternoon.

Miriam, too, was off duty and for once did not want to flop on her bed. She offered Andrea her company. "We could go to Hillington Park. They have a band there Sunday afternoons."

Andrea mumbled thanks for the invitation. "Sorry, but I, er, have to go somewhere else."

Miriam folded her lips inward, then nodded ironically. "I get you. The boyfriend who sent you the note."

"Perhaps we could go together some other time?" Andrea did not want to offend the other girl.

"Huh! When he's taking out one of his other glamor girls?"

Andrea dared not ask Miriam the way to Barnbattle Green, but luckily she remembered that not far from the hotel and outside the town hall was a street map of Millbridge, the kind enclosed in a glass case. She twiddled the knobs until she found the right section and was relieved that the place was only a short bus ride away.

The street of closely packed, red-brick houses seemed to stretch endlessly, but at last she found the right number.

"I'm Huguette's friend, Andrea," she told the woman who opened the door. "She asked me to come."

"Oh. That's right. Come in."

The woman, short and plump, her curves overflowing from a red dress a couple of sizes too small for her, led the way into a back sitting room where Huguette lay on a settee. She was still wearing the dress Andrea had noticed yesterday, a deep rose silk dress cut with Parisian elegance, but now a heavy coat covered her legs and feet.

"Oh, Andrea, it is so good that you come."

"But what's happened? Are you ill?"

"No, no," replied Huguette. "A small accident, that is all. But you must meet my friend, Bobbie Gray."

Andrea was introduced to a gaunt-faced young man in a dark red shirt and black jeans. He returned her greeting with a muttered "Pleased to meet you" and a wary glance, then went quickly from the room.

Huguette grasped Andrea's wrist. "Listen carefully. There is something you must do for me."

"Of course. Anything I can." Andrea promised rashly.

From under the coat the French girl pulled out a bundle of silky dark brown fur. "I borrowed this yesterday, but you must please return it for me. Will you?"

Andrea gently touched the luxurious ermine cape stole. "This is what you had on under your raincoat, isn't it."

"But naturally. I told you I did not want to spoil it."

"That's understandable," commented Andrea, "when you'd borrowed it. It's beautiful. Who's the lucky owner?"

"Miss Jensen, the Danish lady."

Andrea gasped and took her hand away from the fur as though it had stung her. Huguette continued quickly, "This must be back in her wardrobe before she finds out."

"Before—? You mean she doesn't know you borrowed it?"

Huguette's pretty mouth curled in derisive amusement. "Do you think she would be charmed to lend it to me?"

"I don't understand—"

"Listen to me. It is simple," declared Huguette, but Andrea's senses were benumbed by the enormity of her friend's daring action.

"Why can't you bring it back yourself?"

"I have hurt my foot. Bobbie took me to a party last night and he was driving me back and we crashed."

"Then perhaps you ought to be in hospital?"

"No, no, it is not serious. I can walk, and later Bobbie will get me back to the Belvedere."

"Why can't he bring you now? Then you could replace the fur yourself."

Huguette shook her head in desperation. "What an imbecile you are, Andrea! Bobbie cannot use his car, so he has to wait until later when one of his friends will come. And the stole must be replaced while Miss Jensen is at dinner or it is likely that she might miss it."

"Then couldn't I give it to Margaret or one of the other girls to take in? I'm not supposed to be on that floor."

Huguette laughed with considerable ill-humor. "Margaret! She would enjoy herself very much, that one, if she could go to the May Queen with a nice tale about me."

"The May Queen? Who is that? Oh, you mean my . . . Mrs. Mayfield." Andrea was conscious of the slip she had almost made, but fortunately Huguette was too intent on her own troubles to notice.

"Please listen, Andrea. When you are sure Miss Jensen is at dinner, you go to her suite. You know it is the one called Norfolk. You put the stole on the right-hand shelf in her wardrobe. At the bottom, behind some coats, you will find a polythene bag. Put the fur back into that, then on the shelf."

"But how on earth can I walk about public corridors with a fur coat over my arm or under my apron?" Andrea asked.

Huguette banged her fist on the other girl's arm and wailed with exasperation. "Could anybody be more stupid than an English girl? You put the fur into a pillowcase, of course, and who would then notice a maid carrying a pillow?"

Andrea's eyes opened with surprise. "Oh, I see." She was beginning to see more than this one incident, and wondering how many other articles Huguette had temporarily borrowed and replaced unobtrusively without the owner's knowledge or consent.

"That's how you took it from Miss Jensen's room, I suppose?"

Huguette produced a passkey and flourished it like a conjuror drawing rabbits out of a hat. "Here it is. Do not lose it."

Andrea was now frightened as well as appalled. "But we're not allowed to take passkeys out with us. How did you know you'd be wanting it?"

Huguette grinned complacently. "There are times when one forgets to return it."

Andrea stood up. "I'm sorry, Huguette, but I can't do as you ask. If I were caught, I'd be in trouble and so would you."

"I shall be in trouble if Miss Jensen finds her fur is missing." Huguette's lips quivered. "And I am ill and my foot is hurt," she whispered sadly. "It is now that I need a friend, but you will not help me." She dabbed her eyes with a handkerchief.

Andrea weakened.

"How are you going to manage about your foot? Is it badly hurt?"

"It is painful, but I shall manage." Huguette raised her head and wore her martyrdom proudly.

Andrea sighed with vexation. "Oh, I suppose I'll have to help you."

Huguette gave her an angelic smile and patted her hand. "That is a good friend to me."

"How will you be able to go on duty if your foot is damaged?" Andrea asked.

Huguette shrugged. "Every day people are falling downstairs somewhere in the world. Why not Huguette Cloubert who, perhaps tomorrow, will fall down some stairs in the Belvedere?"

Andrea was shocked at Huguette's oblique principles, but also attracted by her audacious charm.

The French girl had not really intended to steal the fur,

only to wear it for a short time, but the car accident had delayed the return.

"All right. I'll help you this time, but never ask me again. I won't encourage your vanity like that."

"Please! I am too tired to listen to sermons." Huguette waved her hand wearily, but the next moment she was all energetic animation as she directed how the fur should be wrapped in brown paper.

"It's going to look odd—taking a parcel like that into the hotel on a Sunday." Andrea objected. "I can't make it look like shopping."

"Is it not possible that you have been out to visit your dressmaker and collect a garment? The English have no imagination at all!"

"And the French have too much! Some of them want to be fine ladies in other people's belongings!" retorted Andrea.

Huguette's answer was a monkey-face grimace.

It was easy enough for Andrea to secrete the parcel into her bedroom, when she returned to the hotel. The difficulty was in knowing exactly when Miss Jensen was at dinner in the restaurant, or even if she'd gone out elsewhere for the evening. *If only I had a fellow conspirator among the waiters!*

But Andrea soon stopped thinking like that. She was falling into Huguette's amoral attitudes.

She walked along the second-floor corridor to see exactly where the Norfolk Suite was located. It would never do to be caught looking for the right rooms with a pillowcase full of ermine in her arms.

A casual query to one of the other maids confirmed that Miss Jensen was not in her suite, and Andrea hurried up to her own room and unwrapped the parcel.

She shook out the fur and stroked its rich, sensuous silkiness.

In spite of herself, she could not resist trying it on, although it looked comical over her black dress and white apron.

She had to use the pillowcase off her own bed, for to obtain one from anybody else would only arouse suspicion.

She crept cautiously down each flight of stairs, her heart in her mouth lest one of the floor housekeepers, or even her aunt, the May Queen herself, should appear and demand what she was doing on the wrong floor.

She knocked on the outer door of the Norfolk Suite, inserted the passkey, which seemed to be burning her hand, and went through the hallway to the bedroom. The sight of masculine pyjamas folded on the bed momentarily checked her.

One glimpse into the wardrobe and she shut the door in panic. It was full of men's clothes. She was in the wrong room.

But Huguette had said the Norfolk Suite. Here were the blue satin headboards, the Wedgewood blue carpet, the pale honey-color furniture, just as the French girl had described. Besides, the passkey had fitted.

Andrea decided to escape immediately and take the stole to her own room until she found out exactly where Miss Jensen's suite was.

Before she could move, the door leading to the sitting room opened suddenly. Mr. Holt stood there. Andrea gave a small, frightened gasp.

"Sorry. Did I startle you?" He half smiled. "I heard you come in."

"I—I thought this was Miss Jensen's suite."

"So it was, but she changed into another one today. And as somebody else has my usual one, I'm here instead."

Could any move have been more disastrous? She cast a hunted glance toward the outer door, but in the most casual manner he seemed to be barring the way.

"Did you want something?" he asked kindly.

"No, sir." To herself, she added, *Yes sir. A nice big hole in the ground.*

She swallowed what seemed like an enormous obstruction in her throat. "I . . . I just brought an extra pillow for Miss Jensen. I'll take it to her."

"I see." He stared at the pillowcase in her arms. "It seems that Miss Jensen has an odd taste in pillows."

She followed his gaze and saw with shocked horror that several dark furry tails had escaped from the pillowcase.

Mr. Holt took the bundle from Andrea's petrified grasp and shook out the stole.

"Could this be the fur that Miss Jensen declares is missing?" he asked. "Or is there a simple explanation of how you come to be carrying this about in a pillowcase?"

CHAPTER THREE

THERE WAS NO END to the shocks, Andrea thought. So Miss Jensen had already discovered her loss!

"It was not stolen," she managed to say at last. "It was borrowed . . . for . . . for just an evening."

"By you?"

"No. A friend. I was hoping to return the fur before Miss Jensen discovered it was missing."

In this moment of shame, Andrea wished that she had refused to help Huguette.

"This is very interesting," Mr. Holt commented. "Come and sit down and tell me about this practice of borrowing hotel visitors' clothes."

Andrea said quickly, "It isn't usual. This was an exceptional case."

He gestured toward an armchair in the sitting room, but she merely sat on the extreme edge.

"In what way—exceptional?" he wanted to know.

"Well—perhaps more daring than most of us." Andrea was trying to put Huguette in the most favorable light, without at the same time casting a slur on the good name of all the rest of the staff.

Mr. Holt smiled. "But not daring enough to come and replace the article she borrowed."

"She was prevented. That's why I came instead."

Although her face was turned away and she could not meet his eyes she was aware of his glance.

"Aren't you the girl I knocked through the main entrance a few weeks ago?"

"Yes, sir."

"Tell me your name."

"Andrea Lansdale."

"Lansdale? I heard about a Charles Lansdale when I was at Cambridge. A first-class scholar everybody thought him."

"He was my father." Andrea now spoke with a certain defiance. Sooner or later her aunt would hear of this escapade, and that would be the finish of any hotel career for Andrea, so there was now no point in not being proud of her father.

"Then what are you doing here, working as a chambermaid?" Mr. Holt demanded.

"I have to earn a living. My father was killed in an accident a short time ago. So I'm training for hotel work and everybody has to start as a chambermaid and learn all branches."

"I'm sorry about your father." There was a long pause and his hand rested on the ermine stole. "Now, what are we to do with this?"

"I must take it to Miss Jensen," Andrea decided, "and face the consequences."

"And what will happen to you?"

Andrea realized that her future prospects were just about as bad as they could possibly be, so she began now to feel annoyed at Mr. Holt's persistent effrontery. But for his interference, she reflected, the fur would have been safely back in Miss Jensen's wardrobe and in the correct suite.

"I expect I shall be dismissed," she said firmly and this time met his glance squarely.

"Then perhaps we can manage the situation better than that." He began to laugh. "I'll admit now that when you first told me the story of borrowing the fur, I didn't really believe you. It sounded like an invention by a girl caught in the act of trying to put back something she'd helped herself to."

Andrea wondered what kind of small boy Mr. Holt had once been; evidently the sort that speared small insects with a pin and watched them squirm and wriggle.

"But I'm convinced now that you're telling the truth."

"Thank you—sir."

Her irony was not lost upon him and he noted the rebellious set of her mouth. "I'm quite sure," he continued, "that Charles Lansdale's daughter would not plant blame on somebody else in order to save her own skin."

Her eyes softened. Perhaps she had misjudged him.

"I will deal with the fur and its return," he offered. "But you realize that I'm now an accessory after the fact, and you must be more careful in future, even in pulling friends out of the scrapes their vanity leads them into."

"Oh, yes, sir. And thank you. May I go now?"

"Yes, but take my advice. When you're in the mood for a spot of self-sacrifice, see that the cause is more worthy."

When she had gone, he grinned at himself for sounding so pompous. Probably he would have dealt differently with any ordinary chambermaid, but it had been surprising to find Professor Lansdale's daughter working on that level.

There was still Miss Jensen's fur wrap to be disposed of and he telephoned Mrs. Mayfield. "Could you please come and see me as soon as possible? I'm in my room and I've something to show you."

He and the housekeeper were old acquaintances, for he had been staying at the Belvedere on frequent occasions over a period of more than two years, supervising the various tall blocks of shops and offices now being erected by his company.

"I'm very relieved that the fur has been found," Mrs. Mayfield told him, "although I can't think how it was overlooked when Miss Jensen changed suites. These little mishaps are very embarrassing to us when they occur in the hotel."

"And I suppose the owner was very angry and wanted to call in the police?" Keir Holt asked.

Catherine Mayfield smiled. "Actually, no. She was certainly annoyed, but the first thing she did was examine her insurance policy. I was glad she took the affair so calmly." Then, as an afterthought, she asked, "But how did you know that something of Miss Jensen's was missing?"

"I heard her say so," he answered. "So when I saw the stole lying at the bottom of the wardrobe, I thought it was probably hers. I know she usually has this suite when she's here."

Mrs. Mayfield made no further comment about the matter. "I'm sorry we couldn't let you have your usual suite, but it will be vacant in two days' time. Everything all right here?"

"Yes. Everything."

Miss Jensen was resting in her sitting room when the housekeeper restored the ermine stole to her.

"Oh, I am delighted!" The slim Danish girl with silky blond hair unwound her long slender legs from under her. "Where was it found?"

Catherine Mayfield was reluctant to admit a reflection on the honesty and efficiency of her staff. How could anything so conspicuous as a large fur stole be overlooked when a maid cleaned and dusted a room ready for the next occupant, especially the Belvedere's premier suite?

"I'm afraid it had been accidentally caught up in the blankets when they were taken out of your room to be sent to the cleaners." Mrs. Mayfield hoped this sounded like a plausible explanation.

The Danish girl was examining the fur for signs of damage, but seemed satisfied. "I am so terribly fond of my furs," she sighed, caressing the silky folds of the stole.

In the seclusion of her own sitting room, Mrs. Mayfield pondered over the mysterious affair. She was convinced that somebody had either intended to steal or else "borrow" the fur and then, as soon as the theft was discovered, had surreptitiously put it back, but unfortunately in the wrong room. That meant it would be somebody who did not know that Miss Ingrid Jensen was no longer in the Norfolk. So that ruled out Miss Deakin, the assistant housekeeper on second floor, and all the maids under her.

Mrs. Mayfield was not satisfied. Maids on other floors could be suspected, or even other hotel guests who might have had access to Miss Jensen's room, and the housekeeper was determined to find the real culprit.

When Andrea went to the women's staff hall for supper, she was still smarting with shame and anger that another girl's escapade should have led her into a foolish predicament.

Miriam was full of teasing remarks, but Andrea was in no mood to enjoy them. "Did you have a good time with him this afternoon?" Miriam nudged two other girls. "Our Andy has soon got herself a boyfriend."

But Andrea paid little attention to the chatter around her. As soon as she was free she sat in her room, her mind churning all kinds of wild possibilities. Supposing Aunt Catherine heard about it? Well, she was sure to know about the affair if Miss Jensen had already complained of a loss. Then supposing she discovered that Andrea was concerned in it? The very thought of Aunt Catherine's face made Andrea shiver with fright. Only now did she realize how doubly careful she must be at every step, much more than other trainees, not to put a wrong foot forward.

Huguette limped into the room, groaned and muttered with pain, then flopped on her bed. Her ankle was swollen and bandaged.

"Oh! Your ankle!" Andrea exclaimed. "Why didn't you let me know what time you'd be back? I'd have come down to the staff entrance to meet you and help you up the stairs."

"Tell me—did you return madame's goods?" Huguette asked tersely.

"Everything went wrong." Andrea related her misadventure. "It would have been all right if Miss Jensen had not changed suites today of all days."

Huguette flung up her arms. "*Mon dieu!* And if I had not been in the car crashing, I would have been here this morning and put back the stole, whether she moved her suite or not." Huguette leaned forward and tapped Andrea's arm. "Andrea, it is extremely lucky that Monsieur Holt caught *you*, instead of me, red in the hand."

"Red-handed, you mean. And why lucky? Any moment tomorrow I shall expect to be on the carpet with Miss Wyvern or Mrs. Mayfield. I was absolutely petrified with fright. I thought he might even hand me over to the police, especially as Miss Jensen knew the fur was missing."

"That is not good. But Monsieur Holt knows you, and

perhaps he thinks he should protect you because he knocked you down.''

Andrea sighed. She thought Mr. Holt had tried to help her solely because he had heard of her father. ''Well, please, Huguette, in future don't help yourself to the guests' finery and expect me to get you out of trouble. Once is enough.''

She helped Huguette to undress. ''Shall I put a fresh bandage on your ankle?''

''You are very kind, Andrea. I am very grateful.''

Next morning, Huguette's ankle was definitely worse. ''You can't go on duty like that,'' Andrea protested. ''Let me go down and tell Miss Deakin you're ill.''

But Huguette refused to listen. With Andrea's help, she put on her uniform and reported for duty. Andrea was worried, certain that the French girl would do still more damage by walking around when she ought to be resting the foot.

While Andrea was breakfasting in the staff hall, a girl came rushing in with the news that Huguette Cloubert had fallen down a few stairs and sprained her ankle. Andrea managed to appear suitably surprised and concerned, but most of all she was surprised at herself, reflecting that one deception inevitably led to a dozen other subterfuges.

''Poor Huguette!'' she exclaimed. ''Where is she?''

''In the May Queen's room.''

Andrea wondered apprehensively whether expert examination would reveal that the sprain had taken place the night before last, and anyway, how did one sprain an ankle in a minor car accident? But there was no sense in going to meet trouble; Andrea found that trouble advanced rapidly toward her of its own accord. Her aunt sent a message commanding her to appear at once in the housekeeper's office.

''Sit down, Andrea. When did Huguette injure her ankle?''

The girl lifted startled eyes to Aunt Catherine's face. She was unprepared for so direct an approach. ''I—I thought this morning.''

Mrs. Mayfield moved away toward the window of her office, looked out, then swung back toward her niece. ''If you're going to be any kind of success here, Andrea, there must be complete honesty between us. Most of my staff know my demands—efficiency, willingness and that they should take an interest in their work. But most of all I demand truthfulness, and I have been known to overlook many petty offences—if only I'm told the truth."

Andrea's face flushed. "I'm sorry, but you can't expect me to tell tales."

"Huguette's ankle is telling tales enough. Quite obviously, she did not damage it this morning—or even last night. It's badly bruised and must be very painful for her." Aunt Catherine paused and as Andrea did not reply, continued, "I understand your sense of loyalty to a fellow worker, but there is also loyalty due to me, not because we are related, but because I must put the interests of the hotel first. You'll help Huguette far more by telling the truth, Andrea."

"Haven't you asked Huguette herself when she hurt her foot?"

"Yes. She told me that it happened on Saturday night."

Andrea gasped. "Yet you pretended—not to know!"

"Not at all. I hoped you would tell the truth the first time I asked."

Andrea's anger overcame her prudence and she forgot the respective positions of herself and her aunt. "I don't like your detective methods, Aunt Catherine. You tried to trap me."

"You must please forget here that I'm your aunt. As I've pointed out to you, if our relationship is known, your position here will become very uncomfortable indeed. The girls won't talk to you. They'll suspect, however wrongly, that you've been planted among them to carry tales to me. Those in the higher grades will look upon you with a certain jealousy in case you may be given the promotion that they've earned and deserve. Only the manager and the staff manager know that you're my niece, and I'd advise you, for your own sake, to keep quiet about it."

Andrea burned with resentment. "It might be better if I left as early as possible and—earned a living some other way."

She was not looking at Aunt Catherine, but became aware after a moment or two of the older woman's cynical regard.

"You promised to stay at least twelve months," her aunt reminded her, with a cold smile, "but I doubt if I could hold you to that. Only you can know whether you have sufficient backbone to stay the course, or whether at the first sign of discomfort you give in and follow your . . . natural inclination to evade responsibility. The choice is yours, Andrea, but you must make up your mind now—because not only is this Monday morning and the busiest day of the week, but I have plans for you—if you are staying. If you're leaving, then there's no point in our discussing them."

"I'll stay," she said quietly, and knew that she was sentencing herself to almost a year's self-control and restraint for the sake of vindicating her father's reputation as a man who dodged responsibility and followed only his own desires.

"Good!" Aunt Catherine's approving voice broke in on Andrea's thoughts. "Then I'm giving you a change of work. Reception is very shorthanded—one girl away on holiday, one ill—and your shorthand and typing should be useful there."

Andrea was amazed. To be given what amounted to a promotion immediately after the stormy scene of a few moments ago was almost incomprehensible. But she was learning slowly that Aunt Catherine was a strange woman, ruthless but just.

"Thank you very much," was all Andrea could whisper.

"Finish your duties for today and report to Miriam and then to Miss Wyvern," her aunt instructed.

"And Huguette?"

Catherine Mayfield smiled. "I like you, Andrea, for that. It's a good thing not to forget one's friends on any level. Huguette will be properly looked after. Don't worry."

Only when Andrea had resumed her tasks in the bedrooms on the fourth floor did she wonder how much Aunt Catherine knew about Miss Jensen's fur. Supposing Huguette had confessed everything? But no, that couldn't be true, or the cross-examination would have been much more thorough. The secret knowledge of her own part in the deception gave her twinges of shame, but there was nothing she could do without involving Huguette—and, of course, Mr. Holt.

Miriam was eager to know why Andrea had been kept so long in the May Queen's office.

"I'm to work in Reception—only temporarily—while some of the others are away," Andrea explained.

Miriam slapped down a pile of linen onto a stripped bed. "Huh! So I suppose you think you know all there is to know about our work!"

"I shall be sent back again when the other staff comes back."

"I'll bet you won't!" Miriam punched a bolster unnecessarily hard. "I suppose it's that pretty face. Shame to hide it up here on fourth when you could be down on the desk smiling at all the men!"

Andrea laughed. "I doubt if I shall be given a chance of smiling at the men. I'll be kept too busy in the background."

Miriam sighed. "Or perhaps you're the manager's niece or something, eh?"

Andrea was glad of her newly found self-control. She saw how even a single move that might spell promotion was open to misunderstanding. "No, not even his daughter or anything like that."

Miss Wyvern's reaction was neither as blunt nor as friendly as Miriam's.

"Are you still sharing Huguette's room?" she asked.

"Yes, as far as I know," Andrea replied.

"Oh, I thought perhaps you were, er, being separated. We usually try to keep troublemakers apart."

Andrea wanted to flare up, but again she curbed her impulses. "Are we considered troublemakers?"

Miss Wyvern's fair, slightly discontented face became a mask. "You know best whether any trouble has occurred. When you come on duty tonight, please be punctual. On several occasions you've been late."

She hurried off down the corridor before Andrea could frame a reply, or at least one that would not be deemed insolent.

Huguette was in bed, but not asleep, when Andrea went off duty.

"How is your foot?"

The French girl smiled. "Much better. Miss Deakin is very good at first aid. She has certificates, she says. So she has bandaged me once more and given me some pills if I cannot sleep."

"How lucky when you get on so well with your floor housekeeper," Andrea commented. "Mine—Miss Wyvern—dislikes me very much."

"You are too pretty. All the time she is getting old and she would like to marry someone before it is too late."

"Old?" queried Andrea. "She's not more than thirty. Or perhaps thirty-two."

"You are without brains, my child. To marry after one is thirty, one must be so beautiful that it is clear one is taking a long time to choose—or else one must be magnificently rich. Wyvern is not very beautiful and not rich."

Andrea laughed. It was impossible not to be amused by Huguette's philosophy.

"Well, I shall escape her for a while. I'm going down to Reception tomorrow."

Huguette almost sprang out of bed, then winced as she moved her ankle. "Reception? You are promoted?"

"Only for a time, while others are on holiday."

Huguette sank back on her pillow like one of Dumas's dying heroines. "You travel fast, Andrea! Down from fourth to ground floor—just like that. By the elevator! Oh, you will not be seen talking to me now, a mere chambermaid, even if we're on the private suites."

"Nonsense! I'm still the same, whatever position I take—and I did come here as a trainee. From now on you must speak French to me every night. I might need it down there."

After she was in bed, she said, "Huguette, how much did you tell Mrs. Mayfield? She guessed about your ankle."

"How could she fail when the bruises were like ripe plums?"

"Then what was the point of pretending you had tripped here in the hotel?" Andrea queried.

"I told her I had been in an accident yesterday, but I did not wish to be neglecting my duties, so I tried to start work this morning—and I fell. That was true, entirely true!" declared Huguette.

Andrea gave up trying to follow the torturous lines of her friend's reasoning.

"Then she doesn't know about Miss Jensen—or the fur?"

"Naturally not. Let us forget the affair. Miss Jensen has her ermine—I have my damaged ankle—and tomorrow you will meet the millionaire who will be dazzled by your lovely eyes. Good night."

CHAPTER FOUR

As AUNT CATHERINE had pointed out when Andrea first started, the Belvedere's rush period was from Monday to Friday, when the businessmen, the sales representatives, staff managers and executives of all kinds were in. Unlike seaside or resort hotels, weekends and holidays were much quieter.

Andrea found that working as a chambermaid in the seclusion of a bedroom floor and especially during the absence of the occupants was like living in a gentle backwater compared with the hectic demands of Reception. In addition, with so many businessmen in the hotel and Millbridge the center of a large industrial area, there was a great demand for personal secretarial services. Somebody would need correspondence attended to, or stock lists retyped or a précis report of men interviewed for positions in the district.

She had not realized that so much business was conducted in the hotel. To cope with social functions such as luncheons and dinners, which every hotel took in its stride, the Belvedere employed a banqueting manager with a small staff of his own.

But lunch or cocktail parties were combined with displays of products set up in a private room; conferences, meetings, film shows, property sales, all were governed by a strict timetable. A weekly functions list and then a daily list in greater detail were circulated to all departments, and Andrea began to catch a glimpse of the enormous amount of organization involved.

"In my ignorance," she told Jill Brookman, one of the

permanent receptionists, "I just imagined that salesmen stayed here for a week or fortnight, toured the area selling whatever their goods were, or supervising other salesmen, and then went off to the next town."

"If you work down here a bit longer," Jill replied, "you'll come up against some of the fantastic affairs that happen here."

When the telephone rang, Jill answered, then looked across at Andrea. "Mr. Holt in the Somerset wants someone to do a report for him."

"But at three o'clock I have to help Mr. Watford check his cosmetic samples in the stockroom."

"I think you'd better go to Mr. Holt," Jill decided. "I'll explain to Mr. Watford."

Andrea had not seen Mr. Holt since the occasion when he had caught her with Miss Jensen's fur stole and she was not anxious to meet him again now, but it was wiser not to argue with her superior.

He seemed surprised when Andrea entered his sitting room.

"I understand you want a report typed," she explained.

"Can you take it down—in shorthand?" From his great height he looked down on her as though she were an inefficient ant.

"Yes, of course. I was a stenographer before I came here."

"Oh, I see. I didn't realize that you were no longer acting as chambermaid."

"I'm temporarily in Reception," she told him.

The report was a long one, complicated by sets of figures and building terms, which he explained. At the end, he said, "This is extremely confidential."

"Yes, sir, I understand that. I'll be very careful."

She picked up her notebook and the folder of papers he had given her. As she reached the door, he said, "I did the best I could—to get the fur back to its owner." The faint hint of a smile played around his mouth and reached his eyes.

Andrea longed to ask him by what methods—direct to Miss Jensen or through some third party—but decided that this might not be discreet.

"Thank you. It was kind of you," she murmured.

As she worked on the report, she reflected on how uncomfortable and ill at ease she became in Mr. Holt's presence. She hoped very much that she would not have to do further work for him. Even over the fur, he managed to remind her of the incident in the most embarrassing way; anyone else would either have kept silent or made a joke of it.

But even he, it seemed, had his difficulties. As Andrea typed from her notes, she saw that the report was a survey of the stoppages, minor strikes, accidents and near accidents that had taken place on the block of shops and offices that Mr. Holt's company was building.

"Even after due allowances has been made for the normal troubles of building operations, it seems to me that certain disruptive forces must be at work to account for the delays, the inconveniences and for the lack of precautions that have resulted in so many accidents."

When the long report was finished, Andrea decided she had better take it personally to Mr. Holt. On the stairs she met Mr. Selborn, a sales representative for a plastics firm. Middle-aged, slightly bald, with a kindly smile, he had given Andrea various batches of correspondence during the past fortnight.

"Finished for the day?" he asked.

"Not until eight," she replied.

He walked beside her along the corridor.

"Excuse me," she murmured, as she approached the Somerset Suite. "I have to take some papers to Mr. Holt."

"I'm on my way there. I'll take them for you."

"I'd rather take them in myself, thank you."

He smiled and made no comment, but followed her into Mr. Holt's suite.

"Thank you, Miss Lansdale. Oh, come in, Selborn. Help yourself to a drink while I read through this report."

Returning to Reception, Andrea felt rather foolish. Evidently the two men knew each other quite well, probably because both of them stayed so often at the Belvedere.

Mervyn Watford stood at the reception desk.

"So there you are!" He wagged a playful finger at her.

"Who was the man who filched you from me this afternoon? I demand to know!"

"I, er, thought Miss Brookman explained, sir, that I had another call."

"But mine was first," he declared.

"I'm sorry—but I just have to go where I'm sent. I've no choice in the matter." Andrea raised her gray-blue eyes toward this middle-height, fair-haired, dapper young man who, by all accounts, was rising rapidly in the cosmetic world.

"Ah, but if you had a choice—then you'd undoubtedly come to me?"

Andrea skilfully slid through the opening by the porter's desk and around the corner to the center of Reception. Now a width of mahogany counter separated her from Mr. Watford and she could at least assume a businesslike manner with a guest and it would not look as though he were trying to flirt with her.

"Can I help you now, Mr. Watford? Or is it too late?"

"Never too late. But work can be skipped for another day. When are you off duty?"

"Eight o'clock," she answered.

"How about having a little snack with me somewhere—if only to make amends for letting me down this afternoon?"

Andrea flushed. At least one, if not two, of the hotel porters must be hearing every word of this conversation and probably chuckling to themselves and each other behind the evening paper.

"I'm terribly sorry, but I've things to do—"

"What about tomorrow? I know you're off duty," he persisted.

At this moment, Jill Brookman appeared. Andrea gave Mr. Watford a half-hostile, half-apologetic glance and scuttled behind the partition into the inner office.

She was busily checking the following week's reservations when Jill came in sometime later.

"Why don't you go out with Mervyn Watford tomorrow? He'll give you a good time, and probably a tiny sample vial of his firm's latest concoction labeled Moon Dusk or Spring

Fantasy. Everybody goes out with Mervyn. He's good fun. And by no means a wolf.''

Andrea glanced up at Jill, then away. "I don't know. I've only spoken to him about three times.''

Jill giggled. "Listen. We once had a girl here on Reception. Two days after she came, a guest staying in the house took one look at her—just one—invited her to dinner, married her three weeks later and whisked her off to Brazil. He turned out to be a multi-millionarie and had a title—count or baron or something.''

"Does that mean that we all ought to accept invitations, in case the man's a rich tycoon?" Andrea asked.

"Entirely up to you.''

On Saturday morning, Mervyn renewed his invitation and Andrea thought it was babyish to refuse.

"Would you like to walk in the country?" he asked her. "Tea and crumpets and blackberry jelly at an inn?''

"Yes, I'd like that.''

Mervyn appeared so entirely the epitome of urban sophistication that Andrea was surprised to find how much she enjoyed the warm pleasant September afternoon walking with him along lanes and footpaths, and telling him of her own early life, mainly at school, then in a country village.

"I like extremes," he told her. "Absolutely rural or right bang in the center of a city. What I can't stand are the great wastes of suburbia—unhappy hodgepodge of town and country. When I was young I lived in a long street of houses, every one of them alike. My mother painted our front door yellow—possibly so that she could pick it out on a foggy night—and the neighbors were shocked. All the other doors were brown varnish. I had to knock down a boy who shouted at me that I was yellow, like our front door.''

They had tea, as he had promised, at a small inn, where the crumpets were delicious, the oak beams and paneling genuine seventeenth century and two huge Labradors gently toasted themselves in front of a log fire.

They returned eventually to Millbridge by train, Mervyn declaring that it was a welcome change not to be chained to the wheel of his car.

"What would you like to do? Have a quick dinner and see a film afterward? Or anything else you'd like?"

"After all those crumpets and cake, I can't eat dinner so soon."

He knew of a small cinema in a back street where they showed interesting, out-of-date films. "But it's too soon. Come and have a cocktail in the Prince's."

In her pleated skirt and cream jacket, Andrea felt self-conscious and countrified as she and Mervyn went down the thick-carpeted staircase, but by the time he had ordered drinks she realized that other people's dress styles varied considerably, from dinner jackets to thornproof tweeds and cotton dresses.

When the drinks arrived, Mervyn raised his glass toward her. His round placid face beamed. "To you, Andrea. We must do this more often."

Andrea smiled, sipped her martini and looked quickly away to avoid Mervyn's foolishly intent gaze. She found herself staring across the room straight into the eyes of Mr. Holt. He gave her a faint smile and nod of recognition, then turned back toward his companion, whom Andrea now recognized as Mr. Selborn.

Hot color swept up into her face, yet there wasn't the slightest reason why she should feel ashamed at being seen in another hotel with a friend. When Mervyn suggested that it was time to leave for the cinema, she was glad to go and very careful not to look again in Mr. Holt's direction.

The Italian film was short and charming; afterward, Mervyn took her to a snack bar where the crowd was noisy, but the sandwiches and coffee excellent.

It was still not quite eleven o'clock when he brought her back to the Belvedere.

"And this is where you disappear into your secret hide-out." He waved toward the unobtrusive staff entrance.

"Thank you, Mr. Watford, for a very pleasant outing," Andrea said. "I've enjoyed it."

"Good. When is your next free day? We'll fix up something, eh?"

Miss Wyvern chanced to pass at that moment. She gave Andrea a slightly contorted smile and a curt "Good night."

"Was that Laura Wyvern?" Mervyn asked quietly when the assistant housekeeper had entered the Belvedere.

"Oh, you know her, too!" Andrea mocked.

"I know everybody in the Belvedere worth knowing."

Up in her room, Andrea eagerly awaited Huguette's return, for the French girl had also been off duty today. Huguette came in later with a most melancholy expression.

"If I were in Paris," she exclaimed, "I would throw myself into the Seine."

"Well, there's a river here in Millbridge. Won't that do?" inquired Andrea.

"So small and dirty!"

"What does it matter how dirty it is if you're going to drown yourself? What's wrong?"

"Bobbie," snapped Huguette. "He is gone."

"Gone where?"

"Disappeared! Perhaps he is in prison."

Andrea was alarmed. "Why should he be in prison?"

Huguette shrugged. "He is sometimes lucky to keep out."

"But what does he do? What are his crimes?"

"He likes good cars and he cannot afford them. So—he takes one that he likes—and drives away. Sometimes he brings it back, sometimes not."

Andrea gasped. "That's what happened when you were hurt! He was driving a stolen car and smashed it!"

"You are quite a lady detective!" was Huguette's sarcastic comment. "I will tell you the rest of the story. He crashed into a lamp post. Quickly he lifted me out of the car and carried me into a small, dark street. But nobody came to see what had happened. So then he went to find a telephone booth to ask a friend to help him."

"You mean he left you, knowing that you were hurt?"

"Could he carry me on his shoulder while he looked for a telephone? He told me what to say if the police should come—that I had been knocked down by the car and the driver had run away. But nobody came, and then Bobbie came back to me and later his friend brought a car and took us to Bobbie's sister's house—that was where you came for the fur."

Andrea was silent for a few moments.

Then she burst out angrily, "Why d'you trouble with a . . . a car thief?"

Huguette smiled complacently. "Bobbie is very nice and he dances divinely."

"Yes—when you're *able* to dance and he doesn't smash your ankle for you!" Andrea retorted.

"We were to meet tonight, but he did not come. Oh, it could be that he is tired of me. So I went to his sister at this Barnbattle Green and she was worried, also. He has not been seen for three days."

"Does he live with his sister?"

"No, I do not think so. But she knew, that one, that there is something wrong." After a pause, Huguette asked, "Did you go out today?"

"Yes . . . with Mervyn Watford." Andrea deliberately added no further explanation just then so that she might see Huguette's reaction.

"Ah! Mervyn Watford," muttered the French girl. "He is a pretty man."

"Pretty? What an extraordinary expression!"

"He has pretty manners, too. Somewhere I think he has also a pretty mother and he will never marry because all his life he likes to take out pretty girls."

"Has he taken you?"

"But naturally. Everybody—unless they are so old and ugly that he cannot be seen with them."

Andrea felt deflated. "And I suppose he took you to a film?"

"Yes, a very good French film," agreed Huguette cheerfully.

"And did you walk in the country first and have crumpets at an old inn?"

"*Mon dieu!* No! Walk in the country? It would kill me. What are these crumpets at the inn?"

"Some other time." Andrea brushed the query aside. "And what perfume did he give you in a little sample bottle?"

"I forget. But it was not as good as Chanel."

Andrea held out her own tiny pyramid of Summer Enchantment. Huguette whisked out the stopper and sniffed.

"Not bad—for English scent," was her verdict.

When Andrea was summoned the next day to her aunt's office she wondered what new crime she had now committed.

"Andrea, I'm not trying to organize your free time for you," Mrs. Mayfield began, by which Andrea knew that this was exactly her aunt's intention, "but perhaps a little friendly warning about Mr. Watford . . . ?"

"What about him?" Andrea asked cautiously, but coldly.

Aunt Catherine smiled. "Just not to take him too seriously, that's all."

"I know already. He takes everybody out and it doesn't mean anything." Andrea's indignation bubbled inside her, not because of Mervyn who poured out his universal charm without much discrimination— Jill Brookman had warned her about that—but who had tattled about Andrea's companion or how she spent her free time? It might have been Jill, but that was doubtful.

Mr. Holt had seen her in the Prince hotel with Mervyn. Then there was Miss Wyvern, who had passed them at the staff entrance. Andrea thought she was the most likely talebearer.

"Working here will possibly give you opportunities of meeting all kinds of men," Aunt Catherine continued, "and men whom you wouldn't normally meet. But as long as you remember that usually they are here for a very short time, you'll be all right."

Andrea was still ruffled when she went back to her work in Reception.

Certainly, as housekeeper, Aunt Catherine was more or less responsible for the moral welfare of her staff and doubtless she intended to take that responsibility very seriously where Andrea was involved, *but need she treat me like a half-wit*, the girl asked herself.

Andrea was putting in a short spell on the reception desk a few evenings later, while Jill went to supper. This was the first time she had been in charge alone and hoped no visitor would ask her conundrums she couldn't answer, but the two porters were at their own desk and she knew they would try to help her.

She answered queries, handed on messages, confirmed reservations and appointments, answered the telephone. Then somebody said, "Why, Andrea! So this is your hotel!"

Trevor Dennistoun had detached himself from a small knot of men who stood in the entrance hall.

"Hello, Trevor—oh, I mean, Mr. Dennistoun."

"You've always called me Trevor."

"Yes, but I'm supposed to address everybody in a proper, formal way when I'm on reception duty."

"I see. How d'you like it here?" he asked.

"Very well. It's good experience."

He glanced over his shoulder toward his companions. "What time are you off duty? Come and have a drink or a coffee with me in the lounge."

Andrea became aware of two other men who were patiently waiting for attention.

"I can't go in there, I'd get shot. Nine o'clock. Please excuse me," she murmured hurriedly, and turned toward the other waiting guests.

As she attended to the new arrivals and gave the room number to the porter, she had time to observe that almost as soon as Trevor went back to his friends, the party was joined by three ladies.

One of the ladies was Miss Ingrid Jensen, who was back again in the hotel after an absence of a week or so.

Andrea cast a glance down the register, but Trevor Dennistoun's name was not among the day's arrivals, so perhaps he was staying in another hotel, or he might only have come to Millbridge to see his friends.

She did not see him again until the following evening.

"Andrea!" he whispered urgently. "Is Miss Jensen here? Ingrid Jensen."

"I think she left this morning."

"Where has she gone?"

"I don't know."

"But you'll have her forwarding address," Trevor persisted.

"I'll see if I can find out from the departure list," Andrea promised, then glanced up at him. "Why d'you want it?"

Trevor smiled dreamily. "I simply must see her again."

In a few moments Andrea returned to the desk. "Miss Jensen left for Paris this morning. No forwarding address."

Trevor slumped like a man dealt a mortal blow. "Will she come back here?"

"I don't really know. It's possible, but I don't know when." She smiled mischievously at him. "If you'll keep it a secret and not land me in trouble, I can give you her bank address."

He took the slip of paper and impulsively squeezed Andrea's hand.

"Good girl!"

Andrea watched him as he walked quickly out of the hotel.

Poor Trevor! He was obviously dazzled by Miss Jensen's exquisite beauty and charming manner, but he was setting his sights high. She would have to be very attracted, indeed, to marry a young man whose main financial asset was a comparatively modest store in a provincial town, but Mrs. Dennistoun might react very favorably to a daughter-in-law whose father was reputed to be one of the richest men in Denmark.

When she turned back to her work, Andrea saw that Mr. Holt was standing by the porter's desk and had just picked up an evening newspaper.

She met his glance and was puzzled by the intensity of his stare, unsure whether he was regarding her or concentrating on his own thoughts.

It was quite probable that he had witnessed the little free-and-easy scene between her and Trevor. He wouldn't know that they were old friends; he would, no doubt, see a young trainee receptionist flirting with every man who came near her.

The sudden clang of an ambulance outside in the street

broke the trancelike moment and Mr. Holt moved quickly to the entrance. Andrea blinked and went into the inner office.

An hour later she saw the connection between the ambulance and Mr. Holt's quickened interest. The latest edition of the evening paper carried a headline: MORE ACCIDENTS ON CENTURY BLOCK.

CHAPTER FIVE

ANDREA HERSELF took the telephone message when Keir Holt asked for a typist to take a report.

"If she's free, I'd rather have Miss Lansdale," he said curtly. "I don't want to explain technical terms all over again to somebody else."

"This is Miss Lansdale speaking," she answered coolly, hoping he would be abashed, but he merely told her to come to his suite at once.

"How discreet are you?" he greeted her.

"I—I don't know what you mean," she stammered. "It's part of our training—to learn not to talk."

"That last report you did for me ... its contents were known to a rival firm of contractors before my own directors knew."

"But I brought the report straight to you as soon as I'd finished it. You're not accusing me of . . . ."

"Oh, no. I'm just wondering how these things leak out. What about your shorthand notebook? D'you leave that about anywhere? Could anybody else read your notes?"

Andrea considered for a moment. "I'm told my shorthand is rather copperplate-like, so I think it could be read, but my notebook is put into a drawer when I leave Reception."

"Locked?"

"No. Other girls use my table when I'm not there."

He paced around the room. "Then we'll cut out the shorthand. Could you have a typewriter sent up here and take the report straight on it?"

"Oh, yes. Easily."

Before he had finished dictating, his telephone rang. "No, I've no statement to make to the press," he snapped. "And please don't put any further calls through to me until *I* tell you," he added to the switchboard operator.

Andrea sympathized with his shortness of temper. This morning he had been to the hospital to see the three men who had been injured in yesterday's accident, one of them very seriously. He had then spent a long time inspecting the partly erected buildings, and the information he had been given formed the substance of his present report.

"Now the men on the fifth-floor levels threaten to strike tomorrow," he told Andrea. "So that will mean further delays and cost us still more money for penalty clauses in our contract. Then, of course, the insurance company is raising the premiums for possible damages for injury. We already have four cases pending and the three men in yesterday's affair are bound to claim compensation."

Andrea sensed that Keir Holt was in effect talking to himself, speaking his thoughts aloud, and she was not expected to make conversation, but she ventured to ask, "Could it be that all this trouble is caused by a rival firm of contractors?"

His unrewarding glance convinced her that she had said the naive thing. Then his dark eyes softened and almost twinkled. "Well, of course, that is our opinion, Miss Lansdale, but opinions are not facts. There are half a dozen firms who would like to absorb us, and if we can be shown to be inefficient or careless about protection for the men or-unable to avoid delays, then our prestige goes down and soon we might be without contracts at all. If that happens, then the take-over price would be extremely low."

Andrea's business experience had, until now, been limited to a small-town estate and house property agency and it was not too easy to follow very closely Mr. Holt's lines of thought. She could grasp the general implications, but she had not realized that the manipulation of affairs, which eventually were reported on the financial pages of newspapers could involve such dangerous hazards and even men's lives.

When she returned to Reception, she found Dick Palmer,

a local newspaperman, leaning on the desk. She had met him several times, for he was engaged to Jill Brookman and often came in for a drink and any morsel of news he could pick up.

"Hello, Andy!" he greeted her. "What's the latest news?"

"How should I know? That's your job."

"Nobody fallen out of a top-story window or drowned himself in his bath? No thrilling fights on the fire escape? No rumors to be denied about that South American actress being secretly married to the Norwegian scientist?"

Andrea shrugged. "Sorry, Dick, but nobody tells me anything."

"Fortunate for us chaps that some people really *like* talking."

"Some people talk too much," she retorted, and vanished behind the partition to the inner office.

During her free time next day, Andrea was impelled to go and watch some of the work on the Century block. The contractors had provided an observation platform for the benefit of all idlers who enjoyed watching other people work. She didn't know whether the threatened strike had taken place, but plenty of activity was going on. Far below street level men looking like pygmies moved around banging girders into place or pouring concrete into foundations; another part of the block was nearer completion and slabs of facing stone were hauled up by crane and guided to gangs of men working on narrow scaffolding. It needed little imagination to see how swiftly and easily a single careless action could bring disaster.

She half turned to move away from the little group of men on the observation platform, when somebody at her elbow spoke to her.

"You're at the Belvedere, aren't you?"

"Hello, Mr. Selborn. I didn't know you were here."

He gave her his slow, benevolent smile. "Everyone ought to spend a little time standing and staring. It's good for the soul." He sighed. "Pity about all those accidents, though. Can't make the men feel very safe when they don't know from one minute to the next whether a few tons of stone or girderwork will come crashing down on them.''

"No. But in a way I suppose they get accustomed to taking *some* risks—like motorists, or sailors,'' Andrea said. "You couldn't go through life and be certain that nothing at all would ever hurt you. Even nurses and doctors take the risk of catching diseases from their patients.''

She didn't understand what forces urged her to minimize the accident risks of a profession about which she knew so little, and suddenly she flushed and thought how foolish and ignorant she must sound to Mr. Selborn, who was blinking good-naturedly at her.

"That's absolutely right,'' he agreed, "and maybe it's only just bad luck that this Century block seems a bit— fated.''

She nodded. "Perhaps it is. Excuse me, I have to go back on duty.''

On Friday, Miss Jensen, back from Paris, appeared suddenly and demanded her usual suite, the Norfolk.

"Yes, madam.'' Andrea who happened to be on the desk, examined the reservations book. "I think the suite is vacant, but I'll make sure.''

At weekends, most of the expensive private suites were usually free but the Norfolk might be rebooked for next week.

"How long will you be requiring the suite, madam?'' Andrea asked.

Ingrid Jensen turned the full force of her eyes like blue fire, intensified by a white hat and honey-gold hair, onto Andrea. "I have no idea. A few days. Perhaps a week.''

Jill Brookman came to Andrea's assistance. "We have a booking of the Norfolk for Wednesday, madam, but we can probably switch if you still require it.''

When Miss Jensen and her suitcases had been conveyed to the Norfolk, Andrea breathed more freely.

"I find her rather overpowering,'' she confided to Jill. "Not because she must be fabulously rich—anybody who can pay the Norfolk Suite prices must be rolling in money— but because somehow you feel that she radiates electric sparks and any moment she may switch on extra power and burn you up."

"You have the most beautiful thoughts, Andy," Jill commented. "But I know what you mean. She's almost too beautiful to be true. And by the way, did you notice her suit? Paris in every line. Oh, what wouldn't I give sometimes to be wearing some really interesting clothes instead of these dowdy little black dresses!"

"And what would the May Queen say if she caught you wearing cerise ninon and distracting the distinguished business clientele?"

Lately, Andrea had acquired the habit of talking about Aunt Catherine using just the same kind of derogatory terms as all the rest of the staff. It was important to divert the slightest suspicion of her relationship.

Andrea wondered if it would be doing Trevor a good turn or a bad one if she telephoned him the news of Miss Jensen's return, but eventually decided against doing so. If Trevor chose to put himself in the way of getting consumed by Miss Jensen's flaming personality, that was his lookout.

Huguette, at least, was delighted at the return of the Danish girl, for she usually acted as lady's maid and received generous tips.

"Almost I wish I had not tomorrow off, but no matter." she told Andrea.

"Are you going out with Bobbie?"

Huguette squealed with laughter. "He is not the only man in my world. I have other fish to bake."

"Other fish to *fry!*" corrected Andrea. "And I thought you were heartbroken because you hadn't seen him."

"That was a long time ago. He had gone to Scotland."

"In a stolen car?" queried Andrea.

Huguette pouted. "You are not kind. Pouf! What does it matter?"

"It matters a lot. That young man is no good to you. You don't want to be mixed up with a gang of car thieves."

Huguette laughed wickedly. "Or perhaps you do not like to be mixed up with a . . . a fur borrower!" she finished dramatically, rolling her eyes upward.

"Once is enough. It makes me shiver even now when I

think of that awful moment when Mr. Holt caught me with the wretched fur in my hands."

"Ah, but think how it has put you on the map. Mr. Holt thinks of you always as the little heroine who made a great sacrifice for her injured friend. Now you are in Reception he specially wants you."

"Only because I happened to go the first time and some of the other girls are away."

Huguette peeled off her stockings. "Oh, no, *chérie*, it is not so. He likes you. Tell me, what does he do when you are locked with him in his suite?"

"Dictates long reports about his buildings," Andrea answered.

"Does he never come behind you and put his hand on your shoulder or kiss the back of your neck?"

"Certainly not!" Andrea's indignation was genuine enough.

"Ah, but I think you would wish him to do these things."

"If you were there instead of me, you'd be sitting on his knee all the time, I expect."

Huguette sighed with ecstasy. "How exquisite that would be!"

"You're not in love with him, are you?" demanded Andrea.

"No, but I think he would be an excellent lover. That is not the same thing."

"I'm not interested in his capacity as a lover." Andrea yawned and made her voice deliberately sleepy. "I'm tired. It's been a long day and I want my sleep."

Huguette eventually switched off the light. "Ah, it is always the long day if you work in hotel. But I think now that I was foolish not to take the advice of my father and learn to play the typewriter. At least one would sit down sometimes—if only on a man's knee!"

But Andrea was not to be drawn in again. She feigned sleep. Yet she was amused by Huguette's ideas. Keir Holt was surely the last man in the world to perch a girl on his knee or kiss her by stealth.

On Saturday afternoons the atmosphere at the Belvedere was usually so hushed that one could stand outside the lounge bar on the lower mezzanine and listen to the silence. The business clientele were home for the weekend, and the few remaining visitors were either out or asleep. The bars were closed and in darkness; the kitchen staff rested between the hectic rush of lunch and the time to prepare for dinner, chambermaids stretched out on their beds and waiters went home or dozed in obscure corners. Occasionally the elevator gates clanged softly, but apart from the power-plant's rhythmical purring far below in the basement few other sounds disturbed the lull.

But today a sibilant whisper traveled along the grapevine. Andrea was alone on Reception and her attention was first caught when the porter made some obviously significant remark to the waiter serving teas in the lounge. Then the assistant manager came hurriedly out of his office and disappeared into the elevator. The switchboard operator called Andrea to know if Jill Brookman was on or off duty.

"Off for the rest of the day," Andrea answered. "Miss Cameron will come in at six. Why?" But the operator cut off without further reply.

Andrea, impatient to share in the suppressed excitement beckoned the porter over.

"What's up?"

"Nothing. Why?"

"You told George something as he took in that tray of tea."

The porter winked at Andrea. "Yes, miss. The winner of the three-thirty race. He backed a loser."

"Rubbish! What is it really?"

"Somebody's come out in spots." He pointed a finger at her. "Now you'll have to be vaccinated."

She laughed. That was the stock "scare" story for every mystery that took place in the house.

"Something to do with Miss Jensen," he whispered.

"Is she—ill?"

The porter shook his head. "She's healthy enough. It's her temper that's bad."

"But what's happened?"

"I don't know. Mrs. Mayfield is finding out."

Andrea could discover nothing further until one of the

girls in Control, the department responsible for checking that every expense was charged, brought her a tray of tea.

"And what's the latest news?" Andrea asked casually.

"About Miss Jensen, you mean? Oh, there's a terrible shindy going on up there. Miss Jensen says she's had a necklace stolen."

Andrea choked as she sipped her tea. "She's only been here since yesterday." She spoke calmly, but her heart was thumping like mad. Huguette attended to Miss Jensen and Huguette was off duty today. Was this another of the French girl's "borrowings"?

"Miss Jensen says she knows that she had the necklace last night," the other girl said.

"Why on earth doesn't she put her valuables in the manager's safe instead of leaving them lying about loose in her suite?"

Andrea was indignantly annoyed that visitors such as the wealthy Miss Jensen left their property carelessly available to be a temptation to girls like Huguette.

A few minutes later the switchboard operator asked Andrea to go at once to Mrs. Mayfield's office.

"But I can't! I'm alone on Reception."

"Hold on a moment and I'll put you through. . . ."

Aunt Catherine's voice sounded almost immediately.

"Andrea, ask the porter to take over at Reception for a minute or so and I'll send somebody else down."

In her aunt's office, Andrea faced not only Mrs. Mayfield and the assistant manager, but Miss Jensen, as well.

"Miss Jensen has lost a valuable necklace—diamonds and sapphires. . . ."

"And aquamarines, also. And a pearl clasp," Miss Jensen added.

Andrea gazed from one person to another. "I'm sorry—I mean, I'm sorry it's been lost—but I don't understand—"

"Have you any objection to your room being searched?" Aunt Catherine asked.

The girl's face flamed. "Does that mean that I'm suspected of stealing the necklace?"

"Not necessarily. Various other rooms are being searched."

Miss Jensen bounced up from her chair. "Oh, what is the use of searching rooms? First it was my fur stole—" she turned toward Mrs. Mayfield "—as though I can believe your story that the fur was mixed up with the blankets! Now it is my necklace! Next time it will be my rings, my bracelets, my mink coat. But I do not stay for that. Today I leave here and find another hotel."

"No, no, Miss Jensen," the assistant manager implored. "Please give us a chance to try to clear the good name of our hotel."

"You must call for the police," the Danish girl snapped.

"Not yet." Mrs. Mayfield's quiet authority was stronger than the assistant manager's protests. "You must give us time to question our own staff before the police come into it." She turned toward Andrea. "Have you seen the necklace?"

"No, madam."

"Have you entered Miss Jensen's suite?"

"No, madam." Andrea considered that the occasion when Mr. Holt had occupied the suite did not count. She was puzzled by her aunt's reasons for the questioning; several other people had much easier access—chambermaids, the assistant housekeeper for that floor—even a waiter who might have served a meal or cocktails in Miss Jensen's sitting room. It could only be that Mrs. Mayfield connected Andrea with the temporary loss of Miss Jensen's fur, so that now she was the most obvious suspect for a real theft.

Miss Wyvern waited at the foot of the stairs leading to the staff wing, and Andrea felt that she was almost a prisoner in the charge of two wardens as Mrs. Mayfield preceded her two subordinates into Andrea's room.

Andrea watched Laura Wyvern opening dressing-table drawers, searching under handkerchiefs, shaking out clothes, examining the pockets of dresses and coats in the wardrobe, tilting the toes of shoes. Since Andrea shared the room with Huguette, all the French girl's possessions were also exhaustively scrutinized. Then the assistant housekeeper stripped and inspected the beds, and the curtains, turned back the carpet.

With her conscience clear on this occasion, Andrea could feel contempt curling inside her and sensed, too, that her aunt found the task necessary, but distasteful. It was quite evident, though, that Laura Wyvern was filled with a malicious delight.

"I think that will do, Miss Wyvern," Mrs. Mayfield said, and turned to go.

"Don't you want me to search Lansdale herself?"

Andrea's chin tilted up. "I'm quite willing," she said proudly, but her defiant look shot out at Miss Wyvern.

Mrs. Mayfield sighed. "No, I don't think that will be necessary."

Andrea could almost hear the clamor of Miss Wyvern's disappointment.

"I'm sorry we had to do this, Andrea, but I'm sure you understand," her aunt continued. "You may go back to Reception now, but come and see me when you're off duty. And please don't talk about this."

Andrea's thoughts were tumultuous when she took over from her relief receptionist. There were so many possibilities and it was frustrating not to be able to discuss them with someone. There was Huguette, of course, who might have "borrowed" the necklace. Then Miss Jensen might not have lost the necklace at all. Perhaps she had mislaid it. Or the whole affair might be a publicity stunt, a fake theft for the sake of a newspaper headline.

As she checked the accommodation plan for next week, Andrea mused about Miss Ingrid Jensen. Why would such a beautiful Danish girl, said to be the daughter of one of the richest men in Denmark, stay so often in a provincial town like Millbridge? One would have imagined that Miss Jensen would favor a luxury hotel in London, or rent an apartment there. Even an expensive one would be cheaper in the long run than the Belvedere's high price for their best private suite.

In addition, Andrea wondered what sort of social life Miss Jensen could enjoy in Millbridge. Or was she escaping a whirl of parties and gaieties that would be expected of her in London? Yet she visited Paris, Copenhagen, Brussels—all cities with considerably more entertainment to offer than Millbridge had.

"Hello, sunshine!" a voice called to her from the reception desk. "Keep frowning like that and you'll be a wizened little old woman before you're twenty-five."

Andrea smiled as she saw Dick Palmer, but then the thought came immediately that Jill, his fiancée, was off duty.

"Jill isn't here," she told him. "Didn't you know she was free today?"

He pushed his hand through thick brown hair. "Yes, I knew. I thought she might be somewhere around, though. We had a bit of a bust-up this afternoon. . . ."

Andrea's face showed concern. "You and Jill haven't come unstuck, have you?"

He grinned. "I'm not sure. She hasn't wrenched my ring off her finger and thrown it in my face with a dramatic gesture, but that may still come."

"Oh, no! Jill wouldn't do that."

"No? You should have seen and heard her this afternoon when I told her my editor wanted me to cover a story out in the suburbs—two schoolgirls mysteriously disappeared three or four days ago, but when I arrived, they'd been found and were tucking into platefuls of fish and chips with ice cream to follow. So there wasn't much of a story in it." He sighed exaggeratedly. "Oh, well, if Jill comes in, give her the tip that I'm down in the cocktail bar."

Andrea promised to do so, but didn't see how she could know if and when Jill returned. Still, she would do her best for both of them.

As soon as she had finished duty, she passed on the message to Miss Cameron, the head receptionist, and then presented herself in Aunt Catherine's office.

"Come through into the sitting room," her aunt invited. "We won't be disturbed there."

Andrea sat down where Aunt Catherine indicated. "I'll come straight to the point," Mrs. Mayfield began. "You were telling the truth when you said you hadn't been in Miss Jensen's suite?"

"Yes, of course. I had no reason to go in there."

"No. But my information is that you were seen coming out of the Norfolk Suite just before two." Aunt Catherine's voice sounded uncompromising and harsh.

"I certainly wasn't. I was nowhere near there."

"Where were you?"

Andrea hesitated. Today, of all days, Miriam, the head chambermaid on fourth, with whom Andrea had first worked, had asked her to stay in the housekeeper's station on that floor while Miriam nipped down to the staff entrance to have ten minutes' conversation with the current boyfriend. "Just in case someone telephones or rings," she had said. "Someone always does when there's nobody on the floor to answer them. And then there's the the devil to pay."

So how could Andrea now disclose that she had helped Miriam, a head chambermaid, to flout the house rules?

"I had my lunch in staff hall and then—went up to my room to tidy myself." This was true, except that Andrea's statement omitted the quarter of an hour just before two.

Aunt Catherine's level glance measured Andrea for a long moment.

"Could I ask who is—supposed to have seen me?"

"At the moment, I can't tell you."

Then Andrea remembered that as she had descended the back stairs and reached the second floor, Keir Holt had been walking along the corridor. Of all the sneaks! Of course it was he who had given Aunt Catherine information about the fur. He had evidently tattled about seeing Andrea in Mervyn Watford's company. Now he had directed suspicion toward her over the latest incident. But why? Did he want her to lose her job? No, she realized she was not as important as that. Besides, he would have to explain his technical building terms all over again to another girl.

Aunt Catherine sighed. "Strange things seem to be happening."

"You mean—since I came here?"

"I'm not blaming you, Andrea. That's just coincidence. But the good name of the hotel means a great deal to me. Please don't discuss this necklace affair with anybody. With luck, we may be able to hush it up and pacify Miss Jensen.

She's agreed to give us until tomorrow to find the necklace—before she tells the police."

"But whoever has taken it—whether it's one of the guests or a member of the staff—will surely have time to dispose of the necklace if she doesn't call in the police until tomorrow."

"It also gives the—thief—an opportunity to return it." Catherine Mayfield smiled at her niece. "But I'm glad you said that—about the delay in calling the police. You've convinced me that you had nothing to do with it. Otherwise, you'd have been in favor of the longest possible delay."

Andrea was in bed some time before Huguette returned.

"Enjoyed yourself?" Andrea asked. "Where did you go?"

"A new dancing place just opened. You must go there one time. It was very gay." Huguette was putting her coat away in the wardrobe. Then she turned, and the light glinted on a sapphire and diamond necklace curving against her young white throat.

Andrea gasped and cold shivers tingled her spine.

"The necklace! *You* took it!"

CHAPTER SIX

HUGUETTE STARED at Andrea. Then she gave an apologetic laugh. "Do not be cross with me. I only borrowed it for tonight. You did not mind?"

"When did you take it?" Andrea managed to ask.

"When I was ready to go out after lunch. This dress has a low neck and needs a pretty necklace. I had nothing of my own—so I thought you would not mind if I looked in your drawer to see if you had anything suitable." Huguette perched on Andrea's bed. "Could you please undo the clasp?"

Andrea's fingers fumbled at the pearl clasp described by Miss Jensen. "You don't believe it's mine do you?"

"Why not? It was in your drawer."

Andrea pressed her fingers into her forehead and temples. "I must be going mad." She swallowed hard, then said, "That's the necklace Miss Jensen has lost—or had stolen—this afternoon."

"This? Miss Jensen's?" Huguette gave a prolonged shuddering exclamation. "Then it is real—diamonds and sapphires—and those others, what do you call them?"

"Oh, never mind what they are. Aquamarines." Andrea spoke irritably. She grabbed Huguette's shoulders. "Tell me the truth—how did it get into my room if you didn't put it there?"

"Someone else did. That is plain."

"That's an easy way out," retorted Andrea. "You took it from Miss Jensen's room. Now you pretend that you found it here and thought it was mine. How in the world did you think I possessed diamonds and sapphires?"

"Truly, Andrea, I did not believe they were real diamonds. I thought they were just pretty stones."

"Well, the May Queen ordered the room to be searched and stood by while Wyvern went over it with a fine-tooth comb."

"You mean they have searched our room? Oh *mon dieu!*" Huguette hastily scrabbled in her own dressing-table drawer.

"What else have you got hidden?" Andrea demanded.

Huguette brought out a photograph. "Only a portrait of Bobbie. I do not want anyone to find that."

Andrea was too worried about the necklace to bother about Huguette's obscure reasons for hiding a young man's photograph.

"Well? What are we going to do now?" she murmured, as much to the air as to the French girl. "I can't take it back for you as I tried to replace the fur you'd borrowed."

"For me?" echoed Huguette. "But it had nothing to do with me. It was there, in your drawer. I swear it. All the time I have attended to Miss Jensen, I have never seen her jewelry except when she wears it. No doubt it is locked away in cases."

"I would like to believe you, Huguette—"

"I speak the truth to my friends, Andrea. I was off duty. I did not go in Miss Jensen's rooms at all today."

"Then someone else did," Andrea said slowly.

"It could be Miss Jensen who wishes to do me a bad injury," Huguette suggested. "Perhaps she has found out about the fur and now she wants to make me lose my job here."

Andrea shook her head. "I can't really see Miss Jensen walking about in the staff wing. If one of us asked her what she wanted what could she say?"

"That she is looking for Huguette, of course. Simple."

"No, I'm convinced it was somebody who has a grudge against *me*, not you," Andrea said. "A woman, of course, because it would look suspicious if a man were wandering about our staff wing. A woman who would have the right to enter our room."

"There is Wyvern. She does not like you."

"And she'd have the opportunity," agreed Andrea. "Also she hates the sight of me, although I don't really know why."

Huguette gave her friend a sidelong glance. "No. You would not understand, perhaps. But there is also the May Queen. She could have put it here."

Andrea was shocked. "Oh no! Not the May Queen. She couldn't do that to me!"

For the first time the thought had flashed into the girl's mind that her aunt might possibly have been in collusion with Miss Jensen and planted the necklace in Andrea's room where it would be found by Miss Wyvern in the presence of both Andrea and her aunt. In the face of that evidence, there could be no alternative to dismissal. Was Aunt Catherine as anxious as that to get rid of her niece? If so, why had she encouraged Andrea to come to the Belvedere in the first place? None of it made sense.

"How can we return the necklace now to Miss Jensen?" murmured Huguette.

"This time we'd both better tell the truth. Give it to me. I think I ought to take it down immediately to Mrs. Mayfield."

"Are you mad, Andrea? That way we shall both jump into prison!" Huguette shivered. "And me—I shall be sent back to France."

A sudden knock at the door sent Andrea's heart into her mouth. Huguette had the presence of mind to push the necklace out of sight under Andrea's bedclothes and then call out "Come in!"

Miss Wyvern poked her head around the door, and Andrea was terrified in case the assistant housekeeper might insist upon a further search for the missing necklace.

"Everything all right?" she inquired, half smiled, then glared at Huguette's provocatively low-cut dress.

"Everything is fine!" Huguette answered cheerfully.

When the assistant housekeeper had gone, Andrea groaned. "Heavens! I thought. . . ."

Huguette immediately hushed her. "She may be listening at the door." She pulled her dress off, slipped on a dressing gown and cautiously opened the door.

"Ah, nobody there."

"The necklace was nearly burning my hands," Andrea whispered. "Gosh! Now I know what they mean by 'hot stones.'"

"What does it mean?" Even in a crisis, Huguette was always eager to learn new phrases or slang.

"Oh, a term used by criminals," Andrea answered. "I've read it in mystery stories."

The French girl snatched the necklace from Andrea's hands. "Come, give it to me. It is too dangerous for us."

Before Andrea could stop her, Huguette had wrapped the precious necklace in several thicknesses of tissue paper, opened the window and dropped the package out.

"There! Now we are safe!"

Andrea panicked. "You fool! Now it'll be really lost. Somebody in the street will pick it up . . . ."

"Imbecile! Are we so favored that we have a room overlooking the street?" demanded Huguette. "Below is the roof of the kitchen, and if someone should look they will find Miss Jensen's pretty beads. More than fifty windows look down upon that roof."

Andrea had, for the moment, forgotten the layout of the Belvedere. From the streets it appeared a solid block, but the glass-roofed kitchens were in the center of the second floor and the floors above formed a hollow square. As Huguette pointed out, sixty or seventy windows overlooked the well.

"Now go to sleep and forget it," advised Huguette. "In the morning all will be well."

Andrea wished she could take these critical situations in Huguette's easy, lighthearted way, but that was impossible. In any case, she was more deeply involved.

Huguette had not been a very accurate prophet, for in the morning all was not well. One of the Sunday papers carried half a column giving an account of a jewel theft from Miss Ingrid Jensen, staying at the Belvedere. The necklace had disappeared, Miss Jensen claimed, while she was at lunch. No, nothing else had been stolen, although other pieces of jewelry were in her suite.

Andrea's spirits sank to zero. Miss Jensen had failed to keep her promise not to call the police until the following day in case she recovered her property. She must have told the newspapers last night.

"Quite a sensation, isn't it?" commented Jill Brookman, when Andrea joined her on duty in Reception. "The boss will throw a pink fit when he reads this, and the May Queen has shut herself in her office and is reading every single newspaper."

Later in the morning, however, Jill was less jaunty.

"Dick's just telephoned asking if there are any further developments about the missing necklace. He says Miss Jensen herself gave him the whole story."

"When?" asked Andrea.

"Last night, apparently. But I'm appalled that he gave it to his paper. He knows quite well that publicity of that sort is the very last thing the Belvedere wants. I can't understand him—unless, of course, he did it to spite me. We quarreled—but I didn't think he'd be mean."

"Oh, no, he wouldn't do that. It's just bad luck that he happened to be in the house when Miss Jensen decided to talk."

Inevitably, Andrea was summoned to her aunt's office.

Mrs. Mayfield was surrounded by newspapers. "Did you talk, Andrea?" she said without looking up.

"No, I did not."

"Or drop a hint in the direction of one particular paper?"

"No. I said nothing at all." Andrea was irritated by her aunt's implied accusations and readiness to believe the worst of her niece. Impulsively she added, "Miss Jensen herself seems to have given a very detailed interview."

Mrs. Mayfield looked at Andrea then. "Perhaps you're right. Fortunately the account appears only in one paper, but tomorrow's paper will pick it up, no doubt."

During the morning, most of the staff knew that plain-clothes detectives were unobtrusively searching the hotel for Miss Jensen's jewelry, and when Andrea went to her lunch the news was that the necklace had not yet been found. Or at least nobody knew for certain.

"Think of all the places where it might be!" exclaimed one girl. "In the stockpot among all the bones—or inside

one of those fancy *gateaux* made by the *pâtisserie* chef.
Gosh! That'd give you a shock if you caught a bad tooth on
a diamond."

Andrea bent her head over her plate, although the food
tasted like absorbent cotton and she had little appetite. How
near these random guesses were to the truth! A kitchen
hand or apprentice cook had only to glance upward to catch
sight of the package. Unless—Andrea caught her breath at
the thought that already, perhaps, somebody else had found
the necklace and secreted it. Huguette should never have
thrown it down into the well, although Andrea was uncertain what else could have been done. *I ought really, though,
to have had the courage to take it down to Aunt Catherine
myself and face the consequences.*

The girls around her were still chattering of hiding
places.

"In the linen room tied up in a tablecloth."

"Or what about the flowers? Anyone could drop it among
the foliage or shove it inside a vase."

After her lunch, Andrea felt impelled to look out of one
window giving a view over the kitchen roof. Where would
the package have fallen? There had been rain in the night
and she could see some fragments of sodden tissue paper
clinging to a sloping corner of woodwork, but no sign of the
necklace.

"Taking the air, Lansdale?"

In her haste to withdraw, Andrea banged her head on the
side of the window frame. It was one of Miss Wyvern's less
attractive characteristics to address all junior staff by their
surnames, when even the May Queen herself either used
Christian names or preceded a surname by "Miss" or
"Mrs."

"I was just looking out," Andrea answered.

"Anything interesting down there?" Miss Wyvern's
smile was no more than a movement of facial muscles, for
the light blue eyes were filled with malice.

Andrea was sure now that Miss Wyvern had planted the
necklace in the drawer and no doubt had been considerably
disappointed when it was missing during the search of
Andrea's room. She couldn't have guessed that Huguette

would unwittingly have borrowed it so her plans for exposing Andrea as a thief had misfired.

"I don't know," Andrea murmured uneasily. Then, with a sudden spurt of courage, she added, "All kinds of rubbish get thrown down there, I expect, but then you would know that Miss Wyvern. You've been here much longer than I have."

Andrea marched away without waiting for any dismissal by the assistant housekeeper. In any case, the girl was at present in Reception and not under Miss Wyvern's control.

At four o'clock she was off duty for the rest of the day and had just gone up to her room and thankfully kicked off her shoes when a chambermaid rapped on the door. "You're wanted, Andy! Down to the May Queen!"

"Oh, not again!" Andrea muttered, but nevertheless tidied herself and shot downstairs, apprehensive of some new development.

She was surprised to find Mr. Blake, the assistant manager, having tea with Aunt Catherine in the latter's sitting room.

"I thought you might like to know, Andrea, that Miss Jensen's necklace has been found."

"That's good news, madam. Where was it?" she asked, steadying her voice.

"In the eaves trough by the glass roof that goes over the kitchens. Almost anybody could have put it or thrown it down there from dozens of windows. So you've nothing to worry about."

"Miss Jensen seems to be careless about her possessions," Mr. Blake commented. "If she doesn't like to use the manager's safe for her valuables, she has only herself to blame if they're lost."

"I apologize for having your room searched," Aunt Catherine said, "but many other rooms besides yours were searched. You realize that?"

"Of course, madam."

Perhaps Sunday afternoon teatime was an occasion when Aunt Catherine relaxed. Today she looked positively gay, in spite of the hotel's ups and downs. She seemed younger, too, and a delicate flush glowed in her usually pale cheeks and her dark eyes were luminous.

Afterward, Andrea reflected that possibly it was easier to relax in the sitting room of a comfortable apartment, with delicious food on the table. Dainty sandwiches and luscious little cream cakes were a far cry from the plain, substantial fare provided for most of the hotel staff. One of Aunt Catherine's privileges as head housekeeper was to order her food from the restaurant menu, and it was always very specially served by a floor waiter.

Eventually, Andrea went out for a solitary walk. She needed something to soothe the jangle and fret of the day, and she had discovered that hotel life was not altogether conducive to the formation of firm friendship, either among the staff or with outside acquaintances. Invariably, one's off-duty times rarely coincided with anyone else's.

So when Trevor Dennistoun telephoned her later in the week, Andrea was pleased to accept his invitation to a meal. He took her to a Chinese restaurant recently opened in Millbridge.

Although he spent most of the evening talking of Ingrid Jensen, Andrea enjoyed being with him.

"Do you know when Ingrid is coming back to the Belvedere?" he asked.

"You've really fallen for her, haven't you?"

"Oh, yes. I don't mind admitting it. It isn't that she's one of the most beautiful girls I've ever seen. She has more than that. Vitality, sense of humor, charm. . . ."

Andrea gave him an amused but friendly smile. "I hear also that she has a very rich father. Does that help?"

Trevor screwed up his face. "Not much. Fathers of heiresses become darned choosy about their daughters. No man is good enough to be their son-in-law. They don't always consider their daughter's happiness. All they think about is whether the chap is a fortune hunter."

"Well, nobody could consider you a fortune hunter. You have your own business."

"It's not particularly flourishing, though." Trevor played with a fork on the tablecloth. "Oh, it isn't that we're losing money. We're really doing very well. But my mother doesn't seem to understand that sometimes you have to put money back into a business instead of taking it all out and spending the lot. When my father was alive, the money was there and mother grew accustomed to having anything she wanted. I simply can't make her see that you've got to expand your business these days if you want to keep going. Alterations, new windows, better layout of the departments and so on.'' He grinned at Andrea. "I'm sure she thinks we're still living in the old days when the drapery sales assistants wrapped up money, put it into a little box, pulled a handle and sent it traveling along overhead wires to the cashier's desk.''

Andrea had long ago acquired the art of listening to men thinking aloud. Her father had often wanted an audience to whom he could project his thoughts and from him she had learned when not to interrupt or sidetrack, when to make a casual comment or ask a relevant question. So now she encouraged Trevor to speak his thoughts, judging that among his circle of acquaintances there were few others with whom he would feel so safe.

"But about Ingrid?" He returned to his most important topic. "When will she be back? Where has she gone?''

"She's coming in tomorrow, but I'm not sure where she's been staying in the meantime. London, maybe. She goes to Paris quite often. . . .''

"If I give you a note for her, will you give it to her the moment she comes into the hotel?''

His eagerness saddened Andrea, for she foresaw that his infatuation was doomed to end unhappily. Ingrid Jensen would take whatever devotion he had to offer, she would dazzle him with her smiles, her charming airs, but that would be the limit.

"I'll do anything I can for you, Trevor,'' Andrea said now, "but I might not be on Reception when she comes in. I could put it with her other letters.''

He walked back to the Belvedere with her and as they passed the half-built Century block, she thought suddenly of Keir Holt. Trevor paused to inspect the window displays in the completed part. "I wish I could use my space as lavishly as that,'' he murmured. "Two handbags, one umbrella, two hats and a wicker cage . . . everybody in Stowchester would think I'd nothing much else to sell.''

"Why don't you try putting in one handbag, one hat and a pair of gloves and leave a large space of gray carpet? Let the people of Stowchester have a taste of modern window dressing.''

His quick smile was appreciative. "M'm. Perhaps I might.''

Out of the corner of her eye, Andrea was vaguely aware of a tall, lean figure watching her and Trevor, but when she looked squarely in that direction, the man had disappeared. She couldn't be sure whether she had really seen Keir Holt or only imagined it.

CHAPTER SEVEN

NEXT DAY she made sure that Trevor's note would be handed to Miss Jensen, although she herself was not on duty. But he telephoned her in the late afternoon.

"Would you like to come dancing, Andrea?" he asked.

"I thought you were taking—someone else." She discreetly avoided mentioning names.

"The arrangements got muddled. You don't mind being a sort of stopgap, do you?"

She giggled. "I'll put up with it from you. But I've nothing to wear. I don't possess a smart evening dress."

"Oh, this isn't a smart place at all. Sort of country club. Girls wear all kinds of dresses—you know, short, wide skirts and all that."

"All right. I'll come. What time?"

"Eight o'clock all right? I'll call for you."

"Come to the staff entrance," she reminded him.

In the car, Trevor was noticeably silent and Andrea thought it would be unkind to ask him why he was escorting herself instead of the ravishing Ingrid. She hoped that the country club was not too smart a place. Men were notoriously vague about women's dresses. They told you to come in a simple cotton and when you arrived you found everybody else in elegant, full-length creations and you felt as though your proper place was in a suburban dancing academy on a midweek practice night.

The Polonaise Club was a converted old house with a spacious ballroom, a riotously decorated cocktail bar and a more subdued restaurant. When Andrea joined Trevor at the entrance to the ballroom and a waiter escorted them to a table, almost the first person she saw was Ingrid Jensen. Her first thought was to warn Trevor so that he would be prepared for the shock, but the next moment she herself received a much greater shock. Ingrid's companion was Keir Holt.

"Come on, let's dance." Trevor's words jerked Andrea out of her momentary trance.

As they circled the room, she realized that within a short time he couldn't fail to recognize Ingrid, but before she could formulate the right words to say, he gave her a friendly hug and whispered, "Will you mind very much if I dance with Ingrid—that is, if I can cut in on her?"

"You knew she was here! I thought you'd be shattered."

"No. She told me she was already engaged for the evening, but I wormed some information out of one of the maids, a French girl."

"Huguette?"

Trevor shook his head. "I don't know her name, but she evidently knew that Miss Jensen was coming tonight to this place."

Andrea could see looming up before her a dreaded possibility, and Trevor's next words confirmed her suspicion.

"Her escort looks a sober type. Perhaps you can cheer him up." He chuckled. "If Ingrid doesn't like it, that's too bad. I shall enjoy stirring things up. I simply must show her that she can't ignore me."

"But, Trevor, you don't understand. Dance with Ingrid all the evening if you like, but that—that man—well, I know him. . . ."

"Fine! All the better."

"He's Keir Holt."

"Who's he? Anybody important?"

"He stays at the Belvedere quite a lot. He's on construction work, that big new block, the Century building in Millbridge."

"Then you'll have something to talk about."

Trevor was as unfeeling as a brother can be when he wants to get the better of his superior sister and watch her discomfiture.

Andrea would have liked to escape, but her arm was firmly linked in Trevor's as he marched toward the table where Ingrid sat with Keir.

The Danish girl, in an exquisite ballerina dress of lilac tulle embroidered with rainbow sequins, immediately made Andrea, in a simple green-patterned cotton, feel dowdy and insignificant.

With swaggering bluntness, Trevor introduced the two girls and Ingrid had no choice but to introduce the men to each other.

"What a wonderful surprise to find you here, Ingrid!" Trevor would have sounded insincere to a twelve-year-old schoolgirl, let alone to a polished cosmopolitan such as Miss Jensen. But Andrea was pleased that he didn't cringe.

Ingrid stared with the full blazing intensity of her blue eyes at Andrea, whose confidence faltered a little.

"I have seen you before somewhere?" Ingrid queried.

"Yes, at the Belvedere."

"Oh, of course. But you are not a guest there."

"No. I work in the hotel." Andrea experienced a tiny dart of triumph. The Danish girl was trying to put a humble hotel employee in her place, in the presence of two men who already knew the truth; but then Ingrid could not know that.

"And you were suspected—mixed up—in the affair about my necklace that was stolen."

Andrea was instantly aware of Keir Holt's quick turn of the head.

"I was not, I think, suspected, Miss Jensen, but my room was searched. So were many other rooms."

"Well, the necklace was discovered," Keir put in, "and the affair gave you a spot of publicity, so you and your insurance company should be well satisfied."

"Shall we dance, Ingrid?" Trevor stood up. He had not taken considerable trouble to follow Ingrid to the Polonaise merely to listen to acid-edged chatter.

For a moment or two Ingrid hesitated. Then she rose and allowed Trevor to whirl her away on the dance floor.

Andrea glanced down at her hands clasped in her lap. Then she looked directly at Keir Holt. "Please don't think

I—arranged this. I had no idea that Miss Jensen—and you—would be here."

An amused smile played around his mouth. "Do you mind?"

"No. Why should I?"

"I'm sorry, your partner has temporarily deserted you. Would you care to dance with me?"

Keir was not an accomplished dancer and Andrea was not tall enough to match her step with his, but apart from these physical difficulties, she was aware of a jangling tension between herself and Keir Holt. If Trevor had to use her in this game of chasing Ingrid, then she would have preferred to be pitchforked into the arms of almost anybody other than her present partner.

When he took her back to his own table and ordered drinks, Trevor and Ingrid were not in sight, but on one of the vacant chairs lay a handsome fur stole, to which Andrea's glance was drawn. She looked up and caught Keir's eye.

"Is it the one?" he asked.

"I think so."

"We'd better take care of it for Miss Jensen," he advised.

"Oh, no! I prefer not to touch any of her possessions," she answered hastily, "Or I might. . . ."

"Or suspicion might rest on you? Tell me how you came to be mixed up in the necklace affair."

She gave a mild gasp. "You seem to think all these incidents are huge jokes, Mr. Holt. I can assure you that it isn't at all pleasant to be involved." She colored at the thought of how closely she had been involved—with the necklace planted in her dressing table ready for Huguette to take it out during the crucial time.

"But I was sympathetic about it—" he began.

"Sympathetic? But it was you who told Mrs. Mayfield that you saw me come out of Miss Jensen's suite."

He seemed startled by her accusation. "I certainly didn't see you—and I wouldn't have mentioned the matter even if I had."

"Oh!" she muttered lamely. "I apologize, then."

He smiled at her. "Shall we forget about Miss Jensen's losses and dance again?"

Somehow the rest of the evening raced by. With practice Andrea was able to swing her steps with his and he managed to hold her in such a way that her nose was not buried in his shirt front. Dancing with tall men was an occupation that always made Andrea regret her lack of height, but tonight with Keir, after the initial awkwardnesses, there was no disadvantage. He seemed younger and, perhaps, relieved to be able to shed his business anxieties for even a few hours.

When he told her that it was nearly midnight, Andrea was startled. "It can't be! I ought to be going back to the Belvedere."

"I brought Miss Jensen here, so I must at least try to find her."

"I think Trevor will look after her and take her home." Then she blushed, for it sounded in her own ears as though she were angling for Keir to take her instead.

"You're probably right," he admitted.

As Andrea collected her handbag, Ingrid appeared, and Andrea's spirits fell.

"Thank you so much for taking care of my stole," Ingrid settled the fur around her beautiful shoulders. "Trevor tells me that your father was a professor at Cambridge."

"A brilliant man," Keir added.

But Andrea was not really interested in the obvious fact that her status had been raised in Miss Jensen's eyes.

Trevor whispered to her, "Let this Holt chap take you home. I'm taking Ingrid."

"You hope!" whispered Andrea, but was surprised when it turned out that way.

In Keir's car she wanted the journey to continue endlessly and fought the heady elation that had been steadily mounting in her all the evening. She chattered about trivial matters to cover the long silences that might otherwise have occurred, for Keir was certainly not talkative. Perhaps, she thought, he liked to concentrate on his driving.

His sudden question startled her. "Are you in love with Trevor Dennistoun?"

She turned her head sharply and caught the outline of his profile against the dim reflection from the headlights.

"No, of course not. I've known him a long time."

She could not understand at first why he began to chuckle. "Does knowing a man a long time then entirely preclude falling in love with him?"

"Well, no. But Trevor is the son of Mrs. Dennistoun, who was my father's employer—and—and we're just friends." She could say this truthfully now.

"But you like him?"

"Yes, I do."

"And you like being taken out by him?"

His questions were becoming a catechism and a spurt of irritation forced impulsive words out of her. "It might be truer to say that Trevor likes taking me out sometimes so that he can talk about Ingrid. He's infatuated with her." She caught her breath. "Oh, I'm sorry. I shouldn't have said that—about Ingrid. That was gauche and stupid of me."

"Why? Isn't it the truth?"

"I think so. But you brought Ingrid to the club and she was your guest."

There was a long pause before he answered. "Miss Jensen asked me to take her to this place, the Polonaise, and I realized that there was somebody else she wanted to meet there. It was really no hardship for me to leave her in the care of Dennistoun, if that was what she wanted."

Andrea sighed with relief. "Then that's all right. We're a pair of outcasts, you and I. Unwanted partners."

Again she was convinced that she had said the wrong thing, for he did not reply. She was glad when the lights of the city center appeared and she waited for him to turn the car along the street at the side of the Belvedere.

"Thank you very much, Mr. Holt, for bringing me home," she began primly, as he switched off his engine.

His arm slid around her shoulders, his mouth rested gently on hers, and in that brief moment a dozen emotions struggled to assert themselves in her consciousness, but she crushed them down. Time enough for sanity after this moment of madness was over.

"Good night, Andrea," he murmured, and opened the car door on her side.

Speechless and shaken, she scrambled out and ran inside the hotel entrance. The night porter took her late pass to check it with his list.

"Had a good night out, miss?" He winked at her.

She forced a smile and nodded, but hurried away toward the service stairs. Was there something in her face that showed she had been kissed?

Huguette sleepily opened one eye. "Where have you been? With who?"

"*Whom!*" snapped Andrea. "With an old friend, to a dance club."

"The Polonaise!" Huguette bounced up in her bed like an animated toy, her dark hair flattened into a nylon hairnet, her face unglamorously shiny. "Tell me, Andrea, all that went on."

As Andrea rapidly undressed and paid no attention to Huguette's demands, the French girl supplied her own answers. "You went with this nice Trevor, your old friend. But was the beautiful Ingrid there, also? You see, I heard her telephone to someone—a man, of course—that she wished to be taken to the Polonaise. So, when Monsieur Trevor telephone, I am able to tell him that Miss Jensen is going to this place."

"But, Huguette!" Andrea could no longer ignore her companion. "You shouldn't interfere in the affairs of the hotel guests like that! Why, anything might happen."

"*Pouf!* One must always make the situation more intriguing and dangerous, if it is possible. Otherwise, of what use is it to be alive? Or perhaps you wish always to be sober and serious, like all the English."

Huguette shrugged her pretty shoulders with such abandon that the top of her flimsy petunia nylon nightdress slipped below her breasts.

Andrea laughed. "At this moment you look intriguing and dangerous and not at all serious, with your nightdress half-off. Are you expecting a fire alarm? Or d'you think you're back in Montmartre?"

Huguette covered herself as far as the exiguous nightdress

would allow. "You are trying to change your subject,
Andrea! What happens when Monsieur Trevor arrived—
with you?"

"Oh, nothing. We danced."

"But Miss Jensen was there? What was her dress?"

"Lilac tulle and sequins. Very beautiful. Now, for heav-
en's sake, let me get to sleep."

"Oh, but no. You have not told me about the other man,
Ingrid's partner—the man she asked to take her there. What
was he like?"

"Tall, dark—and rather ugly." Andrea had determined
that not all the tortures of seven hells, in addition to
Huguette's persistence, would make her divulge that Keir
Holt was that other man.

"His name?"

"He hadn't one. He said to call him Joe."

Surprisingly, that last remark seemed to silence Huguette
for a few moments. Then she said, "He does not sound
suitable for you, Andrea. I am surprised that Miss Jensen
should ask him to take her places. But perhaps he is very
rich."

Andrea, longing for darkness and silence, repressed an
almost uncontrollable urge to shout with laughter, but when
at last Huguette was quiet except for an occasional gentle
snore, Andrea could relax from the unbearable tension of
the last half hour or so.

Why had Keir Holt kissed her? He, of all people, knew
her circumstances. Or was that perhaps the answer? Give
the little hotel girl a thrill when you kiss her good night.
Make her think that you're treating her as though she were
the debutante type. Yet he had never seemed to Andrea to
be that kind of man. Not like Mervyn Watford, for instance,
who obviously set out to treat a girl in the way he thought
she expected to be treated.

Now she knew that she was on the threshold of something more overwhelming than anything she had ever
known. It might not be love, but only infatuation. It might
be no more than emotional growing pains. Whatever it
might be, she was profoundly disturbed by her own reactions to Keir's nearness. She told herself that she disliked

the man, that from the very first day when he had tripped her in the Belvedere's entrance, he had been a source of trouble and irritation to her, that he was patronizing and overbearing. But now the spark of compelling antagonism had lit a flame of desire within her—a flame that might have to burn itself out.

ANDREA HOPED that if Keir Holt wanted any further secretarial work done for him, he would ask when she was not on duty. But when she came back to the Belvedere one afternoon, and took her place in the office behind Reception, Jill Brookman pounced on her.

"Oh, Andrea, go and keep the man quiet, for goodness' sake. He's been ringing for you since lunch."

"Who?" *As though I haven't already guessed,* she thought.

"Mr. Holt."

"Why couldn't he take somebody else? I'm not the only typist in the house."

"Actually, you are—at the moment," Jill told her. "Everybody else is going mad with all the work on Swedish Week."

Reluctantly, Andrea picked up her notebook, praying that Keir Holt would be summoned immediately to the building site or that some other dispensation of providence would spare her the necessity of meeting him again face to face.

Her heart was thumping like mad and her fingers trembled when she sat down in his sitting room, waiting for him to dictate. After a brief greeting, he turned his back on her and was staring out of the net-curtained window. Then he began a long report, and after Andrea had taken a grip on herself, she thought how ludicrous were her apprehensions. What did she expect? That he would seize her in his arms and cover her face with ardent kisses? Obviously, he had forgotten the incident; probably on the same night while he was putting his car away in the hotel garage.

According to his dictation, work on the Century block, with which he was concerned, was going along reasonably well, if not as smoothly and quickly as he had hoped. There were still minor accidents, although no more serious ones—temporary stoppages, dissatisfaction among the men, important loads of material delivered to the wrong part of the site.

When she had finished typing and taken out the carbon sheets from the foolscap pages, she said, "It might be as well, for the sake of safety, to destroy those carbons. They're new ones, and sometimes it's possible to read what's been typed through them if you hold the sheets against a strong light."

He veered swiftly toward her. "But wouldn't all the words be jumbled if more than one page has been done?"

"Yes, often. But sometimes you can see a few lines here and there. It might be just the important lines."

"Here, give them to me." He switched on a table lamp and examined the carbons. "Yes, you're right, Andrea. It's impossible to read it all, but most of it could be pieced together—by someone who was sufficiently interested."

He glanced across at her and smiled, his eyes warm and friendly. His expression seemed to envelop her in an idyllic glow of happiness, but she schooled herself with iron self-control and gave him what she realized afterward must have seemed like a superior and perfunctory smile.

"Thanks for the tip," he said, almost brusquely. "I'll watch that, in future."

She wanted to tell him that she sympathized with him in his business worries and anxieties, that she'd do all she could to help him, even if it meant spying and snooping around the Century block when few people were around. But she remained silent.

"How d'you think the block is beginning to look? D'you like it?"

"No. I think it's ordinary and commonplace." The words were out before she could bite them back. Appalled, she jerked her head upward toward him and saw his amused mouth and raised eyebrows.

"Fortunately, I'm not the architect. What's wrong about it?"

"I shouldn't have criticized," she mumbled, turning her face away.

"No, go on. I asked you."

"The front part cuts across the corner quite well, but the rest of the block seems squat and massive. It's a cliff with windows in it, and squares of blue and terra-cotta to liven it up."

"You're quite right! You seem to have studied the building rather well. Didn't I see you there one night with your friend Trevor?"

So she had not been mistaken when she thought she had seen Keir.

"Yes. Trevor has a store and we were discussing window display."

In a flash, the magical moment had vanished. His mild amusement was replaced by a sardonic chilliness in his voice when he said, "And how would you like such a block as ours to be built?"

"I don't really know anything at all about architecture," she answered defensively, then added more spiritedly, "But I've seen photographs of Continental schemes, where the frontages zigzag or balconies break up the straight sides."

"I shall have to introduce you to our architect next time he's here."

Andrea bit her lip and was glad when Keir's telephone rang and she was prevented from any further reply. *He shouldn't have asked me for my opinions,* she thought rebelliously, *if he didn't want to hear them.*

When he had finished his telephone conversation and she was on the point of leaving, she decided not to tell him that after tomorrow she was being transferred from Reception to waitress service and would therefore not be available to type his reports. That would sound as though she considered herself indispensable. After all, the Belvedere employed several other quite competent typists.

After Andrea had left his suite, Keir worked for a time, smoking endless cigarettes and filled with a restless impatience to finish the Century job and get away from Millbridge. As Andrea had implied, the block was uninspiring and possibly the construction delays and difficulties were due to his own staleness and dissatisfaction over the job.

He swept all his papers into a heap and pushed them into

a briefcase, which he locked in a wardrobe. Then he telephoned for a whiskey and soda and, out of tune with his own company, decided to dine in the restaurant instead of in his own suite. But he regretted the impulse, for Ingrid Jensen sat at an adjacent table and sent the waiter to ask if she might join him. Or would he prefer to join her? Keir Holt knew that he had little choice either way.

"Tell me about all these big buildings you are working on," she coaxed, giving him one of her most dazzling smiles.

Outwardly polite, he returned her smile, wondering how soon he could finish his meal and plead pressure of work. As Ingrid prattled on in her charming, slightly accented English, he found himself thinking of the young Lansdale girl who had bluntly given her views on his projects, even though her interest was probably more in sympathy with the interest shown by the Dennistoun chap, who owned a store and, no doubt, was eager to improve its appearance.

CHAPTER EIGHT

A FEW DAYS before Christmas, Andrea's aunt asked the girl if she had made any plans for the holidays.

"Mrs. Dennistoun—you remember, my father worked for her—has invited me there for whatever free days I have."

"I see." Aunt Catherine scribbled a note on her pad. "Christmas is a slack time for us here in the hotel, so we usually manage to be generous with free time."

"Yes, the girls have told me that."

"And you'll be glad to see Trevor Dennistoun again, I suppose?" There was neither malice nor coyness in Aunt Catherine's voice, yet all the same, Andrea was uneasy.

"He's always very friendly and he's easy to get along with." Andrea paused. "I've seen him once or twice since I've been here." She decided it was better to admit this instead of waiting until Aunt Catherine taxed her with it.

"Yes, so I understand." Mrs. Mayfield smiled at her niece. "Is there some attachment between you?"

Hot color flushed Andrea's face, but not for the reason Catherine might have supposed. Yet again, Keir Holt must have sneaked information to her aunt.

"There's nothing except friendship between Trevor and me. Mrs. Dennistoun would hardly encourage me if she thought otherwise. She's rather ambitious for her son to look higher than a girl like me. In any case, he's very much in love with someone else, but that's his own business."

"I'm sorry, Andrea. I apologize. Forgive me if I sound prying. But I feel at least partly responsible for your future and, quite naturally, I take an interest in all the girls here in my charge."

Andrea still prickled with anger, but all she said was a dutiful "Yes, madam."

"Ask Miss Wyvern for your pass in the usual way. Tell her that you may have one extra day—if she agrees, of course."

After Andrea had gone, Catherine Mayfield stared at the litter of papers on her desk. Although she tried to be kind, something went wrong every time she spoke to the girl, it seemed. Andrea was always on the defensive, but, Catherine reflected, perhaps she herself was to blame.

Resentment had crackled between them from the start and Catherine admitted now to herself that it had been a mistake to invite Andrea to the Belvedere. She should have allowed the girl to potter along happily in her job at Stowchester or change it and go elsewhere. Sooner or later, there would have been some suitable young man whom she could have married and Catherine's voluntary responsibility for her sister's child would have been ended.

All she had succeeded in doing was to prize Andrea away from her own modest, comfortable background and transplant her into one which was unfamiliar and apparently unsettling. Her blushes seemed to disprove her denials that she was not particularly attracted to Trevor Dennistoun.

There was another aspect; meeting Trevor as the son of her father's employer, Andrea would scarcely have indulged in romantic longings with a fairy-tale ending, but now, working in a hotel with plentiful opportunities of meeting many kinds of men, the girl might easily consider that her status had risen and that there was every chance of the fairy tale coming true.

Catherine sighed. No doubt there would be a few other young people at the Dennistouns' Christmas parties, and perhaps Mrs. Dennistoun would be wise enough to provide Andrea with other partners.

Andrea, on her part, was still full of resentment, not against her aunt, for she recognized that a head housekeeper in charge of a number of girls needed to acquaint herself with much of their private business, but nobody except Keir Holt could have given Aunt Catherine an inkling that Andrea had been out two or three times with Trevor.

Why did she have to ask Miss Wyvern for her social Christmas pass? Had Aunt Catherine forgotten that she was now working as a trainee waitress and came under another department?

"You're very lucky, Lansdale," Miss Wyvern told her, as she made out the pass, "considering you've only been here such a short time. Not many girls would get nearly three whole days at Christmas. You must be a special favorite of somebody."

Andrea momentarily started. Did Miss Wyvern suspect that Mrs. Mayfield was Andrea's aunt?

"And may I have the address where you're staying?"

Andrea knew the rule that addresses must be given for weekend and other stay-out passes, but although she hesitated now, there was no point in arguing.

"Howden Hall, Knight's Croome? That sounds most impressive. Is it a hotel?"

"No. A private house." A foolish spurt of defiance made Andrea say, "My father and I lived there at one time." Then, noting Miss Wyvern's surprised expression, she added, "He worked there." Inwardly she challenged her superior to ask, with her usual curiosity, in what capacity Mr. Lansdale had served.

"Oh, I see." Miss Wyvern did not rise to Andrea's bait, but signed the pass without further comment.

In the crowded train to Stowchester, Andrea looked forward again to meeting Trevor in his own home. She had eagerly accepted his mother's invitation, reasoning that a brief return to familiar surroundings and a change from the ceaseless activity of hotel life might enable her to get matters into perspective.

She had seen Keir Holt only once since the night he had brought her home from the Polonaise Club, and only then because he required her secretarial services. She saw now that she had magnified the tiny incident of a good-night kiss into a mountain of importance. He would probably have kissed Ingrid in exactly the same way if he had taken her back to the hotel after a dance.

So now she and Trevor could resume their old friendly, companionable footing and Mrs. Dennistoun need fear no complications from Andrea. But even that thought brought her to a sharp halt. Was she able to regard Trevor only as a friend again because he was madly in love with Ingrid, or because she herself was attracted in Keir's direction?

Andrea decided that she knew too little about love to be able to answer such a question. To allow herself to fall in love with either Trevor or Keir would lead only to insurmountable obstacles—in the one case, Mrs. Dennistoun's opposition; in the other, a futility of wasted affection on a man who was too wrapped up in himself and his own concerns to bother about a foolish girl in a hotel where he stayed.

Her father had often told her that in order to cope with mental problems, it was sometimes an advantage to relax and let experience wash over you, taking each minute as it came and not worrying apprehensively about what the hours or days could hold in store.

At Stowchester, she looked around in case Trevor had come to meet her, but it was unlikely as she did not expect him to be there. There was no sign of him, and she waited for the bus to Knight's Croome.

As she walked up the familiar driveway of Howden Hall, an overwhelming sense of loss engulfed her when she remembered her father. Now another man was in his place, driving Mrs. Dennistoun's car, occupying the apartment over the garages.

Mrs. Dennistoun herself showed Andrea to her room, for which the girl was grateful. Trevor's mother was a kindly, sympathetic soul at heart; she could hardly be blamed for wanting her son to make a happy marriage that would also be a financial success.

"It's very kind of you to ask me here for Christmas," Andrea said. "I appreciate it very much. It's the first since my father . . . ."

"Yes, I know, my dear." Mrs. Dennistoun patted Andrea's shoulder. "Christmas can be a very lonely time. It takes a little while to adjust to changes. Do you like the work you're doing?"

Andrea answered more enthusiastically than she intended about the delights of working at the Belvedere. Not for anything would she allow her hostess to think that she was whining or discontented at having to leave Howden Hall.

"You know your way about the house, Andrea, I'll leave you to come down when you're ready. There'll still be some tea for you."

Andrea stopped only to tidy herself and renew her lipstick. She wondered how many other guests were staying for the holiday.

The sitting room where tea was usually served was dim, lit only by fireglow and two shaded wall lamps, and at first Andrea saw only Trevor as he stood up to greet her. Then in the depths of an armchair, she saw Ingrid's pale gold hair.

Trevor spoke before Mrs. Dennistoun could introduce Andrea to Ingrid. "You know each other, of course."

"I don't think so," Ingrid answered with lazy offensiveness.

"This is Miss Lansdale," Mrs. Dennistoun put in briskly. "Andrea, Miss Jensen."

"Oh! Of course! Now I remember." A spurt of firelight caught a flash of fire in Ingrid's blue eyes as she glanced at Andrea. "Your father used to drive a car here."

"Andrea's father was more than my chauffeur. He was a very good friend."

Andrea took the cup of tea from Mrs. Dennistoun and was glad to sit down in a more shadowed part of the room. How naïve she had been! In offering Christmas hospitality, Mrs. Dennistoun's motives had not been unmixed. She was taking the opportunity to demonstrate to Andrea that Trevor's future lay in a direction far removed from a hotel employee.

Trevor, too, might have had a similar motive in his mind. Andrea must not be led to think that he was trying to progress beyond friendship merely because he took her to a dance or out for a meal.

Probably he had now invited Ingrid here because he wanted to show her his home, his background, although Andrea wondered if this was wise. Would Ingrid be impressed with a modest country house in a quiet village and a small department store in the nearby town? Perhaps he was defeating his own purpose, but at least he was honest in not pretending to be a wealthy financial magnate.

At dinner, Ingrid pointedly tried to exclude Andrea from the general conversation, but Mrs. Dennistoun did her best to prevent the girl from feeling left out.

"Have there been any more jewel robberies at your hotel?" Ingrid asked.

"Not as far as I know."

"Or furs?"

This time, Andrea could not prevent color rising to her cheeks. She shook her head, "I haven't heard anything."

Ingrid turned toward her hostess. "Most surprising things happen at that hotel. Nowhere else, wherever I have stayed in Europe, is so dangerous for the valuable things that one has. They disappear, and when they come back—" Ingrid shrugged her beautiful shoulders "—nobody knows where they have been."

She related the incidents of the fur and the necklace, and inwardly Andrea shivered.

"They must be—what you call—inside jobs?" queried Ingrid finally.

Trevor laughed. "But you've got everything back. Even your insurance company isn't going to worry, as long as they don't have to pay out."

"But one day I think I lose my jewelry and it will not come back."

Mrs. Dennistoun gave Ingrid a puzzled glance and then turned toward Andrea. "We're giving the usual children's party on Boxing Day. Will you help?"

"Of course. I enjoy them very much. Last year's was wonderful." The unworthy thought that this time Ingrid was left out of some family association with the Dennistouns gave Andrea momentary satisfaction.

After church on Christmas morning, Andrea was putting the finishing touches to the giant tree in one corner of the drawing room. Colored fairy lights had already been fixed and Mrs. Dennistoun had given her a large box of tinsel, silver stars and rainbow-hued balls and trinkets. She clam-

bered down the stepladder and stood back to admire her
efforts, when the door opened suddenly and Mrs. Dennistoun came in.

"Oh, that looks lovely! Andrea is so clever at this sort of
thing."

She turned to see the person to whom Mrs. Dennistoun
was extolling her, and immediately a silver ball she had
been holding dropped from her hands and crashed in
fragments on the parquet floor.

"This is Mr. Keir Holt. Andrea Lansdale is staying with
us for the holiday."

"Miss Lansdale and I have already met on several occasions," Keir said coolly.

"Oh, I see. At the hotel where Andrea is, er—"

Andrea smiled. "Mr. Holt knows that I'm training at the
Belvedere and work in the most humble capacities." She
flushed because her eagerness not to let Mrs. Dennistoun
think that she had masqueraded as a guest had now made
her words sound rude. "I'm very sorry that I've broken one
of the glass balls," she hurried on. "It was careless of me."
She bent down to pick up the scattered pieces.

"Don't bother about it. I expect it was cracked already.
They've been in use for many years." Mrs. Dennistoun
murmured something vague about tasks in the kitchen and
went out.

"Were you surprised to see me, Andrea?" asked Keir.

She straightened up and faced him. "Yes, of course. You
were the last person I expected to see."

An amused smile played around his mouth. "You don't
seem at all pleased that I've come."

"Mrs. Dennistoun invites her own guests, of course.
Excuse me, I must throw away these pieces of glass."

She escaped before she made matters worse, but as she
collected a dustpan and brush from the broom cupboard,
she wondered why on earth Trevor had invited Keir. Surely
not for Andrea's benefit, to make a foursome, for if so, the
foursome would develop into a most inharmonious quartet.

Trevor and Ingrid came home only just in time for lunch
and Ingrid greeted Keir with gushing affection.

"Oh, it is so charming to see you, Keir! And now you are

away from your muddy building, you look like an English country gentleman.''

He gave her a mock bow. ''I'm afraid I have a tendency to go about with cement in my hair and odd bits of wood sticking out of my pockets.''

After lunch, an uneasy meal during which unspoken queries hovered over the table, Ingrid annexed Keir on the pretext of showing him the wonderful Christmas roses and winter jasmines in the garden.

Andrea decided to go out for a walk, but on the porch Trevor caught up with her before she could slip out unobtrusively.

''You didn't tell me that Holt was coming,'' he said.

''Not tell you? But you invited him.''

''I certainly did not. What sort of fool d'you take me for? I asked Ingrid because I wanted to give her a sample of an English Christmas in the country. She's never been in England before at Christmastime.''

''But I was taken by surprise when Keir walked in this morning,'' Andrea confessed. ''I thought you'd asked him because you knew that I'd met him at the hotel. Didn't your mother tell you he was coming?''

Trevor raked his fingers through his hair. ''No, she didn't. Well, at least he can provide you with a bit of company. You like him, don't you?''

''No.'' Andrea bit off the word as though it were a piece of celery. She pulled up her coat collar, stuck her hands in her pockets and marched off down the driveway.

A misty sunset tinged the overcast, faintly pink sky and as she walked along the familiar lanes in the afternoon dusk, the nagging suspicion grew in her mind that in some tortuous way Keir had been asked here so that he could more or less spy on her. Was this another of Aunt Catherine's welfare methods?

She kept to the roadways, for short cuts across the fields would undoubtedly be muddy, and on the homeward journey she paused by the stone wall that had been the scene of her father's death.

Across the road there were lights in the cottage windows, flickering Christmas trees, glimpses of balloons and paper-chain decorations. When she had lived in the village, she had never thought of herself as an outsider—although she knew that one must be born there to "belong"—but circumstances had changed her life so that now she was a stranger everywhere. She wondered if she would ever fit into hotel life, but after the year's training she might know the answer.

A tall figure came toward her from the direction of Howden Hall, and Andrea needed no second glance to see that it was Keir. *Perhaps,* she thought impishly, *he'll take me for a villager and call out a jovial "Happy Christmas" as he goes by.* But he stopped in front of her.

"Were you sent to escort me back?" she asked.

"I thought I might meet you on the way home."

As he made no move to continue his walk, she took the initiative. "We'd better go back, then, or we'll be late for tea."

The wind sighed gently through the trees and somewhere along the top road a motorcycle clattered, yet a silence as thick and oppressive as a physical barrier hung between Andrea and this man by her side, this man who had the power to disturb her with his presence, to fill her with resentment and hostility.

"It was not a good place for you to choose to spend this Christmas," he said at last, as though he had spent time searching for an innocuous opening.

"You mean because of my father?"

"Yes. And perhaps other reasons. But why did you invite me here when you—"

"Invite you?" she interrupted, stopping dead in the middle of the road. "But I . . . how could you think that I asked you?"

"I gathered that from Mrs. Dennistoun."

His voice came back to her from several yards ahead, for when she had stopped, he had continued walking a few steps. Now she marched furiously toward him.

"I think the truth is that Aunt Catherine had a hand in it. She sent you here to keep an eye on me and see that I don't get into mischief."

"And do I know your Aunt Catherine?"

Andrea regretted her impulsive outburst. "No, of course. Please forget what I said. I apologize."

"You're telling me that Mrs. Mayfield is your aunt."

"Then will you please keep that to yourself? My aunt thought it would make an embarrassing situation for me at the hotel if other members of the staff knew. So please don't tell Aunt Catherine or anybody else."

In the darkness Keir smiled at her. "I'll keep your secret," he promised, "but it was foolish to let your own temper give it away."

Andrea swallowed that well-deserved rebuke in silence.

"And what makes you think I like to keep an eye on you? Or would you prefer the word 'spy'?" he asked.

She gave a half-sigh, half-grunt. "I suppose it's really the hotel grapevine, but somehow my—Mrs. Mayfield—always seems to know everything about me: what I do, where I am at any given moment."

"But I thought a good hotel housekeeper was in effect an all-seeing eye. Otherwise she can't really control her staff. And why should you feel particularly persecuted? Doesn't her supervision extend to all the other people in the hotel?"

Andrea did not answer for a moment. Then she admitted, "Yes, you're right. I suppose I'm extra touchy."

They were walking up the driveway to the house and lights from the windows streamed out. In the large drawing room, the Christmas tree blinked its fairy lights, and Andrea shivered slightly, not with cold, but from the realization that she was on the outside looking in.

At the front door, Keir turned toward her. "Andrea, are you a good actress?" he asked.

"I don't know. I've never tried."

"Nonsense! Every woman is an actress. Just for once, tonight, play the part of a girl who might even like me a little—however much you really dislike or even hate me. You never know, it might work wonders in unexpected directions."

"But why?"

"You don't want the whole Belvedere to know you're the May Queen's niece do you?" His dark eyes sparkled at her in the hall lamplight.

"Blackmail!" she whispered, and suddenly a happy mood bubbled up within her.

She put on her new dress, a green velvet cut with youthful simplicity to enhance the beauty of the material and her own white neck and throat, and eyed her makeup critically in the dressing-table mirror. The afternoon walk had given a glow to her cheeks and she carefully blotted her lipstick. Perhaps a further touch of eyebrow pencil? She decided against it. Keir would not want her to be too dolled up, and anyway she would never be able to compete with Ingrid either in beauty of feature or dress, so she might as well look reasonably natural.

Mrs. Dennistoun had invited several other guests for dinner and some of these Andrea already knew slightly. Among them was Eileen Stanton, Trevor's private secretary at the store. She seemed surprised to see Andrea.

"Are you staying here for the holiday?" she asked.

Andrea explained that Mrs. Dennistoun had invited her.

"That's entirely the sort of thing that Trevor's mother would do," Eileen said warmly. "She really is a thoughtful soul. She liked your father very much." Eileen lowered her voice. "I gather the new chauffeur isn't quite such a success. Or perhaps it's his wife."

Andrea hadn't yet met the man who had taken her father's place, but there was no more time for conversation now. Keir appeared at her elbow as her dinner partner. Tentatively she rested her fingers in the crook of his arm.

"You look enchanting," he whispered, as they followed the others.

"Is that compliment part of your act?" she asked with her new-found gaiety.

"I'm not acting. I'm just going to be my natural and genial self."

"Genial?" she echoed, then drew in her breath with remorse. "Sorry, I forgot my lines."

The dinner-table setting evoked delighted exclamations and when Andrea caught sight of it she, too, gasped with admiration. Black tableware of elegant, asymmetrical design stood on a golden cloth. Tall red candles grouped at intervals, and a centerpiece of golden tinsel were the perfect foil for crystal goblets and slender wood-handled cutlery.

Mrs. Dennistoun graciously received the compliments that flew toward her, but waved a disclaiming hand.

"You must compliment Eileen. Her ideas, not mine."

Heads turned toward Trevor's secretary, who colored slightly under the impact of so many expressions of pleasure. Then, in a fractional lull, Ingrid's voice came clearly. "It is no doubt a good advertisement for the shop. Do you do this kind of work every day?"

Eileen, off her guard, stammered that design was only a sideline for her. Then she braced herself and looked squarely at Ingrid. "But you know, of course, that I'm Mr. Dennistoun's secretary at the store." She emphasized the last word.

Andrea gave Eileen an approving nod, and as the chatter of conversation began afresh, said, "It's the most beautiful Christmas table I've ever seen."

During the leisurely meal, Andrea had little chance of acting her role of being manifestly pleasant to Keir, for Ingrid on his other side monopolized his attention and almost ignored Trevor. Andrea chatted politely at intervals to her other neighbor, an elderly Major who lived at the far end of the village. But the Major's chief interest was in horsebreeding, and, as Andrea knew none of the finer points of either riding or breeding, the conversation flagged.

She lapsed into a reverie, trying to understand Mrs. Dennistoun's motives in bringing together at one table so many of Trevor's possible and eligible brides. Eileen, who adored her employer; the Major's tomboyish daughter, Claire; two other girls who had long regarded Trevor with loving admiration. Perhaps his mother had hoped to show him the contrast between any one of these girls of his own circle and the diamond-hard brilliance of Ingrid, whose icy perfection held no hint of love or human warmth.

Keir's voice roused Andrea from her thoughts. "Forgive me, Andrea. I've been neglecting you."

Andrea turned her head toward him and around the curve of the oval table saw Ingrid's face as she stopped in

midlaugh. The laughter had not reached the Danish girl's
eyes, and now the glance she gave Andrea was of concentrated hate.

In a flash, even while she listened to Keir's remarks and
answered lightly, Andrea guessed that it was Ingrid who
had prevailed upon Mrs. Dennistoun to invite Keir for the
sport of playing him and Trevor off against each other.

Andrea's conjecture was proved later that night. After the
party was over and the dinner guests had gone home, she
lay in bed, reveling in the rare luxury of being in the
Dennistoun home, and mulling over the evening's events.

She had acted pleasantly toward Keir, as instructed, but
after a while her behavior acquired a natural and spontaneous gaiety that had surprised her. But, she reflected, that
sort of thing was a two-way street. While Keir was so cool
and dour, she herself could feel only a stupid prickliness.

On two occasions Ingrid had tried to butt in on a
conversation between herself and Keir, and each time the
Danish girl had been politely but firmly cold-shouldered.
Andrea smiled at the memory of that thrill of triumph.

A knock on the door now startled her, but before she
could call "Come in!" Ingrid had already entered.

"You have, perhaps, some face tissues I can borrow? I do
not wish to disturb Mrs. Dennistoun."

"Of course. There's a box on the dressing table." Andrea
trembled a little under the bedclothes, for she knew that
Ingrid had not come for so trivial a purpose.

"Miss Andrea—what is your other name? I forget."

"Lansdale."

"Yes, of course. Your father was the chauffeur here." She
had not yet picked up the box of tissues, but was peering at
her own face in the mirror. "Miss Lansdale, I would like to
be your friend."

"Thank you." Andrea's voice remained wholly polite.

"But you are young and you must not take the attentions
of men so seriously. Or your heart will ache."

"You need have no fears for me. I shall not forget my
humble position."

Ingrid sighed. "So difficult for you, when you are pretty."

"Please, Miss Jensen, it's not at all necessary for you to

bother about me. I am learning hotel work and we are also instructed about keeping correct relations with the men guests we may happen to meet. After tomorrow, I shall be back at the Belvedere and you will not see me, except as a waitress like a dozen other girls in the hotel.''

"But you will still be glad that Mr. Holt stays at the hotel?''

Andrea shifted her position among the pillows and leaned forward toward Ingrid, who now sat on the dressing stool. "Why did you ask him here for Christmas if you thought he was so dangerous for me?''

"I knew he would be lonely wherever he was, without me.''

Andrea nodded, her guesswork confirmed. "But you did not know that I would also be here?''

"No, I did not,'' Ingrid snapped. "And I think Trevor should have told me. I do not expect him to flirt behind my back with a chauffeur's daughter.''

Andrea opened her mouth for an angry retort, but stopped in time. Whatever she said would make no difference, and Ingrid would only complain to Trevor or Mrs. Dennistoun that Andrea had insulted her. She saw, too, that temporarily Ingrid realized she had lost the initiative and had admitted that Andrea's intrusion had been disconcerting and unforeseen.

So now she said quietly, "Trevor and I are old friends, but although my father was not always a chauffeur, I hope I have enough sense not to imagine foolish things.'' She was surprised at the calmness of her words; now for the first time she had been able to see her childish leanings toward Trevor in their true perspective and openly admit that she no longer cherished hidden ambitions of marrying him one day. Even after Ingrid had gone, forgetting in the end to take the face tissues she had come to borrow, Andrea lay awake a long time. Perhaps the warning about Keir was necessary, even though it came fron Ingrid, who was not concerned with Andrea's welfare or heartbreak, but only her own dominance and ability to keep two or more men on the seesaw.

Next day Andrea was busy helping with the preparations

for the children's party in the afternoon. Mrs. Dennistoun usually made this a combined Boxing Day party for the village children and members of her staff, although Mrs. Whitton, the Dennistouns' cook-housekeeper, grumbled that it wasn't usually much fun for the staff, doing all the work beforehand, making the little brats behave themselves at the feast, and then clearing up the mess afterward.

"Still, the children probably do behave better if a few grown-ups are here," Andrea said, as she and Mrs. Whitton set the tables with jellies, trifles, iced cakes and all the other gaily colored eatables that children love to gloat over.

"It must be a sad Christmas for you without your father here," Mrs. Whitton murmured. "Have you met the new chauffeur yet?"

"No. What's he like?"

"Not as clever as he thinks he is. As for his wife—" Mrs. Whitton's disapproving sniff conveyed a whole world of unspoken aspersion. "Gorham has a roving eye for a pretty face—likes a joke with the girls—thinks they'll run after him if he so much as winks an eye at them. That fair upsets Mrs. Gorham. She likes to keep him on a tight rein."

Andrea remembered Mrs. Whitton's comments later that day when the party was in full swing. Jennifer Carter, the child who had unwittingly robbed Andrea of her father, had fallen over a stool and her loud howls were almost unheard in the general din of shrieking children, squealing whistles and toys, and the popping of balloons. Andrea bent down to pick up the child and dry her tears. Mr. Gorham knelt down, too, rubbed Jennifer's knee and coaxed a smile from her; then lifted Andrea to her feet with an embracing gesture that in the eyes of Mrs. Gorham, standing near, could only have appeared flirtatious.

Andrea murmured hasty thanks, took Jennifer's hand and led the child to another part of the room on the promise of a red balloon. Keir was there, engrossed in blowing up a further supply of balloons, which the children clamorously demanded.

"Can't keep pace with the little devils," he gasped between puffs.

Andrea began to giggle. "Your eyes are coming out on stalks. A bicycle pump's the thing."

He, too, laughed in midblow and the embryo balloon collapsed into a puny, wrinkled piece of colored rubber. "There! Look what you've done!"

"I didn't know you were here this afternoon," she said.

"I'm not in the prohibited class, am I?"

"I didn't mean that."

"It's a long time since I was at a kids' party." He resumed blowing up the balloon and gave it to Jennifer, who toddled off happily clutching it for a few seconds, until one of the bigger boys knocked it out of her hands and immediately burst it.

Keir and Andrea exchanged glances. "I shall need that breath when I'm old," he declared.

"All wasted now in your misspent youth. But what would be the use of trying to save what we squander and put it away in a freezer for our old age? It wouldn't be the same or have the same quality of our youth."

"I didn't realize you were such a philosopher," he said, after a moment's pause.

Two small children tugged at Andrea's skirt, begging her to give them the fairy doll now soaring on the pinnacle of the Christmas tree.

"You must wait a while, darlings," she told them. "Soon everybody will have their presents off the tree."

"But I want the dolly!" "No, *me*, I want it," they chorused.

"Be patient and wait and see if you get it," retorted Andrea firmly.

They looked hopefully up at, to them, Keir's immense height, as though willing him to reach up and unhook the precious fairy with her star, but finally toddled away in search of some more cooperative grown-up.

"Mrs. Dennistoun never lets them have their presents from the tree too soon. Otherwise most of the gifts are knocked about or lost before the children even get them home to show their parents," Andrea explained. "Last year, one boy opened his jigsaw puzzle, somebody else capsized it for him and all of us were hunting for the pieces."

More games were being arranged and Andrea and Keir found themselves in a long line where couples stood facing each other. To her dismay, Andrea found that her partner was Mr. Gorham, the chauffeur, and although she did not know the game, she was fairly certain that somewhere a kissing forfeit would enter into it.

Gorham grinned at her with a saucy rakishness that she hoped his wife would not see. She looked behind her, wondering if she could change places with someone else in the line, but two small boys and a girl were wrestling for position and by that time the game had started. "Take your facing partners . . . two steps to the right . . . two to the left. . . ." Oh, well, this was simple enough, thought Andrea. "Now turn and kiss the person behind you. . . ."

But instead of the small eight-year-old boy Andrea had expected, there was Keir. He lost no time in seizing her by the elbows and planting a kiss on either cheek for double measure.

"You cheated!" she whispered.

"What of it? As it happens, I didn't. The youngsters lost their places; they were too keen on squabbling with each other."

A delicious little tremor of excitement ran through her and color mounted to her face. He *had* maneuvered his place in the line-up, to be near her in case any kisses were going begging. Had he come into the party this afternoon because he knew she would be there? Or merely because he was bored and had nothing better to do?

For the rest of the evening her head was in a small, rose-colored cloud. Her spirits reacted blithely to every request made to her and were not even quenched when, inevitably, one child who had eaten too much had to be rushed off to the bathroom.

By nine o'clock when the last batch of children had been taken home, Andrea was ready to collapse from exhaustion. Even so, if by some magical chance Keir had asked her to go dancing or walk through the moonlit countryside, she would not have hesitated.

But she did not see him again that night, and supposed

that he had had a surfeit of company, including her own, and had probably gone off somewhere by himself.

Trevor and Ingrid had been out all day, and it was unlikely that Ingrid would have put in an appearance at the children's party.

Next morning Andrea packed immediately after breakfast, for she was due back at the Belvedere for duty at six o'clock. By the time she had found Mrs. Dennistoun to thank her for a wonderful Christmas holiday, there was still no sign of Keir and she wondered if he had already left the house.

"Gorham will take you to the station," her hostess said, and Andrea felt disappointed out of all proportion. She had been cherishing a secret hope that Keir would be leaving at the same time and drive her back to the Belvedere. But probably he would be staying a day or two longer and Ingrid would be able to divide her time diplomatically between him and Trevor.

Then, as she entered the long black car, Trevor came from the garden.

"Goodbye, Andrea! Hope you've enjoyed being here!" he called in a loud voice. Then he added in a whisper, "I might see you again soon at the Belvedere. Bless you, Andrea, I should never have met her but for you."

Andrea smiled and waved to him as the car sped down the driveway. In the end, only Trevor could discover for himself whether it was a good thing or a bad one to have met Ingrid.

In his smart dark green uniform, Gorham looked more handsome than ever, but his demeanor on duty was irreproachable. At Gloucester station he conducted her to the platform, touched the peak of his cap to her and then gave her the merest suspicion of a wink.

"A pleasant journey, miss. He went off early this morning, but I expect you'll be seeing him again."

Andrea reddened, partly out of confusion, but more because she was annoyed with herself for making it so plain the previous night that she was delighted to be in Keir's company. Evidently that delight was not reciprocated, for he had escaped from the Dennistouns's house at the earliest moment.

The train was halfway to Millbridge before she suddenly realized that even Ingrid's presence had failed to make him stay. The thought lightened the rest of the journey and made Andrea eager to return to the busy routine of the Belvedere.

CHAPTER NINE

HUGUETTE DEMANDED to know every detail of Andrea's Christmas visit. "Was there a big party? Who was there? Who made love to you?"

Andrea thrust out her hands as though to fend off the French girl's questions. "One at a time, and the last one first. Nobody made love to me."

Huguette's eyebrows shot up almost into her hair. "Then you have wasted your time."

"There was only a small party in the house and a large party, mostly children, came on Boxing Day."

"Oh! Children! Sometimes they are in the way and do not help."

"Don't be unnatural. What sort of mother are you going to make if you talk like that?" Andrea teased.

"You have not told me about the men who were there," Huguette insisted, undeterred by any criticism of her maternal instincts.

"Don't you want to know about the women?"

"No. They are not important."

Andrea smiled, admiring the other girl's superb self-confidence where her own sex was concerned.

"Trevor Dennistoun was there, of course, in his own house. But you were wrong, Huguette. There was one important woman there, Ingrid Jensen."

"Ingrid Jensen?" Huguette's mobile lips formed into a soundless "Oh!" and she nodded wisely. "Then she is chasing him, and that means that your friend Trevor must be rich. Why did you not secure him first?"

Andrea giggled. "You speak as though a girl had only to

fasten a collar round a man's neck and drag him wherever she pleases.'' But she saw that it was better to keep Huguette's attentions away from other visitors.

"Was that all? No more men?"

"Only those who came to the parties." She was determined not to tell anyone that Keir had been a guest for a couple of days. Besides, he might not want that broadcast all over the Belvedere, whether he had been invited by Ingrid Jensen or not.

"My poor Andrea! So dull for you."

"Tell me about your own Christmas, Huguette. Did you have a good time?"

The other girl's eyes sparkled with merriment. "At first it was all dull and no excitement going on anywhere, but last night I went to a carnival dance—a costume ball, you understand?"

"Fancy dress. Yes, go on."

"And—" Huguette's hands gestured expressively "—one of the men I meet is so charming. He insists that I see him again tomorrow."

"Good. Does he live here in Millbridge?"

"No. He travels to many parts."

"Oh, my poor Huguette!" Andrea mocked. "Once more you've given your heart to a fly-by-night who will swear eternal love and devotion to you alone and the very next morning leave for Manchester or Huddersfield, where he'll start the same game all over again. He's probably married already with four charming children."

"Married, perhaps. I do not think he has children," was Huguette's reflective opinion.

"All right. I'm only warning you. After all, you've given me plenty of advice whether I want it or not." After a pause, Andrea asked, "What was your costume at this ball?"

"A Japanese shepherdess."

"Japanese shepherdess? There isn't such a thing. I've never heard of sheep in Japan."

"What matter? A friend lent me the dress—it was like a painting by Watteau. He was one of our famous painters, you know."

"Yes, yes. I'm not entirely ignorant."

"But there was no bonnet or headdress. So I put a flower in my hair and make my eyebrows long and slanting, and *pfui!* I am Japanese."

"I wish I'd been there to see you."

"And I won a prize. Chocolates."

"That was because you were the best freak in the show. Neither fish, flesh, nor fowl, nor good red herring," teased Andrea.

"Why do you say I am like a herring?" Huguette was indignant and forced Andrea to explain the meaning of the idiom.

"And your partner? What did he wear?"

Huguette shrugged. "Dinner jacket and black tie. Englishmen do not like to dress themselves in foreign ways. Listen, Andrea, you must help me if it is necessary."

Andrea was immediately alarmed. "Not another case of borrowing, I hope?"

"No, no, no! But he asked where I live and I said the Belvedere, which is true indeed. So he comes home with me and I sail through the front door because I have a late pass and it is now two o'clock."

Andrea glanced at her friend. She did not need to be told the inference, but asked for confirmation all the same. "So he thinks you're a guest staying here, instead of a saucy chambermaid?"

Huguette nodded. "So you see I must arrange to meet him somewhere else. I cannot let him see me come out of the staff entrance."

"That's all right, then. No difficulty about that."

"Yes, but if he should ask for me at Reception, you must give him a message that I will meet him at the place we arranged."

"But I'm not in Reception now. I'm on waitress service."

Huguette's face clouded. "Yes, I had forgotten."

"You could tell the girls on Reception," Andrea suggested.

"Too dangerous. They will make a special point of telling my friend that Hélène Cluny is not here—only a French girl Huguette Cloubert, a mere chambermaid."

"So you gave him a false name, too? Still, what does it

matter? Isn't he attracted to you for what you really are, apart from being a Japanese shepherdess?'' Andrea could not help giggling.

"Did I laugh when you were in trouble with the necklace that somebody had hidden in your dressing table? No,'' Huguette snapped the reply to her own question. "I helped you get rid of it.''

Andrea gaped in astonishment. "You were the one who borrowed it. *And* then flung it out the window.''

"Lucky for you I did so, my good Andrea. If not, it would have been found in your drawer. And what could you have said?''

Long after Huguette had turned her back huffily on her roommate and gone to sleep, Andrea reflected in the darkness that so far there had been no satisfactory explanation of how Miss Jensen's necklace had found its way to Andrea's room.

But there was little time to dwell on past unsolved mysteries, for during the next week preparations had to be made for New Year's Eve celebrations and then Swedish Week. In the last few years the hotel management had collaborated very successfully with international trade organizations to give displays and exhibitions of a particular country's products. The January week for Sweden was followed by other Scandinavian countries in February and March; French Fortnight came in May and other countries took part when instructed by their governments and according to their trade agreements. Undoubtedly the Belvedere had made itself the focal point for these activities in the Midlands, and in addition to successful business there was no lack of gaiety.

Special exhibitions of produce were attended by ravishing girls in national costume; mayoral lunches, cocktail parties, film and television shows, gala balls, all lightened the dark months of the year and encouraged the interest of other visitors staying in the hotel as well as elsewhere in the town.

But for the staff of the Belvedere life became one long rush period. Andrea was thankful that she had already had some practice in waiting on tables before Swedish Week arrived, although she did not yet know which department she might be working in. At any moment, Aunt Catherine might transfer her somewhere else.

She hoped she might still be on waitress service, for this was one of the liveliest departments where one could see something of the day's events.

But just before the Week was due to begin, Andrea's hopes crashed. She was serving lunch in the stewards' room where the seniors and official staff took their meals. This was the recognized training ground for table service, both for girls and young-men *commis*, although the latter had the additional opportunity of being allotted to a station waiter in the restaurant.

Today the stewards' room was shorthanded, and Andrea had to cope as best she could with only one other new and very nervous trainee boy to help her. Twice he nearly collided with her as she hurried down the length of the narrow room to serve the staff manager. "Try to keep to the left, Donald," she warned him the next time she passed.

But Donald was apparently a boy who did not know his left from his right, for he turned quickly a few minutes later and, with head down, cannoned into Andrea. Her carefully balanced plates of soup, roast beef and dishes of vegetables crashed to the floor in an indescribable mess.

The boy's face crimsoned as he muttered apologies, and Andrea bent down to wipe up the debris.

From the corner table, Miss Wyvern's voice came toward Andrea. "Surely you've had enough practice by now to avoid accidents like that."

On many occasions, Andrea had been able to dodge serving Miss Wyvern, but her luck was out today. Then, too, she knew that the accident could have been minimized, if not altogether avoided, if she had been carrying fewer dishes.

Now, after sending Donald for cloths and mops to clean the floor, Andrea had completely forgotten what Miss Wyvern had ordered.

"I'm sorry, but would you tell me again—" she began.

"My dear girl, I've told you twice already. Can't you memorize your orders?"

"Was it the kidney sauté?" asked Andrea.

Miss Wyvern sighed in exasperation, then nodded. But when Andrea brought the order and was about to place it carefully in front of the assistant housekeeper, Miss Wyvern savagely caught Andrea's wrist. "I did *not* order kidney sauté!" she muttered.

Then in a flash, further disaster happened. The plate had tilted and pieces of kidney in a mush of gravy were spilled on the tablecloth.

"How could you be so careless!" Miss Wyvern exclaimed in a loud voice. She jumped up, shaking her skirt, but as far as Andrea could see, no damage had been done to Miss Wyvern's clothes. "Don't stand there like an idiot! Do something to clean up the mess."

Andrea's eyes blazed with fury and her breath was choked. The accident was not her fault. At the moment when Andrea's control of the plate had been relaxed, Miss Wyvern had deliberately twisted the girl's wrist, so that the contents of the plate had slid off. As she fled to bring more towels for mopping up, Andrea wished impiously that she had tipped the plateful clean into Miss Wyvern's lap. One might as well be hanged for a sheep as for a lamb.

But, as she well knew, the incidents had repercussions, and at the end of the day Andrea was summoned to Mrs. Mayfield's office. Miss Wyvern was already there having, no doubt, given her own righteous version of the affair.

"Sit down, Andrea," Aunt Catherine said, not unkindly. Miss Wyvern appeared outraged, for she was still standing.

Andrea gave her explanation, as briefly as possible.

"Yes, I'm told you were shorthanded there today, but two accidents at one meal—" Aunt Catherine broke off with a half-smile toward her niece.

"I'm sorry about them, madam. Donald is not very experienced yet and he couldn't help crashing into me."

"I'm still waiting for your personal apology to me," snapped Miss Wyvern. "Nobody likes to have a plateful of food tipped into one's lap."

Andrea shot her a lightning glance of indignation. "But none of it went on you, Miss Wyvern."

The assistant housekeeper gave a derisive laugh. "I'm the

best judge of that. My dress was splashed with grease and I had to change.''

This was too much for Andrea. Without stopping to think of the consequences, she protested, ''The accident wouldn't have happened if you hadn't grabbed my wrist so quickly and—'' Caution rescued her from the final accusation.

''Indeed! I certainly had to do something to avoid having the food thrown in my face.''

Andrea glanced down at her hands clasped in her lap. She clenched them until the knuckles showed white. How foolish to think she could fight Miss Wyvern.

Aunt Catherine said quietly, ''Please apologize to Miss Wyvern—and then perhaps we can forget the incident, provided you are more careful in the future.''

The words almost stuck in Andrea's throat, but she forced out an apology, smarting under the sense of unfairness. It was Wyvern who should be apologizing to her.

''And I trust I'm not to have Lansdale back again on my floor,'' Miss Wyvern observed to her chief in that odious way she had of ignoring Andrea's presence in the room.

Andrea waited, tense and hardly daring to breathe. She knew that, despite the assistant housekeeper's defensive tone, there was nothing Miss Wyvern would like better than to have Andrea Lansdale again under her immediate authority, so that she could eternally find fault until nothing short of dismissal would be possible.

Aunt Catherine looked at Andrea. ''No, I think you deserve another chance, Andrea. But you must try to be careful. We don't want our Swedish guests to find our service not up to the standard of their own.''

''But surely Lansdale is not competent enough to serve guests, when she can't even prevent accidents in the Stewards?''

''We shall need all the waitress service we can muster, Miss Wyvern, for next week.'' She turned toward Andrea. ''And I believe you have had some slight experience with the banqueting and dinner-party work?''

''Oh, yes, madam.'' Andrea was relieved that she was apparently not to be banished to the top floor and Miss Wyvern's care.

"Would you please leave us, Miss Wyvern? I have something further to say to Andrea."

The assistant housekeeper hesitated at first, but had no choice but to march out of the room.

Andrea became apprehensive again. What now?

"You must not make accusations against your seniors, even if you think you are justified," Aunt Catherine told her niece. "If you have any reasonable complaint, I'm always ready to listen. I'm sure that was just a slip on your part."

Andrea had enough sense not to argue the point, for she suspected that her aunt was not fooled by Laura Wyvern.

"Yes, madam, I understand. That was foolish of me."

Mrs. Mayfield gave a small sigh. "That's settled, then. Now tell me about your Christmas holiday. I haven't had a chance to ask you sooner."

"I enjoyed it very much."

The housekeeper glanced at Andrea's face, now lit with pleasure. "I suppose Trevor Dennistoun spent the holiday at home? But don't think I'm prying," she added hastily, alert for signs of Andrea's resentment.

"Yes, he was at home. He'd invited a friend to stay, so I didn't really see much of him. There was a dinner party one of the evenings and on Boxing Day a children's party."

Andrea raced on with the details because she did not want them to be extracted from her one at a time. She considered it correct not to mention Ingrid's name as a guest, and likewise, thought she was justified in not disclosing that Keir Holt had also been there. But after she had left Mrs. Mayfield's office, it occurred to her that quite likely her aunt already knew where Keir and Ingrid had spent their Christmas holiday.

At bedtime, when Andrea related the day's misadventures to Huguette, the latter became thoughtful.

"She is determined, that one, to have you thrown out into the street. You have offended Wyvern and she will never rest until you leave the Belvedere. So, my dear Andrea, you must take a good look at all the men you see and find yourself a wealthy husband. Also he should be handsome, if possible—but money is more important."

Andrea laughed. "I don't know which is worse—to be

thrown out into the street by Wyvern or throw oneself at the first rich and available man." But she hugged to herself the thought that Aunt Catherine would never dismiss her solely because of Miss Wyvern's hatred.

The night before Swedish Week was due to begin, Andrea was helping with other waitresses to prepare several rooms for the next day's cocktail and luncheon parties.

The assistant banqueting manager was there to supervise and give instructions, and Andrea's immediate task was to hand out tablecloths of suitable size and shape for the various-shaped tables. Until she had come to the Belvedere, she had not realized that hotels could provide such a diversity of tables. There were, of course, the usual rectangular ones that could be placed in a variety of formations, according to the size of the party and the importance of a head table, but there were also round, oval, crescent and horseshoe tables.

At the moment, somebody had conceived the bright notion of placing horseshoe tables so that they formed a letter "ess." Two waitresses were grumbling as they tried to fix two horseshoes together.

"They're the wrong way round," Andrea pointed out gently. "The "ess" is inside out, backward."

"Oh, I give up!" exclaimed the other girl. "It's a Chinese puzzle to me. The ends don't fit. Somebody's going to lose his soup plate down the crack."

But eventually the letter "ess" tables were fixed and the cloths spread. Then the two head tables had to be formed in the letters "gee" and "bee" for Great Britain. The "gee" was comparatively easy with one horseshoe, several small curved pieces and a square for the base of the "gee". It was the "bee" that gave the trouble.

"How in the world are people going to sit inside those curved pieces?" demanded one of the other waitresses. "They'll have to climb over. I shall tell Mr. Harding that it can't be done."

But Mr. Harding, the supervisor, armed with a completely drawn table plan of the seating, was firm.

"Nobody sits *inside* the curves, you silly girl," he scolded. "Only on the outside. Where's your sense?"

As Andrea commented afterward and out of Mr. Harding's hearing, the best place to see the general splendid effect would be to perch on one of the chandeliers and look down on the symbolic sight beneath.

At last everything was done to the supervisor's satisfaction, the places were laid, the cutlery and glass set and only the finishing touches and flowers remained to be done the next day.

Andrea was on duty at the preliminary cocktail party the following morning, and as she handed around trays of drinks she wished she were slightly taller. She had never before felt so hemmed in by so many massive men. Some of them had a tendency to swing around suddenly, almost sending her and her tray of glasses flying.

When she returned her empties to the bar, the attendants chaffed her. "Gone again, miss? I reckon you found yourself a nice quiet corner and swallowed the lot, eh?"

"I'm lucky to get around the guests without spilling the drinks all over their waistcoats," she retorted, but she did not feel as lighthearted as she sounded. She knew that this was her final chance of continuing on waitress service, and if she muffed it Aunt Catherine would have no option but to take her off and send her to some other department where she could do less damage to guests and the hotel reputation.

The luncheon was an all-men affair, graced by the mayor and other Millbridge notables, as well as the Swedish consul and heads of industrial and commercial concerns from all over the Midlands. Waiters and young *commis* apprentices took over the service, and Andrea and her companions were free for a breathing space, when the last of the men had drifted into the large room.

"There!" exclaimed one of the other waitresses. "I forgot to have a final peep at the tables. Too late now."

"I looked in earlier this morning," Andrea put in. "When Miss Heaton was arranging the flowers. All spring flowers—daffodils, narcissi and small sprays of lilac. And all the placecards have two little flags skewered into them, Swedish and English."

"Oh, well," sighed the other girl. "We'd better clear this mess away. Are you on afternoon tea duty?"

"Yes, I was told so."

"Don't forget to ask if they want tea with lemon," the girl cautioned Andrea. "They can have it that way for all I care. I like plenty of milk and sugar in mine."

The rest of the week was full of gaiety and excitement, although there were many events which, in the nature of things, Andrea was prevented from seeing firsthand. A fashion show was held one afternoon, but Andrea was kept busy elsewhere and saw nothing of it. In some mysterious manner, Huguette managed to get in and plant herself unobtrusively in a corner.

"Yes, yes, the fashion's quite good," she said patronizingly to Andrea. "Much influenced by Paris, of course. But good materials and some quite elegant lines."

"A lot of clothes for winter sports, I suppose?"

"Many. And some of them truly *chic*. None of those thick baggy trousers and shapeless jackets."

But Andrea did manage to see the exhibitions of food and dairy produce, attended by girls in national Swedish costume; the exquisite glassware and pottery and the handsome furniture in woods of incomparable beauty.

Trevor came in one morning, but Andrea had time only to call out a greeting to him before she had to rush away to her duties and leave Trevor to talk with his business friends.

In the shops in Millbridge, special Swedish displays took the dominant places in windows and interior counters, and in her free time one afternoon, Andrea walked through the newly opened part of the Century block. Three new floors were now ready with their merchandise displayed more spaciously than ever before. Here, too, were Swedish glass, toys and textiles, accompanied by smiling Swedish girls as usual.

The local papers had given prominence to the event and press photographers had been busy inside the hotel as well as outside.

Dick Palmer, Jill's fiancé, wrote a column every day for his paper on Swedish Week and each day's special events.

"You find out more about what's going on from Dick's column than you actually know living here," Andrea said to Jill one evening, when they both had a spare moment.

Evidently the engagement was now running more smoothly, even though Jill took a delight in snubbing Dick whenever she could. Still, if that was the way their two temperaments fused together, what did it matter to outsiders?

"Has Miss Jensen come back to the hotel since Christmas?" Andrea asked Jill. "I haven't seen her and Huguette hasn't mentioned her."

"No, she's not in. In any case, she couldn't have had her usual suite or any other of that class. They were all booked a year ago for this Swedish do."

But the next day, Jill had news of Miss Jensen.

"She must be staying somewhere else," she told Andrea. "She hasn't a room here. She came in to lunch, I think. Perhaps she was to meet somebody here. But a curious incident happened." Jill dropped her voice to a whisper. "She was just idly standing over there by the notice board when one of those Swedish girls came through the hall, looked at Miss Jensen and then exclaimed 'Astrid!' Then she spoke in Swedish, or perhaps Danish, I don't know which, and gave Miss Jensen a little curtsey and held out her hand. But Miss Jensen gave her an icy look and said something that sounded like 'I don't know you.' Then she marched off toward the cocktail bar."

"The other girl must have called her Ingrid," said Andrea.

"No, I heard quite plainly. Astrid was what she said. The Swedish girl looked dumbfounded. Then, to top it all, she came over to the desk and asked if there was a Miss Astrid Kerensen staying here. I told her there was nobody of that name and she walked away, still looking puzzled."

"She must have mistaken Ingrid for someone else."

Andrea thought no more of the matter, but she wondered, as she had many times since Christmas, why there was no sign of Keir. Perhaps he had changed his hotel, because Andrea was at the Belvedere and he did not wish to encourage the acquaintance? No, Andrea was not vain enough to imagine that she was important in his life to that extent. It was easy enough for a guest in Keir's position to avoid a humble employee, whether a waitress or chambermaid.

Swedish Week usually wound up with a grand banquet and ball, a gala occasion, which taxed the service and resources of the Belvedere to the full extent. Two famous Swedish film stars and many other Scandinavian celebrities attended and the press photographers were busy all over the hotel.

Andrea had learned that when the balcony overlooking two sides of the banqueting hall was not in use, it was possible to have a good view of the dinner and subsequent dance.

At teatime in the women's staff hall, this was the only topic. Nobody knew whether the balcony would be required for the guests.

"But I shall go up into Fred's perch," said one. Fred was one of the electricians on duty for lighting and microphones.

Andrea was fortunately blessed with the evening off duty and hoped to view what all the girls told her was a grand spectacle.

"Don't forget to take off your apron and anything else white," someone warned her. "Little bits of white show up and give you away, but a black dress hides you. And keep behind the pillars if you can."

Huguette was not off duty, but she vowed that she would find time to appear.

Apparently only part of the balcony was to be used and a few tables had already been prepared for sitters-out when the dancing began.

Andrea arrived just before the dinner ended, when the closing speeches were being made. She hid discreetly behind a pillar in the dimmer part of the balcony and after a while was joined by two other girls.

The guests rose and filtered out of the banqueting hall while the tables were cleared and Andrea found this part of the proceedings fascinating to watch.

Waiters and young assistants literally ran to their appointed positions, and under the direction of supervising head waiters the tables were stripped with incredible speed.

Plates, cutlery, flowers, cruets, glasses were loaded onto carts and wheeled away. Cloths were whipped off, chairs and tables moved to the edges of the room. Then a dozen or so men and boys methodically unzipped the carpet across the middle, rolled it into two immense halves and staggered off with their loads through a service door.

The orchestra took its place on the dais, the electrician tried a few experimental spotlights and color effects, and by that time small tables had been neatly relaid around two sides of the dance floor, and the surplus tables had disappeared.

"What marvelous organization!" whispered Andrea to one of her companions. "I'd no idea carpets could be unzipped like that."

"Brainy, isn't it?" returned the other girl. "All right as long as the zip works and doesn't jam. I think it was old Bradley who thought of that. He's the upholsterer here, mends the carpets and all that."

A sudden wickedly perverse notion entered Andrea's head. "What would happen if one of the boys tripped over and they rolled him up inside?"

"He'd holler, I expect. They say that did happen once to a small kid who'd only just grown out of being a page and started as a *commis* waiter. But I think the men deliberately put him inside to tease him. They took him out afterward before he was suffocated."

The band played two waltzes and a quickstep before even the first dancers sauntered back into the hall, but soon the floor was a brilliant spectacle of whirling figures, women in dazzling gowns to contrast with their partners' black and white, a sprinkling of uniforms and, of course, the gay splashes of colorful Swedish national costumes.

Andrea was so entranced that she did not realize the other girls had gone. But suddenly a voice spoke beside her. "How envious does this make you?"

She turned quickly, recognizing Keir's voice at once.

"I didn't know you were here," she exclaimed.

"I didn't expect to find you here, either, lurking behind a pillar."

"It's forbidden, really, but as long as we don't make ourselves too conspicuous, it's all right, I think."

At that moment, Fred, the electrician, swept a blinding floodlight all around the balcony. Andrea and Keir were caught in its beam and she instantly sheltered behind the pillar.

"I wonder if that was by accident or design," Keir murmured. "Perhaps it's meant to be a hint to wandering menfolk to join the tripping dance."

"Were you at the banquet?" she asked.

"Yes. I managed to avoid most of the other excitements of this festive week, but I had to put in an appearance tonight."

She wondered who his partner was or whether he had come alone in some official capacity connected with his work.

"You still haven't told me if all this makes you feel envious," he repeated.

"Envious?" she echoed thoughtfully. "No, I don't think so. When something is so very far out of reach, you don't usually envy those who have it. It's just the little bit more that you believe you're really entitled to that turns you green."

For several moments he was silent. "You always astonish me, Andrea, by your simple philosophy."

"I've never thought about it. You're probably the only person who asks me questions like that and makes me give the answer."

For a few more moments they watched the dancers below. Then Huguette, minus apron and cap, came toward Andrea, who would have escaped if that had been possible. The French girl would be sure to recognize Keir.

"Who was talking to you?" asked Huguette, and Andrea realized that Keir had unobtrusively walked away.

"Oh, just somebody who came up and spoke to me."

"You should be careful. Imagine if you had been caught by the May Queen or even Wyvern, encouraging the guests to chat with you in a dark corner."

"Well, nobody did catch me."

Huguette's attention was occupied by the dancers. She

murmured comments on the women's dresses, the good looks or otherwise of the men.

Then she said, "Look! There is Mr. Watford dancing with one of those Swedish girls."

Andrea followed where Huguette indicated. "He's enjoying himself," she observed.

"A pity that the Wyvern can't see him. She would probably throw herself over the balcony with jealousy."

"Hush! Be quiet, Huguette! You don't know who might be listening. Talk in French."

"As you please. There is Miss Jensen, also. Yes, a beautiful dress."

"Where?" But at that moment, Andrea saw not only Ingrid, but her partner as well, Keir Holt.

CHAPTER TEN

HUGUETTE RELUCTANTLY ADMITTED that she must return to her duties and Andrea remarked carelessly, "I might as well come along, too. No point in watching other people dance all evening."

But she did not feel casual about seeing Ingrid dancing in Keir's arms. No doubt he'd had a few minutes to waste while Ingrid titivated herself, and, chancing upon Andrea in the balcony, it had suited him to talk to her.

In the women's staff hall at supper, when the other girls asked questions about the glamorous dresses, Andrea answered, but her lack of enthusiasm made the others believe that she envied the wearers.

"These affairs always make you feel worse than Cinderella," observed Miriam, the chambermaid from the fourth floor where Andrea had first started. "Best thing, I always say, is go to the Palais and cheer yourself up."

"How can you do that at this time of night?" demanded another girl. "The evening's over for most of us."

"But I enjoyed watching all the belles of the ball," Andrea protested. "I didn't say I envied them."

On the way up to her bedroom, she stopped to talk to Miriam for a few minutes in the fourth-floor station, where Miriam was checking her early morning trays.

Presently Andrea asked, "I suppose I ought not to ask you this and you needn't answer if you don't want to, but how do you get on with Miss Wyvern?"

Miriam drew her lips inward until they disappeared. "Well," she said, after a moment, "she's not easy, but I've known worse. She fusses and fidgets about some things and turns a blind eye to others. You just have to find out her funny little ways.''

"She doesn't seem to like me very much," Andrea went on.

"Has she got her knife into you?"

Andrea laughed softly. "I don't know whether it's a knife or a sword. Whichever it is, she plunges it in pretty deep. You heard about the day I dropped a plateful of food in front of her?"

"Oh, yes!" Miriam snorted with laughter. "When she got her kidneys shot all over the tablecloth. Everybody's heard about that."

Now, Andrea could laugh, too, over the incident, but at the moment when it had happened, it had not been so funny. If Aunt Catherine had taken a different view, Andrea might not still be here in the Belvedere.

Miriam moved along the dresser shelves to collect a few more cups. "Hullo, hullo! What's going on down there?" She was near the small window of the station, looking down into the well.

"What is it?" asked Andrea.

"Put out the light, Andy."

Andrea obeyed without thinking, then ran to the window and peered over Miriam's shoulder.

"Look! Down there on third. D'you see what I see?"

Across the well, behind a narrow lighted window, Andrea could see two people, apparently talking. One was certainly Miss Wyvern, but it was not so easy to identify the man.

"It's only Miss Wyvern in the station," she said.

"Huh! And what d'you think she'd say to us if we had our men friends along with us in the stations? Isn't it—why, yes, it is. It's that Mervyn Watford who's with her."

Andrea, uncomfortable at the idea of spying on somebody, said, "You can't recognize anybody at that distance. Besides how is it that we can see straight through that window? This one is frosted at the bottom half."

"Oh, I expect you didn't know," returned Miriam. "One of the maids stuck her broom or mop handle through the window and smashed it and it's only a temporary piece of clear glass they've put in." Miriam chuckled. "I'll bet clever

Miss Wyvern has forgotten that, or doesn't even know. That's what comes of being officious on someone else's floor."

"Perhaps she's doing third-floor housekeeper's duty to-night." Andrea was surprised to hear herself finding excuses for Miss Wyvern.

"In two seconds, they'll be kissing," Miriam prophesied. "There! I knew it."

Andrea turned away. But the illuminated little scene was printed on her mind. Mervyn's kindly placating attitude, Laura Wyvern's hands on his arms, then the sudden movement toward him so that their faces touched.

She snapped on the light and Miriam turned angrily. "Don't do that! I can't see what's going on."

But Andrea called out good night and went upstairs to her own room. In spite of the many petty irritations and frustrations that Miss Wyvern had caused Andrea could feel only pity that a woman, no longer a young and foolish girl, could give her devotion to a man like Mervyn Watford. There was probably no real harm in Mervyn, but then there was no real good, either, if a woman wanted more than a pleasant flirtation with him. Laura's attitude had not implied flirtation at all, Andrea reflected. She wished she had not looked out of the window to satisfy her curiosity, but it would have made no difference to Miriam, who would undoubtedly spread her juicy bit of scandal to whoever would listen.

Huguette had already heard the gossip when she came up to bed.

"Well, Andrea, if the Wyvern tries to go too far with you, you can always—how do you say it—practice the extortion?"

"The word is blackmail, but it's an ugly word and I won't be mixed up in Miss Wyvern's affairs."

Huguette shrugged. "Everybody knows that she has set her cap at Mervyn, but it is not a good choice. He is not a man who will marry until he is quite old, and perhaps not then. But he likes to be free to make love to the girls. He would never marry anyone like the Wyvern. He knows that if he came home five minutes late, she would question him, search his pockets for letters and his collar for stray hair. The poor boy would have no peace at all.''

''Neither would Laura Wyvern,'' added Andrea. ''She'd be very unhappy.''

Huguette beamed at her friend. ''Exactly. Then you must give her your good advice next time you meet. You must tell her that Mervyn would make a bad husband and it would be better if she cast her eyes on a middle-aged, sober man who is looking for a quiet life with a well-trained house-keeper-lady.''

''She'd give me a dusty answer,'' commented Andrea, not realizing that she would have to spend the next ten minutes explaining to Huguette the meaning of the phrase.

''I wonder what the May Queen's husband was like,'' Huguette wiped off her mascara and peered at herself in the mirror. ''I would guess that he had to be very precise and tidy and not bring mud into the house.''

''I don't think so. Mrs. Mayfield was young and—''

Huguette swung around. ''You know about the husband?''

Andrea reddened, annoyed with herself for so nearly giving away the precious secret. ''No. Only that he was killed during the war, so Mrs. Mayfield probably had to earn her living.''

''That is sad,'' agreed Huguette. ''But it is better for us that we have a woman who has been married to rule over us instead of one who has not.'' She shuddered. ''If the May Queen should leave and Wyvern should step into her shoes, then we shall be treated like prisoners.''

Andrea laughed. ''How you exaggerate! But surely your nice Miss Deakin would take the May Queen's place before Miss Wyvern would be promoted?''

''Miss Deakin is engaged to be married. Perhaps in the spring or summer she will leave.''

''Oh, I see.''

''But that is a secret. She does not want to be pushed out before she is ready. Who knows? She might yet be jilted.''

Andrea laughed afresh. ''What a pessimist you are about love and marriage! Anybody would think that there's nothing else in life except capturing a man and leading him to the altar.''

"What else could be so important?'' demanded the French girl. "Without a husband—even a not very good husband—a woman cannot hold up her head among her friends. She is not all there.''

"You don't mean that, Huguette. 'Not all there' means a little bit touched, *un peu toqué*. What you mean is that a woman is incomplete.''

"*C'est ça*. She is only half.''

Huguette's ideas about the incompleteness of single bless-edness lingered in Andrea's thoughts as she carried out her work next day. But she was content to mark time, she told herself. There was nobody, not even on the far-distant horizon, who was likely to ask her to share his life, and last night's encounter with Keir and then seeing him dancing with Ingrid was warning enough for Andrea. She would be foolish indeed if she allowed herself to hanker after a man who merely went out of his way on a Christmas visit to pay her polite social attention.

She was on her way down from her room where she had tidied herself after her own lunch, when she saw Huguette emerge from the service elevator on the second floor with a pile of linen.

"Goodness, you have a hefty load there. I'll carry some for you,'' Andrea offered.

"Oh, this morning it is hectic!'' Huguette exclaimed. "Everybody is leaving after the Swedish festival and all new people coming in.''

Andrea lifted a number of sheets from the pile and walked behind Huguette along the corridor. Suddenly the French girl turned back. "Quick, Andrea! Take these! No, give them all to me! No! Walk in front of me. Somebody is coming.''

Andrea, still holding the sheets, was mystified, supposing that one of the floor housekeepers, or even the May Queen herself, was approaching and that Huguette did not want to be seen, but the only person along the corridor was a man strolling toward the two girls.

As he came abreast of Andrea, she stood aside to let him

pass and turned to ask Huguette where the linen was to be put, but the French girl had disappeared.

Andrea returned, peering into any open bedroom doors where Huguette might be. After a moment or two, Huguette's head cautiously appeared around the corner of another corridor and she beckoned to Andrea.

"Has he gone?" she whispered.

"Who? That man? Yes."

Huguette smote her heart and let out a gusty sigh. "That was an escape!" she shut her eyes in an expression of anguish.

"Why? Was he someone you know?"

"But of course. He is my partner at the dance. Oh *mon dieu,* I thought he would see me. So I carried the linen so high that it was above my face and then I came round this corner."

Andrea began to laugh. "He probably saw you anyway, and now he knows you're only a maid—oh, yes, a very pretty French maid—at the Belvedere."

Huguette was momentarily affronted, but then she, too, collapsed into helpless laughter. But while Andrea was still giggling, Huguette became serious and thoughtful. "Then he is staying here in the hotel. Oh, that is good, but dangerous."

"Now you're in the soup. You'll have to find out which room he has and how long he's staying. Then you can avoid him perhaps, but you'll be lucky."

"Andrea, you have no sympathy for me!" Huguette chided.

"Well, you get yourself into such tangles over men. Are they worth it?"

"I vow he will not see me as a maid," Huguette declared. "I will think of some way."

"What are you doing here, Lansdale?" Miss Wyvern's sharp voice broke in on them with a shock.

"I was helping Huguette with the linen, madam."

"And how do you come to be on second floor helping somebody else with duties quite unconnected with your own?"

Andrea, remembering, too, the little vignette last night

where Miss Wyvern had thrown away her pride and even her discretion, answered gently. "I was only on my way down from lunch and Huguette had a very heavy load."

"It was kind of Andrea to help me," put in Huguette.

"Cloubert, you are not under my supervision, so there is nothing to concern me about you, but Lansdale should not be here at all."

Andrea prayed that she would not have to wait upon Miss Wyvern today, after this unfortunate meeting. If she did, the floor housekeeper might even crown her with a plate of soup. But for once Andrea's luck was in, and Miss Wyvern did not appear until Andrea was off duty from the steward's room.

Instead, during lunch, Jill Brookman from Reception asked Andrea, "Are you free for an evening tonight or tomorrow?"

"No. Not until Thursday."

"Can't you change with somebody?"

Andrea smiled. "Why? Something exciting?"

Jill pursed her lips. "I don't know about exciting, but several of us are going out dancing at the Carlton Ballroom and I thought you'd like to come."

"No partner," murmured Andrea.

"That can be fixed. Robert is dying to take you."

"Robert?"

"Yes, don't pretend that you don't know that he's crazy about you."

Andrea had spoken to Robert, the young *pâtisserie* chef, a few times, but she had no idea he was crazy about her, and said so to Jill.

"Well, come dancing with us and get to know him better," suggested Jill. "Tomorrow night is the one we'll probably fix up, so change with somebody on the roster. Have you been to the Carlton yet? It's good fun."

Andrea promised to think about the suggestion and let Jill know later. It might not be a bad idea to join the party, she thought. Since Christmas she had not been anywhere at all exciting and she was beginning to understand the hotel atmosphere and the deadening effect it sometimes had on staff who were forced to watch other people enjoying themselves.

She was able to change evening duties with another girl and gleefully told Huguette.

"Oh, it will be a dull party, with people you can see every day," Huguette jeered.

"Well, at least I can look them in the face and not have to run down a corridor because I see my dance partner coming, and have to hide among a pile of sheets!" retorted Andrea. "I don't pretend to be a countess staying at the Belvedere."

Huguette's eyes flashed with amusement. "I think you will not allow me to forget that matter for a while. But I, too, am being taken dancing. I am going with Noel."

"Is he the man you ran away from?

Huguette nodded. "He is on the third floor, by good luck, so—"

"So you're not likely to have to march in with his morning tea," Andrea finished for her. "Oh, but I would love to see his face if you did."

"Do not taunt me," Huguette ordered. "Help me, now. How am I to meet him if he is living in the hotel?"

"M'm. That's a problem. Well, he'll soon have found out that there is no Hélène Cluny staying here, so that puts you in a difficulty."

"I think Mademoiselle Cluny will have to move from the Belvedere to the Prince's and I will meet him in the lounge there."

"But when he brings you home, he'll take you to the Prince's," Andrea objected.

"One can walk from the Prince's to the Belvedere. It is not far."

Andrea shook her head sadly. Huguette's complicated intrigues were often too difficult to follow.

"What if he sees you come in the Belvedere after he has left you safely at the Prince's?"

Huguette closed her eyes in pained martyrdom. "Andrea, you are a good friend, but—"

"Yes, yes, I know. I look on the black side," Andrea interrupted. "All right. Good luck to you. You'll need it."

Then, as an afterthought she added, "You won't borrow somebody's best evening dress or stole, will you?"

Huguette smiled. "That is a good reminder. I must look in Miss Jensen's wardrobe and see if there is a dress I can select."

"Oh? Is Miss Jensen back here?"

"Yes. Two days ago."

Andrea longed to ask if Keir Holt had also returned, but this was a question she dared not put to Huguette.

As Jill had promised, dancing at the Carlton was good fun and Andrea thoroughly enjoyed the evening. Robert danced well and maintained only a pleasant, friendly relationship. Jill was evidently teasing when she had declared that the boy was crazy about Andrea.

To Andrea's surprise, later during the evening, Mervyn Watford and his partner, a junior from Reception at the Belvedere, joined the party. As he and Andrea danced, he asked, "Why haven't I seen you for ages?"

"My work keeps me in the background. I'm not supposed to be dashing about in Reception, or helping sales reps in the stockrooms."

"Pity. What are you doing now?"

"Learning to wait at table."

"Where do they teach you? D'you have dummy guests?"

She laughed. "No. We have to practice on some of the senior staff. Somebody has to wait on them, so it has to be us. When we've improved a little, then we may be allowed to help the waitresses on breakfast service."

"Oh, yes. They never have men waiters at breakfast at the Belvedere."

"The men come on duty for lunch, but at breakfast there's a special morning staff who come in from seven until about ten. Mostly married women, who've had waitress experience, and do this as their part-time work."

"Have you dropped soup or ice cream down anybody's neck?" he asked.

"Not so far. Although I did have one accident in—" She broke off, realizing that the person involved in that episode was Miss Wyvern. Fortunately the band stopped playing and she and Mervyn went back to their table.

Jill's fiancé, Dick, decided that he'd better look in at his newspaper office and see if anything important had happened, and as Robert lived at home with his parents, Mervyn drove the three girls back to the Belvedere in his car, as they all had late passes.

"Which entrance?" he queried. His long experience in escorting staff had made him familiar with the routine. "Front or back?"

"Main door," Jill told him. "We all have late passes."

Andrea gasped. "All except me," she mumbled. "I forgot to ask for one."

"Oh, never mind. Jameson's pretty easy. He'll turn a blind eye."

Andrea hoped that Jameson, the night porter, would pretend not to notice her, especially if she came in with Jill. After half-past eleven, the staff entrance was closed and everybody had to use the main door so that the night porter on duty could check the staff passes with the list supplied to him.

Mervyn, for some unknown reason, came in with the three girls, instead of taking his car around to the garage or parking space, and as he grasped Andrea's arm and flung his other arm around the junior receptionist, Pauline, Laura Wyvern reached the foot of the main staircase where it curved behind the elevators.

"Ah, Laura!" Mervyn greeted her. "You ought to have come with us. I know you dance beautifully."

Andrea turned hot and cold. Of all the ill luck! Not only to have the floor housekeeper catch her without a late pass, but to be present when Mervyn seemed to be going out of his way to taunt Laura Wyvern.

The housekeeper gave Mervyn a frosty smile, then glared at Andrea and moved to the porter's desk, obviously to check the list.

"No late pass, Lansdale?"

"No, Miss Wyvern. I'm sorry. I forgot to ask for one."

"Andrea didn't know what time we'd be coming home," put in Jill, quite sharply for her, but then she was not under Miss Wyvern's control.

"I'm sure she knows the rules of the hotel."

Mervyn leaned against the desk. "Now, Laura, don't pitch into the young ones. I've brought them all home, safe and in good order and quite protected from all the late-night wickedness of Millbridge, where nearly everything shuts at ten o'clock anyway."

"Very well, Lansdale. You may go. But please in future ask me for your passes."

Andrea was only too thankful to murmur thanks and call "Good night, Mr. Watford" over her shoulder as she and Pauline hurried away to their respective bedrooms.

Apart from the incident of having failed to ask Miss Wyvern for the pass, Andrea felt that unwittingly she had again been placed in an awkward position. Why couldn't Mervyn have put his car away and left the girls to come in by themselves? Then Miss Wyvern would not have seen him with a girl on each arm. She would now almost certainly assume that it was Andrea who had been Mervyn's partner at the dance.

Huguette had not yet returned from her outing with her new friend, Noel, and Andrea was none too pleased at being woken up after two o'clock to listen to Huguette's tangled incoherent tale of the evening's adventures.

"Tell me in the morning, Huguette," muttered Andrea sleepily.

But the next morning there was fresh excitement, for it was rumored that the new uniforms had arrived. Andrea knew that for some time the management had been considering the matter of more stylish dresses for the staff. In fact, a complete modernization program was continuing all the time; a more spacious bar, the main lounge redecorated in up-to-date style, with new carpets in two-tone cherry and handsome curtains of excellent design. New hotels were being built in London and elsewhere, and since a new one was planned for Millbridge, the management of the Belvedere was aware that they must improve the hotel or be outshone by a new one.

In the women's staff hall at breakfast, there was much gabble and speculation as to the colors that had finally been chosen.

"Purple dresses with emerald green aprons, I heard," said one chambermaid.

"And the receptionists are having dark brown with pink belts," added another.

Andrea laughed at all the nonsense and said she preferred to wait and see what was handed out to her. But the morning held only disappointment for her. The chambermaids were still to wear their mauve dresses and white aprons in the morning, but for evenings they had sapphire blue worsted dresses with cream aprons and gold Alice bands for their hair. Huguette tried on her dress and approved, except that she grumbled that the skirt was too long for her and didn't display her legs to their full advantage.

Andrea had already seen the receptionists in their deep blue, elegantly-cut dresses, with silver belts, and when Miss Wyvern, wearing a moss green dress, came out of her office as Andrea passed, the girl thought how much younger Laura Wyvern appeared in such a becoming color.

"I suppose we still have to wear our old, uninteresting black," Andrea sighed, when she was having lunch with her companions. "Just my luck, to fall between all the stools. I'm neither on chambermaid duty nor Reception."

But on reflection she realized that the Belvedere employed very few waitresses, except for those on breakfast service who came in for that purpose alone. In the restaurants, grillroom and snack bars, only men waiters and their *commis* were used. So it was more than likely that no new dresses were going to be provided for less than half a dozen young trainees, such as Andrea.

After she had served lunch in the stewards' room, however, Andrea was told to go to the linen room and collect her new uniform.

"It's already been pressed well," the linen maid on duty told her, "so don't crumple it as you go upstairs. You've all got to parade before the May Queen."

Andrea took the dress on its hanger and folded the apron over her arm.

"Thank you. It looks quite smart."

In her bedroom Andrea was well pleased. The gray dress

with three-quarter sleeves and turquoise collar, fitted exactly. A turquoise apron and a mere scrap of stiffened nylon lace on a headband of practically invisible elastic completed the outfit.

"Oh, very chic!" she said aloud to her reflection. "Wait until Huguette sees this. She'll be green with envy."

She hurried downstairs to Mrs. Mayfield's office, as she had been told, but paused to admire herself again in a wall mirror at the end of a corridor. In the mirror she saw a tall man coming toward her and turned away quickly.

"Yes, indeed, you look charming." Keir gave her that slightly amused glance, which always made her feel like a pet kitten— there to be stroked or patted when he was in the mood and firmly put away when there were more important affairs to be attended to.

"New uniforms," she explained. "Excuse me, I have to go to the housekeeper."

She whisked off and ran down the remaining flight of stairs to the housekeeper's office, leaving Keir Holt staring at her flying figure until she was out of sight. As she went into her aunt's room, Andrea realized that Keir was evidently back in the hotel again. But then so was Ingrid Jensen. But it was surely odd that she had met him on the third floor, instead of second where his usual suite was.

"There you are, Andrea," Aunt Catherine greeted. "Only one more to come. Maureen, I think."

Andrea saw that some of her fellow workers wore gray dresses with maroon collars and aprons.

"How d'you like them?" Mrs. Mayfield asked the girls.

"Oh, very much," they said, practically in unison. As Andrea reflected, it would have been both ungrateful and unwise to criticize the management's choice. Almost any reasonable color scheme was better than a plain black dress and white apron.

"We'll see what Mr. Blake thinks of the aprons," Mrs. Mayfield continued. "It may turn out to be more practical to have them all maroon and the collars to match."

"Oh, no!" exclaimed Andrea thoughtlessly. "Oh, I beg your pardon, madam, I shouldn't have said that."

Mrs. Mayfield smiled at her niece. "But I like people to express their opinions. You prefer the turquoise, Andrea?"

"Yes, madam. That is—unless they show stains too easily."

Mr. Blake, the assistant manager, entered at that moment and saved Andrea from further comment. He asked the housekeeper for her opinion first before giving his own.

"Yes, I think the girls all look quite attractive in these outfits," she said. "But we shall have to decide later on the final scheme."

Mr. Blake smiled and nodded his approval, asked the girls if they liked themselves in the new dresses and waited for Mrs. Mayfield to dismiss the trainees.

"Andrea, will you bring tea for two here in—" she glanced at her watch "—in about half an hour, please."

"Yes, madam."

The girl was pleased at this mark of confidence her aunt placed in her, for so far she had not been allowed to serve any kind of meal to the housekeeper.

Andrea paid meticulous attention to setting the tea tray and asked Maureen, a more experienced girl who sometimes waited on Mrs. Mayfield, if there were any special points to be watched.

"Yes. When she orders for two, she has the complete afternoon tea menu, the same as they serve in the lounge. China tea, though. Don't forget that."

When everything was ready except the pot of tea, Andrea telephoned to confirm it.

"Yes, bring it straightaway," Aunt Catherine instructed.

In the station the floor-service telephone rang and Andrea stopped to answer it.

"I'm sorry, Miss Wyvern. Would you mind waiting a few moments? I have to take tea to Mrs. Mayfield first."

Andrea thought rebelliously, *that's right, Old Wyvern would want her tea half an hour earlier today just because I'm busy.*

She took the tray to the housekeeper's apartment, where her aunt and Mr. Blake were already in the sitting room.

"The cakes look very good," Aunt Catherine commented. "I must remember to tell Monsieur Cassavini to compliment Robert on his pastries."

Andrea waited for her dismissal, but Mrs. Mayfield poured tea first, handed a cup to Mr. Blake, then glanced again at the girl.

"Andrea, on that little matter of late passes, you will remember to ask for one if you may be late in, won't you?"

The girl reddened. "Yes, I'll be careful."

"Mr. Blake and I are very satisfied with your progress here, Andrea," Aunt Catherine went on. "We think we may perhaps eventually turn you into a most creditable member of our staff."

"Thank you, madam." Andrea was warmed by the compliment and still glowing by the time she reached the station again and busied herself with other duties.

When Maureen came back with an empty tray, she said, "Taken Miss Wyvern's tea yet? She's buzzed twice."

"Oh heavens! I completely forgot."

Maureen grinned. "Not even a smart new uniform will make her pleasant to the girl who forgets her tea. Hurry, for goodness sake, or we'll have her bustling around down here."

Andrea apologized for the delay when she arrived at Miss Wyvern's office.

"I've been waiting exactly forty minutes," the assistant housekeeper said icily, with a glance at her watch.

"I had to take a special tray to Mrs. Mayfield."

"Why? Wasn't Maureen Brown on duty? Or a single floor waiter?"

"After the parade of our new dresses, Mrs. Mayfield gave me instructions," Andrea explained.

Laura Wyvern's pouting mouth set in a downward curve. "Naturally, if Mrs. Mayfield chooses to show favoritism and interfere—or rearrange junior staff duties, I can't do anything about it."

Andrea remained silent, realizing that even Miss Wyvern knew that in criticizing her superior she had gone too far and lost a measure of dignity and authority with her own juniors. Andrea was happily at tea with other maids in the staff hall when the intercom rang, and the girl who answered it gave Andrea a message that the May Queen wanted to see her at once.

"Goodness! What have I done now?" she hastily tidied herself, convinced that Miss Wyvern had lost no time in making yet another complaint about the slack ways of young Lansdale.

To her surprise, Keir was in Mrs. Mayfield's sitting room.

"Mr. Holt would like to continue correspondence if you are free to take it, Andrea," her aunt said in what could be described as her coldest official voice. "What other duties have you tonight?"

"Stewards' hall dinner, madam."

"Very well, I'll see that you're relieved."

"Thank you, madam."

Andrea was puzzled by the unmistakable hostility in the room. Keir towered by the window, his back to the light, and Aunt Catherine's mouth was firmly set.

"And should I change my uniform, madam? I've only a black dress, now that I'm not on Reception."

"Why on earth should she change?" demanded Keir, speaking for the first time since Andrea had entered the room. "You look perfectly charming as it is. As I've already told you, when I saw you in the corridor."

Mrs. Mayfield's head tilted up slightly. "Yes, we've made a number of changes in the uniforms." To Andrea she said, "Will you wait, please, in my office until Mr. Holt is ready to go to his suite?"

Andrea obeyed immediately, but as she turned she saw that Keir was about to follow her until a slight, but authoritative gesture from the head housekeeper stopped him. The girl guessed that her aunt might have something further to say to a guest who demanded the services of a trainee, no matter what department she was now working in.

"You insisted and you won," Mrs. Mayfield was saying. "But don't make a habit of it, Mr. Holt, or I might find it necessary to refuse a guest what he demands."

He smiled at her. "Thank you. It really is important to me to have Andrea do those reports. I can't keep on explaining the technical terms to a different girl every time."

"I know that, but it makes difficulties for the girls

themselves if they're singled out and have to be taken off other duties, even though we like to oblige our guests, particularly when they are such regular visitors as yourself.''

He began to laugh. "Don't keep up your official attitude with me. You know that I'm grateful to you when I get my own way, but I'm not impressed by your reasons for giving in. What you're really trying to warn me about is not to have designs on Andrea.''

"Indeed! Such a thought hadn't entered my head.''

"That remark is not flattering, but I'll accept that you didn't mean it that way. But if it will reassure you, I can tell you that while Andrea is very good secretarial help, she has little time socially for dull chaps like me. When we met at Christmas at the Dennistouns's house, she wasn't at all delighted to see me and I had to apologize, almost, for having turned up.''

"You were staying with the Dennistouns at Christmas?'' queried the housekeeper. "I didn't know that. Andrea didn't mention it.''

Keir's dark eyes sparkled with amusement. "There you are. You see what I mean? She didn't even think I was worth mentioning.''

But when he had gone and ostensibly taken Andrea with him to the suite he was now occupying, Catherine Mayfield became thoughtful. She had deliberately asked Andrea to come up to the sitting room while Keir Holt was here so that she might be able to judge from their reactions the kind of acquaintanceship that existed between them. She had not bothered to look at Keir, knowing that he would not give himself away, and that he expected Andrea's entrance, but the girl? Yet Andrea had behaved perfectly with no more than polite surprise at seeing a visitor in the head housekeeper's sitting room and being told that he needed her secretarial services.

Yet Andrea had certainly not mentioned that Keir was at the Dennistouns's at Christmas. True, Catherine had not asked the girl who else had been invited, but it was strange that Keir Holt should be there. Catherine had not realized that he knew the Dennistouns.

The housekeeper possessed an uncanny knack of sensing most kinds of emotional relationships. She invariably knew when her girls had fallen deeply in love; there was a radiance about their faces, a dreamy tenderness in their eyes. Transient flirtations added a sparkle to their personalities and frequently caused them to giggle without reason or burst into song along the corridors.

But at the moment Andrea was a puzzle to her aunt, who decided that the sooner Keir Holt acquired a tape recorder for his confidential reports, the better it might be for her niece.

CHAPTER ELEVEN

ANDREA CONCENTRATED as much as possible on the lengthy report that Keir was dictating to her, but a small part of her mind was engrossed with the extraordinary circumstances of Keir having evidently made such an issue of demanding her for his work. Other girls must have worked for him before she came, for the Century block must have been started at least eighteen months ago.

Perhaps she should not have answered him so brusquely in the corridor, earlier in the day. Maybe he'd thought she was being deliberately offhand, so he was spurred to teach her that she could not so easily ignore him. Underneath Andrea's attempts at a rational explanation, a vagrant little thought tried to surface—the idea that he wanted to see her and talk to her. But she firmly crushed this ridiculous notion. He wanted his professional work done efficiently and she was the nearest person at hand to do it.

When the report was finished, he said, "Will you take the carbons and burn them somewhere for me? In these modern, centrally heated hotels, there's never an old-fashioned grate where one can burn the incriminating documents; all self-respecting spies have to follow the tradition."

"Sometimes they have to chew up the documents and swallow them," Andrea answered carelessly. "Oh, no!" she tried to correct herself hastily. "That wouldn't be pleasant at all, eating typewriter carbons."

In spite of her resolve to be scrupulously businesslike, suddenly they were both laughing.

"Are you free on Sunday?" he asked.

"Yes. If you want to dictate, I could do some typing for you."

"I didn't mean work. If it's a fine day, I wondered if you'd like to come out with me in the car. Somewhere in the country."

Color flooded her face and she could not look at him.

"If you've made other arrangements—" he began.

"No, I haven't," she said quickly, and realized immediately that she had cut off any possible line of retreat. "That is—yes, I'd like to come." Why on earth shouldn't she seize this heaven-sent opportunity, even if it only meant that he had a spare day and was at a loose end for something to do?

"Good. What time will suit you?"

"I'm off duty at ten. I can be ready at half-past." She was already torn between eagerness to spend as many hours as possible in his company and the faintly coquettish attitude, one that Huguette would undoubtedly have adopted, of feigning indifference and making him waste his time.

But reality burst upon her like a blow. How could she walk out of the Belvedere, whether through the main door or the staff entrance, and step into the car of so well-known a visitor as Keir Holt? Tongues would never stop wagging.

But he understood her hesitations and forestalled her objections. "Would you prefer to meet me in the car park at the back of the Town Hall?"

When she smiled her agreement, he thought he had rarely seen her smiling with sincere pleasure. Usually he received from her no more than polite, deferential expressions or she went to the other extreme with angry scowls.

Andrea found almost as much difficulty in burning the carbon sheets as Keir had foreseen. Outside the kitchens was a huge wastepaper bin, she knew. Surely if she shredded the carbons into small pieces and mixed them with the other waste, a person would have to be a very determined Humpty-Dumpty to piece them together again.

She had just finished mixing the fragments with the other rubbish when Robert came along the passage.

"Hello, Andrea, what are you doing down here?"

In his white jacket and apron and the traditional scarf knotted round his neck, he looked taller than usual and his high chef's hat enhanced his height. But he could not be as tall as Keir, she reflected.

"I just came to throw away some wastepaper."

"Sure you didn't come to peep at someone in the kitchens? Tell me his name."

The kitchens were a sacred precinct for those who actively worked in them and were out of bounds to most of the rest of the staff, unless they were sent there on special errands. Sooner or later, nearly everybody managed to creep in on a slack afternoon for a quick inspection, but it was understandable that in the middle of serving lunch or dinner, the kitchens were no place for chambermaids or waitress staff.

"I don't know anybody in the kitchens," Andrea protested.

"I shall have to go back to *Pâtisserie* in a second, but what about Sunday? You said you were off duty. Come out with me, Andrea."

"Oh, Robert, I can't. I'm already—"

"Booked up. I might have known. Who? That Watford chap? The one who came barging in at the dance?"

"No, of course not. He's gone to another town, anyway."

Robert's expression became moody. "So this is somebody else. Anybody here on the staff? Well, I suppose I ought not to be nosey, but—"

"No, Robert. Nobody on the staff. Just a friend I've known for some time."

"When will you get a Saturday or a Sunday again?" he asked.

"I'm not really sure. I shall have to look at the roster."

"I'll bet it'll be six weeks before we're both off on the same day, but I'll change with someone if I can."

Andrea was touched by his eagerness and thought that perhaps there was something in Jill's teasing, after all.

"Let's leave it for now, shall we?" she said gently. "I must fly upstairs again. Bye for now."

But the memory of Robert's face stayed with her as she ate her supper later that evening. If Keir hadn't asked her first, it might have been much safer to have accepted Robert's invitation. No, perhaps "safer" was not the right word. She would be safe enough with Keir, but each meeting with him became a chain reaction of cause and effect.

There was only one sensible thing to do, she decided. Accept Keir's company on his own terms. When he had a spare Sunday and wanted the passenger seat in his car occupied by feminine company, he obviously felt he could choose Andrea without creating complications for himself.

But when Sunday came, Andrea could not help wondering how many other young women had sat next to him in this or his previous innumerable cars. Ingrid, of course. But today Miss Jensen was not available. She had left the Belvedere two days ago, so Huguette had mentioned.

Andrea had done her best not to fall short of all those other girls, although she could hardly hope to compete with Ingrid. Still, in her caramel velour two-piece and cream velvet hat, she knew that she looked at least presentable.

"I thought that as you probably know the Cotswolds inside out, it might be a change for you if we went to Leominster and pottered round some of those little villages beyond," he told her. "Or we could go to Ludlow and over the border into Wales."

"Wherever you like," she murmured happily. "You probably know the district better than I do."

At Bewdley, where they crossed the Severn, mist rose off the river. Pale sunlight flecked the water and washed the old houses with pastel colors.

As he drove along a ridge road toward Ludlow, he said, "On clear days the view from here is worth seeing. Too misty today."

His words echoed in her thoughts. Perhaps her present life was rather like that—a long straight road with the end hidden from view and a misty plain on either side. Yet could one keep stopping to explore the side paths that beckoned but might not be through roads?

At Ludlow they stopped for lunch at one of the most beautiful of all black-and-white timbered inns. Keir guided Andrea across the street so that she could view the inn from the opposite side.

"Handsome, isn't it?" he said.

"All the ghosts from the coaching past must still love to be there," Andrea murmured slowly.

In the narrow entrance hall of the inn a persuasive atmosphere of warmth and appetizing food greeted them, and Andrea, who had a young and healthy appetite for a good lunch, found her enjoyment doubled in such ancient surroundings, although modern trends in service and equipment were unobtrusively apparent.

"How would you like to work in a place like this?" he asked. "Different from the Belvedere, isn't it?"

"It's different, but most of the essentials are the same: I don't suppose the chambermaids run upstairs every morning with hot water in copper jugs and the stable boys have to look after cars instead of horses nowadays."

"Is hotel life going to be your career, Andrea?"

She colored slightly. "I'm not sure, but it'll be useful experience."

"For running a home?"

"Eventually, perhaps, but not yet. I've agreed to stay at the Belvedere for a year at least and might want to stay longer before I decide what I'm best fitted for, if anything." She gave a quiet laugh, more to cover the slight confusion she felt than because what she had said was funny. She did not understand the drift of his questions and dared not probe under the surface. "Mrs. Mayfield hasn't a very high opinion of my sticking powers," she continued.

Keir smiled at her, but she glanced away quickly. "So you're going to prove that you can stick to a job, however much you may dislike it."

"Oh, I don't dislike the life at all," she corrected quickly. "It's much more interesting than most office work and the atmosphere is friendly, except for one or two people. There's so much to learn in all the different departments. D'you know that the head florist actually goes to market every morning and chooses her own flowers? The bills must be enormous."

"No doubt the hotel guests pay indirectly for the choice of flowers in their rooms," he pointed out dryly.

"Oh, there's more to the business than that. When the Belvedere does a really important banquet, the entire staircase to the reception room is banked with flowers. Didn't you notice it when you came to the Swedish ball?''

"I don't think I came in that way. I probably slunk in the wrong door.''

"And everywhere there are plants to look after," Andrea continued enthusiastically. "In the public rooms, the bars, the manager's office, all over the place.''

"I can see that Mrs. Mayfield is going to have trouble in future if she doesn't put you on florist duty. I'd better warn her." His dark eyes mocked her.

Andrea grimaced. "Don't go out of your way to get me in hot water. I can jump into plenty of my own accord. And there wouldn't be a chance for me to get into the florists' department, unless everybody except Head Florist falls ill or breaks an ankle or comes into a fortune and leaves for a world trip. It's one of the most coveted jobs.''

"And then, I suppose, you'd be too busy—or too aristo-cratic—to condescend to type my reports?''

"I expect I'll be there if you want me.'' Andrea bent hastily over her plate. What jeering demon had caused her to utter such a sentence? She hoped with all her heart that he would take the words only literally and not assume that she meant anything deeper. A few mouthfuls of food later, she was scolding herself for being such a ninny. How arrogant of her to believe that he would ever trouble to seek a deeper meaning in what she said.

After lunch they went through Church Stretton, a quiet little town hushed in Sunday calm.

"If I can find it, there's a delightful spot near here, called Carding Mill Valley. In the summer, it's alive with bus parties and hundreds of motorists, but at this time of year it's quieter.''

Eventually Keir turned the car down a lane leading to a narrow valley enclosed by rolling hills. He drove as far as he could along the rough gravel path, then they alighted and walked along the edge of a boulder-strewn stream.

Andrea enjoyed the country in winter as much as in high summer. "You can see more," she explained to Keir. "The shapes of trees and their branches. Birds flying about, even though I don't know the names of many. So much seems to get lost and obscured when green leaves cover it all.''

Keir turned to look at the girl by his side. Under the velvet hat a few wisps of tawny gold hair curled over her pink cheeks, her mouth was a soft, inviting curve, but her eyes were downcast, for she was stepping carefully over the rough ground. He had already noted with approval that she had put on sensible shoes with moderate heels, so that she did not teeter on a couple of spikes, but all the same, he grasped her hand when they came to a large rock, and helped her to the top and down the other side.

She wished she had not been wearing gloves, but the day was cold. It would have given her more delight to feel the warmth of his hand against hers, even though only for the purpose of lugging her over a rock. Then she realized with exultation that every step taken along the valley would have to be retraced before she and Keir could return to the car. Running water chattered noisily over the rough streambed or made miniature waterfalls; a small water animal darted away into the undergrowth, too quickly to be recognized and leaving only a flurry of ripples in a smooth patch of water; a jay screamed raucously and a couple of finches took fright and soared up into a tall birch.

This is a day that will always live in my memory, she told herself. *Even if I never saw Keir again after today, I would still remember this as a happy, thrilling day, when he forgot to be patronizing and arrogant and just let himself enjoy a day in the country, away from his business worries.*

Following a bend in the stream, the path widened out and the sun was sinking behind the hazy hills. Pinkish-golden clouds floated in a pale wintry blue sky, then changed to rose and lavender.

For a few moments Andrea and Keir stood watching the changing colors. Then he said abruptly. "Come on. We must be getting back."

The return journey seemed to Andrea rougher and certainly gloomier now that the best of the light had gone. There was also a subtle change, a coolness in Keir's attitude. He hurried along faster than she could manage, but when she nearly fell, he grabbed her elbow.

"All right?" he queried.

"Yes, thank you. I only stumbled."

For a delirious instant she thought he was going to take her in his arms and kiss her, but he turned his face away and stared straight ahead. True, he was still holding her hand, but that, she thought, was only to prevent her from falling into the stream. That, of course, would be too awkward, for then he would have to fish her out, even though the water was only ankle or calf deep. As soon as they were on more level ground, she withdrew her hand from his, and when they were both settled again in the car, she was relieved. He probably thought she had stumbled deliberately.

Keir thought as he drove along the lanes that he had come pretty near making a complete fool of himself. She was a sweet child, impressionable and untouched, yet with all of a grown woman's capricious and inconsistent ways. He discovered after a few miles that he was driving much faster than necessary, and as he eased his foot off the accelerator, his inward fury abated.

It was too dark, he decided, to see the small black-and-white timbered villages he had intended to show her. "So we'll drive to Leominster for tea," he said. "We might be able to see something of Pembridge on the way, but we've dawdled for too long on a winter day."

Andrea thought there was everything to be said for dawdling in good company, but wisely she kept that opinion to herself.

Over tea in a small, cozy inn, he encouraged the girl to talk about her father.

"Is Mrs. Mayfield your mother's sister?" he asked. "Oh, I know it's all confidential."

"Yes. She doesn't seem to have liked my father at all," Andrea admitted. "He traveled about a great deal—Greece, Turkey, Persia—because he was interested in the old cultures and ancient races, and my mother loved accompanying him whenever she could and many times he would not have gone abroad at all if she hadn't been able to go. But she wasn't strong, and Aunt Catherine—Mrs. Mayfield— blamed my father for her death. But he was the restless, roaming kind of man. He wouldn't have been happy shut up in a university town," Andrea grinned. "Mrs. Mayfield is always on the lookout for signs of restlessness in me. She's quite sure I've inherited those characteristics from daddy. So you see I must make the best of my job at the Belvedere, no matter how much I might want to leave and go somewhere else."

Then suddenly he began to tell her of his own parents, his boyhood in Yorkshire, his love of the dales and the wild, lonely moors. She was surprised when he said that his mother still lived there, although his father had died when he was at school. Somehow she had imagined him without parents or home, a nomad traveling from one luxury hotel to another in the course of business, like a rather patrician gipsy.

"D'you go to Yorkshire sometimes to see your mother?" she asked.

"I try to fit in a visit at least once a month. My sister married an Australian who whisked her off to Sydney, so that leaves my mother alone with a housekeeper to look after her, but she has an enormous number of interests and I don't believe she's too lonely. Whenever I go there, she's always dashing about to some committee meeting or other, or she has to arrange the flower show or meet a speaker for the local guild."

Andrea wondered why he had not visited his mother at Christmas. Surely she would have expected him. Yet he had spent part of the holiday at the Dennistouns's, and that, no doubt, was because he had wanted to see Ingrid there.

He drove home by a roundabout route through Tewkesbury, where they dined leisurely at a hotel dwarfed by the dimly seen Abbey.

"Where would you like me to stop?" he asked, as he negotiated the one-way streets in the center of Millbridge.

"Anywhere not too well lit and within half a mile of the Belvedere," she answered, but immediately regretted that flippant remark, for it made the outing sound like a clandestine affair, even though that was the fact.

He took his car around a small street at the back of the hotel, from which it was easy for Andrea to slip in the staff entrance.

"Thank you very much." She was grateful for his thoughtfulness. At least there couldn't be a repetition of that awful incident with Mervyn when they had all sailed through the front door and been caught by Miss Wyvern. "And thank you again, Mr. Holt, for a wonderful day."

He nodded coolly. "Glad you enjoyed it." He appeared to be on the verge of saying something else, but evidently changed his mind and leaned across to open the door on her side.

In a daze she climbed the dingy back stairs to third floor, emerged onto the main corridor and walked toward the remaining flights.

"My goodness! Where've you been, all dolled up?" Miriam's voice recalled Andrea from her dreams.

"Oh, I was off duty," she explained.

"Well, I didn't suppose you were wearing those clothes just to sit down and read a book in staff hall. Who's this one?"

"Who? Oh, just a friend."

Miriam sniffed. "They fall for you, don't they, Andy?" A sly envy sounded in her voice.

Andrea smiled. "Not really. I'm just a girl who's taken out sometimes when her friends have nothing better to do."

"Huh! Look at the way you went off at Christmas! Some posh house in the country, lording it with dukes and the rest."

"Don't be silly, Miriam. It was only a house in the village where I used to live. And how did you know where I went?"

"Wyvern said you were lucky to have the chance of being invited to such a grand house."

So Miss Wyvern had broadcast that piece of information to Miriam and others. How typical of her to try to work up jealousy between Andrea and some of her companions.

Andrea fidgeted to get away to her own room, but Miriam, who was on duty and had time to spare, walked with her up to her own floor, fourth. "Did I tell you about my latest?" Miriam launched into a long tale about a new acquaintance who had taken her out to dinner at the Prince's, the Belvedere's rival hotel.

"Made me feel like a real lady, that did, being waited on

and all the 'Yes, sir' stuff. The way the waiters look at you in this place, you'd think we were something worse than the stuff in the garbage bins.''

When the two girls came to the station on fourth Miriam said, "I wonder how Wyvern gets on when that Mr. Watford isn't here? You'd think she'd have more sense than to run after a chap like him, wouldn't you? If ever a man was a here-today-and-gone-tomorrow type, he's the one. I wouldn't trust him as far as I could throw him."

Andrea laughed. "I don't suppose he'll ever let you pick him up and try."

"Oh, I could give him the come-hither if I liked," declared Miriam with some indignation. "Did you know that they've put the frosted glass in that window of the station on third? Pity, can't see anything there now except a sort of shadow."

Andrea eventually escaped, only to find that Huguette, although in bed, was wide awake and also needed an audience to listen to a long series of off-duty enchantments. Andrea was content to let the words, sometimes in French, sometimes in English flow over her like a tide. As long as she put in an occasional "*A, oui*" or a vague "*C'est ça!*" Huguette was happy enough to rattle on in her own dramatic way, while Andrea wrapped herself in the happy garment of remembrance.

She knew that it was unlikely that she would see Keir during the coming week, as he had told her he was due in London for the hearing of an action brought against his firm by one of the injured men on the Century site. Although the case would be presented ably enough, he had decided that he ought to be in court at least part of the time.

"The curious thing is," he had told her, "that although we've offered this man a large sum as compensation, larger than any damages he's likely to be awarded in the courts, he's refused to accept. He says it's a bribe to cover up our negligence and he thinks he can do better by bringing an action."

"Isn't this one of the men you went to see in hospital?" she had asked.

"I did go at the time, but this is one of the very earliest

accidents—it happened before you worked on the reports. He's altered his attitude, because at first he was quite grateful for our offer. And, in any case, he's not incapacitated at all. He can work. In fact, he is back at work, but he claims he can't do anything as fast as he used to.''

Andrea hoped that the day's outing had been as happy for Keir as it had been for her. He needed a few hours occasionally to get away from his worries and responsibilities.

The following Sunday, Andrea was off duty for only a few hours after tea, and then only because she had been asked to change with another girl. At first Miss Wyvern had, as usual, tried to create difficulties, but as it was the other girl on second who wanted to change and Miss Deakin had agreed, Miss Wyvern had little choice, particularly as Andrea was only nominally under her authority.

The evening was fine and Andrea went out by herself to stroll around the city and gaze in the shop windows, many of which were lighted on Sunday evenings.

More departments in the new Century block had now been opened, and an arcade of small shops, selling hats, shoes, linen, leather, jewelry, added to opportunities for shopping in comfort and under cover. Andrea idled her way along, selecting hats and umbrellas that she would buy if she had the money.

When she came out at the other end of the arcade and onto the street, several workmen were evidently finishing their shift and others were starting. She knew from the reports she had typed for Keir that the whole project was behind schedule and that delays and strikes had now made it necessary to work continuous night shifts wherever it was possible for the work to be carried on by floodlight and whenever the weather allowed.

She wished there was some way in which she could help Keir, but she knew there was nothing she could do. Besides, as he had pointed out in his reports, there was practically no trouble on projects in other towns. Unfortunately, the Century block in Millbridge was the most important currently being built by Keir's company and it was necessary for prestige reasons that everything should go smoothly, efficiently and according to plan.

Andrea idly walked up a wide passage leading into the interior. Curiosity led her to a dimly lit, brick-walled alleyway and she heard men's voices shouting to each other. But there was little to be seen and she realized that if she wanted to find out what was going on, daylight was necessary. One man's shout was answered by another's, there was a heavy thud, and suddenly, as Andrea had turned to go back to the street, something hit her and she blacked out.

When she recovered consciousness, she was sitting on a rough bench, with several men bending anxiously over her.

"You all right, miss?" One of the men held a mug of scalding tea to her lips and she sipped gratefully.

"Yes, I think so. What happened?"

"You copped a packet from one of those beams. Jim was chucking them down from aloft and some'ow one of them knocked you out."

Andrea rubbed the side of her head. "I'm still all in one piece, I think."

"Did you come to look for somebody 'ere, miss?" one of the other men asked.

Even in the dimness of the passageway, she flushed. "Well, no. I—I was passing—and I suppose I was just interested and, perhaps, rather inquisitive," she admitted.

An older man spoke kindly. "You take my tip, miss. Don't go poking around places like this, especially in the dark. It's not safe for young ladies. The men are used to keeping a lookout and know how to dodge anything that might fall on 'em."

"Yes, it was silly of me. Thank you for being so kind to me."

"D'you live far from here?" the man asked.

"No. Not far."

"Perhaps we ought to have your name and address, just in case. Although, rightly, you couldn't make a claim on the firm, seein' as you wasn't in a place where the public are admitted."

Andrea smiled gently. "Oh, that's all right. It was entirely my own fault. I'm all right now." She rose to her feet, still feeling a bit shaky. "Is that the lump of wood that hit me?" She pointed to a heavy beam, covered with sand and cement.

"Yes, miss. It just tilted over on you. Lucky you didn't get the full weight of it on your napper."

She shivered slightly at the thought of how narrowly she had escaped a serious injury, and again thanked the elderly man, evidently a foreman, for his help.

He walked with her to the street and wished her good night. Two men were standing close by the entrance to the passage and one of them she recognized as the light caught his face. It was Mr. Selborn, the salesman who stayed periodically at the Belvedere and was a friend of Keir's.

But she hurried away now, lest he might find out about her reckless behavior and even mention it to Keir. Fortunately he might not recognize her.

She still felt slightly dazed and decided to get a cup of coffee at a small bar, one of the few open on Sundays. The place was fairly crowded and she took her coffee to a corner table and let the buzz of chatter and laughter flow around her. She was startled when an assistant came to clear the table and said quietly, "We're closing now."

Andrea's head jerked up. She must have been dozing. Other customers were leaving and most of the tables were empty. She blinked herself awake and went out into the street.

The cold night air cleared her head and she began to hurry along the streets toward the Belvedere. Everywhere was in darkness now, the window lights had gone out, and she wondered what the time was. She had forgotten to wear her watch, but when she saw the time on the floodlit dial of a nearby church, she was shocked. Ten past twelve! It couldn't be as late as that. Then she remembered that the café boasted that it was unique in Millbridge for staying open until midnight.

The staff entrance would be closed and she had no pass. What possible excuse could she give this time? She could only hope that Jameson, the night porter would let her slip quietly in at the front door and not make a fuss.

For once she was lucky. "No pass again?" Jameson

queried, and made tut-tutting noises. "Can't think where you girls get to at this time of night. You can't pretend you've been sitting in the pictures. Shut long ago."

"I was delayed," she muttered.

She was uncertain whether to use the back stairs or one of the service elevators. Either way she might meet someone she would prefer to avoid.

"Is Miss Wyvern on late duty?" she asked Jameson.

"No, miss. She was off early tonight. In any case, she'd be off now when it's past midnight."

Andrea scuttled away, but when she emerged from the service elevator on third, she almost collided with Miss Deakin, the floor housekeeper on second.

"Good night, Andrea," Miss Deakin said pleasantly. After all, she was not to know that Andrea wasn't coming in on a late pass. "Oh, have you fallen down and hurt yourself?"

"No, Miss Deakin."

The housekeeper was staring at Andrea's head. "Your face is a bit muddy, and your hat—looks like sand on it."

Andrea put up a hand and rubbed her cheek. "I expect it was when I brushed against a wall somewhere," she said as calmly as she could.

Miss Deakin had spent several years training as a nurse, so, naturally, she had an eye for the slightest hurt or injury. But she had charm and tact and did not go out of her way to pounce on the slightest breach of regulations, or ask the most pointedly awkward questions as Wyvern did.

Huguette was away, so fortunately Andrea did not have to make further explanations to anybody. The French girl probably had no weekend pass, but usually took the risk of staying out until she was on duty on Monday morning. Andrea would never have had the nerve.

She bathed the side of her head and could feel a slight bump under her hair, but nobody would notice, she hoped. *And let that be a lesson to me,* she told herself, *not to go poking my nose in somebody else's business*. All the same, she still wondered why Mr. Selborn had been talking so earnestly to the other man on the Century site.

On Tuesday, Andrea was delighted to be "lent" to the florist's department.

Mr. Jesson, who was in charge of the floor waiters and the trainee waitress staff, told her rather gruffly, "I understand that Miss Heaton's two assistants are both away ill. They live out. So you're to work under her instructions for a few days."

"Thank you, sir. It'll be wonderful experience," Andrea said tactlessly. "Oh, I don't mean that I don't like waiting at table, of course."

She had already discovered that Mr. Jesson regarded the waitress-trainee part of his work as a waste of time. Training young men to be waiters, to rise to head waiter and perhaps restaurant managers, that was a task he liked, but girls didn't take the job seriously enough. Like as not, they'd be off in a few months time, either to get married or take up some different kind of work, selling shoes or soap or making a nuisance of themselves in offices.

When Andrea presented herself to Miss Heaton, she had already remembered Keir's joking reference on warning Mrs. Mayfield how necessary it might be to let Andrea have a chance in the florist's. But surely he couldn't have done so. There had probably been no opportunity, for he had left for London early on Monday morning and he had other more important matters to attend to than Andrea's whims.

Miss Heaton, the head florist, welcomed Andrea. "Thank goodness I've somebody to help. They seem to think here that I've six pairs of hands."

But if Andrea imagined that she was going to be allowed full rein for her artistic arrangement of the flowered staircase for the banquet the next night, she was soon disillusioned. Her main task was to fetch and carry for Miss Heaton, to tend the plants in various parts of the hotel, to collect vases and flowers from guests' sitting rooms so that they could be inspected or renewed, according to Miss Heaton's instructions, and returned to the rooms.

At the same time, although Andrea was tired before lunchtime on the first day and confessed in the staff hall that she must have walked literally miles along corridors and up and down stairs, she discovered that the new work took her into quarters of the Belvedere to which she had previously had no access. The manager's private office, where he and his two secretaries were surrounded with files and enormous registers; the new snack bar and buttery, which had dividing partitions of open flower shelves; the ladies' hairdressing salon where only semitropical plants could thrive in the heated atmosphere.

Aunt Catherine had several bowls of hyacinths just now in full flower and a couple of vases in her sitting room, but these had to be handed to the head chambermaid on third, who personally looked after the head-housekeeper's rooms.

Andrea had hoped to see Aunt Catherine, if only to say she was glad of a change from waitress to florist's runabout, but there was no opportunity.

"When are you supposed to be off duty?" Miss Heaton asked after Andrea returned from tea.

"I'm not down for anything special."

"Good. Then you can help on the banquet or I shall still be working on it at midnight."

A cart of potted plants had been brought to the foot of the stairs and Miss Heaton placed them strategically at intervals on the steps, securing the pots with wire loops fastened to the side of the stairs. Large, dark green containers with wire-mesh tops were filled with water and placed between the pots of plants. Tomorrow the containers would be filled with fresh flowers.

When eventually Miss Heaton released Andrea for supper, the girl was more tired than she had been so far in any other department. In the staff hall, she could only just keep her eyes open and took no interest in the babble of talk around her.

"Well, what d'you think of that? There's shame and disgrace to bring on the old Belvedere."

Miriam was excitedly pointing to an item in the evening paper.

"What is it? Let's have a look! What's happened?" the others exclaimed.

Miriam read out the paragraph, but Andrea wasn't listening. Then the name registered—"Miss Ingrid

Jensen"—and she looked across at the other girls. "What's happened to Miss Jensen?" she asked.

"Haven't I been telling you?" Miriam glared at Andrea. "She was caught by the police in some night club on Sunday night. One of these places where they serve drinks at all hours."

"Oh." Andrea was not very interested. If Miss Jensen liked to go to those places, it served her right if the police made a raid when she was there. No, that was uncharitable. I shouldn't have welcomed a police raid when I was at the Polonaise with Trevor and Keir, she reflected.

Suddenly her mind became alert. Where was the raid? And who was with Miss Jensen at the time, for she would certainly not be at a club alone?

Andrea edged the newspaper toward her so that she could read the piece. The Polonaise! And, further down, among a long list of names and addresses the name of Trevor Dennistoun leaped out of the print.

Poor Trevor! This wouldn't do his business name any good.

"What happens in these cases?" she asked. "They don't send people to prison, do they?"

"Shouldn't think so," said Miriam. "Usually a fine and the club gets its license taken away."

Andrea breathed more freely. Supposing the police had descended on the Polonaise the night when she was there! In that case, with her name in the paper, her address given as the hotel, and her youthful age, any hotel career would assuredly have been cut short. Not even Aunt Catherine could have been expected to overlook such an incident, even if Andrea had merely been drinking orange juice, instead of the champagne which Miss Jensen considered the only proper tribute to her presence.

What a lucky escape, Andrea thought.

She searched the rest of the evening paper, looking for any report of the case in which Keir's firm was involved, but there was only a small paragraph dealing with some of the evidence and stating that the hearing was adjourned until the next day.

On her way up to her room, she saw Mr. Selborn

approaching along the corridor on third. So apparently he was still staying in the house. She stood aside to let him pass and returned his greeting with a polite "Good evening, sir."

But he seemed inclined to chat, asking her about her progress at the Belvedere and what her future plans included.

"Do you still help Mr. Holt on his work for the Century block?" he asked.

"Not very often," she answered carefully. His mention of the Century block flooded her with apprehension.

"Those buildings have gone up remarkably rapidly, haven't they? It doesn't seem long since we stood on the observation platform. Now half the shopping space is open, arcades and all."

"Yes. I suppose modern building methods are much quicker than they used to be."

He stood looking down on her from his considerable height and seemed to be waiting for her to say something more important than a few elementary comments on a subject of which she was almost totally ignorant.

Impulsively she said, "Mr. Selborn, I expect you've heard that I went poking around on Sunday night and a piece of wood fell on my head and knocked me out for a bit. But please don't say anything to anybody else. I wouldn't leave my address because I didn't want to get into trouble here."

She had expected him to smile and say that of course it would be all right with him, but instead, he smiled kindly, then said softly, "I should hardly be in a position to give you away. I didn't even hear about it."

"But—I thought—you were there."

His expression did not change. "I wasn't in Millbridge at all on Sunday."

As she plodded up the top flight of stairs to her bedroom, she decided she had made a mistake in confessing that she had been literally trespassing on the site. If he hadn't been there and she had mistaken someone else for him, then he could be of no help, and might even become the reverse just by making an unwitting disclosure to the wrong person.

She realized that she should have kept silent about the incident.

CHAPTER TWELVE

ANDREA HAD NO TIME next day to dwell on Mr. Selborn's denial or even the police-court predicament in which Trevor and Ingrid had placed themselves. She spent the day in a breathless daze helping Miss Heaton with the banquet flowers for that evening.

Boxes of spring flowers, daffodils, tulips, narcissi and anemones were stacked in the florist's shop at the foot of the basement stairs and in the storeroom behind. There were also great sheaves of mimosa and white lilac and even a few choice late chrysanthemums.

Andrea lost count of the number of journeys she made either by service elevator or stairs, taking fresh supplies for Miss Heaton's nimble fingers.

"The potted cyclamens and cineraria go around the edge of the band platform," she directed. "Then you can start filling the vases for the tables. A few daffodils and narcissi in each. Not the tulips. They're too floppy."

The balcony was also being used this time and more vases were needed for the tables there. Andrea stacked them on a broad shelf ready for the waiters when the cloths had been laid.

Fred, the electrician who would be on duty for lighting and microphones, gave Andrea a wide grin as he went toward his little enclosed cubbyhole, known as his "perch."

"You be careful, tonight, my girl," he warned her. "You never know when the floodlight might come round your way just when you're holding hands with one of the banqueting gentlemen."

"No danger of that," returned Andrea, but she turned

away all the same, remembering how the lights had swung around on that previous occasion when Keir had come to talk to her in the balcony.

Besides, although the new uniforms were charming and popular, some of the girls had already discovered how conspicious a light-colored dress could be when a black one, without apron or collar, would have melted into the shadows.

"We can come in tonight while the dinner is actually being served," Miss Heaton told Andrea as they worked. "I always like to view the finished article when I've spent so much time on it, and without people, the whole effect is quite impossible to judge. So you can come with me, if you like, up to the balcony."

Andrea jumped at the chance, especially as this time she would be there with permission, instead of hiding behind pillars.

The glittering scene below enchanted her. Dresses of gay colors to contrast with the men's black-and-white, animated faces and a barrage of chatter. The lighting was soft and pinkish and, as Fred had been known to say, "kind to old ladies' complexions." The days of harsh white lighting were gone and he took great pride in arranging artistic glows and illuminations.

In their room, at bedtime, Huguette had a voluble flow of gossip to pass on to Andrea, who did not really listen to half of it, but made suitable replies as occasional punctuation, when Huguette paused for breath.

"And in the afternoon, the manager himself, Mr. Drew in person, called to see Miss Jensen," Huguette announced. "Naturally, as you know, he is not pleased that she gives the hotel as her address when she is to be taken to the police station."

"No, not quite. She will be summoned, no doubt, to the police court, but she won't be arrested or taken there," Andrea corrected.

Huguette shrugged. "No matter! She is mixed up with the police and Mr. Drew does not like it. More than that, he wishes her to pay the bill. She says he must wait. But he has not to worry. Her rich father will send her large sums of money, enough, she tells the manager, to buy up all his silly hotel."

"How d'you know all this?" demanded Andrea. "You're making it up."

"True! Every word! They do not know, but I am in the bathroom. I polish the taps, the washbowl, the bath, everything. I fold the towels—and I hear all that is said."

"How could you? The bedroom is between the bathroom and the sitting room."

"The door was open. So now Miss Jensen is very angry with the hotel. And you, my Andrea, were you not lucky to escape being caught at the Polonaise? Your poor friend Trevor was caught, too."

"I've only been once to the Polonaise."

"Ah, but think! One might go there for the first time and—pouf! That is the time the police choose. But what exactly was the crime?"

Andrea laughed, in spite of the fact that the matter was really no joke for Trevor and perhaps for many of the other victims.

"Crime? Well, it's breaking the law, I suppose, but it isn't a crime like robbery with violence or breaking into a bank. I think the Polonaise has a license for drinks up to—oh, probably eleven o'clock. After that, it's illegal to serve drinks, but the club ignores the time and goes on serving. So, one night, the police come in and take the names of everyone who is sitting there."

"Imagine that to happen in France! Everybody can sit in cafés and drink as they choose."

"Until the waiter can't keep his eyes open, I suppose, and starts piling up the chairs on the tables?" Andrea longed for the day when she would be able to visit Paris, not just because the cafés stayed open until early morning, but for all the life and gaiety she had heard so much about.

Huguette had a further tidbit of news next day. Miss Jensen had left the hotel before eight in the morning.

"When I take in her coffee at half-past eight, she is flown," Huguette told her companions in the staff hall. "All is packed in trunks and cases. I look everywhere. Then I tell Miss Deakin, we look at the porter's list for morning calls and breakfast and there is nothing canceled. So Miss Deakin telephoned to find out and it seems that Miss Jensen went very early."

"But she's left her luggage?"

"Oh, she took one small bag with her and said she would have her trunks collected. Me, I am so shocked in case Miss Jensen has fallen out of the windows that I have to drink her coffee to revive me."

The girls laughed, and Andrea joined in. "Pity there wasn't a handy flask of cognac lying around for you," said one.

"What would be the use of returning the coffee to the station? If English people do not mind it warmed again, we French do not like it. So it was not wasted."

Huguette's capacity for avoiding waste, provided that somehow the cost went on the guests' bills, was well known.

In any case, she declared, she deserved some sort of compensation. Miss Jensen had meanly packed all her own clothes, thus depriving Huguette of a properly earned tip, and in addition the French girl had all the extra unexpected work of cleaning the suite, and getting it ready for the next occupant.

Andrea wondered where Miss Jensen had gone and whether Trevor knew of her intended departure or of her forwarding address.

Later in the day, Andrea heard in a roundabout way of a curious incident. Huguette had apparently cleaned and dusted Miss Jensen's suite, after which the floor house-keeper on second, Miss Deakin, had gone in to inspect it as part of her supervising work. Miss Wyvern had been in the sitting room and there had been an altercation between the two housekeepers which was quite unusual for the mild and placid Miss Deakin.

"Margaret told me there was quite a row," Huguette confided to Andrea when they were alone. "I do not tell all the others this, because of Wyvern. But Miss Deakin was most angry that Wyvern should be poking about on second when she is supposed to be concerned only with fourth."

"Couldn't Miss Wyvern give any reason why she was there?" asked Andrea.

"Only that Miss Jensen had borrowed a book from her and Wyvern had come to get it back."

Andrea frowned. "Seems an unlikely tale. I can't imagine any book that Miss Jensen would be likely to borrow from Wyvern. Was she a great reader? The Danish girl, I mean."

"Only magazines. English, American, Continental. She can read in two or three languages."

Even when Huguette had dropped temporarily the absorbing subject of Miss Jensen's hurried flight, Andrea still puzzled over this odd little incident.

Somewhere in her mind the suspicion was forming that there was a link between the beautiful Danish girl and the floor housekeeper on fourth. Yet that was absurd. In social status, they were worlds apart. All the same, Andrea's thoughts often harked back to the episode of Miss Jensen's necklace and Wyvern's apparent disappointment that the jewelry was not found among Andrea's possessions. If Huguette had not borrowed the necklace, thinking it Andrea's, it would have been exactly where Miss Wyvern had expected to find it—in Andrea's drawer. She could only have been so sure if she had placed the necklace there herself. But did Miss Jensen know that? Andrea could not be sure, but it was certainly obvious that she did not like Andrea and had plainly shown that at Christmas at the Dennistouns's, when her plans had gone wrong.

But in a hotel the size and standing of the Belvedere, one small sensation is quickly followed by another and by the weekend the suite was occupied by a well-known actress and film star, playing at one of the local theaters in a prior-to-London production of a new play. Miss Jensen was forgotten and the question of her unpaid bill was solely a matter for the accounts department.

Toward the middle of the week, Andrea was taking trays of tea to various members of the staff when a telephone operator told her that a Mr. Dennistoun was calling and asking personally for Andrea.

"Can you take the call on your corridor?" the operator asked. "But don't be too long. I can't hold the line open for more than three or four minutes."

Andrea rushed toward the alcove on a branch corridor on fourth, anxious not to keep Trevor waiting.

"Are you off duty tonight or tomorrow?" he asked, after the briefest of greetings.

"Tomorrow I have a half day. Why?"

"Would you like to go to the theater with me? There's a new play with a good cast."

"Yes, I'd like that very much."

"I'll be checking in at the Belvedere in the afternoon tomorrow and I'll give you a ring and fix up where we can meet outside for a snack or something."

"That sounds marvelous," she replied with enthusiasm. "I finish duty at three, but I'll wait to hear from you. And Trevor, I'm sorry about that business at the dance club. What bad luck!"

"Can't be helped. It's not all that serious. We shall all probably be let off with a fine and a caution."

She discreetly kept the arrangement to herself.

In the small quiet restaurant where they had tea next day Trevor was obviously ill at ease and at last Andrea, believing that she knew him well enough to ask straight out, said, "What's on your mind, Trevor? Is it this affair at the Polonaise?"

He waved his hand, brushing the matter aside. "No, that's not my real worry. It's rather unfortunate, of course, and my mother isn't very pleased, but I won't be exactly branded for life. As a matter of fact, we had no drinks in front of us, only the dregs, but we were roped in all the same."

Andrea waited for him to continue.

"It's Ingrid," he said at last. "I'm worried about her."

"Yes?" Andrea wondered what worried him most. Was it because Ingrid had been with him at the Polonaise or because she had now left the hotel?

"I've tried to find out where she's gone," Trevor went on, "but all I can get is her bank address in London. I told her not to worry about the club incident, that my lawyer would appear for us both and settle the matter, that she need not appear in court. I tried to reassure her, but she's still an alien, you see, and she has the idea that she'll be arrested or something drastic like that. So now she's left the Belvedere in a hurry and I've no idea where to find her."

If only he knew he was probably better off without her, Andrea thought.

"If I could help you, I would do so. You know that," she offered.

"Would anybody in Reception at your place have an inkling where she really is, do you think?" he asked.

Andrea shook her head. "I don't think so. She went early in the morning before anybody knew—except the porter. She left all her trunks and other baggage and said she would send for them later." Andrea stopped, uncertain whether to say the rest. "They say that she ran up quite a bill, but I expect it's paid by now."

Trevor nodded. "Yes, it is," he muttered, then jerked up his head to stare at the girl.

Andrea stared back at him. "*You* paid it for her."

He tried to laugh, but the attempt was not very successful. "It's only a loan. She was temporarily short of money. Her father hasn't sent her the usual allowance, but she'll pay me back as soon as she has the money."

Andrea was shocked. Rumors had filtered through among the staff that Miss Jensen's bill was enormous. The hotel had allowed her credit because she was a regular guest, occupied one of the best suites and had usually paid promptly in the past. But the amount was said to be several hundred pounds, and that was not unlikely considering the high rate the Belvedere charged for its luxury suites.

"How much did you lend her?" asked Andrea.

"The amount doesn't worry me. Three or four hundred pounds won't backrupt me. But it's Ingrid herself. I can't get in touch with her. I don't know where to start. I've asked the consulates, the embassy even, to try to find her. If she's done something foolish merely because it was my fault she was involved in a trivial police incident, I would never forgive myself."

"You don't mean—she might commit suicide?"

"I mean just that. And if I don't find her, I shall go mad."

"You love her very much, don't you?"

He looked away across the almost empty restaurant. "Yes, I do."

But that slight hesitation, the split second of doubt, set new ideas in motion in Andrea's thoughts. He wasn't absolutely sure, but was trying to convince himself that it was love, not infatuation. Besides, it was extremely unlikely that Miss Jensen was the type to commit suicide, however much she might fear the police or however heavily in debt she might be.

It was time to go to the theater and Andrea collected her gloves and handbag.

"If you hear anything, even the smallest rumor or bit of information, you'll let me know, won't you?" he said, as he helped her on with her coat.

"Of course. Huguette shares my room and if anybody finds out anything at all, I'm sure she'll be the first. She looked after Miss Jensen's suite."

In the crowded foyer of the theater, she and Trevor slowly pushed their way through to the head of the stairs leading down to the stalls.

Suddenly, Trevor whispered, "There's Holt standing over there. I wonder if—"

Andrea waited while Trevor turned and thrust his way against the stream of people drifting toward the stairs. The two men spoke briefly, then Keir was accompanying Trevor back to where Andrea stood.

"Good evening, Andrea. You're looking very smart tonight." Keir spoke coldly, in spite of the professed compliment.

"I thought you were still in London. How did your case go?" She had scanned the papers, but if there had been any report she must have overlooked it.

"Settled out of court. Agreed damages. Exactly the same as we first offered the man, but more costly for us." His glance implied that when he was not available, she accepted the first opportunity to accompany someone else to the theater or any other outing.

Yet inwardly she was amused. In the first place, she was flattering herself if she thought that he displayed the slightest tinge of jealousy, and secondly, nobody need be alarmed by the fact that ~~all~~ Trevor wanted from a girl was a sympathetic audience, and who better to choose than Andrea, who was an old friend and not likely to entertain the wrong romantic notions.

A bell tinkled near the box office and Trevor took Andrea's arm. "We'd better take our seats. Might see you in the intermission, Holt."

Keir nodded and turned toward the main staircase leading to the circle. Andrea was glad that he wouldn't be sitting in the stalls. Then she felt annoyed with herself. Why should she care two pins if Keir sat observing her instead of watching the play?

The play was a light trifle, hovering uncertainly between comedy and farce, but, decorated as it was with star names and a good supporting cast, it was certain to enjoy a long run in the West End.

Andrea was interested enough to watch the leading lady, now staying at the Belvedere, for she had not seen her on the stage before and had not, like Huguette, met her in the hotel. She'd be able to retail to her French friend what she thought of the star's acting and describe her elegant dresses.

After the show, Trevor suggested coffee and a snack in a little restaurant he knew. "I'd take you back to the Belvedere for a meal," he offered, "but I know that would make things awkward for you."

Even now, Trevor returned to the subject of his missing Ingrid. "I asked Holt if he knew anything about her or where she was likely to be found, but he didn't know—or said he didn't."

"Would he keep in touch with her or she with him?" asked Andrea, interest flickering up again.

"He might. He knew her before I did and I don't mind admitting, Andrea, there've been times when I thought she liked him, especially when he came to our house at Christmas. I took good care to keep Ingrid out of his way as much as possible."

"And landed him on me," Andrea chuckled with quiet amusement.

"D'you dislike him?"

She shrugged in imitation of Huguette. "Like? Dislike?

What does it matter? He's just a visitor who stays frequently in the hotel. When he's finished his job in Millbridge, he'll be off somewhere else to Liverpool or Glasgow or Bristol or wherever new blocks of buildings are being built."

"Curious life for a man," he commented. "No settled home. Does he live anywhere besides hotels?"

"I don't know. I've never asked him." She smiled. She was not going to disclose that she knew of his visits to his mother's home in Yorkshire.

Just before leaving the restaurant, when Trevor had switched the subject back to Ingrid, and Andrea was feeling tired of being his inevitable audience, she remembered the snippet of information given her by Jill during Swedish Week. Would it be wise to tell Trevor what was only the merest piece of third-hand gossip?

She decided it might help. "I know it was Astrid that the Swedish girl said at the time. But I'm not sure of the surname. But probably the Swedish girl had mistaken Ingrid for someone else."

Trevor was busy writing down the name in his pocket notebook.

"How long are you staying at the Belvedere?" she asked him.

"Only tonight. I must go back to the grind tomorrow or everything will pile up."

"Your secretary, Eileen, will look after everything most capably for you."

"Oh, yes, she's a treasure."

Andrea remained silent. She was sure that Eileen was in love with Trevor, and how she must hate seeing him in the throes of a wild infatuation for a Danish girl who claimed to be the daughter of a wealthy man, yet had to borrow a large sum of money to pay her hotel bill.

Some day, perhaps, Trevor would recover his sense of proportion and then Eileen would reap her reward. It was strange, Andrea thought, how much she wanted Trevor to be happy, as long as it was another girl involved and not herself. Once, she would have been achingly jealous of all those other girls whom Trevor knew. Now she wanted only to rid him of Ingrid, the wrong kind for him.

Andrea was awakened by a light, persistent tapping on her bedroom door and then a voice. Surely it wasn't time to get up yet and the night porter was never gentle with his knocking calls. As the girls complained, he brought thunder with him.

But now she became aware of Miss Wyvern shaking her by the shoulder.

"Yes? What—what's the matter?"

"Lansdale! Will you get up, please. A visitor in 379 is ill."

Andrea blinked herself awake. "Shall I dress first?"

"No, just put on a dressing gown or coat. It's urgent."

Laura Wyvern was wearing a dark green housecoat, and Andrea paused only to push her arms into her own housecoat and her feet into slippers.

She followed Miss Wyvern down to third and into Room 379, where a young woman lay on the bed, apparently rolling about in pain.

"What am I to do, Miss Wyvern?" Andrea asked in a whisper. "What's the matter with her?"

"I don't know yet. But fetch some water."

Andrea quickly filled a glass and Miss Wyvern lifted the woman and held the glass to her lips.

"Shall I telephone for the doctor?" Andrea queried.

"Not yet. We don't want to bring him here if it's unnecessary."

The woman moaned softly, then pushed back the hair from her forehead. "I feel like death," she muttered.

Andrea, in the role of a spectator with little to do, was now sufficiently awake to ponder over this strange situation. A small clock on the dressing table pointed to half-past three. Why had Miss Wyvern specially asked Andrea to help her with a visitor taken suddenly ill, when the room was not even on fourth? Possibly Miss Preston, the third-floor housekeeper, was away and, in that case, Wyvern would be temporarily in charge of both floors. But why not fetch Miss Deakin from second? She had nursing experience.

"Anything else I can do?" asked Andrea, tired of hanging around.

"Yes. Go to the station and make a pot of tea and bring it here."

Andrea did as instructed, but there'd be a row in the morning if the head chambermaid on third discovered that Andrea, still only a trainee and without even the status of a fourth chambermaid, had been interfering with the neatly set out *mise-en-place*.

Of course there was no milk. A crate of bottles came up in a service elevator in the morning when it was taken out of refrigerators.

She took the tray of tea, with two cups and saucers to 379. No doubt Miss Wyvern would expect a cup to drink in company with the guest.

"There's no milk," Andrea explained, hoping that the housekeeper would not send her downstairs in search of some.

"Doesn't matter." Miss Wyvern poured a cup and held it for the woman in bed. "All right, Lansdale. You can go back to bed now. I think the patient will recover in a few hours."

Andrea returned to the station and set a substitute tray for the one she had used, checked that the gas burner was properly turned off and retraced her steps along the corridor.

The night porter on his fire-patrol rounds grinned at her. "You're flitting about late, aren't you miss?"

"No business of yours," she answered saucily. "You should turn a blind eye when you meet us on corridors."

She left him as he opened a small glass-fronted case on the wall, where he clicked a key that would automatically record the hourly fire check on every floor and thus prevent arguments arising with the insurance company if fire broke out. It was also intended as a safeguard, so that any suspicion of fire could be quickly discovered and dealt with.

Back in her room, Andrea regretted that she had encountered the porter. Why couldn't he have been checking on some other floor or at some other part of the hour?

She tucked herself up in bed again, relishing the fact that two more hours remained before the porter would come thumping on the door at six.

It was just as well that Huguette was away for two nights. This time she had asked for a pass in the proper way, and had gone to London for a French reunion affair. Huguette would have asked endless questions about the woman visitor and her illness and there would have been no more sleep for Andrea.

Miss Wyvern, who usually breakfasted in the stewards' room, did not appear, and Andrea wondered if she had still had to remain with the visitor in Room 379.

Andrea had returned to her waitress duties, and was sorry not to have worked under the florist, Miss Heaton, for a longer time, as she had enjoyed the flower and plant work of the hotel, even though it was probably more tiring and meant more fetching and carrying than waiting at table. It was all good experience. But one of the florist's assistants had now recovered from flu and Miss Heaton decided that she could manage without Andrea, who hardly knew whether that was complimentary or whether she had been more trouble than she was worth.

She was busy laying the staff tables for lunch when the head waiter in charge told her she was to report immediately to the staff manager. When she did so, he gave her a fierce look and told her to go to the head housekeeper.

Mystified, she knocked on the door of Aunt Catherine's office. "Sit down, Andrea," Mrs. Mayfield told her when she had entered.

While her aunt finished writing some notes on a pad, Andrea made a lightning survey in her mind of any misdeeds during the past few days. Her conscience was fairly clear, although you could never be sure, when you were still a trainee, that you hadn't unwittingly committed a serious crime or trodden on the dignity of some senior members of the staff.

Aunt Catherine turned toward her niece and her face was unsmiling, her eyes stern.

"You were off duty yesterday, part of the afternoon and evening?"

"Yes, madam."

"Would you care to tell me how you spent that time?"

When Andrea hesitated, Mrs. Mayfield continued,

"There'll be no compulsion, of course, but I think it would be in your own interests."

"I went out to tea with Mr. Dennistoun, then to a theater. Afterward, Trevor took me to a small place for coffee and sandwiches. Then I came home."

"Alone?"

"No. Mr. Dennistoun came to the staff entrance with me."

"And you knew that he was staying one night in the house?"

Andrea nodded. "Of course." The drift of all this catechizing was obscure to her.

Mrs. Mayfield sighed, then picked up a pencil and twirled it in her fingers—a habit she had when more than usually worried. This action worried Andrea, too, at this moment.

"Has something happened to Trevor?" she asked anxiously.

"No, not as far as I'm aware. But—you—" Mrs. Mayfield broke off, then tried again. "Andrea, I do want the truth. I've been told that you were seen coming out of Mr. Dennistoun's room somewhere about four o'clock this morning."

Andrea leapt to her feet, her eyes blazing, her color rushing to her cheeks. "That's an outrageous lie! I don't even know which room he had or which floor he was on. Whoever told you such a—such an infamous lie is trying to kick me out of here."

"Sit down, Andrea, and try to control your temper," her aunt said quietly.

Andrea's whole body shook violently. Who could hate her so much as to make this monstrous accusation against her? Not even Wyvern could go so far. Andrea's seething thoughts were suddenly checked and a miraculous calm swept over her. This time Wyvern would be her alibi, her savior.

"Miss Wyvern knows where I was at that time," she said eagerly.

"And where was that?"

"In 379 helping Miss Wyvern with a lady visitor who was ill in the night."

Mrs. Mayfield stared in disbelief at the girl. "In 379? But how would you come to be on third floor at all?"

"Miss Wyvern woke me up and asked me to go down and help her. I just assumed she was in charge of third as well as her own fourth."

"What time was that?"

"About half-past three. That was the time by a little clock that number 379 had on her dressing table."

"And how long were you there?"

"About half an hour, I think."

"And what did you do in that time?"

"After a few minutes, Miss Wyvern asked me to make a pot of tea. So I did that and took it in, and Miss Wyvern said the visitor was better and that I could go back to bed."

"Did Huguette know of your absence?"

"No. She's in London."

Mrs. Mayfield nodded. "Did you meet anyone else in the corridors or speak to anyone else except Miss Wyvern?"

"Only the night porter. He was on fire-patrol." With sudden apprehension, Andrea remembered her flippant words to him about turning a blind eye.

"I see," Mrs. Mayfield rose from her desk and walked toward the window. "I shall have to think over what you've told me."

"But it's the truth!" Andrea protested, her voice shrill. "In any case, you have only to ask Miss Wyvern and she'll corroborate everything I've said." In her mind, Andrea added the words "for once she can't deny it."

"You think so?" There was a curious sceptical expression on Aunt Catherine's face and Andrea was disquieted.

"Yes, of course. And there's also the lady in 379, although she might not remember."

"She left this morning. She was here only one night, I understand. Mr. Dennistoun also left this morning, as you probably know."

"Yes, I knew that."

After a long pause, Andrea asked, "I suppose—I mean—you couldn't tell me who gave you the—information about me."

"No. You must know for yourself that's quite impossible.

I can only listen to what my staff chooses to tell me and then try to sort the true from the false. You may go now, Andrea, back to your duties. I may have to send for you again later in the day.''

Andrea felt like a prisoner who is remanded in custody while the judge considers what sentence he will impose for the offense. But there had been no crime, no offense. She had been called out of bed to assist a sick woman, even though it now turned out that the visitor had been suffering only from a slight tummy upset; something she'd eaten had disagreed with her, or perhaps she had taken several sherries too many. Evidently the woman was well enough to leave the Belvedere this morning.

Andrea realized that she still didn't know which room Trevor had occupied, but to ask Reception might be fatal and she could hardly telephone Trevor to ask him.

Dismay at the turn of events grew and magnified within her. She wanted to go now straight to Miss Wyvern and ask her to make the facts clear to Mrs. Mayfield, but there was no opportunity, for the senior staff would soon be coming in for their lunch. Again, Miss Wyvern did not appear in the stewards' room for lunch and Andrea discovered that the floor housekeeper had asked for a tray to be sent to her office, saying she was too busy to come down.

Later in the afternoon the longed-for summons came, and Andrea was glad to meet her aunt again, but Miss Wyvern was also present, and even in her attractive new moss-green dress with a gold belt she looked more like a vengeful fury than a supporting witness.

''Now, Andrea, would you care to repeat to Miss Wyvern what you told me about last night's events.''

Andrea began sturdily enough, but before she had completed three sentences, Miss Wyvern broke in angrily, ''This is just a tissue of lies!''

Mrs. Mayfield held up her hand and motioned Andrea to go on, but the girl knew now the certainty of those doubts which had been gnawing at her since this morning. Far from Miss Wyvern supporting her, the floor housekeeper was only too determined to blacken Andrea in every possible direction.

"I certainly didn't even come near your room. I attended the visitor in 379. That much is true, but if I'd wanted further help, the most natural thing would have been to rouse one of the third-floor maids."

"But you asked me to make tea in the third-floor station!" Andrea was defeated but not entirely vanquished.

"Nonsense! I would never give you such an order."

Andrea gazed helplessly from her aunt to the floor housekeeper. "May I ask you one question, Miss Wyvern?"

Miss Wyvern glanced quickly at the housekeeper. "What is it?"

"When did you see me coming out of Mr. Dennistoun's room and what is the number?"

Miss Wyvern gave a scornful smile. "You must know the number as well as I do. 368 is almost opposite 379. The time was about four o'clock."

Andrea's heart died within her. Surely Aunt Catherine, with her knowledge of hotel life and her experience of women, would be able to distinguish which of the two was lying?

"Thank you, Miss Wyvern," Mrs. Mayfield said. "I would like to speak to Andrea alone."

When the floor housekeeper had gone, Aunt Catherine said, "How much of your story is true?"

"All of it."

"Yet you've heard Miss Wyvern deny that she sent for you?"

"But how else would I have known that the visitor in 379 was ill in the middle of the night?"

Aunt Catherine nodded. "Yes, that's so. But Mr. Dennistoun occupied the room opposite—and in some way you might easily have found out about 379."

Andrea had come to the end of her patience. She stood up and faced her aunt. "I'm not going to do anything further to defend myself. For reasons I don't know, Miss Wyvern has her knife into me, and she's moved heaven and earth to get me out of this place. But unless I'm dismissed for some crime that can be proved, I'm not going to leave. I'm going to prove to you, too, Aunt Catherine, that I'm made of tougher stuff than you think. You never understood my father and you never gave *him* credit for sticking to a job that, at the time, he thought was the best he could do for both of us. But he still had his integrity and his dignity and his pride—''

"Pride? To act as chauffeur, with all the menial jobs that go with it?''

Andrea was calm as ice crystals. "That was the sort of petty pride he'd learned to throw away. He never cared if the village knew that he was a professor. He did a job—with his hands, too—and with that job he gained a roof over our heads as well as time to spend with his books. He was happy and so was I. We both knew that it wasn't a position that would last forever. He used to say to me, 'Choose a husband you can get along with. I shan't want to live with you both, but I might want to sit in your chimney corner sometimes and help my grandson with his algebra.' So I won't give up my job because somebody makes a scandalous accusation against me. I said I'd complete a year and I will!''

Silence followed Andrea's long outburst. Eventually Mrs. Mayfield gave her niece a searching look. Then she smiled. "I find you a very puzzling young woman, Andrea. I'd hoped that during the time you were here we might have come to understand each other better. So far, that hasn't happened, but at least I think you're honest. Please go back to your duties now.''

After Andrea had gone, Catherine Mayfield neglected her work for a considerable time. The girl believed that she was emulating her father's tenacity of purpose, but actually Catherine could almost have imagined that her own sister, Leonie, had been standing there a few minutes ago, asserting a fiery independence and refusing to be pushed aside.

The housekeeper's thoughts turned inward. Had she, even subconsciously, set out to persecute Andrea because Leonie had a daughter and she had none? If Andrea had given up the course and left the Belvedere, she would have been satisfied to have her own theories proved. How far had she been mistaken in having Andrea here in the same hotel? It would have been so much more satisfactory, probably for everybody, if she had placed the girl in another hotel.

Yet there was another side to be faced. Andrea had been

involved in several mysterious incidents. Miss Jensen's fur and, later, the necklace. Somewhere, Keir Holt came into the picture, and the extraordinary disclosure that he had spent part of Christmas at the Dennistouns's when Andrea was there. Now her niece was apparently making the most of a friendship with Trevor Dennistoun.

Catherine sighed. She would have been much more gratified to learn that Andrea preferred the company of Robert, the *pâtisserie* chef. But that reflection caused a smile. Andrea did not entirely realize how much of the staff's personal affairs, their romances and tiffs, their disagreements and friendships, filtered through to a head housekeeper. If the girl had known that her aunt was already aware of Robert's attraction to little Andrea Lansdale, she would probably have danced with rage.

At a convenient time, the housekeeper asked to see Miss Wyvern.

"I've decided to transfer Andrea Lansdale to Control department. As a trainee, she ought to get some experience of that side of hotel work and she'll be under the supervision of Mr. Blake. I've already asked Mr. Jesson for her release as soon as he can spare her."

"I understand perfectly, Mrs. Mayfield." Laura Wyvern's smile was cold. "You think, perhaps, I'm a little too hard on her?"

"No, no, Miss Wyvern. I didn't say that at all. Or mean it." Catherine was too astute to admit any suggestion that she wanted Andrea treated less hard by any of the senior staff.

Nominally, Andrea was not under Miss Wyvern's supervision, as she had now worked in several departments, but it was tacitly understood that where a trainee began as chambermaid, she continued to be under the authority of her floor housekeeper. So now the housekeeper exerted tact by informing Miss Wyvern of the change.

Laura herself was less diplomatic. "I hope you don't think that I was—well, exaggerating the incident we spoke of."

"Since I've been here, I've learned to know when an incident is being exaggerated or magnified. I'm sure you did exactly what you thought correct. We'll say no more about it, shall we?''

Miss Wyvern turned to go, knowing that she had made an error. Nevertheless, the cold smile was still on her face when she stepped outside the housekeeper's office as Mr. Blake, the assistant manager, was just entering.

"Oh, come in, Francis," called Mrs. Mayfield.

When he had shut the door, she sat back in her chair and smiled up at him. "Isn't it fortunate that I have a safety valve somewhere in this place! If you were to gossip and repeat the things I say to you, the whole hotel would blow sky high."

"Miss Wyvern making trouble again?" he asked.

Catherine nodded. "She always has such a grudge, it seems, against the young ones. She's an unhappy, discontented women herself and delights in making mischief for others. Oh, well, perhaps one day she'll get married."

"Have pity for the man," he begged.

They laughed together, and ten years slipped from the contours of Catherine's face.

CHAPTER THIRTEEN

ANDREA LIKED being in the Control department although at first she found the work complicated. At every point of supply in the hotel, whether for meals, drinks or services, dockets were put into boxes and sent to the Control office. Other copies were passed to the cashiers and it was the function of the Control department to check every item, to see that what had been supplied was eventually charged or paid for, and to provide a system whereby turnover and the costs of running each department of the hotel could be assessed.

Matching up little bits of paper and entering figures in columns was still clerical work and very little different from other kinds of office routine, but to Andrea the atmosphere was not the same. Only three of the senior girls were resident; the rest were day staff working normal office hours, and they contributed a flavor of the outside world on a more equal level than the rigid separation of hotel staff and guests.

"Of course, down here we're neither fish, flesh nor fowl," one girl told Andrea on her first morning. "We realize that as office clerks we don't rank as high as the residential ones who lord it over us."

Andrea laughed. "I've long ceased to worry about all the class distinctions in hotels. If you live in, you have to keep the rules."

The other girl grimaced. "I would hate that. I like my evenings to myself. Live in and you're always on duty, at everybody's beck and call, that's what I say."

Andrea found, too, that she had a much greater number

of free evenings, which was sometimes an advantage, especially now that in April there was so much more daylight. At the same time, there was no off-duty period in the middle of the afternoon, which had proved a blessing for shopping purposes. Still, she reflected, one could hardly hope to have all the advantages, and it was a relief to be free of Miss Wyvern.

Mr. Blake, the assistant manager in charge of the Control department, was a quiet, middle-aged man who exerted his authority with a minimum of fuss and bossiness. He knew when to be informal with the staff, when to check slackness, and his reputation for fairness stood very high.

Occasionally Andrea was sent on errands from Control to Reception, to check queries or ask for information, and she never failed to be astonished by the abrupt change in furnishings and decorations dividing the public spaces of the Belvedere from the working quarters.

Thickly carpeted stairs led down from the ground floor to a cleverly lit lower mezzanine where a cocktail bar, a ladies' hairdressing salon and the florist shop encouraged guests to spend their money. A pair of swing doors led past the barman's glass pantry, to a dim, stone-paved corridor, strictly utilitarian.

Offices and storerooms opened on either side. Mr. Blake's small private office was adjacent to that of the staff manager, and often on Monday mornings the corridor was crowded with young men and boys seeking a job in the kitchens or storerooms. Some wanted to work in the hotel for a few weeks, just to tide them over a patch of unemployment when they had been laid off by another industry, such as building or engineering. Others liked city hotels in winter and preferred seaside or holiday resorts in summer.

But at this time of early summer, there was usually only a Monday-morning handful of men, although more than enough for Andrea. Inevitably, she was greeted by catcalls and wolf whistles, and once or twice she took a circuitous route down a service elevator and through the telephone-switchboard room to avoid running the gauntlet.

At the far end of the corridor, a warm smell of oil rose from the basements far below where the Belvedere pumped water from its own well and machinery throbbed away with muted diligence to heat, cool and light the entire building.

The Control office was dingy, not very well lit, and the day girls complained bitterly that their heels caught in the worn linoleum and tattered strip of carpet.

"My sister works in a factory," one of Andrea's companions confided, "where the walls are pale yellow, the machines pale green with all the dangerous bits picked out in red, and the floor is tiled in squares, blue and gray. She says it perks her up no end just to set foot in the place—which is more than you can say for this dump."

But Mr. Blake had promised that in the slacker summer season, the whole office would be redecorated and furnished and other improvements made.

Although Andrea noticed the contrasts in the hotel, she was not depressed by her surroundings. Upstairs she shared a small but comfortable room with Huguette, the food was reasonable, she had free time in the evenings and there was a degree of companionship in off-duty hours.

In addition, she was studying hard for her preliminary examination at the technical college, where once a week she attended a day-release course in catering.

She had seen Trevor only once since the occasion of Miss Wyvern's accusations, and Keir Holt had vanished out of her life and, indeed, that of the Belvedere's. One of his young assistants occasionally stayed in the hotel for a couple of days, but he did not occupy Keir's usual suite, nor were there any long reports to be typed. The Century block was nearing completion, apart from the interior fittings, and Andrea heard in a roundabout way that Keir was now busy on another project farther north.

She was glad of the lull. If Keir were absent long enough she might forget those ridiculous notions that had jostled in her thoughts for so long. Sharp clashes or controversial opinions between two people were far less disruptive of the dream state than mere indifference. Neglect and time built a gray shroud over what she now saw was only a tinsel dream and not the hard gold of reality.

By now, Keir was in some northern hotel, no doubt ruthlessly demanding the services of another regular secretary because she knew his work, taking her out for a day in the country, kissing her good-night. What was so special about Andrea Lansdale that he should remember her?

Unfortunately for her, forgetting was not so easy. Every time she went into the Century shops, she was sharply reminded of him. Here he had walked and talked with men in rough working clothes stained with cement and sand. There he had tramped along scaffolding where now the hidden girders supported carpeted floors displaying hats, fabrics, eiderdowns and toys.

She had made no definite plans for staying at the Belvedere after the completion of her first year, being content to wait until after August before making a decision.

One afternoon after lunch, as she walked along the corridor on third on her return to Control office, she was passing the printing shop when Mr. Chester poked his head out.

"You going downstairs, miss?" he called.

"Yes. I'm in Control office."

"Then you might take this menu down to the chef and ask him to write it out a bit plainer. He's always the same when he gives me a menu in Italian, scrawls it anyhow. I suppose you don't know Italian, miss?"

Andrea smiled. "No, I'm afraid not. French is the only language I know and I'm not at all perfect in that."

"Oh, French I can do all right. And the wines I know, because I get the waiters to let me have copies of the labels, but this—I don't know whether he means 'peperoni' or 'poperini'— and blast if I know which course of the dinner that is anyway."

Andrea took the sheet of paper from the printer's ink-stained hands. "And if Mr. Cassavini isn't there, whom shall I ask?"

Mr. Chester scratched his head. "Oh, ask the *sous-chef*, he'll know. He's a bright lad."

Andrea hurried down the service stairs to the chef's office just outside the kitchens, but Mr. Cassavini was not there. Timidly, she pushed open the steel door and looked for the *sous-chef*, a young man in his middle twenties and reported to be brilliant at his job.

"Mr. Chester isn't quite sure what he has to print on these menus for the special Italian dinner. Could you write it out more plainly for him, please?"

"Yes, I'd better, or Mr. Cassavini will jump in a cauldron of *minestrone* if there's a spelling error. Now—*Peperoni Ripieni alla Napolitano*. What else? Oh, *Scaloppini* has two p's. Has he got the names of the wines correct?"

"Yes, he says he knows those. Thank you very much indeed."

Ironically, just when Andrea was pressed for time, Mr. Chester was so pleased she had helped him with the Italian menu that he was not only willing, but eager, to show her over his printing shop. Few of the staff were ever invited into what he jealously regarded as his own private hideout. He had spent much of his life in a large printing works, but he was proud of the small press on which he printed most of the Belvedere's stationery, menus, tickets and notices, and he loved his quiet, undisturbed job.

Now he displayed his cases of type, showed Andrea how he set the frames, changed the colors of inks, printed from a block some special emblem or drawing. Finally, he set up her name in the most elegant type he had and printed it on several sheets of paper.

"Thank you, Mr. Chester. It's very kind of you. Now I must fly! Or I shall have Mr. Blake sending out a search party for me."

Miss Wyvern passed the open door as Andrea hurried out.

"Good afternoon, Andrea," she said pleasantly, then glanced at her wristwatch, although she could hardly know what time Andrea was due back at her desk.

Andrea returned the greeting and hurried downstairs in the opposite direction. During the last few weeks she had been able to forget Miss Wyvern most of the time, especially as the floor housekeeper had been away on holiday for a week. But it was a pity that Miss Wyvern had seen her coming out of Mr. Chester's printing shop. Still, it couldn't be helped.

A few days later, a wild rumor swept through the Bel-

vedere that Mervyn Watford was about to be married, or
had already taken the fatal step.

Huguette declared that he must have proposed by accident or after the fourth bottle of champagne.

"Who's the bride?" Andrea asked.

"Somebody said she is an actress."

During the latter part of the morning many of the staff
found necessary tasks in and around the entrance hall, for it
was said that Mervyn's wedding reception had been booked
in another name as a luncheon party. Robert had put in
overtime on a wedding cake, and there was no other reception.

Andrea herself eagerly commuted between her own department and Reception and was lucky enough to be
coming up the basement stairs when half a dozen photographers surged into the hall, flashing their cameras at a pretty
girl firmly clinging to Mervyn's arm.

Dick Palmer, on behalf of his paper, had a few questions
to ask, the manager specially welcomed the party, and
finally the bride and bridegroom with their guests were
allowed to drift away to enjoy the wedding breakfast.

"I'd never have believed it of Mervyn," was Jill's comment. "But she's very pretty and he looks happy."

"Well, you don't expect the chap to look mournful on his
wedding day, do you?" demanded Dick. "If he's like the
rest of us, the least he can do is pin a smile on his face for the
sake of the cameraman. 'Bye. Must rush back to the office."

Dick had gone before Jill could hurl a retort after him.

"Mervyn's days of taking out girls in all the hotels he
visits are over and done with," said Andrea.

"Not necessarily. She's an actress. She'll be playing at
Dover or Plymouth when he's in Norwich or Macclesfield."

"That's a fine sort of life for a couple!"

"Oh, well, they both have their eyes open, I hope," Jill
said. "And she'll get free cosmetics for the rest of her life."

Andrea went away giggling at this materialistic view of
married life.

When word buzzed around that the couple were about to
leave after the reception for a honeymoon in Paris, a
number of girls crowded into an unoccupied front bedroom

on third floor, from which they hoped to have a view as Mervyn and his bride walked from the porch to their car. Andrea was unable to be there this time, but Huguette related the incident between bursts of laughter.

"Miriam had a large box of confetti and little silver horseshoes to throw down, but when she opened it—*pouf!*—the wind blew it all over the people on the sidewalk and also back into the bedroom over us. Oh, I laughed! I enjoyed myself!" cried Huguette unfeelingly. "Afterward Miriam had to sweep the whole room with the vacuum, shake the bedcovers and cushions and dust all again, for the girls on third said they had done the room once and it was Miriam's confetti that had filled it everywhere."

Andrea wondered what Miss Wyvern thought of the surprise, and at teatime in the staff hall, Miriam regaled the other girl with the floor housekeeper's reactions.

"White as a sheet she went, and no wonder. Sweet on him for a month of Sundays and a year before that. Kissing and canoodling with him in the station. You saw that, didn't you, Andy?"

"I couldn't be sure. It might not have been either."

"Oh, yes, it was. I'm not blind. Well, I'm glad Mr. Watford's got himself tied up to somebody else."

After Andrea had finished in her department for the day, she went to her room to change her dress before going out dancing with Jill and Dick, Robert and one or two others. As she passed Miss Wyvern's office on the way, the floor housekeeper called to her.

Reluctantly, Andrea entered and waited warily. Miss Wyvern's rounded face appeared blotchy and puffed, as though she had spent a long time crying.

"I wanted to ask how you're getting on now," Miss Wyvern began smoothly.

"Quite well, thank you, Miss Wyvern."

Andrea continued to stall with a few more platitudes, aware that time was flying and soon she ought to be meeting the others.

Then came the sudden question. "Have you seen Mr. Dennistoun lately?"

Andrea's cheeks flamed. "You've no right to ask me such questions and I refuse to answer," she snapped.

She turned blindly toward the door and wrenched it open.

"Are you in a hurry to complain to your Aunt Catherine?"

Andrea swung around, white with fear, and leaned against the inside of the door. "What do you mean?"

Miss Wyvern's smile was ugly. "It's all very plain. You came here as a so-called trainee, knowing that it didn't matter how often you broke the rules or upset discipline. Your aunt was the head housekeeper, so you were safe."

"How do you know this?" Andrea's lips trembled, but she must find out the source of Miss Wyvern's information.

"During my holiday I visited Mrs. Dennistoun and she told me. I don't suppose she knew it was meant to be a secret. She also admitted that she was very glad to send you packing because you were such an embarrassment to her son."

"Then why did she invite me there at Christmas?"

Laura Wyvern's pouting mouth sneered. "She was sorry for you because you'd lost your father."

"I don't believe a word! Mrs. Dennistoun's not like that. She's kind and sensible. I know she doesn't want me to marry Trevor, but there's never been any question of that. In any case, Trevor's quite fond of somebody else."

"Oh? It's quite likely that when you saw you had no chance with him, you were glad to come here where you could meet plenty of men. You can't leave them alone, can you? Visitors or staff, young or old—it doesn't matter. You can't even leave old Mr. Chester alone. You have to waste your time in his printing office," Miss Wyvern's eyes glittered. "You—you're man crazy!"

Andrea almost reeled under the impact of the words that were flung at her, but she was not going to cringe. She advanced toward the other woman. "I know you saw me coming out of Mr. Chester's printing shop, but you didn't see me that night coming out of Trevor Dennistoun's room, because I was never in there. You made that up, to blacken my character." Andrea spoke vehemently, all caution forgotten. "Since the moment I came here, you've disliked me and done all you could to get me thrown out. It was a lucky chance for you that Trevor happened to be in a particular room and you were in charge of the floor that night and had to attend to a woman visitor opposite his room."

Laura Wyvern first reddened, then her cheeks paled, for Andrea had hit on the exact truth. It *had* only been the merest chance that Laura had known which was Trevor Dennistoun's room, and when the woman in 379 was ill, the opportunity to bring down Andrea and have her pottering around in the corridor at four in the morning was too good to miss.

"It's only my word against yours," Miss Wyvern agreed, "but I still have some authority here."

"But I'm not under your authority," Andrea retorted. "I'm in another department and you have no right to interfere in my personal affairs. You can make my position here intolerable by telling everybody that I'm Mrs. Mayfield's niece, but what good will it do you? I'm not in the way of your ambitions. I won't stop you getting a promotion." The angry words tumbled out, for now she had nothing to lose.

Then the most astonishing change came over Miss Wyvern. She stood up and swayed. "Promotion? D'you think I care about that? All I ever wanted out of life was Mervyn, and I had to stand by and watch you—and a dozen other girls—going out with him, laughing and dancing with him. And now he's married a silly little—*actress!*"

To Andrea's horror, the floor housekeeper collapsed in her chair, broke into noisy sobs and covered her face with her hands.

Andrea momentarily panicked. What on earth could she do? "Miss Wyvern," she began uncertainly, "I'm sorry. . . ."

Mercifully, the telephone rang and Andrea picked it up.

"No, Miss Wyvern isn't here at this moment, but I'll find her and give her your message. Yes, I expect she's around somewhere on the floor."

Miss Wyvern lifted a ravaged, tear-sodden face. "Who was that?"

"Mr. Blake. He'd like to see you in his office when you can go down." Andrea hesitated, then added, "I thought you might like a few minutes—before you went." She pulled open the door and fled upstairs to her room. Laura Wyvern hadn't deserved time to recover, but Andrea understood now the meaning and the cause of the unexpected outburst. Mervyn's wedding had finally crushed any slight hopes Laura might ever have cherished.

Another girl poked her head in the door. "Telephone for you—in the alcove on fourth."

Heavens, what now? This time it was Trevor.

"Well, I'm off duty, yes, but I'd arranged to go out with some of the others here."

"I really must see you. I want to talk to you."

Andrea sighed. Once again, she was expected to act as his sounding board while he talked about Ingrid. Yet, after the scene with Miss Wyvern, she didn't really feel like going out dancing with the others.

"All right," she said at last, "I'll come." She arranged to meet him in half an hour at a small restaurant where they had been before.

Then she rang the switchboard. "Would you give a message to Reception, please? I was going out dancing with Jill and her fiancé. If they haven't gone already, tell them not to wait. I can't come this time."

The operator answered slyly, "More exciting date? I understand. I won't give you away."

Trevor's attitude puzzled Andrea. He was neither elated nor depressed. He ordered a substantial dinner including roast duck with orange salad and finishing with Andrea's favorite dessert, *meringues Chantilly*, and his appetite kept pace with his brisk conversation. But he did not even mention Ingrid. Was that episode over, she wondered.

But with the coffee and cognac on the table, he began abruptly, "Seen anything of Ingrid in your hotel lately?"

"No, but I don't know who's in the hotel these days, now that I'm downstairs in Control."

His smile had a bitter twist. "What a fool I was! She was so beautiful that I thought she had a character to match. I went crazy over her and I really thought she liked me a little.

But all she wanted was admiration, a presentable escort— and—" he broke off, with a self-derisory smile at Andrea " money to pay her hotel bills and enable her to run up a few more accounts elsewhere."

"You've seen her since she left the Belvedere?"

"Oh, yes. In London. She wasn't very hard to trace, especially as it occurred to me that she might be using another name. You were right about Ingrid Jensen not being her real name. In London she'd checked in as Astrid Jorgens, but I remembered what you told me when you said somebody recognized her in Swedish Week and called her Astrid."

"Why should she use several names, do you think?" asked Andrea.

"Goodness knows. I suppose it makes it easier when she wants to disappear."

"And she hasn't a rich father?"

He shook his head. "I would hardly think so. Just as well that I wasn't on the lookout for a wealthy father-in-law. Oh, well, I suppose I can count it all as useful experience. I'll try not to make the same mistake again."

Andrea was not tactless enough to mention that the mistake had probably cost him a great deal of money.

"There was another thing that worried me at the time. That Polonaise affair—it was really quite simple and nothing much to be frightened about, but Ingrid panicked, and when they came to take our names, she said she'd write hers down." He looked across at Andrea. "D'you know what she'd written? Your name."

"Mine? Why?"

"She said she'd be in endless trouble because she was an alien, with a foreign passport and all that. But I tried to reassure her, told her my lawyer would see to everything for us, that we need not appear in court, that he'd settle the fines for us and that it was unlikely we should all be sent to prison. So, in the end, she wrote down her name as Ingrid Jensen and that doesn't seem to be the right one either."

"It's not my business, I know, but she didn't seem to me to be the right one for you, Trevor," Andrea said, after a long silence had fallen between them.

"I suppose I was just a handy sucker. Well, it's over now. She's very definitely told me that I'm no more use to her. Andrea, what are you going to do with your future?"

"Do with it? I don't know. Wait until it creeps up on me, I suppose."

"You could marry me."

She stared at him. "Trevor! You don't mean that."

"I do indeed. Oh, I know what you're thinking. That I'm on the rebound off Ingrid, but that was just a crazy madness. I've come to my senses now."

"I've never thought about—marrying you," she said slowly, not looking at him, but at the tablecloth. That was a lie, but she couldn't tell him the truth now about her silly girlish dreams. They were no longer true, anyway.

"Then do some hard thinking about the problem, please." His eyes held kindliness, affection, companionable interest, but was love there?

She shook her head. "If I took you at your word, Trevor, you'd be sorry if I kept you to it."

"But we get on so well together. That's why I asked you out tonight. You're the only one I feel comfortable with."

"That makes me sound like a little pet cat, when you want to rub your face into its fur."

He laughed. "That's exactly what I mean. You're such an easy girl to get along with."

"You don't want a doormat for a wife. You need someone who'll have a bit of spirit now and again and flatly contradict you, when you know you're in the right."

"Is there somebody else? You haven't lost your head over that chap Keir Holt, have you?"

"Of course not!" she snapped, more curtly than she meant—and the damage was done.

He gave her a slow, sweet smile, full of tenderness and sympathy, and if he had looked at her like that a year ago, she would have melted with love for him.

"Dearest Andrea, let's put away our infatuations for the wrong partners. We could be happy together."

"It isn't the right kind of foundation for marriage," she whispered, tears almost choking her voice. "You don't love me. You're just fond of me. And it's the same with me. It isn't enough. In time, it wouldn't be enough for you, either. You'd meet someone else and know instantly that what you felt was real love. Don't let both of us make a mistake.''

"You're a funny girl, Andrea. I suppose that old head on young shoulders comes from having a professor for a father. Is that why he gave you a classical name?''

"The girls call me Andy.'' Dear Trevor! He knew exactly how to lighten the tension with some quite commonplace remark.

During the rest of the evening, Andrea mentioned Eileen, Trevor's secretary at the store, several times. She was really the wife for him, if only he could see straight, and perhaps, in time, they would make a match.

When he left Andrea outside the staff entrance of the Belvedere, he said, "You'll think over what I suggested, won't you?''

"Of course! You don't think I'd be so crude as to throw your proposal back in your face. Besides, it's the first one I've ever had!''

"I'll start hoping that it's the last.''

But her mind was already closed to the proposition, shut as firmly as if an iron door lay between her and Trevor. She would never choose this easy path of indolence.

She had meant to tell him about Mervyn's wedding and Miss Wyvern's subsequent revelation that she knew Andrea to be related to Mrs. Mayfield, but now she was glad that these events, important enough in themselves, had been crowded out of a conversation mainly centering on Ingrid. Trevor would have immediately seized on the advantage that Andrea was now likely to be most unpopular with the rest of the staff at the Belvedere.

CHAPTER FOURTEEN

ANDREA NEEDED very little time to find out that, in a subtle way, Miss Wyvern had made use of her knowledge of the relationship between Mrs. Mayfield, the head housekeeper, and Andrea Lansdale, the trainee. The girls in Control, her own department, no longer boasted of breaking the house rules; in working hours they spoke to her only when she asked something. In the staff hall, both at mealtimes and in the rest periods, sudden silence fell on any group present when she entered.

Miriam declared that she had known there was some tie-up all along. "Why didn't you tell us in the first place, Andy, that the May Queen was your aunt?"

"If I had, you'd have treated me from the beginning, the way you're all thinking of me now—as a tale-bearer."

Only Huguette remained friendly. But even she was not entirely unaltered. "It is good that you are the May Queen's niece. Now I have no need to worry if I commit small crimes. You, dear Andrea, will speak for me in defense."

Andrea bridled. "If you think I'm always going to haul you out of scrapes, you're mistaken."

"That is not gratitude. Think of the necklace and how I saved *you*."

It was impossible to argue with Huguette or to demolish her outrageous philosophy. Andrea was grateful for even a vestige of loyal friendship, even though Huguette's motives were suspect.

Of Miss Wyvern herself there had been no sign since the day of Mervyn's wedding, and it was stated that she was ill and being looked after by a married sister in a nearby town.

Eventually it occurred to Andrea that Aunt Catherine might not know that the disclosure about their relationship had come from the floor housekeeper. She might believe that Andrea herself had made it. She asked for an interview and squarely faced her aunt.

"I have to make this clear to you, madam. I don't know, or at least I can't be certain, where the information came from but I was not responsible."

Aunt Catherine smiled at the girl. "I believe you, Andrea. I have good reason for doing so."

"Otherwise you might think that I wanted an excuse to leave here," Andrea went on.

"You could have made this relationship of ours an excuse a long time ago. I'm aware of that."

Mrs. Mayfield rose from her chair and walked to the window of her sitting room. "Mr. Blake and I have discussed your position, Andrea. Obviously these rumors and little bits of gossip all filter their way through to us, and we wonder if you'd like a change. I could fix up something for you at the Prince's."

Andrea was silent. When Miss Wyvern returned, she would make Andrea's position intolerable. All the long-pent-up venom caused by continual disappointment would be vented on Andrea, because she would be the most vulnerable. Would it be better to go now to another hotel?

"Of course, if you don't want to finish your training—" began Mrs. Mayfield.

"No, no, it isn't that," Andrea replied quickly. "I'm not looking for an escape. In any case, I could do that in another way. Trevor Dennistoun has asked me to—" She stopped. What demon of impulsiveness had led her into that admission?

"To marry him?"

Andrea nodded. "But I don't think I shall." She smiled at her aunt. "There's his mother. She likes me, I think, but not as Trevor's wife."

"Well, I think you should take a little time to make up your mind, Andrea. Don't be in a hurry."

"Yes, I'll go to the Prince's," Andrea suddenly decided. She would probably never have a chance of seeing Keir Holt again, but perhaps that was for the best. She would bury herself in new routines.

"I'll arrange a transfer for you," her aunt promised. "Miss Wyvern has resigned. She's suffering from a breakdown at the moment, but when she's fit again she'll take a post elsewhere."

"I hope she'll be better soon," said Andrea.

Catherine stared at Andrea. "You have a forgiving nature, my dear. Miss Wyvern confessed to me that she'd borrowed a necklace from Miss Jensen to put into your room and accuse you of having stolen it."

Andrea's head jerked up. "She put it there?"

"But it wasn't found there. Tell me the rest of the story. You need have no fear now."

"Apparently it was there in my drawer, but—somebody—borrowed it."

"Huguette?"

"Whoever it was returned it to me thinking it was mine. I knew Miss Jensen had lost it and I wanted to bring it to you, but my friend—well, we both panicked, and flung it out of the window onto the kitchen roof."

Aunt Catherine nodded. "I see."

"But surely it was risky for Miss Wyvern to borrow anything so valuable from Miss Jensen? Something more trivial would have suited the purpose, wouldn't it?"

Mrs. Mayfield gave a quiet laugh. "Evidently it wasn't as valuable as we thought. It was just good imitation. And Miss Jensen's fur? That was also borrowed by your friend and you tried to put it back?"

What was the use of denying? "My friend has never taken anything and kept it."

"I hope not. She may not always find such loyalty as she's found in you."

Andrea waited for her dismissal. Then her aunt said: "I was mistaken in you, Andrea dear. At first I resented you, although I brought you here. You were Leonie's daughter and reminded me of the daughter I never had. But you've worked well and shown that you can hold up your head when trials and troubles come your way. I'm proud of you, my dear." She kissed her niece, and Andrea's heart filled with elation. It was the first time that Aunt Catherine had shown any affection or given her a real compliment.

There was a new softness about Aunt Catherine that Andrea had not noticed until now, or else she had been so convinced of her aunt's hostility that she had blinded herself to it.

So there had been a connection between Miss Wyvern and the Danish girl, as Andrea had suspected. Was that why Miss Wyvern had poked around after Miss Jensen's sudden departure? The floor housekeeper must have been looking for something, or else making sure that nothing was left in the suite that would incriminate her.

Elation stayed with Andrea until her final day at the Belvedere, but when she was confronted at teatime in the staff hall with a magnificently iced cake, bearing her name in delicate green and chocolate letters on top, tears filled her eyes.

"Cheer up, Andy!" the girls entreated. "It's not the end of the world."

"Even though the Prince's is a comedown from our place."

"Look! Robert's made you a lovely cake."

The girls were only too eager for Andrea to cut the first slice, so that they, too, could enjoy their share. It was traditional that a sumptuous cake for teatime should be provided by anybody who was leaving or had a birthday, but when Andrea had asked what the procedure was, the girls had told her that everything was arranged. She realized now that they had ordered and paid for a staff cake for her and she was deeply touched by this friendly gesture.

"Oh, thank you, all of you. It's very kind."

They had forgiven her for being the head-housekeeper's niece.

She found an opportunity afterward to thank Robert for making such an exquisite confection.

"I haven't had a chance to tell you, but I'm also leaving soon. I'm going to Vienna for a year. The old man, Mr. Cassavini, thinks I'm, er, reasonably promising and it'll be quite a good asset for my career to have Continental experience."

"Goodbye, Robert. And I do wish you the best of luck."

Andrea had never really believed all the teasing about Robert's attraction toward her, but she was glad, all the same, that his mind was more set on his career than on dallying with hotel staff.

Huguette was desolated at losing her roommate.

"Now I shall get a suet-pudding English girl who does not understand two words of French," she wailed.

"Suet pudding yourself! How I've put up with you I don't know!"

"But you must take care about the men you meet at the Prince's," Huguette warned her. "They are not so high class as the ones who stay here."

"Snob! I'll take care of myself. You're the one who needs looking after."

"Now I have my Jacques, everything is settled." Huguette sighed with bliss. French Fortnight at the Belvedere had brought Jacques, a young café proprietor from Le Lavandou on the Mediterranean coast, and Huguette had struck up a promising friendship with him. Whether it would develop into marriage remained to be seen, for with Huguette anything could happen, as Andrea well knew.

At the Prince's hotel, Andrea soon settled in at her new post in Reception, for which Aunt Catherine had recommended her. She spent little of her time on the desk, for she was the most junior and inexperienced of the staff there. She had already mastered some of the mysteries of the tabular system of hotel bookkeeping, adding each guest's daily bill to the amount already charged, and thus being able to present a completed bill as soon as it was demanded. In effect, she was back at office work again, but the environment was different from that of the commercial world. Even when you had finished for the day, the life of the hotel still flowed on; people were coming and going all the time on business or pleasure.

The Prince's was considerably smaller than the Belvedere in its number of rooms, although the public rooms were just as spacious and plush. The head housekeeper was an elderly, white-haired woman whom Andrea had so far met only once, and the staff manager was most genial and kindly. Andrea wondered if the fact that she was Mrs. Mayfield's niece secured preferential treatment for her here at the Prince's, whereas it would have been impossible at the Belvedere.

She had not even been reprimanded when, having lost her way in a maze of passages and corridors, dim staircases and unfamiliar doors, she had found herself in a scullery where a boy was diligently shelling peas.

"Green peas for the five thousand," she had murmured to the boy, for she had never realized the magnitude of a task that involved such a quantity of shelled peas in a gigantic bowl large enough to bathe twin babies in, and a dustbin entirely filled with shucks.

After that illuminating little cameo, she thought no more of the monotony of her own job, and only hoped that sometimes the lad had a chance to peel carrots.

She was on duty at the desk one day at lunchtime in the absence of other receptionists when she was startled by a well-known voice.

"Changed your job, I see."

She looked up into Keir's dark eyes. "It's all experience," she answered.

"I have a lunch conference here today," he told her. "When my friends arrive, tell them I'm downstairs in the bar, or send a page for me. Here are the names."

"Yes, sir."

A flicker of amusement swept over his face, but Andrea, busy writing down the names, did not see that.

"Does the Century block still find disfavor with you— architecturally, that is?" he inquired.

"The shops are very good," she told him, "especially the large store. I like the spacious layout and the display equipment. But I still don't like the outside of the building."

He grinned at her. "We're just finishing off the tower block. You must come up to the top sometime with me and see the view over the entire city. Perhaps that will compensate for the ugly cladding that you don't like."

As he walked away and disappeared down the staircase to the bar, she wished with all her heart that he had really meant his invitation to go up the tower block with him.

But other guests soon claimed her attention. When Keir's guests arrived, she was busy on the telephone and had to pass the slip of paper to the other receptionist.

She had almost finished her relief duty on the desk when she recognized Mr. Selborn standing there.

"Any letters for me? Selborn. Why, I know you don't I? I thought you were at the Belvedere."

"I've changed to this one," Andrea explained.

From the pigeonholes for mail she took out three letters addressed to him at the Prince's and handed them to him. The top one bore in heavy black letters the name of a firm of constructional engineers, Keir's company's strongest rival.

"Thank you." He stuffed the letters into his pocket and walked toward the elevator.

She opened the hotel register, saw that Mr. Selborn had arrived yesterday and occupied Room 427. A terrible premonition of danger enveloped her. Selborn was a traveler in plastics. Why should he be in touch with a firm of constructional engineers? She remembered those tiny incidents—when he had offered to take her reports in to Keir; standing next to him on the observation platform; his remarks about the bad luck that the Century suffered and finally, that night when she had seen him talking to a workman on the site. Although he had denied being there, she was sure now she had not been mistaken.

Was it just coincidence that Selborn was in the Prince's today when Keir was lunching with some of his associates?

When the senior receptionist came back to the desk, Andrea was reluctant to leave and return to her own office, but she could give no excuse.

She would not be off duty until half-past five, and that might be too late. Too late for what, she asked herself. She was making melodrama out of a trivial incident. Yet, in some way, she felt impelled to warn Keir. If Selborn was harmless, then Keir would merely laugh and tell her not to be absurd.

She changed her teatime with another girl and went through to the rear of the reception desk.

"Has Mr. Keir Holt gone out?" she asked.

"He's not staying here," the girl answered briefly.

"Probably only in for lunch. Oh, wait—here's a message—something about being at the Century block if he's wanted."

A glance at the key rack showed that Mr. Selborn's key was still there.

The Century was only a couple of blocks from the Prince's, and Andrea, with no clear idea of what she was doing raced along the crowded street. So much of the Century was now completed that it was difficult to find the way in to the works site.

"Is Mr. Holt here with his party?" she asked a workman in dungarees.

The man bellowed to someone else for information.

"He's up on top of the tower, miss," he eventually told her.

"Is it possible to speak to him? It's very urgent," she said breathlessly.

"Well—I dunno—oh, I suppose you'd better go up. Who are you from?"

With an intuitive flash she gave the name of Keir's company.

"All right. Go up in the elevator. But it only goes up to seventh floor. They're still working on the top floors. You'll have to climb the stairs after that."

She thanked the man, stepped into the unfinished elevator and at the seventh floor clambered out onto a planked floor, then mounted several flights of rough wooden steps.

She saw Keir with his friends in a room close by. Now she realized that he would imagine she had taken his invitation to come up in the tower block quite literally and at the earliest possible moment.

His hands held a large plan, and as he turned to point out something, he caught sight of Andrea, and frowned in surprise.

She ran toward him. "Can I speak to you—privately?" She was past caring what the other men thought.

"Why have you come up here?" he asked, intense but controlled anger in his voice.

The other men had moved away a little. "You're in

danger!'' she told him breathlessly. Even in her own ears, the words sounded ridiculous. "Mr. Selborn!''

"What about him?''

"He's staying at the Prince's. He had a letter from that other firm. I'm sure he's the one who's caused all these accidents.'' The words tumbled out.

Keir was silent for a few seconds. Then: "Thank you for coming,'' he said.

"But he knows you and your friends are up here now. I think he's planning something. Please take care,'' she implored.

A curious change came over Keir's face. He looked like a man who has seen through an open door a most glorious prospect.

Then his face clouded, as though that door had been shut in his face.

"All right. I'll look out. Now go down to ground level and safety. This isn't the place for you.''

He accompanied her to the top of the first flight of stairs down. "Be careful.''

Well, she had done her best for him, and if he thought her a fool, it was too bad.

At the foot of the last flight, a man stood between her and the elevator.

It was Mr. Selborn.

"We meet in the most unexpected places,'' he said pleasantly.

"Excuse me.'' She tried to edge nearer the elevator.

"You'll have to wait for it to come up,'' Selborn told her.

There was only a vast gaping hole down the shaft, lit by one naked electric bulb.

"The most wonderful view over the city.'' he said. "Come and look at it from this side.'' He moved toward an open window.

"I haven't time now. Another day.''

"The elevator will be a long time coming.''

Fear fluttered inside her and she noticed that his usual kindly smile did not match his eyes.

"I'll wait,'' she snapped.

"Waiting can be a very dangerous occupation."

"Especially on a building site? I think you know a great deal, Mr. Selborn, about the causes of so many accidents here. But I've warned Keir."

He continued to smile.

"You're not clever enough, little girl. Run away home and don't try to interfere in matters that don't concern you. I think I hear the lift coming up."

Then everything happened at once. Andrea felt herself twisted in Selborn's grasp so that her back was toward the elevator shaft. She tried to scream, but a hand was clamped firmly over her mouth. Then it seemed that her back hit an iron bar and she rebounded and was sent spinning into darkness.

There were shouts and crashes, and then—there was nothing.

When she opened her eyes, she was sitting on the floor in the room where she had spoken to Keir and he was kneeling beside her.

Everybody else had disappeared.

"Andrea, darling, are you all right?" he asked urgently.

She blinked at him. "Yes, I think so. What happened?"

"There was nearly another fatal accident, but it was all my fault, I should have gone right down to the bottom with you."

"But it was Mr. Selborn who—"

"Yes." Keir passed a hand across his forehead. "I was more intent on catching a criminal than, God forgive me, looking after your safety."

"You knew he was causing the accidents, then?"

"More or less. But we couldn't prove it. At last he walked into a trap, but I'd no idea you were going to walk into danger, as well. But, my darling, the most wonderful thing that ever happened to me was that you came to warn me about him. Oh, God, what am I supposed to be saying to you?"

"Go on, Keir. Say some more," she whispered.

"But what's the use? I suppose you'll marry that Dennistoun chap and live happily ever after."

"No! I'd like to live happily ever after, but I'm not marrying Trevor."

He grabbed her to her feet. "Andrea! Don't you love him?"

"No."

They stared at each other for a long timeless pause. Then she said, "I'd been hoping that—you—"

"Of course I love you!" He was exultant. "How could you be so blind? I loved you long ago, at Christmas, when I had to beg you even to pretend that you liked me. Perhaps even when I saw you with somebody's fur wrapped up in a pillowcase."

"Oh, Keir!" she sighed. "Why didn't you tell me?"

But the long, sweet kiss he gave her was a better answer than words.

"What about Mr. Selborn?" she asked, eventually remembering the world around her.

"He'll be taken care of. He deserves to be in hospital, if not worse. I knew he was a fool to act as go-between and take bribes, but I didn't realize he was dangerous, too. Thank God, I pulled you away from the elevator in time. Don't waste your sympathy on him."

After a long pause, he said:

"You must leave the Prince's at once, and I'll take you to my mother and then we'll be married as soon as you're ready."

"I can't leave until I've finished my year," she protested. "I promised Aunt Catherine—"

"Your Aunt Catherine has her own affairs to look after. She's getting married herself very soon to the assistant manager, what's-his-name, Francis Blake."

"That's good news! I'm sure she'll be happy, and she's been a widow long enough. But I must still finish my year. I can't let her imagine that I couldn't stick it out, even to marry you."

"All right, you can have those few weeks."

With his arm around her, they walked across the dusty floor of the empty, unfinished room to the window. "Look, darling, at the marvelous view over the city. When I told you about it, I didn't know I'd be showing it to you so soon."

He gazed down at her in her plain black hotel dress to which the evening sunshine added a nut-brown tinge.

After a glance at the clustered buildings, the church towers and steeples, the chimneys and factory stacks and the faint lavender line of distant hills, she looked up at his face, the face of love.

"Yes," she said softly. "The most wonderful view in the world."

Harlequin

COLLECTION
EDITIONS OF 1978

Harlequin's Collection 1?

ANDREA BLAKE
**Night of
the Hurrica**

Harlequin's Collection 106   1.25

ANNE WEALE
**If This
Is Love**

**50 great stories
of special beauty
and significance**

$1.25
each novel

ORDER FORM
Harlequin Reader Service

In U.S.A.
MPO Box 707
Niagara Falls, N.Y. 14302

In Canada
649 Ontario St.,
Stratford, Ontario, N5A 6W2

Please send me the following Harlequin Collection novels. I am enclosing my check or money order for $1.25 for each novel ordered, plus 25¢ to cover postage and handling.

☐ 102	☐ 115	☐ 128	☐ 140
☐ 103	☐ 116	☐ 129	☐ 141
☐ 104	☐ 117	☐ 130	☐ 142
☐ 105	☐ 118	☐ 131	☐ 143
☐ 106	☐ 119	☐ 132	☐ 144
☐ 107	☐ 120	☐ 133	☐ 145
☐ 108	☐ 121	☐ 134	☐ 146
☐ 109	☐ 122	☐ 135	☐ 147
☐ 110	☐ 123	☐ 136	☐ 148
☐ 111	☐ 124	☐ 137	☐ 149
☐ 112	☐ 125	☐ 138	☐ 150
☐ 113	☐ 126	☐ 139	☐ 151
☐ 114	☐ 127		

Number of novels checked @
$1.25 each = $ _____
N.Y. and N.J. residents add
appropriate sales tax $ _____

Postage and handling $ ____.25

TOTAL $ _____

NAME _____
(Please Print)
ADDRESS _____

CITY _____

STATE/PROV. _____

ZIP/POSTAL CODE _____

OMN 19 (318)

Offer expires June 30, 1979

In 1976 we introduced the first 100 Harlequin Collections—a selection of titles chosen from our best sellers of the past 20 years. This series, a trip down memory lane, proved how great romantic fiction can be timeless and appealing from generation to generation. The theme of love and romance is eternal, and, when placed in the hands of talented, creative, authors whose true gift lies in their ability to write from the heart, the stories reach a special level of brilliance that the passage of time cannot dim. Like a treasured heirloom, an antique of superb craftsmanship, a beautiful gift from someone loved—these stories too, have a special significance that transcends the ordinary. **$1.25 each novel**

Here are your 1978
Harlequin Collection Editions...

Original Harlequin Romance numbers in brackets